PENGUIN BOOKS

THE KNIGHT, DEATH AND THE DEVIL

Ella Leffland is the author of three previous, greatly acclaimed novels: *Rumors of Peace* (a Literary Guild selection), *Love Out of Season*, and *Mrs. Munck*, as well as an equally praised collection of short stories, *Last Courtesies*.

THE KNIGHT, DEATH AND THE DEVIL

Ella Leffland

PENGUIN BOOKS

PENGUIN BOOKS
Published by the Penguin Group
Viking Penguin, a division of Penguin Books USA Inc.,
375 Hudson Street, New York, New York 10014, U.S.A.
Penguin Books Ltd, 27 Wrights Lane,
London W8 5TZ, England
Penguin Books Australia Ltd, Ringwood,
Victoria, Australia
Penguin Books Canada Ltd, 2801 John Street,
Markham, Ontario, Canada L3R 1B4
Penguin Books (N.Z.) Ltd, 182–190 Wairau Road,
Auckland 10, New Zealand

Penguin Books Ltd, Registered Offices:
Harmondsworth, Middlesex, England

First published in the United States of America by
William Morrow and Company, Inc., 1990
Reprinted by arrangement with William Morrow and Company, Inc.
Published in Penguin Books 1991

1 3 5 7 9 10 8 6 4 2

Frontispiece: *Knight, Death and the Devil* by Albrecht Dürer (1471–1528), German
engraving, courtesy of Fogg Art Museum, Harvard University, Cambridge, Massachu-
setts. Gift of William Gray from the Francis Calley Gray Collection.

Excerpts from *Nuremberg Diary* by G. M. Gilbert. Copyright © 1947 by Gustav Mahler
Gilbert. Copyright renewed © 1974 by Gustav Mahler Gilbert. Reprinted by permission of Farrar, Straus and Giroux, Inc.

Grateful acknowledgment is made for permission to use material from Philipp Fehl's
"The Ghosts of Nuremberg," which appeared in the March 1972 issue of *The Atlantic
Monthly*.

Excerpts from *Germany Reborn* by Hermann Göring are reprinted by permission of
Gordon Press.

THE LIBRARY OF CONGRESS HAS CATALOGUED THE HARDCOVER
AS FOLLOWS:
Leffland, Ella.
The knight, death and the devil / Ella Leffland.
p.   cm.
ISBN 0-688-05836-1 (hc.)
ISBN 0 14 01.4537 0 (pbk.)
1. Göring, Hermann, 1893–1946—Fiction. 2. Germany—
History—1933–1945—Fiction. I. Title.
PS3562.E375K55   1989
813'.54—dc20   89-33836

Printed in the United States of America

To
Harvey Ginsberg

Author's Note

THIS is a historical biographical novel. In using this form I went by my feeling that the novel, with its layered interworkings of meaning, was the only form appropriate to the complexities and incongruities of Göring's character. I had no doubts on this score, but if I had, they would have been laid to rest in the course of an interview with Albert Speer, himself a key figure in the Third Reich. When I mentioned that someone had said to me it was probably impossible to know certain aspects of Göring's character—for that matter, of the characters of all who figured in the National Socialist leadership—Speer replied, "This is what you are trying to work out with your writer's sensibility. I think the novelist's way is the most reasonable approach to these questions." I might also have kept before me the words of Robert Amen, head of the Interrogation Division at Nuremberg, who, after the testimony of Reich Security Chief Ernst Kaltenbrunner, remarked, "It would take a novelist to understand the truth about Kaltenbrunner."

But if the novel offers a dimension of human truth which the work of history cannot, it will fall short of its purpose unless it is rooted in fact as a plant is rooted in the soil. I was therefore as scrupulous as humanly possible in adhering to the facts, in staying within the evidence.

Scenes that are imagined—usually those of the fictional characters, private individuals having no bearing on Germany's official history—

are an organic part of the actual times and the actual circumstances of such individuals. This is also true of imagined scenes in the lives of Göring and other historical figures. These scenes take place only on the private level, and are at one with the established surrounding facts of the character's situation.

Scenes on the historical level are dramatized, since this is a novel and not a historical record, but these scenes do not alter or depart from the facts as presented in the historical records.

These historically or biographically authenticated scenes are interwoven with the fictional private scenes, and interwoven so closely that it would be difficult to separate them into the two threads of fact and fiction; for the factual has gone through the creative imaginative process, while the fictional has been built out of facts.

In a work dealing with the subject as it does—particularly in the section leading up to World War II, and World War II itself, both of which have been thoroughly, not to say exhaustively, documented—it was not possible to avoid using secondary sources. However, apart from Göring biographies, primary sources were the chief material of my research: memoirs and diaries (usually out of print): articles from fifty- and sixty-year-old newspapers and journals; documents, letters and unpublished papers housed in the Munich Institut für Zeitgeschichte; visits to the cities, towns and villages (and if still standing, the buildings and rooms) in which the scenes in the book take place; and not least, personal interviews. For assisting my pursuit of vividness and a sense of immediacy, I am indebted to the people I was able to talk with: Albert Speer, former Minister of Armaments; Adolf Galland, former Luftwaffe Commander of Fighter Forces; Göring's nephew, Klaus Rigele; elderly village people who had known Göring in his youth; and Göring's former personal bodyguard, Werner Hohmann, with whom I had numerous long conversations.

—E. L.

As I write, highly civilized human beings are flying overhead, trying to kill me.

They do not feel any enmity against me as an individual, nor I against them. They are "only doing their duty," as the saying goes. Most of them, I have no doubt, are kindhearted law-abiding men who would never dream of committing murder in private life. On the other hand, if one of them succeeds in blowing me to pieces with a well-placed bomb, he will never sleep any the worse for it. He is serving his country, which has the power to absolve him from evil.

—George Orwell, *The Lion and the Unicorn*

Master, I am in great distress!
The spirits that I conjured up
I cannot now get rid of.

—Goethe, *Der Zauberlehrling*

THE KNIGHT, DEATH AND THE DEVIL

Chapter 1

H<small>E</small> was struck by the dramatic effects accompanying his entrance: the massive boom as the door slammed shut, the clangor of keys turning in locks and of bolts being shot, the abrupt, absolute fall of silence—ein ironisches Meisterstück—and was engulfed in a reek of disinfectant mixed with age-old hints of stale urine, rank armpits, hawked phlegm, of generations of sour-clothed convicts whose heads, he saw, had left a long greasy imprint on the wall alongside the cot.

It was a steel cot, chained and bolted to the stone floor. There was a flimsy table of raw wood, a chair; in a shallow recess, a toilet without lid or seat. Daylight came through the dirty glass of a narrow barred window set high in the wall.

He stood a few moments longer, suitcase in hand, surveying his final home: a stone hole, and a stone hole in Nuremberg. No question about it, for a pack of Ausländer they had a grasp of irony—a much surer, finer grasp than the fools themselves knew, or would ever know. Turning to the table, he dumped down his suitcase. The table swayed under the impact, apparently designed to collapse should you try to stand on it in order to hang yourself from the bars of the window. He saw that the dinginess of the walls was set off by fresh white patches of plaster where clothes hooks and shelf fittings had been ripped out. Such precautions were understandable, if in his case pointless. He snapped open the suitcase, making two pinging clicks in the silence, and took out a large meerschaum pipe, which he laid on the table. Giving a look at the door, he began to inspect the cell.

After a while he straightened up from crouching beside the toilet and stepped back to the meerschaum pipe, into whose bowl he dug his fingers, presently withdrawing a small object covered with blackened tobacco, which he brushed off. This, a tubular metal container about half the length of his thumb, he brought back to the toilet. Crouching again, he reached deep inside the interior, far back along the under-side of the bowl, and pressed the container up, sideways, into a groove which his fingers had felt there, wedging it in firmly.

That done, he stood up and wiped his hands with his hand-kerchief. In his months of captivity he had come to feel a strong bond with the little vial, almost as if it were part of his flesh—he had in fact hidden it sometimes in the flesh of his thigh, pressed into a fold of scar tissue, although usually it was secreted in his pipe or a rent in his mat-tress. Such refuges had served in the interrogation camp and the hold-ing center, but they would not serve here.

Returning to the table, he pulled the chair away and began un-packing the rest of his things. One silver-backed ebony hairbrush. Three small photographs in dark blue leather frames. One pair of blue silk pajamas and some underwear. Two tablets of writing paper, a bot-tle of ink, a fountain pen. One toothbrush and tube of toothpaste. One prison-issue sponge and cake of brown soap. One matchbox containing two buttons.

Shutting the empty suitcase, he dropped it to the floor. There was nothing further to do.

He sat down on the cot, stirring a musty smell of old straw from the mattress, at one end of which lay two U.S. Army blankets, neatly folded. His fingers drummed on his knee. The silence had a density, like sand sifting and humming. After a while he turned and looked at the long greasy imprint on the wall behind him. Close up it was black-ish-brown, gritty, with a dull sheen. He turned back, his fingers still drumming, and gazed up at the narrow rectangle of blue midafter-noon sky. It was warm September weather, but the cell held an edge of a dampness already sending twinges through the mass of old scar tissue. He got up and walked to and fro, but the echo of his footsteps annoyed him and he sat down again, only to rise and begin pacing once more, four steps to one end of the cell, four to the other, the echo of his boots ringing in his ears. The boots were high, of maroon leather, worn with a badly wrinkled dove-gray uniform stripped of insignia. Suddenly he lunged and kicked the chair so violently that it slammed with a crash against the wall, and, lunging again, he gave the wall a battery of kicks.

He stood regaining his breath. Then he smoothed back his hair, set the chair upright and, feeling more at his ease, sat down on the cot.

* * *

Each morning at half past six a panel in the heavy oaken door was opened and through it was passed a bucket of cold water to wash in. At seven, oatmeal in a U.S. Army meat can was passed through. At half past seven he was shaved in silence by a German prisoner-of-war barber, an American guard with a truncheon standing over the man as he worked, in order to prevent conversation and possibly a throat slash. Whether such a slash would be of a compassionate or vengeful nature was something he contemplated beneath the deft strokes.

One evening a week he was taken to a crude wooden shower room to bathe beneath a dribble of lukewarm water; and here, too, the prisoner-of-war attendant, under the guards' surveillance, regarded him mutely with no expression that he could gauge. Respect? Loyalty? Hatred?

In the afternoon he was allowed thirty minutes in the exercise yard. The sky was sudden, vast. Followed by armed guards to ensure silence, he and his twenty-one fellow captives walked back and forth. The only sound was the crunch of gravel.

At irregular intervals there was a cell and body search during which he was stripped and probed and everything in the cell was turned upside down, inside out, and left scattered. The inspection of the toilet was consistently and gratifyingly unproductive.

Also at irregular intervals he was handcuffed and taken to the interrogation room, where an interpreter sat between him and his questioners.

"How do you like it here, everything to your liking?"

"I have no complaints."

"A matter of curiosity—what do you think of that rubble outside, used to be a city?"

"I think you did a thorough job."

"Is that all?"

"A magnificent job?"

"Let me put it to you this way—what do you think of tens of thousands of people killed?"

"Shouldn't I be asking you these questions?"

"What do you think of tens of thousands of people killed?"

"A great number of people."

"And six million, what do you think of six million people killed?"

"A great number."

After three or four hours of interrogation, the silence of his cell was strange to him, and took time to get used to, and when he was used to it he had no sense of its having been interrupted. On occasion he thought his mind was affected by the humming vacuum, for it happened that he suddenly lifted his head to the sound of march music, a startling burst of trumpets, drums, Glockenspiele, and through it the stiff, slamming-down thud of boots and the roaring of the crowd. Then, as abruptly as it came, it was gone.

He was served the indictment against him. It was as he had anticipated, except for some glaring errors which he slashed through with his pen. When asked the next day to set down his response in the margin, he wrote: *Der Sieger wird immer Richter und der Besiegte stets der Angeklagte sein!* The victor will always be the judge and the vanquished the accused!

A psychiatrist, a young German-speaking captain in U.S. Army Intelligence, had begun visiting each of the twenty-two prisoners in their cells. Some of the prisoners were vacant, disheveled, swollen-eyed, as if given to silent sessions of weeping; a few were in a state of hysteria, racked by visions of Christ and riddled with psychosomatic symptoms: stomach cramps, impaired vision, irregular heartbeats; others were quite normal, in good physical shape and mentally alert, if deeply dispirited. All welcomed the diversion of the psychological tests, and all were grateful that the young captain stayed and conversed with them, pressed as they were by the loneliness of solitary confinement, and by the need to unburden themselves. Afterward, as soon as he had stepped out of the cell door, while his memory was still fresh, the captain would open his notebook and make notes of everything that had been said. At the end of the day, using these notes as a basis, he would report to the prison commandant. If the captain felt like an informer, which he did, his conscience was not troubled by this, although he was very deeply a man of conscience.

He had left Cell No. 5 to one of the last, perhaps to get his sea legs, or perhaps to express a disregard for rank, he was not sure which. He introduced himself to the man inside, who had risen from his cot, and though the notorious bulk had decreased drastically, there was a larger-than-life quality projected, something powerful and disturbing, and this was so even though the face beamed with pleasure and welcome.

"So you have come to probe our souls, have you? And here I thought we hadn't any, or ersatz, ja? Sit down, Herr Doktor! Bitte, be comfortable! Is there light enough?"

The captain seated himself on the cot, and felt the weight of the prisoner sitting down next to him. Taking his tests from his folder with hands that had grown damp, he cleared his throat and began explaining the procedure.

Extremely competitive, struck fist on knee if answer didn't come to him at once—but very pleased, as if engrossed in a game. Said when finished: Very entertaining! I hope you will bring me more. Told him I'd be coming on reg. basis, which pleased him. Asked if there was anything he'd like to talk abt & he

*launched into long reminiscence of his exploits as a fighter pilot in WWI—
narcissistic attitude toward wounds sustained then, upper leg, recounted exact
no. of splinters removed, gave length & width of scars, etc. Pleasant voice,
accustomed to holding forth. When asked if he'd like to know how his colleagues
were doing, tone switched to contempt: I see them in the exc. yd., I know how
they're doing.*

   Indiff. to discomfort of surroundings, no mention.

   *Says he's beginning to look on me as father confessor. Follows this with
smiling suggestion: You shld take out yr pencil during our chats, Herr Dr., why
depend on memory? Take notes, feel free. I assure you it won't detract from our
cozy atmosphere, I shall remain as open & loose-tongued as ever.*

   Very pleased with this jab. Takes great satisfaction in his wit.

   *I asked how he sleeps, said he slept well. Asked if he had dreams, Said alas
no. —Why alas? They might be unpleasant. —Well I will try for one, then you
can dissect it. —Do you ever think of what's outside these walls? This city where
you held yr great rallies? —Herr Dr. you are so obvious and so naïve. —Why is
that? —Why is that? How shld I know, am I examining you? —My point is
that it's rubble. —I realize that's yr point, rubble, everyone talks of the rubble.
—There's a lot of it, that's why. I wonder what you think of it. —There's a lot
of it.*

   *Eager for trial to begin, wks every day on his case with supplied documents.
No question in his mind that he'll receive death sentence. Considers it foregone
conclusion. His terms for the trial: burlesque & farce. Says: I challenge the
right of any foreign tribunal to try me. The entire proceeding is illegal & invalid. That has been my official statement from the start, & the official statement
of all the prisoners. —With some exceptions. —I spit on the exceptions. —Why
then are you preparing a case for a trial you consider invalid? —What wld you
do, give them the final word? Turn yr back & say lick my ass? Lick my ass, Herr
Dr., a majestic & time-honored phrase, if you have read yr Goethe. Except that
it cannot serve in this situation.*

   *Was sitting with prisoner when I learned of the suicide in Cell 11. A guard
brought a note in & handed it to prisoner, who read it with no affect & cont'd
conversation. Only when I expressed curiosity did he speak of it & hand it to me.
I read it & asked if he had any comment. —Abt what, him? —Him, yes, the
man's just hanged himself. —A good thing. Imagine how he wld have conducted
himself during the trial. That bombastic ass, brain half rotted by drink. Much
better this way. —But I should think, as a comrade —Bitte, use the word comrade sparingly in our conversations.*

The note had also informed the prisoner that security measures
would henceforth be tightened. Already that afternoon the glass in the
barred window was replaced with a square of gray celluloid, and the

overhead light bulb removed. The panel in the door was unhinged and taken away. All towels, belts, suspenders, shoelaces and sharp objects were confiscated.

In the now open panel of the door was heavy wire mesh, through which a guard's face stared into each cell twenty-four hours a day. The guard was changed every three hours; the one on duty at dusk switched on a lamp attached to the mesh, directing its beam into the cell to provide light. At half past nine the lamp was set at a less glaring angle so that the prisoners could sleep but would throughout the night remain clearly observable on their cots, where by requirement they now lay on their backs with arms outside the blankets.

Yr compatriots complain of frostbitten hands at night. They say if it's this bad in Nov. what will it be like in midwinter? —For me the complaint's crapping in public. But I try to look at it in the best possible light. After all, didn't Louis XIV do everything surrounded by observers, even evacuate his royal bowels? I've told myself I must consider it a sovereign honor. —There are worse things than being stared at. Wldn't you agree, as founder of the concentration camps? —And of the Gestapo, don't forget. Also Supreme Leader of the SA, not to mention General in the SS. You realize these things actually stand in the indictment? Yr Internat'l Tribunal had better get its facts straight or it will sound like a pack of ignoramuses.

He did in fact dream. Often at night, and sometimes during the day. With the two Army blankets wrapped around his legs, he would sit working at the small wobbly table, his face turned away from the observing eyes behind the mesh. And sometimes, in the humming silence, his hand would stop writing, and he would sit looking at the wall, seeing shapes where the paint had flaked away, a hand, a tree, a house. The cell had a twilight feeling, the square of gray celluloid admitting a somber cathedral hue, and he would lean back in his chair and close his eyes, feeling a slow, then a swift falling away. They were short dreams, and they always began with a sense of height, of wind rushing.

I've found a patch more interesting than yr inkblots, Herr Dr. On the wall there by the door. What do you take it for? —Nothing, really. It doesn't lend itself to a configuration. —I see Germany. That is its exact shape. —Is it? —It is Germany & nothing else. You cannot see that, & that is the diff. between us.

It's clear that he intends to take the stand as the great patriot. He has enormous energy & will, a highly persuasive manner, & a mind of the keenest order. Am certain he'll have damaging effect on his codefendants when trial begins & rules of sol. confinement are lifted. Believe that outside the courtroom he shld remain segregated.

* * *

Calls prison commandant Chief of Fire Brigade because of penchant for wearing camouflage-painted battle helmet. I said he had quite a sartorial reputation himself, owning over a thousand uniforms each of his own design. This caused big belly laugh. —Yr own propaganda. When wld I have found time to design or even wear a thousand uniforms? How can you be so naïve as to believe something like that, Herr Dr? I think you like caricatures. But take no offense, with my demented vanity I am able to extract satisfaction even from being caricatured. —That can only be because you haven't seen yr foreign caricatures. —I've seen plenty. Fat of course. Very fat. Mark my word, even when I've peeled down to twenty kilos they'll still be calling me fat. —Yr image is something that concerns you very much. —So you have mentioned so often. All yr inkblots bear you out. Who am I to argue with inkblots? —But you wldn't argue, wld you? You've admitted yrself that being No. 1 has always been of primary importance to you. —I never said No. 1. I was never No. 1. —No. 1 in everything after him. Do you know what yr colleagues say? That you expect them to form a retinue for yr grand entrance into Valhalla.

The prisoner had laughed again, so heartily that the captain could see all the gold fillings in his teeth. What tremendous satisfaction the man took in himself, the captain reflected, although if he had had access to a mirror he might be given pause. His complexion had faded to a clayish-gray prison hue, and sixty of his massive 270 pounds had fallen away, leaving his face loose-skinned, deeply lined, giving him a worn, haggard look older than his fifty-two years. Yet in other ways his appearance belied his age: his hair was a smooth, youthful brown; his eyes were of razored clarity and penetration, a startlingly pale blue-green. Perhaps it was just as well that there was no mirror, or he would commune solely with those features that remained in keeping with his idea of himself. As the captain had written in one of his first test reports: *The subject's cynical realism dissolves precisely at the threshold of his self-image.*

The subject was taking his smoking things and leaning back on the cot against the wall, just beyond the long smear of greasy dirt. He was wearing prison-issue carpet slippers, one of which had fallen off as he crossed his legs, disclosing through the stocking sharply bent, turned-down toes, pressed that way from years of tight jackboots. His hands, divested of their several splendrous rings, had once been compared by a foreign statesman to the digging paws of a badger. He stuffed tobacco into the bowl of his big ornate meerschaum pipe and lit a match, puffing slowly, with relish, his very long, supple mouth turned slightly down, a hard mouth, yet sensual, humorous, good-natured. The chin was brutally prominent, the forehead broad and open as a child's. He looked up, smiling, and blew out the match.

* * *

Every afternoon at about four o'clock, the sinking sun hit the gray celluloid in such a way that for a few minutes its network of scratches was brightly illumined. Each day he waited for that moment, and then he would stretch out on the cot, with his arms behind his head, and lie looking up at the brilliant filigree. Sometimes he drifted into sleep, with a sense of rushing wind, up in a plane sometimes, or on a mountain peak, or in the castle watchtower, there at its top in a sunburst of slotted windows, pulling himself up on his elbows into one of the window slots . . . he was small and light, a boy, bare-legged, and he was squinting down at the fields far below, at banners and flashing shields of medieval armies, a clangor of swords ringing up through the wind . . . how green the fields were, how vast and dark the familiar forests, and there in the distance stood the wooded range of hills, and beyond them stood the old imperial city of Nuremberg, but now the vision grew confused, for he was in Nuremberg, he was walking through its winding, Gothic streets, yet the streets were not there, nothing was there, everything was gone—and he woke abruptly, jerking upright on the cot, the window gray and the cell gone dark.

Outside, the sun had almost set, casting a red, surreal haze across the city's flatness. It was a landscape of rubble, heaped bricks, husks of buildings. Here and there people could be seen living in rooms that had been sheared in half. Small fires were alight in the open, where families stood cooking their food. As the sun disappeared and evening fell, these scattered glows were the only lights of the city.

Chapter 2

In the year 914, on a remote, rocky hilltop some ten leagues northeast of the village of Nuremberg, a fortress outpost was built. Its walls, thick, rough and made of clay and fieldstone, formed a crude rectangle around a large dirt yard. Three sides of the hilltop sloped down in rock-ribbed brush, and the fourth fell away in a sheer, jagged cliff from whose very edge the east wall of the fortress rose, so that from the ground directly below it seemed a dizzying continuation of the precipice. Along the top of this lofty wall, at intervals, were rough-hewn slots behind which bowmen stood. Higher yet, from a crude wooden watchtower, flew the three-pronged blue-and-white banner of the Franconian tribal duchy.

The new fortress looked out over a broad valley of wooded hills and rocky outcroppings, green grasslands and great forests of fir and pine. Down in this wildness the silence was of primeval purity, broken only by the warbling of birds and sometimes by a crashing of stags in the woods. When from the Hungarian plains the invaders came, they were preceded by a suspension of birdcalls, a crystalline silence. Then a few horsemen appeared among the trees, then more, until hundreds were spread through the green dimness of the forest, riding at a steady, rumbling jog over the pine needles.

The geographical heart of Europe was bounded in the north by the sea and in the south by the Alps, but in the east and the west there was neither sea nor mountain range, yet this land lying open to both sides had remained intact throughout Europe's long history of Roman rule; for a thousand years earlier, in Teutoburg Forest, Augustus Caesar's legions were destroyed by barbarian forces led by the warrior Hermann, and Rome, colonizing the rest of Europe, never again tried to conquer east of the Rhine. Only in very recent times, in 772—centuries after the Western Roman Empire had crumbled into the Dark Ages, in great part through the barbarian raids of Germanic tribes—had the Rhine once again been crossed by an invading army. It took Charlemagne thirty blood-drenched years to conquer the Saxon and other tribes, and to force baptism upon them under threat of annihilation, after which he proclaimed Christianity the state religion, set up monasteries and bishoprics and built roads, bridges and schools. Yet among the hundreds of tribes in this vast region, each differing from the next in language, law and custom, forever warring with one another, and spread into the remotest areas, there were those who had never heard of Charlemagne, or of Christ either. Human sacrifices were still made to pagan gods, and the forests were held sacred, above all the great oaks. If man or child peeled bark from an oak, his stomach was slit open and he was pulled round and round the trunk as his intestines went winding round and round the trunk's wound, binding it and restoring it with fresh life from the dying culprit, as was only just.

When Charlemagne died, Emperor of the West, and Roman Emperor crowned by the Pope, his empire too crumbled away, broken up among his heirs and swept by savage hordes of Vikings, Saracens, Slavs and Hungarians. Among the German tribes there were strong chieftains who put to use the ancient tribal consciousness, instinct for battle, and deep, mystical Lokalpatriotismus in undermining royal authority; in time they assumed the title of duke, and came to rule large regions known as tribal duchies. By the year 900 there were five great tribal duchies, Saxony, Franconia, Lorraine, Swabia and Bavaria, and it was the powerful tribal dukes, not the weak Carolingian monarch, who took responsibility against the increasing Magyar invasions from the east, and who began rearing up burgs along the eastern marches.

Massacring, plundering and burning as far as France, the Hungarian scourge was not crushed until 955, in a single, decisive battle with King Otto of the Germans, son of the Saxon tribal duke who had succeeded to the Carolingian line when it died out. It was the greatest victory of the age, and Otto was acclaimed—except by the tribal dukes, who fought Saxon rule as they had Carolingian—the greatest king in Europe. Having already conquered Lombardy and taken the title King of Italy, Otto now returned to Italy in force, rescued the Papacy from its enemies, and was hailed by the Pope as Roman Emperor, direct successor of Charlemagne, Constantine and Augustus Caesar. And so it was that in 962, when the Pope placed the imperial Roman crown on Otto the Great's head—a crown made of gold, and thickly set with enormous uncut jewels, at its center the huge and priceless Stone of Wisdom above which rose the gem-clustered cross of the True Church—the German wilds became the Holy Roman Empire.

The burg on the Franconian hilltop would not have known this. For almost fifty years it had been seasoned by the elements and by man, and as the decades continued to roll on, it was weathered by the same cycle of sun, rain and snow, and scarred by the same outbursts of battle. If the men inside were still fighting eastern marauders, or if they were vainly battling for Franconian independence against the Saxon monarch, or if they now belonged to some local lord and were fighting other nobles for local supremacy, the fortress walls could not tell, all arrows leaving the same pockmarks and all blood the same stain, bright crimson at first, then fading to brown, and eventually to a faint stippling like specks of rust.

The fieldstones of the burg were insensible to the universal kingdom of God, as embodied by the succession of Holy Roman Emperors, but the stones would have known when a powerful crossbow came into use, for under the onslaught of its bolts they grew more thickly and deeply pocked. They would have known, in the mid-ten-hundreds when masonry had grown more refined, that a stone tower was built to replace the many wooden ones preceding it—for whenever the gate had been pounded by a battering ram and the planking had splintered and given way, everything wooden in the dirt yard was fired and the watchtower left a roaring torch.

Germany by the mid-ten-hundreds was a true monarchy, the tribal dukes having long since lost their battle for supremacy. Yet it was in no true sense a kingdom, a nation. It might have been had the Holy Roman Emperors, embodying the universal kingdom of God, ever given evidence of their bodies; but each had been more often absent than present, more often fighting to keep control of Italy than at home ruling Germany. Ruling in the Emperor's stead were hundreds of regional noblemen, of whom all, from the greatest to the smallest, were equal in their direct relationship to that chimerical bodiless being the Holy Roman Emperor. Thus it was that the German peoples gave their allegiance to no flesh-and-blood king, but to the universal kingdom of God. They were God's chosen, and they composed a kind of geographical mosaic in which a holy, crusading sense of Christianity overlaid an ancient, mystical bond with the local soil; and thus it was they were both regional and universal, much less than a nation and much more than a nation, but not a nation.

By the late ten-hundreds, in the valley below the burg, serfs with oxen could be seen tilling the fields of feudal manors, while to the southwest, beyond a wooded range of hills, the small town of Nuremberg was growing rapidly. A hundred more years passed before Nuremberg evolved into a thriving center of trade, and another hundred before it stood a free imperial city of towers and soaring spires.

By then the old fortress on the distant cliff, like many others built in the time of the Magyar invasions, had fallen into disuse, a crumbling relic from another age. Local people called it Burg Veldenstein, but the source of the name was lost from memory; perhaps it was an archaic form of the word "fieldstone."

In 1279 the dank, bitterly chill old ruin was taken over by the church and ensconced with priestly functionaries. Parts were rebuilt, vegetables planted in the dirt yard, new sheds constructed for farm animals and new stables for garrison horses, and for almost two hundred years, as a small village took form on the south slope, the crumbling structure served as an episcopal administrative castle. In the war between the princes and the cities it was attacked, and again during the Hussite wars, when it was badly damaged and finally abandoned. A few years after this, the Prince Bishop of Bamberg, seeking a new site for his residence, appropriated the property to be expanded and rebuilt to his taste.

On its completion in 1468 the ancient bulwark stood enriched by arches, battlements and round turrets with red pointed roofs. Over an arch was an engraved stone tablet, which read: *Master builder Erhart has made these walls, towers and doors. May God and the heavenly hosts protect them. Amen.* Where the crude walls had crumbled or been damaged by cannonballs they had been rebuilt with smoothly mortared squared stones. A massive gate had been set in, its enormously thick planking studded all over with burnished nailheads. The dirt yard, greatly enlarged, flourished with formal gardens where peacocks strolled, while at its far end plump cows grazed in the deep grass and greyhounds sunned themselves among the wildflowers. Under the auspices of God and the heavenly hosts the grounds were permeated by an air of ease and well-being, which faded beyond the gate where the stench of the village began.

When the peasants rose up in 1523 the gate was pounded by a battering ram but refused to give way; and instead of clashing with the Prince Bishop's mailed soldiers, the rebels, armed with pitchforks, clubs and cleavers, swarmed down the hill to find other heads to split. A dented gate was Burg Veldenstein's only memento from the bloody Peasants' Rebellion, which ended inside a year with the peasantry thrown deeper yet into serfdom. Throughout the next years, filled with upheavals caused by the heretic Luther, throughout almost a century of religious, territorial and dynastic civil wars, the castle of the Prince Bishops stood fast; but when the long strife finally exploded against the ruling house of Hapsburg, not a hamlet escaped. With north set against south, with regional kings, princes and dukes backed by the armies of foreign nations, the rebellion developed into a general European war in which Germany became a crossroads of perpetual slaughter.

By this time heavy artillery had grown sophisticated, and light artillery come into use; battles were deafening, and thick with the stinging fumes of powder. Attacked early on by a plundering outlaw army, Burg Veldenstein was left with chunks bitten from its walls and half its massive gate reduced to splinters; walls and gate were patched up, and during the years that followed, as the country became a wasteland of burned fields and leveled towns, as the populace began eating its infants and ripping warm corpses from gallows, the burg fought off sporadic attacks by marauders and foreign armies until finally, heavily damaged in a battle with Swedish troops, it was conquered and fired by an army of Bavarians. The great smashed gate stood open to the burned slopes and charred remains of the village; inside the courtyard the trees and gardens were burned black, as were the stables and service buildings at its far end; the stone manorial residence was a bombarded, burned-out shell, and high above the east wall the ancient stone watchtower stood in half-demolished silhouette against the sky.

The war lasted another decade, ending only in 1648, having spanned thirty full years. Over the ravaged German countryside wandered the diseased and starving survivors of a population diminished by two thirds. Below the ruin of Burg Veldenstein, the broad valley had long since returned to its original purity of silence. Great estates, villages, all lay burned to the ground. Stags, wolves and wild boar again roamed where they would, and sometimes one of these creatures prowled through the brambles of the castle courtyard, more than once terrifying some starved band of wanderers sheltering in the gutted residence. Then, as the years passed, as grain fields supplanted the burned farmlands and new dwellings were raised along charred village pathways, the wild creatures returned to the dim green interior of their forests.

With the passage of time the surface scars sank away, but the country was horribly crippled and lagged far behind the rest of Europe. For Germany, the eighteenth century opened to a bitter sense of impotence, and to a corrosive distrust and envy of its powerful neighbors.

The ruin of Burg Veldenstein stood forgotten for decades, until a Prince Bishop again took interest and decided to restore it. Work was begun during the rise of that strange, spindly-legged phenomenon of the north Frederick II. Prussia, as Napoleon was later to say, was hatched from a cannonball. After centuries of destructive quarreling among the German states—by now having devolved from the five great tribal duchies into nearly two thousand independent kingdoms, principalities, duchies, ecclesiastical states, city states and landgraviates, some of these domains so small that they consisted of one ruling prince and twenty subjects—and after as long a history of foreign interference and invasion, nowhere more evident than in the long savage darkness of the Thirty Years War, a darkness not yet lifted, one of the poorer and least significant kingdoms now suddenly wrenched Silesia away from mighty Austria and shot toward the front ranks of European power.

In 1756, Saxony joined with Austria, France and Russia in trying to bring the upstart Prussia to her knees. For seven years the fighting went on, mostly in the north. Elsewhere throughout the empire, life took its ordinary course, as in the little village of Neuhaus beneath Burg Veldenstein, with its half-timbered houses set hugger-mugger between cowsheds and pigpens, its steep earthen streets pungent with drainage. The great charm of the village was its hillside setting, green with clustered trees and flower-dappled grass, and crowned by the burg whose restored tower, soaring from above the cliff, was once again a landmark for great distances around. In the old courtyard new trees and gardens had been planted, and by the time the scrawny figure in the three-cornered hat was known as Frederick the Great, with the triumphs of the Seven Years War, the partition of Poland, and the Treaty of Teschen behind him, the gardens were growing lush and mellow.

When at seventy-four old Fritz lay dying in his Potsdam palace, his last words were that a weak king could ruin the Prussian state in thirty years. It took only twenty. With Frederick's iron hold removed, the foremost military power in Europe declined so rapidly that by 1806 it had been totally crushed by Napoleon, along with the rest of the empire.

After almost a thousand years, the Holy Roman Empire was cast into its grave; and from it, under the aegis of Napoleon, there emerged a new mosaic no more politically united than the old; but Napoleon had sown seeds of great hatred, and for the first time the word "Fatherland" began to be heard in the many disparate states, and especially was it heard in Prussia. Rebellion erupted in 1813 with the War of Liberation; two years later Prussia joined the British in crushing Napoleon at Waterloo; and then the great mosaic, under the joined hands of Britain, France, Russia and Austria, became the German Confederation, a shrunken number of states to be governed by a Diet possessing no central authority and under Austrian presidency.

During these times Burg Veldenstein passed from the church into private hands; but after a few years, its upkeep proved too expensive and it was left untenanted. The gardens again began going to seed, grass and brambles grew high. No sound was heard except the wind in the trees, and sometimes the shouts of village boys playing on the other side of the gate, reenacting battles of old.

By the time of the liberal revolution of 1848, which brought the states together only sufficiently to squash it, the pointed red roofs had rotted. Still, they remained picturesque, as did all the towers and turrets throughout the area, and foreign tourists could now be seen bumping along the roadways in dusty carriages, off on a day's sidetrip from the medieval splendors of Nuremberg. The German lands offered much to the sightseer, with their enormously varied scenery, customs and dialects, almost as if one traveled through small separate countries, which was more or less the case, their only common feature that of poverty and impotence. Fragmented, old-fashioned, too weak to cause anyone trouble, they inspired a universal fondness, an almost protective benevolence—"Our dear little Germany" as Queen Victoria warmly expressed herself.

In Prussia, Crown Prince Wilhelm impatiently waited to inherit the throne, already having begun a series of visits to the Krupp works in Essen. Crowned Wilhelm I in 1861, he appointed as premier the shrewdly brilliant Bismarck, with his oddly high, whiplike voice, which reinforced the king's own sentiments: "The unity of Germany is not to be brought about by speeches, nor by votes of majorities, but by iron and blood." Within ten short years, Schleswig had been wrested from Denmark, Austria permanently eliminated from German affairs and France stupendously defeated at Sedan. In 1871, in conquered Versailles' Hall of Mirrors, to a roar of cheers and a flashing of swords unsheathed, King Wilhelm of Prussia was proclaimed Emperor of the German Reich.

The fragments had closed ranks with a vengeance. Every town throughout the new nation bore its Sedanstrasse, and the fanatic patriotism of the latecomer ran rampant. But if Europe, stunned by the French defeat, feared further aggression from the Kaiser's superb army, it was soon relieved of its apprehensions. Bismarck ruled supreme, and, having settled the matter of Germany's military power, wished only to further solidify his country within its natural borders. Under his piercing, heavily ringed eyes, Germany evolved with phenomenal speed into an economic wonder, outstripping every nation in Europe. By the closing years of the century the German people basked in a power and prosperity never before known on the continent.

It was at this time, on a warm autumn morning in 1897, that a carriage drawn by two fine bays could be seen making its way up the ancient dirt road leading to the ruin of Burg Veldenstein. Seated inside, jolting over the potholes, was a stout, imperious-looking gentleman with flowing black mustaches. This was Hermann Ritter von Epenstein, a wealthy surgeon already in possession of one castle, in

Austria, but wishing for certain reasons to own another. The gate had been pulled open by the caretaker, and when the carriage stopped inside the brambled courtyard, the Ritter von Epenstein was helped down by his liveried driver and began walking through the weeds, swinging his cane from a gray-gloved hand. Two hours later, having made an extensive tour of the property, he climbed back into the carriage with the decision to purchase. Soon after, he paid out twenty thousand marks and set in motion the repairs necessary for occupancy. Early in August of the following year, he traveled up from Austria to welcome the family he had invited to move in.

Chapter 3

"So, my dear Heinrich," he asked, "it meets with your approval?"

"Curious phraseology," the old Reichskommissar muttered sharply, but his caustic tone did not affect the ponderous, absent expression that had come to characterize him; and as he walked alongside von Epenstein in the sun, with his hands clasped behind his black quilted morning coat, his chin sunk upon his chest, he gave an impression of surveying his feet rather than the crumbled splendors of his new surroundings. This was partly because the sun's glare bothered his eyes under their pince-nez, and made them sting and water. Now and then he stopped and rubbed them, and each time he wished deeply that he might go back inside. But after a while he bestirred himself, and commented, in clipped Prussian tones:

"I see there are roses."

"I had a few put in," von Epenstein said with a nod, looking across the extensive beds.

"In Berlin I missed my bit of gardening. I shall enjoy getting back to it. I may do some riding as well."

He would do neither, as both knew. He was an old man who drank too much and liked his nap and his game of skittles; falling silent again, he walked on with his friend through the sweet-smelling grass of the courtyard, across which several peacocks strolled; and the sight of these exotic creatures, set against the backdrop of the castle walls, seemed suddenly to break something in him, so that his brooding face took on a tremulous expression embarrassing to see.

"Come, it's ridiculous," von Epenstein admonished, taking his friend's arm and sitting down with him on a small rustic bench. "The whole point, as I have said again and again, is that it will be standing empty eleven months of the year. For me its only purpose will be to stay in during the season at Bayreuth, and for some shooting now and then. Otherwise it will just be standing empty. Why shouldn't you have the use of it?"

The old Reichskommissar, with his cropped gray head bent, sat gazing down at the grass. At length he nodded.

"And after all, Heinrich," von Epenstein said, "you need plenty of room."

The Reichskommissar looked over at the great elaborate baby carriage—von Epenstein's gift—where the infant lay sleeping under an elm; and then at the four older children playing nearby. He nodded again, taking off his pince-nez and slowly wiping them with a corner of his white linen handkerchief. A government pension did not stretch far when one had so many children to provide for, not only these five, but five others from a previous marriage. Returning the pince-nez to his nose, he sat looking down at the grass again.

"We are grateful, Hermann," he said at length.

"There is nothing to be grateful for."

And to this the old man also nodded.

The sun drew beads of sweat from the Reichskommissar's face, but he was too correct to remove his morning coat. Von Epenstein, on the other hand, though a Berliner born and bred, affected a loose, flowing peasant blouse open at the throat, which he wore with a pair of coarse breeches and knee-length red stockings. He liked variety, and traveled with four trunks packed with casually flamboyant and impeccably formal garb, and was also fond of appearing in the dress uniform—very tight now—from his past service with the Danzig Death's Head Hussars. Though short and stout, he carried himself with overwhelming aplomb, his dark, almost black eyes smoldering, his double chin either settled grandly upon itself or lifting with sudden, startling effect. Now, taking a flat silver case from his pocket, he opened it and lit a cheroot, and even so small a gesture as this was executed with a grand flourish. Shooting two streams of smoke down his great black mustaches, he leaned back on the warm bench and stretched out his legs.

The yard was as pleasant as a country field, dappled with the shade of elms and fruit trees; and then, in contrast, where the bright grass gave way to tangled dark undergrowth, there were the damp, time-worn passageways and crumbled arches; and from the top of the east wall there was the unbelievable drop of the cliff, its jaggedness recalling the gloomed, macabre etchings of Dürer, setting him musing, as he sometimes did, on *Ritter, Tod und Teufel,* that anarchy of craggy rock and overhanging roots, of pikestaffs, skulls and salamanders, with only the knight on his arch-necked mount shown clearly, cast against the snarled gloom like a medallion. . . . It was a pity that the old man at his side could not be moved to some similar fancy by his surroundings, but probably the only thought he entertained was that here he would run to final seed and be buried.

One could hardly recall him any longer as the first governor of Southwest Africa, the man who had shaped that harsh and backward territory into a colony of the Reich. That he had done so by the most enlightened and diplomatic means was quite astonishing; for though a friend of Cecil Rhodes, he seemed never to have been influenced by the repressive methods of the British, but had labored long and earnestly to establish a policy of rapport with the native chieftains, bringing in doctors and medicine to their tribes, and demanding that the Germans under his jurisdiction treat them with the same civility they would Europeans. It was in the barren, dust-whitened frontier settlement of Windhoek that von Epenstein, a passionate traveler, had first met and become friends with Heinrich, who even then showed the rigors of his work, his face appearing much older than its years, eyes sun-faded and skin deeply crosshatched. His labors were eminently successful, and one assumed that he would receive the recognition he deserved, but though he had been personally appointed by Bismarck, he had never enjoyed the enthusiastic support of the Chancellor, who displayed a marked disinterest in the country's expanding colonies. To Bismarck's way of thinking, the Reich was complete, and all he wished was peace and power within it. Toward this end he had made himself supple enough to bend with the changing winds, and as the country grew more industrialized and the Socialists more vociferous, he tried to cut the ground from under their feet by legislating a series of pioneering social security and labor laws. His entire concern lay in domestic issues, and when Heinrich, with his second wife and three young children, returned from Africa in 1889, there was no dazzling promotion; after a few months of waiting, he was appointed minister to the remote nullity of Haiti. Over the next few years, during which Bismarck was dismissed from office by the young and bellicose Wilhelm II, the ex-Chancellor's conciliatory reforms began stirring strong reactionary currents throughout Germany. Anyone with a progressive tinge was looked upon as an incipient supporter of the Social Democrats; and when Heinrich had returned with his family from Haiti two years ago, in 1896, his reputation for liberalism had put the final damper on his flickering career. There was no further appointment, not even to another backwater. Retired at fifty-six, he moved with his family into a small Berlin apartment, where he was at a loss to know what to do with himself. Sometimes he opened the closet door and stood looking at his officer's uniform from the Austrian and Franco-Prussian wars; other times he would settle into an armchair with the faded volumes of Kleist and Goethe which had held some fascination for him as a young student at Heidelberg; now and then, as a former judge, he evinced interest in some current legal affair; but as time went on, he sank into a routine of schnapps-drinking and long stupefied naps, punctuated by a game of skittles at the local Wirtshaus.

Perhaps he would like to go down to the village now, von Epenstein thought, and look over the skittles ground of the old inn. It was on the tip of his tongue to suggest this, but he refrained. Instead he snapped his fingers at the children, who came running over and lined up before him according to size: first the older boy, twelve; then the two girls, ten and eight; and lastly the five-year-old, von Epenstein's namesake, Hermann. They stood in silence, awaiting his command, which was a request to describe which feature of their new home they liked best.

When the older three had enthusiastically spoken of the dark passageways, the peacocks, the farm animals, von Epenstein looked with slightly narrowed, expectant eyes at his favorite.

"I like the cliff best. I shall climb it."

"Ach, du lieber Himmel," sighed his father, whose voice was drowned out by von Epenstein's burst of laughter as he pulled the child to him with a rough pat of his cheek. "I shouldn't wonder if you could," he said. "Still, you had better wait a few years."

"But no, Pate, I mean today—"

"Did you hear me?"

"Ja, I did, Pate, but I—"

"Did you hear me!"

The child gave a curt nod.

"Then say so."

"I heard you, Pate."

"Gut." He waved the children away. The boys bowed, the girls curtsied—an obeisance on which he insisted from godchildren—and returned to their play, the youngest rushing directly to a pear tree and scrambling up its trunk with a defiant look over his shoulder.

"He is too willful," the old man said.

"Spirited."

No, willful, impossible to control. The fates had conspired to make him so. Haiti, with its earthquakes, its scorpions, its giant ants, had been even more primitive than Windhoek, too primitive for the accouchement of a European woman, or for the raising of a child in its first tender years; and so when Franziska had become pregnant with this child she had made the long voyage back to Germany for her lying-in, and when the infant was two months old she had left it in the care of friends and returned to her husband and three older children.

When the family came back to Germany three years later, they met the child for the first time. He had sobbed mightily, and struck his parents in the face when they tried to embrace him.

Until then the Reichskommissar had been what might be called a father typical of his time and his class, somewhat distant, kindly, always just; but for this child, from the first moment, he had felt an absolute love, deep, poignant, fraught with the understanding of what it was to be abandoned, forgotten, resentful. Gradually, with soothing patience, he had coaxed trust from the small, closed face, and released an unexpected and overwhelmingly affectionate nature. "I'm my papa's darling!" the child was soon calling out to strangers whom they passed on the street, and though he quickly became warm and open with all the family, his father remained the adored one. They were always together. Hand in hand they walked every day to Brandenburg Gate and watched the military parade, for the child loved the rousing music with kettledrums booming, the slamming thud of boots, the spiked helmets flashing. At home he pestered his father to take out his old uniform, which he touched and smelled with awe. Sometimes, when there was a party, the Reichskommissar would even instruct the servant to bring into the child's bedroom the caps and swords of military guests, so that he might admire them while lying in bed, a treat he begged for. He wanted toy soldiers, and was presented with the very best, bright and shiny, row upon row. Whatever he wished, he received.

It was wrong to blame the fates. He himself had sunk into a swamp of sentimentality and indulgence, and the boy was now horribly spoiled. Not that he was a bad chap—that was the problem, you could never be angry with him; he was such a generous, good-hearted little soul, such a pleasure to be around, with his cheerful, handsome little face, so open and earnest in his ways—but headstrong, exhausting. Now he leaped down from the branches of the tree, tearing a long rent in his blouse, and charged off with an imaginary rifle in his hands.

"If I were you," von Epenstein remarked, "I'd bundle him off to a military academy."

"My dear Epenstein, the boy is five."

It was like von Epenstein to forget such small things. There was not a practical bone in his body, though God knew he tendered advice on every possible matter, writing constant letters to the parents of his many godchildren—a confirmed bachelor, he had set himself up as patron saint to other people's offspring—instructing them on how to educate their sons, marry their daughters, invest their money. If they took offense, it made no dent on him. What a marvelous nature to have been blessed with, and everything fallen into his lap—family, title, wealth; and then to be an excellent surgeon as well—he was retired now, though only in his forties. How sweet to retire because you wished to. . . .

"Does it really seem right," the old man asked suddenly, his voice sharp with grandiloquent self-irony, "that in our thriving, our pulsing, our magnificent Fatherland, filled from one glorious end to the other with opportunities such as have never been seen before, does it really seem right—"

Von Epenstein had heard these words many times; they were justified, but tiresome. "Think of it as God's will, Heinrich," he broke in, not unkindly, but succinctly. "There is no point in carrying on."

The old man rubbed his eyes, which were watering again, and after a space of silence asked if the tour was finished. If so, he would return to the house.

The residence was built into part of the east wall, with its rear windows overlooking the valley. Though some of its stonework remained from the residence of the Prince Bishops, most of the building dated from only eighty years before. It was a long two-story manor house of simple, even plain appearance, newly whitewashed, with a sloping red tile roof and two rows of windows bright with potted geraniums. Inside, von Epenstein had had the rooms furnished to create the heavy medieval atmosphere he felt most at home in. The furniture was dark, massive; the walls were hung with tapestries and weapons; full suits of armor stood in corners. An eclectic leaning was evident in the Oriental carpets and crystal chandeliers, yet in no way did they disturb the oppressive Gothic harmony throughout.

Though not arrayed in the elaborate court uniforms of the retainers in von Epenstein's Austrian castle, the servants at Burg Veldenstein were dressed in tasteful light-blue-and-black livery, and went about their duties with the quiet efficiency that marked their role in life. It could not be told by their expressionless faces, but they were greatly relieved to find that they were not to serve the demanding von Epenstein, but rather the couple who had arrived just before him yesterday, an oddly matched pair united only by a pleasantly unassuming manner. The Frau Reichskommissar was at least twenty-five years younger than her husband, and by her accent and demeanor a very southern Bavarian. Robust, full-breasted, fresh-faced, with luminous green-blue eyes, her rich dark blond hair worn up in a fashionable frizz, she had an easygoing manner almost masculine in its heartiness. But there was nothing else masculine about her, and as the day wore on it became increasingly clear that she was Ritter von Epenstein's mistress. Not that the least hint was revealed by glance or gesture; the fact was simply there, as if in the air, one of the many kinds of invisible situations one had grown sensitive to over years of mute, watchful service. One noticed that the old Herr Reichskommissar lived in his own little world, that he was a failure of some sort, and that he obviously had a good deal of melancholy recourse to the bottle. With his stiff, formal manner he was a typical Preusse, but he was courteous and seemed kind, and one had felt a certain sympathy while showing the old cuckold to his room, one of the smaller ones, the master bedroom having been reserved for the Ritter. But when it had spread through the servants' quarters that the youngest child, the infant, in an unvaryingly blue-eyed, fair-haired family, was the image of the dusky von Epenstein, the sympathy had turned to cheerful contempt. They had gotten up a bet last night that the Frau Reichskommissar would lose her way in the unfamiliar dark halls while seeking the master bedroom, and that she would be found at dawn still wandering in circles, frozen to the bone. But apparently her sense of direction was as solid as the rest of her, at least according to the upstairs maid who had this morning set to rights the great, silk-canopied, wildly disordered bed.

Chapter 4

For the gardeners and handymen it was a jolting experience to see someone racing along the walls and leaping across apertures—a child's small, speeding form silhouetted against the sky. Each day he was reported to his parents, scolded, punished; and the next day was back on the ramparts.

"Have you ever seen an egg that has been dropped from a great height, Hermann?" asked his brother, Karl. "Do you know what it looks like? That is what you will look like one of these days."

To the child, it seemed that that was what Karl would look like were he to run along the walls, because Karl was not a boy who knew what to do with his feet.

"I won't fall," he said.

"How do you know? What if you jumped into a river because you thought you wouldn't drown?"

The little River Pegnitz wound past the foot of the cliff, green and shimmering, and there he went the following day, slipping out through the burg gate and hurrying down the steep cobbled streets of the village. Along the bank he stopped, pulled off his blouse and shoes, held his breath and made a flying leap, landing with a splash and sinking like a stone. Before his lungs burst he popped back up and began thrashing his arms and legs, which was how people were said to swim. He managed to keep afloat, if swallowing a good deal of water, and

even found enjoyment in his furious white splashing; t
churned his way into the muddy reeds, he climbed out and
self down, panting and satisfied.

The sun sprayed through the trees, dappling the earth   , on,
and bringing into his mind another, earlier patch of earth. That was in
Fürth, where he had lived with the people on whose doorstep he had
been thrown. In their garden he had had a patch of ground that was
his alone, no one could pry him from it. He had been especially fond
of the fallen walnuts, he had fed them and talked to them, put them to
bed in small holes and in the mornings wakened them with loud greetings. One day he was torn from his patch of ground and taken to a big
town called Berlin, where he was to meet those who had thrown him
on the doorstep. During the whole train trip he had sat huddled up,
refusing to speak. He had himself, and in his pocket one hastily
grabbed walnut.

He seldom thought about those days. Because suddenly there had
been something like a giant somersault, and from then on he woke up
every day wondering what marvelous thing he could do for his Vati. If
he could only fight for Vati in a battle, lay down his life for him; instead, for Vati's birthday, he spent laborious hours cutting out wonderful stars, elephants, cats and swords from colored paper. Vati and he
were always together. They sat side by side on the sofa. They took
walks. Almost every day they went to Brandenburg Gate, a big arch
with a chariot and horses on top, and watched the Kaiser's army march
by with drums booming and black boots slamming down in the
Stechschritt, the stab-step. On his last birthday he had been given his
own Hussar uniform. It was covered with gold braid and had a cape
folded smartly over one shoulder. He dressed in this whenever they
went to Brandenburg Gate. He would very much miss the Kaiser's
army, but to live in a fortress castle was even better. In the Berlin
apartment there had been nothing to climb but the banisters.

He discovered that the door of the watchtower creaked open if
you pushed your whole weight against it. Inside it was black. He
groped his way up a ladder built into the wall, and at first he could
hear birdcalls and voices from the yard coming through the half-open
door below, but then, as he climbed higher and higher, there was absolute silence. The blackness never changed, nor the stale, close air. Then
suddenly, on the sixth, the final, landing, he stood up in a shock of
light. The windows were blinding slots. Sunlight poured through with
the four winds. The winds whirled, keened, whipped his clothes. Hoist-
ing himself into one of the deep, stony slots, he leaned into the battering wind and saw below him a green and startling vastness. He had
traveled in trains and carriages, and had seen trees and fields go by,

but he had not known they were connected in a hugeness, or that such hugeness could fit into your own two small eyes.

One day he and his two sisters came upon a plaque set above an archway. It was dated 1468. The older of his sisters, Olga, squinted up at it for a while. Then she read haltingly:

"'Master builder Erhart has made these walls towers and doors. May God and the heavenly hosts protect them. Amen.'"

"Amen," he said.

"That's a coat of arms," she said, pointing above it.

"What's a coat of arms?"

"It's a family's special sign."

"Is it ours?"

"It must be."

Karl liked to lie on the grass reading. Sometimes his younger brother would come rushing over and fling himself down to talk, and although he was well coordinated for his age, direct and certain in his movements, he was nothing more than a five-year-old in his conversation, and given to high, piping exclamations of *Quatsch!*—rubbish—when he disagreed with what you said. His great subject was soldiers and war, and before succumbing to impatience and turning back to his book, Karl would try to instill in the naïve mind his own solid and clear-cut beliefs.

"War is a thing of the past, Hermann. Running around shooting at one another is primitive. We have advanced beyond that stage."

It was evident that if Hermann did not understand each word, he nevertheless took in the idea, for there came the high, piping "Quatsch!"

"It's called progress. There's no longer any use for war."

"Quatsch! I saw the Kaiser's army in Berlin, with sabers and rifles, and they've got cannon too."

"They'll never use them. They're just symbols of a bygone era."

Hermann went to his father and asked him.

"Karl is an optimist," his father said.

"What does that mean?"

"It means he's wrong."

The child's face lit up. "Oh good! I'm glad, aren't you, Vati?"

"No, I'm not glad."

The child's face fell. "But why not?"

His father sighed. "It would be too hard to explain, Hermann."

He and Vati still took walks together, across the lawns of the courtyard; but Vati's step seemed slower, and he said little. He did not seem happy here in their burg. Mutti was always happy, and she was happiest when Pate visited, which was easy to understand. Pate was strict, but he lit everything up. Pate was a *Ritter*, a knight, second only to the Kaiser. And when Pate came last time he had brought him fifty fine Prussian Guardsmen, so that he now possessed almost a thousand lead soldiers. He loved their smell of lead, and the heavy lead weight of each in his hand. He used complicated strategy, frowning and setting them this way and that, and then, when the time came, he banged them together with splendid hard clunks. He found that if he took the mirror down and propped it next to them, he could double his forces.

In the autumn Karl went off to boarding school in Leipzig and the girls began attending the village school and he was alone. Every day he climbed the watchtower and sat in one of the narrow slots at which a flesh-and-blood bowman from long ago had once stood watch. He knew about bowmen because of the history books Vati read to him from. He knew that history went far, far back, and that the burg did too, and that it was already very old when Master Builder Erhart made new walls and arches. Vati said the burg was built a thousand years ago—a thousand!—when many fortresses were set up against Magyar invasions, and he said history went back even before that, another full thousand years before that, and Vati read aloud from the history books all the things that had happened in these many many centuries.

At the start stood Germany's savior, Hermann. Hermann, as the child saw him, was dressed in a bearskin and had great curved horns coming out of his head, and both he and Pate were named after this powerful being; then came the bowmen, and then knights in armor seated on plunging chargers, and then kings, many of them, in powdered wigs, in silk sashes and furs, with one hand pointing to the flames of battle and the other resting on the hilt of a saber, and then came the soldiers of Kaiser Wilhelm I, all the brave Hussars galloping to glory through bursting shells—and it was all connected, from the very beginning up to this very minute, and it was all Germany; his first patch of ground in Fürth, that was Germany; and the long parade street in Berlin, that was Germany; and this greatness of forests and fields below, that was Germany; and the stone of this slot he sat in, this very wind that whipped his blouse and roared in his ears—all was Germany.

One day he saw a battle unfold on the fields below. It was a battle of knights on chargers, and it was not made of thin black lines as in the book illustrations, but was solid and filled with color: bright shields of every hue, long flapping banners, broadswords that flashed in the sun, and in his ears came the rumble of hoofs, the clashing of metal; then suddenly it was gone, and the fields lay still and green.

Chapter 5

I N the summers, if Pate was not off traveling somewhere, they stayed with him in his castle in Austria. They went the first time in the opening year of the new century, 1900, when Hermann was seven and a general of the Boers. On his head was the Boer slouch hat Vati had given him. It was cocked at an angle, and tied smartly at the chin with a leather thong. Vati himself looked fresh and snappy in a white linen suit and broad-brimmed straw hat—it was what he must have worn on his voyages to Africa and Haiti, his outfit for adventure. In the dark foredawn chill, with the servants standing in a row before the door, waving, the family climbed up and settled themselves into two carriages, the drivers cracked their whips, and the great journey began.

Along the steep, twilit streets of the village a few people, already up and about, turned and bowed as the carriages clattered past them, down to the little brick railroad station where there was a yawning wait until the local train came puffing in. Inside, he threw himself down by a window and flattened his nose against the glass. Wreathes of mist hung between the dark pines slipping by, and mist rose like steam from the river, still sleepy and black with night. Now and again, silhouetted against the gray sky, high on a dark fist of rock, a ruined castle traversed the window, while in between there flashed the damp greenness of meadows with birds fluttering up. It was strange to be deep inside his view from the tower. Everything was close and detailed—a single bird taking wing, a green branch quivering—and soon, in less than an hour, there would be the same astonishing deep-insidedness of Nuremberg, hidden just over the wooded range of hills.

But there was no imperial city to be seen, nothing but brick factory buildings and gravel and train tracks, and then, with a screech of whistles and a jolt, a sooty brick station. "Never fear," said Vati as they climbed out into a din of whistles and hissing steam. "Come. We must be quick." And everyone hurried after him. Mutti and the nursemaid whisked Albert, the two-year-old, along between them, while Mutti's personal maid, Nikki, carrying a big wicker basket, brought up the rear. Karl was told to help her, and he fell back coldly to do so—he disliked servants, but who could ponder that while hurrying with such excitement behind Vati's heels? They pressed through crowds, around piles of luggage, down passages and up stairs, and then, all at once, they stood in the open doorway of the station. Vati pointed. There, across the street, colossal and washed to purest gold by the morning sun, was the ancient city wall with two round towers, while behind it soared the palisades of the city itself, a wonder of towers and pointed roofs and spires, all drenched and glittering in the fresh early light. Hermann had only a glimpse, then they were hurrying back through the crowds and climbing aboard a longer and more serious-looking train than the local one.

He fell asleep under Vati's arm. When he awoke, the red plush compartment was warm and everyone was reading or dozing. The countryside was flat, like a plate. The wheels clicked, clicked, and every once in a while the train gave a whistle that rose straight up, high, and then fell sharply back in the wind like a shot soldier.

The Munich train station was a cathedral; and when they climbed out and looked up, the vaulted ceiling of pale green glass was so high that you felt dizzy, and the crowd's noise bounced and echoed all around. After they were settled into another train there was a long wait. Albert fussed in the heat, while Hermann and Paula and Olga drew pictures with melting crayons. Then there was a jolt and they were off again, still heading south.

"Now we go east," Mutti said suddenly. She got up and cranked the top half of the window down. It was her home country, and as he and the other children crowded around her, as he held on to his Boer hat and peered into the bright sunlight, she leaned out pointing and describing everything. The big green hills and blue lakes made Mutti happy. Her high-piled blond hair came undone in the wind, but she didn't care. "That's where you were born, Hermann!" she cried as they passed a town called Rosenheim. "Home of the Roses! Did you know that?" He didn't know. He stared as the town went by. "And down the other way—oh, I wish you could see Bad Reichenhall, Berchtesgaden, so beautiful! Oh the view, the air, the appetite it gave you—oh we must

eat, Nikki!" she cried, laughing, and Nikki threw open the wicker basket and began passing napkins around. As if on a picnic, hungry, and
with much chatter and laughter, they ate sliced ham with chunks of
dark bread, drank apple juice from collapsible silver cups, and finished
up with sticky imported dates and oranges. He kept his eye open for a
sign saying Austria. There was none, but soon after Nikki had packed
the remains back into the basket, the train stopped before a small
flower-bordered station and they were in Salzburg.

While the others sat on benches, he and Paula went off to explore.
They came back with a small motheaten dog, and persuaded Nikki to
give it what was left in the basket. Nikki was not young, but she was
loud and jolly as a schoolgirl, and she often fell in with your plans.
"Nikki," he whispered, "we want to take him with us to Mauterndorf,
and then home to Veldenstein."

"Well, you can't. If it was up to you the house would be stuffed
with dogs and cats and sick chickens. Where would the rest of us live?"

Mutti was rising from her bench. "Hermann, Paula, say goodbye to
the dog—please don't carry on. Everyone, we must go—the train is
coming. Heinrich, wake up—wake up, the train is coming! Gott, how
the man can sleep!"

He and Paula tried to squeeze their bedraggled friend into Nikki's
basket, and when that failed, explosively, with ringing barks and clattering silverware, the two of them were dragged off, bereft and tearful.
In the train it was hot, and they slept.

When he woke, Vati was carrying him across a dusty village square.
There was a white church with a top like an onion, and hazed blue
mountains rising straight up. Surrounded by a group of gaping, barefoot children, Pate's great open carriage stood waiting.

They started the last leg of the journey. The horses clopped out of
the square toward the mountains, which grew clearer and greener all
the time. They began to climb. They stared up at the woods and meadows that clung to the slopes. The meadows looked like velvet, a burning green-gold, and they were so steep you wondered how the cows
could stand there, but they did, casting long violet shadows like ribbons. "This is nothing yet, you northerners," Mutti laughed, opening
her big needlepoint satchel and distributing shawls, because the air was
growing cool. The wind grew stronger and stronger until his teeth
chattered and the valley they had come from lay far, far below.

Everything was crude and savage at the top, rocks and gravel,
boulders big as houses, coarse brown grass whipping in the wind,
blinding patches of snow, and the sky huge, pure, so blue and brilliant
your eyes hurt. He wanted to bang open the carriage door and leap out
into that great windy glare, but already they were descending; the
brown grass turned gradually green again, the wind softened, and over

the side of the carriage he could see another deep valley appear, caught like a shield in the sinking sun.

The road curved down and down, and after a while they took off their shawls. When they reached the floor of the valley the sun was gone, and the heat of the evening hung dusty and blue around them, like smoke. They drove alongside the dark mass of a forest, and they could smell the biting tang of pine. Then they turned a bend, and before them, pale and soaring in the dusk, stood Schloss Mauterndorf.

The carriage rumbled over a wooden bridge into a stone courtyard filled with the splashing of a fountain, and, so tired they could hardly move, they climbed out to the boomed greetings of Pate, standing with arms akimbo at the top of the stairs. Then there was a confused bustle, a bite to eat, and Mutti sent them straight off to bed. Vati said he was tired too, and came with them, his nice white adventure suit wilted and wrinkled from the trip.

Each day dinner was announced by the blast of a hunting horn, and down great halls you hurried to be on time, otherwise Pate was angry. The dining hall seemed about the same size as the Munich train station, and the table as long as a train coach. There was a gallery overhead where musicians, dressed as minstrels, played and sang while you ate. A footman, in velvet coat and breeches and powdered wig, stood at attention behind each diner. Pate ate a great deal of food. He finished every course and at the same time he gave all his views on politics and history and also managed to keep the footmen on their toes by barking at them. They went meekly. Everyone was meek with Pate, even Mutti, who was always so spirited and outspoken. She sat eating quietly, smiling, her cheeks pink.

Vati's wineglass kept filling up. There were many different wines, and after the meal brandy was served, and since Karl was fourteen he was allowed the great treat of a drop, which unfortunately he hated but which he drank or else Pate would be offended. Servants came around with silver boxes of cigars, cheroots, cigarettes; Mutti lifted out an oval perfumed Turkish cigarette, and the servant, bowing, struck a long matchstick with a breathtaking flourish and lit it. Then, bowing again, he lit Vati's cigar and Pate's cheroot, and Pate leaned back in his polished throne of a chair and continued his speeches. By that time Hermann and his sisters and brother were numb in their behinds from having sat so long, but they kept their spines straight and continued looking attentively at Pate.

At home they went to the village church every Sunday and sat in the front pew. This was because if you lived in a castle you sat in the front pew. Here at the Mauterndorf village church they sat with Pate in the front pew, and he himself sat beside Pate because he was the favorite. This filled him with pride, but did not help to make church less tiresome. When he was twelve he would have to decide if he wanted to be a Catholic like Mutti or a Lutheran like Vati, but he could not imagine wanting to be either, since he would rather spend his Sundays playing outside. On the other hand, one was obliged to keep up traditions. There was no way to avoid church if you lived in a castle and were connected to history. It was one of the things you must bear without a twinge, like getting wounded in battle.

You could wander at will through Mauterndorf. Some rooms held drums, lionskins and spears that Pate had brought back from Africa. Others were filled with strange objects from places like China, Ceylon, Iceland, and the walls of some rooms bristled with antlers, and the walls of others were hung from top to bottom with gloomy paintings in heavy gold frames. You could spend a whole day looking, but the outdoors tore you away early.

There were picnics on mountain slopes, with the soft distant clunk of cowbells, and an abundance of Sachertortes. There were excursions in Pate's white Benz motorcar, horribly exciting even though the machine could not be opened up to its full speed on the rough country roads. There was a party in the meadow below the castle, a feast with suckling pigs on spits, to which all the neighbors came, from the biggest estate owners to the poorest peasants with their big red hands and drawling speech. The peasants had many children, and he played wildly with them into the night, while a brass band filled the starry sky with music and the grown-ups danced polkas and waltzes, their figures lit red by bonfires.

There was a shoot, too, toward the end of their stay. The party set off before dawn and came tramping back before noon, Pate striding ahead of everyone in his medieval hunting costume—deerskin vest and white blouse with flowing sleeves, a jeweled dagger in his broad black belt. The beaters were in medieval costume too, and looked splendid in their peaked green caps with long feathers. But the deer were tied to poles by their hoofs, and were carried along with their fine small heads dangling just above the grass. As his eyes had followed the dangling creatures across the meadow, he had felt a great hope that they would come back to life later on, but when he had expressed this hope to Pate that evening, he had received a lecture. The animals had been killed quickly and cleanly. There were amateurs, Pate said, who came down in droves from Vienna and mangled their quarry. *That* was monstrous. To kill cleanly was not. There were honorable rules of conduct in the forest, just as there were on the battlefield, and the wild creatures were noble adversaries whose skill deserved the honor of your own skill.

One thing was certain, Pate ended, there was no room for sniveling on either side.

Karl said it was a lot of blather, Pate just liked to collect heads, look at the walls filled with them. But Karl was not a boy who knew things. His nostrils could never sniff an approaching thunderstorm. His eyes never saw a cow pie until his foot had stepped in it. And his ideas about war had already been squashed by the Boers.

In the evenings there were sometimes musicales. Pate got famous singers from Berlin and Vienna, friends of his, to come and fill the music room with their voices. The music room was gold, with scenes from operas painted on the walls. The guests sat on chairs and settees with pale green velvet seats, and there were pale green velvet drapes at the tall windows, through which, while you listened, you could see the mountain peaks turn blue with dusk. The singers from Vienna sang gaily, those from Berlin sang Wagner. Most of Wagner was so excruciatingly dull that he feared he would become insane sitting motionless and silent in his spotless white sailor suit. Yet sometimes there came a part that was towering, burning, wild, and he listened with indrawn breath. He described everything from the musicales to Vati, because Vati did not always attend, although he loved music and was known to have had one of the finest baritones in his regiment. You might never see Vati's face except at dinner if you did not go to his room every day, fearing that he was lonely. He said he liked to stay there, to catch up on his reading. He must have read many books by now. Mutti, on the other hand, had no time to read. She was hostess at every social event, and in fact she did not even sleep in the same wing as the rest of the family, but in a wing closer to all that was going on. It was an honor to be hostess at Mauterndorf, his sister Olga said. One had to have taste, charm and a strong constitution to keep up with the pace.

He and the other children spent much time in the meadow below the castle. Little Albert came along with Mutti's maid, Nikki, because the nursemaid was distressed by thistles and bugs, and by the birds that aimed their droppings directly at her fine straw hat. But Nikki liked everything, and she chased Albert through the grass, and gathered wildflowers with the girls, and joked and laughed and squealed. Karl would glare over his book and mutter, "That Dummkopf. That Possenreisserin!"

"I like Nikki!" Hermann protested.

Karl would ignore him, and keep glaring. One day he called to Olga, who came running over. "What is she always laughing about?" Karl asked her. "Does she talk to you about Vati?"

"Vati? Why should she talk about Vati?"

"Because she's an idiot. Does she?"

"Talk about Vati? What do you mean?"

"Nothing. Go and play." He turned back to his book, smacking flat the pages, and Hermann, looking at him, felt a peculiar blow to his heart. He had no idea why this should be. He scrambled to his feet and walked off alone. The air, so hot, quivered like water; in it quivered birdcalls and the droning of insects, and through it quivered the blue-hazed mountains; and after a while he forgot the lingering heaviness in his chest and chased Paula at top speed through the grass, until they fell sprawling and laughing in its hot green pungence.

At night, through the windows of his bedroom, could be heard a gay and distant thumping, which was the brass band playing in the village square. And often there was music from inside the castle, too, the sound of a big party. When Mutti came in to say goodnight before one of these parties, she looked wonderful in a long gown that trailed behind her, her gold hair piled up in ringlets, and her eyes, which were a beautiful green-blue color, filled with little lights of excitement. She sat on the bed and talked with him, in her jolly, beaming way, then she hugged and kissed him goodnight, and he lay back and closed his eyes, savoring the lingering scent of her perfume. He was asleep before he knew it, and already waking to the pleasures of the new day.

But by the long summer's end he was happy to have come and happy to be going home again, to his soldiers and his tower.

Chapter 6

Two months later von Epenstein received a brief note from the old Reichskommissar: Hermann had started school in the village but he was not flourishing there. Although seven was a young age for boarding school, he and Franziska had settled upon an establishment in Fürth. With respectful regards.

Von Epenstein sat back with a pitying shake of his head, yet at the same time could not keep a laugh from setting his stomach awobble beneath his satin dressing gown. Every line was a perfect marvel of self-deception, but "not flourishing"—that was a masterstroke, considering that the boy had been permanently expelled and was now driving a tutor to the point of madness.

The Ritter and his beloved carried on a voluminous correspondence, erotic, sentimental and not without its practical side, Franziska unburdening herself of household and family problems and von Epenstein replying with avalanches of advice. Not long ago Franziska had written, "Hermann seems to think himself appointed from on high to destroy the entire British army. This was also the schoolmaster's opinion when he asked us to remonstrate with the boy, canings and lectures having had no effect on his Boer zest, which apparently whipped his comrades into such melees that the other children ran shrieking to the four corners of the schoolyard. The master was dreadfully sorry to trouble us, oh so dreadfully respectful—I sometimes find the respect that surrounds us odious, why didn't he just say the boy was impossible? I love Hermann dearly, but I would have had to agree."

Von Epenstein sent her a list of punishments, but her next letter informed him that Hermann had led a schoolyard battle in which a boy was knocked so hard to the ground that he sustained a concussion. "That was the end of school, of course. Heinrich gave him *such* a thrashing, but it hurt Heinrich a good deal and Hermann not at all, since he is insensible to pain. At present we have a tutor for him, but the poor young man exerts no authority. Hermann pays no attention to him except to talk about the Boers or to explain the maneuvers of his toy soldiers, and if the tutor insists on schoolwork Hermann simply lies down on the bed and pulls the covers over his face. Yet, for all this, the poor crazed fellow is genuinely fond of him. I am very much afraid that this will always be Hermann's problem."

"I am very much afraid," von Epenstein had written back, "that Hermann's problem is due for a change of scene. Heinrich must make arrangements at the following school in Fürth, which is of good reputation, and no great distance from Veldenstein, so that you will be able to visit him from time to time. . . ."

The cliff had had a wild, dry, crumbly smell. It was ancient rock, eaten by wind, shattered everywhere by deep brooding wrinkles. It had long gnarled roots clamped tight to it, like ancient fingers, dusty and fibrous, and there were broken shells, fragments of speckled brown which were ancient too, the splattered eggs of medieval hawks. When he had looked down over his shoulder at the broadening valley below, his hot face felt a high rippling freshness, and when he glanced upward he saw the burg wall soaring straight up into the blue sky. Once he had slipped and almost fallen, had laced his arms with red and felt a sharp bitterness like metal in his mouth, and that was the taste of death, a sharp metal taste. At last gaining the top, climbing up onto the narrow ledge from which the burg wall rose, he stood up and turned around, trembling with exertion, and gave a salute to the great distances below.

He had done that, and he had that to remember. He also had one soldier, a battered grenadier, who sat deep in his pocket. Mutti and Vati were with him, but he did not look at them. He looked out the train window. Harvested fields slipped by, trees with yellow leaves. The Pegnitz had yellow leaves floating on its surface. Soon they would stop at Nuremberg, but he would not be getting off there. They were taking him to the black hole of Fürth.

In mid-December he was back on the train. Black Fürth grew smaller and smaller. The wheels clicked, snowflakes whirled past the window. Mutti and Vati were again with him, but there was no conversation, because other people sat in the compartment. In silence he looked out at the snow lying thick and smooth across the fields, covering the roofs of cottages. As they drew nearer and nearer to home, lights began going on in the villages, clusters of warmth in the swirling dusk.

There had been a sickness in him these past weeks that made him weep shamedly under his blankets at night, a horror that they would vanish while he was gone—Mutti and Vati, especially Vati, he would die because he was old, and never would they see each other again. But there had been no joyous reunion when his parents came to the school to take him home. Only sternness and silence, and here the train was pulling into Neuhaus's little brick station and they were still stern and silent.

In the study Vati went over to his desk and sat down, while Mutti walked restlessly around the room picking dead leaves from plants. It struck him that that was how they always were: Vati sitting still and Mutti moving, and a whole room always between them.

Finally Vati spoke, listing the reasons for his expulsion. His voice was hard, and he bent a finger back with each reason until all five fingers were bent back. Fighting. Interrupting in class. Low grades. Two attempts to run away. And the final, unforgivable incorrectitude, when, in answer to the headmaster's question as to whether or not he intended to carry on this way, he had answered, "Ja, Herr Direktor. Ganz." Absolutely.

The old Reichskommissar continued looking with severity at his son when he was finished. The child's face bore a properly serious but rather abstract look of wrongdoing, while underneath this expression was something not abstract, something deeply unhappy mixed with something begging to be deeply happy. It was a thin, finely sculpted face, slightly marred by large outstanding ears like the Reichskommissar's own. Below the short-cropped fair hair the eyes were Franziska's pale, brilliant blue-green. The mouth was long, at the moment mute and as compressed as his own. For the Reichskommissar had no idea in the world what further to say. All he wanted was to draw the boy to him in an enveloping embrace, to let him stay and grow up like a savage if he wished, for he was too tired, too miserable, to cope with the future of anyone, not even that of this most precious small being who stood before him.

Mutti's voice finally broke the silence. "You will only be sent to another school. Don't you realize that, Hermann?"

"But not till after Christmas—?" he asked quickly, turning to her with a stab of bleakness. "Please can't I stay just for Christmas? Please, Mutti, I should so like to—"

"But how can you ask such a silly thing?" she asked sharply, as if pained. "Did you think we would throw you out into the snow? Ach, Hermann, really—"

And suddenly the reunion he had longed for was real, for Mutti was coming over to him, kissing him and ruffling his hair, and with an exasperated shake of her head was sending him over to his father, who was sitting forward from his chair with arms outspread—two hops and into his lap, his beloved Vati, alive and real, with his sorely missed Vati-smell of cigars and talcum and schnapps, the unbelievable happiness. . . .

At six o'clock on Christmas Eve, he and his sisters and brothers, sitting in their finest clothes on the stairway, heard the long-awaited voice of Nikki calling that all was ready. Jumping up and dragging Albert along, the others ran pell-mell—even tall Karl—to the drawing-room doors, which were being opened wide. Quiet now, flushed with excitement, they walked into the room. Mutti and Vati stood together by the tree, a great fir lit by hundreds of burning candles, filling the room with an overwhelming sense of forests and stars. Everyone joined hands, family and servants, forming a circle around the tree, and their voices lifted in "Stille Nacht, Heilige Nacht," while beyond the burning candles, and the bright chandelier, and the fire crackling in the grate, beyond the tall windows, with their blue velvet drapes drawn back, the snow fell silently, with a feeling of something eternal, down the ancient, dark face of the cliff.

New Year's Eve was clear as glass, black, filled with frosty stars. All the villagers came tramping into the courtyard, some of the men tipsy and singing, everyone bundled to the ears and breathing out white puffs. Yellow lanterns beside them, retainers had the fireworks ready as Hermann studied the minute hand of Vati's pocket watch, holding it tensely before his eyes. Vati, standing behind him, had said he could call out the moment.

Hermann's forefinger went up slowly.

"Now!" he cried. "Mitternacht!"

There was an upward hissing and whistling, and to the sound of a collective "ah," the black sky flared with gold, blue, red, with sweeping arcs and umbrellas of embers, so many that you hardly knew where to look, and as soon as one went out another burst in its place, shooting bright filaments that dropped in showers of sparks to the snowy parapets. When the last one had spun itself out and the new year in, there was a great cheer, a glorious roar of "Hurrah! Hurrah!" and caps flew high into the air. Vati lifted him up in his arms, and from that high place, he too cheered, and flung his snowcap high into the sky.

And there, in the darkness, his cap hung suspended for four years, or so it seemed to him: the fireworks gone out, the new year not yet dawned—a black, freezing, permanent midnight of boarding schools.

28 March 1901 "'We hereby inform you that your son Hermann was the instigator of a food strike, during which victuals were hurled across the room and plates banged with great unrestraint upon the tables. He is, with our regrets, dismissed.' Well, Hermann, what have you to say this time?"

"Nothing, Vati. Only I don't know why they mentioned the plates. They didn't break."

8 June 1901 "'With the exception of history, Hermann's marks fall lamentably below our standards. We are sorry to ask that he be withdrawn at term's end.' Well?"

"Well anyway, my history marks are the highest in the class."

27 November 1901 "'. . . he is a disturbing and destructive element, a boy who literally knocks his classmates' heads together if his ideas are not immediately followed. It is impossible for us to further tolerate this kind of behavior.'"

"Ja, but Vati, they were such a bunch of slowpokes."

4 April 1902 "'Hermann is a good fellow, but a bit difficult. This is a boy who likes to have his own way. He is a born revolutionary.'"

"I think this one's quite nice, Vati."

"A dismissal, nevertheless."

At some point his acute homesickness had passed, but he remained hateful of the schools. They were the best in the country, but so drab and stingy that it was clear their only purpose was to make you as miserable as possible. Breakfast was black bread with lard, washed down with malt coffee; for dinner there was watery potato soup and tough Rindfleisch. The dormitories were bare and drafty, and you were required to sweep and mop them yourselves. He hated the strict silence and stuffy smell of the classroom, the absolute rule of the master in his chalk-dusted black suit, the crushing seriousness with which grammar and sums and French declensions were treated. He intended to enter a military academy when he was eleven. There was no need to waste time on these pointless subjects.

He knew that Pate was deeply displeased with him, and he counted it a blessing that his godfather's travels prevented a summer visit for two years running. When the family went back, in 1903, he climbed out

of the carriage with a knot in his stomach to face the resplendent figure
on the steps.

"So there you are—come up here, you miserable disgrace! Im-
proving, are you? Thrown out only once this year? Wunderbar!—we
must be thankful for small mercies!" And Pate was actually laughing,
shaking hands with him and sending him inside with a crashing slap to
his bottom.

Chapter 7

THAT summer he grew to understand Pate better. Pate admired a rebellious spirit. Certainly he did not admire quiet Karl, who, apparently realizing this, had not even come along this year but had taken himself off on a walking tour through the Schwarzwald. Nor did Pate admire little Albert, a pale, housebound child prone to asthma. Pate admired someone who broke rules, as long as they were other people's rules. In Pate's presence, of course, absolute obedience was demanded. This made perfect sense; the Kaiser also demanded absolute obedience.

Pate had been to royal fêtes in Berlin, had actually chatted and laughed with the Kaiser. Sometimes at dinner he talked of these occasions, and once a foreigner had asked some idiotic things. To his knowledge Hermann had never before seen a foreigner; this was a vacationing American who had come down from Munich with some friends of Pate's, a young man of earnest appearance who used the same fork for each course. He spoke a fantastic German, enough to make you burst into laughter except that to do so would have been rude. This young man, with his earnest face and wrong fork, had turned to Pate at the head of the long polished table and said, "Baron von Epenstein, does one think after these years that your Wilhelm, to dismiss Bismarck was not wise to Germany to do?"

One expected Pate's voice to splatter the young man's face like a cannonball. Instead, he had replied with the thrilling lightness of a saber slash.

"Bismarck was right for his day. The Kaiser is right for his. The Kaiser, incidentally, is not referred to as Wilhelm, unless one happens to be the Kaiserin."

The young man's face turned red, but he went on. "Is it not so, however, that when it was the Boxer Rebellion the Kaiser have called his soldiers Huns and have greatly cheered them to disport itselves like the Hordes of Attila?"

Even then Pate did not grow angry. "The Kaiser speaks impetuously. It is his character."

"He speaks much of encirclement, this is a word what I am everywhere in Germany hearing. Who, I beg to know, encircles you?"

"Pray ask fewer questions, my young friend, but continue your tour of Europe. Travel. Look. Listen. You may in time find yourself relieved of your oppressive ignorance."

That ended the questioning. The red-faced young man went back to his food. It was a shame to see his embarrassment. *Einkreisung.* Encirclement. Everyone knew what that meant. If children were not forbidden to speak at the table, he would have explained to the poor fellow using the wrong fork that all other countries wanted what Germany had.

He had learned a great deal the past few years. For one thing, he had seen a lot of his country, because he had attended so many schools. He had observed and listened, and found words taking root in his mind, like *Einkreisung,* and *Klasse,* and *Juden. Juden* was not an important word; *Juden* were people who were neither Catholic nor Lutheran, and though this irritated some people, he himself could find no interest in the matter. *Klasse* was more interesting, not really a word you heard, but something built like bone structure into life, exceedingly complicated and absolutely inflexible, such as a mathematical formula that could not be altered in the slightest way. First there were families like his own, who were wealthy and lived in their hereditary castles, then came people who might be wealthy but who were in business, then came shopkeepers, carpenters, and so on down to the poor. Yet professors were extremely high, even if they were of modest means, which was why the masters were accorded such great respect. But army officers were the highest of all. Officers could do no wrong whatsoever. And this was so even if they lacked money and title. Yet titles were the greatest thing of all, like Pate, a Ritter and a von. If you had a von you could be a little penniless seamstress and still be high. It was almost too complicated, and he wondered about people like Nikki and Pate's Jagdmeister, both at the bottom, one a servant and the other a peasant, yet both high in his own estimation.

He was spending much time this summer with the Jagdmeister,

learning to shoot, and under his blouse he had accumulated gray bruises, like medals, where the gun kicked painfully against his shoulder. They practiced with targets in the meadow, and when with its violent recoil the rifle went off in his ear, the sound was a thousand times louder than he had dreamed, a shattering explosion that moments later came echoing back from the blue haze of the mountains. The Jagdmeister never spoke, but chewed silently on the stem of his long meerschaum pipe, which wafted a pleasant odor of tobacco through the mixed perfume of grass and nitrate. The Jagdmeister was brown and hardened, like an old tree, or like an old creature of the forest, somehow noble and wisely powerful, with his inward, watching silence. He never explained, he never commented. He showed, and then he watched. Only at the end of the summer, when the boy lowered his gun after the final lesson, did the old man move the pipe to the corner of his mouth and nod.

"Born to it, Junge," he said in his slow mountain dialect, and that was all.

The words still rang in his ears the day of leavetaking, and Pate's congratulatory slap still rested warm between his shoulder blades. Then everyone was climbing up into the carriage, they were clattering out the stone courtyard, rumbling over the little wooden bridge, and he was pointed back to the darkness of school.

He came to understand everything that year, in 1903, when he was ten, but the understanding had already begun the year before, on a rainy spring day when the Boers' defeat appeared in the newspapers. He had been in a school near Bayreuth, and he went to bed and pulled the blankets over his head, refusing to get up or to speak. For two years now, in half a dozen schoolyards, he had fought to the death for the Boers. He believed utterly in the Boers, whose land, belonging to them for centuries, had suddenly been laid claim to by the ravening British. Never once had he thought that these brave, righteous soldiers in their slouch hats could be beaten. The world had been flung upside down; and all morning he lay fuming with misery beneath the blankets, refusing to say anything even when the doctor came, pulled back the blankets, and checked him for some dreadful illness. Then in the afternoon he had suddenly jumped up and departed; hurried to the train depot and bought a ticket home—it was no great distance—where Vati would explain to him this horrible outcome.

He found Vati in his study, asleep in the big carved chair he favored, which was dark and polished, with lion heads at the ends of the arms. His legs were outstretched on the Oriental carpet, pages of the *Berliner Tageblatt* lying by his feet. His pince-nez had slipped off, and there were gray cigar ashes down the front of his morning coat. He slept deeply, with his mouth slightly open. There was no color in his face, except for his closed red eyelids and the broken veins that covered his nose. He smelled faintly of schnapps, and he looked small and shrunken in the big chair. Because the fire had gone out in the grate and the room was cold, Hermann took a coverlet from a settee and spread it gently over Vati's legs. Then he stood looking at his father again, and after a while he went out.

That evening at supper—and there was no talk of the Boers, but only of his breach of conduct in leaving school without permission—he was struck by the way Mutti's words came rolling out full and round, in the easy southern way, while Vati's had the sharp cutting accents of the north. His classmates said he talked sharp, like a Preusse, but they also said he talked a lot, which was like Mutti. He had Vati's ears and Mutti's eyes. He was part of them, but they were not part of each other. They did not even like each other very much.

Afterward, banished to his room, with the rain pouring down the leaded diamond-paned windows, he sat reading one of Karl May's adventure books to Albert, who was always following him around. Albert was not especially interested in adventure stories, but Hermann was fond of his younger brother and believed he would be happier if he could get excited over Karl May the way Hermann himself did. Instead of becoming excited, Albert fidgeted and yawned in his chair, and for some reason Hermann was struck by the darkness of those sleepy eyes and tousled hair, and it came to him that in some peculiar way this was not the child of Mutti and Vati, who did not like each other, but of Mutti and Pate, who did; and he understood this without any sense of astonishment, but as if he had always somehow known it.

Now, after his summer in Mauterndorf, he was at a school in Würzburg. In history class one day they were asked to write an essay on the figure whom they considered to be the greatest of all Germans. Just to upset the master, who was a Frederick the Great fanatic, he chose Pate as his subject. The next day he was called into the headmaster's gloomy office and handed a gloomy-looking book. It was entitled *Almanach de Semi-Gotha*.

The headmaster said: "You will find listed in this book all titled German families of Jewish blood. You will copy out every name from A to E, ending with your von Epenstein. You will then copy down, one hundred times: 'I will not write pieces in praise of Jews.' You will have it on my desk by tomorrow morning."

"But I beg your pardon, Herr Direktor, Herr von Epenstein is Catholic."

"Natürlich! He could not hold a title if he were not a convert. Do as I say."

The headmaster indicated the door, and Hermann went out leafing through the book, still not expecting to find Pate's name there. It was there, however, and he pondered what it meant that Pate was a Jew. All he really knew about Jews was that there were some people who didn't like them, and he had thought this was because they were neither Catholic nor Lutheran. But even when they were Catholic or Lutheran, apparently some people still didn't like them. But Saxons disliked Bavarians, and Bavarians scorned Saxons, and neither could stand the Prussians. Monarchists hated Social Democrats. Those who favored Schubert often despised Wagner. Someone always disliked someone. In any event, he would not write a syllable against Pate.

That afternoon he realized the story had leaked out when a dozen classmates came running over to him in the schoolyard, holding a placard scrawled with *Mein Pate ist ein Jude*. Grabbing his arms and holding him pinioned as he struggled, they hung the thing around his neck, and so decorated he was pulled through the yard until a master interceded with a shout. Pulling off the placard, he began a furious chase to overtake his persecutors, but he saw that they had already vanished; still he kept running, until he was back in the dormitory, where he grabbed a chair and swung it against a window.

Mutti was not delighted to see him walk into the house the next day, dismissed once again. But this time when he told his story, she told him he was in the right.

"I wouldn't want you in that kind of school. Imagine a headmaster with opinions like that, and the students no better. Why, it doesn't sound like Germany at all, but Poland or France. Such an unenlightened attitude. But if you *will* bounce from one school to another, I suppose you are bound to come up against all kinds."

And Vati, when he came home from his skittles at the inn, gave a thoughtful nod.

"You should have said to the headmaster, 'If Epenstein is good enough for the Kaiser, might he not be good enough for you?'"

"I should have struck him!"

"Certainly not! Nor can I countenance your breaking that window. That was sheer primitivism, Hermann. And we shall have to pay for it, you know."

But Vati would not pay a pfennig for that window. He understood all at once, as he listened to Vati's voice rambling on about the impropriety of explosive tempers, that everything was paid for by Pate, that everything was owned by Pate, that Veldenstein—the tower, the ramparts, the cliff—was Pate's, not theirs; and again it was as if he had somehow always known this, and he was not astonished, and yet as it came absolutely clear to him he felt that the ground was breaking beneath his feet, that he was floundering and falling, and yet even as he was falling he was somehow struggling back up and standing steady again, the awful moment behind him. For it was Pate he belonged to. He loved Vati very much; but for a long time now, ever since that rainy spring day the year before, it had been a strange, pitying kind of love, as if Vati had grown smaller and smaller and smaller, until he was smaller than he himself, who was only ten.

And so he came to understand clearly all the murky family things that Karl had used to mutter about and think the servants were gossiping over; and he came to terms with these things and put them in their place and had no interest in them; and Karl had no interest in them either, all he cared for was books and theories; and so there was not much for them to talk about when they saw each other that Christmas. Christmas was almost the only time Karl came home. He had changed a good deal from the year before; he was eighteen now, a university student, a tall stooped fellow in suit and vest, with a cigarette always streaming from his fingers. His hair had grown very long, like a bohemian's, and he pushed it back often, with a world-weary gesture. That was what Olga called it, "world-weary." She was sixteen now, she and Paula were at a girls' school, and she was annoyed that Karl did not consider her a grown-up person like himself, and perhaps world-weary in her own right. But Karl lumped his younger brothers and sisters together as small children.

Except one day when he invited Hermann into his room for a chat.

"Have a seat," he said, and Hermann even thought for a moment that he was going to be offered a cigarette. But Karl merely lit one for himself, blew smoke through his nostrils, and looked at him with great seriousness.

"I've been observing your rambunctious approach to life, Hermann. You don't seem to get any better as you get older. It seems to me that you're interested in nothing but climbing and jumping and scraping your knees. Whenever I hear a sound like thunder outside my door, I know what it is. It's you galloping down the hallway like a horse. Whenever my ears are assailed by loud ringing laughter, I know what it is. It's you, having found something to be hilarious. Too many things strike you as funny, Hermann. Not that there's anything wrong with a cheerful disposition, but you'll be eleven years old in a couple of weeks, and it's time you took serious stock of yourself. I understand that you're between schools at the moment, is that correct?"

Hermann nodded.

"May I ask how many you have now been dismissed from?"

"Rather a lot."

"Rather a lot. Well, let me tell you something. Things don't go on forever. You're a fool to squander a good education. You had better start buckling down and taking advantage of it. That's my advice to you, because we neither of us know when it might be pulled out from under our feet."

"What do you mean, pulled out from under our feet? Nothing's going to be pulled out from under our feet!" And he stamped his foot resoundingly on the floorboards, as if in illustration. "Quatsch!"

"I don't mean literally. And there's no need to squeal."

"I wasn't squealing, I was shouting!"

"Well, don't. Let us discuss things quietly."

Giving another stamp of his foot on the burg's old floorboards, Hermann got up and went over to a window. His high child's voice was calmer.

"Anyway, I don't see that there's anything to discuss. Because I hate school and I just want to be finished with it. And that's all there is to it."

When in June of the following year—he was in a dreary establishment in Ansbach—the long-awaited last day of school arrived, he hurriedly packed his things in the noisy, jubilant dormitory, everyone mad to be off, and suddenly throwing his head back he cried "Mitternacht!" and his old snowcap came falling down from the skies while the long, suspended darkness was swept with fireworks, with the light of life resumed.

Chapter 8

"COULD one have foreseen that our wild, obstinate Hermann would ever do us such credit?" the Frau Reichskommissar wrote von Epenstein when, at sixteen, her son graduated from Karlsruhe Military Academy to the Imperial Cadet College in Berlin. "I still marvel that the hardships he loathed in one boarding school after another he accepted in much severer form at the academy, and not just with good grace but boundless enthusiasm. What a relief it has been to know that he has found his place and is happy. I have said all this before, I know, but I am delighted by the fact—he will of course write you himself—that he graduates with high marks in all his subjects. Even, if you can imagine, in discipline! The report calls him an exemplary pupil, and says further, 'In his five years with us Hermann has developed a splendid quality that should take him far: he is not afraid to take a risk.' I think this is not a quality Hermann actually found necessary to develop, but I am extremely pleased with his accomplishments, and I know, Liebchen, that you will be too."

The Frau Reichskommissar was a youthful forty-three, a vivid, exuberant woman who rose early each day for a brisk canter through the valley, efficiently managed the house, designed her own flamboyant hats, attended plays in Nuremberg and concerts in Bayreuth, and entertained often. Her passion for von Epenstein had been violent, and even now, after fourteen years, though he was growing increasingly rotund and dyed his hair and mustaches—the color came off on the pillowslips—his imperious manner still stirred her satisfactorily. With her large store of common sense she knew the liaison had endured precisely because they saw each other seldom, and she had no quarrel with the faint pang of separation that sometimes visited her. She kept busy and happy, and wrote him with faithful regularity. Having finished and blotted her letter, she took up a recent photograph of Hermann to send with it. A three-quarter-length studio portrait, it showed him with one hand resting stiffly, as if placed there by the photographer, on his hip; the lapels of his military coat had been artfully parted to disclose the two rows of brass buttons and high collar of his tunic; and again as if arranged just so by the photographer, his large, black-visored military cap sat squarely centered on his head. One rarely caught a glimpse of Hermann standing still, and his expression was unexpectedly pensive, quite uncharacteristic, as was so often true of posed pictures; but the rather sad, Hamlet-like gaze did emphasize the unusual beauty of his face—still that of a boy, slender and smooth, though with pronounced chin and square-cut jaw. The nose was slightly curved, the mouth very wide, strongly and beautifully chiseled, its upper lip like a long pair of wings. In the high cheekbones there was perhaps an ancient admixture from East Prussia, as in the faintly Slavic angle of the eyes, which in the gray tones of the photograph showed startlingly light. His one unfelicitous feature was his big protruding ears, which, bracketed to the slender boyish face, gave him the look of a starveling, a waif. Yet even with the ears, it was the face of an unusually attractive youth. Epenstein would be happy to receive this further testament to the general excellence of his namesake, his favorite, the perhaps only true apple of his eye.

The ears, about which the boy had never been sensitive, withdrew from prominence as his face filled out and matured. During his three years at the Imperial Cadet College at Lichterfelde, in the suburbs of Berlin, he developed from a wiry adolescent into a slim, broad-shouldered young man with musculature hard as rock. The shaved head required at the preparatory academy was now allowed a less convictlike appearance, and he sported a glossy crop of dark blond hair parted on the right with military precision. With his lean good looks, his wide spontaneous smile and his impeccable future officer's manner, he made a strong impression on the young ladies whom he met, although he met them under such rigorously formal conditions he had no suspicion of his impact. He was completely without conceit, but was filled with a brimming, somehow detached arrogance, a kind of animal self-certainty so natural, so unconscious, that it had an engaging and tonic quality. Vivid, warm, sure, with his fresh high color and brilliant blue-green eyes, he seemed to emanate an actual physical radiance.

"Mein Gott! Behold the dazzling creature!" he heard someone remark on the street one day, an incredible rudeness which he properly ignored, only to feel a hand grasp his arm and pull him around.

"For such familiarity I await decapitation!" his brother Karl said, smiling and standing back to take in the flared, ankle-length cadet coat, the spotless white gloves, the hilted saber hanging, tasseled, at its elegant angle. "Who is this paragon? Can it really be that little scrape-kneed savage I used to know? This resplendent warrior? This strapping Siegfried?"

"You haven't changed," Hermann laughed, shaking his brother's hand. "Still as sarcastic as ever."

"Ah, but that doesn't mean I'm not impressed. I may dislike the military, but I'm able to appreciate the *beau idéal* in any sphere."

"What rot—either you dislike something or you don't. That's how I feel. Anyway it's wonderful to see you. What are you doing in Berlin?"

"Sitting in at some lectures at the university." And saying this, Karl quickly lifted his hands in mock self-defense. "I know, His Majesty's intellectual regiment of the guards. Home of Hegel. Of Treitschke, God help us. But don't forget Mommsen, don't forget Dilthey. There's been a free voice at Berlin University from time to time. And there's another now—this Troeltsch, the historian. You should hear him, Hermann, you should see him; you'd hate him. When the noise of the parade march comes blasting through the window, he stands utterly still and shuts his eyes. I tell you it's wonderful, that look of pained forbearance until the bloody ruckus has passed."

Hermann had forgotten how didactic Karl was, always launching into a lecture at the drop of a hat. Even now, when they had not seen each other for some two years, here he stood on the sidewalk with people surging around them, delivering a sermon on some professor.

"Come on, let's walk. Tell me about yourself, I don't care about your professor with his pained forbearance."

"Most tolerant of you."

"If I said he should be kicked out on his ass you wouldn't like that either. Anyway, I don't want him kicked out. I want everyone to be happy. Everyone should be happy on a day like this."

It was one of those rare days in late October when midsummer seems to have come back again, the sky to shed a shimmering benevolence over everything. Along Unter den Linden, where they walked, the trees had turned the color of gold, and beyond Brandenburg Gate, stretching to either side, you could see the massed amber and red of the Tiergarten treetops. The broad avenue reverberated with a spacious sound of traffic, with the deep, two-note klaxon of motor cars, the sharp ringing of bicycle bells, the clopping of horses drawing hansoms and wagons, while from the cross streets came the pealing, make-way clangor of the new electric trams. Only this year had horse-drawn omnibuses been replaced by these fast, smooth-moving trams, and faster and smoother yet, beneath the city, hurtled the trains of the new U-bahn, the first section of which was now complete, and whose further ramifications were apparent wherever you saw workmen industriously tearing up the streets. Such commotion had been a traditional feature of Berlin since 1871, when, in order to honor the new national grandeur, there had begun a feverish razing and reconstruction—unseemly buildings knocked down and replaced, streets enlarged, monuments erected. The city might lack the splendors of Paris, but it possessed its own somber, uniquely Wilhelmian majesty, with its vast gray squares upon which sat its vast gray palaces and state buildings, ornate with heavy gold fretwork and parapeted with heroic statuary. To the foreign eye, the imperial center of Berlin was perhaps both grim and showy, as was the whole crude, expanding city, but no one could deny Berlin's life force, its zestful satisfaction in its booming industry and ceaseless construction, its superb public services and free hospitals, its clean streets and its abundant trees and parks so tenderly cared for; its huge palatial department stores—you could now buy Spanish tomatoes at Wertheim's—and its twenty legitimate theaters playing night after night to capacity crowds; its well-dressed burghers and busy sidewalk cafés; its richly mixed strains of church bells, organ grinders and parade fanfare; its massive bronze sculptures in triumphant stance; and its all-pervasive sense of the Kaiser ensconced there in the imperial palace, reigning over a nation of incomparable wealth, over the strongest military power on earth. Filling the air was an enormous pride, a kind of intoxicated success which, on days such as this, seemed to combine with the heavens in a simple, sun-drenched statement of God's grace.

"... a complete sociological paradox that even a city as freethinking as Berlin is possessed by this nationalist fever. Look at its population, sixty percent workers, strictly Socialist, but you step inside a hod carrier's flat—"

"You've been inside a hod carrier's flat?"

"No, of course not, but I've heard. And you'll find a picture of Marx on the wall, but next to it will be one of Bismarck. And they'll cheer themselves hoarse at a glimpse of that imperial yellow-and-black motorcar, and they'll stand there at the Gate by the hundreds drinking in the lordly likes of you stomping through *en masse*."

"I don't think that's so odd. The colors are always inspiring. It's true in any country. And if it's truer here, is any working class better off than here?"

"Certainly they're better off. What does that prove? There's still an abyss between them and us."

"And you want it nice and gray and level. It only proves that they have more sense than you."

"I see where it's headed, this Army-Kaiser hegemony. I see that everything, all this"—he gestured at the street—"is going to be staked on war someday. Don't you realize that? It may all be swept down the drain."

"Quatsch!"

"You know something, Hermann?" Karl stopped to light a cigarette, squinting through the smoke at the face beside him. "You know the sun pours from your eyes?"

"It does?—mein Gott!"

"Ja, absolutely. When I saw you I said to myself, here is the quintessence of the Fatherland, so strong, so proud, so dazzling—"

"What are you talking about? You're embarrassing."

"I've given you thought, Hermann, though you may not know it. I've thought of you snorting up those Austrian Alps, dislocating your shoulder in your passion to be first to the top. I've thought of you on your shoots, slogging along stinking of sweat and stag blood and no doubt imagining yourself draped in a bearskin, spear in hand—the true romantic Teuton. And your tender concern for animals, those you don't kill: so tender, so desperately sentimental. And so disciplined! All straightness and quiver, all aquiver for glory. A clash on the fields of death—that would be the ultimate joy. You're irradiated with the holy ideal, Hermann, you're the *chevalier sans reproche* of the Holy Roman Empire, ach ja, absolutely. But all the same, you're nothing but bits and pieces. You don't know *what* you are—pagan, medieval, Wilhelmian. Just fragments pretending to be whole. Well, that's our Germany, isn't it? 'Germany, the light of the world!' 'The German soul is God's soul!' 'Ye alone are God's representatives on earth!' Up in the clouds somewhere, that's where the Fatherland is—while your feet are floundering around on a patchwork of geographical, religious and class divisions. Look at you, you're even cracked parentally down the center, half Prussian and half Bavarian, half Protestant and half Catholic, and that piece of ground you like to call your own, that historic pile of stones you happened to have been brought up in through pure fluke—"

"I'm flattered by all this analysis, and bored shitless. Why do you stand there blathering? You're obstructing people!"

"What are you, eighteen? Amazing what a whipcrack they can make from a young voice."

"Why don't you leave off!"

They walked on in silence.

"I'm sorry, Hermann. It comes of sitting in lecture halls all one's life. One's critical faculties become . . . I don't know, overdeveloped; one tends to fly off on wings of theory. Look, I was just going to hop a tram somewhere for a bite to eat. Have you time?"

"I have the time, but—"

"But you can't. Of course."

He had forgotten that cadets were forbidden to use public transportation, nor were they allowed to eat in any but a handful of select restaurants. Much was forbidden to them. They could not remove their white gloves outdoors; they could not even stretch their necks to remove the pressure of their suffocatingly tight collars.

"Poor fellow, don't you envy me my freewheeling Adam's apple? Never have an urge to jump in a tram, pop in somewhere for a sausage? What do you do, walk and starve?"

"More or less."

Like most cadets, he was usually short of money. Even the largest allowance, and his was not large, was stretched thin across the obligatory manner of life at Lichterfelde: the purchase and upkeep of uniforms; the expensive cadet societies; the opera and theater tickets, for box seats and orchestra only. There was horseracing at Karlshorst, formal bridge parties where debts were incurred, discreet visits to bordellos; there were the engraved vellum calling cards, the flowers and baskets of fruit that must follow any visit to a private home, and the occasional dinner at Kempinsky's or the Hotel Adlon. Only beer-drinking revels were cheap, and only swimming parties on the Wannsee free. There was always some arid stretch when lunch or a cab were beyond one's means; if one was unable to borrow, one skipped lunch, and one walked.

"I'm strapped today, but what about next week? Maybe we could meet somewhere."

"Good. That's what we'll do."

Karl had put out his cigarette, only to light another as they walked along. His fingers were nicotined, his shoulders stooped. He was twenty-five, with degrees from Jena and Heidelberg, and still he dipped into one university after another, his long pale hair already receding, his well-cut clothes stamped with the untidiness of the scholar. He turned around when they came to Brandenburg Gate, and with gloomy eyes stood looking back down Unter den Linden, surveying the flags, the traffic, the bustling crowds.

"These smug, self-satisfied faces . . . every last one is stamped with materialism. Where have their souls gone to? There's nothing left but the pursuit of prosperity and the cult of patriotism."

Hermann sighed.

"I sometimes think, so what if it should all go down the drain?" Karl went on. "What would be the loss? Rootlessness and speculators, machines and commerce, something so sick at the center . . . Have you see *Elektra*? It has lines that stay with you. 'Can one decay alive like a rotten corpse? Can one fall apart while awake, like a dress eaten by moths . . . ?'"

"Come on, you're not as bad as all that." Hermann gave the stooped shoulder a clap. "Just straighten up and get yourself a haircut."

Karl looked at him with a little smile.

"You're developing a nice wit, Hermann. No, no, don't look so contrite, my feelings aren't hurt. It was as good as I gave. But anyway," he said, taking out his pocket watch, "I'm afraid it's getting on. I've got to eat and get back to class. Keep well, old man."

They shook hands, and Karl walked back down den Linden, disappearing in the crowd. Hermann turned and walked on past the Gate toward the Tiergarten. They had forgotten to make plans for lunch next week. They had forgotten because they had no more to say to each other. It was sad in a way.

He walked along the Siegesallee toward the Spree. He enjoyed walking around the city when he had time away from the barracks, nor did he mind knowing that he cut a superb figure of a cadet. Even when his clamped collar made his neck itch madly, when he longed to tear off the choking band, he maintained the smooth crisp step and erect bearing of the future officer, and took pleasure in the tightness of his uniform beneath his greatcoat, aware of its perfect smoothness except for the permanent horizontal crease made by bowing from the waist.

Autumn in Berlin could be marvelous, winter was always miserable; summer was stifling, but spring took your breath away. Still, Nuremberg in any season was his city; nothing could wrench that soaring medieval beauty from his first memory. Newly arrived at Lichterfelde, he had written his parents with high emotion: "The medieval rituals and codes of behavior make me feel that I am the inheritor of all the chivalry of German knighthood." It was what made the grinding harshness of cadet life far more than bearable, but inspiring. The Imperial Cadet College was a barren red-brick complex of buildings filled with long gloomy corridors. It was familiarly known as Hat Keinen Ausgang—No Way Out—and Homeopathische Kuranstalt—Homeopathic Sanatorium. They rose at five and ran for fifteen minutes outside, then came back and washed under an icy shower. After dressing, if your cot was not perfectly made, so as to appear an austere work of art, you were ordered to climb the high dormitory wardrobe fifty times without stop, hauling yourself up by the arms, struggling onto the top and jumping down the other side, over and over again until you reeled, and felt that every muscle in your body was screaming. At the preparatory academy a loose button was torn off and thrown to the floor for you to pick up and sew back on. Here they sewed it back for you, not onto your tunic but to your bare chest. But the high collar was the worst. Still, you took pride in the fact that you bore its iron grip lightly. Collar and all, he would not have exchanged his years at Lichterfelde for any other existence in the world.

* * *

Half a year later, in the spring of 1912, the nineteen-year-old cadet graduated with *des Kaisers Belobigung,* the commendation of the Kaiser. Commissioned as a second lieutenant in the Prinz Wilhelm Infantry Regiment 112, he was gazetted to its headquarters at the frontier garrison town of Mülhausen, in Alsace. He would have preferred—he wanted very badly—a commission in the cavalry, but that was reserved for the sons of nobility, and even a brilliant cadet record combined with the influence of von Epenstein could not get him in. He took the disappointment with good grace, and in answer to a rare letter from Karl, studying now in Bologna, he wrote: "I'm known chiefly for my common sense, believe it or not, so I find no point in brooding over what can't be changed. I'm happy enough with things as they are. (Incidentally, if it's true—as you're so fond of saying—that in Germany the human species is considered to begin with the lieutenant, what is it I've stopped being and you still are, a primate or an amoeba?) Well, you were very much missed at the celebration I was given at Veldenstein. I don't think the place had seen such a festivity for five hundred years. I enjoyed it greatly, but was sorry to find Vater more aged than ever, uses a stick now, shuffles around muttering darkly to himself. I was home a week, afterward went down to Mauterndorf—Pate older too, immensely stout—then off to the Hohe Tauern. Climbed the Grossglockner again, didn't dislocate my shoulder this time—your snorting (was that the word?) brother is maybe learning patience, but also there was too much snow to make time. It was hard going altogether, but those who didn't turn back enjoyed a tremendous experience, at least I enjoyed it. Imagine a faint, then steadily growing rumbling and trembling, and all at once a mighty avalanche of snow and boulders roaring down almost on top of you. It was marvelous, that blinding white mass thundering by just a hairbreadth away, one's not usually treated to such a close look. Now I'm getting a close look at the opposite, a garrison town. Nothing duller. But the life's pleasant enough, first-rate Offizierkasino, and thank God since it's a border post there's at least some hint of urgency in our drills. You can't have the French frontier a kilometer away without feeling a constant sense of the enemy. Here I see your hackles rising, but even you must know that we're encircled by enemies whose pacts and plots will one day force us to take up arms against them. I say that day can't come soon enough, for then will Germany march forward to wrest out what she must have once and for all, the incontestable security of world power status. Now I see your hackles flying off (what are hackles, anyway?). Well, be assured that your letter roils me as much as this roils you, but have no doubt of my abiding affection. . . ."

Chapter 9

Nikki cleared a space on the cluttered table where the Frau Reichskommissar sat with Hermann, and silently set down a tray of tea things. Albert, summoned home from boarding school, was asleep in the next room. The girls, Olga and Paula, would arrive with their husbands tomorrow. Karl was traveling abroad and could not be reached. It was almost midnight, and the silence was very great. All you could hear was the shuffling of papers—family documents, old letters, photographs—that littered the table. Nor was the disarray limited to the table: the room, a parlor of modest dimensions, carpetless, without curtains, was a welter of trunks, boxes, piles of books, odds and ends wrapped in newspaper. Nikki was not surprised that disaster had befallen them, for it was 1913, and thirteen was the unluckiest of all numbers. She had seen omens from the year's start—two moths flying backward, an odd reddish star one night—and indeed the catastrophes had come, one on the heels of the other: first the loss of Veldenstein, and then, scarcely had they moved in here, the death of the old Herr Reichskommissar. She poured the tea, looking at her mistress's face, which was drawn and colorless above her black frock. Since Hermann had arrived this afternoon on compassionate leave from Mülhausen, the two of them had been sitting here by the fireplace sorting out the old man's effects, and it seemed to Nikki that everything had come to an end. She turned and looked sadly at the fireplace, where, from time to time, the flames received a handful of old receipts or a yellowed calling card. Then, leaving the parlor, she plodded along the bare floorboards of the hall to her bedroom, though she knew she would not find sleep there, or anywhere.

Hermann slowly refolded a letter and put it back with a sheaf of other old letters, retying the narrow faded red ribbon around them. There was a constant burning under his eyelids, a hot film that sometimes brimmed and threatened to seep, so that he was obliged to draw in a deep breath through his nostrils. He did so now, as he placed before him his father's African diaries, bound in dusty calfskin, and opened the first one, which disclosed the rust-colored strokes of a bold, slanting hand.

Abruptly he pushed back his chair and threaded his way through the clutter to a window, where he stood with his back to the room and with a brief, covert gesture wiped away with his palm the wetness on his cheeks. There was a purity of silence behind him, as if his mother had lowered the papers she held, and was regarding his back.

"Never think, Hermann, that I lacked pity for your father...."

He gave a faint shake of his head. "I have never thought that."

There was another silence. "When we came back to Germany ... to see him sink away as he did, to see him simply give up ... I did pity him, Hermann, I did, very much, but pity is a bad companion."

He nodded, still looking out the window. Pity was a companion who did not wear well, who thinned and frayed to impatience, condescension, who kept no memory. In his fingers he could still feel the affectionate, good-natured boredom that had so often been communicated to Vati as they shook hands goodbye. So many times, and the last time, too.

A door opened. He heard Nikki plodding back in, sighing, fussing over their not having touched the tea, sighing again. She and Mutter had been run ragged these last few days, so much to befall a family all at once; and he lowered his eyes from the night sky to the unfamiliar Munich street below, narrow, lined with brick apartment buildings. It was as if he could not absorb the fact that Veldenstein was gone. Only Vati's death was real, and the hours ahead that must somehow be got through. He turned and threaded his way back, catching his boot on something and tripping. "How are you going to live in a hole like this?" he asked irritably, sitting down again.

"I shall manage very well," his mother replied, and her face, in spite of its tired lines, was strong in the glow of the lamp, resilient. "And seven rooms do not constitute a hole, Hermann."

"Many have it worse," Nikki agreed, although her heart was not in this statement. Indeed, her heart was flattened. Tiredly, she took up her bag of knitting and sank onto a sofa, having to push aside a heap of household items wrapped in newspapers. It was a blessing that in such adversity and disorder the Frau Reichskommissar was so level-headed. And so she had been from the very start, when rumors first came floating up from Austria that Epenstein had gone off his head for some snip a third his age. It was said that the old rhinoceros was putty in her hands; no surprise to Nikki. You take a big loudmouth like Epenstein—a Jew after all, it told—always stomping and blustering about, when he gets old and flabby and dyes his mustaches, then suddenly he'll lose his senses to some smirking little idiot who's supposed to bring back the hard muscles and black hair. Except that this snip was no idiot—holding out for marriage, and had a strong head for finances; she disapproved, so it was said, of the Ritter's generosities not directed to herself. And so when Epenstein came to Veldenstein to announce his marriage, it was possibly to announce a few other changes as well. But if so, he never got to them, because the old Reichskommissar had all at once, astoundingly, flown into a rage. Why, after so many dim, puttering years, he should take it into his poor head to fly apart just then, no one could know. No one could have dreamed of the violence in the man. He screamed that his friendship and honor had been betrayed, that Epenstein was a swine—Schwein and Schweinehund, he had actually cried—and that he would not allow his family to remain a moment longer in the house of a swine, and all the while he had beaten Epenstein's chest with his fists, like a crazed person. And Epenstein was speechless for once, openmouthed. Then he had stormed out, and later sent a short note saying that if the Reichskommissar felt as he did, he would not stand in his way; he would expect the burg to be vacated promptly. Nikki had to admit that Epenstein could do nothing else, considering how vilely, if properly, he had been insulted. Honor was a great thing to people of standing. In olden times they had shot each other dead in duels; nowadays they broke off with an icy note, or else they brooded for years like the old man, and finally went berserk. Honor to them was everything, but to her it was Quatsch—it plunged you into an upside-down set of rooms in a big unknown city. What matter if her mistress pointed out that they could get along on the pension, and that there were investments as well? Such practicalities were of no real comfort, could not be, in such a year. If only 1913 were over, but they were scarcely into May; she could not even knit properly, see the mess she was making—and she lay her needles down with a sigh.

Hermann and his mother looked up a few moments later, a sharp intake of breath having filled the room. Nikki was rising from the sofa, clutching a crumpled newspaper in one hand.

"'An end . . . an end is come upon the four corners of the land,'" she read breathlessly, her other hand pressed outspread to her aproned bosom, "'for thou hast gotten thee riches and hast gotten gold and silver in thy treasure and thou hast said thou art God—therefore will I bring strangers upon thee, the terrible of nations, and they shall draw their swords against thee, and bring thee down into the pit—and thou shalt die the deaths of them that are slain in the midst of the seas.'" She stood staring at them. "It is an omen, an omen . . ."

"It is not an omen," Hermann said. "It is *Die Zukunft*."

"I don't know . . ." She stared again at the newspaper. "Ja . . . ja, *Die Zukunft* . . . but it is an omen that they have printed, that I should suddenly pick it up like this . . ."

"What they print is trashy political opinions. Biblical passages, anonymous poems, they haven't even the guts to sign their names."

But poor Nikki was deaf to reason, her eyes wide and beseeching. His mother went over and settled her back on the sofa, coaxed the newspaper from her hand, spoke soothing words; then she returned to the table, and after a while the faint click of knitting needles could be heard again.

It was a blessing, Nikki thought, that those around her were not as unstrung as she. And yet that did not help—for it might well be true that the whole of Germany was going to sink into a pit, and that everyone would be slain, just as in the Bible.

On the long train ride back from Munich, across the flat green plains to the west, into the mild rolling hills of Swabia, and then along the southern edge of the Schwarzwald, its dark pines silhouetted against the deepening afternoon sky, Hermann saw over and over the severe black rectangle that had been cut into the earth. His long-held control had begun to crumble as the coffin was moved over the rectangle; and as it began its soundless descent, he had broken beneath an uprush of childhood memories, like an unbearable rush of sunlight. The sobs had shamed his uniform, but he had known this helplessly and without caring; and now the grief, still raw in his chest, spread up into his throat and eyes whenever he thought of Vati's suffering existence, his humiliation, his loneliness. It was Vati's loneliness that was hardest to bear; why had he not spent more time with Vati when he was home? Why had he not thought to talk about those old days that had meant so much to him? Why, instead of offering an affectionate, preoccupied smile, had he not been attentive? Now it was too late to ease the misery of his father's life, although he knew, sensibly enough, that Vati's debased situation was Vati's own doing. No human being could be forced by another to act against his own will; the will has gone first, has softened, disintegrated, become something that can be twisted any which way. And when the will dies, the man dies. A husk. You can love a husk, even deeply, but what is there left to respect, to speak with, to be attentive to? And these thoughts, so unwanted and disloyal, increased his sorrow. But one thing comforted him, that Vati had died in a strange place, beholden to no one. He was glad for that. He was glad for the fury that preceded it, and only hoped that in Vati's eroded, pandemonious mind he had somehow believed that his violence was taking place fifteen years earlier, on that warm summer day when he had first been shown through Veldenstein's courtyard.

Yet this comforting thought brought its own pain; for he himself had never hated Pate, and did not hate him now, but mourned his loss too. And the loss of Veldenstein—all at once it came to him fully, clearly, like the earth giving way, a jolting emptiness. And then there were only the mahogany walls of the train compartment, the glow of the small, red-shaded reading lamps, and a cigarette that had burned out between his fingers.

They crossed the Rhine into Alsace. The sky had darkened, and held a few pale stars. He sat looking out at them, seeing Vati's dead face in his bier, his marble, impassable stillness.

On his twenty-first birthday the following January, he woke very early. He lay gazing up through the darkness of his barracks room, and it came to him that this year he would not be receiving Vati's long, sentimental greeting. The pain flooded back, intensely, and then subsided. He thought too of Veldenstein, and that he would never again return to his tower and his cliff. Then he pushed aside that brooding knowledge, and concentrated on the crowding urgency of the world around him. There were the Bernese Alps for climbing, only three hours by train whenever you had a day or two free; there was his leave this coming summer, during which he planned to climb in the distant, virginal Caucasus; there were wonderful nights in Freiburg and Basel, girls and bedclothes mixed up in blissful scraps of memory; there were pleasant formal dinners at the Offizierkasino, followed by the heart-swelling harmony of drinking songs around the piano; with no love of liquor, he could outdrink everyone in the room and hold it like a gentleman—he prided himself on his iron constitution—although he much preferred marzipan to schnapps, and haunted the Mülhausen sweetshops along with the local schoolboys. Karl, who was now teaching at Marburg, "where the usual climate of aggressive patriotism is mercifully lacking," as he had written in his dry fashion, accused him of being un-grown-up. Not, indeed, because of his sweet tooth, but because with teasing delight he had sent off an account of having brought down a sword of iron upon the heads of three Frenchmen.

". . . not that it was exactly a sword," he had written, "or that they were exactly Frenchmen. They were German, in fact, and that's what galled me—German blood, French loyalties. And so, you will be fascinated to know, I dragged the three of them off to a pigsty—a wonderfully mucky one, both the pigs and the smell knocked you down—and over their howling protests locked them up with their brethren overnight. You must agree that it was apt. . . ."

"I agree," Karl had written back. "Apt behavior for an overgrown adolescent. I cannot even accuse you of following in the steps of the Zabern affair, since you draw the parallel with such blithe innocence. It is to your credit that you did not split open an Alsatian head with your sword, as did the fine officer in Zabern, but confined your exuberance to a pigsty. It is to your credit that you have more regard for human beings than did the Zabern garrison, although no doubt you are crowing in abstract ecstasy over the outcome of that monstrous business. To think that when a nation is rocked to its depths by such a scandal, when a united liberal front has forced the issue right up to the Reichstag— that nothing, nothing at all comes of it. Acquittal. Congratulations by the Crown Prince. To think that in the best-educated nation in the world there sits a parliament with no more power than a girls' finishing school—all authority vested in Kaiser, Chancellor, Army General Staff. Why do we write each other? Are we so limited to our own respective types that we can find only each other to argue with? Well, go back to your pigsty games. You have conducted yourself as a juvenile, which is the least offensive thing that can be said of the officer corps. You are also, the tone of this letter notwithstanding, my very dear brother. . . ."

If he was a juvenile, Karl could use a drop of less than sclerotic blood in his veins. What was the use of mooning about like a ninety-year-old? Did Karl ever find anything to spark him into joy? He himself, even in the routine dullness of garrison life, could always find something, even if it was only contradicting the senior subaltern and watching his eyes pop. No one admired Frederick the Great more than himself, but sometimes he could not bear to hear the same old fusty legends, what old Fritz would have thought, what old Fritz would have done—then out snapped an irreverent remark, out popped the senior officer's eyes: "Um Gottes Willen! How dare you!" followed by a stream of furious rebuke. It was good fun but could not be done every day. More often the days passed peacefully, with just enough international tension to give one hope that peace would not continue forever.

From home—although he could not really call the Munich apartment home, for he loathed it—Mutter wrote that she had made the place "cozy and charming," and that she was enjoying its warmth, for in all her years at Veldenstein she had never gotten used to its terrible dampness. "Nikki," she went on, "is her usual cheerful self again, now that this sad year has drawn to a close. Or perhaps it is due to the presence of a cook and second maid, who have largely relieved her of her impossibly inept running of the house. All goes well. I am getting along splendidly. I never look back, only ahead. . . ."

There was everything to be said for that; he too looked ahead, and on this particular morning, which brought him to the estate of manhood, he could scarcely contain himself for looking ahead. In a single bound he was off his cot and at the window, flinging it open.

He stood looking out, charged with the knowledge of some high destiny awaiting him. Snow gleamed white from the trees, the air was keen, fresh, and the sky overhead as pure as only a dawning sky can be.

Chapter 10

THE spring in Europe that year came with exceptional warmth, and unfolded to a green luxuriant June perhaps more beautiful than any within living memory. In Munich, Nikki often took herself by tram to the Nymphenburg Gardens, where she strolled among the flowering trees with her parasol, or sat beneath its iridescent shade on a bench with the gossiping nursemaids. She made a very good appearance, dressed in one of the Frau Reichskommissar's eyeleted muslin frocks from some seasons back, and a dark blue straw hat, bedecked with paper roses, perched squarely on her head. She was sharp-nosed, rawboned and ruddy, but this was a look that had always become her, one of conclusive plainness that set her cheerfully above the complications and battles of beauty. She was in fact at peace with the world. Last year's unhappy events had receded, the heart-fluttering year of 1913 was gone, and the sun shone once again. The sky was silken, luminous. Flowers grew in extraordinary abundance, overflowing in every hue from the borders of the paths, drenching the air with sweetness. Sometimes, as she sat on her bench, it seemed to Nikki that this lovely weather embodied her whole life, for she and the Reich had been born together in 1871, and the two of them had known only peace and constancy ever since; a peasant girl gone very early into service, she would have had to invoke an endless, golden afternoon to describe her life, a steadfast, sunlit day of good manners and regular habits, of mellow tradition and new-grown comforts, of drawing rooms upholstered in velour, agleam with crowded bibelots.

Basking beneath her parasol in the full flood of contentment, Nikki liked to recall the triumphs of her life, which for some reason usually had to do with Karl. Most often she summoned up her great triumph of 1905, the year those mujiks in Russia had revolted and set Karl off with his big words—how the German workers would take fire now, and the Socialists would lead them in rising up and overthrowing the whole system. She had broken right in and informed him, and with what sacrifice to her pride, that *she* came from the lower orders, what did he know?—and she, Nikki, had no truck with foreign abominations like revolution, she liked things as they were, and he could put that in his pipe and smoke it. Ja, and that was exactly what he had had to do, because he and his windy likes had not found a soul to lead in over-throwing anything. Life, as he could not help but see, went on exactly as always.

Her later triumphs over Karl, though smaller, were nevertheless satisfying. On his infrequent visits to Veldenstein he did not include her in his conversation—that was quite all right, guests did not, and he was more guest than family—but she punctured the droning voice any-way as she passed by with a tray or sat knitting in a corner. That time he had gone on about France, how the statue in Paris representing Strasbourg still stood draped in black mourning. Fine! she had told him over her clicking needles, what was wrong with that? A good thing they remembered 1870. Besides, though she had not gone into it, she had no use for foreigners. Here in the park there were a few too many of them, gabbling and gesticulating and carrying on—not the En-gländer, of course, a cold and dreary lot; about them Karl had once said that they were displeased because Germany was growing stronger than they on the sea and in world trade, and to that she had said good! England was a tired old empire on the way out—and small wonder, she said to herself now, with such pale, constipated-looking citizens. No fear of confusing them with the Russians promenading past her bench, beautifully dressed but with a wild look in their eyes; scratch them and you found a pack of savages, backward as the day was long—not even an organized army, look how they had been squashed by the clever Japanese, no bigger than dwarfs. Yet on his recent visit to the Munich apartment Karl had shaken his head over Russia, and sighed that it wanted the Bosporus and the Balkans—sighed over places in the back of beyond. Why, let them squash each other. That was what she had said. What had they to do with the civilized world?

One afternoon during that visit, when Karl was talking with Albert and filling the boy with misery, Nikki had gone over and confronted him. "I know about foreign countries," she had told him, stammering a little, for he turned his eyes full upon her, such sad, hooded eyes, like those of a mortician. "I know about their pacts and alliances," she had stammered. "I know that we're encircled, but don't you see, they will never dare to do anything, because we're the strongest. We are the strongest, and we are lovers of peace. If *we* don't want war, there will *be* no war."

Karl had surprised her greatly. He had answered at length, the drooping cigarette in his mouth moving up and down with his slow professor's voice. "Ja, we want peace, but we want something else, too . . . and I don't even think we know what it is. And we're not the only ones. No, we're not the only ones, but we're the loudest. If you traveled in foreign countries as I have, you would see, side by side, this love of peace and this seething toward something else. It's like a decaying, it's like a fermenting that eats up all question of choice. It's everywhere, but it's nowhere worse than here. Isn't there something beyond choice in a country that is one vast garrison? Or in a Kaiser who deeply and sincerely wants peace, who detests the idea of disruption, yet who cannot prevent himself from boasting and shouting and rattling his damned saber until the world's eardrums are bruised?"

Poor little Albert had no reply, but she—the Kaiser shouting and rattling, what a way to speak of the Kaiser! And garrisons, what was wrong with garrisons filled with fine young officers like Hermann, with drums and flags and plumed helmets?—"It is . . ." For a moment she vainly sought the word; then she found it, her stammer gone. "It is glory."

Karl could find nothing to say to that; he had just looked at her with his mortician's eyes, and after a while had slouched off to some Schwabing café.

Such triumphs Nikki reflected upon beneath her parasol, not that she wished Karl ill; she merely wished he would stop talking. Hermann talked a great deal too, but one loved that, one enjoyed Hermann because he so enjoyed himself. In August he was traveling to the Caucasus, wherever that might be, and she looked forward to his visit on the way; but she was not pleased that he was also invited to Mauterndorf, and that he was quite open in his intention of going. The Frau Reichskommissar did not care. It will give Hermann pleasure, she said cheerfully, and if it gives Epenstein pleasure too, that cannot be helped. But she, Nikki, was not so easygoing as her mistress, and she would express some strong thoughts on the subject when she saw Hermann. But just as she was sinking into this scene and selecting her words, a youth came huffing importantly along the path, pointing over his shoulder and yelling about a royal assassination in Austria.

Nikki collapsed her parasol at once and hastened out to the street, where already people stood in shocked clusters. It had not happened in Austria, but in Bosnia-Herzegovina, one of those back-of-beyond Balkan places. There, on a state visit, Archduke Franz Ferdinand and his wife had been shot in their carriage. There had been a lot of political murders all over Europe the last few years, anarchists floating around doing whatever came into their heads, so that you were almost used to the idea of assassination—but the heir apparent of Austria! Nikki was outraged. At home her mistress was outraged. The cook and maid were outraged. Next day in the park everyone there was outraged. The newspapers printed the world's outrage.

And then after a few days the subject wore itself out and life went back to normal. July had come in, and the days were growing hot, the sky intensely blue—an arch of purest azure from one end of the continent to the other, as one newspaper item described it. The end of the month they were going on holiday to Berchtesgaden. The Frau Reichskommissar loved the mountains, though Nikki herself preferred the lakes. On her bench she discussed the merits of both with the nursemaids, and the days grew hotter and hotter, and gradually she began hearing talk of the assassination again, of complications that had arisen from it. It had been the Serbs who were behind the murder. Epenstein, she couldn't stand the thought of him, but he had used to say that Serbia was Austria's eternal pain in the neck, always fussing and fuming over some idiotic thing like the export of Hungarian pigs. But now the fussing was over something much bigger than the price of bacon. Crowds began standing around the news kiosks. Every day the crowds grew bigger and more anxious, and she was among them, craning and squinting. The sense of tension grew almost unbearable, and more so when newsboys began shouting extras from morning till night. The Frau Reichskommissar was constantly sending the maid downstairs to snatch up an edition as soon as it came out; she had canceled the Berchtesgaden holiday; Nikki felt a rising hysteria, which she tried not to show.

If only she could figure it all out, but no one was able to. Austria was going to punish Serbia, which was the correct thing to do. And the Kaiser had promised German support to Austria. That was also correct, since they were allies. That was all clear and simple, and the Kaiser had gone for a holiday cruise, and everything had been fine. But now, less than three weeks later, a continental war seemed to be rumbling toward them. It was those Russian savages lusting after the Balkans—Karl had said so—screaming that Austria must leave Serbia alone. It will be war, everyone said; and war with France too, since France was Russia's ally. And, ja, Nikki could see the scheming Frenchmen rubbing their hands together and hurrying to tear that black shroud from the Strasbourg statue. All because of miserable, no-account Serbia. The confusion of it: Austria, Russia, France, England, Germany, telegrams crackling among them; conferences, messengers, ambassadors running to and fro—and that was the most confusing thing of all, that no one wanted war. No, every government, even that of Russia, was doing all in its power to keep war from happening. It was beyond comprehension, a chaos, and as the days grew hotter, the suffocating air was filled with rumors of cavalry patrols already stationed at every frontier, of huge armies preparing, and this while their governments struggled frantically for peace. No, it could not be grasped, it was a whirlpool, something mad and rushing, a collapse of nature.

On the 28th of July, Austria declared war on Serbia. "It will be a localized war," said the Frau Reichskommissar, sipping iced tea in the stifling parlor. "It is between Austria and Serbia. Russia has no place in it, and she will abide by that." And yet the Frau Reichskommissar kept turning the glass in her hands, and after a while, not bothering to call the maid, she herself went down to the street to join the crowds waiting for the next extra.

Nikki went to the window and moved the lace curtain aside, and stood looking out at the sky. She began to cry, because she knew that the long, golden afternoon was coming to an end, and because the Bible had said so on that crumpled piece of paper—had said that they would sink into a pit of death; and it seemed so unfair that God had let her forget, but that He himself had remembered.

In Berlin the heat was stupendous. On the morning of August 1, a sweltering mob of thousands gathered before the gray imperial palace. Two days previous, Austria had bombarded Belgrade, at which Russia had mobilized along the Hungarian frontier; at twelve o'clock last night, Germany had issued Russia an ultimatum to demobilize within twelve hours. An unbearable anxiety hung over the crowd as morning moved toward noon; like Nikki, for all their pride and patriotism, they could not conceive of war, it had been too long gone from them. Yesterday the Kaiser had announced: "The sword has been thrust into our hand." But the sword was heavy, cold, a strange and terrible weight. And now noon came and passed. The ultimatum had expired.

Still they waited, hoping with increased agitation that the Russians would yet answer. At five o'clock a policeman walked out to the palace gate; stood there as the noise subsided.

"Mobilmachung!" he announced in a sharp, carrying voice. Mobilization!

A stunned hush fell over the square as the word sank in. Hats were slowly lowered, and slowly the thousands of voices began to sing the national anthem, "Now Thank We Our God," the enormous sound spreading through all the streets. At the anthem's end there was another long silence, and then, as if swelling from the bowels of the earth, a massive cheer went up, hats flew high in the air, arms waved wildly amid cries of "God protect Germany! God protect Kaiser, folk and country!" People shouted for a glimpse of their Kaiser, others ran through the streets spreading the news. When toward evening the Kaiser and Kaiserin appeared on the balcony, the mob had reached a pitch of delirium that carried all the way to the Siegesallee, where officers stood up in racing motorcars, waving scarves and handkerchiefs, crying, "Mobilmachung! Mobilmachung!"

By August 4, Germany was at war with Russia, France and Britain. The old hatreds were rapturously unloosed on France, the hereditary enemy, and on Russia, with her Slavic hordes—but for England the hatred was new and even stronger, perfidious England who had leaped on them for no reason at all except that for tactical purposes the German Army had had to pass through neutral Belgium. Russia, France, Britain against them—and Italy had broken her pact; it was encirclement indeed, nor was the rest of the world disposed to favor them. It was said that a government official had sighed, "Is there no one friendly to Germany?" and received the answer, "Ja, Siam seems friendly." The feeling of isolation only whipped spirits higher. Everywhere there was a sense of fiery purpose and sacrifice, all differences of rank and class swept away by passionate love of country. In this moment of the Fatherland's need, even liberals and pacifists set aside policy and those of fighting age hurried to join the colors. People gathered in churches to sing "A Mighty Fortress Is Our God." Merchants stamped "God Punish England!" on envelopes. Regimental barracks were madhouses of activity. Horse-drawn cannon rumbled across cobbled village squares while townspeople leaned from their windows cheering and waving flags. The columns were now in field gray, not Prussian blue, but the sun flashed from their spiked helmets as it had forty-four years ago at Sedan, and as the marching and singing and excitement grew, there grew with it a feeling of a quick, fresh, happy war. The exultant youths in feldgrau hung from the windows of flower-garlanded troop trains, and at every station were greeted by brass bands, by crowds pressing bouquets and fruit and chocolates upon them, joyously cheering the mightiest army on earth. Then the train would pull out, the band still playing, the crowd cheering and waving, the young soldiers hanging from the moving windows, waving back. The Kaiser said they would be home before the leaves fell, but the young soldiers hoped it would not be quite that brief a contest.

Chapter 11

ALREADY on August 2 the Prinz Wilhelm Infantry Regiment was on the march—but eastward, falling back behind the Rhine; and on August 8, French cavalry troops galloped into evacuated Mülhausen to reclaim the city as their own. The retreat to the Rhine, no matter its tactical necessity, had been a profound letdown for Hermann, a drab, ignominious start to the war he had so long awaited. He felt desperately thwarted by the daily standstill, and when on the 8th he was detailed to reconnoiter the Mülhausen area with a six-man patrol, his exhilaration was so great that as he gave a smart heel click he feared a dizziness of joy could be seen on his face.

They set out at dawn, by the unprepossessing means of bicycles, but as he zipped ahead of his men along the familiar back roads, yellow haystacks and rows of smoke-blue cabbage stretching to either side, everything quivering in the early-morning heat, his mind churned high above the handlebars. It was at breakneck speed that the seven young feldgrau figures cycled into Mülhausen's fringes, immediately drawing fire from a French outpost but careering unscathed around a corner, the baptismal fusillade pounding in their blood, intoxicating, dynamizing. The streets they sped through were deserted—everyone was apparently gathered in the town square; propitious, yet galling to their need for terrified eyes, feet scrambling to the curb, and all the harder they pumped toward the center of town, slowing only once, the men in a frenzy of elated impatience as their lieutenant, leaping from his bicycle, ripped a French flag from a window and threw it to the gutter. Then they were off behind him again, crouched flat over their handlebars, certain that he meant to take them straight into the heart of the French forces and wishing for it, lusting for it.

But in a narrow street leading into the square the lieutenant slowed down and motioned them to a halt. Dismounting in the sudden, still heat, to a blare of music, removing their rifles from over their shoulders and keeping close to the wall, they advanced behind him toward the crowd: varicolored backs of townspeople; close by, a red-trousered French soldier standing with a horse. Through the spaces among the backs could be seen the troops on review, a splendor of gleaming breastplates and black horsehair plumes. The air throbbed with the ringing brass and emphatic tempo of the "Marseillaise." "Don't they have anything better than that done-to-death old tune?" Hermann murmured to himself, but his chest was a tumult, and the music swelled the ecstasy of the wild ride, so that he felt melting, exploding, yet at the same time as oddly detached as a bird. His rifle held at the ready, he carefully counted the strength of the French troops for headquarters' edification, then picked out the military gentry who stood in a vivid clot before the little sweets shop where he had so often bought marzipan, the green wooden sign, he noticed, having with judicious haste been altered from Georg Greiner to Georges Grenier. Centerforward in the clot—he was so sure that a zing went through his trigger finger—stood the resplendent figure of General Bonneau himself. How easy it would be to send a bullet through that smug Gallic head— but cheap, underhanded. Glancing around again, he drew in a sharp breath as a plan unfolded before him. Turning, he gave a whispered order to his men. They would cover him as he leaped upon the nearby mount to gallop past the astounded general, sweeping up this dazzling prize into the saddle and tearing out of sight before an eyelash batted. Without wasting another moment, the unholy beauty of his plan reflected in his men's faces, he slung the rifle over his shoulder and began running crouched toward the horse.

Seconds later—a too zealous finger behind him splitting the air with a rifle crack—the horse reared, heads swung around, and he was dashing back to his bicycle. In fury and humiliation he fled the commotion, pumping through back streets and alleys until the patrol was safely in the outskirts, where he looked at them in silence. They were hot, dusty, their ardor spent. "Come on, you assholes!" he snapped. "Los!" And he pedaled directly on to the outpost that had fired upon them, approaching it from its unsuspecting rear. The men behind him exchanged looks. Coming had been one thing, but going seemed very different. Why risk disaster by wobbling up to an armed post on seven spindly bicycles? But here they were, halting now, in open view of anyone who cared to look. And the lieutenant, bold as brass, maybe crazy, yes, crazy, was getting off his bicycle and walking over to four tethered dragoon horses. He gave them a leisurely lookover; handsome beasts, black, big, their trappings glistening in the sun. Unhurriedly, with pats and murmurs, he untethered the first horse; in the same leisurely manner he led them, one by one, over to the patrol, taking three or four excruciating minutes at least. Then on they proceeded with the horses in tow, their hooves making a terrible racket on the cobblestones. With backs rigid, anticipating a puncturing barrage, the men glanced continually behind them; but the lieutenant did not look around once, and they wondered if he was showing bravado, or if he actually felt himself invulnerable to bullets. Whichever it was, they began to feel it take possession of them, like a draft of wine spreading through their blood, and before they gained the end of the street their back muscles had relaxed, and they looked around only to savor their captured horse-flesh. Twenty minutes later they were deep in the peaceful countryside.

Hermann was pleased by headquarters' warm reception of his troop count and booty, relieved that his gross disregard of orders—he was not to have penetrated Mülhausen proper—was looked upon as a daring act of initiative, and elated, two days later, to participate in the recapture of the city, earning in the fray his first medal, the Iron Cross Second Class. But nothing could rid him of the rankling knowledge that he had failed to start his war in the right way, on a rearing steed, with a captured French general slung across his pommel.

The fifth element, said Napoleon, is mud. Hoof-chopped mud; encrusted mud covering barricaded sandbags; trench sides a blackness of clods saturated and crumbling. In it they did little; they waited, while the boards of the dugout trickled in the light of a slush lamp. He had had a small print propped on his table, but it had begun to spot with mold. Pate had sent it, Dürer's *Ritter, Tod und Teufel,* and had written: "It is a picture I have gazed at often, and whose truth I know by heart. See the chaos of jagged rock, and see that only the brave knight on his mount is shown fully, cast like a bright medallion against that chaos, the only true ideal in this, our strife-torn world. Cherish that ideal, Hermann, let it lift you and carry you forward, and may God keep you safe until victory is won. Your proud and loving Pate."

Dear innocent Pate, you will find here only bundled figures trying to keep warm. In this war, I am afraid the Knight develops mold and ends up back in the knapsack, wrapped in a pair of underpants . . . He did not write that; it was not something to write, or even to think. You had to look farther and higher than a hole in the ground.

Toward Christmas of 1914 he was helped through the sludge like an elderly wreck, stiffened by acute arthritic inflammation of the leg joints. In the Freiburg hospital, touching the excruciating ankles and knees and hip sockets that refused to work, he saw himself falling farther and farther behind in this war, as if dragged at every turn deeper into a tunnel.

"Scheisse," he said bitterly to Leutnant Bruno Loerzer, his closest friend from Mülhausen days. "What am I doing in a military hospital? I should be in an old people's home."

Loerzer found himself repressing a look of amusement. He admired Hermann's mountaineering exploits, his capacity for carousing, his French dragoon horses, and the enormous delight Hermann took in these things—but the other side of the coin was the flawless, crisply upright bearing, from which he seemed to draw an almost holy satisfaction; that, of course, being a state of grace which could be achieved only by way of nine years of military academy. He himself was a regular; no slouch, but free from the exaltedness that would make a touch of rheumatism too humbling to be borne—the end of the world, an old people's home.

"Come on, half the cases here are rheumatism. The trenches are full of it. It's more popular than the clap."

Hermann said nothing, unwilling to speak the words "degenerative arthritis," a term he could not bring himself to attach to the pain that worked around and around inside his right hip socket. The hips were the worst, harder to move than the knees or ankles; when he walked, with the help of two nurses, it was with the stiff, shuffling steps of a mechanical toy.

At length he smiled. "You look like the painted whore of Babylon." Loerzer was attached to the fledgling Imperial Air Force, training as a pilot just outside Freiburg. Under the blond hair the fair, broad-nosed face was windburned, cheeks two flaming circles. But Hermann realized that he had already made this joke, and that his humor had gone flat. He was relieved when the visiting period was over.

When Bruno stepped through the door on his next visit he was stunned to see that the blanket was drawn over his friend's face. He stared with thudding heart. A nurse, tending one of the other men, called over to him.

"He's not dead. I don't know what he is." She looked at the covered form over her shoulder. "He's been like that all morning. Don't go over to him—I speak from experience."

"Won't he suffocate?"

"I hope so."

In the darkness he could hear them, voices of no consequence. "Unfit for further duty in the field" was the verdict he had heard today; he was to be posted behind the lines as soon as he was up and about. He, with strong, rock-hard legs that had always served him perfectly; it was unbelievable that they would rust up at the first bite of damp, and rot away for good in their sockets. It was unbelievable that he was without power over his own destiny, helpless as a paralytic swooped down on and stolen from, picked clean. It was unbelievable, but it was so: his future had been taken from him. And there was no past either; not a pinch of earth did he possess from his home, not a chip of stone from the tower, nor a thread from a tapestry. Null. If he were to pull the blanket from his face, there would only be a nickel-plated bed, some bottles of medicine, and the gray drizzle beyond his window.

It was a week before Bruno was able to return to the hospital. Just coming away from Hermann's bed, the recently aggrieved nurse was now a picture of smiling indulgence. He must be back to normal, having no trouble charming the birds from the trees. He didn't even work at it, and was possibly unaware of it—something bright, sunny, alive; the birds were of both sexes and every age, and Bruno himself was one. He was delighted to see the broad smile, but it was the last thing he had anticipated.

"You must have had some good news," he said as he sat down.

But on the contrary, the verdict his friend had been given was sobering. Poor wretch, Bruno said to himself, to be finished at twenty-one, and not even a bullet hole to show for it. What was he so happy about?

"I've written my reserve commanding officer, Bruno. I've requested transfer into the Air Force."

Bruno considered this. "Your chances aren't exactly . . . stupendous." For a medical washout designated for rear-line work, they were in fact zero.

"Quatsch. I explained to him that sparrows don't get swollen joints. Off the ground I'll be all right."

"Vielleicht. Just don't get your hopes up too high."

But on each visit Hermann's hopes were higher, and Bruno found himself infected, talking enthusiastically as he snailed up and down the ward with his future air comrade, who had by now graduated to a cane and poked stiffly along in a gray hospital robe, his face beaming.

The reply from the commanding officer was long in arriving, and was a refusal. Bruno came down with a thud, but from this time on his friend existed in a fantasy world, like someone with a high fever. He would fill out the application form himself, and forge the commanding officer's signature. He would sign himself out of the hopsital, simply depart without medical leave. It was all simple, and he would do it.

"Are you crazy? That's desertion. And forging transfer papers—are you crazy? You're talking about criminal acts, court-martial offenses—"

"Do you think for want of some stupid signature I'll give up everything? Do you really think that? Because if you do, *you're* the one who's crazy!"

He turned and limped on, speaking more quietly. It would be weeks, maybe months, before the forgery caught up with him. He would be flying by then, and he would be too good to be court-martialed, he would be too valuable. It was all simple, and he would do it.

A week later, newly qualified as a pilot, Lieutenant Loerzer took off from the Freiburg airport in a gray drizzle, headed for Darmstadt Air Force Depot. There he and his craft would be assigned to a base at the front, and there at the front God knew what would become of Hermann, who was painfully but happily squeezed into the observation cockpit.

Chapter 12

O<small>N</small> a day in early August 1918, Nikki went into her room, closed the door, and, going over to a picture postcard pinned on the wall, folded her hands in prayer.

Unser erfolgreicher Kampfflieger
Oberleutnant Göring

This was in white lettering at the bottom: Our successful fighter pilot, First Lieutenant Göring. Above it he stood in dress uniform, decorated with the Iron Cross, First Class and Second, the Hohenzollern Medal with Swords, the Karl Friedrich Order with Swords, the Zähring Lion with Swords, and the Silver Flying Medal, while from around his stiff collar hung the highest of all military honors, the Pour le Mérite, awarded for long-proven qualities of leadership and gallantry. He had been awarded the Pour le Mérite in June, shortly before taking over von Richthofen's squadron command. Nikki was desperately proud of him, and desperately worried that he looked much older than he should, like a man in his thirties. They all did—Udet, Loerzer, Buddecke, all of them; Richthofen had; Loewenhardt had; young men of twenty-two, twenty-five. She had once heard that a pilot going up the first time had a life expectancy of three weeks. No wonder they aged, those who lasted in the face of such odds. And as the months and years had gone by, and the odds had steadily mounted, she had grown steadily more anxious. Whenever another postcard immortal went down in flames, as Loewenhardt had done today, she stood before Hermann's picture and prayed for his safety.

Young girls found him the most eye-filling of the Heldenflieger. "Ach, a god!" she had overheard more than once. No one agreed more heartily with this than Nikki, but for all the bold handsomeness of his face, with the pale, startling beauty of the eyes, and the hair, darker now as a grown man, brushed straight back and smooth as a tango dancer's, it was somehow a terrible face. A terrible face for a terrible war. One eyelid was a fraction lower than the other, and it gave the eye a hooded look, cold, razorish. The wide mouth, with its long, strongly curved upper lip, bore the hint of a smile, but it seemed distant and hard-set. Along either side of his jaw ran a line of strain.

What violent happiness she had felt at the war's start, after the first shock had passed; it was an exultation, like wine in her veins; that was four years ago. Now she was tired. Sometimes she felt like weeping, it was all so different from what she had expected. A slaughterhouse, and the boys were sent into it younger and younger, and the men older and older; and along with lives, the war consumed everything that could be eaten, worn, or melted down for munitions. The Allied blockade had reduced them to making flour from chestnuts. In some places people ate berries and nettles. Infants and old people were starving to death in the thousands. And strikes and riots everywhere. When she dwelled on the death and turmoil and hardship, she saw God and the pit, and she prayed to God, for no matter if it was He who had ordained the pit, you had only Him. She prayed at night, and she prayed during the day, and it had actually begun to seem—dare she let herself believe it?—that God had begun to love them again. It started with Russia's capitulation last year, for then the war had at last become a one-front battle, and now Major General Ludendorff had opened a huge offensive and had driven the Allies back almost to Paris. Everywhere you went you felt a sense of renewed energy and hope, almost a certainty that the victorious end was finally drawing into sight. She hardly dared give way to such certainty—that was bad luck—yet her spirits had begun to climb; but then, as had happened today, one of the air heroes fell, and as she read of it in the newspaper all her anxieties came rushing back.

She was not a good Catholic, she never went to mass; but she had her deep, anguished bonds with God, and it was with anguish that she prayed for Hermann, remembering piercing things from the old days, a dog in a picnic basket, fireworks in the snowy courtyard, his sweet, open child's face. She prayed with her whole soul, with all her deep and special connections to God; and yet, as she gazed at the pale, hard eyes, she confessed to herself that things got strangely mixed up, reversed, and that it was not she who was irradiating Hermann with protection, but quite the other way around.

Chapter 13

T HE Order of the Pour le Mérite had been personally founded by
Frederick the Great, and bore his signet. It was an elegant medal in the
shape of a Maltese cross, its flaring, deep-forked arms creating eight
points, starlike. Between the arms of the cross was worked the gold
filigree of four spread-winged eagles. The cross itself was deep blue
enamel, finely edged in gold. Against the blue, in upraised gold, above
the words *Pour le Mérite,* stood the Hohenzollern crest and the initial *F.*

This, in a sunny outdoor ceremony in Berlin, had been placed
around Oberleutnant Göring's neck in the presence of his Kaiser. The
medal resting freshly against the cloth of his tunic, he had remained at
rigid attention, eyes forward, as the Kaiser raised his hand to his ornate
spiked helmet and saluted.

It was, as he later wrote to his mother and to Pate, the most moving moment of his life. But—he did not write this—the Kaiser's appearance had shocked him. His eyes were hollowed, his face drawn,
and the hair at his temples had gone white, quite white.

The room Oberleutnant Göring sat in was of collapsible corrugated tin, furnished with a camp bed and some shelves, and resounding with the tin rattle of autumn rain on the roof. On the table stood a
spirit lamp, against whose base was propped his small engraving by
Dürer, the room's only ornament apart from a Sèvres cup and saucer,

deep blue with a floral border, purchased in Antwerp at too high a price, but an abiding pleasure to look at. He sat back, closing his eyes and feeling Karl's presence strongly. Two years dead now, he who had been meant to grow into a venerable Akademiker with a walking stick and square gray beard . . . to have ended instead an artillery officer with the Turks at Gallipoli . . . and if I punched that shabby back one of the last times we ever saw each other, that day on den Linden, and made light of you, you must know it was just my stupid way . . . and you did know, because in spite of everything we understood each other, we were the same. That was the strange thing, we were the same. It was as you wrote me the second day of the war . . . our love of our country runs deeper than our differences, you wrote. We will never agree on anything about Germany, Hermann, except that it is our beloved homeland, and that in its time of need we will defend it, and defend it with our dying breath if that is what must be. God grant us a swift victory. God grant that we may meet again. . . .

He sat for a while with his eyes closed; then, rubbing and opening them, he took from a small box on the table a cigar made of bay leaves. Its taste was putrid, but would help keep him awake. It was very late, and his mind kept drifting away from the papers before him.

Everything had been so simple in the beginning—flying off with Bruno from Darmstadt as his self-appointed observer, and at the front, with hip sockets still aflame, hanging by his mountaineer's legs from the cockpit as the plane swooped low over enemy territory and pointing his camera straight down in the tearing wind, snapping picture after picture of gun emplacements as the guns crackled up from the ground, sounding like chestnuts popping—in time this daring if peculiar method earning him, much to his pleasure, the soubriquet the Flying Trapezist, and, as he had foreseen, the court-martial proceedings spluttering away to nothing.

Later, when he became a fighter pilot and the planes were small, fast, and mounted with machine guns, he found the challenge far more gratifying. He possessed neither Richthofen's shooting savagery nor Udet's superbly instinctive handling of a plane, but he was a better flyer than Richthofen and a better shot than Udet, and above all suicidally reckless.

Those were the days of the lively, merry air war when you flew into combat wearing silk pajamas under your flying suit, and a bright silk scarf, and even bracelets, even an earring in one ear—maybe to show Fate you were still alive—and your jaws were nonchalantly stubbled and your hair untrimmed. A variety of indulgences was allowed fighter pilots, including choice meals that digested pleasantly in your stomach as you hummed over the sallow, sulfurous mist swathing the trenches and cratered fields below. It was true that these rich digestive juices had an unpleasant way of breaking forth, what with the splatter and inhalation of the engine's castor oil, and that the corpses of downed comrades were usually plastered with excrement as well as blood. Still, one might as well die on a full stomach as an empty one.

But he had never thought much about death. He knew only exhilaration as the mechanic swung the propeller, and as a hacking of the engine gradually took hold, and as his trim Albatros started rolling slowly down the field, bumpily picking up speed until the ground fell away and he was abruptly light. In the steplike V formation of which he was part, the planes' colors were bright and barbarous, like the plumage of exotic hawks. His own colors were green and purple for the wings, jet-black fuselage, tail fin dazzlingly white. The wind flattened and stung his cheeks, the earth grew increasingly pale, and after a while his feet grew numb with cold in their heavy boots, and he took them from the rudder bar and stamped them on the floorboards, not only to warm them, but because he liked the rite of stamping, the rumble of it mixing with the eager, grinding din of the engine.

When he saw the long-awaited dip of the commander's wings, signaling the *Jagdfrei*, the free hunt, he felt himself racing along the burg walls—peeling off in a lateral arc, the motor accelerating in a sharp, downcurving whine before he leveled out in pursuit and opened up his throttle. His habit was to close in on a target with the briefest glance at the sky around, and on one occasion he rushed toward a huge aircraft of a sort he had never before encountered, one of the new Handley Page bombers. He was surprised and impressed to see that it possessed guns both amidship and in the tail, both flickering in pale gold bursts at his rapid approach. Pressing on his trigger release and keeping his hand there, he let off a long, steady return blast, his whole arm feeling the vibration of the guns as the metallic blur of the ammunition clip raced by beneath his eyes. He took his hand away only when the tail gunner fell, and zoomed over the barreling craft with centimeters to spare. Bringing the zoom up and around and down again in a wide-curving dive, he came flashing up alongside the bomber with his hand pressed again to the trigger release, hammering mute the racket of the amidship gun and bursting the left engine into flame. Then, ritually wiping his powder-blackened chin preparatory to the final dive and *coup de grâce*, he was aware of a dozen streaking Sopwith fighters around him, of an intensity of gunfire, of everything ripped into, the smell of fuel gushing, a deadness in his side, the seat beneath him a glimpsed mass of torn horsehair and jagged metal. Automatically he connected the engine with his emergency fuel tank and tried to put the plane into a dive, but instead it slammed into a lurching stall, upsetting the charging case and spilling his ammunition earthward. The deadness in his side began a massive unfolding of pain, yet it had a peculiar remoteness, like that of the racketing machine-gun fire and constant puncturing slams along his fuselage. The wobble stick consumed his whole attention as he worked it vigorously, trying to bring the sputtering engine back to life and finally feeling it catch, take hold—but the pain had lost its remoteness, was spreading in a rapid, diamond-bright flickering behind his eyes, a flickering that began to wheel and wheel, and wheeled into blackness.

Some hundred meters from the ground he regained consciousness, his body pressed back flat in the huge downrushing momentum, his head splitting with the shriek of engine and wires. Lunging with both hands at the stick, pulling it back with agonized strain, he barely cleared the ground and brought the machine up in a low, tilted limp over enemy gunfire, the cockpit sluicing with gasoline and blood, shreds of canvas flapping from the wings. Just over German lines he crash-landed alongside a cemetery, the plane bouncing and thudding and blacking him out again as it slammed to an abrupt standstill against a fence.

Fortune had smiled upon him, he was later told. He would have lived only minutes longer had he not landed almost on the doorstep of a French church pressed into service as an emergency hospital, and been carried, disgorging blood like a pump, directly from his cockpit onto the operating table. Three machine-gun bullets had opened his right thigh and hip, as had numerous vicious jabs from the shattered upholstery. From these wounds, over a period of weeks, was extracted an abundance of deeply embedded metal splinters, horsehair fibers, and slivers of wood. "Fortune smiles on you, too," he managed to joke with the laboring doctors. "What if it had been the other way around? Three bullets in the Albatros and sixty-four in me?"

But the mangled flesh, the bite marks of mortality, brought him a new, strange sense of sobriety. He spent three months on his back, and six hobbling around an officers' convalescent home in Thuringia, at the end of which time he was ordered to report to Böblingen for further treatment. Instead he returned directly to the front, saying in excuse of his disobedience that he hadn't been able to find Böblingen on the map. He returned early in 1917 with a broad, circuitous, twenty-five-centimeter scar mass, angry red in color and of a rough, puckered topography, to find that the air war had also changed, all its silk-pajama gaiety vanished.

When he became a squadron commander, he quickly earned himself a reputation as a harsh and unforgiving martinet. He was sometimes ribbed by Bruno about his demand for absolute obedience, which Hermann admitted was ironic in view of his own high-handed record of disobeying orders. "But that was then. The air war has changed. The only way we're going to win it is by iron discipline. An iron knee in every gut, an iron fist in every mouth. Figuratively speaking, of course."

Bruno knew that Hermann's men were in fact devoted to him.

They found his harshness invigorating, and off-duty there was no jollier companion. But most important, he brought them glory. With enormous energy, hardworking to the point of obsession, he developed a striking ability for ground organization and air tactics, and within weeks of his appointment had made the indifferent Jasta 27 one of the most effective in the Jagdgeschwader. It was no surprise to the men he led into combat when the following year he was appointed commander of the fabled Richthofen Jagdgeschwader. They were as sorry to lose him as the Richthofen group were to have him.

First of all he was an outsider; and secondly, they knew his reputation for domineering, for being a *grobe Kunde*, a tough customer, although his acceptance speech was quiet, gracious and modest. Holding Richthofen's black Geschwaderstock, which had gone with the baron to his death and had been dropped by the British over the Geschwader's headquarters, the new Kommandant spoke gravely of the special honor done to him by His Imperial Majesty in making him commander of the illustrious Richthofen Squadron; he was only too sensible of the fact that there were no better fliers in all the world than those he saw before him now; he hoped he would be worthy of their confidence and their trust.

A few days later they learned that his voice had a biting, metallic quality when raised.

"Four weeks of an interim command, gentlemen, and you've turned into a gaggle of prima donnas. Well, let me tell you that there will be only one prima donna here, and that will be me. I will give the orders, I will decide the tactics, and I will tolerate neither scoreboard rivalry nor sloppy discipline."

Ernst Udet particularly, who had scored almost sixty kills, the highest of any living ace, and who had expected to inherit the black Geschwaderstock, was resentful of the new Kommandant. But Hermann felt an unreciprocated fondness for the little Ernst. Barely twenty-one, short, slight, with the face of a worn-out adolescent beneath already thinning hair, he had a peppery, sardonic personality along with a strong streak of the artist—how wonderfully the fellow dashed off planes, profiles, erotic cartoons, usually on the tablecloth of the officers' mess while knocking back a glass of schnapps. Hermann would often, with rosy conviviality, go over to the sketcher's side and, in the room's pervasive smell of damp wool and sweat, stand looking down admiringly until, after several mutely unresponsive minutes, he departed with a hearty nod.

He understood the man's feelings. His own score, thanks to almost a year out of action, was twenty-two. A prestigious enough number, but it was not only Udet's score that was spectacularly higher. How could such peacocks enjoy being pushed around? But pushed around they were going to be. If the war was lost, what then would individual notches count for? If the war was lost, everything was lost.

Only Leutnant Bodenschatz, the squadron adjutant, was supportive. In this tall, quiet staff officer he had sensed from the first an absolute loyalty. And he was a rock of reassurance. He pointed out that the men could not help but see that the Jagdgeschwader was being strengthened, and that not one of them, not Udet himself, could feel anything but admiration for the skill and courage of the Kommandant's leadership in the skies. And eventually it came to pass that, goggles pushed back, chin blackened, Udet walked over to him on the field to report, and said: "Sixty-first and sixty-second enemy shot down, sir. Myself slightly wounded. Shot through the left cheek. Face undamaged."

They had both laughed and shaken hands.

He had the confidence of his men, but there were fewer and fewer of them. Faces were lined, tempers shredded. Men who had indulged in an occasional cigarette had turned into chain smokers; he suspected that some of them used drugs: cocaine, morphine. You could not fly into combat five, six, sometimes seven times a day, week after week after week, without paying for it in your nerves. There were times when he wanted nothing more than to fling himself down on his cot, pull the blanket over his face, and forget the war.

And there would be an abundance of memories to sink into . . . his trip to Mauterndorf on convalescent leave, all the old sights and sounds . . . hazed blue mountains, the soft clunking of cow bells . . . at dinner the same minstrels playing from the same little balcony, and below it, hung in isolated splendor, the mounted head of his first deer, shot at age thirteen, his name and the date engraved on a silver plaque . . . Pate sitting opposite him with his little consort, who darted flirtatious glances at the guest—depressing, insulting to Pate, who didn't notice . . . hair and mustaches still dyed jet black in contrast to his deeper-than-ever wrinkles . . . but still the same, holding forth on every subject, bellowing orders, stomping corpulently about, albeit with a cane now . . . when they walked together there had been a tapping of two canes, which moved Pate deeply . . . his beloved Hermann shot up so badly, was it still painful? Such concern in those black old eyes, such love, such depths of pride, and when those eyes looked into his, he felt the world of his youth flame up gold within him. . . .

Or he would think of his and Bruno's last fling in Berlin . . . four courses, starting with white asparagus; a string quartet, the scent of cut roses and good cigars and of mouth-watering perfume as mouth-watering women stopped at their table, smiling and rosy, holding out a menu or bit of paper to be autographed . . . cabarets afterward, blue smoke and gravelly songs, and then a revue somewhere, girls screeching and kicking in unison, red flounces, black net stockings, white arms—and white arms afterward, a thorough and marvelous debauch in a couple of seedy rooms off Friedrichstrasse, a naked lamp bulb, red silk scarf thrown over it, and rushing out at dawn into the dark maw of the Friedrichstrasse station, barely catching the train back to the front as all the bright colors of the night receded in memory to a tiny cluster of gems. . . .

No, more likely he would think of something else that had receded—Ludendorff's great spring offensive. That huge and almost victorious push, almost to Paris, close enough to bombard the city with Krupp's giant cannon . . . and then the steady, relentless falling back, until the troops were finally dug in again along their old positions, and now—as freshly arrived American troops kept pouring into the Allied trenches—were fighting on with ebbing supplies, wearing broken boots, subsisting on turnip mash, their wounds bandaged with paper.

Such was the effectiveness of the British sea blockade. But it was not only the blockade that was bleeding them white, it was their own home front. Defeatism, strikes and riots fomented by the Social Democrats; a munitions strike in the middle of a war, it stunned you, a stab in the back of every man fighting for his life and the life of his country; and stupidity everywhere—strike leaders arrested and sent to the front as punishment, but it was no punishment for seasoned antiwar agitators to be flung into the trenches; they had spread disaffection to the point where soldiers' soviets had sprung up, where cases were rumored of men refusing to obey orders, turning on their officers. No, Karl, for all your Socialist views you would not have understood these kinds of tactics, the treachery, the vile underhandedness; filth that has no place in the honorable history of Germany. . . .

The cigar had gone out between his fingers. He set it down in the ashtray, flexing his fingers in the chill of the room, and took up his pen.

It was three o'clock when he put the completed papers together, and, not bothering to call his servant, bent over to work off his boots. He threw them across the room and turned off the lamp, leaning back in his chair with an exhausted sigh. He sat there in the darkness for a while, then, stretching and getting to his feet, walked over to the cot and flung himself down for three or four hours' sleep.

Chapter 14

Wιτн the door of his corrugated-tin office standing open to the November fog as clerks lugged in tables, chairs, and cardboard boxes, Leutnant Bodenschatz was trying to find files and memos in the welter, while having constantly to break off in order to answer the jangling telephone. His eyes were red-rimmed with lack of sleep as he hurried back and forth, and in them, mixed with exhaustion and strain, was a glaze of bitterness. Within a period of only weeks the Navy had mutinied, the Bavarian monarchy had toppled, most major cities had fallen to revolutionary councils, and as of yesterday in Berlin—where truckloads of sailors, soldiers and workers had rumbled through the streets waving red flags—Imperial Germany had ceased to exist. The country having been proclaimed a republic, its delegates were even now meeting with the Allies at Compiègne to hear the terms of an armistice. Only one battle remained—that which would ensue when the Kaiser led what was left of his army back into Germany against the Reds, an act incumbent upon his and the Fatherland's imperial honor, even if he found only a handful of loyal troops to follow him.

Since the Allied breakthrough at the Meuse, the Geschwader had fallen back twice, striking camp at this muddy, rutted aerodrome late yesterday. And while the tent hangars and tin shacks were still going up, a chaos of conflicting orders was pouring in from the High Command: to fall back yet another ten kilometers; to fly all aircraft out to

Darmstadt; to surrender immediately to the nearest Allied forces. The telephone never stopped ringing, and now Bodenschatz hurried once again to pick up the receiver. He stood listening to the voice at the other end, and his hand spread slowly across his eyes, which he felt growing wet beneath his fingers.

"Ja," he murmured at length, and put down the receiver, standing there by the table for some moments. Then he went back through the litter and outside to find his commandant.

Everything familiar was suddenly unendurable to him. The squelch his boots made in the mud, and the dull, distant rumble of cannon, and the fog, which was not gray but brown, dirty, made so by tons of earth blown into the sky for years. Across the fields near the aerodrome there moved columns of helmeted figures in retreat. They were dim in the fog, ghostly. Here and there he could make out rag-wrapped feet thick with mud, moving like clods of earth. He felt that he himself moved as heavily, but when he found the commandant, near one of the tent hangars, he managed to step briskly forward, smash his muddy heels together, and give a sharp salute.

"Sir! I beg to report that His Majesty the Kaiser has abdicated. We are told that His Majesty has left Supreme Headquarters to seek refuge in Holland. Sir!"

Göring's eyes flickered, as if he had been struck, and his face underwent an extraordinary change, a pinching, a wasting, the skin becoming as wax on bone—only for an instant, so brief you might have thought you had imagined it.

"Danke," he said curtly, returning the salute and walking away.

Soon after dawn the next day they received word that the ceasefire would take effect at eleven o'clock that morning. The fog had lifted during the night, giving way to a thin drizzle that continued through the sober, laborious hours as the newly erected tents and shacks were pulled down and piled with equipment into a convoy of trucks, and the planes were taxied out onto the muddy field. Of the conflicting orders the Geschwader had received, only one was acceptable to its members: to fly back to Darmstadt. Surrendering their machines to the Allies they would refuse to do under any circumstances.

Standing in the drizzle, the commandant gave his instructions to Leutnant Bodenschatz, who was to lead the convoy out as soon as the planes had cleared the field. As he talked, the commandant noticed that the men loading the trucks had stopped working and were gazing around as if puzzled. He looked around too, feeling that a strangeness had come over everything, and then he realized that he was listening to an enormous emptiness. For the first time in four years and four months the distant rumble of guns was still. The tortured countryside lay silent.

Nothing was said, and after a few moments the work went on.

*   *   *

Half an hour later, as he was climbing into his cockpit, the commandant saw a staff car plowing toward them through the mud. It halted directly in front of his plane. "Get that damned car off the field!" he cried, climbing down with his black Geschwaderstock clutched in his hand as if to bash in the head of the staff officer hurrying toward him.

"I have—" the officer began, his eye on the stick. "I have urgent orders, sir," and he held out a sealed envelope which was torn from his hand and ripped open.

> Fifth Army Headquarters to Kommandant Jagdgeschwader Freiherr von Richthofen No. I. You will disarm your planes at once and fly to French air headquarters at Strasbourg where arrangements have been made for you to land without hindrance. Acknowledge.

"Acknowledge, my ass! Bodenschatz, get the telephone rigged up! Tell those shitheads we're not handing our planes over to any frogs! And you're under arrest!" he shouted into the staff officer's face. "You'll accompany this convoy as a prisoner—what are you sputtering about? It relieves you of responsibility! The responsibility is mine." And with an abrupt signal to his pilots, his Geschwaderstock still trembling in his angry hand, he climbed back up into the cockpit.

The flight to Darmstadt was made in strong winds and driving rain, and when the Geschwader set down at the air depot it was discovered that one of the groups had gone astray in the storm. Two hours later the missing fliers showed up in the back of a truck, the blinding weather having caused them to mistakenly land at the Mannheim airfield, which was held by one of the Soldiers' and Workers' Revolutionary Councils. An armed troop had hauled them out, stripped them and their planes of all weapons, and shoved the fliers off to make the rest of the way by foot or thumb. This time too outraged to shout, the commandant listened white-faced; then he assembled a flight of nine Fokkers, gave the pilots instructions, and led them on the short flight to the Mannheim airfield, where three planes landed while the other six circled low, banking in the rain.

On the field the three pilots were taken through the milling rebels to the commander, who was presented with an ultimatum. Either all arms would be restored and a formal apology written, or the planes overhead would machine-gun everything on the ground that moved. "Our Kommandant will wait two minutes, no longer," the spokesman concluded, and from his holster withdrew a signal-flare pistol. "I am to fire this if you agree to our terms."

"Fire then—fire!"

The weapons were set aboard, the apology was written, and the three Fokkers took off in the rain to rejoin the flight back to Darmstadt. There, going in first, the commandant set his machine down smoothly, and halfway along the runway put his hand over the side and gave the canvas a tender pat. A moment later he slammed his foot down and whipped the plane around on its side, smashing one wing and tearing up the undercarriage. The other eight pilots followed suit, each wrecking his machine beyond repair, beyond the touch of either Allies or Reds.

11 November. Armistice. Flight in bad weather to Darmstadt. Since its establishment the Geschwader has shot down 644 enemy planes. Death by enemy action came to 56 officers, six other ranks. Wounded, 52 officers, seven other ranks. Hermann Göring, Leutnant O.C. Geschwader.

He was demobilized with the rank of captain, in a small town near Frankfurt, where the remnants of the general staff were gathered, and where, in a paper-making factory on the outskirts, the Geschwader had set up headquarters for its mustering-out process. The formal disbandment ceremony took place in the factory courtyard under the usual drizzle, the wet cobblestones littered with sodden paper. After the brief and simple ceremony, the fliers silently collected their luggage and departed.

"Ich hatt' einen Kamaraden
Einen bessern findst du nicht . . ."

The Bierstube rang with song, shouts, laughter, the clinkings and table thuds of glasses. Determined to go out with a bang, a dozen or so senior officers had gathered here after the disbandment ceremony, but none was as drunk as he wanted to be. The place was freezing, the waiter unfriendly. The townspeople resented the presence of the military, attracting as it did too many troublemaking mobs from Frankfurt—deserters, whores, adolescent louts, roaming the streets in search of officers. Captain Göring, as he sat singing loudly, still felt the shock of "Imperial butcher! Kaiser lackey!" shouted into his face, and the greater shock of having his arms grabbed and his epaulets ripped from his uniform. He had been quaffing one schnapps after another, but was as coldly sober as he had ever been in his life, and felt relief when long before midnight the forced merrymaking wore itself out. He got up and mounted the small bandstand with his glass.

"Gentlemen. The Richthofen Geschwader is no more. But its skill and courage and gallantry were very great, and are respected through-out the world. Only in Germany is its record suddenly forgotten, its name dragged through the mud, its officers insulted and attacked. One can feel only outrage against people who attack those who sacrificed themselves for their country, only outrage against the revolutionary forces sweeping through Germany and bringing deepest shame upon it. The new fight for freedom and principles and morals has begun. We will fight against these forces which are seeking to enslave us, and we will win through. We have a long way to go, but the truth will be our light. We must be proud of this truth and of what we have done. The same qualities that made the Richthofen Geschwader great will prevail in peace as well as in war. Our time will come again."

His voice had grown thick with emotion, tears stood in his eyes.

"Gentlemen. To the Fatherland, and to the Richthofen Ge-schwader."

He drank and threw his glass to the floor with a splintering crash as the others did the same, almost all of them weeping.

The railways throughout western Germany were given over solely to the transport of demobilized soldiers, who hung thick to the sides of the trains and sat crammed along the roofs and were sometimes scraped off and crushed by sudden tunnel entrances. Inside the trains, in a stench of overflowing lavatories, the corridors and compartments were jammed solid. Göring and Udet, returning home together to Munich, stood mashed and immobile in a compartment whose sagging baggage nets had collapsed under the weight of knapsacks, helmets and gas masks. The compartment was barren, every piece of metal having long since been removed to the armaments factories, every leather accouterment stripped away by passengers to make shoes of. From under the floorboards the axles, with no grease to lubricate them, sent up a ferocious grinding and jolting, along with a harsh smell of hot metallic friction. Many of the trains came to a sudden stop be-cause of broken axles, or they ran out of coal, and hours would pass before the men inside, standing upright, half asleep, felt a violent lurch as the journey resumed.

At changing points an exhausted clash erupted between those in-side struggling to get off and those on the platform struggling to get on, a window-breaking pandemonium which, when it was over and the train had chugged away from the station into the distance, was re-placed by an immediately stagnant sense of waiting. An hour might pass, or half a day, before another overladen train heading in the de-sired direction came rumbling to a stop. It was impossible to squeeze inside the station; most had been shot up during the revolutionary skir-mishes, and though the interiors were swept with drafts from broken windows, they were dry, and always crammed to the last centimeter with sleeping men. But at least field kitchens had been set up outside the larger depots; these stood steaming in the rain, presided over by nurses who ladled out a hot, watery, brown substance which might have been soup but which Göring, upon his first taste three days before, had declared to be boiled diarrhea. He drank it anyway, and Udet's as well, since poor Ernst, with his artist's imagination, had taken the remark to heart. What four years of combat had failed to do to Ernst, this demoralizing trip had achieved. He had lost his cap somewhere along the way, and his worn, juvenile face, with its rain-soaked thinning hair and three days' growth of beard, was the color of pewter. He looked seedy, lost, played-out.

Udet thought the same of his companion. The lid of one eye was drawn down with fatigue, his lower face was covered with reddish-brown bristles, and the wet weather brought out a dragging slowness in his right leg as they walked up and down the crowded, refuse-strewn platform. Red armbands of the soldiers' soviets showed through here and there in the crowd, but at none of the stations and in none of the trains did more than an embittered look ever pass between rebels and officers, as though it was agreed that there was too much rain for more than that, and too much weariness.

Toward nightfall a train bound for Munich came clanking in, and the two friends made the last part of their journey hanging on with a cluster of men from the platform of the coal tender. The towns they passed through in the morning were gray and wet. Long lines extended down the streets from food shops. No motorcars were to be seen, only horses and carts. The people were shabbily dressed. They paid no attention to the returning troop train.

He woke in an unfamiliarity of fresh, lavender-scented pillows, and for a moment the sick feeling inside him disappeared as he stretched his limbs, groaning with well-being. Then, throwing back the eiderdown, he stood up in the gray watery light that fell through the lace curtains of his mother's guest room.

Down the hall he washed in a basin of tepid water, there being no heat for a bath, and with his long razor carefully shaved his face clean, afterward dusting talcum powder onto his jaws and wondering if this too would now be considered a crime, since it was a custom of the officer class. Returning to his room, he dressed in a clean if crumpled uniform from his suitcase, and, standing before the cheval glass, briskly smoothed his hair with two silver-backed brushes until it lay flat and glossy. Then he strode down the hall to the parlor.

With a cup of ersatz coffee beside her, a coat around her shoulders, Nikki sat before the fireplace twisting newspapers. These, in lieu of coal or wood, were first dampened and then twisted very tightly so that they would not burn too fast. Though her hands grew dirty from the newsprint, she had come to like the steady, soothing motion of this daily task. Always when she was finished and sat back, it would come bursting in on her again—defeat, riots, cold, hunger, the monarchy swept away, everything swept away—and with her soiled hands she would draw her coat more closely around her and try to make her mind a blank.

Today, however, she had immediately set about laying the newspapers in the grate, having already brought in a tray on which was arranged a little feast of coffee and bread with marmalade. The marmalade was vile, made of turnips and hardly any sugar, but it was the best one could offer. And now as she lit the newspapers she heard Hermann coming into the room and she turned with arms outspread.

"Ach, fourteen hours you've slept, Hermann!"

He gave her a rough hug and thought how exactly the same she looked—red-faced, bony, ageless. Yesterday he had noticed little, but today he took everything in, gazing around the parlor with its Oriental throw rugs and dark mahogany furniture and cherry-red drapes, a pleasant little room that he had never ceased to loathe, and now cold as an icebox, with twists of cloth pressed along the windowsills to discourage drafts.

He turned back to the beaming face beside him. "You're looking well, Nikki. In fact you look better than ever. It's all that turnip mash."

"Doch, get away. If I never saw another turnip I'd be happy. But eat, Hermann, eat!" And she felt lit within by that brisk, hand-rubbing gesture of his when he looked forward to something, and she sat down and watched with pleasure as he poured a stream of chickory coffee from the silver service, and took a slice of the chestnut-flour bread covered with the turnip marmalade. He did not even gag as he chewed, merely made a hideous face, and then ate another slice of bread and drank his coffee, standing, always ready, always up to something. She felt completely happy watching him, not happy in the way she had been yesterday—a joy so mixed with tears it was more like pain—but in the simplest, sunniest way, as if a curtain were now going to rise on something wonderful; and it was absolutely right and wonderful that he walked directly to the gramophone and cranked the handle, and that a moment later the cold room sprang to life with the beginning strains of "Liebe Kleine Nachtigall." She sank back in her chair and closed her eyes, giving herself over completely to the sweet, light-hearted elegance of the song, which seemed to bring back in a rush everything that had once been; and then suddenly she was pressing her face into her hands.

"What's happening here?" Hermann chided, coming over and looking down at her through the muffled noise of her sobbing. "It does no good," he said, giving her shoulder a pat. "It does no good, Nikki."

Poor Nikki, who only three months ago had written him of a

dream in which she had glimpsed Hindenburg and Ludendorff, as clear as could be, striding triumphantly through the Palace of Versailles. "No good," he murmured to himself, and the sick feeling was suddenly so strong inside him, mixed with preoccupation and restlessness, that he began to pace back and forth by the fireplace, which gave off more smoke than heat.

"Where's Mutter gone off to?"

"She knows someone," Nikki brought out nasally, wiping her eyes with the sleeve of her coat. "She's going to have such a feast for you, Hermann. Veal. You can't live without the black market, nobody can. But you're cheated anyway. The bread's full of sawdust." She felt strengthened by her sobs, as if her lungs had been shaken into life. "They're all Jews, these profiteers. And the Reds, everyone in this new government, they're all Jews—what else would they be?"

He gave a short sigh. He loathed this Marxist republic, and there was no doubt that many of its key figures were Jews. But Jew-fuss had always bored him. Half the Prussian officer corps was married into Jewish families. He stood before the fireplace, impatiently rocking back and forth on his heels.

"You should see our fine Bavarian Minister President, Herr Eisner," Nikki went on. "Of course that's not his real name, it's Kosmanowski. And how he looks it. I've seen him in his carriage, a shabby little nothing with a long beard right out of the Old Testament. The man who has taken the place of the royal house of Wittelsbach! A journalist, a Schwabing bohemian who's never done anything in his life but hang about sleazy cafés and run off at the mouth. And what has he done as minister? Ach, let me tell you! First he sat down and composed a hymn called 'The Song of the People' and had it performed at the opera house. Then he got busy and had posters plastered all over— 'Every human life shall be holy.' 'Keep peace and contribute to the rise of the new world.' *What* new world, I should like to know! Everything goes from bad to worse, and this—this numbskull, this insect, can think of nothing better to do than fiddle with songs and posters!"

Hermann was laughing, and Nikki began to laugh too, so hard that she had to wipe her eyes again with her coat sleeve.

The feast that evening consisted of a small cut of veal, turnip mash in the shape of dumplings, a few bluish potatoes, and a bottle of red wine. The cook and second maid had long since been let go, and the Frau Reichskommissar herself had prepared the homecoming meal, and now, seated in an evening dress and winter coat, she presided over the table which Nikki had set with all the finesse of Christmas Eve.

"Nikki," she said suddenly, "you haven't let on about the surprise, have you?"

"I? How could I see it to tell about it? It's too small to be seen by the human eye."

"How can you say that?" the Frau Reichskommissar protested, pleased to discover her maid back in her old state of impertinence, and turned to her son. "It's the dessert, Hermann. It may shrivel your taste buds, but I guarantee that it will dazzle your eyes."

"I can't possibly wait." He smiled. "And you've created this spectacular thing yourself?"

"Ja, from glue and chalk," she answered gravely; then smiled. "No, I think things are bound to improve before it comes to glue and chalk."

"After all," Nikki said, her eyes resting confidently on Hermann, "they can't keep up the food blockade forever."

"No," he agreed. "Not till the end of eternity. That seems unlikely."

His mother gave a bitter shake of her head. "That they have kept it up at all is vile. The war is over."

"And the vile lies they've told about us," said Nikki. "Hammering the tongues of Belgian children to tables, things like that—how could they tell such monstrous lies!"

"Because they're swine," he said shortly. That burned inside him still—the German Imperial Army did not deserve that, though God knew it deserved a bash in the teeth for stupidity; to have slapped down a billion-mark indemnity on the Russians when they capitulated, and forced them to sign away three hundred thousand square miles of territory, that was pure rutting greed, an unforgivable stupidity that had made the Allies resolve once and for all never to submit to a German peace. So much stupidity everywhere, the government throwing antiwar agitators into the trenches, the imbecile U-boats dragging America in—the whole world dragged in; twenty-nine nations they had stood up against—and a food blockade, and an internal revolt, and still they had not been conquered in battle, but had been stabbed in the back by the revolutionary government.

His mother was lifting her wineglass, her fingers red with the room's coldness.

"To our Hermann," she said quietly, looking at him. "We give thanks to Thee, our Lord, for his safe return."

They drank, and his mother lifted her glass once more.

"I believed, and I now believe all the more, and however strangely things may go, or however badly, that I shall remain in the order of the faithful."

Hermann remembered these words from one of Vati's favorite books, a biography of Goethe, in which Vati had drawn a pale penciled star next to this passage. His mother had apparently looked through the volumes in the bookcase for something that would express her feelings on this occasion and had found the staunch, inspired quotation, already marked. He wondered if she had seen the sadness of that mark, for Vati's pale star, far from reflecting the passage, was only a pale, wistful thought. But he doubted if she had taken notice, nor in a way could he blame her; and sinking into the old tangled mesh of loyalties, he took a small sip of wine and set the glass down.

Nikki went into the kitchen to fetch the surprise, which was a gluey little pudding drowned in brandy. She was to set a match to it. In the other room, Hermann and his mother sat talking about Albert, who was also being demobilized—frail and asthmatic, he had been called up toward the end. "That will be another wonderful moment," the Frau Reichskommissar said, smiling at her son from across the table, and thinking how different was his appearance from yesterday. In a fresh uniform, clean-shaven, his hair brushed back smooth, he radiated crispness, vitality, good cheer; but for all that, she could not agree with Nikki that he seemed fit as a fiddle, for she saw that beneath the surface he was torn to pieces. Already she was learning that if conversation was to go smoothly, it was best not to discuss the defeat or the revolution. As for the Kaiser, having brought up his name once, she dared never say it again. They talked about friends, family, everyday things, and it was enough for her just to see him sitting there across the table, and when Albert came home, too . . . then the war would have given her back two sons out of three, for which she must consider herself one of the very fortunate. Her eyes suddenly brimmed with the cruelty of this paradox, and she felt the wound of Karl's death as if it were as keen and fresh as the joy of Hermann's homecoming, and then she could not tell whom her tears were for, looking through them as Nikki came in bearing the little dessert, a blur of flame struggling blue and orange from the silver dish.

Chapter 15

HERMANN stayed in Munich only a week, spending the days walking around the city with Udet. In the summer Munich was in its element, sunny and easygoing, with its innumerable beer gardens, beer halls, beer cellars, its mixed classic and baroque architecture imparting an airy, Italianate flavor, as did its green, lazily curving River Isar. December's drizzle did nothing for all this even at the best of times, and now it fell, with a touch of sleet, on parks raw with the stumps of trees chopped down for firewood, it dripped from the rifles of soldiers guarding the city's half-empty coal dumps, and from the eaves of factory buildings shut down for lack of fuel. It soaked the red flags hanging from public buildings and streetcars, and fell on sodden kiosks where you could buy postcards showing a yellow-bellied Kaiser floating down a Dutch canal, on scavenging mobs with a wild eye out for stray officers, on one-legged soldiers begging from doorways, on sullen, shivering queues before food shops, and on the diminutive Herr Eisner himself, whom the two officers stood watching as he alighted from his carriage and went up the steps of the parliament building. He wore an ill-fitting black frock coat and a shapeless black slouch hat, and his long un-Germanic beard fluttered in the wet wind.

Ernst, taking out his notepad, rapidly sketched a picture of a slouch-hatted flea leaping from an armpit onto a scepter.

"Better show the other vermin leaping behind him," Hermann said, striding on down the street. "He's not going to last long."

"Are we late for an appointment?" Ernst asked, his feet hot inside his boots. It seemed they never slowed down, nor were they headed anywhere. They just kept tramping, usually in circles, while Hermann talked.

"The rest of the government won't do any better than Eisner. A pack of old ladies. Look at the mess they've got in Berlin. Having to call in the Army to put down their own radicals—that's the joke of the century. The Army's what they've kicked *out*. Authority. Force. That's what stinks in their nostrils. They hate the Army like sin, but they can't do without it. And they hate revolution like sin. Do you know Ebert actually said that when he took over? 'I hate revolution as I hate sin.' You know what our Chancellor Ebert wants? He wants a moderate democratic socialist state to spring into existence without his taking steps. He doesn't have a circus monkey's idea how to put his programs into effect. All empty talk, a lot of musical farting. The country's an ash heap and they do nothing. They can't even squeeze a few vegetables out of these filthy little profiteering farmers. Using authority would scare them sick. They've got power in their hands and they don't know what to do with it. They've got no instinct for power. It dribbles through their fingers."

Ernst agreed with all this, but he had heard it so often as they pounded along in their vast circles that he only nodded. He could envision no solution. What solution existed in a nation dictated to by its victors? The Allies had refused to negotiate with the monarchy, only with a democratic government representing the people: the Allies had pulled the Socialists in, and they would see that the Socialists stayed in. The Allies might not like socialism, but they liked the militarist monarchy even less. Already they had interned the Navy and abolished the Air Force. And God knew what spine-crushing economic terms would come of the Paris Peace Conference; you could draw your own conclusions from the fact that they still refused to lift the food blockade, though it was bringing death by starvation to thousands upon thousands of civilians. It took more insight than he possessed—than perhaps anyone possessed—to see where it would all end. Only one thing was clear: Germany was once again to be made a weak, impoverished nation.

"Have you decided what you're going to do?" Ernst asked as they hurried along.

"Weiss nicht. This place—I look around, I don't know it. Red flags. Mobs spitting on you. Germany's gone. Like an avalanche—whoosh! gone, there's nothing left. Nothing to stay in the Army for."

"You'll stay in. I can't see you a civilian."

"I can. One with a lot of sharp ribs. The only thing I can do is fly an airplane. No airplanes. You're luckier."

"A civilian born and bred."

"An artist."

Udet smiled, as he always did when Hermann called him an artist. He considered himself a doodler. But unlike most products ground out like bars of steel from the Prussian military machine, Hermann enjoyed a lively appreciation of the arts, cherished a deep esteem for artists, and insisted that he, Ernst, was one of the anointed. Ernst was not interested in painters, but on leave in Berlin he had been dragged to the Kaiser Friedrich Museum by his enthusiastic commandant, who stood rapt before a huge Rubens while he himself put on his cap and went off in search of a café. During those two days they had never passed an antique shop that Hermann had not pulled him inside, his eyes shining at such massed relics of the past. Opera Ernst disliked and balked at, but he enjoyed their evening at the theater, if not to the same degree as Hermann, excited as a schoolboy as the curtain went rattling up. He was an odd duck, this friend of his, this Prussian paragon—up and down, unpredictable, which was maybe his attraction; he was never boring, the one unendurable thing to Ernst. Still, he could be an intolerable pain, overbearing. Yet even in that there was something appealing, a magnetism. Look how you galloped along at his side, your feet burning. Far be it for Hermann to slow down if he was not in a mood to slow down.

"You know that we're not going anywhere, Hermann."

"True. But why dawdle?"

"Well then, let's take a streetcar," Udet suggested with a broad smile. Since lack of fuel had put cabs out of service, the only way to get around, except on foot, was by public conveyance. But this Hermann could not bring himself to do. It was the principle of the thing, and it vastly amused Udet. He himself had never worn a uniform until the outbreak of the war, and though proud of his officer status, he could not help but think the career officers' code of behavior quirky, extreme and ridiculous. Never to have hopped aboard a streetcar—it was amazing.

"Look here," he said, swinging his arm out as a tram came clattering along, its red banners fluttering in the drizzle. "Avail yourself of life's conveniences. A whole new world opening up before you."

"I'll walk."

And so they walked.

Hermann had intended to go to Mauterndorf to visit Pate, but the taste of defeat was too strong in his mouth. Nor was there anything for him to do in Munich. Perhaps, he thought, if he went to Berlin he would come to some decision about his future. And so he took leave of his mother and Nikki and set off for the north, crammed into a third-class train compartment. He could afford nothing better, and in any case all the compartments were in the same sorry state. It began to snow as they neared Nuremberg.

On impulse, but what impulse he could not say, he got off the train there. He did not go outside the station doors, for he had no inclination to see that medieval glory brought down to beggars and breadlines, but stood smoking a cigarette instead—one of those things so flimsily made that the tobacco, or, more likely, cow dung, spilled out from either end—and then, throwing it aside, went over and bought a ticket home.

It had been six years, but he knew by heart every village the train passed, every field and dark stand of forest, and just where each stone bridge would appear over the little winding Pegnitz. Then, in the distance, faintly through the falling snow, he made out the high red dot of the tower roof. Gradually the tower came clearer, silhouetted against the gray, white-flaked sky, and he could see the south and west walls of the burg and beneath them the hill with all its treetops dusted white. Then the train turned a bend, cutting off the view, and a few minutes later slowed to a stop before the small brick station. He had meant to get out, but he remained sitting in the coach. The burg was rented out to strangers who would show him around his courtyard, point up to his tower, and perhaps allow him a glimpse of his childhood room with its three leaded diamond-paned windows overlooking the fields and forests, with the jagged cliffside falling away below. . . .

With a lurch the train moved on. For a while he sat looking at the palisades of trees passing at his side; then suddenly he rose and opened the window, craning his head and shoulders out into the falling snow. The tower was already distant, and it seemed, as he leaned out gazing back at it, to be gazing back at him. Then gradually it grew more obscured by snow until he could see it no longer.

Berlin was shabbier than Munich, colder, hungrier, crueler. Along Unter den Linden, where traffic consisted of old bicycles and horse-drawn carts, the prostitutes had left their drab posts around the Friedrichstrasse station and now boldly patrolled the city's showcase avenue, where, often in tight trousers and boots, with a leather whip displayed from a back pocket, they competed with scores of war-widowed housewives. These newcomers to the trade were astonishingly brazen, pushed by desperation to the crudest directness, and yet they conveyed a feeling of wretched respectability, for they had developed no sense of dress or makeup. Youths of sixteen and seventeen showed a quicker knack, lips and cheeks brightly rouged; some wore blue sailor suits with short trousers; they stood in doorways, shivering and smiling, batting their lashes. Crippled soldiers and officers sat along the pavement, begging, or trying to sell postcards and trinkets. Most of the buildings along den Linden had been pocked by machine-gun fire. There were boarded-up shop windows where mobs had broken the glass trying to get to the food inside. Overhead, the republic's red flags flapped in the snowy wind.

One of the reasons he had come to Berlin was to attend an officers' mass rally at the Philharmonic Hall, to be presided over by General Reinhardt, whom Ebert had appointed Minister of War. It was said that the general would urge support of the new government and ask his audience to obey the latest governmental edict, which was that officers remove epaulets and all other insignia of rank and replace them with simple blue stripes on the sleeve.

In full dress uniform, displaying his captain's stars and silver epaulets and every last one of his medals, Hermann sat down in the great hall, which was rapidly filling to capacity. Up on the stage sat the newly formed Officers' Society Committee with General Reinhardt at its center, his epaulets gone, his sleeve bearing the government-ordained blue stripes. When the general stepped forward and began addressing the audience, Hermann felt his face flush with anger, and suddenly, blind to his very minor status of captain, he was out of his seat and striding down the aisle. Stepping up onto the stage, he pointedly interrupted the speaker, who turned to him in astonishment.

"I ask your pardon, Herr General," he said loudly. "I knew, sir, that you would be here tonight to address us, but I had hoped that you would have had the good taste to wear on your sleeve a black band, in token of the regret you should feel at the rape of the Army's tradition. In fact, sir, I believe red stripes would be more in keeping with your apparent sympathies."

This was met with a crash of applause from the audience. He called out for silence, and went on.

"For four long years we officers did our duty and risked our lives for our Fatherland. Now we come home and how are we treated? We are spat upon, and our honor, the only thing left to us, is taken from us. But I tell you the people are not to blame for this. The people were with us as comrades, the comrades of each of us, for four long weary years of war. The ones to blame are those who stabbed our glorious Army in the back and thought of nothing but their own wish to rule. I ask everyone here to cherish a hatred, a deep and abiding hatred, for those swine who have outraged the German people and the German traditions. I tell you now that the day will come when we will drive these criminals from the Fatherland. Prepare for that day! Arm yourselves for that day! Work for that day!"

The audience had risen to its feet; there was a deafening applause in his ears. He stepped down to back claps and pumping handshakes, and was carried shoulder-high up the tumultuous aisle.

But as he went to bed that night he knew that his outburst would have no effect on the situation. He knew, too, that he had effectively ended his military career.

Over the next few weeks in Berlin, staying now with friends, now in some cheap hotel room, he watched the country's continued deterioration. In Munich, poor Eisner of the shabby slouch hat was assassinated by a deranged nobleman. Though the people had already voted him out of office, they now wept and kissed the bloodied pavement where he had fallen. In death the fumbling idealist was raised to the stature of martyred saint; having welcomed in the moderates, Bavaria now swung to the left. Here in Berlin, machine-gun fire rattled through the streets for a full week before the Army put down a concentrated uprising of Spartacists. The Spartacist leaders, Karl Liebknecht and Rosa Luxemburg, had disappeared and were rumored to have been shot out of hand.

It was surprising to him that the Spartacists, who designated themselves the German Communist Party, had lasted even a day. During skirmishes in the Tiergarten they had dutifully obeyed "Keep Off the Grass" signs and stayed respectfully on the graveled paths. In one instance they had actually lined up to buy tickets in order to enter and take over a railway station. Except for their red armbands, they had nothing in common with their ferocious Russian counterparts, but were law-abiding Germans at heart. He hated them, as he hated the bourgeois Socialists in power—hated Communism passionately, for its ravening internationalism—but he did not take these German Communists seriously. Their radical aims were alien to the German character, and no matter what mobs they were able to whip up in chaotic times, they would always in the end be rejected like a bad skin graft. It was the Socialists he took seriously, that miserable amalgam of red flags and top hats, of confusion, faintheartedness, and ineffectual discussion. The Army with its little blue stripes would do the dirty work, and with a vengeance; already it had formed Freikorps units to fight the Reds in the Baltic states; and the Freikorps would be sent to Munich, too, where without doubt they would crush the swing to the far left. That was fine as far as it went. They might rip out the Communists, but who would rip out the legally entrenched, Allied-sanctioned Socialists?

He had packed away his uniform and medals, all but his Pour le Mérite, which he kept in its small black leather case and carried in his trousers pocket. He wore a civilian suit made of some flimsy ersatz material, probably processed nettles mixed with wood fiber, and could not get used to the absence of his tight collar or the tight grip of his boots around his calves. The aching scar along his thigh reminded him, every day, that he had survived when two million had not. He had believed that he was marked for a special destiny, and he knew now that that destiny was the vindication of those two million. And yet everything rational in him said that he had no destiny at all. He was without country, flag, or Kaiser. He was an unemployed man of twenty-six, wearing a badly fitting suit that wrinkled like paper.

Eventually he learned that German aircraft manufacturers were being allowed to produce machines on a small scale for the commercial market abroad. Early in the spring of 1919 he left for Copenhagen to demonstrate the Fokker F-7 monoplane at an aviation exhibition.

Chapter 16

Dearest Fanny,

I am wildly, wildly happy!!—oh so homesick for Sweden & all of you & shall always be but that was the choice I had to make & it was the right & only choice. Fanny if you could see me you wouldn't know your Carin, my health is wonderfully sound & I'm brown as a Bavarian farmgirl— we've rented a hut quite high up, just a tiny hunting box really, no glass in the windows just shutters we never close & the nights are so mild & lovely & in the mornings the sun comes flooding in! Weather like midsummer! & we take a knapsack & ramble all over, we're lying on a hillside as I write this, very high & green & spring flowers everywhere—bluebells, yarrow, blazing-red primulas—& cows grazing, & two big caramel horses with creamish manes, & the mountains are hazed a dark greenish blue, so still & majestic, everything is so peaceful here, so high & green & spacious. We take bread & cheese along & we read or write letters, we talk & doze in the sun & then we wander on—oh Fanny to be so in love, to be married and to be here!! I don't feel thirty-four but as if I were twelve, the joy bursts in me & I feel like a child God had been terribly kind to, I feel so dazzled & grateful!! I've written all about the wedding to Mother &

Father so you've seen the letter, but I'm sure I forgot to tell everything—I admit the first few days in our little hut did make for rather a brief note, forgive my crudeness but what glorious crudeness!! Well I like his mother so much, so warm & lively & the sisters too, Olga & Paula, they live in Austria & so does the brother Albert, & then there's Nikki the mother's maid & a family institution, face very like a hatchet but beaming & beside herself & dressed to the teeth, she adores Hermann & now me as well & in spite of the face is a dear, & his flying comrades were there, the great Udet's just a little fellow & very young—travels all over the world, like Hermann he went into stunt flying after the war, & he's witty & nice & quite the ladies' man, two dozen girls on either arm, & Bruno Loerzer was there, another ace, & Hermann's closest friend & former adjutant Karl Bodenschatz, & there were flowers & telegrams & dancing & then here to Hochkreuth!!

Dearest Fanny, we five sisters are bound by an almost mystic love, we have always known that, but even so you & I were always closest & you knew as no one else what my life was like before I met Hermann. I think so very often of the day—no the minute, the second—that my life began, at Rockelstadt, you remember I'd taken the train to visit Mary just for the day but then that tremendous snowstorm came from out of nowhere & the railways shut down, & in the evening Mary & I took supper alone, knowing Erik couldn't get home from Stockholm that night, not even my resourceful brother-in-law could manage to find a way through that blizzard!! But about nine o'clock I was coming down the staircase, & the front door opened & in stepped Erik with another man, both covered with snow & snow blowing in with them, & I paused on the stairs looking down & the man looked up at me—& what passed between us at that moment, Fanny, has never changed.

Then they were gone to get into dry clothes & Erik's teeth chattering so hard he couldn't say a word, & all I knew about this other man was that somehow I had been with him always, & was part of him. And Mary, she'd come down the stairs behind me, Mary said my word that was a fine figure of a man & eyes like turquoise & did I suppose he was an apparition, & Erik too? Because we couldn't imagine how they'd come. Then it turned out he was a pilot Erik had hired to fly him home, & oh I thought what magnificent recklessness flying into the teeth of that storm! & landing right on the tiny frozen lake just outside the castle walls, practically in front of the door! Do you know it seemed to me then & still does that my beloved literally dropped from the skies!! & when we learned that he was the air hero Göring I wasn't at all surprised, or only because he was so natural and unassuming—except when he talked about the Versailles Treaty, the most swinish crime in world history was his least violent term (I think some of the Allied signers themselves say that!!) but what a lovely happy evening it was, & that electric awareness between us, every glance, every smile, every word!! & the four of us sat before the fire & Erik played his

*lute & we sang all the old lovely Swedish & German folk songs—you know
Fanny I so often think of our family's bond with Germany, that it is still so
strong even though the von Focks came from there so very long ago, I feel
as if it were destiny that I have always felt Germany to be my second homeland, that I grew up with all the old German tales & songs—& those songs
were so deeply beautiful that night, everything that night was so beautiful,
& that electricity between us, & when we shook hands goodnight & our
fingers actually touched—!!!*

*Of course I knew that even you were alarmed when I moved in with
him the next week, but I knew at least God understood & that He blessed us
because we were in love, oh so crazily, crazily in love!!! I was a married
woman, yes, & I can say* nothing *against Nils except that when you marry
as young as I did & know nothing of life & nothing of yourself you may be
making the most terrible mistake, & should you be forced to live with that
mistake forever? With no kinship of the soul, no passion of the flesh? You
know it was a life without meaning except for my beloved little Thomas—
but when I met Hermann not even Thomas could keep me, & of course I*
did *have the naïve belief that as Thomas's mother I would be allowed to
have him,* everything *seemed possible those first few weeks, Hermann & I
were so desperately happy in his little flat & if we had hardly any money &
I scarcely knew how to cook a meal it didn't matter, nothing mattered &
least of all the talk—Baron von Fock's daughter an adulteress, how sinful,
how shocking! What small minds Stockholm is full of! What sin? I could
never grasp it—I was doing what my heart told me, there is* no *sin in
that!! & I was so deeply grateful & shall always be that the family stood by
us, that in time all of you came to understand my happiness & that you took
my Hermann into your hearts, that made me so terribly glad. Just to be
together was all we asked, & I would have divorced in a minute but for
Thomas, because at least in Stockholm I could see the child, but to* divorce
& leave*—& I couldn't ask Hermann to stay permanently with only a
future of barnstorming & taxi piloting, he'd been a year in Denmark &
now more than two in Sweden & had stayed on so long only for my sake so
that I could be near Thomas, but Germany was* always *pulling him—you
remember the day I felt I finally had to choose & finally told him he must go
back by himself & I would stay & work out my decision, you remember that
day because he & I were both so miserable, & you remember that when he
had gone from me I knew within the first hour what my decision would be.
Dearest Fanny I can never forget your kindness & goodness during those
long trying months I was seeing through the divorce, knowing that I must
leave my Thomas & at the same time missing Hermann so terribly, the time
seemed endless without him, not a day passed in all those months that we
didn't write, pouring out our hearts to each other, & when the moment
finally came that my train pulled into the Munich station, oh so slowly! &
we saw each other!! I leaning from the train window, & he waving from*

the platform—I know only one thing Fanny, we will never be parted again, except by death, & not even then.

Now of course you will want to know all the practical things, there we are different. Well, financially I suppose we'll manage, there's the divorce allowance, it's small but in foreign currency & with the inflation that counts for everything, & before I came Hermann swallowed his pride & asked a loan from his godfather—you remember that adored godfather he was always talking about, well I've met him & he's the most dreadful old ogre—but colorful!—& Hermann found a tiny house in Obermenzing, outskirts of Munich, so tiny but just built & smells of fresh wood in every room & will be so snug & cozy when my things come from Sweden. Hermann also gets a small salary from the patriotic association he works for, but I had no idea there were so many, dozens in Munich alone & they form & fall apart & apparently it's a constant turmoil but Hermann says this one is going to last, I hope so because he is deeply committed to his work. Fanny, his vision of Germany is clear & driving & passionate, he is an unusual man, a man of greatness, & I think I know this better than he himself. In Sweden he sometimes seemed to lose all belief in himself & his country both, but I knew he was wrong to feel that way, I knew he could accomplish anything he set out to do, & just as my Hermann gave me my life, he says I have given him his. We believe so deeply in one another, Fanny, & this great cause of his is my cause too.

If you could experience how things are here—when I put the postage stamp on this letter you'll see that it cost a million marks!!! People losing their entire life savings—inflation, unemployment, & nothing done about it but what can be done under the Versailles Diktat? It is still unbelievable to me that the Allies kept up the food blockade—70,000 people dead of starvation!!—in order to force Germany to sign the treaty terms, how else could they have gotten the government to sign that crippling piece of infamy? Staggering war reparations, the entire cost of the war—to pay such a debt will keep Germany starving on her knees forever. And to have slashed the Army down to a feeble 100,000 men governed by an Allied Supervisory Commission, and to abolish all armaments while the Allies themselves can build up anew!! And what they've done to West Prussia!! To have given Poland land that's been German since it was settled by the Teutonic Knights and there it sits between East Prussia and the rest of Germany!! Have you ever before heard of a country chopped in two with another country sitting between? And to take away all foreign colonies, has that ever been done before? But to have to accept alone & totally the guilt of starting the war! I think that is almost the worst, for it eats into the very soul. For the Germans there seems no way out of their chaos & weakness & humiliation, & there are a thousand political groups screaming—left, middle, right—all screaming & accomplishing nothing because there are so many.

Certainly it is the worst of times, yet it all seems so far from this high

*green hillside, everything so sunny & peaceful, & I feel almost guilty that
for Hermann & me it is such a happy time. Of course I don't know what
our life will be like when we go back to Munich next week, but the uncertainty doesn't bother me, it's exhilarating! And I know that our future, even
if it should be very hard, will be a good one because we are together!! But
I must end this now, your Carin can't stop once she starts—my health is
radiant, Fanny, you mustn't worry, & we are hoping so much that when
Thomas comes for Christmas—oh I long so deeply for that moment when
I'll see him, & it's so far off!!—you will come too because it's going to be
such a wonderful cozy Christmas in our new little house & it will be all the
more wonderful if you're there too, dearest Fanny I send you & all the
family my abiding love & a thousand warm thoughts & am forever*

Your Carin

Chapter 17

WHEN Hermann had returned from Sweden to Munich, in the fall of 1922, Nikki was still twisting newspapers. The apartment, unheated since the last year of the war, had taken on a permanent damp chill, and from the wallpaper there emanated the faint, sweetish odor of mold. He noticed the smell mostly at night, lying beneath blankets and coats on a horsehair sofa in the parlor. An elderly couple now occupied the guest room, a shoe clerk Nikki's room, and Nikki the sewing room, which was littered with scraps of felt and linen and netting; for in addition to subletting rooms, his mother had put her hat-making talents to use in supplying a neighborhood millinery shop. She had changed little in the almost four years that he had been away; she was perhaps more stout now than buxom, but remained handsome and fresh-cheeked, and as brisk and good-humored as always. Only superficially was she different, her dark gold hair, still without a trace of gray, worn in a marcelled bob, and her dresses hemmed up to the new midcalf length. At night as he lay on his sofa he could hear American jazz coming from the gramophone next door.

Everything had changed, and nothing had changed. He had left a flailing newborn republic, and he had returned to a flailing three-year-old republic, named with hopeful symbolism for the city of Weimar, that great old cultural center steeped in humanitarian tradition, past home of Goethe, Schiller, Wieland, Bach, where in 1919 the new German Democratic constitution had been drawn up, a constitution which for the first time in German history enforced a parliamentary system democratically allowing all voices to be heard. Since that date no fewer than fifteen parties had sat arguing in the Reichstag while the country continued its collapse around them.

When he left Germany a loaf of bread had cost under a mark. Now a stale pumpernickel sold for two hundred. A lump of coal went for thrice that. War reparations, in cash, in goods, in raw materials, were falling behind, with rumors afloat that French troops would seize in payment the coal mines and iron works of the Ruhr—nor had he forgotten Clemenceau's *vingt million de trop* remark during the food blockade, that savage opinion that there were twenty million Germans too many—let them starve, freeze, let them keep nothing, not even a shred of pride, for it was also rumored that the Allies were about to demand extradition of the leading generals of the old Imperial Army, to be tried and punished as war criminals—Field Marshal von Hindenburg himself, General Ludendorff, the heroes of Tannenberg . . .

In the chill gray early mornings, he woke and lay turning these things over and over in his mind. Then Nikki's sharp nose would appear in the doorway, and she would come tiptoeing in, her coat around her shoulders, to twist her newspapers.

"Are you awake, then, Hermann? But need I ask? You always woke before the birds, always outside running and climbing before another soul was up"—sitting down as she talked, lifting the stack of dampened newspapers onto her lap—"and don't you think the air was different there? I always loved the mornings at Veldenstein, everything was so fresh and sweet. There is no air like Franconian air, and that's a fact. Oh, you don't know how often I think of those days, before everything changed, you can't help but think back to them. And I'm not alone in that, I can tell you. Those mobs rushing out to kiss Eisner's blood all over the street, kneeling and weeping and turning him into a saint, *him*, that little Marxist louse! And who are they weeping over now? Their exiled Wittelsbachs! Turned out by the thousands for Ludwig's funeral procession—by the thousands, and *weeping*? Like fountains! It only goes to show. They're tired of twisting newspapers. I tell you, Hermann, everything in this rotten republic is twisted. Jazz clubs and nude revues, and those plays you hear about, ugly and crazy, just like the paintings nowadays. You don't know what you're looking at. You knew what you were looking at in the old days. And there were jobs, and steady wages, and savings in the bank. People *trusted* their banks, they *trusted* their government. If you built a little nest egg for your old age, year after year, you *knew* that it would be there when you reached in for it. But now you reach in for it, your *own* money, and what have they done to it! They have turned it into a pile of—a pile of—"

"Scheisse," Hermann said for her over his shoulder, already robed, his clothes in his arms, heading out the door for the bathroom to shave, dress, and set off for his first day of classes at the University of Munich.

He would be a decade older than the other students, but this very fact—that he would soon be thirty and had not yet accomplished anything in the postwar world—gave his decision an added sense of urgency. From his pilot's salary in Sweden he had brought back savings which, though small, would, in foreign currency, stretch a few months for board and room while he studied political science from the ground up. He was aware of his ignorance in this field. The military traditionally stood above politics; an officer did not acknowledge by speech or even by thought that low form of activity, slimy with opportunism and wholly lacking in the concept of honor; an officer would no more have considered mulling over political issues than he would have considered removing his gloves on the street. But all this had changed since the war. Germany *was* politics, nothing else.

And so he listened carefully in class, took copious notes, and in the evening sat down with his work at the parlor table. Only his long nightly letter to Carin turned him from the pile of textbooks before him; then, afterward, he would change into his pajamas, an old silken pair badly frayed, put on his bathrobe, and on top of that his overcoat, knead the pain in his thigh, and sit down again, lighting a bayleaf cigar called Woodsman's Joy—he had once splurged on a Havana only to find that it was made of cabbage leaves soaked in nicotine—and once more settle down to study.

By the third week his interest had faded, his thoughts centering instead on a small group of ex-officers who had invited him to attend one of their meetings. Reading textbooks was a waste of time. He already had a vision of Germany's struggle, and it was absolutely clear, with two or three outstanding points underlined as if in black crayon. He needed neither professors nor textbooks, whose eternal hairsplitting could only shrivel scope and defuse action. Slamming shut the book in his hands, he ended his university education.

At the ex-officers' meeting he felt a great impatience. "Listen to me, you damned fools," he interrupted, getting to his feet. "Here we are surrounded by burning issues, and you sit about discussing how to get beds and meals for veteran officers. Do you suppose an officer worth his salt can't find a bed to sleep in, even if it happens to be the bed of a pretty blonde? Get your thick skulls out of the sand! There are more important things at stake!" But this opening speech failed to rouse his colleagues' enthusiasm; instead they took him heatedly to task for his insulting manner, at which he walked out.

He was sorry the next morning, and sent a note of apology. But he had no intention of returning. As he walked around the city, with the raw November wind flattening his coat against his back, he knew that the group's concern was needed. The streets were still thronged with beggars in feldgrau, the blinded, the one-armed, the legless, who looked like creatures from Brueghel, half-men, stumps, locomoting themselves along the sidewalk by means of their palms. If even one of these men could be helped with a bed or meal it would be worth doing. But it would change nothing. While you dealt in small measures the wind would still be fluttering the scabs of neglected building fronts, whistling on into the outskirts where families lived in cowsheds, in lean-tos made of cardboard, in abandoned and eviscerated automobiles. An immediate and total overhaul—that was the only thing he could set his will toward. And the Raffkes would be the first to go—those new rich, the confidence men, black marketeers and stock exchange grubbers who, garishly resplendent in dark glasses, wide tango trousers, and checkered wasp-waist jackets, could be seen constantly coming and going from smart cafés and restaurants. They were a parody of themselves, the butt of endless, rancorous jokes—

First Herr Raffke: My house is full of Titians.

Second Herr Raffke: Why don't you call an exterminator?

He could not help thinking of that particular joke as a beaming, chattering pair bustled out from an art gallery and brushed past him to a waiting cab. With a great slamming of doors the cab drove off, overtaking and passing one of the shabby old tram cars. At least red flags no longer flapped from tram-car roofs. From any roofs. Bavaria was glaring White, its government a radical-conservative dictatorship, installed through a military coup and welcomed by a citizenry half battered to death by revolutionary upheavals. The south was a magnet for anti-Weimar elements from all over the country; in Munich alone there existed more than seventy nationalist organizations, ranging from big groups like the Iron Fist down to those of more moderate size, down to those smaller, and yet smaller—so many in all, and in such a continual state of flux, that you could not begin to sort them out.

Also hard to sort out were their so-called private armies, groups of un-uniformed riffraff in armbands whose shared and imbecilic practice it was to tramp along the sidewalk five abreast, scattering pedestrians, while bellowing out slogans and songs which they would break off in order to slap up posters and thrust out collection cups, and, inevitably, to concentrate their real energies on brawling with some identical band of louts for possession of a street corner or square.

Oddly enough, the parties themselves were paralyzingly dull. He had spent his first couple of weeks home attending public beerhall meetings; and whether he listened to parties bearing the stamp of war veterans, or small businessmen, or landowners, or disillusioned Weimar officials, the speeches of each were read from prepared manuscripts in the same steadily droning voice. It was the traditional mode of German speechmaking, borne of reverence for the printed word, but though a traditionalist to the core he found himself kneading his neck with impatience. Nor was it just the mode of address that bored him—and everyone else in the audience, to judge by the unabated, mug-clinking jabber—but the speeches themselves, which, from Bierstube to Bierstube, were fraught with the same narrow biases and mutual denigrations. The parties were nationalist in theory, but in practice each seemed, like its armies, myopically intent on scratching out space for itself, on digging straight down into the yielding soil of Bavaria, there to entrench, to strengthen, and to remain. The great issue which the parties supposedly embodied—the rebirth of the Fatherland—was dealt with only in the form of threadbare negativisms: the parties were against the Weimar Republic, they were against poverty and hunger, against graft and moral degeneracy, against Jews, against Allied outrages . . . but by this time he was usually making his way through the tables to the door.

His walk had taken him to the Marienplatz, the central square of the city, where he stood looking up at the ornate Rathaus silhouetted against the gray of the sky. Every quarter hour, from an upper portal, a group of life-size clockwork figures popped brightly into view, and he could never pass without stopping to wait for them. Now, with a loud click, like that of a child's toybox, the portal opened to the music of the "Defiliermarsch" and on a slowly revolving platform the knights and peasant dancers and robed saints and woodcutters began chopping and dancing and nodding as the clock tower chimed its round notes into the air. Today a mass of leaflets came fluttering down from the figures and were spread by the wind in a white litter across the paving stones. He picked one up and read it as he walked on down Residenzstrasse. It was an announcement that the nationalist societies were going to stage their first mass rally the following Sunday in the Königsplatz, to protest the Allied demand for the extradition of Germany's military leaders.

He dropped the leaflet in a trash bin and crossed the narrow street, weaving through cabs, horse-drawn carts, dilapidated bicycles. The small, exclusive Residenzstrasse shops, their interiors already lit in the early dusk, had a rich, amber glow, and as he passed them, bell-tinkling doors opening and closing, he caught a mingled fragrance of almond soap and cinnamon. Residenzstrasse was one of the few streets still swept meticulously clean, although as he approached its end, where it opened onto the Odeonplatz, he saw another wind-blown litter of leaflets. He walked alongside the Residenz, former palace of the Wittelsbachs, an elegant dark gray building guarded by two stone lions on pedestals, each with its paw lifted and great mouth open, its mane a luxuriance of stone intricacy. Here too, a favored spot of his, he paused for a few minutes. In the Odeonplatz, more leaflets were being showered from the back of a truck rumbling through the late-afternoon traffic.

He reflected that he might as well take himself to the rally on Sunday. Perhaps the groups, coming together at last through a common cause, would do something more than mouth platitudes.

They did not, and he stayed only a short while. A large crowd had turned out, everyone bundled up in the damp cutting wind and milling about as the speakers simultaneously droned their grievances. "The Allied demand is an insult to Germany . . ." "Germany has been insulted too many times . . ." "How long must Germany be insulted . . . ?" Rousingly cheered on by small claques in armbands, they reiterated one another from wooden platforms aflap with party banners and placards. From one platform to the next he went, pressing his way through the crowd, at one point finding himself wedged in before a platform that was empty but nevertheless surrounded by a roar of "Speech! Speech! Speech!" The claque seemed to be directing its cries at a fellow standing quietly nearby, hands folded before him. Hermann ran his eyes up the long black overcoat, past a high celluloid collar, to a shapeless black slouch hat—shades of Eisner—under which he glimpsed a pale countenance stamped with a small tight square of black, then glanced up at the wind-battered platform banners and signs, all in screaming red. The detested color was off-putting, if perversely eye-catching. Less eye-catching was the banners' Hakenkreuz symbol, a decorative Germanic emblem dating from the days of the Teutonic Knights and favored by many of the groups. This group, according to its signs, was the Nationalsozialistische Deutsche Arbeiterpartei, a thorough mouthful, inclusive and contradictory, perhaps hoping to appeal to nationalists and workers alike. If it was a visionary or merely confused title he could not say, but the fellow in black seemed to be designating which it was, unfolding his hands now, lifting and dropping them, and uttering the words "Es ist zwecklos" as the noisemakers, having run out of steam, came walking back to him. Finding the crowd loosening, Hermann moved on as the fellow said again to his claque, again releasing the twang of some local provincial dialect, "Es ist zwecklos. Useless, I've already told you that I will not speak today. I don't want to break up the unity of this pretty, bourgeois demonstration. If I spoke I would ask what good are protests without power behind them—I would only smash the harmony you see here today. I don't want to do that."

Hermann turned in the crowd, almost taking a step back. But the sloppy enunciation checked him, the shabby-genteel look of the man. Big words could fit into any small mouth. Turning again, he moved off, and a short while later went on home. But he found that the fellow's words had stuck in his mind.

The Kindl Keller was hot, loud, and crammed with a cross section of Münchners—ex-officer types, students, workers, people who looked to be of the concierge and small shopkeeper class, youths and girls in Bavarian folk costume. He sat down at a scrubbed wooden table with two colorfully dressed young couples and ordered a mug of beer, handing the waitress five hundred marks in a fistful of bills and looking around him. He had come late in order to avoid the inevitable preliminary speakers, one of whom had just finished and was sitting down next to another on a raised platform at the end of the hall. The Nationalsozialistische Deutsche Arbeiterpartei—or the NSDAP, as it was condensed to on a great placard above the two speakers—appeared to be more concerned with its flag than were other groups. Members of its private army, perhaps thirty or forty, a seedy lot, were stationed on either side of the platform holding rigid a veritable palisade of red banners. Along the dark burnished paneling of the walls hung more banners, unfurled and very large, the black Hakenkreuz on a white circular ground surrounded by vibrant red. And they had their own small brass band, which was thumping out march music through the terrific din of voices.

Munich political meetings were all alike: malt-happy. The same beery hubbub, the same perspiring waitresses running back and forth with three mugs bristling from either fist, the same shouts for refills which never let up from first speech till last. Beer was the main event, and maybe body heat was an attraction too; good sweat-stinking stuffiness in a city of stone-cold living rooms. Smoke lay in a warm blue haze over the noisy tables and the banner-draped platform on which the two speakers sat, neither of whom was the man he had come to hear.

"Where's this Alfred Hitler?" he asked, shouting through the noise at the youth beside him. "I thought he was supposed to be the main speaker."

"Adolf!" the youth shouted back, pointing. "He's coming now."

He was walking rapidly through the tables from the front entrance, bareheaded, in a belted trench coat, followed by an entourage of a dozen men with red Hakenkreuz armbands. The brass band had struck up the "Badenweilermarsch," and to its rousing, annunciatory notes he strode vigorously along, almost at a controlled run. In the Königsplatz, under the drooping rim of his slouch hat, he had appeared middle-aged, but here he looked to be a man perhaps just over thirty. Without the dark hat his face was less pale, his black postage-stamp mustache less severe. His hair was thick, dark brown, neatly brushed. In profile, as he passed Hermann's table, his nose jutted out large and angular, like the exact half of a triangle. He was already unbelting his trench coat; and as he reached his destination, he tossed the coat to an aide and stepped rapidly up onto the platform as the "Badenweilermarsch" beat high to a climactic finale and broke off.

"Who are the other two?" Hermann shouted in the noise. One was young, dressed like an Italian organ grinder in violet shirt, red necktie, tan waistcoat and chocolate-brown suit. The other, getting to his feet, was a grizzled, workmanlike older man in spectacles.

"That's Drexler getting up," the youth yelled back. "He's founder of the party. The other one's Rosenberg—writes for the *Völkischer Beobachter*. Haven't read it? You must!"

The older man had begun to introduce the main speaker, but after listening for a few minutes in vain, Hermann stood up with his beer mug, grabbed his chair, and dragged it along the floor to a table near the platform, where he unceremoniously wedged himself in, beaming at the jostled and annoyed occupants—a stylish lot, slummers—and focused his attention on the platform.

After all his fanfare, the fellow seemed to have reverted to the lifeless figure of the Königsplatz. Standing in a dark blue serge suit and his lamentable celluloid collar, he had begun speaking in a hesitant tone, his eyes wandering around the noisy hall. He used a perfectly good High German, but as he went on Hermann occasionally heard his accent seep through, not a local dialect after all, but provincial Austrian and equally grating—whined vowels, T's flattened to a vulgar D sound. Sometimes he trailed off, as if wondering what to say next; or he would cough against his fist and keep the fist there for a moment, as if lost in mute forgetfulness; then he would start in again, his eyes resuming their vague peregrination around the noisy hall. The speech itself was entirely without interest, a dry enumeration of the events of the last five years. Hermann took a swallow of his beer and sighed, observing that one person had already been put to sleep, a massive figure sitting opposite him at the table. He had a great underslung jaw, which was resting peacefully on his chest, gently rising and falling with it. But not for long; his wife, or girlfriend, wearing a pink silken cloche almost obscured by a fashionably large fox boa, was shaking his arm.

"You were the one who dragged us here, Putzi. It's not fair that we should suffer and you shouldn't."

The huge Putzi lifted a face like that of a kindly gargoyle. Smiling, he peered over nonexistent spectacles at the bizarre Rosenberg. "Perhaps I got it wrong," he said. "Perhaps it's that one there we want to hear. I believe he's a costermonger's donkey."

"We've already heard him."

"Ach, so we did. What did he say?"

"Who knows? Oh, why don't we leave?"

"That one who's talking now, I've seen him before," Putzi mused. "He's a waiter. Ja, he's a waiter. I distinctly remember him standing somewhere with a towel over his arm."

"Permit me," Hermann interrupted from over his beer. "He is a mail clerk. You see the postage stamp beneath the nose."

"Gewiss!" the enormous man said with a laugh. "That's what it is. I thought he'd forgotten to use his handkerchief."

He was using it now, to wipe his forehead. His face was running with sweat. But his voice was growing louder, and harsh, as if something were all at once coming together inside him; his body seemed to be growing harder, straighter, like a hose swelling. Suddenly the room's babble was ground under as the voice reverberated from the walls, a thing of enormous power, resilience, control.

"The Allies are stripping Germany of everything but her war dead, and the November criminals bow, scrape, and make good the Allies' every wish. The November criminals must be cast from our midst, the Versailles chains must be flung from our necks! Not in ten years, not in five, but now! Are we not sixty-three million German people? Are we not bound in our hatred of this vile republic? Are we not greater than this vile republic? Are we not immeasurably greater? We are righteousness! We are vindication! We are power! We will not tolerate the Versailles chains. We will not tolerate the November criminals. We will destroy all that is fraudulent. All that is decadent. All that is bloodsucking. We will destroy all that is not Germany. We will give back to Germany her traditions! Her glory! Her soul! We will—"

But a shattering burst of applause broke him off in midsentence. He stood impatiently waiting to continue, his hair hanging over his forehead in a dark wing, his eyes shining and brilliant. With a handsweep he cut off the applause and went on. It was a harsh graveled voice, yet amazingly flexible, and in perfect unison with his every gesture. Hermann followed with his eyes the pale hand as it stretched out to the audience and returned slowly, palm up, beseeching, and clasped itself to his breast, the other hand pressing upon it; now the arms spread wide and raised heavenward, the face lifting the powerful voice to the vaulted ceiling. The girl in the pink cloche sat utterly still, a cigarette burning down between her knuckles.

For a full hour the speaker held forth, his face pouring with sweat. At times someone in the audience would break in with a question or an opposing sentiment, and he would shoot up his right hand as if catching a ball, and send it flying back verbally. He was as if something electric, a magnetic force.

"For four years I fought at the front, and at the end of that long battle I saw my dead comrades betrayed by a Red revolution. I saw

Germany's great sacrifice betrayed by Marxist Jews. I saw a revolution that was purely destructive. It did not unite the people, it divided them. It brought them bloodshed, turmoil and hardship. A revolution cannot destroy. It must construct. It cannot divide. It must unite. It cannot be a workers' revolution! It cannot be a peasants' revolution! It cannot be a coup of the military! It can only be a movement in which the general marches side by side with the worker, the burgher, the peasant. It can only be a movement in which we are all, *all* of us, involved. *That* will be the real German revolution! When the rotten foundations of the November republic are torn out by the roots! When the Versailles shackles are torn off and flung in the face of the Allies! When the last Communist enclave is torn from its last filthy corner! When the Jews waxing fat on our misery are torn from their carrion nests! When the Reichsmark in our hand is not worth a thousand times less than the paper it's printed on! When there is coal in our stoves! Food on our tables! When we have brought back dignity to our land, and meaning to our lives! *Then* we will have had a *German revolution!*"

The hall exploded with an almost demoniacal cannonade of cheering, clapping and table pounding, in which the blue serge figure stood with arms severely crossed, breathing heavily, hair plastered flat. A moment later he was stepping down, snatching his coat from an aide, and walking rapidly out a rear door. The great roar of the audience went on for another three or four minutes before it began gradually to subside. The palms of his hands throbbing, Hermann pushed his chair back and got to his feet. He saw that the massive Putzi was rubbing his brow with his hand, as if dazed. He was saying, to no one in particular, as if to the air around him, "He is the man. He is the man. . . ."

The man had a room near the Isar. It was a room almost completely occupied by a narrow bed lacking a headboard. Crammed in alongside the wall, leaving exposed only a strip of worn brown linoleum, was a small table, a stool, and a makeshift bookcase. The shelves held Clausewitz's *Vom Kriege*, biographies of Richard Wagner and Frederick the Great, a collection of heroic myths by Schwab, Treitschke's several volumes of German history, and Ludendorff's history of the Great War. When he was alone he would put on carpet slippers, remove his celluloid collar, and in shirtsleeves and suspenders lie back against the wall and read. At night, when he slept, his pillow and head projected onto the sill of the single narrow window. He was content with the room, which was sufficient for his needs, and paid his rent punctually ahead of time. When he went out in the morning, seldom before eleven, he walked rapidly along a narrow corridor, running the nail of his thumb down the yellowed keys of an old upright piano standing there. Outside his front door, in a niche in the rose brick wall, stood a small weatherbeaten statue of the Madonna. Here he would pause and put on his slouch hat before continuing down the street.

It was a short walk to the NSDAP business office, which consisted of two dingily papered rooms—actually one room with a plywood partition—and was still incompletely furnished. They had only one desk. They needed more chairs, bigger filing cabinets, a telephone. It was a drafty office, and it held the dreary bureaucratic clatter of a typewriter. He did not like the place, and dropped by infrequently.

Stepping through the door, he nodded to his staff of three—one pounding the decrepit Remington, the other two talking to someone wreathed in cigar smoke—and passed into his own office behind the partition. His business manager came hurrying in after him, and said in a loud whisper, "That's Hermann Göring out there. He's applying for membership."

He said nothing as he hung up his coat and hat; he had a stubborn disinclination to respond as expected. Sitting down at his desk, he looked over some papers awaiting his attention. "Ask him to step in," he murmured as he read.

A few moments later he rose and cordially extended his hand over the desk. "I saw you often during the war, Herr Oberleutnant, though only in pictures. I am honored to make your acquaintance."

"The honor is mine, Herr Hitler. I heard you speak last night. I was greatly impressed. I agreed with ninety percent of what you said."

"I am glad to hear that. I am sure we will not have to argue about the odd ten percent. Won't you sit down, Herr Oberleutnant?"

"Hauptmann."

He seated himself, glancing at the slightly yellowed celluloid collar, which, through some misguided attempt at fashion, was secured by an imitation gold safety pin. But the man's face itself, close up, held none of the rather hangdog inertia he had glimpsed in the Königsplatz. Neither did it recall the messianic visage of the night before. It was first and last an intelligent face, dominated entirely by the eyes, which were alert, thoughtful, clear blue-gray in color.

"I knew last night, Herr Hitler, that I would apply for membership in your party. I have now done that. There is only one other thing I wish to do: to assure you that if I can be of any use to your cause, I am entirely at your disposal."

"That is most generous of you, Herr Hauptmann. I am most grateful."

He was also grateful that his visitor had put out his cigar in the other room. He disapproved of smoking and did not tolerate it in his presence, but with people of Göring's social class he felt an awkwardness in making his wishes known. Still, this former commander of the Richthofen Squadron seemed a down-to-earth sort, no airs about him despite his officer's bearing, and despite the knowledge that his name would be of incalculable value to any party he chose to join. He seemed a genial, vigorous, blunt chap. What he communicated most strongly—you could sniff it in your nostrils—was energy. A huge, eager drive, waiting for release.

Chapter 18

"I really don't know about his personal life," Hermann said to Olga, sipping his cognac and motioning with his glass, a twinkle in his eye. "You must ask Herr Hanfstaengl here. Herr Hanfstaengl—you see how exhausted he looks—has undertaken to teach him the social graces."

It was mid-August of 1923, and they were sitting with after-dinner coffee and liqueur in the living room of the little Obermenzing house, Hermann and Carin, Hermann's sister Olga—a younger replica of her mother, with whom she was staying on a week's visit from Austria— and Putzi and Helene Hanfstaengl. The immense Putzi was lifting his hand in amiable denial.

"Your brother exaggerates, Frau Rigele. I merely make a small suggestion from time to time. Ach, so small, so small. Yet, if I do say so, my poor hints have on occasion borne great fruit. The semisoft collar that he now wears—that, in all modesty, is my achievement. On the other hand, I once implied that a large honest mustache, or no mustache at all, would be preferable to something which is neither here nor there. 'Don't worry, Herr Hanfstaengl,' he told me, 'I am setting a fashion.' Think of it! One can only stand in awe of such supreme confidence. . . . But none of this is my true function, Frau Rigele. Nein, my true function, if you wish to know, is playing the piano. Ja, I soothe his nerves by bashing out Wagnerian chords. Usually on an acutely disturbed old upright that squats in his hall—"

"Usually on *our* piano," corrected his wife, she of the pink silken cloche in the Kindl Keller. "My head splits right down the middle," she told Olga. "I do admire him, but I sometimes wish I were somewhere else when he comes to the house."

"So unkind," Putzi admonished her. "So unkind, when here he cherishes the most tender feelings for you. And for you, too, Frau Göring . . . I recall that exquisite phrase, what was it exactly?"

"Oh, I'd rather not remember," Carin said, smiling and shaking her head.

"But it was marvelous. You must tell your sister-in-law."

"Oh well. It was just that he once said to me—we had been standing together talking of one thing and another—and he said all at once, very gruff and abrupt: 'Countess. Permit me to say you are like a queen of the northern forests.'"

Olga joined in the room's laughter, very much enjoying herself. She had never seen this Herr Hindler, had never heard his name until tonight, but he seemed to provide both amusing anecdotes and great political enthusiasm. And that was surely an uplifting mixture in these dark times. The little room was filled with life and promise; and the room itself was charming—terribly small, but its polished, honey-colored floor, with its simple Swedish folk furniture, imparted a feeling of airiness. The air held a scent of fresh, new-lathed wood, mixed with the fragrance of Flammenblumen standing crimson and gold in vases. There was also a pervasive sense of romantic bliss. It was not too excessive a term, bliss, for what emanated from the recently wed pair sitting opposite her on the sofa. They were very unlike, she thought. At least on the surface. Her new sister-in-law was as reserved and soft-spoken as Hermann was not; and she was anything but robust, according to Mutter. She suffered a weakness of the lungs; not precisely a tubercular condition, but one which often caused her to run a low-grade fever and made her prone to severe chest congestions. She did not look frail. She was a tall, slender woman who walked with an unusually handsome and free carriage. While not strictly pretty—her eyes were a little too round, her lips a little too full—she was overwhelmingly more than pretty. It was the grace of her bearing, the deep expressiveness of her eyes; and it was the marvelous coloring—dark lustrous hair, black-lashed blue eyes, creamy skin marked on either cheek by a small fever-ish blossom of pink. She wore a pale apricot silk dress tonight, with a long strand of moonstones around her neck. Her husband was in a crisp white suit set off by pale blue shirt and dark blue tie. They made a handsome couple, somehow with the same fresh and seemly aura of the room. And it was true, you could feel it almost palpably, the joy they took simply from being in one another's company, the pure bliss of proximity. What, Olga wondered, must their nights be like? And with an earthy smile, she returned to the conversation, which had gotten onto wheelbarrows.

Wheelbarrows, children's wagons, prams, everywhere you saw people trundling them along, heaped with Deutschmarks, hurrying to buy something, anything, before the mark plunged further. This morning an egg had cost twenty billion marks. By tomorrow it would cost eighty or ninety billion. And it was even worse in Austria.

"The notes fly off the printing presses like scrap paper," Hermann was saying to the Hanfstaengls.

"You wonder where it will all end," Olga said, "or if it will ever end."

"It will end like that," he told her, giving a finger snap. "Overnight. You don't think it's some kind of natural disaster? It's Weimar democracy at its finest. The government itself has devalued the mark; it pays off war reparations and internal debts in worthless money, and the financiers and industrialists pay off *their* debts in worthless money while at the same time slurping up everything around them with foreign currency."

"It's true," said Herr Hanfstaengl, nodding. "The mark will be stabilized when the government sees fit."

"I've heard that rumored, of course," Olga said. "But much as I dislike President Ebert, I can't believe that he—"

"Not he," Hermann said. "You can't include Ebert with the lice around him. He's just a dreamer, a dupe. Weak as water, turn him this way, turn him that. Not that I have anything against paying off the Allies in toilet paper. Except if it's done at the people's expense, and fills the Raffkes' bellies at the same time. I tell you, the name Weimar will stink in German nostrils for a century."

"If I were Herr Hitler, I would make it stink a good deal more," Herr Hanfstaengl told him. "I would pound home this reptilian scheme in my speeches, but he—"

"Is it Hitler?" Olga asked. "I thought you said Hindler."

"Hitler, dear lady—but he seems to think there's more mileage to be got from Allied voraciousness than Weimar escape artistry."

"That's very good," Hermann said with a laugh.

"And it's true," Frau Hanfstaengl said to her husband. "Why waste energy on a *fait accompli*? Nothing will make people hate this mess of a government more than they already do."

"I read in the paper," Carin put in, "that the other day Ebert and his entourage arrived in some city, I forget which, on a state visit; and instead of flags hanging from the windows, people had hung their underwear out. Can you imagine? Bloomers and drawers!"

"Now there is a vote of confidence!" Herr Hanfstaengl said over the room's laughter.

"And it was *raining!*" she went on. "Can you think of a more wonderfully sodden salute?"

Hermann raised his glass. "Let us make hay while the rain falls."

Putzi knew what he meant. When the mark was stabilized, the Party's drawing power would be sharply reduced. And if they were actually going to carry out a revolution, actually march on Berlin—the thought rather dizzied him—they would have to do it soon. Since last autumn the party ranks had swelled unbelievably, along with the inflation. They now had a membership of thirty thousand. Their private army, under Göring's leadership, numbered twelve thousand men. They also had the blessings of General Ludendorff himself, who—the Allied extradition demand having come to nothing—was busily advising and plotting from his tree-bowered villa outside town. They also had Dr. Wilhelm Frick, head of the Political Division of the Munich police, who efficiently squashed every complaint that rose against Party excesses—Adolf's questionable dictum being "We will incite the people, and not only incite: we will incite them into a frenzy." And from the Reichswehr—such was the name given the tiny provisional army allowed by the Versailles Treaty—they had Captain Ernst Röhm, who supplied them with surplus war weapons from hidden depots flourishing beneath the nose of the Allied Control Commission. They had some Reichswehr funds as well, and contributions from a few business establishments and a sprinkling of wealthy families, and from the thousands upon thousands of lower-middle-class members who gave what they could.

All this they had, and yet . . . Hindler, Putzi sighed to himself. Local newspapers, when they did not ignore the name entirely, misspelled it as Hittler, Hütler, Heidler. He himself, that night at the Kindl Keller, had been under the impression that he had come to hear a Herr Hilpert. It seemed a name destined to be misremembered, garbled; and often he felt himself involved in no more than a local sideshow stirring up a lot of provincial dust.

But big things must grow from small seeds. And had they not already made great progress? Although whether Putzi himself was making progress, he could never be sure. Adolf's collar and mustache, and his flattened T's—gratingly reminiscent of New York cabbies' deses and dems—were not Putzi's primary concern. There were larger things to be changed. But the larger the issue, the more difficult it was to tell if one's words sank in. Off the platform the fellow had a strikingly limited range of facial expressions. It was not a cold face, but it held a quality of inner watchfulness, a kind of veiled truculence which revealed very little of what the man was thinking. Unless, of course, he was thinking minor thoughts. Then he could be quite open, and for a man without a sense of humor he could be excruciatingly funny—as when he mimicked the Görings, his voice taking on a honeyed quaver: "My darling Hermann . . . My adorable Carin . . . Oh Hermann, my precious . . . ! Oh Carin, my treasure . . . !" Then the gruffness returned. "It's a real love nest, Hanfstaengl. I have never had such a home, and I shall never have one. I have only one love, and that is Germany." An echo straight from Wagner's *Rienzi,* whose overture Putzi was required to bash out again and again, preferably on his own well-tuned Bechstein grand. It was usually after their piano sessions, as they sat sipping imported Brazilian coffee, which his guest ruined with three heaped spoons of brown sugar, that Putzi tried to make his influence felt.

He had traveled widely in Europe, knew England well, and, as the son of a German father and American mother, had lived in the United States for ten years, graduating from Harvard and afterward managing the New York branch of his family's art reproduction firm. He felt himself to be, as in fact he was, a mellow, civilized, worldly being, and whenever possible he tried to slip a sliver of light into his guest's narrow, closetlike store of convictions. "You know, Herr Hitler, speaking of European affairs, the United States is going to play an increasingly large international role . . ." A sip of coffee, a shoulder shrug: "Weak. Corrupt. Run by Jews." "Really now, how can you—" "Hanfstaengl, I am not interested in the United States. I take into consideration your tender feelings for the place, but I am not interested." Nor was he interested in Britain. As if the Great War had never occurred, as if he were living two centuries ago, he thought strictly along Continental lines, and could quote Frederick the Great by the yard, which was what he did. For ten minutes, or twenty, or thirty, nonstop, until finally he rattled onto some subject which he deigned to invite comment on. "We're getting a nickname, Herr Hanfstaengl, a very good thing. Nazl. Have you noticed?"

Putzi nodded. An abbreviation of Nationalsozialistische, sometimes Nazl, sometimes Nazi, both diminutives of Ignatz and both a Bavarian slang name, something like "Buddy" in America. "I can't say it sets my soul afire," he confessed.

"Why not? One wants a popular handle, something warm and familylike."

"There's nothing very familylike about *Der Stürmer,* which I had the misfortune to read the other day."

"Ah well, Streicher gets carried away. I look past that, Hanfstaengl, to the man's energy. Streicher is simply bursting with energy. I will hear nothing against him."

Putzi was silent. Much as he disliked the racial garbage that poured from the *Völkischer Beobachter,* it could not hold a candle to the putrescence of the *Stürmer;* yet the *Beobachter* was bad enough, and it was he himself who had turned it from a two-page weekly into a full daily, having lent the Party a thousand American dollars for the purchase of two rotary presses. He had been green enough at that time to think he might be given some voice in running the paper, in which case he would have tried to squeeze Rosenberg off the staff. Instead, the Costermonger's Donkey had been promoted to editor and was more firmly than ever ensconced at Adolf's ear—that rigid ear sprouting from the plumber's haircut, temples shaved nude, as if the barber had worked around a bowl; that large, rigid ear, cocked for what it wanted to hear, serenely deaf to all else. Or perhaps not deaf, that was what you hoped. For you sensed the huge potential in him, ja, even as he sat there in his cheap serge suit, tilting his cup for the last drop, his little finger stiffly extended, a small crinkling of the eyes denoting the syrupy residue.

It was a pleasure to know someone in the Party with whom you could be entirely at ease, not only in discussion but in the social sense. He had liked Göring from the start; that night at the Kindl Keller, when the fellow had barged in and made himself at home at their table—so like him, as it turned out—even then, as strangers, they had hit if off. A few days later they had met again, at another beerhall where Hitler was speaking. And a few days after that he had gone along with Göring to the swearing-in ceremony for new members. Greatly enthused as he was by Herr Hitler, Putzi was not by nature a joiner, and he had gone along to watch. It was an impressive ceremony, but he was taken aback by the intensity of Göring's emotions. In stepping forward and swearing himself loyal until death to the person of Adolf Hitler, he had spoken in a voice that was profoundly moved, raised high in volume, and at the same time thick, while in his eyes you could see a gathering shine of tears. Putzi reminded himself that this was an ex-officer of the Imperial Army, whose oath of personal loyalty, sworn in the past to the person of the Kaiser, held a depth and meaning that no civilian could entirely grasp. However, his new friend had certainly expressed himself objectively afterward, as they walked down the street together. "As for the racial-ideological junk, that part he can shove."

There was no faulting Hermann on his candor. When he was introduced to Rosenberg, he had said upon parting, in a voice rich with cheer, "Don't waste your time working too hard, Herr Doktor. You're only going to fall flat on your Balt behind once we get off the ground." His turn of phrase always recalled the fighter pilot—"getting off the ground," "opening up the throttle." You could feel yourself zooming high into the future with him, "blasting out the Weimar rats, blowing a hole through the Versailles Treaty." But he had a practical side as well. "Nothing is certain, Putzi. There will be no revolution unless the Party remains welded together. And the Party will remain welded together only if Adolf remains Party head. And that is by no means certain. There is Strasser, after all. And there is Röhm. Well, we shall just have to keep an eye on them, keep party politics in its corner. I hate all this divisive nonsense. We're out to make a revolution, not to slop around in a lot of stupid Scheisserei."

Barracks-room crudities peppered his speech; from an ex-enlisted man they would have been offensive, but from an ex-officer they possessed the sanctioned glow of tradition. So did an officer's debts. The officer caste had always lived beyond its means, piling up IOUs to friends, tailors, bootmakers, wine merchants, as if it were a point of honor to do so. Nor did the debt holder wax indignant, but waited politely, sometimes forever. The arrogant license of the officer caste had always seemed outrageous to Putzi, as did its self-imposed severities. A gambling loss, for instance, was the only debt that must be immediately honored; if this could not be done, the disgraced officer put a bullet through his head. It all seemed arbitrary to Putzi, and arcane; but if his liberal brain disparaged it, his traditional soul did not, and when Hermann borrowed small sums he gave them with good grace, knowing he would never see them back. In fact he knew this with double certainty, for in Hermann's case tradition was enhanced by an exuberant disregard for bothersome detail. But that was Hermann. You had to take him as he was—see him now, slapping his knees and rising to his feet, urging them all to a songfest around Carin's small white harmonium in the corner. He loved to sing. He had a strong, agreeable baritone which always, in the increasing volume of its pleasure, drowned out everyone else.

It was late when the host drove his guests home, Olga to their mother's apartment, the Hanfstaengls to their *pied à terre* in the center of town. Putzi enjoyed the ride; he missed having his own automobile. He could easily have afforded one, but rode around instead on an elderly Swift bicycle. Seated in his well-cut suit upon the scuffed and wobbly conveyance, he knew that he presented a hybrid picture, but that was what he was, a hybrid, a royalist with a belief in social reform. And the NSDAP was the ultimate hybrid, his logical home, a house of many mansions—capitalists contributed to a movement aimed at wiping them out; socialists thronged to meetings where the Socialist Party was flayed alive; royalists entertained hopes of everything from reestablishing the divine right of kings to the setting up of a constitutional monarchy; and the separatist-minded Bavarian government gave its support to a man who preached the unification of Germany. Here, in all its murky confusion, was the embodiment of the yard-long, catchall Party title. But in spite of these variegations, it was the lower middle class that crammed the meeting halls, spread into the ranks of the private army, gave the movement its mass and power. Some moneyed adherents obviously looked upon this mass as a vehicle, an armored tank that would pave the road with flattened Reds, after which it could be abandoned by the wayside. But for Putzi the terrible plight of this mass was real, so real that he felt it not only ostentatious but shameful to zip around in an automobile. Hermann felt no such inhibitions, and his great pride was the red Benz roadster that Adolf had bestowed upon him for his success in reorganizing the Party troops. Even Adolf himself now owned an automobile, but a modest and ramshackle Selve; no doubt he sensed that whereas a red roadster would fit ill with his own simple image, it could do no harm at all to his flamboyant confrere. Who drove it like a maniac, Helene always complained as they stood teeth-shaken, if safe, on their front doorstep, waving after the departing screech of tires.

The city was dark as Hermann sped homeward, rumbling over the cobblestones of narrow streets and broad empty squares. The cool night air rushed against his face, and all the stars were out, so many that the sky seemed strewn with silver sand. He was happier than he had been for years, married to his Carin, commanding an army, and readying for the great day . . . which had seemed very far in the future on that morning, eight months ago, when he had stood on a stubbled field outside town and observed an odd assortment of store clerks, office workers, Freikorps veterans, farm laborers, jobless drifters. An aide enumerated their functions. They fought Communist and Socialist troublemakers at Party meetings, disrupted the meetings of these groups in turn, smashed the business establishments of local profiteers, and on weekends were put on parade in neighboring towns in order to draw attention to the Party.

"Attention? Attention like that we need like the clap. They look like the French Foreign Legion."

Some were in business suits with leg wrappings, others in Lederhosen and knee stockings, still others in faded Army uniforms. The only note of congruity was an abundance of visored ski caps, which were inexpensive and gave a vaguely military look. They carried no weapons, all arms being forbidden by the Versailles Treaty. Through Captain Röhm they were in possession of several hundred old carbines and revolvers, along with some field pieces, with which they were supposedly given secret training. But the arms were so well hidden, secreted in so many different places, that the men had scarcely been exposed to them. The weapons they used were fists, alpenstocks, homemade swagger sticks, knives stuck in back pockets. They had their own unsoldierly salute as well, something between a casual wave and the Roman greeting of the Italian Fascisti you saw in cinema newsreels.

Standing in uneven rows, some leaning on their alpenstocks, they waited for him to speak. That morning he had put on his uniform for the first time in four years; it smelled slightly of camphor as he stood in it, and slightly of metal polish. The decorations had not needed much rubbing. That was a task he had kept up over the years, bringing them out from time to time, holding each one in his palm while slowly rubbing the cloth until the luster was released anew. He was aware of their familiar weight across his left breast. They had the exact feel of a hand resting there lightly. The band of his officer's cap had settled into its old groove, that slight encircling indentation of hair that had never grown out differently. On his legs he felt the long smooth grip of his jackboots, and around his neck the rigid clamp of his high collar. At his throat hung his Pour le Mérite, taken from the velvet interior of its small black leather box and affixed before the mirror with solemnity.

He realized how ludicrous he must appear to these men, supreme commander of a provincial rabble, standing at attention before them in full regalia. Looking at their expressions, he also had reason to recall the old Bavarian proverb "A Frenchman's ass is preferable to a Prussian's face."

"You are called the Sturmabteilung!" he shouted in his best parade-ground voice, a Prussian whipcrack. "I want to hear you say it!"

Voices went up in a ragged drift.

"Not like a bunch of sick hens—in unison!"

"Stürmabteilung!"

"You were given this name, Storm Detachment, in honor of the crack commando units of the war." He paused for a moment, and smiled. "You are aware that there is a slight, a very slight discrepancy here?"

There was a murmur of amusement.

"It is a discrepancy I am certain you would like to see removed. We can together remove it if we are both willing to work and to work hard. I am ready. And I see on every face that you are ready too, and have long been ready. Also los! We start now from the beginning!"

He had reorganized headquarters on the lines of a divisional staff, with infantry and artillery commanders; had worked out a program of secret arms training in the woods around the city; and had drilled the ragtag group with merciless parade-ground discipline, marching them again and again across the broad stubbled field; while, between these activities, his addresses pounded home the necessity of stamina and loyalty in the building of a new and glorious Germany.

The SA had more than quadrupled in size by now and was an effective paramilitary unit with an esprit and gloss that would almost have done credit to the Lichterfelde parade ground. The Storm Troops' salute, however, remained outside military tradition. It had sprung from the men themselves, it was their own tradition, and he left it as it was. Improvisation of dress also remained, but thanks to a warehouse surplus of biscuit-brown shirts, bought wholesale by the Party, there was now at least the general impression of a uniform. With reluctance, but in the spirit of solidarity, he removed his feldgrau uniform and donned brown shirt and breeches.

Sometimes he managed to rustle up a horse, and he would review his troops at a rapid canter, relishing the clatter of hoofbeats in his ears, a crisp, clean link between past and present. It was true that there was not much historical continuity in the *Saalschlachten*, the beerhall brawls, but he had soon come to realize that they were a practical necessity. No meeting could fulfill its purpose if it was disrupted by hecklers. Nor was he averse to taking a hand in the fighting himself; the sense of immediacy was stimulating—the solid, unequivocal crunch of his fist against nose cartilage, the din of yells, crashing tables, beer mugs shattering against walls. When it was over, he would reseat himself, breathing hard and rubbing his pleasantly stinging knuckles. A job well done, attentiveness restored. At such times he thought of Adolf's theories, expressed in coffee-sipping, hour-long monologues—if you were polite enough to sit listening to the end, which he himself was not. "People want a good scare, they want someone to make them afraid, to whom they can submit with a shudder," which he would illustrate with the fact that after a *Saalschlacht* the audience requests for Party membership invariably doubled. That was so much Quatsch. People applied for membership not because cracked skulls sent them into ecstasies of submission but because they got a good look at Party effectiveness, they saw a winning force. And if Adolf supplied the words, standing there thundering from the platform, he supplied the proof.

And then his mind would wander on to other things, for he no longer listened to Adolf's speeches. They were as impassioned as the first he had ever heard, but the same points were pounded home again and again. And when you could recite these points in your sleep, a place between your shoulder blades tended to itch and your eyes to drift . . . resting for a satisfied moment on the small squad of men flanking the platform, the *Stabswache*, or Headquarters Guard, a group he had recently organized at Adolf's behest, to act as his personal guard; a crack unit, distinguished by black ski caps bearing the Death's Head insignia . . . not exactly the living image of the Death's Head Hussars, but one did one's best, and one's best was not bad at all. He had worked long and hard since that first day on the stubbled field, he had achieved good results, and he had reason to be happy, especially on a starlit summer night like this, roaring along streets becoming leafy as he neared home. The wind stilled as he drew alongside the little house, dark as the trees around it except for the amber glow of the bedroom window.

Chapter 19

Dearest Mother and Father,

I write hardly knowing what I write—Hermann's mother died suddenly yesterday, a massive stroke. We are stunned, we go about in a daze of grief. Only the night before, Frau Göring was here with Olga and as always she was a picture of health and in the best of spirits—it is such a terrible shock, such a grief. The funeral is day after tomorrow, we cannot yet grasp it—I cannot write more now, I know you understand.

Carin

7 September. The hours are long when you lie in bed all day, every day. Time hangs heavily. You think so much. I could not write even to Fanny the thoughts that press in on me, I can write them only here. The doctor says such a severe case of pneumonia cannot help but leave one weak and despondent, especially when it has followed so hard upon a family sorrow. It is true I think much about Frau Göring. I think much about death. About parting. About illness that never ends. This siege has borne in on me that I will never really be well. There will be times when I am better rather than worse, that is all. And those times will become fewer and fewer in the years that are left.

I have always known that I would not have a long life. When you have never possessed good health, it is something you do know. In the old days I lived with this knowledge, and somehow it was almost as if I did not mind. But I mind so terribly now.

The Föhn blows and blows. It booms against the house with a hollow sound. It blew so hard during the burial. It blew the trees, and it blew the wreaths on the coffin, and the flowers on Hermann's father's grave, and I thought it would never die down, the noise of it, and the heat, as if from an oven. I was chilled with sweat, then hot again, I felt my lungs aching even before the service began. My hand was clasped around the beloved one's, I wanted to be strong for him and be his comfort, I tried not to think of the wind, or to look at poor Nikki, or to allow myself to realize that Frau Göring's life was over, that all the thousands of experiences and feelings and thoughts and words that make a human life were finished. So abruptly, like a light snapped off. But I could not help myself, I felt such a turmoil of grief, and that terrible wind blew and blew. Only at the very end of the service did it die away, when the coffin was lowered into the grave. It came to rest at the bottom of the grave, and everything was very quiet, still, and I felt suddenly that I understood. It is peace, I said to myself. It is peace.

I try to remember that, I try to find serenity in it.

I am tired now, just to hold the pen exhausts me.

10 September. When I think that they call him the Iron One, I think how little they know what he is really like. He is so dear and good, the tenderest of nurses. Nothing is too much trouble for him, and he is always at such pains to show me a cheerful face, though he grieves for his mother deeply. I had so wanted to be strong for him at this time, and instead it is he who has had to be strong for me.

I want so desperately to be well, only to be well.

11 September. It upsets me that Hermann neglects his duties in order to be here with me. I know things are beginning to build to a crisis, and that he cannot afford to turn away from all that he has worked toward. He knows it too, and I am sure he is torn. I told him, and it is true, that I am feeling much better these last few days, much stronger, it would be quite enough if Nikki came for a few hours each afternoon. I have done rather more than tell him, I have insisted.

14 September. Nikki looks more sharp-nosed than ever, she looks thin and careworn. She is lonely without her old friend and mistress. I would like to ask her to live here with us, but there is no room in this doll's house. And she won't go to live with Olga and her family in Austria, she won't leave Germany. The end of the month, when the apartment lease is up, she will return to her village near Nuremberg. She says she will be glad to leave Munich. Nikki is a true Franconian, she talks so much about the countryside there, and reminisces over Burg Veldenstein at such length that I feel I have been inside it myself. It is Nikki's great dream that she will one day find herself living there again, her and Hermann and me. I tell her it is more reasonable to hope that someday Hermann and I will have a house with two bedrooms, and then she will come and live with us. This thought lifts her for a moment, but then she is cast down again. This is understandable, but Nikki's sadness is something devastating, it has a peasant woman's abandon in it. I feel as if the plague of the Middle Ages were upon us, or as if we were deep in the darkness of the Thirty Years War, although I am sure Nikki has never heard of either.

The Föhn still blows. Nikki says it is a wind of malaise, that birds sicken and die of sheer sadness, and rivers are tainted with blood, and that priests' urine runs black. I tell her, well then Nikki, we must hope it will soon end.

20 September. I have been up all day for the first time, dressed, actually with shoes on. I felt so frail and light. I took Nikki's arm and went through the rooms slowly, just looking at everything. I even went into Hermann's den, I call it the Plotters' Corner. I think it was meant as a storage cellar, you go down steps. He's fitted it out with dark heavy furniture. Steins, pewter tankards, and crossed swords on the wall. Photographs of the Richthofen Squadron, Dürer's engraving *Knight, Death and Devil*. One small deep-set window. Truly you feel in the bowels of an ancient fortress. Here they gather to talk and argue and plan, to bring into being a strong and glorious new Germany. Afterward we went out into the garden, for the Föhn had died down. The flowers were so beautiful, my eyes ached with their beauty.

27 September. Nikki will never be the same after today. No, she is utterly silent, with the stunned, hoarding look of one who has seen a vision. For today General Ludendorff is here. Nikki herself opened the door and graciously, if with a trembling hand, ushered the legendary hero inside. Herr Hitler came in with him, but Nikki has no use for him, she says he makes himself out as more important than Hermann, she says it is a great crime. I've met the general on other occasions, but I was struck again by his appearance. Strong heavy features, short-cropped white hair, a compelling gaze from under bushy brows. Every inch a general, even in civilian clothes. I must admit that Herr Hitler lost by comparison, and that I did regret an overreadiness with yes Your Excellency, quite so Your Excellency, and the uneasiness of his hands, as if he could not decide what to do with them. I hope he has decided by now, since the discussion is well under way—in the living room, for Herr Hitler whispered to Hermann that the general could not be expected to sit in a storage room. Hermann thought this amusing, but has complied. Nikki and I are upstairs in the bedroom, she sits in her sacred silence at the window, and I am at the little table.

I reread what I've just written about Herr Hitler, and it is wrong, because it stands as if that were all. It is not even anything. Even when he used to address me as countess, rather than baroness, the most embarrassing gaucherie, I would be untruthful if I said that that was what stayed with me, that *that* was real. What is real is the man obscured by the manner. What is real is his great heart, his great vision. And these are in his eyes. His eyes are never obscured. He may use the wrong accent, and even the wrong fork, but his great visionary's soul is there in his eyes. *That* is what one remembers.

I have finally broken Nikki's silence. I said: What are you sitting there thinking, Nikki? Won't you communicate your experience? She replied with quiet dignity: I thought the general looked very well.

30 September. It was sad to say goodbye to Nikki. The doctor said I might go out in the car if I bundled up to the eyes, and Hermann and I drove over to the apartment, nothing in it, everything divided up or auctioned off. Full of echoes as you walked around, shabby-looking. Nikki was in her traveling suit, with a hat that Frau Göring had made for her last year. She wept as she put it on. We took her to the train station with her things, and she wept again as she embraced me, but it was hardest for her to say goodbye to Hermann. I truly believe she loves him as much as I do. We were sad when we drove back. It is not just that Nikki is gone, but as if Hermann's last tie with his family past is gone too.

5 October. The house feels empty without Nikki. The beloved one puts in long hours, is seldom home until late at night. The political situation has gone quite mad. The country is wild with fury that Berlin has declared passive resistance in the Ruhr a failure and has ordered acceptance of French occupation. The second bitter defeat since 1918! And the mark plunges crazily into the trillions, food riots everywhere, Red uprisings in Saxony, separatist uprisings in the Rhineland, and here in Bavaria the government defies Berlin openly. Berlin has lost *all* support, it has had to declare martial law throughout the country. The crisis builds and builds, but the Party has not yet made its move.

So much is going on, and here I sit taking my temperature and my pills. But I am not unhappy, it is wonderful just to be up and about. Mostly I sit here in the window seat in the living room, embroidering or writing letters. Or I just sit looking into the trees, there are hundreds of swallows in them, they have the sweetest voices, crooning, very high, pure, so innocent and excited. I am almost lost in cushions, Hermann has brought every cushion in the house to the window seat and arranged them himself, and I laugh because he is so serious about these cushions of his. You are cushion-mad, I say, and I throw one at him and he throws it back, we're like two children, and our arms are around each other among all these cushions, and it is as if life were beginning again.

I have begun to plan for Christmas, the first in our own home. And Thomas will be with us! I hardly dare think of it, what if it shouldn't happen? I couldn't bear it if after all these months I shouldn't be allowed to see him. But then I think that's ridiculous, Nils has promised, and I even allow myself to believe that he'll stay for good—after all he *wants* to live with us, and Hermann wants to adopt him, and why should it not be? Hope carries me away in a flood!

11 October. The doctor says I can take up my ordinary life again, but there is no ordinary life to take up. Such a turmoil! My beloved returns home usually past midnight and is off again at dawn before I wake. One would think that this pace would wear even Hermann out, but his energy is limitless. His *patience*, however, is not. He agrees with Herr Hitler that before they can do anything they must first come to an understanding with the Bavarian government, but Hermann is all for a confrontation with them *now,* whereas Herr Hitler is undecided. Hermann says he is beginning to see that Hitler is not at his best in a crisis. Hitler told Putzi that when he talks with Hermann it bolsters him, it's like a bath in cold steel. Hermann says fine, but it's time he dried off and did something. But it is all so complicated. The Party doesn't feel it is strong enough to overthrow Berlin alone, it must join forces with the Bavarian government. Some such agreement had existed, and Herr Hitler felt assured that Bavarian government forces would march beside his Storm Troops. But now it seems that Kommissar General von Kahr never considered Hitler more than a useful rabble-rouser, and has no intention of joining his march on Berlin. What's more, von Kahr seems to be planning his own march, and if his forces overthrow Berlin the result will be Bavarian independence, a splitting of the Reich. It is anathema to everything we believe in. We must do something soon! Hermann says if we do not, the SA is going to break away and follow whoever strikes the first blow.

19 October. Putzi and Helene came today. A nice visit, but when we talked about the mounting tension and I said the Party holds Germany's destiny in its hands, Putzi gave me that look of his as if I were overly dramatic. And then he told me about an American magazine he subscribes to, called *Time,* where the Bavarian situation was reported at length, and no mention at all of the National Socialists. We should keep things in perspective, Putzi says. But I say what good is perspective? Think small, achieve small! I *know,* in my *blood,* that my beloved and Herr Hitler are men of greatness, that Fate has brought them together in Germany's direst moment of need, and that they will triumph! As for *Time* magazine, I told him, I have never heard of it. Well, says Putzi, with his mock-serious face, you have convinced me, everything is much simpler than I thought. Oh, Putzi is impossible. Nothing is *simple,* I never said that!

22 October. The most wonderful birthday present yesterday: the whole day together, just the two of us. A long morning walk in Nymphenburg Gardens, the beautiful autumn colors—but of course as soon as we got back someone rang the doorbell with a note for Hermann. But Hermann told him: "Unless the revolution has begun, I am taking the day off. You may wait here with your note and ring again at midnight."

When the beloved one shuts out the world he does so

wholeheartedly, he has a wonderful gift for separating himself from his worries and enjoying the moment for what it is. And we had such a beautiful day, quiet and simple and cozy. He had got me such thoughtful gifts, a pair of moonstone earrings to match my necklace, a lovely blue silk scarf, and the sweetest little wooden troll from Sweden. In the evening we sang our songs at the harmonium.

26 October. The weather has turned. Fog and rain, winter already. The damp season isn't exactly our favorite, I catch colds and Hermann's old wounds ache. What a pair! But he doesn't allow his leg to hinder him, and I am *determined* that I'm not going to be hindered either, I am going to get through the whole winter without one illness.

29 October. I think nowhere in Munich exists a warm room. I wonder when we shall ever see a piece of coal again. I stay in bed most of the time, it's warmest there. I write so many letters home. My thoughts are so much with my dear and faraway family. Hermann says perhaps next summer we can make a trip back. And then I think *next summer*—why, it will be a different world then—we shall have had the revolution—and I shiver with excitement and dread and hope, for it is going to happen any moment! The plan is to capture Kommissar von Kahr, Reichswehr General von Lössow, and State Police Chief Colonel von Seisser—we call them the triumvirate—and persuade them to support the National Socialist march on Berlin, or if they will not be convinced, to imprison them and assume control of their forces! And then—on to Berlin!

1 November. The date is set for Memorial Day, the fourth of this month, when all three will be present at ceremonies outside the Residenz Church. But Hermann says he will go to the Residenz first and rub the lion's paw for luck because he has no faith in the plan, nor has anyone else. The ceremonies will consist of troop reviewing, and it will be like going into a hornets' nest. But once Herr Hitler makes up his mind, nothing on earth can change it. He waits and waits, in a kind of daze, then he snaps to life, makes his decision, and that is that!!

3 November. Last night Hermann came home with Police Kommissar Frick and Captain Röhm. I can never remember how the one looks, and always remember the other too well.

Dr. Frick is just a tall gray filing cabinet. But Captain Röhm is unspeakably and cartoonishly ugly. A face broad and fat like a pear, with tiny eyes, low forehead, with black hair parted right in the center like an old-fashioned Bierstube proprietor, and a nose mutilated in the war, the upper part gone and the end built up in a pointed, shiny red graft. I quite like him, I feel he is a man of absolute courage.

Herr Hitler's deputy Herr Hess *everyone* likes. I think it's because he's not ambitious, that's guaranteed to make you popular. His face is like a fist, knitted brows and clamped mouth, but it's all shyness. When he laughs—that's not often—he shows buck teeth and looks like a country boy. Actually he's well educated, and a hard and able worker. I find him agreeable, but monkish. Also, he's a vegetarian.

Herr Strasser is much more amiable, and a good person I think, even if he does tend too far to the left. He's a big lumbering fellow in homemade breeches and woolen knee stockings and wears a little green Tyrolean hat, and he quotes the philosophers in Greek and has a nice humor. I always enjoy his visits except when he brings along his secretary, little Heinrich, who is a pale youth with no chin and no conversation, *so* awfully quiet although perfectly nice. Several times we've been left alone when the others have gone off to talk and I find the silence excruciating, especially since he sits there so serene, little square spectacles on his nose and hands folded just so in his lap. I pick up my embroidery in order to do something, and I work away with terrific concentration. In fact once I completed an entire rose with leaves, so I suppose he is at least good for something.

Dr. Rosenberg is another who makes the minutes scream. He is as slow and pedantic and dull as his clothes are wild—he dresses as if he were blind, we call him the Costermonger's Donkey. He's a Balt, has spent more of his life in Russia than Germany, a foreign sort, juvenile-looking though thirty, with a round rather handsome face but dyspeptic expression. He drones and drones, he is very sincere, his theories are about race and blood and all that. He is so woolly-minded and ponderous, I don't see that he makes any sense. I think he is a crackpot, even if he does have a degree in philosophy, granted from a Russian university. Hermann loathes him, I think partly because Rosenberg shares his birthday, same day and year, 12 January, 1893. Hermann says it was insulting of Fate to have done that to him, and if they should also die on the same day he will lodge a very serious complaint, but I can't bear to hear him talk about dying, even in jest, and it's no use my scribbling on about this one and that because my thoughts always come back to tomorrow and my beloved's safety. . . .

5 November. It came to absolutely nothing. The street was bristling with troops. When Hermann came back safe, only disgruntled, it was such a relief even though I know it only means waiting all over again.

8 November. Hermann came home this morning at seven o'clock from an all-night meeting, excited and geared-up. They had learned that von Kahr and the two others are to address a public meeting tonight at the Bürgerbräukeller. It's a God-given opportunity, Hermann says, although it allows almost no time to arrange things. There is such an awful lot to do—he could only stay briefly. He had driven home just to be with me for a few minutes, and we sat with our arms tightly around each other, then he was gone.

Afternoon now, gray and wet. Everything is so quiet. It doesn't seem possible that today is really the day. In a few hours the German revolution will have begun. I feel anxiety and fear and faith and hope all rushing around inside me, and I try to calm myself by thinking of Christmas, I start planning every detail—and then I'm looking at the clock again!

It is growing dark outside, only a few hours more. The clock ticks and ticks. I pray that God will keep Hermann safe. I pray for a successful outcome. I pray for Germany.

Chapter 20

IT began with swiftness, with cutting purity—a machine gun quickly set up in the doorway and then they were pushing into the crowd inside and Hitler was jumping onto a chair and firing his gun at the ceiling. "The national revolution has broken out! This hall is occupied by six hundred heavily armed men! No one may leave!" He jumped down, pulling off his trench coat—dressed for the occasion in a black swallow-tailed morning coat of provincial Bavarian cut—and hurried to the platform, where the triumvirate stood staring in astonishment. He brandished his gun and led them off to a side room.

The hall was in an uproar. Captain Göring, in battle dress and steel helmet, leaped onto a table and a second shot was heard.

"There is no reason for alarm! Have patience—everything will soon be clarified for you. It is all being done for a greater Germany! Anyway, you've got your beer, what are you worrying about?"

He was in full spirits. Captain Röhm was this minute marching his troops on Military District Headquarters; in St. Anne's cloister, where troves of arms were hidden, priests were passing out rifles to hurried lines of Storm Troopers. The plan was to take over the Reichswehr barracks and seize the weapons there. Aided by the element of surprise, the Storm Troopers were to get a foot in the door, so to speak, and hold on until something happened. What happened would be determined by the talk now taking place in the side room.

Meanwhile the crowd was beginning to calm down, which was a good thing, since it was three thousand strong. There were a few nervous calls of "Sideshow!" "Mexican Revolution!" Barmaids were going back into action. And no trouble with the police guards; most were sympathizers who had already slipped on Hakenkreuz armbands and were helping round up government officials from the audience and lead them off as prisoners. Everything was proceeding faultlessly, except that General Ludendorff should have appeared by now.

Göring jumped down from the table and went over to where Putzi, Hess, Rosenberg, Drexler and a few others stood grouped by the speakers' stand. Putzi's great face was sweating. "What's happened to Ludendorff?" he cried, but at that moment the old general, clad in a worn tweed hunting jacket, came stomping in past the machine gun, apparently summoned in all haste from his villa. His harsh, heavy face was flushed with annoyance by this careless treatment. It was typical of Adolf, thought Göring, to keep the general in the dark until the last minute; he would have kept everyone in the dark if he could have, that seemed to be his instinct. Reaching the side door, Ludendorff disappeared inside with a resounding slam.

A short while later, Adolf came hurrying out and stepped up on the platform. His face was white, and lit by feverishly brilliant eyes. His voice broke out over the noise of the audience.

"I proclaim a new provisional government for Bavaria! Quartermaster General Ludendorff will head a new national army! I shall take over the political leadership of the new national government! There will be high posts for Kahr, Lössow and Seisser, and for all Bavarian stalwarts of the right! The mission of the provisional regime is to begin with a march against Berlin with all the might of this state, and with the accumulated power of every province in Germany!"

The effect of this short, passionate speech was extraordinary—almost unbelievable—turning the hostile, anxious mood of the audience inside out like a glove, as if magically, and releasing a huge and sustained roar. Adolf shot his arm up.

"In the room behind me three men are struggling desperately to reach a decision! May I tell them that you stand behind them?"

"Ja!" the crowd roared in unison. "Ja! Ja!"

"All that's missing is the psychiatrist!" Putzi yelled cheerfully, wiping his forehead with a handkerchief, and Göring replied with an exuberant backslap, his own brow wet with heat and excitement as Adolf disappeared once more into the side room.

Twenty, thirty, forty minutes of noise, smoke, beer fumes, then the side door opened and the five men emerged and mounted the platform, where they stood in a row. Each gave a brief speech, after which Adolf went down the row shaking hands, his face radiant with joy and gratitude, like a child's, while the audience sent up one roaring cheer after another, until, utterly beside itself, it rose to its feet and broke into "Deutschland, Deutschland, über Alles," although many people were too moved to sing, and stood weeping openly.

As the crowd streamed out into the wet night, Hitler and the others repaired to an upstairs room to discuss the immediate problems of the new government. It was a long discussion, frequently interrupted by this one or that having to leave in order to check things out in the city. Except for Captain Röhm's occupation of Military District Headquarters, no real progress was being made. The surprise element had not been sufficient for a quick takeover of the Reichswehr barracks; outnumbered, and with orders not to shoot unless necessary—bloodshed was to be reserved for Berlin—the Storm Troopers were milling about waiting for the next step. Göring went to see for himself; but he was not unduly worried, since a coordinating order would soon arrive from General von Lössow. But on returning to the Bürgerbräu he found that the triumvirate had disappeared. Left momentarily in Ludendorff's charge, the three dignitaries had politely asked if they might leave in order to get things under way. Ludendorff, with equal politeness, had given his permission, and they had walked off. The old general was now indignant at the expressions of dismay around him. He cut Adolf off in midsentence. "They have shaken hands on the agreement, Herr Hitler! I forbid you to doubt the word of honor of German officers!"

But toward dawn they learned that von Kahr and his two consorts did not consider themselves bound by promises made under duress, and were taking action against the uprising.

Dawn broke, gray and wet, as they sat discussing their next move. The morning wore on. Government posters were brought in from the street, ink still damp, announcing the abolition of the National Socialist Party and charging its leaders with high treason. By forenoon only one thing had been agreed upon: that they could not remain where they were, to be ignominiously surrounded and captured. If they marched into the city they could at least stir up the people, demonstrate that they had the public's support.

Adolf said nothing. For hours he had swung between despairing silence and bursts of hope. Now he was slumped at the table in his formal black morning coat, his face drawn and colorless. Ludendorff, sipping from time to time from a glass of red wine, sat stony-faced under the perfidy of the triumvirate. He wore a heavy, beaver-collared overcoat which had been brought him during the night. His black felt hat lay next to him on the table. He picked it up.

"Wir marschieren," he said.

*   *   *

And so they marched. It was a column of some fifteen hundred Storm Troopers plus an entire Reichswehr regiment of enthusiastic cadets. Hitler had ordered all guns unloaded, certain that the column would be annihilated in the event of a pitched battle. Göring followed this with an order to bring along the government officials taken prisoner the night before, and almost at once, when the column was blocked by armed police at the end of the Ludwig Bridge, he found his purpose served. Stepping forward, his breath coming out white, he spoke to the police commander.

"You see that poor shivering group of elderly gentlemen back there? They're government officials whom we've taken as hostages. If you impede our progress, I've given orders that they be shot immediately. In fact, some of my men are eager to stomp them to death. Of course, I wouldn't want that to happen."

The police fell back and the column proceeded. But Adolf, who had been unaware of the hostages' presence, ordered them returned to the Bürgerbraukeller. "I want no martyrs on the other side," he said, pulling up his trench-coat collar in the wet wind. His step was firm, but his face was haggard with misery and strain, and his eyes moved around constantly, as if he were trying to understand where the column was headed. Ludendorff had not consulted him on the matter.

The old general, his heavy, expressionless face red-nosed in the cold, walked between Hitler and Göring in the front row. Ahead, with bayonet-fixed rifles over their shoulders, walked an advance line of Storm Troopers. The direction of the column seemed to be toward the Marienplatz, from which the sound of a crowd could be heard. People on the street were beginning to fall in alongside the column, cheering and waving and accompanying it to the Marienplatz, where several speakers—among them Streicher, his bald, bullet-shaped head shining—held forth to a wildly excited mass so tightly packed that three No. 6 Sendling streetcars stood mired. The marchers, too, found themselves mired, and a confusion followed in which it became apparent that Ludendorff himself had no idea where they were going. Finally they pressed on in the only direction open to them, up Weinstrasse, their ranks swelling with jubilant hundreds from the square, and voices lifting all through the column in "O Deutschland Hoch in Ehren."

A few blocks up Weinstrasse they sighted a blockade in the distance and made a detour to the right, then turned left again on the narrow Residenzstrasse, and proceeded in their original direction. The column's width became compressed and more forceful within the narrow confines of the street; a thin line of police shouting "Halt! Nicht weitergehen!" was broken through and swept aside, while the massed singing reverberated as if from the bottom of a canyon. Then through the front ranks the singing died away as a platoon of State Police could be seen coming at a run from around the Feldernhalle to form a barrier across the end of the street, where it opened onto the Odeonplatz. Green-uniformed, standing shoulder to shoulder, armed with rifles, pistols, and rubber truncheons, they spanned the narrow passage from the great colonnaded Feldernhalle to the baroque Residenz guarded by its two gray stone lions. The column came to a halt only a few paces before the green cordon, and the advance line of troopers stepped forward with bayonets leveled.

Göring could hear "O Deutschland Hoch in Ehren" still being sung in the rear ranks, which were too far back to see what was going on. The distant sound seemed to underline the silence and uncertainty as the two lines of men faced each other. Pistol in hand, the police commander gave no order, made no move. The wind was wet with drizzle beginning to turn to snow.

Finally the police commander, whose face was so close that you could see white snow particles in his mustache, stuck the pistol in his belt and borrowed a rifle, and with its butt knocked aside a bayonet pointed at him. This broke the tension; it was a sign for the usual streetfighting, a free-for-all, and both lines of men were already hitting out with fists and rifle butts when a shot rang through the commotion, freezing everyone in momentary astonishment. An instant later the green cordon swung up its rifles and fired.

He felt a thud against his body, another as he struck the wet paving stones, and was aware that the racketing din continued, that everyone had dropped flat, like an infantry battalion ducking as one, that through the noise there came the cries of those hit, that someone in a dark coat, Ludendorff, was getting back up, and that he himself was crawling to the side of the street, toward one of the lions, pulling himself along on his elbows, the lower half of his body dragging behind in bright, electric, paralyzing pain.

Chapter 21

—they're all dead but Ludendorff, and he's dead too, standing straight up in the fusillade, a corpse pinned to the air—all I can see is the gray Residenz lion above me as I keep struggling, struggling—

All was a shifting, quaking blur of hospital white as he flung his head from side to side on the pillow, his leg under the sheet so hugely swollen it was a giant sausage about to split. At the juncture of thigh and belly was a green-and-yellow mass embedded with a black tube; a dozen more tubes protruded from the stretched, taut surface of hip and thigh; when he thrashed, all these tubes were yanked out and the jar they emptied into was pulled onto the hospital bed and spewed out yellow pus. All these things he was aware of in some scattered, meaningless way: what was central was this wave of pain that had risen to its peak and vibrated as if it must break and topple, yet never broke, but held itself continually at its crest. Sometimes he was aware of a needle sinking into his arm. It brought vomiting and profound sweating, but no relief.

Then the peak of pain, though not breaking, seemed to diminish in height, for his eyes were focused clearly on Carin's. He smiled at her from the pillow, but saw with a stab that her face, for all the brightness of her eyes, was chalky and ill, drawn with fatigue.

"Why do you look at me that way?" she asked. "I'm very well . . .

oh my dearest, if you keep looking at me like that, I shall think you're not happy to see me."

"Not happy . . . ?" And he could not keep his eyes from filling, nor prevent his hand from drawing her to him in the clumsiest and weakest of embraces.

In the evening the nurse came rustling in. He was lying in darkness. "Herrgott, what a long face," she said as she switched on the light. "You should be happy instead. Do you know you've been shouting about lions for two weeks? Two weeks, but now the swelling has finally gone down, and the fever too. And your wife has finally gone home to sleep. *That* is the surest sign that you're mending."

She rattled on, her face beak-nosed and red, like Nikki's. The two faces had been mixed up in his mind; now they were unmixed; the nurse was Austrian, he was in Austria, in Innsbruck.

"I don't want the injection. It doesn't help."

"Believe me, the pain would be much worse without it."

When she was done she went out, turning off the light behind her. Presently he felt the morphia taking effect: the wave of heavy nausea, his mouth growing dry, sweat breaking out on his brow and trickling down his temples. The reaction was not as severe as it had been, but still he felt no release from pain. After a while he turned on the bedside lamp and lifted the blanket away from his thigh. The flesh was covered with blackish puncture marks left by the tubes. The mass of scar tissue, no longer stretched taut, had resumed its angry red flush. Joined to it, the new wound was neatly covered by a large, palely stained gauze bandage. Two bullets had been removed.

"Fate has no imagination . . . always the same old place. Just nearer the family jewels this time."

He dropped the blanket and lay back again, turning off the lamp. He lay looking across the dark room at the snow drifting down outside the window.

Finished. It was all finished, all lost. The last thing he remembered was lying on the paving stones beneath the stone lion, and knowing through the noise and pain and the sudden dark flickering behind his eyes that they were wiped out, he was dead, they were all dead, Germany was dead. . . .

However, he was not dead. He was not dead because, Carin told him, his men had dragged him to the nearest doorway, where the people inside, the family of a Jewish furniture dealer, as it turned out, had taken him in and stanched the blood. They had contacted Carin, and with the help of friends she had managed to get him across the Austrian border. He was not dead, but the revolution was. Fourteen National Socialists had been killed, and three policemen. Ludendorff had actually walked through the barrage without a nick, only to be clapped into an armored car. Adolf, escaping in the aftermath, had been arrested the following day and imprisoned in Landsberg Fortress. The Party had been abolished. Its leaders were behind bars or in exile. His home, his automobile, his belongings had been confiscated, his bank account blocked. He possessed nothing. Not a suitcase, not a pfennig.

The wound began festering again, and was operated on for the removal of deeply embedded debris. Then there was a second operation, the first having been unsuccessful. His recovery was slow, the injections brought no relief, and he worried constantly how he would pay the mounting hospital bill. At least there was no worry about the hotel where Carin was staying, its National Socialist manager having generously told her they could pay if and when they were able. But her health had been undermined by the strain of the last weeks. She looked worn and ill, even though her cheer was unflagging. He tried to join in her enthusiasm over the encouraging letters and telegrams that poured into his room, and to feel buoyed by the scores of visitors he received— for Austria, like Bavaria, was rife with sympathizers—but nothing could diminish the blow of the disaster.

He managed to answer a letter from Putzi, who had escaped to Vienna, and to write the family in Munich to whom he owed his life, and through a courier to smuggle a note to Adolf, telling him he would return to Germany as soon as he was physically able and stand trial with him and Ludendorff.

One of the letters he received was from Nikki, whom Carin had written. It was a long letter, filled with concern and commiseration, and ended with the amazing announcement that she was to be married.

". . . He is Hans Schmidt, as simple and upright as his name. He is a gardener in Nuremberg. The families he worked for were forced to sell their homes for a song to the Raffkes, so he works for them now, he has no choice in these hard times. He is steady, honest, and good. I was so lonely after your dear mother's death, and I am fond of Hans and respect him. I think we will be happy together, and I hope I have the blessings of my beloved Hermann. . . ."

But Adolf's reply deeply depressed him. It was curt and negative. Under no circumstances was he to return to Germany. His arrest would benefit no one. He would be more useful working for the Party out of Austria.

He was released from the hospital on the afternoon of Christmas Eve, walking with the aid of crutches. As soon as Carin had assisted him from the cab into the hotel and up to their suite, he was overcome by such severity of pain and sweating exhaustion that she had to help him directly into bed. There he fell into a shallow, restless sleep, from which he woke in the evening, his mind filled with the loved, lost faces,

Vati's, Mutti's, Karl's, and he felt that he saw them there in the frosty stars outside the window, he felt himself dissolving with grief, he saw the burg with all its windows lit, and the festive drawing room inside, and the great dazzling fir, he saw the bright little Obermenzing house boarded up and dark, Carin's box of Christmas decorations standing unopened in the closet, and he saw that the streets around the little house were also dark, that all the towns of Germany were dark, all Germany dark, lost, clamping his eyes shut against this sloshing melancholy, wringing his hands as if he would pull the bones apart while feeling a building torment as of worms writhing under his skin, a torment so great that his body shook with it, and with both shaking hands he managed to yank the chain of the overhead reading lamp.

Again and again the needle hit the wrong place before finally plunging into the vein, and he pressed the top of the syringe down, slowly, as he had been directed by the doctor, more slowly than he felt he could bear. When the fluid was emptied into his arm, he pulled out the needle and dropped it on the night table by the hospital kit, a small scuffed container of artificial leather. After a few minutes he felt the nausea spread through his chest, the sweat breaking out; and gradually, by degrees, the tormented nerve endings quieted, the shaking diminished to twitching, and finally ceased. The pain continued as before.

Putzi had sent money for the hospital bill, and a few days after Christmas he arrived in person. Göring, on crutches, dressed in a borrowed suit, greeted his friend with congratulations on his Franz Josef muttonchop whiskers. Under this new-grown foliage and dark glasses, Putzi had sneaked over the border to Munich to spend Christmas with his family. Before returning to Vienna he now came to Innsbruck, bringing his usual good humor and his gossip, but the gossip was not good. It seemed that Rosenberg, nominal head of the dispersed and underground Party, had stricken Captain Göring's name from the membership list. This was not surprising, what was surprising—what was devastating—was that Adolf had been informed of the deletion and had done nothing about it. "But bear in mind," Putzi went on, "that he's preoccupied. He's completely wrapped up in preparing his case. That's probably all there is to it. Unless maybe the triumvirate's doublecross was too much for him. Maybe he's condemned all members of the officer class as unreliable, you included. Who knows with him?"

He felt, like an animal sensing its only salvation, that he must keep moving. Soon after the New Year he began setting up meetings with local National Socialists, arranging to speak to Party cells in Salzburg,

Linz and Vienna, and to meet with wealthy sympathizers in order to persuade them to send funds to Germany for the outlawed Party.

But in Germany a great change was coming about. The currency had been stabilized—overnight, as one had foreseen—when the government reissued the four-trillion-to-the-dollar mark with its string of twelve zeroes lopped off, each bill magically restored to its prewar value of four to the dollar. Simultaneously the Reichskommissar for National Currency, a man named Hjalmar Schacht, had shut off all credit to the speculators who had been allowed to drive the mark into the trillions in the first place. Industrial empires built on the inflation began to topple, and to create an alluring situation for foreign investors. The Bank of England agreed to lend Germany half of the entire capital needed to back her new mark, and other foreign loans would soon come pouring in to launch a boom. The inflation would skid to a halt, and with it the furious cries for revolution.

He began rattling back and forth across the white mountains and valleys of Austria, sitting in third-class carriages with his crutches beside him. He was able to dress presentably, friends having smuggled out two suitcases of belongings from the house in Obermenzing, but the clothes hung on him. Once he had glimpsed a half-finished letter on the little writing desk Carin used: "If you could see him, Fanny, he is emaciated. He looks sick, lost, white as snow. The pain never leaves him, and it is not only the pain of his body. He is so cast down, and so terribly nervous, I hardly know him. But I hope his spiritual balance and old energy will return once he finds his strength again. . . ."

On these long train trips only the thought of returning to Carin gave a sense of meaning to his life. But it gnawed at him that his condition was an added worry to her in her own state of ill health. He tried to control his agonizing nervousness, and to keep the injections down to two a day, but more and more often he needed three, and he felt his willpower growing increasingly feeble, loosening and shredding like the fibers of an old elastic band.

Putzi wrote: "Unlike you, I am not honored as a Putsch leader. Therefore the warrant for my arrest has been lifted. I'm now back in Munich for good, sans facial shrubbery. We're all hoping that the trial will bring an amnesty for those of you still exiled. I think the trial will go all right for Adolf. I visited him and found him in good spirits (the prison authorities treat him like royalty) and indifferent to the fact that the Party is splintering apart under Rosenberg's leadership. Of course, that's why he appointed him. Imagine Adolf sitting in a cell while things outside were taken over by someone who knew what he was doing. That may partly account for your own eclipse. I had to badger him before he agreed to order your name back on the membership role. But I'm afraid it doesn't matter much. I don't think there's a future for National Socialism. Its time came at a crisis of despair, and that crisis is gone now. We are all to be eclipsed, Adolf included. . . ."

The trial took place at the end of February. It was a triumph for Adolf, whose oratory reached spectacular heights even for him, and who was seldom interrupted by the sympathetic judges. For the first time in his career he received national and even international newspaper coverage. Munich itself went wild, and, according to Putzi's letter, you could open a fruit and wine shop with all the stuff people were sending him. "You'd think he had been acquitted along with Ludendorff, instead of getting five years—of course, it will be commuted. Amazing fellow. Do you know what he asked me beforehand? 'What on earth can they do to me? All I have to do is tell what I know about von Kahr and company, and the whole thing will collapse.' Which is more or less what happened, as you know from the papers. Our triumvirate will very likely be forced to resign from office. And the flowers and chocolates keep flowing like a river into Adolf's cell, which is a pleasant three-room suite. He is sanguine to say the least, and is now writing a book of some sort. He's got Hess with him, as you may have heard. Our Rudi couldn't bear the separation any longer, came rushing back from Salzburg and turned himself in, and has already begun pecking out Adolf's dictation on the old Remington from the business office. I don't think he's a good influence. Anyone who lives on lettuce leaves cannot be a good influence. Adolf wants broadening, not more narrowing, and here he is cooped up with a vegetarian and the Costermonger's Donkey, who comes every day. But what does it all matter? The sun has set."

The only thing to do was to continue existing on loans, charity, donations, to go rattling back and forth across the country, organizing cells, raising Party funds, and to keep trying to cut back on his four-a-day injections. In late April his fund-raising tours drew a visit from Austrian government officials, who were unhappy to see currency drained from their country in favor of a foreign movement. He was told to settle his affairs and get out.

Carin made the short trip back to Munich to raise money for their further extradition. She sold their automobile, now desequestered, and withdrew the small savings from their bank account, which had recently been unblocked. They decided to go to Italy. A German hotelkeeper in Venice, a great admirer of the air hero Göring, had written to offer them cut-rate prices at his establishment should they ever come his way.

As the train chugged over the Brenner Pass into Italy, he felt a tearing regret that he had not gone to see Pate. He had been so near Mauterndorf, so often. But the thought of crossing that little wooden bridge into the courtyard had been unbearable to him. Only when he pictured Pate booming down his greetings from the top of the steps did he see himself with absolute clarity—a twitching, pallid washout with sleeves concealing arms like pincushions, the punctures crowded together in rashes oozing pus; a broken-willed addict, living on hand-outs—and he knew he would rather have done anything, anything at all, then stand face to face with Pate.

Venice was like a good dream. Carin's health improved under the warm skies, and though he was unable to cut back on his injections he felt in better spirits. He used a cane, and hand in hand they walked everywhere with a sense of bedazzlement and gratitude. Sunlight shone down on the green canals, bathed the walls of fantastic palazzos, irradiated balconies half lost in purple bougainvillea. Their hotel room, looking out on the domes and spires of San Marco, was old and ornate, a dusky rose color, and in drowzy, love-sated afternoons its high ceiling was patterned with shimmering gold reflections from the water.

They stayed a month. Then, equipped with hotel names given them by their host, they traveled on to Florence, Siena, and finally Rome, where he hoped to negotiate a loan from Mussolini. In Rome they came to an end of hotels run by patriotic countrymen and moved into a cheap backstreet *pensione.* It took weeks of battering persistence to arrange to be seen by the Duce, but when he was finally shown into the vast reception room—his cane seemed to clack across many kilometers of black marble—and shook hands with the thickset, aggressively bald figure, from whom issued a fluent and exuberant German, he felt an immediate warmth between them.

Numerous mutual amenities crossed the great polished desk. He expressed to his host his admiration for the land of Garibaldi, Mazzini, Cavour and now Mussolini. "But I have not come to take up your time with generalities, Excellency. My visit has a purpose."

"Quite so. Your letters have preceded you. You want two million lire, in return for which your Party will publicly support Italy's claim to the South Tyrol."

"Yes, it has long been our wish to cement relations—"

"I do not recall that there were any relations to cement. Forgive me, Herr Göring, but your worthy organization is not really well known to me. You might say I know it best by virtue of its unfortunate conclusion."

"Forgive me in turn, Excellency, but I hope you remember that the Fascisti were once small and unknown too. And we are not concluded, that is far from the case. And we are ready to support your South Tyrol claim, even though it is a very unpopular cause in Bavaria—just think of the difficulties and embarrassment we are willing to burden ourselves with! Think, Excellency, what a bargain you would be getting for a mere two million lire!"

"A novel point of view. We must sometime discuss it further."

The remainder of the visit was spent talking of German and Italian politics. They parted on the friendliest of terms, but there was no invitation to return.

The intolerable white sizzling sky. Cheap greasy pasta, and never enough. One window, an alley view of ulcerous walls and hanging wash. The room dark, sweltering, then an icebox when the rains began. Blankets and coats over Carin in bed with fever. The sound of the window shutters rattling in the downpour. They would rot here, there would never be an amnesty. Why not go back and serve his sentence? A year, if the judges were still so inclined. Five, if not. Five years parted from Carin, five years for something that had been no crime but a righteous action. And the alternative was a life spent moldering in furnished rooms, among alien voices, alien landscapes. You had been torn out of your soil, but your roots were always there, deep, like nerve endings still alive.

Nerve endings, they were what he consisted of; worms crawling from head to foot, the small scuffed kit the center of his existence. Better than any Roman vista did he know the color and texture of that little container, opened six, seven times a day, and the more he pumped into his arm, or thigh, or ankle, the more violent the worms grew after their too brief quiescence. Get out of the room. Spare Carin the pacing, the frenzied chair-kicking. Go to the post office, see if Putzi had sent more money. Go to the museums . . . portrait after landscape after epic battle, even the glut of Christs and Marys and hovering cherubim—in these great rich, somber canvases he was able to lose himself, to feel as if his soul were released into their sublimity, until in a sudden breaking of sweat he could not bear the silence and hurriedly made his way outside into noise and traffic yet more unbearable.

In late spring they once again sat on the wooden slats of a third-class train carriage, money for tickets having been scraped together from Putzi and other friends. Through Italy, Austria, Czechoslovakia, Poland—the more direct route through Germany was barred to them—the countryside spread green and budding. On the third day they reached Danzig and German soil—German, for blood was blood, treaties were paper—and then, standing at the rail of the small Baltic steamer, they watched the German soil grow more and more distant, until finally it disappeared.

When they got out of the boat train in Stockholm he felt the clear northern sunlight reveal him white and soft as a slug. If he had been emaciated earlier, he was the opposite now; too many months of cheap starchy food, of working at nothing. The superb physique was lost deep within a blur of dead flesh. It was apparent that his in-laws did not at once recognize him. And later, in the small flat which they had rented for him and Carin, he saw their many questions baldly summed up in the eyes of young Thomas, who was thirteen, wild with joy to see his mother again and almost as happy to see his good friend Hermann; but in the boy's welcoming eyes there was unconcealed puzzlement. Who was this pale, flabby, unhealthy man with his cane and bad teeth and drooping eyelid? What was wrong with him that his cheek jumped around the way it did?

The family, endlessly helpful, did everything they could to aid him in finding work, but Sweden was suffering an economic slump; and even apart from that, he knew he made a wretched impression. Eventually Carin's father, Baron von Fock, suggested, with great tact, that he put himself in the care of a hospital. But he could not—would not— do that.

And then there was a period when things went better. The Obermenzing house was desequestered, and they arranged to have it sold and their furniture shipped to Sweden. It was uplifting to be financially independent again, with their own cherished things around them; but gradually the money from the house sale dwindled, and reluctant to turn to the von Focks again, they began selling the furniture, pawning clothes, eating one meal a day. Eventually they were back where they had started, living on the kindness of Carin's family.

He kept tramping around looking for work. He had his teeth fixed, some of the back ones pulled. He took care of his Carin, who was so often ill. He read German newspapers. An economic miracle, the United States outdoing Britain in pouring in the gold. Borrowed money—who should know better than he about borrowed money? If for any reason America were to call in her loans, Germany would be faced with bankruptcy. Cabinet crises continued without Ebert, worn out from the strain of his office and dead at fifty-three, and replaced by Field Marshal von Hindenburg; interesting that the hero of Tannenberg had been elected to succeed the paunchy ex-saddlemaker. And what was Hindenburg all about, this aged and thoroughgoing conservative? Hard to tell, except that he scrupulously adhered to the republican constitution he had sworn to uphold, did little to strengthen republican forces, and was having no more luck than Ebert in bringing order to the parliamentary system.

And he? He could not even bring order to his own thoughts. Five, ten minutes of concentration, then crumpling the newspaper, pacing.

Carin was in many ways mystical, as were all her family. They belonged to no church, but worshiped the Christian ideals of purity, truth and love in a small chapel built behind the parents' home. It was called the Edelweiss Chapel, and a vase of the small white-and-yellow perennials stood on the altar between two plain brass candlesticks holding white candles. The walls were whitewashed, and bowls of fresh-cut flowers stood about. The room held a feeling of rustic simplicity, and seemed filled with the air and light of the outdoors. Carin and he had come here often during his first stay in Sweden, to sit quietly together in prayer. And they came now, when Carin's health and his own tense moods permitted. They prayed for strength in this time of illness, poverty, homelessness, and in the fresh, quiet surroundings, with his beloved's hand in his, he felt a sense of peacefulness. Then within hours he would be rampaging through the flat, kicking the walls, beating them with his fists, until the sudden awareness of Carin, cowering and tearful, would throw him into a paroxysm of remorse, an uncontrollable fit of weeping as if his insides would be vomited up.

He was diagnosed as suffering from acute morphine addiction, with a morbid allergy to the drug. He was to be given a slightly smaller dosage each day until he had been tapered off, but the doctors seemed unable to understand the massive amount he was used to, and the first day's allowance was so mild that it felt as if it were nothing at all. The hours passed as he argued, then began pleading, and was finally begging; and then he was lunging at the nurse with his fists clenched and swinging. He knocked her down and would have killed her had not others come running in, a dozen people holding him back until the police arrived with a straitjacket. Struggling, shouting, spitting, he was forced into the garment and examined by two doctors, who formally certified him insane—although he did not know that at the time, only that he was being taken somewhere in a police car, still thrashing and shouting, to be pushed into a cell, where he staggered around trying to claw his way out of the straitjacket. He struck his head against the wall, which was padded with some heavy resilient material, as was the floor; he struck his head on that, beginning to vomit and shake, every nerve in his body sizzling and crackling like an exposed wire, billions of frayed electric ends—stamp on him, grind him out—"Töte mich! Töte mich—!"

He got to know Langbrö Insane Asylum well, spending the entire autumn of that year there. Released as cured, he was back on the needle in a week. And that was the end. The end was when you had crawled up out of the hole, inch by laborious inch, and finally you stood upright—and then you turned and crawled back down into the darkness again. The end was when you knew there was nothing left of you that had once been, that your will was finally and totally destroyed.

Then where did the will come from on that day when he went back, voluntarily, through the Langbrö gates? A shred must have been left somewhere inside him, he thought; somewhere inside that hard, lithe body which was lost from sight within the other, but which still existed. There, inside that buried, suffocated body, a scrap of will still existed too. And months later when he came out through those gates, he knew that he had achieved the greatest victory of his life, though he would never wear a decoration for it. He knew absolutely, without doubt, that he would never return to the needle; and he knew this because, in those terrible months during which he had crawled slowly and steadily up out of the hole, he had regenerated that scrap of will. He had forged and hammered it into an iron wholeness that was much greater, much stronger, much harder, than it had ever been before.

One of the first things he had done was to go to the Edelweiss Chapel and give thanks to God. That evening he wrote to his mother-in-law, and the words poured from his heart. "I do so want to thank you for the beautiful moments I have been able to spend in Edelweiss Chapel. You cannot imagine my feelings in that wonderful atmosphere. It was so calm and beautiful that I forgot all earthly turmoil and cares, and felt as though I were in another world. I closed my eyes, I felt like a swimmer who rests on a lonely island to gain new strength before he throws himself back into the raging stream of life. . . ."

It was late autumn of 1927 when the German government proclaimed a general amnesty for all political exiles. The weather was cold and damp, and Carin was recovering from a lung congestion, but with the electrifying news—they were embracing, laughing and crying at the same time—she looked less ill already; he must not lose another moment, she insisted, he must leave now, and as soon as she was able to travel, in two or three weeks' time, she would join him.

He sent a telegram to Putzi, and two days later was on a steamer bound for Sassnitz. It was an overcast day, with a strong, cutting wind. As the ship neared Germany, he stood at the rail with his clothes flapping and strained his eyes for the first sight of his homeland. The water was green and wild, and the salt wind was keen in his nostrils.

Chapter 22

As the gangplank of the small Swedish steamer was thrown down with a clatter on the Sassnitz dock, a foreign affairs expert in London, sitting at his desk editing a manuscript on Germany, was penning a footnote on the bottom of the page before him.

Hitler, Adolf. Rose to notoriety in 1922 when he founded the so-called German National Socialist Workmen's Party. Concentrated on exploiting the Semitic and Bolshevik bogies. In 1923 he joined General Ludendorff in leading the insurrection in Bavaria, but with its failure was arrested and imprisoned. He was released after serving a year of his sentence, thereafter fading into oblivion.

Hitler, Adolf, was at that moment removing his shoes in his little room on Thierschstrasse, but neither the worn linoleum nor the fact that he was a year and a half from his fortieth birthday stirred him to thoughts of oblivion. He had come out of prison late in 1924 fortified by the knowledge that the Putsch had been no disaster but a gift from God, for the movement now possessed a foundation stone, a blood-red rock of martyrdom that could never be swept away. The Party itself, of course, had been swept in all directions. Ludendorff and Gregor Strasser had taken a large segment into a coalition of nationalist organizations; while Captain Röhm, who had reorganized the remnants of the SA, now wanted absolute authority over them.

His first step was to break with Ludendorff, for whom he had no further use. He then got Strasser out of his hair by sending him off to the northern provinces, where NSDAP groups had begun springing up after the trial's publicity. That left Captain Röhm . . . but he kept putting off a decision. Röhm, the only comrade with whom he used the familiar *du* form of address, he had known since the Party's beginnings in 1919, when it had been no more than a small discussion group under the ponderous leadership of the railroad mechanic Drexler. No other single person, apart from himself, had done more to build up the Party than Röhm, who had supplied funds, followers, arms and advice. But now he wanted the SA. In Röhm's words, it was simply a matter of the SA being on equal footing with the Party rather than subordinate to it; the SA would answer to Röhm, the Party to Hitler, each loyal to the other. So simple, and so impossible. But he kept postponing a reply to his old friend's request. Finally, his silence having spoken for itself, he received a note from the captain, tendering his resignation. "I take this opportunity," the note ended, "in memory of the fine and difficult days we have lived through, to thank you for your comradeship and to beg you not to exclude me from your personal friendship." These words moved him deeply, but he did not answer them either. Some time later he learned that Röhm had gone to Bolivia as an army training instructor.

He also broke with Drexler, long a dangling appendix.

The Party whose reins he was now trying to gather back in his hands was smaller than it had been in 1920, disorganized, and almost without funds. But it was more viable after his small purging, for he meant to start again from scratch. In prison he had undergone a profound change of attitude. He had come to realize that armed coups were useless against the power of the Reichswehr and the civil authorities, that the state could be usurped only by way of the constitution, legally, through votes. That was how he meant to proceed henceforth.

The ban was removed from the Party a year after he came out of prison, and he continued working to regain control of it. By the following year he had achieved this, at least in Bavaria. In the north there were problems with Strasser, who leaned too far to the left, and was too independent. Strasser's new secretary, a young Rhinelander reportedly more radical than Strasser himself, had actually stood up at a meeting in Hannover and demanded that "the petit bourgeois Hitler be expelled from the Party."

The northern situation was a thorn in his side, but he did not yet feel a sense of how to remove it. As for the SA, it existed in a state of suspended animation. Greatly decreased since Röhm's departure, and continuing its existence under its usual guise of sports clubs and glee clubs, it remained under the command of its various local leaders. He was not yet prepared to put it into the hands of another Supreme Commander.

Through Herr Hanfstaengl he had been introduced to Richard Wagner's daughter-in-law Winifred, and to a few representatives from the world of banking and manufacturing. Once out of prison he had reestablished these acquaintanceships and begun broadening his network of wealthy donors. But of Hanfstaengl he saw little, for Hanfstaengl had decided that he would have a Ph.D. from Munich University, and was deeply immersed in the subject of Bavaria and the Austrian Netherlands in the eighteenth century.

"So you have given up on the present, Hanfstaengl."

"Not at all, Herr Hitler. I'm just pursuing a subject that has long interested me."

But it was clear that his large musical friend had lost the spark of faith. His remarks were no longer carefully aimed and carefully shot. He said whatever he thought and let the chips fall everywhere. He was openly critical when Rosenberg was returned to the helm of the resuscitated *Völkischer Beobachter*. He called Rosenberg, Hess and Streicher the "inner circle" and pronounced them suffocatingly narrow-minded. Once he had even taken it upon himself to describe the Party's twenty-five-point platform as an impossible hodgepodge. "It served well enough in the confusion of the past, Herr Hitler, but now that you are aiming at the Reichstag it should be clarified. You should prune it of its contradictions." When Hitler had replied that the New Testament was also filled with contradictions but that this had not prevented the spread of Christianity, Hanfstaengl had sighed loudly through his great nose, as if he found the comparison too fantastic.

Hitler was not bothered by any of this. He was not interested in Hanfstaengl as a political thinker but as an exuberant pianist, and an exuberant pianist he remained.

For years, whenever he was able to take the time, and could manage the cost, Hitler had liked to get away to the Obersalzberg in the Bavarian Alps. Only an hour's drive from Munich, the Obersalzberg was a steep, lushly wooded green hill that rose to a broad summit of meadowland and stands of fir surmounted by great peaks. The area was inhabited by a few mountain farmers, with a handful of hotels, pensions and private villas dotting the slopes. At the foot of the hill lay the beautiful little resort town of Berchtesgaden, with a swift, clear river flowing past it into the nearby Königssee, which was of amazing jade-green clarity. But he had gone to the Königssee only once or twice, for he was not fond of water, and neither swam nor boated. It was the heights he came for. Staying in one of the cheaper pensions, wearing Lederhosen and stout walking shoes, he would hike up to the magnificent outlook from the Obersalzberg summit, where he would spend hours wandering and thinking or sitting in the sun with his back against a tree. In the mountains he felt a great faith in the activity of waiting.

He was still not sure what tack he would take with Strasser when he asked for a meeting with him; he said very little, but found himself taking stock of Strasser's secretary, a young man named Goebbels. He came away with an impression of something auspicious, something in the eyes—very dark, very large and beautiful, in contrast to the rest of the fellow—which had a shining, restless quality. Nothing else about this youthful Rhinelander, who had called for the expulsion of "the petit bourgeois Hitler," was auspicious. He was clearly a man of razor intelligence, much sharper than Strasser. The articles he wrote for Strasser's newspaper, always calling for a heavier Socialist slant in the Party platform, were brilliant. He was said to be an equally brilliant orator. In conversation his voice was rich, fluent, educated. Though reportedly of working-class origin, he held a Ph.D. in literature from Heidelberg, and was addressed as Herr Doktor. A pure leftist radical, he was the worst possible person to be linked arm in arm with Strasser. Yet there was something in the eyes to be pondered.

A few weeks later, Hitler called a general meeting of all Party leaders, taking care to arrange it for a weekday so that most of the northern leaders could not get away from their jobs. With his southern supporters overwhelmingly in the majority, with banners and giant posters in magnificent display and the band striking up the "Badenweiler March," he strode to the speaker's stand and immediately pronounced on the problem of the north. He was the nucleus and leader of the movement, he told the audience, and he would tolerate no split in the movement. The speech was in the nature of an ultimatum—the northerners would either have to reject him outright and break with the Party, or accept him as their supreme leader—and he sat down to tumultuous applause. Strasser, caught off-guard, cut a poor figure on the stand. His sparse hair damp with sweat, he spoke uncertainly and sat down looking crushed. From Strasser's few supporters present there was scattered clapping. His young secretary shouted out a leftist slogan or two, then fell silent.

Soon after, Hitler invited the young secretary, this Dr. Goebbels, to Munich. He allowed him to be the primary speaker at several meetings, again replete with banners, guard detachments, martial music, with all the accouterments of power which the north so conspicuously lacked, and after a few more such visits he appointed Goebbels to the post of Gauleiter of Berlin. The man was not a pure leftist radical. He was a pure radical. It was that which was in the eyes, with their shining, restless quality. It was a searching for the ultimate, any ultimate.

With Goebbels quit of Strasser, he had the two strongest men of the north unlinked and working as rivals. He should be grateful to Strasser for his taste in secretaries—they worked out not at all well for Strasser, but were proving a distinct boon to the Party, certainly Goebbels, and, to a lesser degree, young Heinrich Himmler, whom Strasser had fired for secretarial incompetence but who was showing organizational talent as assistant leader of the erstwhile Stabswache, now called the Schutzstaffel, the elite guard detachment.

Finally, as Supreme Leader of the SA, he selected Captain Pfeffer von Salomon, a former Freikorps man who was practical, a good worker, and, unlike Röhm, unimaginative.

He continued to spend most of his time on the Obersalzberg, where, with the modest proceeds from the book he had published, *Mein Kampf*, he had bought a house near the summit, set pleasantly among maples and raspberry bushes. Haus Wachenfeld it was called, not more than a small cabin really, but with a veranda and superb view. When he had settled in, he wrote and asked his widowed half sister in Austria if she would come and stay as cook-housekeeper.

For his trips to Munich he kept his little room on Thierschstrasse, and it was there in the late autumn of 1927 that he received a visit from his first SA leader. In his brisk familiar walk there was a suggestion of stiffness, more noticeable when—beaming, already talking—he sat down with an absently painful easing out of his right leg. He was greatly altered in appearance. He was a heavyset man now, you might say fat, lacking entirely the elegant, muscular leanness of the air hero Göring. And though the face itself had not thickened, it held other changes. There was a bagginess under the eyes, as if he suffered from insomnia, and a thinning of the long, mobile lips. His skin was pale, unhealthy-looking. But the eyes were as keen as ever, and sparkled with the pleasure of reunion. He gave the impression of having run all the way from Stockholm.

It was a brief meeting. Captain Göring's post in the SA was filled, and beyond that there seemed little to discuss. The man had been gone four years, was out of touch with everything, and was penniless. He brought no assets, neither personal contacts nor money, not even a healthy skin tone. He looked worn out, and walked with a limp.

But he could not very well say these things to his visitor, or that he was permanently soured on the officer corps. After a courteous length of time, he rose and extended his hand to his guest.

"It has been a pleasure to see you again, Captain Göring. I hope you will manage to get settled somewhere. That is what you must do, find a job, put yourself back on your feet. And then perhaps we'll have another chat. Indeed, a pleasure to have seen you."

Chapter 23

"Y OU'RE not the type to commit suicide."

"Who mentioned suicide?"

"You. Just now."

"I don't know what I said—I only know it wasn't what I expected!"

"Haven't you read what I've been telling you in my letters for four years?—Please Hermann, would you stop that pacing? It's driving me mad. I mean it. Take off your coat, for God's sake, and calm yourself."

"Fifteen minutes—who does he think he is, Bismarck?"

"What do you propose to do?"

"Weiss nicht . . . but I tell you this, Putzi, I will not be pushed out the door! I will not be told to go play skittles in some corner!"

"Listen to me, I sent you his book, *Mein Kampf*. Did you read it?"

"*Mein Krampf*? Who can read it?"

"Exactly. Who can read it? It's goulash. If you slog through it, you ask yourself, is this what I've been hanging on to, this völkisch bombast? And I ask you the same thing. What is it you're hanging on to? If this is his ideology—"

"I don't give a damn for his ideology. He doesn't have an ideology—a system of ideas. What he's got is a genius for moving the masses, and if that's goulash, that's fine with me as long as it gets us to Berlin. I want to break the Weimar government. I want to break the

Versailles Treaty. I want a free and powerful Germany. You ask what I'm hanging on to? That's what I'm hanging on to, and no one is turning me out to pasture to play skittles!"

"What is all this with skittles? Hermann, will you *please* stop that pacing?"

"And you, you haven't let go either."

"I know . . . I suppose it's a form of inertia. I don't really have much hope for the Party's survival, you know. From the public's point of view it's just another little no-account group. The public looks past it with complete indifference, at most with a pitying smile for its bombast. But that's not the reason for my inertia, it's that I feel I made no dent on him, and that I never will."

"You've turned into a regular voice of gloom."

"Things have changed since 'twenty-three. He's been cast in his final mold. Ja, I mean it. Narrow. And taking himself very seriously. You ask if he thinks he's Bismarck? Wirklich! He's not Herr Hitler anymore, you know—ach, nein, it's 'mein Führer' now. You may credit our Rudi with that. He started it, and it caught on like wildfire. As for me, I can't bring myself to say it. Well, Adolf doesn't mind. He likes me. It's the piano, you know. But even if he doesn't put on the Führer business with me, I know it's there underneath. And other things too. He's taken a real plunge into . . . what should I call it? Mystic drama? *Mea culpa*, all very Wagnerian. The Putsch he's built up into something right out of Siegfried's death. He got hold of one of the flags carried on the march, the Blood Banner he calls it, and whenever other flags are consecrated—in torchlight ceremonies, I must add, and to a thunderous roll of drums—each flag is solemnly touched with the tip of this Blood Banner. Presumably some mystical force flows on contact. I see you find it amusing."

"Of course it's amusing. Slaughtered innocents, holy martyrs—do you suppose for a minute that all our rifles were emptied of ammunition? If so, how do you account for three police deaths? They didn't shoot themselves. It's anyone's guess who fired the first shot and set the whole thing off. I find it amusing that he's managed to get around that little obscurity."

"He doesn't have to get around anything. Everyone sees things exactly as he sees them. This is how things are now, Hermann. This is what I'm telling you. He's kicked out everyone but the toadies and fanatics. Narrow-minded doctrinaire provincials."

"We'll get rid of them."

"Ach, here you are getting rid of everyone when by your own admission you've just been shown the door."

"I've been shown the door, but I have every intention of reentering it."

19 December, 1927
Berlin

Dear Putzi,

    I've been meaning to thank you for your hospitality while I was in Munich, but have been tremendously busy. Before I forget, did I leave my robe at your place? Red silk, gold dragon on the back—if it's there please keep it for me. It's the one thing I bought in Italy, I shouldn't like to lose it. Berlin's a madhouse—theaters, opera, films, nightclubs, everything going full blast, motorcars bumper to bumper, everyone dressed to the teeth, all resting very uneasily on foreign capital. And the place is a regular thieves' kitchen—gambling, nudism, homosexual dives, a lot of occult hocus-pocus. Well, to each his own, except that the hotel staff keeps throwing whores at me every time I cross the lobby, finally told them I'm studying for the priesthood. The place is a dump off Kantstrasse, but I'm seldom there. Believe me, this scratching around for a stake takes up every hour—doing what I can with the representative's commission I got in Munich with BMW, also trying to set up a salesmanship with Tornblad parachutes in Sweden, also making contacts with Lufthansa. The great thing is that so many of my flying comrades are in Berlin—Udet's abroad, but I've had a great reunion with Bodenschatz and Loerzer. Another, Pilli Körner, I've gone into partnership with. Putzi, what do you think of this! I'm riding around in a Mercedes-Benz. That's Pilli's one asset, his car, so he chauffeurs me to my appointments and we both profit from the splendid impression this makes. As for politics, I have no contact with the Party, and no time for anything but what I'm doing, which is working my ass off, literally—have lost pounds and look and feel better for it. I'm getting back into my old stride, and I apologize for sinking into hellish melancholy, as you called it. No more of that, except that I'm hellishly lonely for Carin. It looks as if it will be weeks yet before she can travel—can't wait that long, so I'm pushing everything aside and going back to Stockholm for Christmas, swimming the Baltic if I can't scrape some funds together. I close now. Don't forget the robe. Don't give it to your maid.

Hermann

P.S. Who is this Goebbels character? According to the papers he wrote an article asking if Hindenburg was alive. Our aged president was not amused, and has filed a suit against him. Apparently the fellow already has six character-defamation suits pending. I suppose it's one way of drawing attention to the Party, if somewhat junky.

Chapter 24

A<small>T</small> fifty-seven, Nikki was a bride of four years. Marriage she had never coveted, for to judge by what went on at Veldenstein, and she judged everything by Veldenstein, the married state was too complicated. Quite without it she had had home, family and a high place in life. But when in middle age she returned to her village, which lay halfway between Veldenstein and Nuremberg, and moved in with a widowed niece living above the ceaseless squawks of a poultry shop, she had only memories.

Herr Schmidt she met on the village square bench, where they fell to chatting. Herr Schmidt came of a Sunday to visit relatives—walking from Nuremberg, he was that thrifty—and before going back he liked to sit in the sun and muse on things. He was a quiet man, a gardener by trade. He had always worked for the gentry, and this showed in several pleasing ways: he was neat and courteous, and he listened with appreciation when she told him of her own background. They began taking a walk every Sunday along the Pegnitz, he in his good black suit, with waistcoat and Sunday watch chain, she in her best dress, which was of fine prewar quality.

Herr Schmidt's personal history was not uncommon, and therefore the sadder. His two sons had fallen in the war, and his wife and daughter had died toward the end of the food blockade. "My wife was frail, and the girl too, a bit tubercular, you see. Otherwise, mayhap they could have made it on the vegetables." For he owned an allotment plot where he had quite a nice little vegetable patch. But they died just the same. "It was a bad time, all four of them gone. Lonely, you see." But one went on. He was a gardener, and he gardened. He moved into the shed on the allotment plot, big enough for one, and no rent. He worked at his job and he saved. He planned to buy half a share in a vegetable stall. Then overnight no savings, and no job either, for who could afford to keep a gardener? It was a bad time, but one went on, one stood in the soup lines. Well then, the Raffkes had moved into the houses he had worked for, and they could afford a gardener, they could afford anything. So he was working again, and even if his wages weren't worth the paper they were printed on, he wouldn't complain. For he was fortunate, you see, to have a job at all.

Herr Schmidt was a thin balding man with a lined, sun-reddened face and a sharp nose. He wore a full-bodied mustache of the old-fashioned handlebar variety, a dignified gray in color, and beneath this his lips often formed a shy smile, which Nikki found herself growing fond of. Herr Schmidt brought her flowers. He was one to take your arm when you came to a bump in the path. One day he kissed her on the cheek, and the idea of marriage began to bloom between them. Nikki felt a great happiness, along with moments of panic as if she would faint. But she and Hans looked remarkably alike, except for the mustache, both of them bony, red-faced, with a sharp nose; this gave her a certain confidence, it made everything seem less a step into the unknown. Also they sprang from the same Franconian soil, and not least, they shared an instinct for the finer things in life. They were practically twins.

It was a good marriage, because they were not twins at all. Hans Schmidt was a man to nod, his wife a woman to talk. That worked out well. He was slow, she was quick. He smiled or frowned, she laughed or wept. He liked her extremes, it was almost like having a houseful of children again. And she liked his solidness, she leaned on him like a bride of eighteen. She said their marriage was a renaissance—Nikki used large words like that—and that God in His infinite goodness had brought them together on that bench. Then again she sometimes called it Fate, for she had seen an S-shaped cloud the morning they met, S for Schmidt, you see. Nikki saw signs everywhere. She brought life, drama, into the house. House he called it, the three small rooms he had built onto the shack over the years, Haus Sonnenblume: that was painted in Gothic letters over the front door, complete with floral border. Around the house were sunflowers, roses, bushes of pink phlox, green rows of vegetables. And what happiness to see Nikki hurrying to the gate as he came walking home from work, what happiness to return to bustle and chatter; not much of a cook, but the table always set just so, and she herself as neat as a pin and in earrings, what fine dresses she owned,

what exceptional hats, what grand tales she told from Burg Veldenstein and Austria and Munich, enough to make you sit back and marvel, if you were the kind to marvel. He was not, but he nodded from
time to time and sometimes put a question.

"What was it that was so bad about him, this von Epenstein?"

"Na, can't you see? He was impossible."

It was frustrating for Nikki to pound Epenstein into the ground
and yet to have to refrain from explaining that he had thrown them
out of Veldenstein and to forgo the juicy mention of his Jewishness.
But these were private matters which she would disclose to no one, not
even to Hans. And so, unless she wanted not to bring up the splendors
of Mauterndorf at all, she had to make do with its lord's shouting and
bossing, yet even here she was inhibited by a desire not to tarnish too
badly her picture of life in high places.

Only when she was out in the garden, vigorously planting and
weeding, did her thoughts spread freely into all the unfinished business of the past. Remember the time the old bastard had trod on her
toes getting into the carriage? Not a word of apology, just a servant as
far as he was concerned. But when he was seated she had looked him
up and down very coldly, very coldly indeed, and he saw it, and he
knew where he stood with Nikki. But her greatest triumph had been
the time she was down in the meadow and he came tramping back with
his retinue from a day of hunting, all dolled up in his costume and
soaked with sweat, stinking like a goat. Well, she gave a loud, disdainful
sniff as he passed, and with eloquent offendedness averted her face.
And he noticed, all right, and if he didn't know anything else, he knew
to this day—old and feeble, and sick too she hoped—how he stood
with Nikki.

She would have been bitterly disappointed to know that von
Epenstein retained no memory of her whatever. He had always lived
for the moment, and at seventy-six this was still so. He sat solidly in the
present, very solidly, since his greatest source of satisfaction was food.
After that came the pleasant presence of his wife, who remained
charming to look upon. Then came an occasional motor trip around
the countryside, though it was a chore to get in and out of the car, he
being immensely fat and weak-legged and requiring the use of two
canes. It was years since he had walked through the entire castle. He
spent most of his time by an open fire in one of the smaller rooms,
reading or dozing. That was what it came to. You owned more rooms
than you could count, and you never saw them. You sat in one of the
smallest, to be warm, with your hands held out to the fire. But that was
all right for a man getting on in the direction of eighty. He still ran the
place exactly as he saw fit—no diminishment of lung power. All told, it
was a decent enough life, and one unclouded by regret. One regret,
perhaps: that Hermann was not his son. But what, after all, were blood

ties? Not much. The tie of the spirit was the real tie; and that was theirs, and would always be, even if they did not see each other for years. Years it had gotten to be. A letter now and then from Sweden, but it was not the same as a visit. He longed for a visit, before it was too late. And it was only then that he really felt his age. When it came to him that he might die without seeing the boy again, his eyes seeped, and he sat wiping them with his handkerchief, like any old doddering fool in a corner.

Both Ritter von Epenstein and Frau Schmidt received a letter from Hermann in March of 1928, one which they had been waiting for ever since the news of the general amnesty. He wrote that he and Carin were settled in Berlin, where he was working as a representative for several business firms . . . Carin was in better health than she had been for years, and they were both overjoyed to be back in Germany . . . his work kept him very busy, and he also planned to run for a seat in the Reichstag come May, but he hoped afterward to get away for a visit . . .

Old Epenstein's eyes seeped happily. Nikki's flooded. All these years she had wept for her Hermann, shot up so terribly and banished from his homeland. How she had worried, and so few letters to tell her anything. When she wept, Hans was so good and kind, and always said, "He'll turn up one of these days, wait and see." Today he smiled as the tears ran in profusion down her cheeks. "Na," he said, when she had dried them and straightened her hair, "didn't I say so? Ende gut, alles gut."

She smiled back, sighed deeply.

"And a seat in the Reichstag," he said. "Just think of that."

"Just think of it."

"He must still belong to that party. One must belong to a party, you know, in order to sit in the Reichstag."

"I am well aware of how the Reichstag is run, Hans."

But for all Nikki's strong opinions on government and politics, she did not really seem to know much more than he himself, who was your ordinary man on the street, he admitted it. Take the Nazis—or rather the National Socialists, for the other was vulgar slang and she was very definite about correcting him on it—she could not explain a thing about them. That had been a bit of a disappointment early in their marriage, just after the Putsch. For he was curious, you see, everyone was. He knew about Herr Streicher, Streicher being the Gauleiter of Franconia, with headquarters here in Nuremberg. He had once read *Der Stürmer,* and had once caught sight of the man himself downtown, both unpleasant experiences. But that was all he really knew firsthand. And here was Nikki, who actually knew General Ludendorff, and Hitler, knew them well, and had herself brought up Captain Göring, and yet she could not tell him a thing about their platform. She said it was confused. Well, it was confused, that was why he asked. All he could figure was that they wanted to overthrow the Weimar government and that they took a hard line on Raffkes, especially Jews. That sounded all right to him, but he would like to know more, he being a monarchist. Would they put a Hohenzollern on the throne if they got in, or would they nationalize everything? Nikki was a monarchist too, passionately so, but she did not know. What difference did it make anyway, she said, the whole thing was kaputt. And so it was. After a year or two you never heard a word about them. They would have passed entirely from his mind except that they scraped together a few rallies at the local stadium, and that he heard that Herr Streicher was still walking around the streets cracking his hippopotamus-hide whip so that people jumped aside. Whatever the NSDAP was or might have been, there was one thing he knew: he did not care for the Gauleiter of Franconia.

Josef Goebbels, Gauleiter of Berlin, sticking his briefcase under his arm, opened up his large black umbrella as he headed down the street to where his used car was parked. "My foot bothers me badly," he had written in his diary as a boy. "I am conscious of it all the time, and that spoils my pleasure when I meet people." The fact was that it spoiled his pleasure even when he was alone. Orthopedic footwear had improved since his childhood, and he had also contrived a special manner of walking which he hoped reduced the obviousness of his limp. But he was aware that nothing could disguise an affliction as pronounced as his, not only a clubfoot but the leg itself shriveled ten centimeters shorter than the other. He was aware of it every moment, as if one part of his mind hung permanently at his side, watching. So it was today, as he stumped down the street trying to hold his umbrella steady in the strong March wind and rain. He lived in Wilmersdorf, a modest section of Berlin. The street was lined with nondescript new apartment buildings of gray stucco, each with its narrow herbaceous front garden black with the long but finally thawing winter. The snow on the sidewalk had turned to brown slush, and was slippery under his feet.

He had no liking for Berlin. "A monster city of stone and asphalt," he had written in his diary the day of his arrival, carrying his one old suitcase containing a few clothes and a copy of *Mein Kampf* inscribed with the words "To Dr. Josef Goebbels, Gauleiter of Berlin, from Adolf Hitler." A prestigious title, Gauleiter of Berlin, but a thankless enough job—stopping a moment to alleviate the distress of a girl struggling with her whipped-inside-out umbrella; nothing to be done, it was broken; but a delicious face, charming smile, though not the best calves in the world as she departed down the street—a thankless enough job to attack this stone monster, "this sump of iniquity," he called it in the first issue of his newspaper, *Der Angriff*, "this morass of dying culture, this gathering place for Jewish literary cosmopolitans, this focal point of intellectual nomadism," this Social Democratic stronghold in which Party headquarters were in a filthy cellar lacking so much as a filing cabinet, just some loose sheets and exercise books lying around. Meetings had consisted of beer drinking and pointless talk, everyone having formed his own individual opinion of what National Socialism was. After his first speech in a hired hall, a third of the Party had drifted away, never to be seen again. He was left with five hundred people in a city of four and a half million. "We must cease to be anonymous," he told them. "Let them curse us, libel us, battle and beat us, but let them talk about us. There are five hundred of us here in Berlin. In five years there must be five hundred thousand."

16 March. Hardly anyone on the street today, a little man with a briefcase limping along under a big black umbrella. Rain and wind, the snow nothing but slush—but I don't care what the weather is, for me it's already spring!

The apartment is really awful with its pretentious "modern look," which just means furniture with rounded edges made from the cheapest possible wood—our fine new age of mass production—and the desk lamp is a hideous brass Buddha holding a lantern, and yet it pleases me because everything pleases me. We eat hardly anything but pea soup with sausages, and that pleases me too, and the woman next door who fancies herself an opera singer, even her screechings please me, because I am listening to them here in Germany where we are free to take up our lives again, to follow our star even if it means more and greater struggle. I feel that the very air in Berlin is charged with life, and my health is testimony to this—no relapse since coming, and no more fainting spells. That makes me think the doctor in Stockholm was wrong when he said my heart was weakened. I think I know more about my own heart than any doctor—I suppose that's silly, and yet I mean it. I feel that my heart, because it is happy, is sound.

The beloved one has regained his health and spirits—the change in these last few months is remarkable. He has lost a lot of the weight he put on, though he has kept some of it— well, he is thirty-five and not a boy, one must describe him as a big man now, powerful and solid-looking. The wound still bothers him, but his limp is hardly noticeable. He says work cures all things. Not that being a sales representative is his idea of important work—hardly—it is only a means to an end, for he must get himself back on his feet before he can do anything else. And how he has thrown himself into it! Biggest calling cards I've ever seen, not likely *they* get lost in the shuffle—and if someone doesn't return a phone call, Hermann simply rings back every five minutes until the secretary is finally driven mad and puts him through—he lets nothing stand in his way, and has already got the agencies for BMW, Tornblad parachutes, and Heinkel Aircraft, and is sure to get Lufthansa. He's got a dingy little office like a closet but has brightened it up with a sword on the wall, and sometimes he sits down there with paperwork till midnight, then up again at six—he can't sleep anyway. Ever since his drug illness he's suffered from insomnia—but he never seems to *need* sleep, he never wears out!

We're fortunate to have such good friends here in Berlin, Pilli Körner, and the Bodenschatzes and the Loerzers—Bruno Loerzer married a very well-to-do woman, they have a lovely home in Dahlem and are wonderful to give luncheons and dinners for Hermann's customers since we can hardly entertain them here—and Prince Philip of Hesse, another wartime friend of Hermann's, he's married to the King of Italy's daughter, Princess Mafalda—and the Princess zu Wied, whom I knew in Stockholm, a warm good person and Prince Viktor too—so it is very different from Munich where our friends were all political and none really close except Putzi—we are always rushing off somewhere. I have to squeeze in my letters home when I can, and this is the first day since I came that I've had time to write in here—it is all hectic, marvelous, and Berlin is unbelievable!!! Alive, alive, especially at night with its cinema palaces lit up, and huge department store advertisements everywhere in colored electric lights, and the crowds swarming along Kurfürstendamm—girls with lip rouge so dark it looks black, and eyebrows shaven and drawn on, and hemlines halfway up the *thigh* and peach-colored silk hose, and fops in loud checkered suits and long pointed shoes and neckties so awful they would make the Costermonger's Donkey's mouth salivate! And women in expensive moleskin coats, furs of every kind, jewelry just dripping! All terribly decadent but so *alive* with the lights and traffic—taxis honking, and doormen tooting, and hurdy-gurdies on corners, and jazz bursting out from nightclubs with nude revues I'm told—there on Kurfürstendamm it's hard to believe a *political* life exists in this city, but of course it does!!! It fills the newspapers, and the radio too if we could afford one, and Hermann follows the papers closely though he has no contact with the Party. Even so, he is determined to run for parliament and already tomorrow leaves for Munich to put his request before Herr Hitler. He is not sure what his reception will be, but I *know* that Herr Hitler in his heart never turned against the beloved one. It was the backbiting talk of people like Rosenberg and Streicher that clouded his thinking. I am sure that this time he will welcome his old comrade with appreciation and friendship. He is too great a man not to.

18 March. Hermann was so eager to bring home his news that he returned straightaway from Munich on the night express, and has now fallen on the sofa for half an hour's sleep before having to rush off somewhere else. The sun is just coming up over the housetops, the most magnificent morning!! And we are so excited, so happy!! And Hermann said Putzi was too, he walked with Hermann to Thierschstrasse and there was snow on the ground, but Hermann said he felt hot as a boxer—a boxer, alas!—and he ran up the stairs two at a time and when his request was not right away met with enthusiasm he shouted that it was no way to treat a man who got two bullets in the stomach at the Feldernhalle and either Herr Hitler would put him up for the Reichstag or they would part forever as enemies—he shouted so loudly that Putzi told him afterward he could hear him from the street. Well, I am sure it wasn't necessary to express himself so tempestuously, but perhaps it did clear the air, for Herr Hitler came around right away. But I know he would have anyway, for I know the bond between these two great patriots is a true one—and this was borne out by their parting warmly as comrades and friends, as in the past. If Herr Hitler wasn't immediately taken by the Reichstag idea, it was for practical reasons, and Hermann is the first to admit that he has been out of things for years and is politically unknown to the voting public. But he has absolute confidence in himself, nor did it really hurt for Herr Hitler to see how completely he has regained his vigor and drive—and so the upshot is that the beloved one has been asked to take up the flag again on behalf of the Party, and to fight for Germany's redemption at the elections in May!!!

I told him I don't care if it *is* early in the morning, we're going to drink a toast! And we got out a bottle of Kirsch and we drank to Reichstag Deputy Göring, laughing because we already had him elected, and because Putzi had thrown a package at him as he left and in it was his Chinese robe, so gaudy with its big dragon, but what fun we had picking it out in Venice that sunny beautiful day!

18 May. All Berlin has election fever, and it will be settled on Sunday. Each day there are clashes between Communists with their red hammer-and-sickle flags and Hitlermen with their red Hakenkreuz flags, so that there is strife, killings and woundings, although Hermann says Dr. Goebbels is great for having bandages colored with red liquid put around the heads of the SA men so they will look like battered heroes, and then Dr. Goebbels marches before them with his limp, like a wounded veteran. Which is what he tells everyone, though Gregor Strasser tells *us* it's a congenital deformity. But *everything* is grist to Dr. Goebbels's mill, I am sure it is his Jesuit upbringing, he is so terribly clever and shrewd. He has dark splendid eyes and a manly smile with rough, deep laugh lines around it, but they're his only good features. His chin recedes, and his forehead too, and he is so skimpily made, a shred of a man. His limp must be the bane of his life—yet women find him irresistible, or maybe it's just that he puts so much effort into their conquest. Rumor has it that his dedication to the Party is equaled only by his dedication to the chase. Apparently he used to live near here, but he's recently moved to a better part of town and has bought a Mercedes, although he is the one to bring in the Berlin working class. (Hermann is going to bring in the higher class, with all his good connections.) We have seen a lot of Herr Goebbels. Wonderful evenings singing around the harmonium. Hermann surprised me with one just like the first, white, it was so dear of him. Goebbels sings well (not so well as Hermann) and is charming and cozy, at the same time so clever and intense, I quite like him though I'm not sure what I make of him.

We have also had Gregor Strasser here, what a pleasure to see this lumbering good fellow again, and quite a good tenor—I suppose it's awful that I drag them all to the harmonium but they do like it. After all, the Germans are supremely musical, and it makes everything so friendly and happy. Both Goebbels and Strasser—who get on very well together, at least here—are running for parliament, and also our gray filing cabinet, Dr. Frick (fine baritone), and General Ritter von Epp (tone-deaf), and others—the hope is that *twenty* National Socialists will be elected, six more than are sitting now! What a pace! We are constantly coming and going, all Hermann's electioneering on top of the usual luncheons and dinners, but I wouldn't miss *one* of his speeches!!

He is *very* good!! He has a natural gift, and expresses himself so straight and honest and deep from his soul, and then of course his humor can be very salty, and altogether the audiences love him, for they're ordinary good folk who appreciate someone human and real and down-to-earth. There are also an awful lot of Party meetings just now. At the one last night who should step over to say hello but—who indeed? I had no idea. I had forgotten him completely, little Heinrich, who used to strain my nerves. Up from Munich for a visit, he said, polite as ever and more socially outgoing, so that it wasn't like pulling teeth to chat. Well, he's grown up, I suppose, now an assistant something with the SS, the Schutzstaffel (founded by Hermann, I should like to remind everyone), but still looking like someone's secretary or a grammar school teacher, folded hands and pince-nez and serenely blinking. A perfectly nice creature, but dreary, and knows it, bowing and stepping back as others louder and heartier came over.

Yesterday Hermann and I made a three-hour car journey to a racecourse for cars where we went around the track at 115 kilometers an hour!! Then back to Berlin for tea at a pavilion on the Wannsee, then back home for half an hour's rest and off to dinner with the zu Wieds at a Chinese restaurant where we ate swallows' nests! And strawberries on sticks! Then to the Party meeting and back here past midnight, and today I'm just being lazy and catching up on things. Wrote long letters to Sweden, and now I'm repeating everything here, but I want to have my own record of these exciting times to look back on. I'm sitting by the open window in my kimono. Spring in Berlin has a special quality, the air seems actually buoyant, radiant, like fresh sparkling water. And hundreds of little crooning, piping swallows in the trees, just as in Obermenzing!!

21 May. *Hermann elected yesterday!!!* Have just sent a cable off to Mother and Father, and am so proud and happy!!! Strasser, Goebbels, Frick and von Epp won seats too, and seven others besides Hermann—only twelve altogether, a far cry from the twenty they had hoped for, in fact two *less* than had been. A bitter disappointment to the Party, gloomy faces everywhere. Well, 3 percent of the national vote is certainly not overwhelming, twelve seats out of 491 are not many, but I say to them, cheer up: Hermann is ten men rolled into one, so you have more than your twenty!!!

Chapter 25

JOSEF Goebbels took a splenetic view of his new status as Reichstag Deputy. "What does the Reichstag mean to us?" he wrote in *Der Angriff*. "We come not as friends but as enemies. We have no intention of wasting our energies and talents in the service of the parliamentary pigsty. For us the appellation 'Member of the Reichstag' means that one is able to attend sessions without having to pay the amusement tax, and that one earns 750 marks a month for accepting the benefits of immunity and free railway travel."

For Göring, the Reichstag perquisites were undimmed by such satirical distancing, and as an early-morning train began pulling out of the Anhalter station he stood leaning from his compartment window exuberantly waving his free railway pass at his friend-chauffeur-partner Pilli Körner on the platform; with a last flourish of the large beige ticket, his face covered with smiles, he shut the window and sat down with his overnight case. The compartment was pleasantly empty at this early hour. His eyes took in the rubiate plush, the small red-shaded wall lamps, the dark gloss of the paneling. He was not sure when he had last sat in an intact first-class compartment—sometime well before the end of the war. The intervening decade did not prevent an immediate sense of familiarity and rightness, as if the torn-up coaches of defeat had not existed, nor all the hard second- and third-class seats that had been his lot since. Smiling, he unbuttoned the smart ankle-

length overcoat he had bought on credit and snapped open his overnight case, from which he took out a packet of congratulatory letters he
had not yet had time to enjoy. Pulling out the little hinged shelf beneath the window, he set out on it a couple of cigars, his cigar cutter, a
box of matches, and a handful of marzipan chocolates in gold foil.
Then, settling back and stretching his legs before him, he began to
read.

Hitler was no poor stick when it came to outbursts, but his had
method, whereas Göring's explosion had seemed native to him and
wild, and as he had stood there in the storm of shouts he knew that he
did not want this excitable fellow, to use the mildest of possible terms,
to leave the room as an enemy. Indeed, it was clear that the man had
recovered in superabundance his single greatest asset: vigor. He had
also recovered his impressive appearance; he looked fit and strong,
healthy, his color fresh and clear. Broad-shouldered, clean-featured,
fair, he was one of the few perfect Aryan types the Party leadership
had ever possessed, and one remembered this, too. And then, in the
long talk that followed, he learned that the captain was establishing
himself in the business world, and had reentered the social circles in
keeping with his inclinations. There was also the fact that he had always had a personal liking for the captain, so that he felt himself stepping back into their shared past, felt a reflowering of comradeship and
warmth. When he shook hands goodbye with his visitor, it was with a
strong clasp, and with the promise that Comrade Göring was to have a
safe seat in the Party.

He knew the epithets he would hear—this superfluous back
number, this arrogant, face-powdering, loudmouth career officer—
and he knew he would be warned to keep an eye on him. And he
would nod agreeably. Certainly he would keep an eye on him, just as
he kept an eye on them all. There was not one—or rather, there was
only one, Hess—whom he trusted completely.

Göring had soon proved himself an effective orator: forceful, direct, with a pungent humor. In spite of his background, it was he who
had the strongest common touch. It was a gift, something warm and
outgoing and not without coarseness, and his audiences loved him for
it. Putting this talent to its fullest use, Hitler at once began sending him
off on tours throughout the country to bolster sagging Party spirits and
bring in new members.

Göring wrote his wife nightly on these trips, sharing with her all
that he observed, from the three worthies sitting opposite him on his
way to Essen, like triplets—each with a black-rimmed monocle in the
left eye, a folded newspaper on the right thigh—to the old plowhorse
that came galloping up alongside his train window near Frankfurt, en-

livened by spring to a racehorse. He wrote of the blossoming cherry trees all through Franconia, and of walking again through the supremely beautiful old streets of Nuremberg—was it Goethe who had called them the folds in a Gothic drapery? He wrote of Hans Schmidt's marvelous mustache and emerald-green thumb. Nikki was knee-deep in fruit and flowers and she looked not a day older, and maybe younger.

He wrote of visiting Putzi in Munich, and Herr Hitler in Obersalzberg, where he was living with his half sister and her daughter in a little villa, magnificent view. Putzi said Adolf was madly in love with the girl and held her in some kind of erotic thralldom, but that would be Putzi's passion for gossip, since "Uncle Dolph" paid no attention to his dreary niece, a hard-eyed little number who sat about sucking loudly on peppermints while her mother did all the work. Of more interest was that he was to be put on the Party payroll at eight hundred marks a month. This, combined with his Reichstag salary and Lufthansa's thousand a month for lobbying, should make it possible for them to move into another apartment.

And he wrote in detail about his trip to Mauterndorf. First the familiar rumbling of the little wooden bridge under the wheels of the car, then the sound of the fountain splashing in the courtyard, and then Pate's voice calling down, and there he stood as always at the top of the stairs. What joy to see him again, and to embrace him, although maybe for the last time, "for he's terribly aged, walks with two sticks, very stout and bent over, and the dyed hair and mustaches are more than ever wrong for his old face. Yet somehow I feel he is still the Pate I always knew, still stamping about bursting with life. That is what he will always be to me, two walking sticks notwithstanding. I can tell you it was a deeply moving visit. I only wish I could have stayed longer than a day, but had to leave for a meeting here at Passau. No time either to cram in a sidetrip to Vienna to see Olga and the others. It's rush, rush, rush, but important and worthwhile work, if only it didn't separate us . . ."

11 October. Four good-sized rooms, lots of windows. The sun comes *flooding* in! Silver birches along the street, and swallows in these too! I love the swallows, I sit here at the open window listening to them. Warm, golden weather. Have been terribly busy furnishing the apartment (and hostessing luncheons and dinners even *before* we were settled in), but now it's all done and it's such a bright, cozy little home, although we never have time just to sit and enjoy it. It's odd, really, that the one thing we most deeply want, to be alone together in our own home, is denied us by the other thing we most deeply want, the resurrection of Germany. But it is a sacrifice we must make, and willingly make, for there is such satisfaction in doing all we can for the cause.

25 December. At eight o'clock Dr. Goebbels arrived to spend Christmas Eve with us. He came loaded down with presents. For supper we had cold meats and fruit. Afterward I played the harmonium and the three of us sang "Stille Nacht, Heilige Nacht" and "O, du Fröhliche, O, du Selige," and we harmonized. The tree was lighted and the presents were handed around. Then I got a shivering fit and it was so violent I had to be carried off to bed, and I had a fever and bad headache. Today it is better, but I feel too tired to write down everything from last night, a beautiful Christmas Eve in spite of what happened.

28 December. I feel all right today, but am lying here on the sofa propped up on a heap of pillows and covered with blankets and shawls, and must remain so all day. Strictest orders from Hermann!!

Reading all morning. One of Hermann's Christmas gifts was Ivan Bunin's latest short-story collection, for he knows Bunin is my favorite of the modern writers. I joke that this is very subversive of me since Bunin is Russian (White Russian émigré, granted) but really it is surprising the bond that has always existed between Prussia and Russia. At least between the officer classes. And it is a mutual respect now strengthened by mutual feelings about the country that sits sprawled between them, says Hermann. And that is understandable, since big present-day Poland is one of the loathsome creations of the Versailles Treaty, and what is more, has a treaty of alliance with France, and is France's vassal. Yet it is ironic that the Reichswehr, the sworn enemy of German Communists, is cooperating fully with the Communist regime in Russia. Hermann says it is a fact, though cloaked in greatest secrecy, that the Reichswehr has since the war been sending officers to help train the Russian Army, while in return the Reichswehr has been given an airfield near Moscow where it is secretly working to rebuild the German Air Force. This, of course, is of great interest to Hermann. He is also extremely interested in the air training going on here in Germany, under the guise of commercial aviation.

Not only in the air is Germany's spirit of regeneration present, but on the ground too. The Reichswehr has constant secret maneuvers with dummy weapons and tanks made of cardboard. The Weimar government knows and approves of these maneuvers, and even the Allies are aware of them, but they don't make their awareness public. Secretly, the Allies are pleased to see Germany strengthen herself as best she can. They want a strong anti-Communist bulwark between themselves and Russia, which they did not even ask to sign the Versailles Treaty. Russia is a world outcast, and so is Germany. That is perhaps the real bond between them.

But Bunin, who started this whole train of thought, is above and beyond politics. He writes simply, solely, and beautifuly of human beings.

21 February, 1929. There has been so much to think about, arrange, attend to! Today Hermann gives his first big speech in the Reichstag. I shall be there in the visitors' gallery. It is fascinating to visit the Reichstag, though dismal to see so many Red Guards, they take up a colossal number of seats. In the opening session they were in their uniforms, wearing Jewish Stars of David, Red stars, it's all the same, and red armbands, etc., young types, most of them, a pugnacious lot, perfect criminal types. And then tonight Hermann speaks at Berlin University before students from all the different parties. Since more than half of them are already ardent National Socialists, I hope he will win over the rest of them! Tomorrow he speaks in Nuremberg and then goes off on a ten-day trip to East Prussia to make twelve different speeches in twelve different places!

4 April. Herr Hitler here last night. He doesn't come often to Berlin, he hates Berlin. Superficially he has changed, is more filled out, and in his manner is more at ease and sure of himself. Yet he is still the same man. You still feel that shy, homey quality, and in those extraordinary eyes there still shines, stronger than ever, the great light of revolutionary ardor.

8 April. Red Berlin it may be, but I love it—the most exciting city in the world! A magnet for painters, dramatists, architects—yesterday we went to some art galleries and saw works by Pechstein, Kokoschka, Hekel, Munch, so fresh and startling and strange! We quite like it, though Goebbels describes it in *Der Angriff* as Jewish degenerate art. I said to him last night: But listen to me, Munch for one is *Norwegian*. Well, he smiled, it just shows how far the Jewish influence has spread. You can't catch him, he's too quick. But I think it's wrong to make a political battlefield out of art. I hate those

Jews politically who support the Versailles government, and I think there are too many of these in the professions making their influence felt, but it's idiotic to write off all Jews as a baneful influence. That is just political haymaking, and especially in art it has no place. Art belongs to God, not to Goebbels. And how art quivers and throbs here in Berlin! A bursting renaissance, everything new and experimental and jolting, some of it is dreadful like Bartok's music which gives me a headache, but there's room for everything and it is all surging and alive, and the air in Berlin is so alive—clear, fresh, sparkling air as you find nowhere else.

29 May. The beloved one on another speaking tour, returns day after tomorrow. Have spent today resting on the sofa, feeling tired. Was going to write in here, but feel like closing my eyes instead.

12 June. Upset, shouldn't be—at the von Ds' reception yesterday overheard two women talking, one said you can see he utterly adores her and the other said yes, odd isn't it, she's so worn-looking. Women can be so cruel, and such *liars,* because I feel healthy, very healthy, and I think I look it—but I can't allow myself to brood over idle talk, there is too much to live for.

30 October. The American stock market has crashed!! It may have worldwide effects, it is frightening.

21 December. For so long the Party talked of its need for a burning issue. Well, it has it now. All Europe has begun to collapse, and Germany is the worst hit because her economy was based on American loans. Now the mock prosperity comes crashing down and you begin to see bitter, despairing faces, just as in the inflation.

Is it true, as Goebbels said the other night, that the German people are united only by war or disaster? In between, he says, Germany is just a worm can of squabbling, self-seeking provinces. He is so extreme. He seems almost *glad* that the German people are being punished for living so high and blindly on a rotten foundation. But you cannot blame people for wanting to enjoy the good things of life after so much suffering and privation.

Hermann says this proposed Young Plan, an adjustment of reparation payments "in view of Germany's disastrous economic situation," is in actuality a demand that the payments continue as before and for *sixty* years! It is like a blow to the neck. The people are enraged that their country forever remains the pawn of international interests and foreign powers.

They have begun coming in much greater numbers to Party meetings. Unfortunately, a lot are also flocking to the Communists. There is such violence between the two parties— bloody street battles every day, hospitals and morgues full. Can there never be a peaceful solution to Germany's tragic problems?

26 February, 1930. Hermann fusses and fusses, I must not do this, I must not do that, I must rest, I must have the doctor, he is so *tiresome* he makes me cry. All morning I cried, first because he wanted me to have the doctor and I don't *want* the doctor, I won't *have* him, and then because my poor beloved had to leave and was so upset he came back up the stairs twice, and I lay here afterward knowing that it is unfair to him because he worries so, but I don't want the doctor, he makes me feel worse, not better, I hate his black bag and his long face and his cold fingers.

4 March. Up and about and feeling fine. I insisted we not cancel our dinner with Goebbels last night, I was so curious about his new amour, apparently it's serious for once. She is Magda Quandt, a lovely woman and an ardent National Socialist. We liked each other at once. It was a pleasant evening, and Hermann and Goebbels were on good terms again after their falling-out over the Wessel affair. He was a young brownshirt killed in a brawl with the Reds. He had written a popular SA marching song and Goebbels thought much should be made of his death—great funeral, orations, Hitler present, etc. Well, Hermann told me it wasn't a political brawl but a feud over a prostitute. A big funeral could do no harm, but he told Goebbels on no account should Hitler come, because the Communists would probably assault the mourners and Hitler's safety couldn't be guaranteed. Goebbels was furious, but the beloved one's common sense won the day. Hitler stayed in Munich, and there *was* a battle at the funeral. Goebbels made a tremendous thing of the clash and he is now delighted. Horst Wessel has become an official Party martyr, and his song, "Die Fahne Hoch," will probably become the official Party song. Hermann says it's not bad even if the melody is from a Red marching song. How mixed up everything is.

And nothing is more mixed up than the SA. Every day it

grows more violent and moblike. Hermann thinks the commander will either resign or be fired, and he is terribly eager
to take over his old job again. He already has a full-time job
conquering the executive suite and drawing room—to lead
the SA too would be a tremendous additional load. But he has
his heart set on it. Hermann is a soldier by nature, not a politician. To lead an army is his true calling. But I tell him not to
raise his hopes too high, for I think we have both learned that
one can never be certain of anything. Nevertheless, he is optimistic.

2 May. Spring came early this year. It seemed to arrive all
in one minute! Warm, bright, intoxicating! What a difference
to one's health the warm weather makes!!

25 May. The last few weeks we've hardly been at home
for a meal, and then only if we've had guests. Wherever we
go, Hermann is bombarded by questions—it is an attempt to
find chinks in Hitler's armor, criticisms of his program, etc.,
and so Hermann must explain, answer, elaborate to an exhausting degree. Many people ask about the Jews, but Hermann can only say that their great influence in political and
economic life should be reduced to a level in keeping with
their percentage of the population (1 percent), but that is just
his own opinion. In the Party everyone sees things his own
way—it is all so unclear and unformed, but no doubt that is a
strength, since it allows for freedom of thought, differences of
opinion.

19 June. A fainting spell last week, since then in bed. The
doctor thinks I should go to a sanatorium for a while. But I
am much better. Today I wrote three long letters home,
whereas last week I was too weak to do anything. But Hermann is so worried—the doctor keeps upsetting him with talk
about my heart. Hermann wants to come to the sanatorium
with me and stay in one of the cottages for relatives, but it is
impossible with the election campaign coming up, and if I'm
so tired it's partly from arguing about this. Anyway, I'm not
going.

The bedroom is so sunny and pretty. Our lives are inter-
twined along the wall. My Swedish scenes, his *Ritter, Tod und
Teufel* and Richthofen Geschwader photo. Pictures of my family, pictures of his. Pictures from our honeymoon. We have
been happy in this apartment. I would be content to live here
forever, to wake every morning in this room with our arms

around each other—women can be so cruel, little knife twists whenever they tell you something nice—you have such a devoted husband, Frau Göring, do you know they call him a eunuch because he doesn't avail himself of the ladies on his speaking tours, my, isn't it terrible the things that are said?—a Party wife, naturally. Some of them are *unbelievable*! Jealous, shoving, two-faced cows, no compliment without its simpering little barb. Well, it's amusing, really, like calling black white, except for the meanness behind it. One must ignore it, like so much in political life.

I wish I could ignore the strife in the streets. Not a day goes by that blood isn't spilled between Reds and Hitlermen. And the poverty—in Berlin's outskirts, just beyond the gray miserable slums, there are actually houses made of old crates and cardboard boxes, mothers trying to take care of children in these wretched holes, fathers who would work but cannot, who are forced to be idle, who must watch their families starve. It is for these people, for suffering Germany, that Hermann campaigns next month. It is for a Germany of health and power and justice that he gives himself totally, and it is for this that the people love him, they see the greatness of his soul. They know he is their glowing shield against the powers of darkness.

23 June. It is useless to argue with the doctor anymore. I know I must go, there is no longer any choice. . . .

16 July. And so it comes, all in one moment. I couldn't sleep this morning, it was about five o'clock, and I got up and sat by the window. The windows are always kept open here, they are great believers in fresh air. Everything was twilit, the long rolling fields and dark stands of fir, the mountains beyond. All across the gray sky there was spread ripple after ripple of pale silvery clouds, like sandbars, just touched with pink. It was so still, so beautiful. I sat there thinking of nothing at all, I felt quiet and at peace. And then I heard myself say aloud, quietly: I am dying now.

18 July. They would not be honest with me if I were to ask. Their opinion is on their faces, but never in their words. A month? Six months? A year? They would not tell me. And I suppose, after all, I do not want to know.

How brief, joyous, and anguished are Hermann's visits. Every Friday night he drives from Berlin in Pilli's car, it takes ten hours. We have Saturday together and Sunday morning he drives back, and as soon as he is gone I yearn so for him. He writes every day, but I miss him unbearably.

I feel stronger than when I came. For a while I had not even the strength to hold a book in my lap. Now I read, write letters, even walk about the grounds. And sometimes the hope flames up in me that I will truly get well. I wish I could recapture the spirit of acceptance I felt at the window the other morning.

19 July. My beloved has written today that he is bringing a surprise with him when he comes on Saturday—Thomas!! He arranged with Nils that the child—the child, who is almost eighteen!—should visit his mother for ten full days! I know what it cost Hermann's pride to ask that of Nils. He is not a cruel man, but he hates, hates Hermann. It must have been as hard for Nils to let the boy come as it was for Hermann to ask him. But together they have made me the happiest woman in the world.

23 July. My little boy is a tall, fine young man. We are together all day, every day. He is so dear, so good, and I cannot take my eyes from his face, or my hand from his hand. I feel as if my heart will break with happiness. On Saturday, when the three of us were together, it moved me so deeply to see my beloved one and my Thomas the same good comrades they have been from the very start. May that always be, as long as they live. It was the happiest and most perfect day, my thoughts went no further than these moments I was sharing with the two beings in the world I love most.

6 August. Thomas has been gone for the better part of a week. It was a hard parting for us both. I know it was in both our minds that we might never see each other again.

I mind leaving those I love, but I am not afraid of death. I am in God's hands, I trust in Him and love Him, and I thank Him for all that He has given me. I have known hardship, and much illness, but I have known happiness granted few mortals. If Hermann and I had been together only a month, still would I thank God with all my heart for that single month, but He has given us ten whole years, that is so much more than I had ever hoped for.

10 August. Everyone is so kind to me, so good. I take walks, play patience, read. I am reading the Russians again—

Tolstoy, Turgenev, Bunin. I am better, but I don't allow my hopes to rise too high.

I am writing this sitting on one of the blue benches outside. The sun is hot, everything is still and peaceful. I am so far removed from everything that is going on, but it is always with me. I want so much to do something, but cannot. I can only pray for Hermann's efforts, for his strong sense of purpose, for his great soul. He is far away now, campaigning in East Prussia, then goes to Rostock, Lübeck, Kiel. A bitter, violent campaign—bloody street battles—the SA is getting horribly out of hand. Hitler must put Hermann back in charge, but he will procrastinate. Hitler is a great man, but a terrible procrastinator.

So quiet all around. There are many birds here, but no swallows.

18 August. In bed all week, exhausted. I live for Hermann's letter each day. I dictate mine to the nurse, and I don't blush for the words of love I send. She is understanding and good.

24 August. The Föhn blows. It booms against the walls. I stay inside, I try not to hear it. I play patience, I read until my head hurts. Bunin says in one of his stories that the eeriest thing in the world is the human soul, I am so tired, so tired, I wish the wind would stop, dear God let the wind stop. Poor Nikki, how it undid her, how she went on with her great-eyed peasant visions—rivers tainted with blood, and birds dying of sheer sadness, poor, poor birds. . . .

4 September. The storm broke and now it is quiet at last, at long last, everything still and calm. I walked outside this afternoon. I do not think my body is mending, it is just my will to live that cannot give up.

15 September. It is unbelievable! From twelve seats to 108!!! The NSDAP is now the *second-largest* party in the Reichstag!!! The Social Democrats have 143. Then come us with 108. Then the Catholic Center Party with only 87. Then the Communists with only 77, and then all the others. Telegrams of congratulation have poured in all day, and flowers, and my beloved left Berlin early this morning and will be here any moment—!

Chapter 26

YOUNG Thomas von Kantzow visited his mother again at Christmas, in Berlin. She was much improved, although she could not yet go outside. She rested on the living-room sofa, a shawl over her legs and her books and stationery around her. A rawboned peasant girl from the Mark of Brandenburg, named Cilly, did the cooking and shopping.

He and his mother talked, or he read aloud to her, or he sat gazing at her face as she dozed. He was perfectly fulfilled by this routine, but he greatly enjoyed his Uncle Hermann's entertainments too; or perhaps it was the affectionate concern he enjoyed, more than the entertainments themselves. One afternoon he was bundled into the front seat of Hermann's long-nosed, powerful black Mercedes, a recent gift from Herr Hitler, and taken on a sightseeing drive through Berlin. Hermann went at a great speed, honking as he shot around cars, and slamming on the brakes to jump out with historical commentaries before the State Opera House, Brandenburg Gate, the Reichstag—this last a massive stone structure rather grimy with age, its roof bristling with dark heroic statuary and crowned by a green glass dome crowned in turn by snow. "I can't take you inside, because it's closed for the holidays," Hermann said as they drove off. "Too bad the zoo is closed too—and that's not a non sequitur by any means." They had lunch at Horcher's restaurant, where Thomas watched the enormous pleasure with which his tablemate put away the imported asparagus with herb-spiced butter sauce, the tender, garnished meat in its bed of crisp new potatoes, and the chocolate soufflé smothered in whipped cream, of which he ate two portions. Hermann was in fact quite hefty these days, though he carried his weight well. A commanding figure, he looked every inch what he was: member of parliament, newly appointed political director and spokesman for the Party, and soon-to-be Supreme Commander of the Storm Troops. This last post was not yet definite, but he sounded very hopeful of getting it. Herr Hitler had fired the commander and was now in charge himself, but he must soon appoint someone, and who would be better than he, Göring?

"We'll drink to it, Thomas. And then we must leave. I'll drop you off at the house. Tell your mother I hope to be home early tonight, and that I'm bringing her a surprise."

The surprise was an enormous man with lank black hair and a homely dish face, apparently an old friend, and one his mother was touchingly happy to see. Dr. Hanfstaengl—such was the visitor's name—was congratulated on his reentry into politics. After the Party's overwhelming success at the polls, Munich headquarters had been flooded with foreign correspondents, and Herr Hitler had asked him to be his foreign press chief. "Now," he said to the Görings, "he is going to *have* to listen to me."

It was a quiet two weeks. One evening a Herr and Frau Bodenschatz, a Herr and Frau Loerzer, and a Herr and Frau Körner came for Christmas Pfefferkuchen and a glass of wine. The talk was of the past, of the Great War and flying.

And on Christmas Eve a Dr. Goebbels came. He was a very small, dark-haired man with a pronounced limp. But more than his limp you noticed his eyes, glitteringly dark, restless, penetrating. Thomas's mother had told him beforehand that Dr. Goebbels sometimes showed a very poetic soul, as when he had once referred to Hermann at a Party meeting as "this strong, pure Siegfried, this upright soldier with the heart of a child."

And tonight, too, Dr. Goebbels was poetic. "'Sterne mit den goldnen Füsschen . . .'" he began, gazing at the window, outside which the snow had stopped falling, and stars now shone.

> "Stars with golden feet are wandering
> Through the heavens infinite,
> Softly, lest they wake the earth below,
> Sleeping in the arms of night . . ."

"Hoppla!" said Hermann, turning to Carin with a twinkle in his eye.

"How beautiful Heine is," she murmured, smiling.

"Of course one is fond of Heine," Herr Goebbels replied, smiling too. "One is not an idiot, after all."

Shortly after returning to Stockholm, in the New Year of 1931, Thomas received from his mother a newsy and cheerful letter. Cheerful except for the fact that Herr Hitler had appointed someone else SA commander.

". . . our Hermann was bitterly disappointed, but it is understandable that Herr Hitler believed him busy enough with his other responsibilities. Like Hermann, Captain Röhm is a strong leader, and I think he will be able to bring discipline back to these wild brownshirts. It is odd in a way that Herr Hitler chose him, for they had a falling-out some years back. But Captain Röhm has close ties with the Reichswehr, and that is important. It is the Reichswehr and President Hindenburg who guard the gates to power. Captain Röhm must open the gates to the Reichswehr, and Hermann must open the door to Hindenburg."

Spring brought a surging improvement to his mother's health. He could tell by the resumption of her exclamation points. ". . . I so wish, Thomas, that you could have been here to meet Ernst Udet!! Neither Hermann nor I had seen him since our wedding, he spends his life making airplane adventure films all over the world, America, Alaska, even New Zealand! He was back in Germany just for a holiday—such a charming, cocky fellow, so carefree, a real bon vivant and not a political bone in his body (sometimes such a relief!!!).

"It was a wonderful evening, but I cannot say the same for Herr Milch's visit! Herr Milch is head of Lufthansa Airlines. *Milch*, the name doesn't fit him. If he is filled with milk it is skimmed milk and ice-cold. A cold little button face and cold button eyes.

"Tomorrow Hermann and I are motoring into the country, the doctor says it is all right. We're taking a picnic!! We are so looking forward to it, but I know it will be sad to see the farms, they've been the worst hit by the depression. And those little towns made of crates outside the city, they are heart-wrenching, and who are the ones to help them with medical care and soup kitchens? The Party! Oh Thomas, I hope the day will soon come that all our ideals and efforts will be realized!! When Herr Hitler was last here at the apartment for a meeting, he took my hand afterward and said, you are the mascot of the Party, Frau Göring, when you are here everything goes well. That has made me so proud and so glad. . . ."

But in the early summer Thomas had a deeply disturbing letter from his Aunt Fanny, who was visiting his mother in Berlin.

". . . I do not know what to tell you, Thomas. Two days ago your mother suddenly collapsed, and lay with her pulse barely detectable, as if in a coma. The doctor told Hermann and me that there was no hope at all, he said it would be a matter of hours. But soon after he had told us that, Carin rallied, and by today she is surprisingly recovered.

"The bond between her and her beloved husband has been forged, not here, but in some holy place. It will not give easily. But I feel it would be a mercy now if it did give. The strain of Carin's illness has been hard on them always, and this last year, it has worn them unendurably. They should be given peace now."

His mother wrote that she had had a small relapse but was feeling fine again. And throughout the summer weeks her letters came regularly, filled with the usual news and gossip. She was glad that Fanny was staying on, they were having such a good long visit. Hermann had been to Rome twice. He got on famously with Mussolini, and was doing much to cement relations between the Fascists and the NSDAP. Back home he kept busy every minute. "The political situation is increasingly a turmoil. Such confusion and ineptitude in the Reichstag, thirty-two parties bickering and yelling. Chancellor Brüning is now governing by emergency decree, which shows how desperate things are growing. President Hindenburg is not happy with him, but Hindenburg will not appoint Hitler his Chancellor, and that is the only solution to Germany's problems. He will not even allow Hitler to be introduced to him. The old Field Marshal is eighty-four now, still a fine figure with his great white mustaches and military bearing, but he is not at all modern. Of course, it is understandable, but it is so terribly frustrating and such a pity for Germany. If only he would sit down with Herr Hitler and discuss Germany's plight with him, he would forget in one minute Hitler's background and accent, and see him for the great German savior that he is. . . ."

In late August, Thomas's mother, accompanied by Fanny, went for a rest cure at a spa in Silesia. She wrote him that Hermann was demanding two full weeks off from his work, and that this had given her such a strong new grip on life that the doctors were amazed. She felt in radiant health, and she had the doctors' permission to take a long, relaxing motor tour—she, Hermann, Fanny, and Hermann's friend Pilli Körner.

Picture postcards arrived from Dresden and Bamberg, and from Nuremberg, where they visited an old family friend who loaded them down with fruit, from small villages through Lower Bavaria, and from Austria, where they stayed several days with Hermann's godfather. Then they had driven to Munich "for a wonderful family gathering. Hermann's sister Paula lives here now, and the whole family came for the christening of her new baby. We also saw Dr. Hanfstaengl, whom you met, and we will also be seeing Herr Hitler."

But in a hasty note written a day or two later, she said, "Herr Hitler's young niece was found dead in her room, apparently shot herself—accidentally or maybe suicide, the Socialist press is turning it into the most lurid smear campaign—incest, jealousy, etc. & not suicide but *much* worse—Herr Hitler was on a speaking tour when it happened, he went into a state of shock & is in seclusion—Hermann saw him, said he looked utterly broken & kept insisting it couldn't have been suicide but had to be an accident for he had done everything to make the girl happy, but Dr. Hanfstaengl said he did rule the girl's life much too rigidly. It is too bad our trip has ended on such a sad note—we return to Berlin tomorrow & your Aunt Fanny travels directly on to Stockholm from there. We are both uneasy over Mother's health & feel it best that Fanny return home at once. . . ."

Chapter 27

Ten days after receiving this note, Thomas, with his Aunt Fanny and his Aunt Mary and Uncle Erik, stood waiting on the platform of the Stockholm train station, holding umbrellas under the late-September drizzle. Three days earlier, Hermann had cabled to say that Carin had collapsed at the news of her mother's death, and was too weak to travel home for the funeral. Then yesterday he had cabled again to say that they were coming.

They would be too late for the service, which had taken place this morning; and it was just as well, Thomas thought, for the strain would have been very great for his mother, whose face he eagerly searched for in the passing windows of the boat train as it came rumbling and clanging to a stop, its hissing white steam mixing with the rain. He scanned the opening doors and disembarking passengers, but when he finally caught sight of her, it was not with the emotion he had anticipated, but with a deep jolt of fear. He could not see her face, for she was leaning against Hermann, but he could see Hermann's face, and it was so taut it looked as if it would break apart. He did not speak or even look up as the youth reached their side; his arms held her fast to him, and with one hand he kept tremblingly patting her green knitted beret. She seemed almost unconscious.

When the little group had gotten her into the car, Hermann drew

Thomas aside. "She pleaded with me—hour after hour she pleaded and wept to go home, I couldn't bear it, Thomas. When I said we would go, then she was calm, she seemed much better. But the trip was too much. I've done the wrong thing."

At the parental home, where after the funeral the family had gathered around old Baron von Fock, Carin was helped to bed and the doctor summoned. When he came downstairs from her room, he said there was no hope.

All night Thomas and Hermann sat by her bed, with Fanny on the other side. It was Carin and Fanny's girlhood bedroom. Blue wallpaper with white birds. Old china dolls sitting with children's books in the bookcase. A fire going in the *Kakkelovn,* the tile stove. In the lamplight Carin's face, with her dark hair massed against the pillow, was absolutely white; every breath was labored and knifelike, and was repeated in a small blanching in her skin and lips, a steady, suffering wearing away.

In the morning Fanny turned out the lamps. At noon the doctor came. He was astonished that the patient had held on. That evening she rallied; her eyes opened, her breathing was less harsh, she took a little broth. The next morning she spoke a few words with them, and said she felt stronger. A few hours later she seemed suddenly to be slipping away. And then she came back. The doctor could tell them nothing. Her heart was so weak, and yet somehow she held on. The third day her breathing was ragged, terrible to hear. The fourth she was better. And so a week passed, as she sank and then rallied, her face becoming small with her struggle, pinched, darkly circled beneath the eyes.

Hermann scarcely moved from her side. He sat with her hand in his, and from time to time, with his free hand, would stroke her hair, or gently wipe the perspiration from her brow. His eyes were swollen red. In the mornings stubble covered his jaws; then he would steal away for a few minutes to shave and wash and take a bite of food.

The second week the weather turned bright and crisp, and Fanny drew back the curtains so that Carin could see the sun. One morning when Hermann had left the room and Thomas sat alone with his mother, he saw her eyes open slowly, very blue in the sunlight.

"I am so tired," she whispered. "I am so weary, Thomas . . . I want to follow Mama . . . she keeps calling for me. But I cannot go. As long as Hermann is here, I cannot go . . . I cannot bear to leave him . . . I cannot bear it . . ."

Thomas sat holding her hand and remained silent for a long moment. He did not know if he should, or if he could, say this thing. He felt very small, like the smallest child, utterly lost.

"Hermann has had a telegram, Mama."

"A telegram . . . ?"

"From Herr Hitler. President Hindenburg has granted him an interview. But only . . . only if Captain Göring accompanies him."

"He will go . . . ?"

"He will not go, Mama. He is not going to tell you."

The room was silent. When Hermann came back in, Thomas got up and hurried past him out into the hallway, where he stood leaning against the door, his whole being lost in pain and confusion. Through the closed door he could hear their voices, then he thought he could hear the sound of sobbing, and then he heard nothing.

His Aunt Fanny came along the hall, carrying a tray. She opened the door and went inside; he stood looking in from the half-open door. A great change had come over his mother. She was very calm, very controlled. She looked over at Fanny from her pillow. "Hermann has been called back to Berlin . . . he is needed urgently there. You must help him to pack his things." She put both her hands to her husband's wet face. "It will only be a short while, my dearest one. Thomas will look after me until you come back. . . ."

President Field Marshal Paul von Beneckendorff und von Hindenburg received his two visitors in his dark-paneled presidential study. Immensely tall, solid, as if carved from oak, and utterly without expression as he briefly shook hands, he seated himself stiffly behind his large rococo desk. His old eyes were slits, from which some blue still glittered; his head, square in shape, looked bald from a distance, but was covered with short-cropped white hair; beneath his blunt, square nose the two wings of his full white mustache curved down well below his jowls. The Bohemian corporal, which was his private term for Herr Hitler, seemed badly ill-at-ease. The President watched coldly as the man crossed his legs in his chair, thought better of it and uncrossed them, folded his too-white hands in his lap, gave a nervous clearing of his throat. Captain Göring, who was at least a gentleman, a former career officer and a Knight of the Order of the Pour le Mérite, looked a complete wreck despite his satisfactory bearing. Haggard, with heavy bags under inflamed eyes, his very wide mouth compressed with strain, he seemed hard put, beneath his alert expression, to rid himself of some private preoccupation. That was no matter; it was the one with the mustache who had come to talk.

And who, once he was given leave, talked without stop, like the street-corner orator he was. Too polite to order him to be quiet, the President began drumming his gnarled fingers on the desk top. When at long last the man was finished and the room silent, the old fingers continued to drum. Herr Hitler, with no other recourse, said a perfunctory goodbye, and the two men left the room.

"Make him my Chancellor?" the President said aloud to himself, when the door had closed. "I'll make him Postmaster, and he can lick my face on postage stamps."

On October 17, while hurriedly packing to return to Stockholm, Göring received a telegram saying that Carin had died that morning.

Chapter 28

Aᴌᴛʜᴏᴜɢʜ it was only early June, the weather had suddenly turned
hot and sultry, and Frau Goebbels had dressed in an ice-blue gown that
left bare her broad, very white and beautifully molded shoulders. Sitting before the mirror of her bronze-and-glass dressing table—even
glass felt warm—she was selecting a necklace, lifting up one, then another, and holding it contemplatively to the moist hollow of her throat.
The spacious bedroom, with its lime-and-cream décor, was as stifling as
a closet; and as she finally encircled her neck with a string of amethysts,
she realized that the heavy air had grown gray with dusk. She turned
on the lamp beside her, aware of the click it made in the silence. It
always hurt her a little that she and her husband did not dress together, cozily, as other couples did; but she understood his extreme
sensitivity, which was such that he left on his sock and garter even in
bed, and in weather like this. She dabbed a tissue to the beads of
moisture along her upper lip. Her skin and her eyes were radiant with
approaching motherhood, but in no other way did she appear pregnant, certainly not in her sixth month. Nor did she suffer any discomfort, except for an aversion to shellfish, sugared almonds and
sometimes champagne. It was because she was built to bear children—
effortlessly; and often, she hoped, for though she had one child from
her first marriage, she had always longed for many. She began putting

on a pair of amethyst earrings, then smiled and turned in her chair as
her husband came through the door.

"Oh, Engelchen, no!" she murmured, on learning that the first
guests were already arriving. Carefully she adjusted the earrings, then
lifted her fingertips and gently patted the blond waves that framed her
face. She was not a vain woman, only incapable of hurrying.

Just as they reached the drawing room, her husband snapped his
fingers.

"We forgot to order something, Magda."

"Did we? What?"

"Oats."

She repressed a little burst of laughter; both of them were smiling
as they entered the room, where newly appointed Chancellor von Papen and his wife sat waiting. With the graciousness for which she was
known, Magda greeted her guests, apologized both for her tardiness
and the heat, and introduced the couple to Josef. Of the six guests
invited tonight, only two were friends of theirs: Captain Göring, who
would be coming alone; and Magda's former sister-in-law, who would
round out the odd number. The von Papens Josef did not know, and
she herself knew them only slightly, from her first marriage; and General and Frau von Schleicher—the maid was showing them in now—
neither she nor Josef had ever met before. There were more greetings,
introductions, exchanged comments about the weather, and as she sat
down chatting, she hoped that the dining room, with its bare parquet
floor and the white arctic light of its chandelier, would provide at least
an illusion of coolness.

After her divorce Magda had wandered through these ten rooms a
good deal, not knowing what to do with herself. Suitors she had, including the nephew of the President of the United States, but she was
not really drawn to any of them. And being a virtuous woman, she
would not enter into an affair unless her heart was deeply stirred. She
had not expected it to be stirred by Dr. Goebbels, although it was his
voice ringing through the Sportpalast, extraordinarily rich and vibrant,
that had moved her to join the Party—an act which had upset her
friends; they had taken her to the Sportpalast as to a boxing match or a
Moabit dive, to be revolted and entertained; one did not join forces
with ear-shattering music and proletarian-red Hakenkreuz flags. Nevertheless, in her calm, assured way, she looked with pleasure and a
sense of proper destiny at her membership card: the entrance to something extraordinary, something absolutely new and breathtakingly
alive. She became dedicated. She made monetary donations. She read,
or tried to read, *Mein Kampf,* and Alfred Rosenberg's *Myth of the Twentieth Century.* She joined the West End Women's NSDAP Auxiliary; and
one day, sent by the auxiliary to help with some clerical work at the

regional office, she met the man whose voice had so impressed her at the Sportpalast.

There was a time, after she had given her heart to Josef, that she felt she would like to take it back and give it to Herr Hitler. This was a troubling time for her, for she was a loyal and honest woman. Yet she felt that she was in love with the Führer; in his presence her pulse raced, her cheeks burned, and she even entertained fantasies of being married to him. Then she came to understand that he was a political being entirely, that he had no personal life, and that he would never marry; and in her calm, unruffled way, relieved to have the problem solved, she returned Josef's embraces with tested and renewed love. Since that time, her feelings for Herr Hitler had been only those of deepest, purest admiration. And how profoundly happy she had been when she realized that she was becoming a special favorite of the Führer's; realizing too, of course, only too keenly, that his official favorite was Frau Göring—but one could not feel rancor toward Frau Göring, who was so kind and so pleasant, and who suffered so much, always so terribly ill, poor woman. Surely her death last autumn could only be seen in the light of a blessing.

Neither Magda nor her husband, seated at opposite ends of the long table, was eating much of the *chaud froid* of chicken garnished with crayfish and stoned cherries. In Goebbels's case it was because he preferred talking to eating; in Magda's because of her temporary distaste for shellfish. Toying with her fork, she noted with an irrepressible smile that the Chancellor was discussing horses with her sister-in-law.

It was true that a bag of oats under his chin would not be amiss. Not only did Herr von Papen's life revolve around horses—he was a crack gentleman rider and polo player—but with his long narrow face he greatly resembled one. A thoroughbred, to be sure, for it was an aristocratic countenance, and he was the most urbane of men, so debonair in fact that he always struck one as hopelessly frivolous. She, along with all Germany, had been astonished when President von Hindenburg had suddenly fired Brüning last week and replaced him with this beautifully tailored nonentity. His dark pinstripe suit, worn with a natty bow tie, was of exquisite cut. His long distinguished face was set off by perfectly matched hair and mustache of smooth glossy gray. He was a charming light conversationalist, and his laugh—he had turned now to listen to one of Josef's *Blue Angel* anecdotes—was clear and rippling as a brook.

Josef's favorite nonpolitical topic—and it was an absolutely nonpolitical evening—was films, and his favorite of all films was *The Blue Angel*. She herself had found it too harsh and twisted; she preferred a happy musical, as indeed did the Führer; but Josef adored *The Blue*

Angel, and adored repeating the amusing stories he had heard about its making.

There was laughter around the table, except from General von Schleicher, who responded only with a brief half-smile. The general, chief military adviser to Hindenburg, seemed a man not easily roused to merriment; convivial, and not without humor, yet rather the restrained officer type. He was very straight, with a bald head tanned the color of café au lait. His dark narrow eyes were sharp, as was his small bony nose, beneath which sat a clipped salt-and-pepper mustache. His wife looked much younger than he, and Magda sat trying to assess the age difference. Frau von Schleicher was probably in her late thirties, she decided, but with her fair hair worn in a simple bob, and her shy manner, she seemed younger. She hardly said a thing unless one took the trouble to draw her out, as her table partner, Captain Göring, was doing. They seemed to be comparing notes on the merits of baked trout over steamed.

With the passage of months Göring had become more his usual outgoing self, at least superficially; for Magda knew from experience that his eyes were apt to drift away in the middle of a conversation, as if into some other world, and then you were very much aware of the black mourning band around his sleeve. Josef said his private life was a running sore. He lived cooped up in rooms at the Hotel Kaiserhof, where, on a table surmounted by Carin's photograph, he had set out her comb-and-brush set, her silver letter opener, favorite books, a silken scarf, a little Swedish troll—Josef said it was morbid, and *dumm,* since you could not resurrect the dead. Josef had no patience with things that did not bring results.

Josef had gotten to Marlene Dietrich's first film test, and was taking the pose of a director slowly scratching his head. Magda winced, knowing what would come next.

"Der Popo ist nicht schlecht, aber brauchen wir nicht ein Gesicht?"

It was an idiosyncrasy of Dr. Goebbels's to deliver at least one small, humorously wrapped crudity when with members of the so-called upper class in order to express his feelings for them. Both his contempt and his mirth were sharply increased when they laughed along with him, as they did now, too courteous or too stupid to do otherwise. His large white teeth still showed in a smile as the next course was served and the talk passed onto the *Graf Zeppelin's* latest accomplishments.

Magda was used to his little social blunders—that was what she thought they were; but this one was discomfiting, for it revived in her mind a nasty piece of gossip she had recently heard. She had brushed it aside at the time, and she was inclined to do so now, turning her attention back to the table talk.

". . . a great step, regular passenger and mail service to South America."

"Even without helium from Herr Hoover."

A liaison with some minor film actress . . . could it be true of her Engelchen? Certainly she knew his past reputation . . . but she also knew that they lived in a jungle of Party malice; Göring over there, impotent or else he would have taken a mistress by now; the Führer, incestuously involved with his niece—there were still those who hinted at that; and she, Magda, racially tainted, when everyone knew that it was only her stepfather—her beloved stepfather, she might add—who was Jewish. No, the only thing to do with gossip was to ignore it, and turning to the Frau Chancellor, she agreed that she would not care to go up in a balloon.

"Airship, Frau Goebbels," Captain Göring corrected her.

"A balloon, you see, is more like a polo ball," the Chancellor explained.

Frau von Schleicher contributed little to the conversation. She was not at her best in groups. She much preferred to be passed over, although her table partner had won her heart with his discussion of baked trout, her great talent and hobby being cooking. She was relieved that there was no talk of politics, a subject which she knew nothing about and found tedious. Her husband left politics at the front door. With their small daughter they led a quiet life in their pleasant villa by the Griebnitzsee . . . and it was true, she had to admit it: even at the most pleasant gatherings, and this one was very pleasant, she found herself wishing for her own familiar surroundings. It was so much cooler at the lake; here in central Berlin even the silver and glasses were warm. Every now and then one felt an unladylike trickle of perspiration down one's forehead, and had unobtrusively to blot it with the napkin. She did so now, smiling at her husband through the buzz of voices.

"If you will just listen to Kipnis's lower register—"

"No, I will stay with Mayr—"

"I agree, what of Mayr?—"

"Ach, no comparison! When you consider his lower—"

Dr. Goebbels was less interested in opera than he was in films and theater, so he took no part in this discussion. He sipped his wine instead, moving his eyes from face to face. At the other end of the table, down the length of flowers and crystal, Magda raised her glass in a little private toast. Smiling, he returned it. He was faithful to Magda, which surprised him very much, and made him happy. He did not pretend she was pretty; the length of her nose, coupled with a rather heavy chin, gave her face a matronly cast. Nevertheless, she was beautiful, a woman you turned and looked at, glowing and fair, and marvelously elegant. And while possessing a lively wit, she also possessed an almost Buddha-like calm. He found that deeply attractive. Their life together was like a smoothly running machine.

The same could not be said of his work. Everyone was worn down to bare nerves. It was obvious that the great number of parties in the Reichstag would forever preclude a majority vote for any one party, even the largest. There were ways around this, but all were blocked. There was armed revolt; Röhm, of course, favored this, but not Adolf Légalité. There was the chancellorship; but President Hindenburg remained inflexibly hostile to the idea of Hitler as his Chancellor. And there was the presidency; but when Hitler ran against the old cretin, he had lost by seven million votes. He, Goebbels, had written in his diary after that election: "We are beaten. Terrible outlook. Party circles depressed and dejected. We can save ourselves now only by some clever stroke."

Instead, they had been dealt a further blow, a crushing one. Chancellor Brüning had outlawed the SA; and without the SA to battle the Communists' Red Front and the Socialists' Reichsbanner, electioneering would be hopeless. But at this very dark moment there came the interesting news that General von Schleicher "did not approve of Brüning's action." Meetings between Schleicher and Hitler followed. A bargain was struck. If Schleicher could get the ban lifted from the SA, Hitler would support the new government that Schleicher wished to set up.

No one knew how the general meant to go about achieving his ends, but his reputation already marked him as an exception to the politically obtuse officer corps. First he circulated a few lies concerning the scruples of his superior, mentor, and closest friend, General Gröner, long Hindenburg's chief military adviser. Gröner in short time was called before the scandalized Hindenburg to turn in his resignation, after which Chief Military Adviser von Schleicher set about gnawing away at the old man's confidence in Chancellor Brüning, whom Schleicher himself had helped to power; and as soon as Brüning fell he paraded von Papen before the old rheumy eyes: splendidly tailored, of noble birth, had sat in the Prussian Landtag, what more could the Old Gentleman want? Nothing. It was love at first sight. And thus the ban was now being lifted from the brownshirts, compliments of freshly appointed Chancellor von Papen.

Who, engaged in some banter with Magda, was laughing his mellifluous burble. He was almost a caricature of the bon vivant, thought Goebbels, this political amateur who for years had been hopping about like a cricket trying to land in a bit of limelight. As Schleicher was reported to have put it, "He doesn't need a head. His job is to be the hat." Through this hat Schleicher would set up what he hoped to be a strong Rightist cabinet, and what Hitler hoped would be a colorless, transitional government. Meanwhile the Party would keep on working, struggling; it was a great boon to have back the SA. It was interesting that Schleicher, who had managed this for them, was now having secret little meetings with SA Commander Röhm. It was interesting that the bald brown head, perspiring in the heat, looked to be carved from hardest wood, while its interior was so infinitely flexuous.

The head was now turning in Goebbels's direction, with its quick half-smile and a genial inquiry.

"Ja," Goebbels replied, "Frau Goebbels and I find it the best of both worlds. We are in the very heart of the city, a stone's throw from the Chancellery, yet we're also in the country."

"You can't imagine all these old back gardens, Herr General," Magda told him. "They're quite wild and beautiful, and reach all the way to Friedrich-Ebert-Strasse, just like flowering meadows."

"Indeed? How very pleasant."

Indeed, how very pleasant, Goebbels said to himself. It was all very pleasant, a very pleasant evening, but he had no illusions as to why they had accepted his invitation, the most powerful man in Germany and his polo player: Schleicher out of amused curiosity, Papen because he knew and liked Magda. Their reasons were unimportant. What was important was that his image within the Party would be several degrees enhanced by having had the pair feed off his table.

But the keen edge of his pleasure, which lay in his exclusion of other Party leaders, was blunted by Göring's presence. "Party comrade Göring must be there," the Führer had insisted when giving permission for the dinner. That had cut Goebbels to the heart. When you revered someone, loved and worshiped him, it was terrible to be treated as untrustworthy. He comforted himself with the knowledge that the Führer's suspicions were at least democratic; for if it had been Göring's gathering, he, Goebbels, would doubtlessly have been sent along to keep a sharp eye out. A sharp eye, however, was not one of his friend's distinctions. As a watchdog, Göring was much better at lapping up the food than observing.

General von Schleicher, dipping his spoon into his dessert dish, which held fresh pineapple steeped in Schwarzwald Kirschwasser, was not unhappy that the last course had been reached. The heat was unbearable, the chitchat tiresome, and his host had early ceased to interest him. He had come through an inclination to look at this curiosity here, this sawed-off, howling propagandist who in person could be summed up as pleasant, glib, not badly dressed. Extremely well turned out, in fact. One was always surprised when they dressed well. How could Captain Göring, a Knight of the Order of the Pour le Mérite, have gotten himself mixed up with this pack of louts? But then Göring was a lout himself. When you were with him socially, you forgot how obnoxiously the man sometimes carried on in the Reichstag, ignoring rules of conduct and shouting people down in ungovernable fits of temper—a violent, fist-pounding savage. Sunny chap otherwise. Liked his food and wine, liked his simple pleasures.

A very different type was Goebbels. The crippled little monkey didn't know what he was eating. Brain always working. The cerebralist of the Party. In the land of the brainless, the three-quarter brain is professor. They were all intellectual children, Corporal Hitler and his people; small boisterous children who must be led by the hand. And by the hand he, Schleicher, would lead them. Into his new goverment, where an eye could be kept on them. The SA must also be led into a corner where it could be controlled. If the ambitious Captain Röhm was only a fraction as naïve as he appeared, this could be done. Meanwhile, the general had finished his dessert, and, having set down his spoon, he flicked a smile at some joke of Göring's that had sent the table into hysterics.

Chancellor von Papen was enjoying himself thoroughly. A toast to his chancellorship had been the only political note of the evening, and that was fine with him; the dinner table was a place to savor good food, fine wine and a pleasant flow of conversation. He was aware that this talent for enjoying himself was one of several things that gave him an air of frivolity. He knew he was already nicknamed "Herr Luftikus," and the "Top Hat Chancellor." No one took him seriously, least of all his good friend Schleicher. But Schleicher had one very grave weakness, in that he was incapable of taking anyone seriously, underestimating even the most formidable personalities. It was a weakness no schemer could afford to have, and it was one which Papen himself did not suffer from.

"No, it does not bother me," he said in response to a comment by his hostess. "One was used to much worse heat in Palestine and Turkey."

"And did one also find Washington hot?" his host asked.

"I found it a delightful city, Herr Goebbels. The cherry trees were a sight to behold."

And so are you, Göring said to himself over his second helping of pineapple. If Papen was remembered for anything it was for his ignominious expulsion from Washington, where, as a military attaché during the war, he had been involved in some unfortunate scheme to blow up bridges. The man's self-possession was of an order all to itself. They said he had been more astonished than anyone by his appointment as Chancellor, but one could bet that this astonishment was already a thing of the past. One could bet that Papen's talent lay in instant, effortless adjustment to new situations.

One could bet on very little these days. It was somehow hard to understand that the closer you got to the peak, the more fatal was failure. And yet he knew from his mountain-climbing days that this was so. A stumble on the slopes was nothing; from the top it meant death. On its way up, a political movement could afford grave setbacks, but near the peak there was no tolerance for defeat. If in all its strength and success a party began slipping, the public saw this as evidence that it could never do better. The public would not allow it another climb back.

Why he still drove himself day after day, he no longer knew, except that it was worse not to . . . and Carin would have wanted him to. And Putzi, whenever he was in Berlin, always brimming with advice. "You've got to put your life back in order, Hermann. Working day and night isn't the answer." Putzi had found him an apartment on the Kaiserdamm, and he had finally agreed to take it. He realized he could not live in a hotel forever, but a hotel room without Carin was somehow more bearable than an apartment without her. Her cheek, when he stroked it, was very smooth and hard and cold . . . her hands, lying folded, were white as the white satin lining around her. . . .

"I asked, Captain Göring, if you would be so kind as to pass the cigars."

"Of course. Forgive me."

He took one himself and passed on the silver box to the general. Coffee, brandy and liqueurs were being served, and little dishes of Lindt's bitter chocolates, here at the table rather than in the drawing room, for it was too oppressively warm to move. He was not sorry to see the evening end. He wanted to get out of his sweaty clothes into a cool bath, as indeed must everyone, except Papen, of course, who did not sweat. Even the beautiful Magda in her ice-blue gown looked wilted. And Schleicher's bald head shone wet in the white light of the chandelier. Schleicher, backstabber of old comrades, a prime example of what was happening to the Army's leadership. Early on in the republic, the Army had recaptured its prewar domination over government policy by meddling in politics; now it actually had a Political Office, of which Schleicher was head. A Political Office of the Army—it was unthinkable. Greatness could not survive in an army that involved itself in politics. Crooked as a corkscrew, Schleicher was, with that crooked little half-smile. How had he ever gotten hold of this charming wife here, with her quiet, serious discussion of trout, fresh-faced as a schoolgirl, and full of fond glances for the man? Of course, it was possible that he was a loving soul in his own home. People were never cut from whole cloth.

Conversation began to flag. The heaviness of the air had increased as the night wore on. Frau Goebbels apologized for not owning an electric fan.

"Living in Berlin, one should really invest in one," she said. "Although our weather is generally so lovely."

Everyone agreed with this, and then there seemed no more to say. Presently the party broke up, with many thanks and pleasant leave-takings.

Chapter 29

THERE was another heat wave in late June of 1934, just over two years later, and as Frau von Schleicher took down her family's bathing things for their morning plunge, handing them from the clothesline to her small impatient daughter, she recalled that stifling dinner party and how she had longed all evening to return here where it was cooler. Even on a day like this, ninety degrees and not yet noon, the air was occasionally stirred by a breeze from the lake, which was already filled with Saturday boaters, with white and yellow sails silhouetted against the heat-hazed blue.

"Will Fräulein Güntel swim, too?" the child asked as they went back to the house to change, and her mother smiled.

"You know we cannot get Fräulein Güntel into a bathing suit; she considers it an undignified costume for a governess. You ask that every day, and every day it's the same answer."

Coming into the kitchen, the little girl began industriously flapping the bathing garments, shaking sand out all over the floor.

"Not on the floor, dear. Take them back outside and do that."

She had closed the door behind the child and was crunching across the linoleum for a broom when she was startled by the sound of a sharp blast. Running out through the dining room and through the open doors of her husband's study, she screamed as she caught sight of him on the floor and heard another burst of gunfire. One bullet struck her in the temple, two in the chest.

Fräulein Güntel, who had answered the front doorbell and been brushed aside by a half-dozen men in belted raincoats, stood rigid with shock as they now emerged from the study, walked past her again, and shut the front door quietly behind them. "Keep the child out—" she managed to whisper as the maid came creeping, white-faced, down the stairs; and suddenly shaking uncontrollably, Fräulein Güntel made her way into the study and kneeled down by the two figures, around which the rug was already soaked dark.

Some ten or twelve days later, an obscure governess disappeared from the rooming house into which she had just moved, was found strangled in a nearby wood, was registered by the police as a suicide, and was duly buried, thus joining belatedly the many people who had been laid to rest a fortnight earlier. No exact count had been made, and the events of that weekend had already moved into the past with the oppressive weather.

Berlin was bright and clear as an open gray Mercedes passed through the northern outskirts of the city into the countryside. Göring, seated next to his chauffeur, unzipped his briefcase and withdrew a small, red-bound book recently sent to him from London. Holding it on his lap, out of the wind, he opened it and looked at the title page.

GERMANY REBORN
by
General Hermann Goering
Prime Minister of Prussia

Turning the page, he read his Foreword.

> I welcome this opportunity of presenting to the English-speaking peoples a few of my ideas about the struggle of the German people for freedom and honour. I hope that these words will also be accepted by our opponents as a frank expression of my boundless love for my country, to whose service alone I have pledged my whole life.
>
> Berlin, February 1934

Turning more pages, he skimmed passages here and there. Though unable to speak English fluently, he understood the written language; and then of course the contents of the book were more than familiar to him. It was because he knew his subject so thoroughly—the Great War, its aftermath, the Party's long struggle and final victory—

that he had been able to start and finish the book in one afternoon of vigorous dictation. He leafed through the rest of it, then dropped it into the open briefcase beside him, catching the tail end of a scrutinizing glance from his chauffeur.

"Stop bullying me, Kropp. You're worse than a Feldwebel."

Kropp, who was also his valet, nodded in agreement. His master was an easy man to work for, but he had one trying characteristic, which was a dislike of sitting still while people fiddled over him. This meant that it was hard to get him to submit to a haircut. Kropp, always keeping a vigilant eye on the growth rate just behind one of the large ears, would finally call in a barber, who would usually sit waiting for hours in an outer office until Kropp rushed him in at an opportune moment, then rushed him out afterward with a generous tip both for his long wait and for the squirming session. No doubt if the Minister President could cut his own hair, he would. He cut his own nails. He shaved himself, too, using an old-fashioned straight-edge razor and afterward patting dry his skin with powder, an imperial-era custom of which Kropp approved. The Minister President also drew his own bath, and dressed with lightning speed. He made few demands, except that he was an insomniac and in the small hours of the morning, when one was sleeping soundly, he was liable to ring: "Kropp, I'm hungry—bring cheese, sausage, cakes and plenty of beer!" But just now he was on one of his frantic weight-losing regimens, which consisted of almost no food at all, slimming pills, harsh gymnastic workouts, Turkish baths, and pummeling massages. All his clothes had had to be taken in. Unfortunately, they would all have to be let out again in due time.

Villages passed by, copses of birches, wheat fields stretching flat into the distance. The sky was clear and very blue. From under the heavy tires there came a sudden smooth zinging sound.

"They've done a good job," Göring remarked, taking up his book again and leafing through it.

"So they have, Excellency."

This stretch of the highway, like many roads in Germany, had for years been in a state of neglect. Now, having been under repair for some weeks, it was paved smooth and even.

. . . The year 1932 will always be considered one of the most important turning points of German history. . . . There was one election after another; the avalanche of meetings rolled over the country. On the one hand we had the National Socialists passionately attacking, stirring up and firing the masses; on the other hand the Communists attacking too, and desperately resisting; the other parties hopelessly trying to defend themselves. . . . One government decree followed another, each one being more stupid than the last. Once more they thought it would be possible to hold back the mighty millions of the National Socialist movement with ridiculous attempts at suppression. . . .

In our ranks there were those who were discouraged and thought that further suspense would be unbearable, that the Storm Troops could no longer stand further persecution, further terrorism and suppression. But the Leader knew better; he knew that the mood of the Storm Troops would always remain the same, always as resolute and unafraid as the mood of the Leader himself. . . .

And so the struggle of the year 1932 continued. . . . There was only one possible solution, and that was to make Hitler Chancellor. . . . We proclaimed that anyone who stood between us and this goal of ours would be passionately attacked. We proclaimed that anyone who thought to draw his sword against us would be ruthlessly pushed aside. . . .

After a few months Papen fell, as had been foreseen. That had to be, for first of all he had the whole National Socialist movement against him, and secondly he had the Minister for Defense, Schleicher, apparently on his side. But any Chancellor who has Herr von Schleicher on his side must expect sooner or later to be sunk by the Schleicher torpedo. At that time there was a joke in political circles. "General Schleicher ought really to have been an admiral, for his military genius lies in shooting underwater at his political friends!"

. . . Strasser, up till then one of the most powerful men in the Movement, worked with Schleicher against the Leader, and in the middle of the fiercest battle attacked his leader from behind. . . . The Movement can pardon everything except faithlessness towards its Leader; it never forgives disobedience, indiscipline or treachery. . . .

The scenery was gradually changing. Villages lay farther apart, the soil was dryer. Rifts of white sand gleamed through sparse vegetation, and here and there, in the strong sunlight, there shone patches of reddish-purple heather. The flatness began to be broken up by great rectangular blocks of pine woods, and the whining screech of a sawmill flew by with a raw, sweet whiff of new-cut wood. They were nearing the Schorfheide, a vast terrain of forests and moors stretching north to the Baltic and east to the Polish frontier.

The masses participated perhaps more passionately than ever in the meetings and electoral battles; the government was attacked still more hotly, and ever and again they and their party confederates were driven into a corner. More and more did the people come to realize, and the old Field Marshal came to realize it too, that Chancellor Schleicher's government was incompetent and impossible. . . .

And so the year 1932 came to an end in such a turmoil of political passions as the German people had never before experienced. The suspense was almost unbearable. . . . The beginning of the coming year would either bring collapse or recovery. . . .

January 1933 began, the month which for long will be reckoned as perhaps the most memorable in German history. . . . There was feverish activity on all sides. . . . From January on I was, as political delegate, in constant touch with Herr von Papen, with Secretary of State Meissner, with the leader of the Steel Helmets, Seldte, and with the leader of the German Nationalists, Hugenberg, and was discussing with them future developments. It was clear that our goal could only be reached by the union of the National Socialists with all the remaining national forces under the sole leadership of Adolf Hitler. And then it was that Herr von Papen, against whom, for political reasons, we had once been forced to fight, now realized what a momentous occasion this was. With sincere cordiality he entered the alliance with us, and became the honest mediator between the aged Field Marshal and the young lance corporal of the Great War. . . .

On Saturday, the 28th of January, 1933, I could report to the Leader that in its essentials the work was finished and that now at last one could count on his being appointed. . . . On Monday, at eleven o'clock in the morning, Adolf Hitler was appointed Chancellor by the President and seven minutes later the Cabinet was formed and the ministers sworn in. . . . With the words of the aged Field Marshal: "And now, gentlemen, forward with God!" the new Cabinet started on its work.

. . . How wonderfully had our luck changed at last and how wonderfully had the aged Field Marshal been used as an instrument in the hand of God. . . . Outside in the streets of the capital, and in all the towns of Germany, people were rejoicing, were embracing each other, were happy in the intoxication of a great and noble enthusiasm. . . . In Berlin, the crowds streamed in. Storm Troops, Guards [SS], assembled in close columns at the various meeting places, lit their torches, and then marched past the President's palace in such a procession of thanks as had never before been seen in the history of the capital. There, at the lighted window of the palace, stood the aged and venerable Field Marshal and, deeply moved and filled with gladness, looked down upon a people that had become free and happy again. And a few houses further on there stood, motionless, the man who had earned the thanks of the whole people—the man who had never weakened in the bitter, unceasing struggle . . . who, through thick and thin, had always remained true to the people—the Leader of the German people, its Chancellor, Adolf Hitler. . . .

They had turned off on a side road, and were driving through a flickering greenness like that of an aquarium. The beech trees, with their thick, perfectly straight trunks of olive-gray smoothness, were like a forest of pillars. Their clear green leafage formed a vast canopy that met overhead above the road. A forester's hut came into view and passed. Farther along, a deer bounded through the dimness. Gradually the beech trees gave way to pines, closer together, darker, and more solemn, and to clusters of ancient, gnarled oaks, the holy trees of the German forest.

. . . The Leader appointed me a member of the new Cabinet. Before my appointment I had already been speaker of the German Reichstag and I was to continue to hold this office. But the Leader gave me the Prussian Ministry of the Interior, above all things in order that I should overthrow and crush Communism in this, the greatest State of the Reich. . . . An enormous task lay before me. . . .

To begin with, it seemed to me of first importance to get the weapon of the criminal and political police firmly into my own hands. . . . Out of thirty-two police chiefs I removed twenty-two. Hundreds of inspectors and thousands of police sergeants followed in the course of the next months. New men were brought in, and in every case these men came from the great reservoir of the Storm Troops and the Guards. My task was to inspire the police with an entirely new spirit.

In one of my first big meetings in Dortmund I declared that for the future there would be only one man who would bear the responsibility in Prussia, and that one man was myself. Whoever did his duty in the service of the State, whoever obeyed my orders, and took severe measures against the State's enemies, whoever ruthlessly made use of his revolver when attacked, could be certain of protection. . . . I declared then, before thousands of my fellow countrymen, that every bullet fired from the barrel of a police pistol was my bullet. If you call that murder, then I am a murderer. Everything has been ordered by me; I stand for it and shall not be afraid to take the responsibility upon myself. . . .

From time to time, with a flood of sunlight, the forest gave way to sandy fields of heather, or to expanses of rugged marshland from which the squalling and chattering of waterfowl could be heard, or to green glades thick with wildflowers. They passed a small rush-fringed lake, the first of many scattered through the Schorfheide like fragments of mirror.

Finally I alone created, on my own initiative, the "State Secret Police Department [Geheime Staatspolizei, or Gestapo]." This is the instrument which is so much feared by the enemies of the State, and which is chiefly responsible for the fact that in Germany and Prussia today there is no question of a Marxist or Communist danger. . . . I am kept daily, I might say hourly, informed of everything which happens in the vast Prussian State. The last refuge of the Communists is known to us. However often they change their tactics and change the names of their couriers, a few days later they are tracked down, watched and arrested. We had to proceed against these enemies of the State with complete ruthlessness. . . .

Concentration camps were set up, to which we sent first of all thousands of officials of the Communist and Social Democratic parties. It was only natural that here and there beatings took place; there were some cases of brutality. But if we consider the greatness of the occasion and all that had proceeded it, we must admit that this German revolution for freedom was one of the most bloodless and most disciplined of all revolutions in history. . . . Certain unpleasant and undesired phenomena are the concomitants of every revolution. But if, as in this case, they are so few, and if the aim of the revolution is so completely attained, nobody has any right to work up an agitation about them. . . .

It very soon became clear to me that it was absolutely necessary that I should, besides being Prussian Minister of the Interior, also be Prime Minister. Only if I had this post could I properly carry out my task of exterminating subversive ideas, doing away with Middle Class Parties and bringing in the new order. . . . I got Herr von Papen, as had been previously arranged, to retire from his post as Commissioner of Prussia in order that the Leader could give the post to me. . . .

It very soon became clear to me that it was absolutely
I had the fate of Prussia in my hands and was conscious

of being able to take part, from the most important position in the Reich, in Adolf Hitler's great work of reconstruction. For Prussia has had at all times a mission and responsibility beyond her own borders, and that has been "The Solution of the German Question." Laws passed in Prussia often serve as a pattern for other States. . . . For this reason I tried as soon as possible to put through the National Socialist principles into practise in Prussia. . . .

This was made possible through the creation of a totalitarian State, that is, by the victory all over Germany of the National Socialist Party and its continuance as the sole political organization in the country. It was also made possible by the Leader giving me full authority. I joyfully undertook the mighty task of turning a Prussia which had become rotten through Marxist misgovernment into a new State inspired by the spirit of Frederick the Great. . . .

Special departments were put under my direct supervision, such as the State and Municipal Theatres. . . . I had always been interested in forestry, and now was supervisor of the greatest forest estate in Germany, namely the Prussian State Forests. . . .

Along the roadside there grew blossoming Faulbäume, thick clusters whose whiteness was repeated in an occasional glimpse of swans gliding across the gray-green of a small lake. Wild boar were also native to the area; the European brown bear had once roamed here, and elk and bison. He had begun to reintroduce elk, which he imported from Sweden along with bison from Canada; the wild swans, too, were his doing, and the waterfowl and a variety of small game: dying species, overhunted or poached nearly to the point of extinction. All of the Schorfheide he had begun to restock, as well as Rominten Heath in East Prussia.

"Never hunt, do you, Kropp?"

"Not I, sir. I'm not a sportsman. Although I used to like a bit of fishing when I was younger. Trout."

"Trout . . ." the Minister President murmured, looking away.

"Trout, ja. Trout fishing was something I used to enjoy. There is nothing like catching and cooking your own fresh trout. That's what I always used to—"

"Ja, ja," the Minister President replied shortly, flattening the open pages of his book with his hand.

. . . As a former airman I was given yet another sphere of work. . . . A new Air Ministry was formed and the Leader appointed me its head. He gave me the task of making the German air service the best and safest in the world and of raising the commercial air fleet to a new pinnacle of importance. . . .

It also seemed to me absolutely necessary to convince the other powers that Germany too had at least a right to a defense air fleet. Germany, surrounded by Powers bristling with armaments and herself completely unarmed, does not possess even a single chaser machine or a single observation plane. . . . The world must at last awaken to the fact, and nations must be made to realize, that to grant Germany a small army and navy for her security is a mere mockery so long as the vertical line of attack is undefended and open to all attacks. It is therefore my task to go on exhorting and demanding until Germany has at last obtained true equality and security. . . .

For ten months Hitler has ruled Germany. How short a time, but how great the achievement! How much has happened! In all spheres an advance has begun. . . . The German peasant, up until a few months ago without rights and liable at any time to be turned out of house and farm, now stands fast once more on his hereditary land. His land is no longer a commodity, it has been removed from the clutches of speculative usurers and has again become sacred and inviolate. Nearly seven million unemployed looked expectantly and with despairing eyes at Adolf Hitler. Today, after ten months, nearly half of them have work and maintenance. . . . Thousands of kilometres of great new roads for motor traffic have been planned and work on them has already begun; new canals are to be made, the motor tax has been abolished, insurance premiums lowered. The completely corrupt and almost bankrupt Old Age Pensions Scheme has been abolished by a boldly conceived law which at the same time saved the members' contributions. . . . But the most important thing, the greatest and most wonderful of ideas, has become a reality: Hitler has achieved what seemed impossible. Out of the divisions and disunion of the German people, out of all its parties and classes he has made a united people.

. . . Germany is, and will remain, the heart of Europe, and Europe can be healthy and live in peace only when its heart is healthy and intact. The German people has arisen and Germany will again be healthy. For that we have the guarantor who is Adolf Hitler, the Chancellor of the German people and protector of their honour and freedom.

He closed the book on his lap, and after a few moments turned his attention back to the drive. There was another long cool stretch of

aquarium green, then sunlight and they were passing through the
stone gateway onto the entrance drive. A few minutes later they pulled
up inside the courtyard. Not one for protocol when off duty, the Prime
Minister threw open his door himself and climbed out, filling his lungs
with the fresh piney air as he hurried up the single step to the massive
double doors, which were already being pulled open for him.

Chapter 30

Here had stood an old hunting box which Göring had used on shooting trips, and whose surroundings he had fallen in love with. Here, he decided, his home would stand. With the aid of two Berlin architects he had devoted his every free hour to the project, a project inhibited by no money problems, since, as a ministerial residence, it would be built at state expense. He himself had planned and designed everything down to the shape of the smallest door handle. Construction had begun in the summer of 1933, and with round-the-clock shifts of workers was completed in the gratifyingly short space of ten months.

No visitor was ever able to determine what style of architecture Carinhall consisted of. Hitler's personal architect, young Herr Speer, described it with amused acerbity as "pure Göring, which is all things squashed together in one fistlump." The fistlump, combining elements of hunting lodge, baronial hall, rustic farmhouse and medieval fortress, was a broad, massive structure with high, steep thatched roofs. There was a main building with two shorter wings extending forward, enclosing a courtyard on three sides. The walls, bordered by flowering hawthorn and young birches, were made of huge blocks of Brandenburg granite—gray, pink, red, greenish—alternating with half-timbered white plaster, each wall decorated with a row of antlers above windows whose shutters, in rustic tradition, were painted blue and white in diagonal stripes. In austere contrast stood the great jutting block of the entrance, with its human-dwarfing double doors set between two black wrought-iron torch holders.

Anyone who had ever seen Veldenstein would have found repeated here both the massiveness of the burg itself and the simple lines of its stone manor house. Indeed, for all Carinhall's peculiarities, and in spite of Herr Speer's remark—or perhaps bearing it out—the building possessed an undeniable and robust unity, and seemed almost to have grown as organically from its Germanic soil as one of the ancient oaks around it.

Göring had also designed the burial place by the edge of the small lake that lay behind the building. Rough stone megaliths ringed a forest clearing whose sandy earth had been mixed with Swedish soil, and at whose center lay a great rectangular block of polished red granite. Steps led down from this into the crypt below, of mortared stone, illumined by a small window whose pane was inset with an edelweiss flower of white stained glass. In the center of the crypt stood the double pewter casket—this too designed by Göring—in which Carin's body had been transferred from Lövo Cemetery in Stockholm, and which, when the time came, would hold his own body as well. The room contained one decorative object, a simple blue-and-white bowl that had once stood in the little house in Obermenzing. This was always filled with fresh flowers.

Some people wondered how Emmy Sonnemann liked her situation, which Goebbels called a *ménage à trois* (the blond one, the fat one, and the dead one), hinting that a third of the bed was occupied by Carin's ghost. But those who knew Emmy Sonnemann knew that she accepted the hovering presence with equanimity. "I should consider it strange, and callous," she said, "if a man could quickly forget someone he had loved so deeply. What's more, I think a heart that loves deeply is a large heart, and in a large heart there is always room for more love."

As Göring came through the front entrance, Emmy Sonnemann was having afternoon coffee on the flagstone terrace behind the house, sitting at a round white wicker table with her old friend Rose Korwan and Hermann's stepson, Thomas. Although Emmy had met Thomas only a few days before—Hermann having avoided bringing them together for more than a year, as if he feared Thomas would resent his having taken another woman into his life—a closeness had already grown between the quiet Swedish youth and herself. Far from resenting Hermann's romance, the youth seemed to understand that life had a way of reflowering as time went on, that it should, it must, or the gift of life itself was wasted. Yet, understanding this, he seemed himself never to have known even a first flowering; Emmy felt that he was one of those people who have slipped directly from childhood into middle age; she was touched by his dry, worldly-wise manner, his beautiful courtesy, his faintly wistful onlooker's gaze. She felt protective toward him. They got along very well, and they were both enjoying Rose, who in her vivid, descriptive way was recounting tales from the days when she and Emmy had been struggling young actresses together. Then Rose broke off in the middle of a sentence—she had that habit—and raised her eyebrows extravagantly. "What is that huge affair?"

An enormous man was wandering around the far end of the terrace; but Emmy did not know him; he could be the King of Bulgaria or an authority on hoof and mouth disease. "Don't ask me," she said cheerfully. "People come and go—it's like a train station."

"I think I've met him," Thomas said as the man came wandering in their direction. "He's a great friend of Hermann's." And as the man grew near, deeply absorbed in his own thoughts and exhibiting a distinctly seedy look, as if he slept in his clothes, Thomas rose courteously.

"Doctor Has . . . Haf . . . ?"

The man stopped irritably. "Neither. Han. Hanfstaengl."

"Thomas von Kantzow."

"But of course." The man's face softened, and they shook hands; but he seemed completely harried and preoccupied, and he bowed wearily as he was introduced to the two ladies. "Won't you sit down and have some coffee, Herr Hanfstaengl?" asked Emmy, whose first inclination was always to give aid. He accepted, and sank into a white wicker chair that creaked under his weight.

"I've just been having a walk around," he said. "I haven't been here before."

"Oh, you must see it all," Emmy told him. "Herr Göring will take you on a tour. He loves to take people on tours."

"I believe he's expected shortly?"

"I think so. Would you like me to ask if he's come in?"

"Please don't trouble yourself, Frau Sonnemann."

"It is no trouble," she said, reaching down and taking up a telephone whose cord was apparently plugged into the terrace floor. "I find it so strange," she confessed, pressing a button, "to talk on a telephone while sitting outside."

If he had not been so tired, Putzi would have smiled, for one of Frau Sonnemann's crimes, according to Party gossip, was her haughty and overbearing manner. She was also, if he remembered rightly, whorish, scheming, stupid, untalented, and a Jew-lover. He stretched his back under his gray flannel suit jacket and fought down the urge to smoke yet another cigarette.

"They say he's just come in, he has gone to change," Frau Sonnemann told him, replacing the phone. "Now you must have your coffee."

She poured, and handed him a small flowered cup and saucer that flared in the sun and hurt his eyes. He saw that his nicotined fingers were trembling as he lifted the cup. He felt exhausted, crumpled, badly out of sorts, and was not at all sure that Hermann would welcome his unexpected visit. He had been back in Germany only four days, having sailed off three weeks ago to the United States for the twenty-fifth reunion of his Harvard class—something he had long looked forward to and refused to miss, even though the atmosphere here at home had grown heavily charged. The reunion was a great success, and, taking advantage of his holiday, he had also attended the wedding of his old friend and classmate John Jacob Astor. It was during the church ceremony that someone came creeping hurriedly down the aisle and thrust an Associated Press news release under his nose with an urgently whispered request for comment. Stunned, then shaken, he had managed to get passage aboard a ship sailing for Bremen the next day. In Berlin he could pry no facts from Hess or his staff, whose offices were next to his own, and he had immediately entrained for the Baltic resort where Hitler was on holiday with the Goebbelses. But there, met by a lightly sociable, utterly deflective look from Hitler, he had not dared even broach the subject. Nor could he worm anything out of Goebbels. Putzi had gone back on the next train to Berlin, where, still shaken, and beleaguered by the foreign press, he had been running himself ragged pestering everyone he knew for information, and receiving only the same official statements that had been given in the newspapers and over the radio. Hermann he had not been able to get hold of, a very busy man these days. Finally, with a sleep-starved sense of desperation, he had climbed into his roadster and made the long drive to where he was now sitting, and where, unable to resist any longer, he was bringing out his cigarette case. His throat was raw from chain-smoking, and he grimaced as he inhaled.

"Mind you don't fall in again!" Frau Sonnemann called, and he saw that two young boys were playing a little distance away, by the water's edge. "They're Herr Göring's nephews," she told him. "Jolly boys, but always up to something. This morning Fräulein Korwan had to fish them out with her parasol."

Fräulein Korwan laughed, and related how she herself had once fallen into the Spree. ". . . and it was so cool and lovely, you know, that I just stayed in and had a nice swim."

"Rose would do that, you see," Frau Sonnemann explained. "Rose is a free spirit."

"I may have had a few spirits in me, for that matter."

Putzi laughed too, feeling himself relax for the first time in days. He had a strong wish to stay all afternoon in this pleasant, easy atmosphere, sipping coffee, basking in the warm, pine-scented air. He even accepted one of the rich little Sahnetorten Frau Sonnemann offered him, though his stomach had been in a knot since he got back. His hostess appeared to have eaten a good many Sahnetorten in her time, and verged on plumpness, if of a stately variety. She had an attractive face, rather long, but with delicate features and the fresh, evenly pink skin of very blond people. She appeared to be about forty, and at the corners of her blue eyes small, friendly lines fanned out. Her hair was waved; she wore a white sundress. She gave the impression of an easy-going sort of woman, completely lacking in the feverish intensity that had always shown through Carin's reserve. Apparently she lacked Carin's political predisposition as well, for she was telling young Kantzow, with an amused headshake at her own ignorance, that when she had first met Göring she had mistaken him for Goebbels.

Putzi found himself laughing again. "That is a hard mistake to make."

"Oh, not for us. We in the theater are all political imbeciles. Isn't it so, Rose?"

"It may be so, but surely there's a more attractive term than 'imbeciles,' Emmy."

"Artistes," young Kantzow offered.

"Artistes, much better," Putzi agreed, stretching his legs out under the table and leaning back in his chair just as a Schutzstaffel orderly stepped onto the terrace and gave a sharp heel click.

"The Minister President will now see you."

Chapter 31

HE was led briskly down a hallway and shown into a spacious study. The door shut behind him.

The sunlight, pouring through an enormous window that looked out across the little lake, burnished the auburn, elegantly diamond-shaped paneling of the walls and struck gleams from two bronze chandeliers hanging from slender bronze chains. He stood on a sapphire-blue Oriental rug that seemed lit from within, and walked across it to a long polished desk, behind which, covering almost the entire wall, hung a superb medieval tapestry in jewellike blues and reds. He lit a cigarette and stood looking at the tapestry, wondering how long it would please the Minister President to keep him waiting. After a few moments, annoyed by the tremor of tension and exhaustion in his fingers, he stubbed out the cigarette in an ashtray; then turned as a side door opened and Hermann came striding in, greatly reduced in girth, clad in white ducks and navy-blue polo shirt, followed by a loping young lion.

"Wie geht's, Putzi!" he called, smiling, and pausing to settle the lion on the rug, then crossing the room with hand outstretched. "I thought I'd be seeing you one of these days—Pilli tells me you've been driving him crazy. Welcome to Carinhall," he said as they shook hands. "What do you think of it?"

"Very nice."

"Ach, don't sound so constipated," Hermann admonished, taking his guest warmly by the arm and leading him toward a pair of leather armchairs by the window. "Shall I live like Mahatma Gandhi? Isn't it enough that I look like him?"—a clap to his reduced stomach. "Anyway, it all goes to the state on my death, all perfectly proper. Will you have something to drink? A gin and tonic?" He pronounced it *chin taunich*. "You must know it well, Putzi, a good Yankee drink. I was introduced to it the other day."

"Nothing, thanks," Putzi replied as they sat down. He would not have minded a gin and tonic, but he knew the ice would rattle delicately in his glass. He stretched out his legs in an attempt to relax, and tried for an easy conversational tone.

"Well, I must say your State Secretary is a regular *tabula rasa*."

"Pilli? What else should he be? What had Pilli to do with it?"

"What had anyone to do with it? Frankly, that's been my impression since I got back."

"Mein lieber Putzi," his host said good-naturedly, "if you want to stay on top of things, you shouldn't lead such a flighty life. Sailing off into the blue like that—one must stay put when the pot begins to boil."

The criticism was annoying, mainly because it was just. "Well, rest assured that I'm being punished for my sins. I've sailed back to an unholy mess, I can tell you. I've got the entire foreign press on my back."

"Shit on the foreign press," Hermann replied equably, then beamed as the lion came loping over and flopped down with a thud between their chairs, Putzi hastily drawing his feet back.

"Ja, you know where you want to be, don't you, Caesar?" Hermann asked it indulgently. "Such a pet she is. I settle her somewhere, a minute later here she comes. She's got to be right on top of you."

"So I see."

"Well, we've been together since she was a little cub. I used to feed her with a baby bottle. Isn't that right, Caesar?" he crooned, leaning from his chair and fondly petting her flank.

"She's not exactly a cub anymore."

"No, she's really getting much too big to keep. I'll have to give her back to the zoo pretty soon. We'll miss each other, won't we, Caesar? Ach ja." He sighed, rubbing and patting the tawny fur.

"Hermann, do you very much mind taking this beast away?"

Hermann looked up, surprised. "No, of course not. But why?"

"Why? Why? Because I'm not used to sitting around with some—some damned *lion*. Is that so odd? Look at her, look how she keeps staring at my feet—"

"Probably's never seen anything like them. Have you, Caesar? The eighth and ninth wonders of the world!"

"I mean it, Hermann—!"

"All right, come on, Caesar, you're not appreciated," he said, getting down from his chair onto his knees. Rolling the lioness over onto her back, he scratched her belly and played with her, then crawled off and patted the carpet. "That's right, come over here and lie down. Take a nice nap, Caesar, dream of what you've seen." And with a final patting, his face wreathed with affection, he got to his feet, looking very fit indeed, the tight polo shirt revealing a hard muscular chest and almost flat belly. He must have lost sixty pounds, Putzi thought, watching him come back and sit down again. Either he was on one of his maniacal weight-losing regimens, or else the strain of the last weeks had taken its toll. But Putzi doubted that; everything about him radiated fitness, health, good cheer. It was only his own nerves that were frazzled to the point of breaking.

"Listen to me, Hermann," he began again. "I've got correspondents in my hair day and night. I haven't had a moment's rest since I got back. There's been a terrific uproar abroad. A terrific uproar. And it will go on unless there's proper justification for what happened. What was the authority behind it? Who signed the execution warrants? They want to know if"—he saw that a coldness had replaced Hermann's amiable gaze, but he could not break off—"if there isn't at least a complete list of the people killed. You give out a figure in the seventies, but they're putting their own lists together and they say it's beginning to look more like a thousand. I tell you, Hermann, this agitation abroad will never die down unless they're given the correct information in black and—"

"The correct information has been given," Hermann cut in. "It has been given not once but many times. But I will give it again. The SA planned an armed revolt. We took immediate steps against it. It was necessary. It was done."

Then in a sharper tone, getting up from his chair, he went on.

"What are you asking me, anyway, sitting there behind the skirts of the foreign press? Whose agitation are you talking about? What do you want me to tell you—that I had nothing to do with it? I thought that was what you were tired of hearing. Is that what you want to hear? I have stated openly, to our own press and to the foreign press, that I and Reichsführer Himmler carried out the action here in Berlin, and that I take full responsibility for my part in that action! You know it, everyone knows it! So why are you sitting there with that weakpiss look on your face asking these stupid questions? If you've got something to say, say it!"

His voice had risen to an angry shout.

"Say it! You'd have done differently? It was a national crisis. In a crisis you strike first and ask questions later! You've been running around like a fly in a bottle, Hanfstaengl, you don't get answers, and you don't get answers because the Röhm file is closed! Can't you get that through your head? It's closed! But I'll tell you this much—when I saw things were getting out of hand I went to Adolf and demanded they be stopped, and they were stopped! Certainly there were excesses, there were bound to be. But a thousand? Quatsch! My list contained thirty-two names, and in Munich Adolf had twenty-odd on his. What does that make? Even with some excesses, seventy or eighty at the most. I know nothing of these other lists you speak of. If your ausländische shitheads have come up with a thousand, I can only say they're better informed than I! Listen to me—they carry on because it pleases them to carry on. But it's none of their damn business! There is no more to be said on the subject. I have given the information."

He walked over to the window and stood looking out, his hands locked tightly behind his back.

Shoot him! And him!—shoot them!

All afternoon of that sweltering Saturday, in his Leipziger Platz Palace office, he had worked over the list of names before him. Throughout the city the Berlin leadership of the SA—in uniform, in business suits, in white flannels—were pulled off beaches and playing courts, out of homes, offices, cafés. One had even been hustled from church where he was in the process of being married.

Shoot them!

They were scum, vandals, would-be ruiners of all that had been so arduously won. So enraged were his orders that whenever they ceased he heard a deep chop of silence despite the hectic bustle of ADCs, SS, Gestapo, hurrying in and out with messages, footsteps ringing, faces wet. His own face was wet. His hair hung wet over his eyes, so that he had constantly to whip it back. The white tunic of his uniform was soaked in gray patches. The heat was what he remembered most clearly from that day. The windows were shut and the drapes partially drawn, leaving the room twilit. From the courtyard below, swarming with police, there came a steady din of trucks and shouted orders. Between the drapes was a glare of roofs bristling with machine guns. The sky was hazed, colorless, boiling. A platter of open-faced sandwiches had been brought in, and he would take a hasty bite while conferring with Himmler and Himmler's young deputy, Heydrich, the three of them passing reports and notes across the increasingly littered desk, their fingers leaving prints of sweat on the paper. His typewritten list of names, many of them by now slashed through with red pencil, was smudged and dog-eared with handling. He remembered the sweat, the dimness and bustle, the odd scrap—Himmler's taut unshaven face, and his hand white and slender as a girl's, with delicately traced blue veins, hanging poised in the air before descending on a liver-paste-and-beet sandwich; Heydrich taking a sip of coffee, a face like two profiles pasted together, eyes so close-set you couldn't get a finger between them, small eyes, small intelligent icy holes; the click of the cup on its saucer, the nibbled liver-paste sandwich set down, the resisting clatter of feet as a brownshirt was brought in, fury seizing him by the nape: "Straighten up, you pig! What have you got for a backbone, potato mash? Stand up! Come forward!"

By the end of the afternoon he stank with sweat, as did his two confreres. The entire area around the desk seemed thickly malodorous. On their departure he went immediately to his private quarters and showered.

Bathed, shaven and talcumed, splashed with cologne, dressed in a fresh uniform, he then left to conduct a foreign press conference at the Chancellery, where he answered the turbulent rush of questions directly and briefly. On hearing General von Schleicher's name brought up, he gave a brisk nod. "I know you people like a good headline. Well, I will give you one. General von Schleicher plotted against the regime. I ordered his arrest. He was foolish enough to resist. He is dead." With that, he left for Tempelhof Airport, where Adolf's plane from Munich would be arriving shortly. The drive was stifling; his fresh uniform was already sticking to his sides. The evening sky was luridly, bloodily red.

Later that night, Adolf, he, and Himmler sat down together in an upstairs study at the back of the Chancellery. The heat was still oppressive. Through the tall windows, the night sky was hazed a dark copperish gray. Adolf's face was drawn, his eyes looked almost extinguished. His voice was flat. His first statement was that Röhm was alive, locked up in Stadelheim Prison in Munich. In response to their questioning looks, he warned them that he was not going to have Röhm executed, and that he would not discuss the matter. He went on to the business of Schleicher and his wife.

"That was a grave mistake," he told them.

"I understand that he reached for a gun," Göring said, with a narrow look at Himmler. He, Göring, had ordered Schleicher's arrest, but the order was carried out by the Gestapo, and the Gestapo were no longer his. First his concentration camps had gotten into this dry turd's hands; now his Gestapo, along with the rest of his Prussian police forces—

"A grave mistake," Adolf repeated, his eyes resting on Himmler's pince-nez. "It will cause a storm of protest from the Reichswehr."

"So far there has been no protest, mein Führer," Himmler replied. "So far."

Himmler folded his slender hands on the table before him. "I must point out to the Führer that the Reichswehr interceded several times today on our behalf, most conspicuously during the action in Breslau. I feel sure that this is an indication—"

"Vielleicht," Adolf said shortly.

But it was not Schleicher whom Göring wished to discuss, it was Röhm. That Röhm remained alive was shocking, fantastic, utterly wrong. He knew that Adolf was not in a frame of mind to listen to reason—Adolf had had many of his old comrades killed today, and the burden weighed heavily on him—but the issue of Röhm could not be left hanging.

"I realize you don't want to discuss Röhm, but—"

"I am pardoning him."

They both looked at him incredulously.

"But surely," Himmler said, "surely the Führer cannot mean that. I beg the Führer to consider the repercussions. Think of the Reichswehr's dissatisfaction with such a situation. Think of the charges that Röhm could make against us. . . ."

Göring had gotten up in a cold fury and gone over to one of the windows, where he stood tapping his booted foot on the floor. Outside, under the hazed night sky, old gardens stretched away to Hermann-Göring-Strasse, formerly Friedrich-Ebert-Strasse, its streetlamps glowing in a converging row to the lights of Brandenburg Gate.

"Perhaps all that we have gained would be lost," Himmler went on. "Surely that is the main consideration."

"My main consideration," said Adolf, "is Captain's Röhm's long service to us. That is my *only* consideration—lieber Gott, he has been with me from the very beginning."

"But he is not with you now!" Göring said, turning around. "He has almost brought about your ruin! If you let him go, then I must ask what we have been doing. Many people have been killed—many people! Have we shed so much blood only that he himself should go free? He must be killed! He must be killed at once!"

"I will not discuss it!" Adolf replied with a cutting stroke of his hand. The room was silent. He sat back with a deep sigh, rubbing his eyes. "I am too tired to talk now. I must have some sleep. You will both return tomorrow morning at eleven."

The remainder of the night and the early-morning hours Göring spent in his hectic palace office, going through the sealed communiqués that had come in during his absence, and then conferring with the Lichterfelde Barracks commander, whom he had telephoned to report to him with an account of the SA executions.

It was three in the morning when he pulled the blankets off his bed and threw himself down in his underwear on the taut, warm silk sheet. It was too hot to sleep. And his mind was too active. The Röhm issue should have been settled tonight. And not only the Röhm issue, but everything. He should not have to wait until eleven o'clock to confer with Adolf, and he felt a surge of anger for his leader's work habits, his Austrian Schlamperei, never rolling out of bed till nine or ten or later—he himself was always up by half past six. On this day Adolf should be up at dawn, to put an end to the whole business.

But Adolf had had to be dragged all the way. It was his nature in a crisis to lose sight of the essential thing. Once Röhm had made it clear that he wanted the Reichswehr it was clear that Röhm must be ground into the dust, and that this was the only essential thing. But Adolf brooded over a thousand details. Could he afford to expose a split in Party solidarity? And if he got rid of the SA, what would he use as a counterweight against the Reichswehr? And did he not owe the brownshirts everything? Were they not his beloved children, his old comrades? And was not Röhm his oldest comrade? So he pondered, while his oldest comrade was busily cutting the ground from under his feet.

Röhm was without a shred of sense. He could not see that if he plunged the regime into the abyss, he himself would plunge along with it. He could not see the one simple, glaring, dangerous fact that the regime had not yet consolidated its power. As long as the Chancellor was dismissible by the President, and as long as the Army swore its loyalty oath to the President, Hitler was without full power. He could be toppled. The regime could be toppled. And on this delicate, infirm ground Röhm was trampling like a large animal showing off its might. At this vulnerable moment, when Hindenburg's failing health would soon make the matter of his succession a reality, when Hitler must lay the groundwork to merge the offices of Chancellor and President, when the conservatives must be given no reason to indulge their inclination to set up a Hohenzollern regent as head of state—at such a moment Röhm was displaying the power of his troops in giant parades and marches and calling for a second revolution. He encouraged his men to run wild in the streets, he refused to tone down his homosexual orgies, and he openly stated his intention to incorporate the Reichswehr. And the more he frightened and antagonized the conservative bloc, the deeper were the cracks he struck through the Party's hope of achieving the last, necessary step to absolute power.

Adolf tried to reason with him. He explained that the new army must be gray, not brown; a civilian militia would never be suitable for national defense. He explained that a second revolution, that all further social reform, was not feasible until they had recovered from the past years of economic disaster, and that in order to create employment they must rebuild the armed forces, and for that the support of the industrialist-conservative bloc was essential. He explained that the brownshirts' street violence was intolerable, and that Röhm's private life was creating a scandal, and that these things were alienating the people not only from the SA but from the entire regime.

The talks were useless. Röhm went stomping off in his own direction, and Adolf sat down to brood some more. It seemed to Göring that Adolf would sit there procrastinating until the earth caved in beneath him. Only something extreme might jolt him into action, such as the knowledge that his old comrade was plotting an armed revolt.

There was no actual evidence that an armed revolt was being

planned, but there were abundant rumors, and using these, Göring did all he could to whip up the necessary atmosphere of imminent threat. He was assisted in his endeavors by Himmler, whom he loathed with good reason, but who was eager to squash Röhm's four-million-man army, since his SS was part of and subordinate to it. Goebbels, too, contributed his talents. Goebbels was Röhm's friend—Röhm's only friend in the Party aside from Hitler; and Goebbels, as an old leftist radical, had taken up Röhm's cry for socialist fulfillment; but then, intelligent creature that he was, he had had serious second thoughts when he smelled which way the wind was blowing.

Göring had always found the fruits of his wiretapping fascinating. In talks between Röhm and his Berlin SA chief, he was variously referred to as Herr Reaktion, the old clotheshorse, and the pig Göring. Now, as tension began mounting, he read his wiretapping reports with even more fascination. "I will personally," said the Berlin SA chief, "cut slabs of flesh from his fat body until he is half his size, and only then will I stick my knife in his throat." "Do that," Röhm replied, "but don't eat any of the cuts. Forbidden meat!" And whether the words implied actual homicidal intent or were so much colorful fantasizing, it made no difference. If Röhm was plotting to overthrow the regime, or if he merely intended to pursue his crashing, pigheaded course, it made no difference. He must be brought down with an ax chop.

But time was running out. Every day Adolf was brought warnings of armed rebellion, even handed falsified documents provided by Heydrich. Still he wavered. Then Vice Chancellor von Papen—von Papen, of all people—gave a speech at Marburg University that rocked them on their ears. He attacked the new regime's single-party system, its control of the press, its racial bigots and doctrinaires, its restrictions on the church, and went on to scourge Hitler for tolerating Röhm and his violent Marxist brownshirts. On the heels of this, Hitler was informed by the Minister of Defense that if he could not control the present intolerable situation, Hindenburg would declare martial law and turn the job of control over to the Reichswehr. And on the heels of this, they learned that Papen meant to force the issue of the President's succession by slapping Hitler with an ultimatum at the next Cabinet meeting: either Hitler suppressed Röhm or Papen and his fellow conservatives would resign from the Cabinet. In this event the government would fall, Hindenburg would hand over full executive power to the Army, and on the old Field Marshal's death a Conservative candidate would step into the presidency. If Hitler did nothing he was shorn of power. But if he acceded to an ultimatum, he was also shorn of power. He must act now, on his own, before the ground beneath them was split wide open.

And finally he was prepared to do so. For he was now convinced, or perhaps not convinced, but feeling it was best to be convinced, that the SA was on the very brink of armed rebellion, and must be crushed flat. Nor was this conviction altered when Röhm put his men on a month's leave, and himself went off to Bad Wiessee, near Munich, to take the waters.

The Gestapo and SS stood ready. The Reichswehr had provided extra arms and an assurance of support. Everything was prepared. And Adolf fell into another torment of indecision, so that it was necessary to fan the flames of threat even higher. For three excruciating days everything hung in the balance. Then suddenly Adolf made up his mind once and for all, flew to Munich, released the code word, and at last, at long last, the collective ax chop was delivered.

There was no deliverance from the heat. The silk sheet was wet with sweat and twisted from his constant turning. He got up impatiently and paced around the warm rug in the darkness, aware that the rage that had pulsed through him for weeks, and which had reached its peak yesterday, was gone, dissipated like smoke. He felt only impatience now, that the thing was not yet finished; that he must argue further about Röhm; that the Army's reaction to Schleicher's death was still unknown; that the executions at Lichterfelde had not been completed, but would resume at dawn; that the early-morning sky outside promised no breath of wind.

Pulling on a robe, he went out onto the balcony, feeling the air as heavy and close as in the room. The building's roofs bulked black against the dark copperish sky. The silence was immense. He turned back to the door, feeling a desire to go into the room where he kept Carin's things, where every day he secluded himself for a little while, opening the closet door to gaze at her dresses, to bring their still faintly perfumed fabric to his face, to touch the keys of the small white harmonium, on whose rack her favorite sheet music still stood open . . . the old songs, the old voices . . . Gregor Strasser, dispatched with a bullet to the back of the neck . . . and he turned around and remained where he was, other names and other faces fluttering down inside his head. Papen's private secretary, author of the Marburg speech, gunned down at his desk . . . Frau von Schleicher, gunned down with her husband . . . two obscure restaurant waiters, perhaps having once overheard some confidential tabletalk, hauled off into the woods and killed . . . an SA leader overtaken in his car with his son and chauffeur, all three shot . . . Dr. Klausener, head of the Catholic Action Group, on whose behalf he had twice interceded earlier this year, shot together with the Catholic Youth leader . . . a music critic named Willi Schmid, mistaken for a brownshirt of the same name, killed in error . . . a village goatherd held down in a pond till drowned, allegedly a Marxist agitator . . . Kommissar von Kahr, betrayer of the 1923 Putsch, old now and long retired, taken to the marshes outside Munich and hacked to pieces . . . big people and small, grudges, expediencies, mistakes, like Frau von Schleicher, the downward flicker of her face, a flickering-out . . .

He turned from the balcony and went inside. Pulling off his robe, he threw himself down again on the wrinkled, damp sheet, resuming his twisting and turning as the bedside clock ticked away. The sky through the windows was growing a shade lighter. Dawn would soon be breaking over the palace roofs, and over the brick barracks of Lichterfelde, those austere buildings of his youth. The Imperial Cadet College, away from the center of town, enclosed by high walls, shut down by the Weimar government, had stood empty for years until he had reopened it to house a contingent of his police troops. It was the logical site for the SA executions, and had been his own suggestion.

There had been a sour edge to the Lichterfelde commander's voice tonight, as perhaps befitted his marginality in an action overseen by the SS, but his description had been thorough. The prisoners were held in the old coal cellar. Beginning late in the afternoon, at intervals, they were taken out four at a time and stood in a row against a wall. An SS man pulled down the shirts, and around each left nipple drew a circle with a piece of charcoal. Eight SS men with rifles stood at a distance of five meters—rather too close, according to the commandant, for when the order to fire was given, the bullets tore out through the backs and splattered chunks against the wall. The wall was not hosed off between executions, and it grew thickly plastered with these blood-ied scraps of flesh and darker pieces of internal organs. This was an unnecessarily cruel sight for any man being led to his last moment, the commandant complained. Also, it created dreadful strain in the firing squads, so that they lost accuracy and inadvertently injured rather than killed, and had frequently to be changed. The commandant would like to add that none of the prisoners requested a blindfold; for the scum they were, they died well. As for disposal, he did not know. From time to time the corpses were thrown into a horse-drawn, tin-lined butcher's cart and taken off somewhere.

So ended the report. The commandant would like to transmit an order that the wall be hosed down before the last batch was lined up at dawn. By all means, he agreed, that should be done; and he had writ-ten out the order . . . but they could hose till Doomsday, he would never again be able to think of those hallowed, imperial buildings, the heart of his youth, except as a stretch of intestine-splattered brick wall by the old coal cellar.

He woke to a flood of hot white light. The clock said half past six. Kropp came in with a tray of coffee, set it down, and picked up the green satin robe from the floor, holding it open for him as he got out of the rumpled bed. "Too hot," he said, pushing it aside. "This damned weather! Bring me some ice water, Kropp, and tell them I don't want any breakfast."

"But you ate only a sandwich yesterday, sir. You've hardly had more than that for days."

"So? I'm on a diet, aren't I? Stop badgering me to get fat again! Ice water, that's all I want! Water out of the tap, with ice in it!"

At seven, showered and dressed, drinking his ice water, he turned on the radio to hear what Goebbels had to say.

". . . by a life of unparalleled debauchery, by their parade of high living, by their feasting and carousing, they have damaged the principles of simplicity and personal decency which our Party supports. They were close to tainting the entire leadership with their shameful and disgusting sexual aberrations . . ." That was Goebbels's particular line of attack, the debauchery. His own was armed revolt. Others would stress the Marxist threat. Still others the public rowdyism. All coming together in one badly needed sweep of the broom. ". . . millions of members of our Party, of the SA, of the SS, congratulate themselves for this storm of purification—" He clicked off the voice, recalling its burst of laughter on the occasion that Röhm had stated in a speech, with deep seriousness and unfortunate sentence structure, "It is our great dream that from every Hitler Youth an SA man will emerge." He too had found the remark uproariously funny. Well, he still didn't care if the SA leadership had a taste for youths and pheasant tongue, but all things must be used in a time of crisis; and after pacing around the room he went down the broad alabaster staircase to the already bustling office floor.

The first thing he did was to check on Papen's welfare, learning that the Vice Chancellor was still safe under house arrest, protected by his, Göring's, staff guard. That he had had to put Papen under protection yesterday was grotesque in retrospect—the Vice Chancellor nervously pacing his living room floor while his two persecutors, Himmler and Heydrich, sat smelling up the air in Göring's office . . . a malodorous pair, but it had been necessary to use them as allies, the only people with manpower; the SS, the Gestapo, the State Police—*his* Gestapo, and *his* State Police, all secured by Himmler now except nominally. How rapidly that little turd had built up his police empire throughout the rest of Germany until he lacked only the Prussian police. And how he, Göring, had fought tooth and nail to keep what belonged to him, but he had finally made Himmler Chief of the Gestapo, to strike a bargain, to make an alliance, for he saw that an alliance with the SS was necessary in the face of the growing might of the SA. And little Heinrich would have gotten the Gestapo and the rest of the Prussian police anyway, eventually, for Adolf was in favor of it. Germany's police must ultimately be centralized, put under one authority: Himmler's. Göring, after all, had so many other things to keep him busy. That was what Adolf had said once before—one did not forget, one had never forgotten, one had rankled with it for three long years—when he had given the SA leadership to Röhm. It was Adolf's instinct: a lopping-off of power here, a bestowal there, an adroit twist of the scales, and you never knew when. . . .

Meanwhile, the incoming reports showed that the night had been as active as the day preceding it. Schleicher's former assistant, General von Bredow, had been shot; and Dr. Beck, president of the International Students' Exchange; and Papen's State Secretary—

"Tell him this Schweinerei has got to stop!" he shouted into the phone.

"Ja, Herr General," came Himmler's quiet voice a few minutes later. "We are trying to bring the action to a close."

"What does that mean, trying? Do it!"

But at eleven o'clock, when he and Himmler met at the Chancellery, Göring did not bring up the subject. It was necessary to present a united front, and as it turned out it took them two solid hours to make Adolf see that his sentimental bond with Röhm was outworn, unfitting, impractical and dangerous. Only at one o'clock did they extract the promise they wanted, and depart.

But Göring's tension, like the hazed white pressing heat, did not diminish. He had meant to confront Adolf with the continuing murders, but had been aware that the right psychological moment was hardly at hand after having badgered him for two hours to kill Röhm. He must now wait until three o'clock.

At that time, having again showered and changed his soaked uniform for fresh, he returned to the Chancellery to attend the garden party Adolf was giving, as a gesture of normality, for diplomats, ministers, and high-ranking Reichswehr officers. Filling the sidewalk outside the Chancellery was a crowd chanting for a glimpse of their Führer on his concrete balcony, which, for just such joyous occasions, had been appended to the old building by Herr Speer. A spontaneous cheer of "Unser Hermann!" went up as his car rolled into the courtyard, but he was too preoccupied to feel his usual full-bodied pleasure at the cry. When the car door was opened for him, he climbed out in a rush and strode hurriedly into the garden.

The first face he caught sight of was Goebbels's, cheerful but still tight with strain as he played with his little daughter on the lawn. He had stuck like glue to Adolf these last few days, hung on to his coattails for dear life—and with good reason, for as an ex-radical who knew but that he himself might not have fallen under the ax he was helping to wield? Frau Goebbels, with the new baby on her lap, sat next to him in a lawn chair beneath a striped beach umbrella. She looked almost serene, but not quite, not quite, and one sensed that this had less to do with the tumultuous events than with the fact that her husband had reverted with such zest to his former habits that he was now known as the goat of Babelsberg, the German film center. Pressing on through the clinking of cups and chatter of voices, past bright summer frocks, white linen suits, feldgrau uniforms, he found Adolf, whom he took aside. Adolf's eyes were still tired and grave; he shaded them with his hand as he listened.

". . . if things are allowed to go on like this, we will be accused of greater crimes than those we have put down. We will have replaced the excesses of the SA with those of the SS. . . ."

Adolf nodded, taking his hand from his eyes and squinting in the sun's glare. The nod might indicate agreement, or it might only indicate that he had heard. More than that you could never be sure of. A few moments later he left to make his appearance on the balcony.

Göring stayed only long enough to exchange a few pleasantries with the Reichswehr officers, leaving with a feeling of certainty—it was a savage feeling, half triumph, half bitterness—that there would be no outcry from the generals on behalf of Schleicher and Bredow. Whatever stuck in the Army's craw would stay there till it rotted. They would not spit out anything now. They would not spit out anything ever again. The German officer corps had made its bargain and broken its own spine.

At five o'clock he learned that Adolf had given orders for the bloodshed to cease.

At seven o'clock an airplane courier from Munich reported to him the news of Röhm's death.

He listened keenly, in silence, nodding from time to time. Röhm had been handed a gun in his cell, loaded with one bullet, and told to use it on himself. He was then left alone for half an hour. Nothing happened. He had thrown the gun to the floor. If Adolf wants to kill me, he said, let him do it himself. It was very hot, and he had no shirt on. He stood with his fists on his hips. A moment later he was gunned down.

"Gut." Göring gave a clap to his thighs and stood up. "Gut. You may go."

The heat of the evening was intolerable. Again the sky was blood-red, and the heat, beating down through the red, seemed compressed by it, as if held down by a red ceiling, growing and building and pressing, like the heat inside an oven. Even when the red had sunk behind the horizon, the oven pressure remained. It remained through all the conferences and telephone calls, and through the late hours of the night as the hectic bustle of the last two days finally drained from the corridors, and as he went up the broad staircase to his bedroom. He showered again, scrubbing himself with the harsh bristles of the bath brush until his flesh stung. As soon as he lay down, the sweat began pouring from him again, the sweat of heat, and the sweat of utter depletion. He had hardly slept for a week, hardly rested, hardly eaten. He lay for a long while in the reek of his sweat, looking up through the dark oven heat of the room. Finally his eyes closed, and he saw again, as if inside his head, flickering bits and pieces of faces. But then he slept.

He felt something at his shoulder, and groggily brushed at it, opening his eyes by degrees to see Kropp standing over him.

"I'm sorry, sir, but I felt certain that you wouldn't wish to sleep longer. It's half past nine."

He sat up, kneading his face, then climbed to his feet, sensing at once a lightness all over his bare skin. He saw that the sky was a clear, regal blue.

"Much nicer today, sir. The heat wave has finally broken."

"Ja," he said, looking at the windows. "Ja, it is finished."

Slipping into the proffered robe, he went out onto the balcony, where he drew in a lungful of the fresh, clear air. Exhaling, he strode back in, heading for the bathroom to shower and shave.

"Will you have something to eat this morning, sir?"

"The whole works."

Half an hour later he sat down in his dining room to a breakfast of Bratwurst and Kartoffelpuffer, rye bread and cold sliced meat, soft rolls spread with smoked breast of goose, an egg whipped in cream, a bowl of Italian peaches, and a steaming pot of coffee.

While he ate, a telegram was brought to him on a salver.

MINISTER PRESIDENT GENERAL GÖRING BERLIN

I WISH TO EXPRESS TO YOU MY GRATITUDE AND RECOGNITION FOR YOUR ENERGETIC ACTION CROWNED WITH SUCCESS IN THE CRUSHING OF THE ATTEMPTED HIGH TREASON. WITH COMRADELY THANKS AND GREETINGS.

HINDENBURG

Chapter 32

H<small>E</small> stood looking out the window at the shimmer of the little lake, the deep green of the forest, the clear blue of the summer sky. He turned and walked back to his chair.

"Certainly, Putzi, I'm aware of how important is the attitude toward us abroad," he said, sitting down again, "but they'll soon find something else to sell their newspapers with. You'll see. Things have already died down here. People are relieved that the brownshirt danger has been done away with and civil war averted. Listen to me—the events of June thirtieth are in the past. We can't undo anything. We can only go ahead. The thing to remember is that there was absolutely no way of avoiding the choice we made."

His tone was conversational, but Putzi could still hear the voice from some minutes ago hanging furiously in the air; so, apparently, could Hermann; apparently it bothered him.

"Look here, Putzi, I'm sorry I shouted. But verdammt! If you've got something to say I wish you'd say it. Straightforward, it's the only way to be. You know I don't believe in mincing words. Listen to me. Do you think the brownshirts weren't warned in the bluntest terms? I even stated in a national broadcast that anyone who eroded confidence in the Führer would pay for it with his head. His head. How much clearer does one have to be? They were given plenty of opportunity to fall into line. Nein, we had no choice, the crack had widened too far. Factionalism, it's been our biggest problem from the start. We both know that. We've stood on cracks and fissures from the start. And we've worked hard to close those cracks, so that Germany might be whole. And now we've closed the last crack, the oldest and deepest of them, and we've shut the last chapter on factionalism. The ground is solid. Germany is solid. For twelve years we've been climbing from one ledge to the next—"

"You're mixing your geological metaphors," Putzi murmured.

"—one ledge to the next, never knowing a minute of rest. Twelve years, pulling ourselves up, climbing, sweating—"

"It's your métier, Hermann, it's what you thrive on."

"—always knowing we could be back at the bottom overnight. One minute nearing the top—the next, maybe whoosh! But we've gained the top. We've arrived. And for the first time we can straighten up and let out a long breath."

His soliloquy, undeterred by the two sour little interruptions, concluded with a deep intake of breath and a long, illustrative exhalation. Indeed, he looked the very picture of arrival, Putzi thought: his face, all lit by the sun, was clear-eyed, fresh-cheeked; the long hair, smoothly brushed back, shone like bronze; the hard, muscular body, for the first time in years completely free of its excess weight, was relaxed as a sunwarmed animal's. Prime Minister of Prussia. General der Infanterie. Reich Aviation Minister. Reichstag President. Reich Forestry Minister. Reichsmeister of the Hunt. His bare, hairy arms, gilded by the sun, rose in a powerful stretch, followed by a clap to his thighs. He got to his feet.

"Up, up, we take the tour."

"Nein, I've got to get back."

"Nonsense. You'll stay and eat."

"I *won't* stay and eat," Putzi told him, rising, and the snappish little phrase, which was meant to express the depth and vastness of all that he had not said, pushed him suddenly to the brink of tears. He was growing infantile with fatigue, and he lowered his tremulous face as he stood smoothing and straightening his jacket.

"Well, if you can't stay for supper," said Hermann, taking his arm, "at least you've got time for a tour," and Putzi was enthusiastically conducted across the room and out the door. He was glad, at any rate, that the beast did not wake to accompany them.

"Here is where I sleep."

Putzi glanced around the room for an ashtray, having stopped along the hall to light a much-needed cigarette, but he was at once too humiliated by the trembling of his fingers to take another puff. He stubbed the cigarette out in an ashtray standing on a small rococo desk of exquisite workmanship, of gleaming mahogany inset with endless intricacies of bronze scrollwork. It looked as if it might have been lifted right from Frederick the Great's bedroom-study at Sans Souci. Perhaps it had been.

"I read your opus," he remarked, picking up a small red-bound book lying by the ashtray with papers and briefcase.

"Oh? What did you think of it?"

He tossed it down again, an amalgam of brutal candor, deep romantic patriotism, and Party-line claptrap.

"Like your geology—a mixed metaphor."

"Probably," his host agreed, beckoning him to come look at the bed. Canopied, with heavy curtains drawn back, it was a massive piece of furniture with a gloomy, medieval flavor. Hermann stood beaming at it.

"What do you think? Isn't it nice? It's exactly like the one that stood in the master bedroom of my home."

"I'd suffocate in it."

"Here is where I read."

They stood in a large, well-stocked library. Putzi glanced around at German classics, George Bernard Shaw in translation, Karl May's adventure books, books on wildlife, on art, on history. On one wall hung a portrait of Bismarck; on the other, Frederick the Great. There was also a tapestry featuring maidens and unicorns, which Hermann drew his attention to, pointing to one corner which appeared to have been rewoven.

"The only Gobelin I salvaged from the Reichstag fire."

"Such a pity," Putzi replied, wondering if Hermann would launch into his set piece, but he did not. He would be tired of repeating himself by now. A year and a half had passed since the night of that expedient conflagration, supposedly set by Communists as a sign for uprising. It had allowed Hermann to lock up thousands of presumably insurrectionary Reds, while Adolf invoked a state emergency decree suspending personal and civil liberties in order to deal with the alleged crisis; this in turn—with most of the Communist Reichstag deputies imprisoned, and with the support of the crisis-cowed Nationalist and Center parties—giving him a Reichstag majority sufficient for the passing of an Enabling Act which in effect buried the constitution.

For months afterward Hermann would protest to anyone at the drop of a hat, with a wounded expression: I am no arsonist. That is entirely foreign to my nature. And think of the Gobelins that hung in my office—am I likely to have plotted a fire that would destroy my own Gobelins? Of course not! Ridiculous! And now look, we have to hold our sessions at the Kroll Opera House. Don't you suppose as an opera lover I would much rather have left the Kroll to its proper function? Of course I would! They were feeble protests, in contrast to his violent behavior at the trial, during which he screamed insults and threats at the three accused Communist leaders, thereby losing a good deal of prestige, particularly since the three were finally acquitted for lack of evidence: no thread could be found linking them to the Dutch transient who had confessed to the crime, and who, in due course, was separated from his head by an ax—Hermann having revived this medieval and picturesque form of execution. The trial had been murky and inconclusive, but world opinion was not: it laid the crime at Göring's door, and however much he went on about his Gobelins and the Kroll Opera House, he could not deny the underground passage— so convenient for a little dark-of-night arson—that connected his Reichstag President's residence with the Reichstag building. It was the underground passage that had convicted him at the mock trial in London. That had infuriated him. But time had rolled by, and now he apparently limited himself to the sad display of this poor patched tapestry. Yet, as Putzi followed him from the room, looking at the rims of the large ears, and at the nape of the thick neck where the hair grew down to a point, he was very glad that those ears had not gotten wind of the opinion he had so often aired among intimate friends—for he found it hard, as a raconteur, to resist a good session of gossip, although this was an increasingly unwise self-indulgence. "Of course it was Göring. No question about it. No question at all." He had said that many times.

"Here is where I sit and think."

It was a small room with a low wooden ceiling and bare floor, deep-set mullioned windows, and a table and chair of beautiful rustic simplicity. A monk's room.

"*Saint Jerome in his Study*," Putzi commented dryly, and added yet more dryly: "You even own the right prop to complete the scene. I suppose that presence is *de rigueur* while you contemplate?"

"Caesar, you mean?" He gave a laugh, looking at the room. "But I lack the wolf. And the skull."

"Do you?" Putzi murmured.

However, there was no faulting him on his knowledge of Dürer.

"Here is where we come after a shoot."

This being the original hunting box around which the rest of the house was built, a timbered room hung with antlers and hides, bearskins on the floor, a rough-hewn table with benches, a crude field-stone fireplace. An earthy, acrid smell of hides was mixed with a suggestion of grimed boots and sweat-soaked jackets. Hermann's love of hunting had become his trademark. Even in the States, by way of the cover story in *Time*, Hardboiled Hermann—such was the sobriquet—was known for the jovial pleasure he took in leading his titled, polyglot hunting guests into his vast and well-stocked forests. Putzi himself did not hunt and was always hard put to reconcile the dichotomy of hunters, that urge to kill what they seemingly held some kind of strong love for. In Hermann's case, as Reichsmeister of the Hunt, he was in a position to fully satisfy both sides of his nature, richly stocking his private preserve while at the same time outlawing all practices which he deemed cruel and unsportsmanlike. Horse-and-hound hunts, shooting from cars, claw and wire traps, artificial lights to attract quarry, the issuing of licenses to poor marksmen—all these things were now banned by law, and throughout Germany the breaking of these new laws was punished by the harshest penalties. He had also set up regulations protecting work animals, and had in one sweep abolished vivisection. Wer Tiere quält, verletzt das deutsche Volksempfinden—He who tortures animals wounds the feelings of the German people. That was his motto. It hung framed in his Master of the Hunt office.

"And what are your other mottos?" he murmured.

"Wie, bitte?"

"Nothing. I'm dead on my feet, Hermann. I must go."

"Ach, nein, not already?"

They walked on in the direction of the front entrance, going along halls laid with Oriental runners, passing elaborately carved chests, glass-fronted cabinets holding porcelain, and a servant or two in black-and-pale-blue livery; then they turned into a broad parquet-floored hall lined with paintings in heavy gilt frames. Hermann's hand went up, pointing, as they walked.

"Cranach. Cranach. He is my favorite. Hobbema. Guardi. Memling. He is also my favorite. Claesz. Pontormo. Cilly—you remember Cilly? She is head housekeeper now," and he smiled at the girl, who had come stepping out through a door reading a list in her hand.

"Cilly, here is Dr. Hanfstaengl, who sees Carinhall for the first time. Now he meets the one who keeps it all going."

"Doch . . ." she murmured, serious, bashful and adoring, and with a bow at the guest hurried on.

"The country air has done Cilly good. It does everyone good. Altdorfer. Gossaert. Cranach. He is my favorite. They are all my favorites. What a joy it is, Putzi, to track down and purchase for yourself some painting that you have long loved!"

Or else, thought Putzi, to commandeer it as a permanent loan from the Kaiser Friedrich or the Deutsches Museum.

They turned down another hallway, heels ringing on the shining parquet. "And here—slow down!" Putzi felt himself pulled by his arm to an entranceway. "Here you see the banquet hall."

A long gilt-and-pale-green room, tall windows, gold brocade drapes. The table, seating perhaps fifty, stood bare at the moment except for a silver candelabrum and a lovely ink-blue porcelain vase filled with white roses.

"Isn't it nice? And down here . . ." They continued along the hall, meeting more people now, servants, uniformed adjutants, tanned houseguests in casual summer clothing. "Down here—down here, you see—here we are, here you see the reception hall."

It was a room of vast proportions, soaring as high as the nave of a church. Tasteful contemporary furniture stood about on an immense expanse of Oriental carpet. Along the sides of the room, lined with low, brass-studded rustic chairs, the hardwood floor was bare and shining. There were few decorations: two great tapestries, a life-size wooden Madonna and Child. The massive fireplace and the walls were white, and the walls, in keeping with Hermann's eccentric architectural ideas, slanted gradually inward as they soared, creating a pyramidic shape crossed by a series of dark wooden beams. From the very top there hung down below the beams two great chandeliers like silver wheels, like huge silver bracelets. It was all curiously well integrated, which fact shone from Hermann's face as he stood gazing in at it from the entryway. Lifting his hand in a wave to guests at the far end of the room, he turned and proceeded with Putzi toward the big double doors.

"Now you must see the animals," he said as they stepped out into the courtyard.

"I'm too tired, I can't walk another step."

"You don't have to, I'll stick you in the dogcart."

"I don't want you to stick me in your dogcart. I want to go home."

"But you should see them, Putzi, and the fowl—I've got every kind. You should see the falcons! Come on, I'll stick you in the dog-cart."

"I'm telling you I'm too tired!"

"All right. But there is one last thing that you must see. I want you to. It's not far."

Putzi felt relief at coming back up the steps of the crypt, having endured two or three minutes of the gloomed chill while Hermann stood lost in his own thoughts. They walked slowly back across the clearing, past the great stone menhirs, in the same silence that had prevailed in the tomb. There Hermann's mind seemed to remain. He suddenly looked his forty years, middle-aged, hands joined behind his back, head lowered as he walked slowly along. At the edge of the trees, he turned and stood looking back.

"I'm sorry you couldn't come to the interment. It was a very beautiful ceremony."

Putzi nodded as they turned and walked into the woods; but from what he had read and heard, he was not sorry that he had been abroad at the time. It was a state funeral, with all the heavy, traditional pomp of such occasions, and a good deal more. Ceremonies had begun in the Baltic, where Hermann rode out in a boat to meet the steamer bearing Carin's casket from Sweden; then came a railway trip, the entire train bedecked with wreaths and greenery, which ended with a ceremony at Eberswald railway station—flaming torches in black obelisks, a military band playing "March Funèbre" as the casket was lowered into an open horse-drawn cart; then a long procession to Carinhall, the flower-strewn caisson followed by a convoy of mounted Reichswehr officers, followed in turn by a cortège of black funeral cars, along roads lined with solemn countryfolk. Finally, in the little clearing by the lake, came the interment ceremony itself; more torches, a muffled rolling of drums as the casket was carried in by eight helmeted soldiers, a Lutheran graveside service, and at the very end, the ancient, doleful cry of a hundred hunting horns sounding from the opposite shore.

"We're strange creatures, we human beings," Hermann murmured, as they walked along. "Ceremonies, wreaths . . . we're like children. We believe, we're obedient . . ."

Putzi nodded. "I suppose it's true."

"It's true."

They were again silent, in the softly crackling sound of pine needles underfoot, and Putzi felt something untightening in him, as if his companion's quiet, philosophic mood were somehow restoring the old familiarity between them. The woods were still. Broad shafts of sun fell through the trees.

"This is everything that Carin would have loved. I come down here, I walk through these trees . . . and sometimes, Putzi, I feel her hand in mine."

"I'm glad for you," Putzi said, remembering the stark, inconsolable wretchedness of the man when he had expressed himself once, and only once, about Carin's having died without him, without his hand around hers.

"You were always a good friend, Putzi . . . you were always our good friend. Carin would be sorry to know we had drifted apart. I'm sorry too."

"And I."

"Perhaps it can't be helped."

"Perhaps not. Perhaps we're just too different."

"I suppose that's so. You were always the Questenberg in the camp. Well, that's your nature . . . everyone has his own nature. Only you shouldn't gossip so much, Putzi. You shouldn't tell people I set fire to the Reichstag."

Putzi's eyes swung to the profile beside him.

"Believe what you like, only don't talk about me behind my back. Well, now you've seen most of what there is to see," he went on in the same quiet tone. "If you were going to stay longer, we could take a walk around the lake. You used to be a great walker, you old horse box. Do you remember when you went from Vienna to Munich for Christmas? In your dark glasses and muttonchop whiskers? And walked across the border?"

Putzi nodded, with a feeling of deep relief. "Rather. It was freezing. Snow to my knees."

"It was a terrific snow that year."

"We had all the luck that year."

"It could have been worse."

"I don't see how."

"I don't either. Well, you could have been arrested as an escaped lunatic."

"Not at all. Carin said I looked fetching."

"Carin would." Hermann smiled.

Those early days, and all the experiences they had shared, seemed to join them in warmth as they walked along, and Putzi felt the great rankling unsaid thing inside him freeing itself, and coming out in a quietly spoken question.

"How could it have happened, Hermann?"

Hermann gave a silent shake of his head.

"Here. In Germany. This is what I can't grasp. Not in some godforsaken jungle, but here."

"It happened. It could not be avoided."

"You've changed Germany now. You've changed Germany forever."

"Don't overdo it."

"I'm not overdoing it. Something has been broken. Defiled."

"You must know I regret it," Hermann said, stopping and turning to him, so that they stood facing each other. "I regret it, Putzi. I will tell you that. I regret it deeply."

"That's hardly enough."

Hermann stood looking at him a moment longer.

"It will have to be enough," he said shortly, turning and going on.

Putzi, swallowing the rest, followed him with a footcrunch of pine needles.

His dark blue roadster was parked by the north wing of the house, not far from where they emerged from the woods. He was glad to see it, for he felt much more exhausted than when he had arrived, and at the same time furious with himself, confused, and anxious to be alone. He nodded without reply as Hermann, again the cordial host, pointed at a flowering lime tree. "You must smell it," he said, taking his guest by the arm. Putzi smelled it. "And I put flowering hawthorn here," he went on as they walked down the broad sandy path alongside the build-

ing, "and birches too, you see," he said, pointing, but Putzi did not
look. They came to where the car was parked. "Well, so our tour is
over. You didn't like any of it."

"I'm tired, that's all."

"Nein, it's true. You didn't say one nice thing. Ah well, I'm glad
you came anyway, Putzi," he said, smiling and shaking hands. "Next
time stay longer."

But in spite of the smile he looked disappointed, like a child whose
great surprise has been a dismal failure. And in spite of everything, as
Putzi recalled the bursting pride and joy with which he had been
dragged from one room to another, he suddenly could not bear to
leave him standing there like that.

"I thought it was beautiful," he said as he climbed in behind the
wheel. "Wonderful, all of it."

His host's smile expanded, his whole face brightened. "Well, it's
not a bad little place," he said over the sound of the motor, and he
stood waving as the car pulled away.

"Auf Wiedersehen, Putzi!"

Chapter 33

T HE roadster shot along through the rapid alternation of tunneled green and flooding brilliance. Only when the driver heard a frantic blare and swerved around an oncoming red Bugatti was he startled into awareness of his fatigue and preoccupation, and in a seemingly endless deceleration brought the car to a standstill at the side of the road.

In the green, rustling silence he closed his eyes, but he was too boxed-in and uncomfortable to doze. He brought out his cigarettes only to put them away again, denied even that small comfort, for to light one was punishable by jail. The Reichsminister of Forests was very serious about his work. He had set up drastic regulations for the prevention of fires. He had also pushed scientific research to come up with a chemical spray that was doing away with parasitic grub growths. He had passed special laws to protect ferns, bushes and trees in danger of becoming extinct. He had put irrigation schemes into effect, had inaugurated plans for the manufacture of synthetic products from wood pulp, had planted green recreational belts around industrial cities and a thousand square miles of new trees from the Baltic to Austria, and had made jobs for hundreds of thousands of the unemployed, who were now building hutments and barracks, making roads, digging dikes, learning woodcraft and lumbering.

The unbelievable energy of the man, Putzi thought as he climbed stiffly from the car and plodded in among the trees, looking for a spot where he could stretch out. The unbelievable energy . . . too bad it isn't limited to trees and animals. Still, he's had to accept some limits. Some amputations, in fact. I'd have given money to see his face the day his camps were incorporated into Röhm's and Himmler's. Not that it was a great day for his inmates, either, though you could hardly say they were living it up in holiday resorts. Rehabilitation Centers for the Politically Misguided, that was farfetched enough. Still, you had to grant they weren't like the illegal camps. The rumors were substantially different. Now the illegal camps are the legal ones, and the only ones, and the rumors are all alike. Such as lowering the testicles into boiling water, peeling off the skin, and lowering them into iodine. No, throw that one out, with rumors you have to use some judgment. Not that the credible rumors aren't bad enough. But should I congratulate him for having broken only a few heads? Look what he's opened up. That seems to be the fate of all his brainstorms. The camps, the Geheime Staatspolizei, the purge. He sets things up and swings them into motion, and they go swinging out of his hands into little Heinrich's. Why does everyone call him little Heinrich? He's of normal height. It's a mistake to call someone little who isn't little. It means you see them as little and treat them as little, and if they're not little but you think they are, it means you've been hoodwinked, it means they wish to be little, little enough to slip through keyholes, which is what they do. . . .

The beech trunks around him were thick and smooth, silverish, and rose like pillars into the thick rustling of leaves above, from which fell chinks and pencils of sunlight, sharp as metal in the cool aquatic gloom. It was too damp to lie down. His trouser cuffs were wet from brushing through dewed ferns. Blowing out a deep sigh, he turned and began plodding back to the car.

Not that you could have fallen asleep anyway. You won't sleep until you've done what you should have done a long time ago.

I tell you I'm tired of going over it. I've made my decision. If we moderates all jumped out of the boat, who would be left to provide a voice of reason? It's a matter of duty. I've gone over it and over it, I've discussed it with Schacht, I've discussed it with Neurath—

And if you take your dutiful friend Schacht and boil down that long intellectual neck and that nostril-quivering contempt for the Party, what have you got left? A broker with one client, Germany. Who doesn't mind hanging a diamond Hakenkreuz on his wife's bosom for Chancellery soirées. And what of Neurath? How long has the good Neurath been a member of the diplomatic corps? Since the Kaiser was young? Doesn't that create a slight habit? Wouldn't you say the baron would rather lose an eye and an arm than spend his sunset years pruning roses in his garden? And what of Hanfstaengl? Hanfstaengl is addicted too. Hanfstaengl loves being at the center of things, he craves it, he laps it up, he loves the excitement, the throb of power, and above all he loves knowing things, because above all Hanfstaengl is a gossip. In the field of gossip, there lies *his* particular vanity and ambition. Reich Raconteur! Aflame with the glory of the inside track! Take a good look, Hanfstaengl, that's what you boil down to.

You'd better give me more credit than that. Vanity, ambition— you'd better throw out every great statesman, every great soldier, every great patriot who has ever lived. Vanity and ambition have never precluded love of country. Listen to me, I have always worked to do the best for my country. I have not ceased and will never cease to be a voice of reason.

Are you joking? What are these delusions of grandeur? Since when have you had a voice? The last time you dented Adolf's consciousness was when he got rid of his celluloid collar back in 'twenty-three. Why are you still with him? You should have resigned after the Enabling Act. What good did it do to hang on? Why didn't you resign after the camps were set up? After the Jewish boycott? After the book-burning? Devour, flames! How much clearer does something have to be? You said back there to Hermann that you couldn't grasp how this purge had happened. What is there to grasp? It was perfectly logical in terms of what preceded it. What is there to grasp, you blockhead? That's right, keep plodding in circles, now you can't even find your way back to the road.

The beech forest had imperceptibly merged into a forest of pines mixed with old gnarled oaks. His feet and calf muscles ached, he was sweating heavily, yet at the same time felt chilled. In the vast green dimness, he took a handkerchief from his pocket and blotted his brow. He tried to be calm. After a few moments he chose a new direction and set off again.

You're a jackass, Putzi. You have an unfailing instinct for the ridiculous. Six months from now they'll find your bones scattered among these trees just because you felt like a snooze. Just because you had to come out here to Carinhall in the first place. What did you think you'd accomplish? Whatever it was, you gave a sodden performance. What were you afraid of? Why didn't you open your mouth? He told you to speak out.

Speak out? Just to be shouted down? What was the point? I spoke when I knew I would be heard.

That's right, when the nostalgia and sentimentality were so thick they oozed. Then it was finally safe to venture a few words. Very few, as it turned out. Hardly enough—but they'll have to be enough. Tell me what you were afraid of, Hanfstaengl. Did you really think he'd turn you into one of those misnomered suicides that keep cropping up in the obituaries? You know that's not him, it's the one who goes through keyholes. You didn't have to fear for your skin. What was it, then? He's become a very powerful man, despite those amputations you like to dwell on. Maybe you weren't prepared for that quality of power. Was that it? Almost tangible, wasn't it? Tingling in the air around him. In such close quarters maybe you were dazzled by that five-rank leap from captain to general? No? You say you're not impressed by Hindenburg's promotions? Well, maybe in such close quarters you found it off-putting to look upon that magnet of manly sobriquets. The Iron Man. The Prussian of Prussians. Hitler's Fist. Hardboiled Hermann. Not too strong a glare for your eyes? You say, what glare? You say he was perfectly pleasant, except when he shouted. Yes, that was unpleasant. Paralyzing. You say you weren't paralyzed, merely circumspect? That was why you kept your mouth shut all afternoon except for that aborted blurp at the end? I ask you again what you were afraid of. Was it all those things or none of them? And I'll tell you that you don't even know what you're afraid of, because you're afraid of everything. You no longer have any idea of what you can say, where, when, how much, to whom. Your frame of reference has corroded into uncertainty, guardedness, suspicion. You call it circumspection, I call it fear. Even in your candid talks with Schacht and with Neurath, none of you was really all that candid. Weren't you discreet to the point of toe-dancing, of dogs sniffing at each other? You've all degenerated to that level, and now since the purge you're a thousand times worse. Listen to me, there will come a day when you won't feel free to talk openly with anyone, not even your most trusted friends. Drive back now to Berlin and resign. Get out now.

I can only do what I feel is right. I'm obliged, it's my duty. There has to remain some moderating influence.

You keep talking in circles, just as you keep walking in circles. You're lost, you fool. Land of oaks and stupidity—Heine knew of which he spoke.

Nevertheless, he loved that land. As I do.

Not enough to stay, he didn't. But you will. You'll keep stumbling around in circles until you fall down and die under these sacred oaks of yours.

Very amusing, very romantisch . . .

But he was fighting down a sense of panic, so exhausted that every step jolted up through him, as if his knees had locked to bear his weight. With heaving sides he stopped to regain his breath, feeling an overwhelming desire to throw himself down and rest. But he dared not, in case he could not get up again. Yet he was too exhausted to go on. He kept standing as the harshness of his breaths subsided, leaving only silence. And as he stood, he felt the hairs of his neck rising in this dark, vast stillness, which, for all he knew, stretched unbroken to Poland. He closed his eyes, trying to force down a fresh surge of panic, and then opened them with horror, for he thought he heard, very faintly, what seemed to be many voices singing; a celestial choir, a heavenly chorus that was swiftly growing nearer and louder, terribly near and terribly loud as he stood staring around him with horror, and then the singing reached a peak of intensity that made him clutch his head, and then the sound faded by degrees until again there was only silence, and tremblingly he took his hands away.

With a deep sudden sigh of realization, he plunged off to his left, moments later stumbling out onto the gray asphalt, far back along which stood his parked car. He had been walking parallel to the road all the time, but he was too relieved to feel embarrassed, and too weary, and too dazzled by light, for across from him lay a broad, sundrenched clearing of sand and heather. He had to wait a moment before crossing, as another chorus was upon him: a lusty, earsplitting crescendo as the truck passed, singing sunburned faces, blowing hair, hands waving—young forest workers returning from their labors at the close of day. But it was only technically the close of day; summer evenings in the north were long and luminous as morning, and he was already struggling out of his jacket as he plodded across the road.

Collapsing to a sitting position against a lichen-covered rock, he removed his shoes, stockings and garters. His great naked feet throbbed. He stretched his whole stale, aching body and leaned back, closing his eyes, and lay staring into the bright sepia of his shuttered lids.

Of course you can't sleep, I could have told you that. You know what you must do before you'll be able to sleep. Listen to me—

And you listen to me. I'm trying to look coolly and dispassionately at the situation as it now stands. One, the radical socialists are finished. Two, the conservatives are also finished—they thought they had Adolf buttoned into their pocket but instead they're buttoned into his, and in the other pocket he's got the generals. Three, the presidential succession is assured, and should bear fruit very soon, since Hindenburg's practically dead. . . . A dreadful story I heard the other day, somehow it struck me; it was when Adolf last visited him, a week or so ago—he's begun to fail, very dim, his mind wanders, and what I heard was that throughout the visit he addressed Adolf as Your Majesty . . . Majestät, think of it. All cracks are closed, the ground is solid. I don't need Hermann to tell me that. The struggle is over. It's the irony that leaves a bitter taste. Because the purge was the final upheaval of the struggle, and when the dust of the purge settles, it will settle on a very different picture. The head-cracking days will be done with, respectability will set in. The whole regime will turn from its narrow upward struggle to take its place at the table of nations. And with this there is bound to come a broadening, a balancing, a more hopeful climate for those of us who hold moderate views.

If I may be permitted to say something. I thought your great statement to Hermann was that Germany of old has been broken, changed forever.

But to abide by that? To abide without hope? Without hope there is no hope. We who hold to the ideals of our fathers must do all we can, or who will? If the winds are in fact going to change, we must be there to give the helm a decisive touch, and we cannot do that from our rose gardens. This is what I must and will abide by . . . and now, let me have some sleep at last. . . .

Chapter 34

IF, in the deep blue foredawn of September 5 of that year, 1934, a bird had been circling over the old quarter of Nuremberg, and had glided down and settled on some high tower or church spire, it would have sensed nothing unusual from below, no sound or movement in the silence to indicate that the city's population had been swelled overnight by half a million souls. The little River Pegnitz, winding in from the fields and forests of the east, and winding out again to those of the west, still ran black with night, wreathed in mist. The city squares lay empty, their fountains splashing patient and unheard in the cold dark blue air. The mazelike crooked streets, deep-cleft and murky as canyons, were steeped in slumber; down the dark fronts of their old half-timbered buildings ran long black rectangles, immense long banners hanging in the silence, only rippling faintly now and then in the night air, with a faint scraping of cords.

Gradually, as the sky began to pale, there came echoes of footsteps, a voice or two, the grate of a shutter opening, sounds that had already multiplied into a great bustle by the time the sun broke over the horizon, flashing gold across towers and spires, and releasing color from bastions, gateways, statues, from overhanging gables and flowering windowboxes, and from all the immense long banners, heightening to brilliant red. By the time the orb was climbing into clear

brilliant blue, the streets and squares were a mass of humanity and the
bird had long since soared away to some less tumultuous place.

If it had flown over the camping grounds in the outskirts of town
it would have found no calm green sanctuary below, but sixty thousand
swarming dots whose clamor would have sent it speeding on in the
direction of open country, perhaps, on its way, winging over the city
stadium, from which it would have heard nothing at all, for there was
only a handful of dots on the great lozenge-shaped field, the dot at its
center being Herr Speer, standing alone with his hands clasped behind
his back.

It had been Herr Speer's task to replace the old wooden bleachers
with a permanent structure, and to have it finished for this fourth annual National Socialist Party Day Congress. He had built it of white
granite, a broad and mighty flight of stairs not yet given its final height
by the great colonnade he planned, but already its ultimate length,
which was twice that of the Baths of Caracalla, along which workmen
were affixing garlands of fresh green laurel leaves. Even without the
colonnade, it was a magnificent structure: dazzlingly white in the morning sun, flanked by two mammoth granite eagles, and crowned by a
single unit of three red Hakenkreuz banners more than a city block in
height.

Tilting his head back, he gazed into the morning blue, where, during night festivities, pillars of white light would shoot straight up into
the darkness for kilometers, creating the effect of a huge cathedral of
ice. It had been an extraordinary inspiration, but one almost squashed
flat when General Göring had refused him the antiaircraft spotlights
necessary, saying that they constituted the entire strategic reserve. Herr
Hitler, however, had intervened, and all 130 spotlights now stood in
place.

Turning slowly around, he took in the bright encirclement of flags;
then, heeding a call from one of his assistants, he turned and gave a
final look at his edifice twice the length of the Baths of Caracalla and
set off across the field, a tall slender young man not yet out of his
twenties, dark and glossy-haired, with regular features bearing a
mellow, well-bred expression of thoughtful reserve. For today's occasion he had been obliged to put on the brown Party uniform, an outfit
in which, as an architect, an artist, he usually felt acutely uncomfortable; but on this morning he was too busy for that feeling, and too
exhilarated, although his high spirits could be seen only in the long
strides he took across the sunlit expanse, hands still clasped studiously
behind his back.

The week-long festivities, which Herr Speer and so many others
had labored to bring about, were to be recorded by the lenses of a
movie camera. One sequence—that of the Hitler Youth in the camping
grounds, a kaleidoscope of tanned, healthy adolescents involved in ex-

uberant preparations for the day's events—had already been shot, and the filmmaker had now driven back to the old quarter of the city, where she and her assistants were busy setting up their equipment in a thronged little street opposite the Deutscher Hof.

Fräulein Riefenstahl had also filmed the previous year's rally, but since Captain Röhm and Herr Strasser had figured so prominently in so many scenes, the film had been recalled from all cinemas and the entire footage junked. This year's rally in any case was planned on a much grander, an epic, scale, and might well result in a film that was a great work of art. Pulling off her jacket, the morning having grown increasingly warm, she studied the design of light and shade on the flower-garlanded hotel, carefully adjusting the angle of her camera in readiness for the moment when the Führer would step forth from the door.

The Führer would appear later than his young film director or the impatient crowd expected. On great public occasions he conserved himself until the last possible moment. It was as if he drew a shade down before him. He sat reading over some papers at a small table in the bedroom of his pleasant, provincially furnished suite, the sitting room of which was packed with members of his entourage. If he was not unaware of their nearby presence or of the noise in the street, he was indifferent to both.

The crowd outside suddenly glimpsed a window opening, and all heads lifted, seeing the face of the Minister of Propaganda and Enlightenment. There was no increase in the volume of noise, no pointing of fingers or waving of hands. The Minister of Propaganda and Enlightenment did not expect that there would be, for he took professional pride in knowing the exact spot each Party leader occupied in the hierarchy of crowd response. Only the Führer, who was unique, who existed above and beyond all that was ordinary, a remote, austere, ungraspable figure, could throw crowds into frenzies simply by appearing. Göring, too, had tremendous impact, almost as great as the Führer's, but of an entirely different nature; the roars he inspired had nothing frenzied or ecstatic about them, but were a kind of huge rushing flood of fondness, robust and proprietary, almost familial. From Göring's extravagantly high level of popularity there was a good drop to Hess, a well-liked figure who drew his own share of vigorous response. Below Hess came all the others in descending order, with himself, Goebbels, at the bottom.

He struck no response at all in the masses, except when he was delivering a speech. As a creature without words, only a face regarding them, he elicited nothing. For his was a face too much its own, too separate, too intelligent; and very likely, he thought, as he stood looking down at them, they could sense in it how strongly, how deeply, how totally, he despised them.

He stood assessing their level of excitement, which was very high, an emotional climate that promised electric, week-long success. He was not in charge of the rally this year, other duties having crowded it from his grasp, and suddenly he felt himself seized by regret, by a passionate longing that brought rushing back the words he had scrawled in his diary after the first rally—Hitler, loved and gentle shepherd of the flock! Your praise for my pageant at Nuremberg was like honey in the drought of my life! I grovel before thy mighty generosity, the gift of thy thanks, O Führer!—and yet, with a mighty generosity of his own, he felt it mattered not who created the epic about to unfold, as long as it was created for the worship of the Führer.

Filled with this high emotion, he closed and turned away from the window to see that his wife, with characteristic poor timing, had got the clasp of her necklace caught in her hair and had come out of the bedroom to ask his help. Yet he went to her ungrudgingly, almost warmly, and with gentle fingers worked at the clasp. The wall of ice between them was melting away here at Nuremberg. He knew, of course, that it would form again afterward, for she bored him unbearably with her preoccupation with social life; nor did he even enjoy her beauty anymore, that lovely golden glow that turned people's heads, but had come to loathe it, as if somehow its brightness darkened and shriveled him.

What Magda herself felt, she never said, for they discussed nothing. But she was a simple woman, and wronged daily, and he saw clearly enough that she hated him; hated him with a simple, wronged woman's hatred, at once wounded and hard, an expression in the eyes that put him in mind of rained-on rock.

But since arriving at the hotel yesterday they had entered upon a truce, all differences bridged by this time, this place, this celebration whose keystone, heart and pinnacle were the Führer. That they both loved Hitler more than they had ever loved each other was the bond that made him adjust the necklace gently on her smooth neck, and her turn to him with shining eyes. Then she was hurrying back to her dressing table for a few last touches, and he was returning to the window and opening it again to the roaring of the crowd.

A few doors down the street, in a small bar filled with British and American newspaper correspondents, Foreign Press Chief Hanfstaengl, attired in the outfit that had earned him the nickname "the Chocolate Soldier"—a beautifully tailored uniform of magnificent dark brown English gabardine, set off by gold buttons and delicate gold epaulets—was catching up on the latest American gossip from some of his more warmly disposed journalist friends. He had given offense the night before, especially to those correspondents fresh to Germany, when, at the official press gathering, he had urged them to draw inspiration from the moss-covered moats and dreamy portals and splashing fountains of Nuremberg, and to report on affairs in Germany without trying to interpret them, since history alone could evaluate the events now taking place under Hitler. The newcomers were not used to this mixture of romanticism and arrogance; they had found it odious and were not disposed to exchange pleasantries with the towering hulk in his operetta costume as he leaned against the counter, chatting and sipping from a glass of beer. But their more seasoned colleagues, who had come to know him well, understood that his personal attitudes did not necessarily correspond to those he expressed officially; in private, the small shrugs and eyebrow lifts and oblique comments were his form of detached criticism, and communicated the patient irony of a man doing his civilized best by a post which, after all, might well have been filled by some doctrinaire slogan-slinger. In their wry, pragmatic way, the journalists were appreciative of this fact; they were grateful to their Putzi, who was at least urbane and witty, and spoke perfect colloquial American—which was being shouted at the moment; everyone had begun shouting in order to be heard over the noise of the crowd outside, some of whose backs were pressed like sardines against the bar's well-polished, lace-curtained windows.

One of the backs, clad in a sober, square-cut suit long out of fashion, belonged to Hans Schmidt, who had lost Nikki somewhere along the way. Being short, thin and old, he was having a hard time extricating himself from his squashed situation while holding high his hat for Nikki to see, wherever she was. They should not have come. But Nikki had wanted to see what was going on. What was going on was a lot of pushing and yelling, and he was not much for that, being a quiet sort and getting on for sixty-seven as well. But Nikki was only sixty-three, and still chipper as they made them. Doubly chipper since their visit to Carinhall. A grand visit, even though he had felt out of place. But no side to their host; you wouldn't know he was Prime Minister of Prussia. Downright and jolly, full of pep—bighearted too, always was, look at Nikki's handsome pension. Showed them a really grand time, and Nikki had lived high on it ever since they got back, Hermann this, Hermann that, Hermann the next. Epenstein too—still a big subject with her, even though he was no longer of this world. He had died earlier in the year, and it was very hard, she said, to have to listen to Hermann reminisce over him. Hermann had always been fond of the old horror, but she herself had better judgment, although of course she did not say so to Hermann, for it was wrong to correct another's sorrow. "Nevertheless, Hans, it was hard to have to sit there listening. For I disliked Epenstein greatly, as I have mentioned more than once, and believe me I let him know it. If there was one thing he knew, it was where he stood with Nikki." It was wonderful, really, Nikki's energy to chew on the same thing over and over. Never wound down, whereas he never wound up . . . not the sort to enjoy being squashed in a yelling mob. But Nikki wanted to see Hermann in the motorcade. Hitler she didn't care about. As for himself, he would rather be working in his garden.

His large white mustaches were becoming twisted and ruffled as he kept laboriously wedging himself forward, still holding his hat high and at intervals uttering "Entschuldigen Sie, bitte, entschuldigen," although nothing could be heard above the din. And what was all this din about? He should know if anyone on this sidewalk should know— three days a guest at Carinhall, and would be sitting today in the honored guests' section of the stadium. Amazing, when you thought of it. Still, he had no clue to the fuss around him, he felt separate from it. He'd been disappointed when Hitler became head of state. Many people thought right up to the last minute that they would have a monarch again. It was a letdown. Not that he didn't give Hitler credit for a few things. The way he squashed those brownshirt brutes on the eve of their revolt, that was good work. And it was good work that the Jews were being taken down a peg or two. But that a low sort like Streicher was still allowed to run around publishing Schweinerei and cracking his whip, that was not good work. Nor did he take to all this saluting either, every last person in the country having to stick out an arm when they greeted each other, that was tiresome and embarrassing, and he noticed no one bothered with it at Carinhall. Still, you couldn't deny that there was a lot more order now, and cleaner streets and better services. But on the streets radio loudspeakers were forever blaring political speeches. That was not orderly, that was noisy and upsetting. On the other hand, what did any of these annoying things amount to when you considered that the country was being put back on its feet? People had jobs, food on their tables. That was the important thing. On the other hand, why couldn't they have jobs and a monarch too?

Suddenly there was Nikki's furled pistachio-green parasol sticking into the air just ahead of him, and with glad hoots of reunion, waving their beacons, they pressed on toward each other.

A few kilometers to the west, Göring's open gray Mercedes was speeding toward Nuremberg from the country estate of friends where he always put up during the congress. Sitting next to Kropp, he was dressed in the drab biscuit-brown uniform of the Old Fighters, which was *de rigueur* during these six days. Only for the Armed Forces Review would he be in feldgrau. He looked forward to that, but to little else in this annual marathon of rallies, speeches, meetings, processions. He took no part in the beery socializing among the Old Fighters, attended only the functions that required his presence, and each day departed as early as possible from the jammed city with its plethora of brown, its stifling sense of the Party wherever you turned. Nuremberg was no place for a mass gathering. It was a medieval town, its streets were too small. It was a matter of annoyance to him that this annual affair was not held in his own bailiwick, Prussia; Berlin was the logical place for it. But Berlin lacked the historical mystique. Nuremberg could be plucked endlessly of plums, like a fruitcake. One of last year's plums was an oversized print of *Ritter, Tod und Teufel,* presented to Adolf in an elaborate ceremony after which the picture was projected onto a screen and its heroic symbolism explained at length, with the aid of a pointer.

His blouse under the tight Sam Browne belt flapped in the wind, while below his brown kepi his hair whipped, drawing a squint from Kropp. But it was only an empty habit, for the valet had come to realize that all the old Heldenflieger, bald Udet included, had a built-in resistance to barbers; it was a carryover from those scruffy silk-pajama days of daredevil glory, and what could one do against that? One was inclined to give up, and take comfort in the heroic source of the growth.

Kropp turned off the narrow country road and barreled down the highway; at the start of his service he had tended to drive too slowly, but had soon learned never to go moderately when it was possible not to, and to make generous use of the siren in cutting a path through heavy traffic. He doubted if there would be need for the siren today, since every suburban thoroughfare leading into Nuremberg was prohibited to ordinary vehicles. Five or ten minutes and they would be there, and Kropp would be glad, for he ended every journey with the depleted sense of having run a racecourse.

It was unlikely, Göring was thinking, but not impossible . . . a risk, but no way to avoid it: fifty thousand brownshirts with Adolf standing before them. It was essential that Adolf address them, that he show publicly that he was master of the SA and that unity had been restored. But was it true? Who knew but that those massed thousands might not be united by a passion to avenge their slain leaders? And if so, who could guarantee Adolf's life? Certainly an uprising seemed unlikely . . . but unlikeliness was only a point of view. One should remember that for those on whom the purge was sprung, it must have seemed not only unlikely but beyond the realm of imagination.

And that little Austrian swine Dollfuss! Why did he have to get himself shot just as the dust of the purge was settling? It had kicked up another international howl of outrage . . . the bloodied little corpse was a handy club to hit Adolf over the head with . . . as if they were likely to instigate an Austrian purge before they had even recovered from their own. It would have been one thing if the Austrian National Socialists had managed a real coup, but the assassination was extreme, unnecessary, the whole action a piece of bungling incompetence.

Germany's own procedure would be very different. They were in no great hurry about Austria. She had wanted union with Germany since the end of the war, had voted for it and been overruled by the Versailles dictators. It was only a matter of waiting for the propitious moment, and all would unfold peacefully and joyously. But as far as the foreign press was concerned, one sniff of blood and off it went with its howls of *furor Teutonicus*. It was aggravating in its untimeliness, since the chief aim of this congress, this first great gathering since the consolidation of the regime, was to express to the world Germany's desire for peace both in its own land and abroad.

And that other little swine, Goebbels. Now was a time for rebuilding, for constructive activity, and where did that leave him? He only knew how to attack and tear apart. That was where he shone—blazed. And how was he to continue blazing when there were no political opponents left to attack? Yet the weaker his limelight, the sharper his incisors. So there you were with his teeth clamped into your back, and into Emmy's too. The delicate fellow was shocked to death by their liaison. That the Prime Minister of Prussia went about openly with his mistress—shamelessly, brazenly—where in this scandalous behavior were the principles of personal decency which the Party upheld? No, it was too much for Goebbels, he all but foamed at the mouth with outraged sensibilities. Fortunately to no effect, since Adolf was fairly broad-minded sexually . . . for which Goebbels should consider himself very lucky. Still, it was galling to know that Emmy's absence at the rally would be construed as a major Goebbels victory, when in fact it was due to her rehearsals at the Berlin Staatstheater.

He was pulled from his vexed thoughts by the low groan of the siren starting up. And as the streets grew peopled, as he caught the first strong whiff of excitement, as cries broke out and arms waved in a flurry of welcome, he began brightening and beaming. The car had reached the West Tower Gate, and was rolling through a crowd which was exuberantly parting and shouting, "Der Dicke! Der Dicke! Unser Hermann!" He swept off his kepi and waved it as everything grew noisier and happier yet—people grabbing onto the screaming car, running alongside it cheering as it made its way through the great ancient gate into the old quarter and the heart of the tumult.

Another thirty minutes passed. The crowds lining both sides of the deep-cleft little streets, clamorous and impatient, craning their necks in the direction of the Deutscher Hof, grew louder with every minute. Suddenly a cavalcade of open cars came into view. The noise heightened to a deafening roar, flowers began flying through the air, and the police guards spread out their arms to hold back the pressure of bodies.

Under the rain of flowers, sitting erect in his brown Party uniform, the Führer wore a small contained smile, just touched with jauntiness, as he turned his face from one side of the roar to the other, at intervals extending his arm in salute. Now and again there would be an ecstatic surge against the guards' strained, outspread arms. As the motorcade turned onto Königsstrasse, a joyous flood of bodies broke through, rushing past the guards, who, pushed and buffeted, their own faces wreathed in smiles, tried uselessly to hold them back. Thronging around the Führer's car, which had come to a stop, they pushed one against the other, mostly women and girls. Their faces were rapturous, many ran with tears, temples were clutched frenziedly; then they were all being shepherded back to their places, all but one woman who was being helped up from the cobblestones, having either fainted from emotion or, in a spirit of hysterical sacrifice, tried to throw herself beneath the wheels. Then she too, casting back a wild, tear-stained look, was returned to the crowd, and the motorcade moved on through the roaring and the shower of petals, which had not ceased in the interim.

Except for one afternoon of drizzle, the fine weather held all week. Sunlight flooded down on flowered dresses and the embroidered frocks of children, on white linen suits and tweed knickerbockers, on the dark cutaways of foreign dignitaries, on folk costumes of every bright hue, on brown uniforms and black and on their medals, badges and scabbards; on gorgets and gonfalons, on eagles, Hakenkreuze, flags, and long banners, and on gold-tasseled trumpets swinging skyward in piercing fanfare; it flooded down on the superb drummers of the horse-mounted Reichswehr band, their great kettledrums mounted on either side of the saddle, their arms swinging high in swift, elaborate parabolas between each thundering cadence; and on the youngest drummers, those of the Hitler Youth, who proved themselves masters of the fiery tattoo, the cheeks of their small faces shaking with the vigor of their attack. There was a pervasive rapturous vigor, something dazzling and highly charged, and the Riefenstahl could be seen everywhere capturing it.

Goebbels having soon recovered from the fit of magnanimity that had overcome him in his hotel room, Fräulein Riefenstahl was beset by the bewildering problem of brownshirts tearing up her camera stations. But she quickly hit on the idea of having her crew dress in the SA uniform, which caused sufficient confusion for the harassment to cease. With similar ingenuity she dealt with each technical difficulty as it arose, feeling herself keyed into high, unremitting inspiration, over and over capturing the brilliant spirit of youth which was the leitmotif of the congress. At the Hitler Youth rally her camera moved with loving gratification among the rows of cleanly chiseled, tanned young faces, serious and uplifted beneath the carrying passion of their Führer's words.

"We wish you German boys and girls to absorb in your mind all that we expect of Germany in times to come. We want to be a peace-loving people, but also brave. We want our people to be honor-loving, and that is why you must learn the concept of honor. We want a people

that is not soft, but hard as flint. We shall pass on, but Germany will
live in you. You are the flesh of our flesh, blood of our blood! . . ."

The Riefenstahl was much interested in bodies, in those that were
tanned, lithe, smoothly muscular, and she found ample opportunity to
film the regime's craze for physical fitness, for there were always gymnastic exhibitions in progress. She was less interested in paunchy middle-aged men delivering speeches. She filmed them duly, but many
wound up on the cutting-room floor. She also scissored out as a matter
of course all anti-Semitic harangues, considering them jarring and unartistic.

The day she filmed Hitler's address to the SA she was aware of an
electric tension around the speakers' stand. The line of guards had
been doubled. She trained her camera on Hitler's face as he took the
rostrum, and saw a tautness around his eyes, though his stance was
bold, as was his voice. The tension remained almost palpably in the air
throughout his entire speech, during which he referred to the purge as
a black shadow that had crossed the National Socialist movement but
had left it more united than before. In his harsh, carrying voice, with
its timbre of absolute certainty, he concluded:

". . . comrades, I give you new flags, convinced that I am giving
them to the most faithful hands in Germany. You have in the past
proved your faith a thousand times, and it *cannot* and *will not* be different in the future! And so I greet you, my old and faithful Storm
Troopers! Sieg Heil!"

Only then was the long tension broken, as there came a returning
roar of fifty thousand voices.

"Sieg Heil!—Sieg Heil!—Sieg Heil!—"

Visitors from other countries, many of them, found the continual
roars unsettling, as they did the phenomenon of outstretched arms.
Old arms, smooth youthful arms, children's little arms. Extended with
flat-palmed rigidity, in the old Roman style. When foreigners observed
this imperial salute exchanged between passing matrons or slips of
schoolchildren, it seemed peculiar enough, but to behold it expressed
by massed thousands of such arms, all straight as lances, accompanied
by those deafening roars of *Heil Hitler!*—this went beyond peculiarity
to something that shook the senses, and there were those foreigners
who felt themselves seized and swept up like chips, as if into a vortex,
and began to *heil* and *heiled* until their throats were raw and their arms
ached; and of these some felt only embarrassment afterward, others
were angry with themselves, and others yet, with radiant astonishment,
felt themselves reborn.

The power of the roar was great in the streets, and was great inside the meeting halls, but it was greatest at the stadium. When half a
million people gave voice to *Ein Volk!—Ein Reich!—Ein Führer!* it was a

sound that rose slow and vast, like a gigantically amplified groundswell, so multitudinous and monolithic at once, so colossal, so prolonged, that it seemed it must be reaching the heavens themselves. And at night the heavens were reached by blazing white beams of light. Herr Speer's 130 columns, soaring straight up into the darkness, created an ice-cathedral even more awesome than its creator had dared hope. And inside this cathedral, on its floor, were the lights of fires everywhere: red tongues leaped from braziers and sconces, ceremonial torches were carried in pagan scenes of flaring, wind-swept flames and swirling smoke. And out in the campgrounds was the blaze of hundreds of bonfires, and in the dark skies over the city were magnificent fireworks, and one night there was a great torchlight parade which seemed, from the crowded heights of the Castle Hill, a slow-rolling river of molten, bright-bubbling lava.

The sun disappeared on Army Day. But in spite of the drizzle a crowd of three hundred thousand filled the stadium, for this was the first time military exercises were to be performed at a Party Day Congress, and the first time since the signing of the Versailles Treaty that people would be able to see a large contingent of their army in action.

Although the weapons consisted only of those small defensive arms permitted by Versailles, there was little doubt in the minds of the crowd, including those of foreign dignitaries and correspondents, that the forbidden kinds existed as well: tanks, heavy artillery, airplanes. Meanwhile, as helmeted cavalry galloped past the green-garlanded reviewing stand, in which could be seen the brightly observing, turning faces of the Führer, General Göring, the Reichswehr Commander, and the Minister of Defense; as galloping horses pulled swiftly rolling, rough-jouncing field cannon behind them; as mock battles and artillery demonstrations unfolded; as stab-stepping troops paraded to the sharp, sunny tempo of fifes and Glockenspiele, bassoons and trumpets—as all these things followed one upon the other, the stadium's roar reached heights surpassing any that had been heard on previous days, became a veritable fury of exultation that finally drove the foreign dignitaries to press their hands to their ears.

Hans Schmidt, too, put his hands over his ears. Next to him, under her damp pistachio-green parasol, Nikki was utterly beside herself, pounding her foot and screaming *Bravo!* and *Hurrah!* as her eyes flew from flags to slamming boots to Hermann's feldgrau figure in the reviewing stand, his face beaming above the massed splendor of his decorations. But Hans Schmidt, who was not one to shout or to enjoy the sound of shouting, sat silent with his hands over his ears. It seemed to him that everything he had grown up with and knew and understood had been swept into darkness that November of 1918, as with a finger snap, and that now before him, as if with another finger snap, it had all been swept back, unbelievably—his Germany of old, her splendor and power and joy—and though he sat silently with his hands pressed to his ears, tears of pride and happiness were coursing down his stolid, contorted old face into his great white mustache.

Finally there was the Great Parade through the old quarter. The Führer reviewed the marchers from his flower-garlanded open car, standing for long stretches with his arm thrust out, then snapping back his hand to his chest. From time to time, his thumb hooked over his belt, he would chat with uniformed officals who stood around the car, or he would throw a greeting to someone among the marchers; then cries could be heard from the crowd: "Look, the Führer smiles!" "Look, the Führer laughs!" "Look, the Führer waves his hand!" After a while he would thrust out his arm again, for as long as a quarter of an hour at a time. There were stories that he wore a collapsible spring device under his sleeve to achieve this feat, but the stories were false; the straight, unwavering arm was the product of the same will that had brought him to this moment—to this endless column of marchers, this massed and ceaseless roar, these flowers strewn before him so thickly that they blanketed the cobblestones.

For six hours the groups marched by, each in their thousands: the Labor Service with shovels glinting over their shoulders, the Storm Troopers, the SS in their new black uniforms, the League of German Maidens in white, the Hitler Youth, the Reichswehr, and many others. The sun poured down as they marched through the ancient banner-blazoned streets under a rain of flowers. And all the while as they passed their Führer, all facing smartly right, there was the roaring, the music, and the magnificent Stechschritt of the military groups, the high, stiff slamming-down of boots in perfect, thousandfold unison.

Dusk fell, the moon rose. There was a final grandiose display of fireworks. There was a farewell serenade of folk songs for the Führer, who stood at the open window of his hotel room. And there was a good deal of Stiftkeller carousing among the Old Fighters, which lasted well into the small hours.

After which, over the streets and squares of the old city, there once again descended the pure, ink-blue silence of foredawn.

Chapter 35

T HE night was clear, with a moon just rising, and so still that it seemed unearthly. The little lake lay almost frozen, in a pale gray encroachment from around its edges. You could almost hear the ice particles forming, the slow, relentless increment making a faint clicking sound, like a ghostly tremble of glasses on a tray. Then again there was only silence, and the dizzying sky—incredibly vast, pierced everywhere by stars. Across the lake the steep thatched roof, white with snow, bulked against the sky's glitter. Masses of white lay tumbled on the terrace and enveloped the trees along the lake, turning them to a cliff of chalk.

Göring had ordered the weather for this first Sunday in Advent. So he said, and it could not be more perfect, the mantle of white and the clear starry sky. He had had the drapes removed from the windows of the reception hall, so that the beauty of the night could be seen without impediment. Inside, the chandeliers were unlit, and at one end of the room stood an enormous tree lit by hundreds of candles and strung with slender chains of white lilies; red Advent candles, set in circlets of holly and berries, glowed in the soft ambience of lamps; thick boughs of fir decorated the walls, a great fire leaped in the fireplace.

Frau Rigele, Göring's sister, was greeting the arriving guests, for the host was not present. Where was the host? The host had vanished.

People stood admiring the tree, conversing in quiet tones—members of the diplomatic corps, various state secretaries, high-ranking members of the unofficial Luftwaffe, their wives, sons, daughters. Everyone turned as a cloaked and hooded figure, heavy staff in hand, came in through a side door and progressed through much merriment and clapping. A few moments later there emerged from the garb of the Weihnachtsmann a radiant Göring greeting and shaking hands with everyone: the vital spark—now everything sprang to life. A musician in evening clothes struck up a medley of carols on the grand piano, people sank into sofas and armchairs conversing with animation, footmen glided among them with silver trays of champagne glasses.

The event of the evening was to be a concert of Christmas hymns performed by the Berlin State Opera Chorus, and presently the choristers came in and gathered before the tree. Guests who had been standing seated themselves, conversation died away. There was a space of silence, then the voices rose, rose in such a purity of beauty that tears came to the eyes of the audience.

After the concert, Fräulein Korwan, in a white satin gown, a tiara of pearls in her bright chestnut hair, took her place before the tree to recite Christmas poems. Her voice, soft yet rich, filled the room with words so old and familiar and moving that again eyes grew moist before the fall of silence, the ardent clapping of hands. Then the chandeliers came on in a flood of brilliance, the pianist struck up his carols, people began rising and drifting over to the refreshment table.

At some point in the evening, Thomas von Kantzow left the party and slipped outside. Each breath he took stabbed his backbone, came out in white smoke. He was bent over with shivering, his hands ached, he brought them to his mouth and breathed on them. One of his aunts had once said they were a surgeon's hands, but he had no desire to cut people up. Someone else had once said they were a musician's hands. Closer, that. He played the piano, a little. And sketched, a little. Wrote, a little. His father and grandfather had been army officers, but he had never felt a calling in that direction. He felt no calling in any direction. In the new year he was going into a Stockholm business firm as a clerk . . . and if he was freezing to death, what of it? The sorrow that had been there for him all evening, just beneath the surface, pulled him on, a wound breaking open at the most beautiful, soaring moments, the grief of his mother lying under the snow in the darkness, away from the songs and warmth. It was cruel of God to make the dead so lonely.

When he finally reached the tomb, he was startled to see someone standing there.

"You should know better, Thomas, a good Norseman like you."

Holding something out, an overcoat. He took it with hands so stiff and shaking so hard that he could not put it on. Hermann helped him with it. He was blurred and fragmented in the bits of ice around Thomas's eyes. "I saw you leave," Hermann said, pulling up the heavy coat collar. He smoothed the frosted, windblown hair back from Thomas's forehead, and gave a small, rough pat to his cheek. Then he took him down the snowy steps of the tomb.

The door closed behind them. The crypt was black, more bitterly cold than the outside, with a deep, close, underground coldness. Thomas heard a match being struck, and in its small light he saw Hermann take from the pocket of his overcoat a red Advent candle. He gave it to Thomas, and from his other pocket brought out greenery. With both shaking hands, Thomas placed the candle on the window ledge. He watched Hermann light it; then together, with care, they arranged the holly and berries around it. The ice prisms in Thomas's eyes were melting. He wiped them with his numb hands. The candle spread a soft, rose-gold light through the small chamber. The pewter casket, in which his mother lay, was suffused by the warm glow.

They stood together quietly for a few moments; then they went out, closing the door gently, in order not to disturb the flame.

4 December, Tuesday. Frau Rigele is Hermann in skirts, he is Frau Rigele in trousers. Twins, except she's not so stout. He has put on a great deal of weight since I was here last summer. He has always fluctuated, but now he has really gone to an extreme. He's taken to wearing big roomy dressing gowns around the house, gold, burgundy, rose, etc., some in velvet, some in quilted satin. They give him the look of a big beaming Renaissance prince. Today the Loerzers came with their small daughter, Renate, and Hermann strode forward to meet them in his long rose-colored velvet gown. The child's eyes went round as saucers, you could see the parents were on pins and needles—what mortifying thing might she pop out with? But it was a piping little voice of purest bedazzlement: "Ach, bist du schön!" Hermann was delighted. "There, you see? They're all against my house suits, Renate, you're the only one who understands. I shall have a dress made for you of the same stuff. Now come with me, we must get to know each other better." And off he took her by the hand, and for a quarter of an hour they sat deep in conversation.

He left this evening for Berlin, will be gone a couple of days. The house is enormous, but you feel his absence in it everywhere. As if its central force had dissipated.

5 December, Wednesday. Fräulein Korwan left this morning for Weimar. I had coffee with Emmy in her sitting room and she was glum, unusual for her.

E: It's just that I enjoy Rose's visits. I miss her when she goes.

T: I know you're very close.

E: She is one of my dearest friends.

T: But Hermann could easily have the Weimar Theater moved here to Carinhall. Why don't you ask him to do that?

She snapped at me not to be clever, then apologized, said she was distressed that Rose's reading of the Christmas poems had gone wrong.

E: You think you know your guests . . . but there are bound to be some, when you have so many. Or so it would seem.

T: What would seem? I'm afraid I don't follow.

E: That it was Rose who read. It's reached the wrong quarters.

T: I'm sorry, I still don't follow.

E: Ah, Thomas, I forget you're from abroad.

T: I realize we Swedes have a reputation for denseness.

E: You ridiculous thing, you know I don't mean that. Well, at least you've made me smile. Come, let's finish our coffee and go downstairs.

Evening. A new arrival. He is soft-spoken, leisurely, and dark. For these reasons one wouldn't expect him to be Hermann and Frau Riegele's brother, but such he is. He lives in Vienna. So does Frau Riegele, but she spends more time here and in Berlin than in Vienna. Since Hermann is unmarried, she acts as his official hostess at state affairs. Our New Arrival greeted her with a deep bow.

He: Hohe Frau. This is a great honor.

She: What an idiot.

He: But do I not address the First Lady of the Reich?

She: Herr von Kantzow, this is my brother Albert, unfortunately.

We shook hands. I was embarrassed.

She: And how long are you staying, Albert? Half an hour, one hopes?

Upon which they laughed and embraced.

6 December, Thursday. In the place of our absent host, I took Herr G for a walk around the grounds this morning. On our way out, in the main hallway, he paused before the bust of Hitler which occupies a prominent place there. It is new since I was here last summer. Of white marble, rather more than life-size.

Herr G: He used to paint picture postcards in Vienna,

you know. By all accounts he lived in a flophouse with holes in his socks and bugs in the bed—though the bugs may be apocryphal—and drove everyone mad with his political harangues, shouting and carrying on just as he does now. So it's said, at least. Well, with or without bugs there he sits. Austria's revenge on Prussia for Sadowa.

Herr K: Shall we go on?

Herr G: I take it you're one of the smitten. No doubt you've met him socially. I understand he can be charming.

Herr K: I've met him once, at my mother's interment. He was warm, sincere and kind.

Herr G: There you are.

Herr K: Where, if I may ask? Everyone was warm, sincere and kind. That's how people are at funerals, except at their own. No, I'm not smitten. I'm not anything.

Herr G: I should think that was an attitude hard to maintain here.

Herr K: Politics are not discussed here. I could count on the fingers of one hand the times Hermann has mentioned politics.

Herr G: You are fond of our Hermann. Well, who isn't? I am, certainly, although I visit him rarely.

Herr K: It's a distance from Vienna.

Herr G: It's not the distance. No, I will tell you. When I was small, Hermann used to set me on his lap and read me Karl May. Now, I didn't care for Karl May, but because Hermann loved Karl May he was sure I must love him too, because that's how Hermann is. And I might fidget and yawn, but on he went, all certainty and zest—and sure enough I would suddenly feel myself swept up, totally enthralled in spite of my own preferences. And that is quite a phenomenon. I will tell you one thing about the sun, Herr von Kantzow, it will always sweep you into its own orbit. And it can warm and cheer you; it can inspire you to great heights; it can also blind you; it can burn you to a crisp. And you may not even know which of these things is happening. No, I find it much simpler to keep to my own dim, distant course.

Herr K: What do you make of these tracks here?

I don't like to hear people discussed behind their backs, not even in a tone as well disposed as Herr G's. He looked at the animal tracks in the snow but couldn't identify them.

Herr G: All my family are great hunters. Hermann, of course, but even my sisters are good shots. And our father had some fine heads from Africa. Our godfather too was a passionate hunter. I was surrounded by it, but it never took.

Herr K: The same with me. In fact, I developed a dislike
for all guns. In fact, I'm a pacifist.

Herr G: Herrgott, how do you breathe here in Germany?
Or don't you ever step out of this fairyland once you arrive?
Never gone into Berlin, or any town or village?

Herr K: Of course I have.

Herr G: But it escapes you? Regimentation, militarism,
uniforms everywhere?

Herr K: It doesn't escape me, but I'm a foreigner; it isn't
my affair, it's the Germans'. And thus isn't it your affair, Herr
Göring? But I understand if you prefer the fairyland of
Vienna.

He wasn't offended, only smiled dryly. Some fairyland, he
said.

Night. Very late, reading in bed. Hermann is back. There
came a sound from outside, a slamming of car doors in the
courtyard. It's as if the house has now had its center restored.

7 December, Friday. A day packed with dialogue between
the two brothers. Brother Albert was Albertian, Brother Hermann Hermannic.

I came down to the terrace where the two were having a
snack, and sat down with my book.

Herr G: What's that you're reading, Herr von Kantzow,
Thomas Mann? But isn't he consigned to oblivion? How is one
to understand that, Hermann?

H: How is one to understand what? In the first place it's
Heinrich Mann you mean, not Thomas. In the second place,
Heinrich, Thomas or whoever, one may read whatever he
wishes in this house.

Herr G: I should think the Czar of Prussia would weed
out his library into a shining example of the principles upheld
by his Party.

H: The Czar of Prussia will keep Karl Marx in his library
if he feels like it. Eat your blinis, Albert.

Herr G: Please don't tell me to eat my blinis, Hermann.

The three of us and Emmy took a walk around the lake.
The paths had been shoveled clear and covered with wood
chips. Everything was white and sparkling. Emmy was telling
Herr G how she fell in love with Vienna when she worked
there at the Staatstheater some years ago. He agreed that it
was a delightful city.

Herr G: It's especially delightful in the Christmas season.
And this year we have some wonderful ornaments. In fact, I
brought one with me, because I thought you might like to see

it, Hermann. An old woodcarver made a few last Christmas, and they caught on so well that the stores are filled with them this year. Here, isn't it charming?

Hermann took it and held it up by its bright red-and-gold string. It appeared to be a little gallows with a little long-bearded figure hanging.

H: Why do you wish me to see it?

Herr G: I thought you might like to know how well the National Socialist gospel is doing across the border.

H: What are you trying to do, make me laugh? Since when has Austria needed encouragement? Austria could give lessons to Streicher.

Herr G: I don't deny that. I am only saying, in my clumsy way, that what is second nature to our little old woodcarver is the German regime's official doctrine.

H: Is it? What is official about it? Has there been any legislation against the Jews' rights as German citizens? No. And there will be no such legislation. And let me tell you this, Albert, you will not find trinkets like these in German stores, because no German would buy them. Take your little obscenity back to Vienna, where it is at home.

Herr G: I should perhaps remind you of the large obscenity who emerged from Vienna.

H: I should perhaps remind you to speak more plainly, Albert. It's very hard for me to point out the sights and figure out your allusions at the same time. You must forgive my limitations.

At dinner—there were only the four of us and Frau Riegele—I was talking about my trip back to Stockholm next week by Lufthansa.

Frau R: The idea makes me queasy.

E: The idea makes Thomas queasy too, but he's determined to try it.

Herr G: And why is that, Herr von Kantzow?

Herr K: I don't know, really, I suppose I'd just like to try it.

Frau R: He is taking advantage of progress. I shouldn't care to fly, but I can see that it is progress to be able to go by boat, train, motorcar, or now by airplane. Think of the poor cave dwellers who had hardly a choice in anything.

Herr G: Ja, think of the poor cave dwellers, Hermann, in the great darkness of primitive times, who had no choice in anything.

H: Mein lieber Bruder, have a little patience. We are only now standing on solid ground. We must have solidity first, then we'll see to alterations and reforms. But solidity first. It cannot be the other way around. The other way around was the republic. Limitless choice, and limitless chaos.

Herr G: Chaos may only be the second worse condition to live under.

H: What are you anyway, Albert? Not a republican, certainly.

Herr G: Of course not. You know what I am. I am what our family has always been and what you should still be: a monarchist.

I was surprised to see Hermann's face redden. I think it's the only time I've ever seen him embarrassed. Herr G pointedly led the conversation into hunting, guns, militarism, etc.

Herr G: Tell me, Herr von Kantzow, have you ever discussed your view on these things with our host?

Herr K: Uncle Hermann knows I'm a pacifist.

Herr G: (Turning to Hermann) So? And what do you make of such an attitude?

H: All for it. I'm a pacifist myself.

Herr G: Please, Hermann, you'll give me heartburn.

H: It's a well-known fact. Are you the only one who doesn't know it? You think it inconsistent with pacifism to want to arm Germany? That's nonsense. Germany must achieve equality of power with other nations or she will have no voice in maintaining the peace of Europe. Certainly I want Germany armed, and armed in all ways. If a nation is militarily weak, industrially weak, psychologically weak, she's screwed like a halfwit schoolgirl. That's common sense. I'm no warmonger. I had my fill of war, and so did everyone else. But I want a strong self-sufficient Germany, and so does everyone, and so do you.

Herr G: That may be, but I don't want the regime.

H: You won't get the one without the other. But think as you want, that's your right. Only I'm sorry you're not happier with the soup. I asked for it especially because it's your favorite.

Herr G: Why must it always come back to food, Hermann?

H: Why? Why not? You've never learned to experience each moment to its fullest, Albert. Here you have a delicious cream of artichoke soup before you which you derive no pleasure from, because you're too busy thinking up things to say, which you derive no satisfaction from. That's poor management.

This was said good-naturedly and received in the same

spirit, and I wouldn't be giving an accurate account of these
dialogues if I didn't mention their fraternal tone. Nevertheless, this seemed to mark the end of Herr G's table commentaries.

Afterward we joined the other guests for a sleigh ride,
about fifteen of us in three sledges, everyone bundled up under furs and blankets, and it began to snow. Sleigh bells, hoofs
thudding, much singing and laughter, afterward cherry
brandy by the tree and Hermann played his accordion. Then
a late supper and Hermann led the way to cognac and bil-
liards for those so inclined. Inclined to the former if not the
latter, I sipped and watched. About midnight the game broke
up and I went over to say goodbye to Herr G, who's leaving
early in the morning. I wished him a good trip. He wished me
the same, and joked about my queasiness.

Herr G: You know, of course, that if you don't want to fly,
there's no reason why you should.

Herr K: Why do you say that? Of course I want to.

Herr G: Gewiss, gewiss. I wish you well, Herr von Kantzow.

9 December, Sunday. Weekends Hermann eats breakfast
around ten, though he's been up as usual since half past six.
I'm a coffee and toast man myself, but enjoy watching him put
away potted meats, stewed sweetbreads, soft rolls with
Spickgans, eggs done up in cream, coffee with whipped
cream, and a glass of sherry. Afterward a brisk stroll outside.
On Sundays one may make use of the chapel, a small room on
the ground floor. An organist plays. There are always people
there, such as Frau Rigele, a devout Catholic. The chapel is
Lutheran, but one may pray as one wishes. I entertain
thoughts instead. In the afternoon everyone goes his own way.
Both afternoons this weekend Hermann was busy setting up
an enormously elaborate model railway in the attic. I went
with him and helped him, although even as a child I was never
a toy-train addict. I can't say I enjoyed the trains themselves,
or crawling around on my knees, which is ridiculous for a man
of twenty-three and more so for one of forty, yet I say without
reservation that they were two of the happiest afternoons of
my life. The sense of working together, just the two of us, and
talking about everything under the sun—and then his enthusiasm for everything he does, cigar clamped between his teeth
and his movements so quick and agile for someone his size,
now he crouches and pulls this lever, pushes that button,

whips the cigar from his mouth and with beaming face throws
his arm around my shoulder as we both sit back and watch—

In the evening everyone gathered in the small salon. I
played chess with Herr Bodenschatz. Hermann stood over us
and advised us, although he admits he's never learned the
game, being too impatient. Other guests played cards, or sat
talking. Music from the gramophone, *Rosenkavalier*. A pleasant
evening and early to bed. A weekend that passed too quickly.

Chapter 36

10 December, Monday. Hermann has let me have the use of his den for my "writing." I suppose I've given him the impression I'm involved in some great work.

Honey-colored wooden floor, Scandinavian throwrugs. Built-in bookcases, a fire crackling in the fireplace. Before me on the desk are: a vase of luminous tangerine-colored roses, an antique dagger letter opener, six small eighteenth-century porcelain soldiers, and an array of framed photographs. Among the faces is my own; I'm next to a portly, black-mustachioed gentleman whom I don't recognize. Mother is here too, of course; and Hermann's parents, Emmy, others whom I don't know.

The photograph of Mother is very lovely. Hermann has even had a painting made after it, which hangs on the wall. But the photo is lovelier. And very familiar to me, since it was I who took it, during those days we had together at Kreuth. It was one of those good days Mother sometimes had. She sat on the sanatorium lawn in a flood of sunlight, gazing off to one side with a beginning little smile. There was a doctor, old Dr. Müller, totally humorless, monumentally dignified, and passionately attached to his vegetable garden, it was his only conversational topic, and we had a private name for him; and as I gaze at the photo I can't help but think that whoever else may gaze upon it, it is only we two, Mother and I, who know that as I click the shutter she has just caught sight of old Herr Doktor Eggplant on his way to his garden.

As for the painting, it's not bad if not Rembrandt. Hermann has had the lawn turned into a mountain slope with soaring peaks behind. No doubt he wished to recreate their Alpine honeymoon retreat where they reached such extraordinary heights of rapture.

Well, let us get on with our itemization. In addition to *Alpine Rapture* there are several other paintings, mostly seventeenth-century Dutch genre. On the mantel stands a bronze figurine of Frederick the Great with his two greyhounds, and framed group photographs of the Richthofen Squadron. Above these hangs a sword. Finally, on the wall behind us, above the desk, is Dürer's *Knight, Death and Devil*, which Hermann packed around with him throughout the war, and which, due to creases, spots and waterstains, must look older than the original.

Very quiet. The big pendulum clock in the corner ticks, ticks. In the air is a faint lingering aroma of cigar smoke.

12 December, Wednesday morning. I sat down there again yesterday but couldn't write anything at all. It is better up here in my own room.

Thaw the last couple of days. A steady splatter of snow dripping from roof to terrace, and you can see the green darkness of the trees again, wet and glistening, and rivulets and puddles shimmering from the ice of the lake. Everything melting, breathing, stirring, as if it were the breakthrough of spring, when of course it's only that the elements are taking a final stretch and yawn before settling for good into long, dark winter.

Poetic. The weather here does that to me, though it's no different from the weather at home. For which place I must depart on Friday, since I commence my career a couple of weeks hence. Yes, Kantzow will soon be joining the ranks of Bob Cratchits in their little knitted black shawls, sitting hunched and mute over their ledgers in an eternal scratching of quills. If not in actuality, then in essence . . . Essence of

Embalming Fluid, the clerks' scent. Cologne of Corpses . . .
Eau de Styx . . .

Some Thoughts on Outside Matters

I put on my coat, go out the front door, and begin to
walk. I walk down through Germany and Austria, across the
corner of Italy into Yugoslavia, down into Bulgaria and continental Turkey, then up through Rumania, Hungary, Czechoslovakia, Poland, Lithuania, Latvia and Estonia, and never
once—Czechoslovakia excepted—do I walk on the soil of any
but some kind of dictatorship. People lump these countries
together as fascist, but only Germany and Italy are fascist,
and Germany more truly than Italy; the others are just quasi-
and semi-dictatorships grafted onto traditional systems where
power remains in the hands of the usual elite. But people
sloppily use the term "fascist" for any repressive method of
governing, forgetting that by this definition they must include czarist Russia, British imperial rule, Bolshevism, etc.
Still, I admit it's hard to say what fascism is. If you want to be
academic, you can define it as a corporate economic state,
roughly a system of guilds whose profits are under state control, this being Mussolini's program. But that illuminates
nothing. Nor can you go by land reform and a classless society, since these two great shibboleths of fascism have triumphed less notably in Italy and Germany, where the
nobility is allowed to keep titles and land, than in Eastern Europe. Anti-Semitism is least of all a descriptive feature, since
it is absent in Italy, the original fascist state, while natural to
Eastern Europe, where it seems part of the cellular structure.
No, I think fascism itself doesn't know what it is, except that
it is against our age. Our age, which differs from all ages of
the past—the first in all of history to hold as its faith man's
material progress. And does our age have any concept of
what it is? Has it ever seen into itself since it first came into
existence a century ago? I grab it at random—say 1890—I
slap it into human form and poke a mouth in its face.

"Why should I find fault with myself?" it asks in a pleasant and reasonable tone. "I leave faultfinding to the poets and
philosophers. They enjoy it, they've done nothing else for
years. And yet why? Ask them what other age has been
marked by the spreading light of literacy, by every kind of
humane amelioration, and by such extraordinary achievements as the locomotive, the electric light bulb and the five-

floor department store. Of course, they'll answer that literacy has spread but there's no light in it, for it's only used as another means to get ahead in the world. But ask them if they would prefer the black shroud of ignorance that smothered the world of the past—good gracious no! And see how they mourn the church, they deplore its having gotten so thin since the idea of God was removed from it. They are saddened that it's so light and nimble and agreeable; but ask if they would like to feel its old stranglehold around their throats—oh heavens no! And they tell me that I have put through my great work reforms only in order that the wretches' backs, upon which I have built everything, will neither collapse nor rear up *en masse;* but ask them if the spirit of improvement, whatever its motive, is not a great good in itself, and a great good unique to me—yes, just ask them if they would really like to trade places with some superstitious, bug-ridden yokel of yore permanently mired in his niche, squashed between his feudal lord and his Holy Lord, subject to rotting teeth, scabies and early death through an infected carbuncle. It is I who have given these complaining poets their dentists, I who have brought them absolute certitude that they will never be felled by a caprice of their appendices. And they know it, don't fool yourself, they know it. They don't want to go backward any more than the rest of us do. You stick a poet on a pin and hold him up to the light, and that's what you'll see. Certainly they carry on—'purposeless progress, hollow values, spiritual decay'—melancholy sentiments are their stock in trade, you see. As a businessman I respect that. I don't hold it against them."

How gracious of you, you bureaucratized fungus, you toadstool of standardization, you urban stench of underpaid masses producing more mass goods in order to create more mass taste in order to create more mass goods ad infinitum.

"I respect your sentiments, sir, but forgive me if I rush off. Time is money."

And off it strides, briskly twirling its cane, a thrumming, progressive, bourgeois society going industriously about its business. Not until the turn of the century does it begin to feel a kind of malaise, a strange combination of satiety and emptiness, a kind of weariness and hunger it can't define; it feels a drawing toward something, and it can't define this either, but it is very strong, this pull toward something, and it begins to walk faster, like Frankenstein's monster clumping toward the abyss, like a sleepwalker with arms outstretched, clumping faster and yet faster until it finally reaches its goal and bursts apart in a lava spew of blood and intestines and rot.

One can be academic. One can look at the century-long multipower competition to expand economic empires and increase world markets, and assign this as the reason for the Great War: inevitable when so many commodities must find so many purchasers. Yet wasn't this war a suicide pyre? Or some kind of crazed bid for regeneration? Hadn't that great body finally asked, in its horrifyingly dim way: "Is this all?" And wasn't its explosion the ultimate rejection of itself? That world-shaking holocaust of perfectly calibrated machines? We may wonder if it meant to destroy itself utterly, or somehow to achieve rebirth through the fires of sacrifice, but we know it accomplished neither thing. All it managed to do was to slaughter on a scale undreamed of before, to obliterate everything it most cherished, and to leave intact the thing that created it. For that was not destructible: industrial economy had become the condition, the iron framework of man's existence.

Fascism shines a torch into that opaque despair. The fascist rejects all utilitarian motives in favor of acts in which no economic motives play a part. Fascism believes in holiness and heroism. Hitler has no economic ideology. This is what fascism means. The state not as an economic fact but as a spiritual and moral entity. A soil-rooted Germanic culture restored in the place of artificial modern civilization. It is the Rhine, after all, where the West has always drawn to a conclusive stop. If anyone ever doubted that, it should be clear as I return from my long walk, frostbitten and footsore, to report that Czechoslovakia is the sole reminder of Versailles' attempt to liberalize all Europe.

Of course, in resettling frontiers, the Allies were trying to make it possible for ethnic minorities to live under their own national regimes, but it's unfeasible in an area as ethnically mixed as Eastern Europe. They suffered from demographic dilettantism and in the process chopped off a full 70 percent of the Austro-Hungarian Empire.

I've just walked through the resultant treaty states of Yugoslavia, Czechoslovakia and Poland. There in the east a country was suddenly made big and strong, and it wants to stay that way; or it was made small and weak and doesn't want to stay that way. Power, that's all that matters. Still, I can't deny the Allies' idealism in their concern for mi-

norities, or in their desire to democratize every country they
set their hand to. They may have been unrealistic in reshuf-
fling borders and imposing democratic rule overnight, and
they were certainly too intent on consolidating their own
position, but I insist the component of idealism was also at
work.

Yet idealism doesn't exist as a component. It is not an
also. If it works along with something other than itself, it
ceases to be itself. I should cite an example of true idealism
which I saw in the newspaper this morning. "Farewell,
lemon, we need thee not! Our German rhubarb will take thy
place fully and entirely. It is so unpretentious that we overlooked and despised it, busy with our infatuation with foreign things. Yet we can have it in masses, the whole year
round. Slightly sweetened, it provides us with delicious refreshment, and what is more, it is a blood-purifying agent
true to German type. Let us make good with the German
rhubarb the sins we have committed with the alien lemon!"
One must call this fanaticism, but isn't true idealism always
fanaticism?

What a contrast Germany is to the dust all around! The
air is charged with vigor and purpose, you feel that the very
atoms are dancing with bright hope, with common endeavor
and great good works. It's as if everything were united in a
single soaring will—it's exhilarating, and not only to me but to
countless visitors who come to condemn and are converted instead. And I, I wouldn't even *have* to be converted, for there is
in me such a powerful longing for the absolute, the *Absolute,*
and don't ask what the Absolute is, because it can't be defined.
It's like a wonderful joke, like God and Truth. Upon such in-
substantialities are built our great philosophies—one could die
of laughter, but I'd rather die otherwise. For in me is this
longing *not* to see, *not* to laugh—the longing for the in-
controvertible kiss of the Absolute, for the Ultimate Heights
of Blinding Holy Heroism, and I would not have to be converted, only released. Then why *can't* I be released? Because I
persist in seeing. I'm all eyes, like Argus. Only I guard nothing, I merely see. And here in Germany I see on the one hand
this exhilarating spirit and drive, and on the other the most
unjustifiable tyranny and crushing excess. And I see that they
both derive from the fanaticism, or impassioned ardor, of
which I gave an example from today's newspaper. And I see
that revision and reform may begin to take over now, and
things may begin to straighten out; that's what all good people

hope, and I must include myself among them. Yet I also see that in order for the excesses to disappear, so must the great passion.

There's England, lethargic, mediocre, frightened. It's partly the depression, and I have to express a certain satisfaction at seeing unemployment and stagnation there, where all that economic glory first came steaming up from those new-locked, pumping lovers, the machine and the pocketbook. But her dusk is due to more than economics. It was the war; she hasn't gotten over that. Almost her entire young manhood vanished. It broke her spine, it made her stop loving herself. And there she sits guilt-ridden, shamed and frightened.

Over in France we find that they fear war in a more concrete way than the English; a fear directed at the abuttment of Germany, against whom they feel they can never build up enough security. It's curious that France even more than England is aware of the Great War's monstrousness yet feels no shame. It's because she is France, the acknowledged jewel of all that's intelligent, cultivated, life-loving and balanced, the perfect flower of European civilization. By comparison England, for all her splendid pomp, is a clodhopper; well might England sit crumpled with shame and doubt, brooding over her true qualifications as a highly civilized creature—but France? France would never stoop to self-doubt, she would never question herself. But in place of self-questioning something else has grown, something unwholesome and dank, a kind of decay of the will, a kind of spiritual gangrene. If England is dull-eyed and torpid, France is atwitch with maggots.

These are the victors. What of vanquished Germany? There is one thing to be said for defeat: it simplifies things. What room is there for soul-searching, conscious or otherwise, in a country whose only sensation is that of a boot pressed on its neck? Shame? Guilt? Self-doubt? All such debilitating complications are squashed to nothing by the solid simplicity of resentment, hatred, self-pity, self-righteousness. What a marvelous four-pronged tool for turning up new earth, plowing fresh furrows to be seeded with the hard shining kernels of change. That's the great difference: the victors settle back, they've made the present and they belong to it; but the defeated can only belong to the future—to the single, simple necessity for change. We've already discussed Germany, we know the rhubarb fields are thriving, those decent, honest, upright plants. We know the country is filled with the enthusiastic figures of American industrialists, British bankers, French and Belgian socialist intellectuals, and pacifists from all over. Some hurl obloquies at Germany with one hand, while with the other embrace her as their bulwark against property-devouring Russia. Others are sincere and hopeful souls impressed with the good that National Socialism has achieved, and confident that the excesses will now dissolve. Still others are those strange creatures afflicted with the voluptuous infatuation of the weak for the powerful. All, in any event, give one the hopeful feeling that communication, discussion, mutual enlightenment can only be for the good. But look there to the West, in whose image our century is made. Behold the great body that came crawling out of the smoke in 1918. It's still crawling. Wherever it's going this time—and is there any doubt that it's going to the same place?—it won't rush headlong; no, it will crawl sideways, like a crab, but it will get there. Because in its dim, pitiful way it fears and broods and questions as it crawls along, but the one thing it never questions is the Iron Framework of its existence. Are we not looking at something grotesquely familiar? Nor can I even place hope in National Socialist Germany, although she does question the framework—more than that: despises and rejects it. Rejects the economic ideal, rejects the enshrinement of industry and technology. Rejects them, but will never be able to do without them, because she too is a creature of our century. Do you know what I think about our Iron Framework? I think it is so endemic, so entrenched, that it will consume every social system and form of government in the world until it's the only thing left on earth, a slab of towering steel in the ruins and terrible silence. . . .

13 December, Thursday. Woke early and was restless, thinking about departure tomorrow. Put on my robe and wandered around the house, still dark, no one up. Thought I might have coffee with Hermann, even though it's when he studies the foreign newspapers. A polyglot aide goes through them first and marks in blue pencil what's of political interest and in red any references to Hermann. While he reads he listens to gramophone records. Herr Kropp judges his morning mood and puts on a record in keeping with it. Everyone knows his early-moring routine and no one ever interrupts. I did consider it this last day, but at his door Kropp was coming out with a gramophone record and shaking his head as if it were a highly peculiar object. What have you there? I asked him. Why, it's just Schubert's *Trout.* It's one of the Minister President's favorites, or so at least I thought. But I no sooner put it on than he said take that thing off and take it out of here, and was annoyed. It only goes to show that you can never be sure of anything. If you'll excuse me, sir, I must take this somewhere. So I went back to bed instead, got up late. This evening when Hermann returned from Berlin he was in good spirits, no trace of musical annoyance. He said I'd have a good flight tomorrow, clear skies. As Supreme Chief of the Weather Bureau he knows these things. I said I was glad. And so I am. It annoys me to recall Herr G's implication that Hermann is pushing me to do something I don't want to. It was my own idea entirely to fly back. And why should I be queasy?

14 December, Friday. Stockholm. Is it possible that only five hours ago I stood at Tempelhof Airport with Hermann? He was very proud of the plane, a trimotor Junkers 52, and pointed out all its features, but I didn't see a thing except that it was silver, corrugated, and had a Hakenkreuz on the tail fin. All I wanted was to stay with my two feet on the ground. I confess that I felt sick. But I managed a warm farewell and went up the boarding stairs waving, face wreathed in smiles. There were about fifteen passengers. They all looked perfectly relaxed, even an old lady of probably eighty. And I, the color of pewter. Ah, God, I said to myself, why have I done this? Then there was a terrible clatter, a roar of propellers, everything vibrated, and we were moving. Again smiling, going to my death, I waved to Hermann from the window. We were going faster and faster and suddenly we were off the ground and in the air, climbing, and I was soaked with sweat, but I no longer felt sick. I felt wonderful. I watched the square roofs of Berlin growing smaller, and soon all I could see was snowy plains far below. Everything fascinated me and filled me with pleasure. Amazing, the combined power and lightness of an airplane; so heavy, yet it quivers with every windstir. I felt absolutely fearless. I even enjoyed a windstorm over the Baltic, everything bouncing and shuddering. Over the coast of Sweden we ran through banks of cloud like snow sculptures; then all was crystalline blue as far as the eye could

see. Ha, Herr G, I said to myself, you should see how I'm
enjoying this. A born flier!

It was an absolutely splendid trip. And at least I'll have
that when I join the Bob Cratchits. Comes Heldenflieger von
Kantzow!

And the old lady in her hat with the cherry cluster, she is
a Heldenflieger too?

Chapter 37

Lɪᴋᴇ most people, Rose Korwan had one physical feature of which she was vain. It was not her slim waist, clear complexion, or bright chestnut hair—she gorged on pastries, kept monstrous hours, never went to the hairdresser's—but her white, white teeth, small and exquisitely proportioned. They had the radiant gleam of pearls, and at the same time were iron-hard; not one had ever known the smallest pinprick of a cavity—in short, they were extraordinary, imperishable teeth; nevertheless, three times a year she took the train from Weimar to Berlin to have them checked by one of the best dentists in the capital, who, stepping into the operating room where she sat bibbed and waiting, always greeted her with, "Ah, Fräulein Korwan, here you are again, and for no reason at all except to provide me with a few moments of incomparable joy." That was how he spoke, a true poet of the human tooth; and as he peered and delicately probed, his thick salt-and-pepper eyebrows would go slowly and admiringly up and down, while from deep within his throat she sometimes heard a low, engrossed murmur of almost amorous gratification. After each checkup he informed her with regretful honesty that she really need not return for a year, if ever, but she was always back on the dot four months later.

So it happened that on a rainy Saturday afternoon in mid-March of 1935, sitting bibbed and waiting, Rose beheld Herr Doktor

Weinblatt coming in through the door with a jubilant step, his face shining with happiness, clearly elated by something even greater than the prospect of examining her teeth.

"Then it is really true!" she exclaimed.

"I've just heard this moment, Fräulein Korwan. Yesterday it was only rumors, but today—they say the Wilhelmplatz is bursting with crowds!" And he paced excitedly about before settling to work with a clink of instruments, his eyes brimful with joyous tears.

Tactfully, in case they spilled over, she looked aside. Mute, wide-mouthed, she sat gazing past the rim of his ear at the rain that lashed the tall window, with its fan-shaped top of stained glass. It was an old-fashioned room, for he had inherited it from his father, who had inherited it from his; a high-ceilinged little chamber richly paneled, its tall particolored windows looking out on the venerable Singakademie, though all you could see now was rain battering against the glass, streaming down in a chaos.

At length, having been pronounced the paragon she was, and having exchanged a warm handshake with him, along with congratulations on the breaking of the Versailles Treaty, she departed through the ornate old waiting room, always well populated. His clientele was large and distinguished, Berlin's cream of the upper middle class, mostly second- and third-generation Weinblatt enthusiasts.

Outside, turning up the collar of her trench coat—naturally she had left her umbrella on the train—she went off down the stormy street in no great hurry. She was already soaked by the time she reached the corner and turned down Unter den Linden, across which, through the downpour, shone the tawny marble of the State Opera House, where tomorrow would take place the commemoration of Germany's two million war dead. It was right that the breaking of the Treaty should coincide with Heldengedenktag. The papers tomorrow would be filled with the news that Hitler was restoring universal conscription, and that Göring had announced to the foreign press the existence of an air force. The Versailles shackles were broken, and she was happy, deeply happy, because she loved her country and because honor had been restored to it; and it was a simple feeling, so simple that if she had tried to express what it was that honor had been restored to, she could only have said it was a field of orange and yellow Ringelblumen stretching from her childhood window.

People plowed along under blowing, rain-pounded umbrellas. The budding trees shook. Water splashed high from under zipping tires, drenching her further. Shoes sodden, coat soaked, hair plastered— what matter, she would hop into a steaming bath at her boyfriend's. Then they would fling themselves into bed. That was how she liked it, spontaneous. She had no wish, even at thirty-nine, for the dull habits of marriage. A free creature going her own way, she liked everything about her life, and not least her work, and without cherishing any illusions: good enough for good secondary roles in a good provincial theater. Ambition did not increase talent, why be burdened with it? Why be burdened with an umbrella, when the teeth of a storm felt so good? Why climb into a tram to sit encapsulated and clammy, when you could walk free and wet instead? She would walk the whole way and battle the Tempest's breath and plunge where Shipwreck grinds his teeth, and Faust plunging her back to that moment three years before when Emmy had come through the door of their boardinghouse room exclaiming, "It's ridiculous that a performance of Faust should be canceled for politics! Why can't they hire a hall for their electioneering? Ah good, you're making coffee, I bought some Nusstorten on the way home. You should have seen how they infested the theater, they were everywhere. We were introduced to the main one, Hitler—if you'll hand me a plate I'll put these on it—and to that other one, what do they call him, Goebbels. I must say neither struck me as a good reason for canceling Goethe."

"How many did you get, only four? You're not taking into consideration my passion for Nusstorten, Emmy."

And the next day: "The most wonderful thing has just happened, Rose! Here I am sitting with my coffee and he comes into the café and right over to my table, he remembered me from yesterday he said, and he is a real lover of the theater and we had such a nice chat, and he—"

"Who? Who are you talking about?"

"That one I met yesterday, Goebbels, only he is Göring. But you're just rushing out, don't let me keep you—"

"Heavens no, I must hear! Your face is like the rising sun."

"There's nothing to tell, really, just that he walked me back from the café, and there was such a feeling of understanding between us, Rose, and I told him all about darling Mutti and he told me all about his wife—she too died only a few months ago."

"Doesn't sound very cheerful."

"I don't mean that was all we talked about . . . but that he's so sympathisch, so warm and real. He's someone who fills you with a feeling of—I don't know, something so wonderful. Oh Rose, I like him so much! I feel we are already friends, good, good friends."

"Friends? If you could see your face, Emmy. Wirklich, he's had an effect on you! It will be a great romance! I feel it, I predict it, I must fly—"

Weeks passed, but Captain Göring did not return to Weimar. Emmy, being of a patient disposition, did not say much about this. But one day she expressed herself sadly.

"I think I'll never see him again, Rose. I think he mourns his wife so deeply . . . I think no other woman can leave him with any memory but the most fleeting."

"I think that's nonsense. Do try to remember, Emmy, that the country is collapsing. It's practically in a state of civil war. Consider that the man might possibly be busy."

And then one day, to Emmy's joy, he reappeared. They took a long walk through the beautiful Buchenwald, green and rustling and romantic; but it was a romance slow to bloom, for his visits were few, and his attentions more companionate than amorous. In time, however, this changed; and by the spring of the following year, in 1933, the National Socialists having meanwhile come to power, an incidental occurrence as far as Emmy was concerned, she was taking the train to Berlin whenever her schedule permitted and staying nights or weekends with her lover. In the fall of that year, standing in the doorway of their boardinghouse room, she and Rose embraced. "I'll miss you so much, Rose—and everyone, and everything. But to be so near Hermann, and then to be working with *them*, oh, it's almost too much!" *Them* being the Prussian State Theater, whose august director had invited Emmy to join that august company. She was moving to Berlin, to a small apartment near the Tiergarten.

Where, on Rose's first visit, she was greeted by a distraught face. "I'm absolutely sick, Rose. I've found out that the invitation was made at Hermann's request."

"But how can that be? Aren't the theaters all under the clubfoot?"

"*No*—I thought so too, but the Prussian State Theater is under the Prussian Prime Minister. I'm so upset, so disappointed—and he can't understand why! Do you know what he tells me? But you're so splendid, Emmy, you deserve to work in the best theater, they were bound to ask you sooner or later and I just sped things up. But I'm *not* splendid, although when I was invited I naturally thought . . . well, what would one think? But it was ridiculous of me, but to Hermann I'm Duse! The trouble with Hermann is that if he cares for someone he is absolutely blind. I can't tell you how *happy* he is for me."

In time, Emmy too became happy. Not least because her colleagues, after initial resentment, accepted her as a hardworking, thorough professional. More than that she was not. She was a few cuts above competent, and she was dedicated. Since a brief marriage in her youth, she had lived entirely for the theater. She loved and respected it, and it was her world.

And now, Rose thought as she walked along in the rain, Emmy would be giving up that world to become Frau Göring. Rose, who was unable to equate love with matrimony, nevertheless acknowledged this equation as a universal poem of some sort, and she was happy in her friend's happiness. And she was sorry, when she had seen Emmy last, to know that there was a cloud that marred that happiness.

"I can't help wondering if he really wanted to ask me. I don't mean that he doesn't love me . . . but marriage? For him there was only one marriage. I've told you often enough how strong her memory is in him. Sometimes it's almost as if she were alive."

"But I've always thought you were far too sensitive about Carin."

"Sensitive? You say sensitive? My dear Rose, if I were sensitive I would be in a mental institution by now. No, I am understanding of it, I am, truly. I think I'm able to see it in perspective. I'm only saying that perhaps he didn't mean to remarry yet. Perhaps he never meant to, I don't know. But our relationship has been criticized so much, and I think maybe he was told to legalize it, either that or break off."

"Well, what of it? Did he break off? No. You see which choice he made when he had to make a choice. Some people are like that, they must have a jolt. But I think you've created this whole thing in your own mind, Emmy. And do you know why? Because otherwise you might be too happy, and the gods are jealous of that."

That visit had taken place at Carinhall. But following the Advent party last December, there had been a period of weeks when Rose had not gone to Carinhall. Emmy said they suspected someone on the house staff of reporting Rose's reading of the Christmas poems, and that it might be best to stay away until the culprit—a footman, as it transpired—was winnowed out and dismissed. And so Rose had. And such a lovely party too, and some spying idiot should think it not lovely: "I tell you it's true, the woman recited *Christmas* poems!" "What? You mean to say he's permitted such a thing in his own home? That's going too far, even for him! A mockery! Revolting!" "If you could have seen! Everyone present collapsed in a dead faint, the floor was littered with victims of shock! Ambulances came from as far as Berlin!" And what, as she had stood there before that great tree, might have set her apart from any German woman of Lutheran faith, minor but genuine emotive gifts, and exceptionally fine teeth?

Along Friedrichstrasse the buildings stood out against a clearing sky. The rain was letting up and the wind blowing stronger—huge gusts of bracing Berlin air, sweet as wet flowers and knife-sharp, intoxicating to the soul, whirling you high in a kaleidoscopic vision of all good things, of amour, of dancing, of swimming in summer and skiing in winter, good food and drink, a career you loved—Halt! Halt! Bitte, whirl yourself back down to the hard fact that you've kept your job only because you have a powerful protector in Göring. Keep in mind that you are fortunate. Yes, she was fortunate. Yet why should she have to feel fortunate to keep a job she fulfilled perfectly well? A ridiculous question, but she could not answer it. If she had been an Eastern Jew, one of those thousands who came flocking in from German Poland and Galicia after the war, that might have been a different matter, for one thought of them as Ausländer, and she resented them for stirring up violent völkisch feelings that went rushing out over people more völkisch than anyone. Lieber Gott, if German Jews had one conspicuous feature—and Herr Streicher should really get hold of it, he would find it much more helpful to him than his noses and bow legs—it was love of Germany. By that you could tell a Jew: "Achtung! Observe on the forehead the mark of the Fatherland!"

One's thoughts became as stupid as the regime's. Except that the regime's thoughts were stupid and swinish both. But it was curious, the less swinelike the swine sounded, the more swinelike they smelled. When you heard such highflown official phrases as "irregular antecedents" and "national elevation," when you heard such pompous abstractions, it was like hearing someone in fastidious formal attire whose armpits overwhelm. Cousin Otto had been overwhelmed by more than smells—"It will be a bloodbath now they've come to power. They'll unleash the SA thugs by the droves"—and he was soon on a ship to New York with his family and two fox terriers. She supposed she wished Otto well, yet no swine could make her scurry from her country in the interests of national elevation. Nor could she get worked up like Cousin Max, who had run around organizing anti-emigration meetings. Anyway his meetings sloughed off as emigration decreased by itself, there having been no bloodbaths, no unleashing of SA thugs, no sort of blanket policy, all those things predicted by Cousin Otto, who now, two years later, was contemplating a move back. There was no pleasing Cousin Max. "He'll be like the others. They come running home and kiss the ground, they settle back in and then they say, 'Oh, but it's still not nice.' Of course it's not nice. We've been sticking it out while those softbellies have been lounging about abroad. I have no use for them." He had a hard militant streak, Cousin Max, being a much-decorated war hero, possessor of the Pour le Mérite and of a back filled with shrapnel still working itself out in bits. She was not harsh and unforgiving like Max, but she understood him. She did not understand Otto, who had felt that circumstances defined him, who had said yes it's me you mean, I fit your description, and so I will pack my bags and vacate my country, thereby contributing to your efforts to raise the quality of the German people. He truly baffled her. For the foundation of reality was oneself, not politics. She had always been who and what she was and nothing else. It was so during the monarchy and under the Weimar Republic, and it was so now, and would be so under whoever came next. Governments came and went dressed in a little brief authority, as the good Shakespeare said. The point was that the real things never changed. It was the unreal things that would change, seep away like a bad dream. It was all like a bad dream, absurd, meaningless, bizarre was the word, or hallucinatory, not fitting with real life, a passing hallucination with smells. If Göring were head of state he would make it pass more quickly, but as only second-in-power he couldn't bring his foot down and squash fanaticism flat. Hardly, or he would have squashed whatever element had planted a spy in his own house. Imagine, the Prime Minister of Prussia himself being observed and spied on. Still, it had come to nothing.

She squelched along the street both chilled to the bone and exhilarated by the cutting wind, through which she could now hear the crowds in the Wilhelmplatz. Turning down Mohrenstrasse, she saw that the crowds had overflowed from the square into the street, filling it from the Hotel Kaiserhof to the Chancellery, where those massed below the balcony were strenuously chanting for their Führer. It was a sound she could do without, and did, pressing in among the sea of figures along the street, from whom rose a more generalized exultation, a tremendous uplifting roar joined by her own cheers as she made her way through, eventually emerging with lungs and throat wonderfully fulfilled, and striding on in a windsweep of sun and flashing rain.

She was pulled from sleep by a loud crackling in her ear. Fire—no, the Sunday paper . . . and she turned sleepily to the whiskered jaw beside her for a warm and scratchy kiss, closing her eyes again. They'd had a lovely time yesterday afternoon, during which her clothes had dried on the stove . . . then a theater party, and early-morning breakfast at the Adlon bar, and now she lay in the full-bodied light of noon, opening her eyes again with a yawn. There was another crackling as Bodo turned a page.

"What does it say? It's definite?" she asked, stretching.

"Definite? Ganz." He began reading parts aloud. "'. . . With the present day the honor of the German nation has been restored. . . . We stand erect as a free people among nations. . . . We are now a sovereign state. . . . Honor . . . freedom . . . freedom . . . honor . . .' et cetera, well, it's all very fine but they've forgotten one thing. The Great Powers won't take it lying down. All they have to do is send in a few troops, we're weak as water."

"They won't do that."

"No? If you know that, you're the only person in the country who does."

"What are you worrying about? They won't do anything. I'll bet you a full year's salary. Oh, Bodochen, put the paper away, bed's no place for reading."

At the Opera House, where at that moment the Heldengedenktag ceremonies were commencing, the British, French and Russian envoys were conspicuously absent. The audience, consisting mainly of old officers in polished imperial-era spiked helmets, sat in inspiredly somber silence as the orchestra played the funeral march from Beethoven's *Eroica.* In the first row there could be seen the only surviving field marshal from the Great War, old von Mackensen, like an apparition from centuries past in his Death's Head Hussars uniform, black, with an overwhelmingly complex adornment of gold braid, and under his arm his great fur headdress. Also in the audience was the Crown Prince and a large representation of the aristocracy. The royal box was occupied by the head of state, who on this occasion did not speak. When the funeral march came to its somber end, the principal speech was made by Minister of War von Blomberg, who stood before a vast curtain hung with a vast black-and-silver Iron Cross.

"The world has been made to know that Germany did not die of its defeat in the Great War. Germany will again take the place she deserves among nations. . . . We do not want to be dragged into another world war. . . . Because all nations have equal means at their disposal for war, a future war would only mean self-mutilation for all. We want peace with equal rights and security for all. We seek no more."

At the end of the indoor ceremonies the audience joined the throngs that had gathered along Unter den Linden—throngs unequaled in numbers or jubilation since 1914, twenty-one years earlier—for the reviewing of the troops.

And the next morning a squadron of the new Luftwaffe roared in formation over the city.

And by the end of the week it was clear that the Great Powers were not going to do anything.

Chapter 38

10 April, Wednesday. Arrived Zoo Bahnhof early this morning. Heavy rain. Car waiting, was whisked off to Hermann's Berlin residence, the Leipziger Platz Palace. Streets decorated, everything drenched, unbrellaed crowds already waiting. At palace the butler whisked me off to Uncle Erik & Aunt Mary & Aunt Fanny, saying the Count & Countess von Rosen & the Countess von Wilamowitz-Moellendorf wish you to know, sir, that they are risen. (An even holier day than we realized, I replied, but joke was lost on him.) Took coffee with them, they'd motored down from Stockholm earlier in week. Uncle Erik said maybe everything would have to be changed because of the rain, I said maybe just closed cars instead of open. Hermann came in & said: Neither, the rain must stop. Warm embrace, but expression in the eyes. Apology? Why should I object to his marrying? He was in resplendent blue-gray uniform of General der Flieger, diagonal broad red sash for state occasion, all medals present. Now the rain must really stop! he said again, at which it did.

Bridal procession. Long line of open cars. Drizzling a little but no one cared. People lining streets in thousands, like gathering of mass family. Our Hermann! Our Hermann! Bridal car smothered in pink tulips. Emmy radiant, Hermann too, both beaming and waving. Civil ceremony at Rathaus, then on to Protestant cathedral. Crowds surging against police cordons. Unser Hermann! Hoch Hermann! Hoch Emmy!

Church ceremony. Afterward couple goes down red-carpeted cathedral steps under crossed sabers, trumpet fanfare from Wehrmacht premier band, overhead a roaring salute of low-flying fighter squadron.

Wedding banquet at Hotel Kaiserhof. Three hundred guests, recognized some. Udet, the Bodenschatzes, Frau Riegele, the zu Wieds, Pilli Körner & wife, the big one, Dr. Hanfstaengl, Hitler at Emmy's right. String orchestra, endless toasts, press cameras flashing. Champagne, lobster, turtle soup, etc. & ices of every flavor. Observed Herr Hitler ate two ices, both raspberry. Looked as if he would have liked three, but too polite. Didn't eat much else. Possibly annoyed by so much extravagance. An ascetic himself. Or maybe just doesn't like big gatherings, Mother used to say that. Shy, no social lion. The eyes, she used to say, there you see the lion. Looked at his eyes across table. Not to find lions, but her. Eyes that had looked on hers. I do that with people she used to know, ludicrous, what for?

Dusk when we got back to Carinhall. New bride a gracious hostess, new husband nowhere to be seen. Was gone more than an hour. Knew in my bones where, am sure she did too.

Wedding gifts filled two entire rooms. Frl. Korwan said if one wanted to look at them all, better have a camp bed brought in, would take a week. Think she's much occupied with beds, would like to get her into mine. She wasn't at wedding. That surprised me, thought she'd be maid of honor. My dear, I could never stand still that long, she said, & true she's an active creature but even so. Had boyfriend with her, actor, big blond fellow named Bodo, pleasant.

Hermann finally returned, in very quiet mood, but became himself as evening wore on. Emmy re-radiant, much talk about honeymoon, Adriatic villa, shimmering sea. E aglow & all smiles, & he too with arm around her waist, both 42 but seemed 22, how really beautiful are people who are happy.

11 April, Thursday. Couldn't sleep till daybreak. Then Kropp rapping on door: the car is waiting, you'll miss your plane! A man of affairs after all, important duties await—Bob Cratchit leaps to, attacks face with razor & crashes down stairs with bits of bloody tissue stuck to cuts, whizzes to Tempelhof & collapses snoring into plane seat. Woke up a while ago, apparently snoring into seatmate's shoulder to judge by his distended nostrils. One of your old monocled types. Probably thinks I've come from a brawl.

Baltic below now. Terrific air currents, plane lurching & shaking, sounds like giant bucket rattling. Monocle beginning to look around with severe concentration. Isn't thinking anything now except plane is going to break apart. Don't worry your head about it, dear fellow, do as air hero von Cratchit, whose lids are closing, closing. If we go down what difference, a long sleep instead of short.

As if to make up for the wet spring and summer, September was beautiful. Hans Schmidt took full advantage of the sunny days to work in his garden, and when the NSDAP rally week arrived, his wife could not tear him away. Army Day last year had moved him deeply, and with the regime's breaking of the Versailles Treaty his last uncertainties had gone sliding over the side. Even so, he had had enough of crowds and noise last year. Nor had he found it a great treat to sit in the honored-guest section of the stadium. He was a gardener. He was not comfortable sitting among diplomats, counts, foreign dignitaries. The classes should keep to themselves. That was order. His wife was a different kettle of fish, she had a high background, one of those backgrounds that was sometimes the strange destiny of a country lass gone into service. Let her go and sit there, for she fit in, but let him stay here and attack his weeds. And so, with her pair of week-long complimentary passes, she went with a neighbor friend instead, a small stout woman, pleasant enough, whom Hans Schmidt liked. Nevertheless, as he stood in his garden watching them depart, his eyes narrowed with opprobrium, for the round little person had bought an enormous cartwheel hat and elbow-length white gloves, and both her chins were lifted high. She was an impossible sight. She was a railroad conductor's wife, and a huge new hat and long gloves would not change that. Would not, could not, and should not. He creaked down on one knee by his heliotrope, but then, because he had the troublesome habit of thinking on after annoyance was spent, he felt a little sorry for her. No doubt she expected to attend a dozen events at least, but Nikki had no use for any event in which General Göring would not figure. A very few outings were all that big foolish-looking hat would get, and it must have cost a pretty penny.

Frau Schmidt was four times gratified by the sight of General Göring, whose mobile, sunlit face was constantly kept framed in the lenses of her opera glasses, but the most important event in which he figured she did not attend. This, an event unannounced and unprecedented, was a special session of the Reichstag, which had been summoned from Berlin to assemble in Nuremberg's Kulturvereinshaus. The opening of the session was preceded by a fanfare of trumpets. Reichstag President Göring rapped his gavel.

"The Führer will now present to the Reichstag, for its judgment as to ratification, the new laws for the protection of German blood and honor. To our Führer! The savior and creator! Sieg Heil!"

"And of course I won't be able to marry Bodo now."

"Oh, Rose, I had no idea that you—"

"I don't want to marry Bodo. That's not the point."

Frau Minister President Göring, cut off again in midsentence, remained worriedly attentive. Now and again as she talked Rose disclosed her beautiful, white, imperishable teeth in a contemptuous smile. Rose's line was clearly one of hostile irony, while her own—she could take no line at all; she felt properly rebuked for whatever she said, she felt helpless.

"I broke off with Bodo weeks ago, I'm involved with someone else. As you know. Or as you may not know. You have so many other things to occupy your mind, I can hardly expect you to recall the trivialities of my love life."

"That is untrue, that is unfair," Frau Göring murmured.

"But then, so much in life is untrue and unfair," Rose agreed with her bright contemptuous smile, taking a sip of coffee and ignoring the plate of Nusstorten between them. The little thoughtful cakes, her favorite, annoyed her; Emmy's brow annoyed her, corrugated with patience and commiseration; and her eyes annoyed her, those candidly unhappy blue eyes, waiting, waiting for her, Rose, to do something real—to burst out angrily or burst into tears—something that would clear the air and bring them close again. Well, it would not happen. She set her cup down with a sharp clink in the silence she commanded. They sat in Emmy's writing room at the Leipziger Platz Palace, a small, exquisitely furnished study in pale blue and gold, and it was as if she were the presiding hostess and Emmy the guest. She continued speaking.

"Bodo was well equipped in one area, I will say that. You may presume which area."

Frau Göring, with her unhappy corrugated brow, nodded politely at this crude lapse of taste.

"Even so. He was beginning to bring up marriage, it was time to move on. But the point is, Emmy dear, if I had wanted to marry him— if I decided this moment that I wanted to marry him—I should be able to. Do you agree?"

"But of course," Frau Göring murmured, looking more unhappy and helpless than ever.

"For that matter, why do I talk about marriage? Sex—simple sex,

Emmy dear. If I hadn't quit Bodo's bed of my own accord, your husband would have yanked me out of it last week."

"Rose, really—"

"Were you there, by the way?"

"You know I don't go to the rallies. I—"

"Oh, that's right, you don't like them. But you would have liked this. Such an impressive ceremony, from all accounts."

"Rose, really—"

"How could he stand there? How could he do it!"

Frau Göring looked at her friend a moment, unsure if she was meant to answer, or if she would be cut off again. "It is what I have been trying to say, Rose," she ventured. "As Reichstag President he must announce whatever bills come before the assembly; it is his function. But it doesn't mean that he himself advocates them. He does not advocate these Nuremberg Laws. He did not sign them. He did not put his name to them."

"Oh, that is wonderful, wonderful. This is such an entertaining visit. Why doesn't he resign from the filthy government if he disapproves of its filthy laws!"

"Rose, really—"

"Don't keep saying 'Rose really'! It makes me sick!"

"But Rose, dear, if he did, what good would it do anyone? You yourself?"

"I? Oh yes, I should be grateful to him. For what? Every Nazi has his pet Jew, it's no skin off his nose and none off yours either. That's right, break into tears! Am I being unfair? Everyone knows Emmy is the patron saint of Jewish actors, always interceding on their behalf with her husband, and he, good soul, always seeing to it that these poor unfortunates with their irregular antecedents keep their little jobs or are helped with a little money or with some little papers or whatever— that's a fact, and Rose is harsh and unfair, so unfair, what's unfair if not *this*? Protection of German blood and honor! *I* am German blood and honor! —Oh, you see how stupid you make me sound, stupid, everything is so stupid! It's all so stupid, what does it mean? Shall I not decide whom I'll marry, whom I'll fall in love with? How dare these swine tell me I'll pollute—*pollute*—German blood and honor? How *dare* they?"

Tears of anger stood trembling in her eyes. She brushed them roughly away, giving vent to a deep, shaken sigh. Emmy was wiping her eyes with her napkin. Slowly, she refolded it, and laid it on the table by her plate; she too released a long, shaken sigh. Neither of them spoke for a while.

"Is it never going to change, Emmy?"

"Oh, Rose, I wish I knew."

Again there was silence.

"Please, won't you stay for dinner?"

"No, I don't want to see him."

Rose did have one Nusstorte, and when she left she embraced her friend with customary warmth. Frau Göring felt that their friendship had weathered the storm, but she also felt sadly certain that Rose would not be coming to visit as often.

Rose too felt this certainty, but it was not borne out by time. As she gradually came to realize, and as Cousin Max expressed it, the Nuremberg Laws simply formalized measures which had already been taken. If anything, they gave stability to the Jews' position by reducing the scope for arbitrary actions. The laws clarified what had been shifting and confusing; and until the entire repugnant lunacy had spent itself, it was a practical advantage to know where one stood. Cousin Otto felt the same. Cousin Otto had returned from New York during the summer, and when the new laws were announced she was sure he would again take flight; yet it made sense that he did not, for it had been the murky uncertainties that had sent him fleeing in 1933. Also, Cousin Otto had come back to resume his business, which was flourishing, one of the odd inconsistencies that abounded being that many Jewish retailers were doing better than ever before.

And so, Rose found, life went on. The new laws forbade her to hold public office, but that was hardly her ambition. They forbade her to vote, but she never voted anyway. And they forbade her to have carnal intercourse with any Aryan, but the lover who had replaced Bodo happened to be Jewish. It continued to be possible to lead an ordinary life within a bad dream, to exist as oneself inside a hallucination. And when she went back to Dr. Weinblatt for her November appointment, he too was as always, except that his bushy eyebrows were perhaps a little whiter.

In late February of the new year of 1936 there was a sudden increase of aircraft displays at the various airfields in the environs around Berlin. And because the public always turned out in great numbers for such exhibits, because people were so interested and so enjoyed themselves, it was arranged that they would be able to attend every display if they wished, for each would be held on a different day. In this way no one would have to miss one exhibit because its timing conflicted with another.

This thoughtful arrangement was much appreciated by the crowds, who, at one airfield after the other, enthusiastically milled about the many machines lined up along the field, row on row; but of these throngs of people only a microscopic number of individuals concerned Göring, those being a presumed dozen or so foreign air attachés whose eyes, always so intent on gauging Germany's air strength, were on each occasion observing exactly the same planes they had observed on the occasion before.

What no one in the crowds could know was that the insignia of each plane were hurriedly changed after each display and the cowlings repainted in new colors, and the planes were then flown in the dead of the night to fill up the field of the next airfield. Nor could anyone know that the planes were mostly training machines, and that the fighter pilot training school had been stripped so thoroughly that it was rendered inoperative for the time being. Also unknown to the onlookers was the fact that not one of these planes lined up along the field could give combat, their guns at this point lacking the synchronization gear necessary to fire through the propeller. The abundance of pilots, strolling about or posing in groups for press photographs, was due mainly to mechanics dressed in flying clothes, for if planes were scarce, trained pilots were scarcer.

All these lacks—for the benefit of a few foreign eyes, specifically those French—had not only been cleverly disguised but magically turned into their opposite; the hope being that on the morning when the French woke to find German troops marching in to reoccupy the demilitarized Rhineland zone, they would have been given reason to think some very vivid thoughts about the numerical strength of the Luftwaffe.

Nevertheless, on the cold drizzly dawn of March 7, as three ill-armed German battalions marched rumblingly across the Rhine bridges, there was a feeling of enormous tension in the pilots flying cover overhead. One thing was to hope that the powerful Armée de l'Air would not come roaring out of the gray skies toward them, another to face the possibility that it might. If it did, there would be no hope for survival. One might manage to ram an enemy plane before going down, that was all.

Tension ran nearly as high in the Air Ministry in Berlin. Only Generalleutnant Milch, bearing out Göring's assessment of him as a man who pissed ice water, remained a model of cool efficiency, his button face undisturbed by the least sign of anxiety as staff officers, standing clustered around the telephones, answered each ring with a hand-pounce. Chief of Staff Wever worked off his anxieties by pacing. Colonel Bodenschatz dealt with his more unobtrusively, showing only by a sporadic rippling along his jaws that his teeth were being ground. Generalleutnant Udet could be seen chain-smoking and continually running his fingers through his thin hair. And Commander in Chief Göring, though the day was damp and chill, sweated through three uniforms in twelve hours.

But when dusk fell, not a breath of opposition had come from the French.

At midmorning the next day, General von Blomberg, Chief of the

High Command, in a state of extreme agitation, was shown into Hitler's Chancellery office. Tall, silver-haired, as impressive in appearance as he was not in personality—for his dependable pliancy, wits had dubbed him Gummilöwe, the Rubber Lion—the general approached Hitler's desk with a face white and taut with recrimination, a tic galvanizing the flesh beneath one eye. The general had just learned that the French were rushing thirteen divisions to the Maginot Line.

"This is what comes of our rash move, Herr Chancellor," he began at once. "We must withdraw immediately. If we wait to retreat until the French actually march, if we fall back without giving battle—as we must, since we are not equipped to give battle—it will be a shattering, an unqualified, military and moral defeat. We will lose nothing by withdrawing now. The operation will be seen as an admonitory gesture. We will have shown that we have no intention of sparking off hostilities, but only that we are making a demand for negotiations. There is time yet to save the situation, but very little time. If we are to avoid total disaster, we must withdraw the troops immediately!"

The Chancellor was as white and drawn as the general. His eyes were swollen with lack of sleep. He had been advised by everyone—Blomberg, Göring, Army Commander in Chief von Fritsch—that the armed forces were still too weak to fight should France resist. Everything had depended on France's not resisting.

The general, his face still twitching, waited for an answer. If they did not withdraw at once there were two possiblities: surrender or slaughter. Neither Hitler nor his regime could survive such a debacle. Surely that would guide his decision.

Sitting at his elaborate eighteenth-century desk, where Bismarck in his time had sat, the Chancellor crossed his hands on the polished dark wood, tightly interlacing his fingers. Through the tall old windows, with their fan-shaped tops, a gray rainy light fell on his face.

"So they are sending a few divisions to the Maginot Line," he said. "Very few. And the—"

"Very few? What is very few when Germany possesses only one division? One! France can mobilize a *hundred* divisions, and if she calls on her Czech and Polish allies, *two* hundred—"

"They are sending a few divisions to the Maginot Line. And the Maginot Line is in France. We should remember that. If they are manning it, they are making a defensive move. If even that. They have no stomach for fighting, defensive or offensive. The position most comfortable to the French, the one least painful to their decayed backbone, is one of cowering. You may depend upon it, Herr General, they will not come into the Rhineland. They will not take one step in our direction. We have only to stay put."

"I beg you to listen to reason—!"

"We will stay where we are!"

When members of the General Staff were shown in, the Chancellor, his fingers still tensely interlaced, was confronted with the same words he had just heard from General von Blomberg.

During the course of the discussion, Colonel Jodl stepped out of the room on some official pretext. He walked down the marble hallway, his boots ringing out. SS guards in black, huge creatures, each chosen for his extreme height, white-gloved, with a gun on either side of the belt, stood at rigid attention along his route, even lining the long staircase, one on every third step.

At the bottom of the staircase he went into the men's lavatory and lit a cigarette, but took only a few nervous puffs before stabbing it out. Bringing out his pocket diary and a pencil, he wrote, standing:

They have ceased putting their case to him; he cannot be moved. I think he is right. My own belief is that it would be the ultimate in cowardice to pull out now. But the strain is intolerable. The atmosphere in the room is like that of a roulette table when a player has staked his entire fortune on a single number.

He put the diary back in his pocket and lit another cigarette, only to stub that one out too. Then he went out the door and back up the staircase.

In the Rhineland the populace continued its frenzied welcome. Wherever the troops settled in, people cheered them wildly, they wept, they threw flowers, and priests came hurrying to bless their saviors. Rain dripped heavily from helmets and rifles, and from the massed umbrellas, but nothing could dampen the radiance of joyous greeting.

As Lord Lothian said in London a few days later, "The Germans, after all, are only going into their own back garden."

Two weeks later, the Chancellor put the peaceful and victorious reoccupation of the Rhineland to a national referendum. It was not the reoccupation itself the people were to vote on, but whether or not they approved of him as the creator of that action; in short, they were to decide if they wished him to remain their Führer. He slept soundly on his narrow bed the night before the balloting. The next day 99 percent of the German electorate voted in his favor.

The Rhineland takeover was a watershed in his life. The last shreds of Versailles were shaken off. The League of Nations was shown up as a shadow. France and England were exposed as henhearted, so fearful of war they collapsed at a sneeze. To his generals he had proved that his instinct was more reliable than theirs. And to the people he had proved the quality of his leadership. His popularity leaped from immense to extraordinary.

Chapter 39

Herr Speer saw everything with the eyes of an architect. Herr Hitler he viewed entirely as an architect, an artist, a man whose early dreams had not been realized but whose private passion was still the drawing of buildings and floor plans, whose talent was very great and who had chosen Herr Speer to carry out his astounding plans for the re-creation of Berlin. The entire center of the city would be rebuilt, "for Berlin must change its face in order to adapt to its great new mission. It will all be in granite, so that it may endure, and may transmit my spirit and the spirit of the times to posterity." There would be a Domed Hall twice the size of St. Peter's in Rome, a Triumphal Arch to dwarf the one in Paris, a new Opera House and Soldiers' Memorial, new ministry buildings, and all these structures would be standing a thousand years from now, and all would have been built by himself, Albert Speer, who was scarcely out of his twenties. Meanwhile in Nuremberg he was already building a new Kulturhalle, and a processional avenue six times the breadth of an ordinary boulevard, made of heavy granite slabs to bear the weight of tanks. He would also be setting to work on a new Chancellery building, Herr Hitler being dissatisfied with the old one, saying that it was fit for a soap company.

Haus Wachenfeld too, the Führer's little house on the Obersalzberg, having become too small for his entourage and too humble for the receiving of foreign dignitaries, had been rebuilt over the past few years as an official summer residence. In late May of 1937 the main section was finished, and although Herr Hitler had used the house as always during its enlargement, and his guests and associates were as familiar with it as himself, he was so pleased with the thought of his officially completed home—this fine three-story villa now called the Berghof—and so inspired one morning by the splendor of the weather that he gave a spontaneous tour to all who happened to be present, as if the house had just that moment been taken from its wrappings like a sparkling gift. Herr Speer with Herr Bormann and the photographer Hoffmann, the Führer's ordnance officer and chauffeur and two private secretaries, all went along behind him as he climbed stairs, opened doors, and pointed out this feature and that, his face beaming under the onlookers' unfailing response of pleasure and admiration.

On the top floor they were even shown the Chief's bedroom, which was small and plain, almost a monk's cell, but which nevertheless drew comments of "original" and "charming." There was a collective upward look through a window that gave onto a particularly fine view of the cragged gray mass of rock and glacier, striated with snow, that towered behind the villa. Then they were led downstairs again, into the salon, which everyone knew well but which elicited glances and comments of fresh appreciation.

The Chief walked to the picture window, his particular pride, and pressed a button. The huge glass—it was a window of such great size that fifteen people could stand alongside it without touching elbows—came slowly down with a muted rumbling and disappeared from sight. The outlook was magnificent, with its sense of extraordinary height and vastness, and again, as the small group stood leaning out into the view, there was a feeling of everything being seen for the first time. A faint haze imparted a soft golden cast to the hills and valleys far below, and to the mountains that composed the horizon, grayish blue, with broken patterns of gleaming snow.

"You see the Untersberg over there," came the Chief's voice. "It is no accident that I reside exactly opposite it."

There was a silent nod of heads as they all looked at the highest peak opposite, where, according to tradition, the Holy Roman Emperor Friedrich Barbarossa sat sleeping in a cave, awaiting the day he would rise up to restore the glory of the medieval German Empire.

The Chief turned and led them through the side door onto the long stone terrace, with its potted flowers and white garden furniture and its view as splendid as that from the window. Pausing and turning, he greeted someone coming up the steps.

It was Göring, in Lederhosen and a short green Bavarian jacket, big as a whale and puffing from his climb. He carried a stout alpenstock, which he thrust under his arm like a baton as he strode forward, red-faced and catching his breath, but brisk and light on his feet, smiling and clearly in fine fettle, to shake hands with his neighbor. For Göring too had a summer residence on the Obersalzberg, only five minutes' walk from the Berghof. He turned with a friendly nod to the others, and seeing Herr Speer, whom he knew personally, if not well, extended his hand.

Herr Speer, uncertain after shaking hands if he was meant to stay and chat or to take his leave, decided it was the latter. With a courteous nod, he turned and walked back to where the chauffeur and the photographer Hoffmann were sitting down.

He tried to enjoy the sun's warmth, but was frustrated to be stuck here with these people. They had nothing against idleness, whereas it ate into him like acid, he wanted to get on with his work. But he could not get up and leave without the Chief's permission. And if the Chief wandered off somewhere with Göring, Herr Speer might be sitting here another hour or two.

Göring's deep flush from his climb had disappeared; his color was clear, his eyes were brilliant blue-green in the sunlight. The Führer was in a sociable mood today, and apparently full of humorous anecdotes, for Göring now and then burst into laughter. Well might he give vent to that potent sound of pleasure, thought Herr Speer. His Luftwaffe, sent to Spain last autumn to support the rebelling Nationalist forces, was proving itself a formidable air power; and formidable Göring himself, in November, had surprised the world by stepping forth in yet a new role, added to all the others: Plenipotentiary of the Four-Year Plan, virtual dictator of the German economy.

A movement from above caught Speer's eye. In a window on the third floor, above a wooden balcony holding potted geraniums, the curtain had been drawn aside and then fallen to. He always felt somewhat sorry for Fräulein Braun, a simple and unassuming girl caught in the life pattern of a preoccupied public figure who, while undoubtedly fond of her, found it necessary to maintain his image of solitariness. Only with the regulars, the family, so to speak, was she free to show her face. She was always relegated to the upstairs when Göring or Goebbels or Ribbentrop or foreign dignitaries came, swept out of sight as if she had scurvy. She would have to sit there behind those curtains knowing she could not come down and join them until Göring was gone. On the other hand, she must take satisfaction in knowing that half the female population of Germany would be ecstatic to find themselves in her position, restrictions and all.

Chapter 40

Herr Hanfstaengl had not been seen since February of 1937.

He had been sitting at his desk one February day, in the study of his Munich home, and because the wintry afternoon was darkening, and because he would soon be turning fifty, his thoughts had taken a melancholy turn. He thought of his wife, who was no longer his wife . . . his work had come between them, his association with "that man," as she had come to call Adolf; she had finally left him, and the irony was that Adolf had finally left him too. How slowly and yet quickly a thing could change. He had always been able to express a difference of opinion to Adolf, level a criticism, and if the fellow had grown less and less patient with him, wasn't he less and less patient with everyone and everything? One had never expected that suddenly one's office would be moved from the liaison staff to an obscure building much farther down Wilhelmstrasse. The snap of a finger, no explanation. Weeks had gone by with no invitation to the Chancellery, weeks that had turned to months, and how long was it now since he had seen or heard from Adolf, since he had had any opportunity to be of the slightest influence? Almost two years. And so why had he kept working? What was he hanging on for? He could scarcely harbor hope of reinstatement at this point. His hanging on was simply a form of inertia. So he sat brooding, with the half-century mark soon upon him, and his gaze on the darkening sky of evening. When the telephone shrilled at his side, he answered irritably.

"Ja, what is it?"

"Hier Reichskanzlei. Dr. Hanfstaengl? You are urgently requested to report to Berlin. The Führer wishes you to see Herr Wiedemann as soon as it is possible for you to get here."

The first morning flight from Munich had him at Wiedemann's Chancellery office by midday. Wiedemann, Hitler's aide-de-camp, was one of the few members of Adolf's staff with whom he had been on good terms, and they shook hands warmly.

"Herr Hanfstaengl, the Führer wishes you to fly to Spain to protect the interests of our press correspondents there. Apparently they're having difficulties, and it needs someone like you to set things right."

Hanfstaengl's high spirits collapsed. What had he anticipated? He was not even sure—but something with the bright unequivocal sound of ice breaking: a welcome back, a reentry to the seat of power. True, that Adolf wished him to do anything at all was a change, but one apparently signifying very little. What he resented most was all this urgency. Had he got up at the crack of dawn only to be confronted by this distant dreary errand involving some no-account press problems?

"So what's the hurry?" he asked, sitting back in his chair and disgruntledly lighting a cigarette. "Day after tomorrow is my fiftieth birthday, and I have a family party down in Munich. Surely this business can wait until after that."

"No, you're to leave at once. Tomorrow. Check in with Ministerialrat Berndt over at the Propaganda Ministry; he'll give you the details. It's not a small matter, apparently. And I'll tell you something in confidence, Hanfstaengl: some of us have missed you badly around here. If you make a success of this mission, I have no doubt that the Führer will have you back here again. And your influence would be very valuable."

"Our people are having problems with the Franco authorities," said Ministerialrat Berndt, head of Goebbels's press division. "They are getting no assistance, and are having every sort of difficulty thrown in their faces. Ambassador Faupel—you know him well, don't you?—is willing to help, and you must get him right onto it. Report to him as soon as you get to Salamanca. You'll fly there directly and stay at the Grand Hotel. You'll be using a false passport, traveling as a Herr Lehmann, so send me a couple of photos as soon as possible. I'll have your papers in order by tomorrow, and I needn't add that for security reasons you mustn't discuss the mission with anyone. You'll be traveling by military plane, and we'll send a car at three tomorrow to pick you up and take you to the airfield. You can expect to be gone two or three weeks, maybe a month."

"Look here, Berndt, how can I leave for that length of time at this notice? Even if I abandon my birthday jubilee—and I can tell you that my aged mother is going to be very disappointed—"

"Ach, Hanfstaengl, really—"

"—even apart from that, I'll have to make all kinds of arrangements. And what am I supposed to wear? Most of my clothes are down in Munich."

"Get them sent up from Munich by plane. That's simple enough."

"More arrangements," he grumbled, scowling and getting to his feet, but in fact he was less annoyed at having to rush around than he was gratified by the mission's importance. He took his leave full of complaints, sighs and vitality.

The clothes arrived at his apartment the next day only an hour before his departure. He packed hurriedly, as he had done everything since his arrival yesterday: arrangements with his office staff, telephone calls to Munich, and this morning a quick trip over to the Air Ministry to see Göring, who had asked to talk with him before he left.

"So you're off to unsnaggle the journalists. Well, you can manage it if anyone can, Putzi."

"No doubt, but I can't say I enjoy being rushed off like this. Do you realize I'm having to give up my fiftieth jubilee tomorrow?"

"Don't brood over that. It's all going to go very well, I'm sure of it. And I'd like you to do me a favor. Bring me back an unbiased view of the political situation there. You know what we get from our press, snaggled or otherwise: Goebbelsdreck. So do me that favor, will you? Frankly, I wish I were going myself. I never get to go anywhere these days."

"Be glad. I've still got a dozen things to attend to, and hardly any time. I'd better be going."

"Well then, *bon voyage*," said the general with a hearty slap to his guest's shoulder. "And watch out for the ladies!" he called after him in his boisterous way. "Half my Luftwaffe personnel's got the clap already!"

And now it was three o'clock. Having barely finished his packing, he hurried down to the car Berndt had sent for him, climbing in beside a Propaganda Ministry functionary called Neumann, and an untidy-looking young man in a camel's-hair coat with a camera slung around his neck, who introduced himself as Jaworsky.

"I've been attached to you as your personal photographer, Dr. Hanfstaengl. And I can tell you, sir, that I know Spain like the back of my hand."

"You will find our Jaworsky indispensable," said Neumann. "I've been there recently myself, and I know what it's like. The conditions are very dangerous."

"Ach, nothing dangerous," countered Jaworsky with a shrug. "No defined front lines, that's all. Never know when a Communist patrol might pop up in front of you, but that's the only thing."

"Our little Jaworsky has a sense of humor," Neumann explained with dry distaste. "Still, I'm glad not to be going back myself. Civil wars are always brutal, but this one seems to be outdoing itself."

"Brutal?" said the youth. "I'll say it's brutal. Take a look at these. I haven't been photographing bathing beauties, I can tell you that." And he brought out a sheaf of pictures which he showed Neumann, pointing with a black-rimmed fingernail. "Here, look. And this one, what do you make of it? Man or woman?"

"Really, Jaworsky," Neumann protested, pushing the photographs aside. Hanfstaengl could see that they were pictures of mutilated bodies; and when Jaworsky offered them to him, he turned his head away, determined to give the boot to the ghoulish youth in Salamanca.

It was with relief that he got out of the car into the cold clean air at Staaken Military Airfield, and greeted Berndt, who stood waiting with his papers, and Colonel Bodenschatz and the station commandant. He shook hands all around, his suitcases were taken aboard, he was put through the rigmarole of trying on a parachute, and finally, disencumbered, he climbed inside the plane, a light bomber. Sitting down in a nook on a seat of bare metal, he arranged his great body in the tiny space and thought what a way it was to spend nine hours. Jaworsky climbed in, followed by an individual in a belted trench coat who was shoutingly introduced, over the roar of the motors, as a courier returning to Spain.

In his rush he had not thought to bring anything to read. Nor was it possible to look out the window, because there were no windows. The roar of the engines was deafening, everything vibrated. It was not exactly a luxury flight, but it possessed the charm of novelty, he decided, and arranging his bulk in the cramped space, he put on the earphones and tried to be entertained by the pilot's weather and location reports, which came at long, crackling intervals. By the time they had passed over Magdeburg, Göttingen and Kassel, his boredom weighed so heavily that he almost welcomed the sight of Jaworsky making his way to his side.

"The captain wants to see you," the photographer shouted over the roar, and Hanfstaengl unfolded his legs and hunched his way forward through the obstructed, low-ceilinged cabin into the cockpit, where the pilot gestured at the copilot's seat.

"Sit down, Herr Lehmann," he shouted. "I'm Captain Frodel. I thought you might like a change for a while. Pretty boxed-in back there."

"Something like being in a clothespress," Hanfstaengl shouted back, sitting down and drinking in the vast reaches of sky all around. It was growing dark, and far below he could see the clustered lights of towns and villages. "Clear as a bell," he shouted. "You should make good time. What is it to Salamanca, about nine hours?"

"Salamanca?" the captain shouted back. "I don't understand. I have no orders for Salamanca. I am to drop you over the Red lines between Barcelona and Madrid."

Hanfstaengl swung around in his seat, for a moment too stunned to speak.

"But that's a death sentence! What are you talking about? Who gave you such orders?"

"My orders are from General Göring himself. They're signed by the general in person. But I don't understand why you—"

"Göring!"

"But you've volunteered for this mission, Herr Lehmann. I don't understand what the problem is."

"Volunteered?" he yelled. "To parachute into enemy territory? To be shot as a spy? Are you crazy? Listen to me, my mission has been arranged by the Führer himself. I'm to report to Ambassador Faupel in Salamanca. I am Foreign Press Chief Hanfstaengl!"

"I'm sorry, there's no mention of that name in my orders. The name in my orders is Lehmann."

"Of course it is, it's a false name! I have a false passport! Ask that photographer, he knows who I am—no, don't. Gott im Himmel, what's happening? Listen to me, you've got to put down somewhere and call Berlin so we can sort this out!"

"I can't just put down somewhere. I have my orders."

"But you don't understand!"

"I understand what's in my orders. I'm sorry, Herr Lehmann, there's no use asking me to disobey them."

Unable to make sense of anything, the engines roaring in his ears, his throat raw from shouting. Hanfstaengl got up and made his way back from the cockpit, passing Jaworsky and the individual in the belted trench coat. He squeezed himself onto the hard metal seat of his nook, feeling stupefied.

They mean to kill me, he said to himself, with a flush of embarrassment, for the words had an absurd sound. I don't understand. I don't understand. . . . It will all go very well I'm sure, *bon voyage*! The swine, the incredible lying swine! Why is he doing this to me? And Goebbels too . . . the arrangements were made by the Propaganda Ministry, Berndt did the papers . . . and the car ride, all that talk between Neumann and Jaworsky, the atrocity photos, it was all planned.

Let him have something nice to chew on when he finds out where he's going. Send him up to the pilot after a couple of hours, let him know well in advance, let him suffer. And I suspected nothing . . . I who know I'm on a dozen blacklists, who've grown suspicious of everyone and everything, as soon as Adolf called I came running like a dog, slavering with expectation. What have I done to deserve this? Ah God, I have talked. I have talked against the Rhineland reoccupation, I talked against rearmament, I talked against this intervention in Spain, I never stopped talking. And why did I think Adolf would tolerate it forever and even ask me back? Because I used to play Wagner for him? Because he used to dandle my boy on his knee? Ach, Putzi, you fool, *this* is how it ends. The trench coat will see that you get into your parachute when the time comes. If you refuse, he'll shoot you up here. If you jump, the Reds will shoot you down there.

But I must do something! What if I talked to the pilot again? Maybe now that I've collected my wits I could get through to him—

As he got up and began making his way forward, the trench coat got up too, and almost casually, without expression, blocked his way.

He felt for the first time a coldness drop through him, an icy prickle in groin and armpits. Turning, he made his way back in the steady, vibrating, deafening roar and sat down again in the cramped nook, which suddenly took on the appearance of a coffin. He saw himself squeezed inside his own deafening, onrushing metal coffin, and he thought of that time he had gotten lost in the forest, how he had heard a thousand angels of death descend upon him—the suddenness, the unreasonableness, the horror—and afterward realized that it was his exhaustion and overwrought state, for they were only a truckload of singing workers, but he knew now that that hallucinatory moment had been his one clear grasp of truth—suddenness, unreasonableness, horror—and it seemed an astounding thing to him, astounding, and pitiful too, that he could ever have doubted it.

He was yanked from his thoughts by a brief clatter followed by a decrease in the roar's intensity. He heard the captain shouting from the cockpit that there was no reason for alarm; one of the engines was giving trouble and he would have to land somewhere and have it seen to. Hanfstaengl sat pondering and confused. Could it be that the captain, a decent soul after all, had concocted engine trouble for his sake? Or was there actually something wrong? What difference did it make as long as they set down? But no, he could not believe they would set down. Were they even descending? It was impossible to tell in this blind enclosure. But his fingers, more hopeful than his mind, had already buttoned up his overcoat. They had put his hat on his head. They lay spread on his knees.

There was a bump, then another, and minutes later he was climbing out with Jaworsky and the trench coat, and everything went very

fast after that. They were in a small airfield surrounded by pines, probably somewhere between Kassel and Frankfurt. The captain went off to
scare up a mechanic, while he and his two companions walked over to
wait in a small dimly lit canteen, where, with an expression of rising
vomit, confessing to airsickness and in the same breath clapping his
hand over his mouth, he made a staggering retreat down a passage to
the lavatory, which he continued swiftly past. He went through a
kitchen and out the back door into the pine woods, feeling his way
forward in the darkness, stumbling in snow, coming suddenly upon
railroad tracks and jogging alongside them until he saw a country depot, where, with hardly any breath left, he asked for a ticket to the
nearest town—Leipzig it was, there would be a train in four minutes—
Leipzig? That couldn't be, he was hundreds of kilometers from
Leipzig. Nevertheless he was in Leipzig half an hour later. It made no
sense, it was as incoherent as the rest of this insane night; but he would
waste no time wondering. He bought a ticket for Munich, arriving
there early the next morning—his fiftieth birthday, and it was festivity
enough to be breathing—found that there was a train leaving for
Zurich in three quarters of an hour, made a mad taxi dash home for
his passport and visas, a mad dash back just in time to catch the train,
and three hours later was safely across the Swiss border.

Days went by filled with frantic, covert efforts to arrange for his
son in boarding school to leave Germany secretly and join him where
he was holed up in a Zurich hotel, from which they would take further
flight to England. Snags turned the days to weeks, to a month, then
finally he was able to expect the boy daily. When one morning he hurried to answer a knock at his door, he was stunned to see not his son
but the tall figure of Colonel Bodenschatz, that good fellow, as he had
always seemed, with his long, pleasant, honorable face, who had so
viciously bundled him off in the bomber. Between astonishment and
outrage Hanfstaengl could only stare, as the colonel, with a murmured
word of greeting, held out a letter. He took it curtly, slammed the
door, and tore open the envelope. As he read, his face turned crimson
with fury.

Dear Putzi,

   You should have worn your Franz Josef whiskers, because someone
recognized you in the foyer of your hotel. The police have now issued orders
for your arrest and your property is being seized as recompense for flight
from the Reich. Why did you run away? The whole thing was a practical
joke! Just a prank to make you reconsider some overaudacious remarks that
had been brought to the Führer's attention. The plane was never more than
a hundred kilometers from Berlin, because it was going in a circle. It was

to circle around Berlin for five or six hours while you listened to false location reports, just to shake you up a bit, then you would be set down at Staaken Airfield right where you'd started. Didn't I hint broad as day that everything would be fine? Why didn't you remember that? If you hadn't bolted, you would have been back in Munich in time to celebrate your jubilee in the bosom of your family! There was no reason for you to flee the country and make such difficulties as have now arisen. But I am writing to tell you that I will straighten everything out for you. I can assure you on my word of honor that you may return in perfect freedom under my personal protection. I expect you to accept my offer.

Göring

He crumpled the letter. A joke! He had been the butt of a joke! And it rang true, for he had never been able to fathom the peculiarities of their route. A filthy prank, and not a word of apology, the insufferable swine! No, *I* have made difficulties for *myself*.

He paced the room, trying to calm down. But to have been used so cheaply, so unseriously! It was worse than if they had been in earnest. The sheer pervertedness of taking so much trouble for so little reason, the gratuitous cruelty of it. The whole thing stank of Goebbels. No question who had brought those remarks to the Führer's attention . . . "brought to his attention," what a euphemism—flapped in his face by that damned dwarf. The dwarf fans the flames, the mustache gives the order, the fat one sees to it—Gott, and that's my homeland! And he expects me to come back? Ach ja, and with gratitude! The overbearing bastard, he *expects* me to accept his offer. What kind of bullying threat is that? But it's pure unadulterated Göring. I have no doubt he's sorry and that it would do his heart good to make amends, and by God he'll have his heart done good to even if he has to drag me back by the scruff of the neck. Well, it's no go, Hermann. There's no way you can drag me back. I have money here, I have money in England, I'll survive. And before I leave here, God willing tomorrow, I'll have put this billet-doux of yours to its proper use as a piece of toilet paper. And I'll now present that fact to your worthy shadow out there.

But as he reopened the door, feeling himself so near the final lap of his flight, he was instinctively hesitant to make waves. He would say that he had to consider the offer, that would be the most sensible response. With frigid dignity he looked over to where the colonel stood leaning against the wall of the corridor, his fedora in his hand. His features had the grace to express abashment as he came forward.

"Well then, Dr. Hanfstaengl. Now you see what the situation was."

"Ganz. I see what morons you Luftwaffe people are. I should have thought you had better things to do than fly around in circles."

The colonel gave an embarrassed nod of agreement, and then—one could hardly blame him—took cover in his official role. "I'm supposed to take back an answer. What shall I say your reply is?"

"What? I should reply just like that? Why, the thing is an absolute scandal, Bodenschatz! I've been treated in a disgraceful fashion. I'll be damned if I'll be pushed. I want time to think this offer over."

"Well, that's understandable. What I'll do is go up to Arosa for a couple of days and do some skiing. We can talk again when I come back."

Watching his visitor depart down the corridor, Hanfstaengl had no expectation of seeing him again. But his son did not arrive the next day or the day after that, and he began thinking how he could put Bodenschatz off a second time.

"Does Göring's guarantee protect me against attacks from Goebbels?" he asked himself aloud as he stood shaving before the bathroom mirror. "Goebbels and I have had some nasty run-ins, I don't have to tell you that, Bodenschatz. We had one a few months back, and I see its significance now. I place that dirty little demon squarely behind what happened, and he's not the sort to let go once he's got his teeth in. What's to keep him from persecuting me in my job, or even personally? I feel the Führer has turned his back on me. That's a reasonable assumption, isn't it? He kicked me down the street a couple of years ago. Who took over my office? Ribbentrop. That's the direction of foreign policy now. Ribbentrop's the coming man, the Führer's fair-haired child. I'm out, Rosenberg's all but eclipsed—well, that's no loss—but wait and see, Neurath will be next, he's too much the old school for the Führer. Ribbentrop's angling for his job, and I'll bet you good money he'll have it inside a year. Can you imagine him our Foreign Minister?

"No, I shouldn't have been surprised to find myself down the far end of Wilhelmstrasse. And now the Führer's made himself unequivocally clear by ordering this piece of dirty work perpetrated against me. He has closed the door. And that will leave only Göring to keep Goebbels off me, and he can't even keep Goebbels off himself—you know what that jungle's like, nothing but backstabbing and Schweinerei. . . ."

The Reich's raconteur again, he had rambled on, lost to all but the flow of his words while his half-shaven face waited patiently. He returned to it, warning himself to stick to the point when his visitor reappeared.

He managed to do so, although it was not easy after weeks of addressing only desk clerks and waiters. Over whiskey and soda in the sitting room of the suite, Bodenschatz replied that he knew nothing about the details of the offer. He would report back to Göring and ring from Berlin in a few days.

Fully expecting to be in London by then, Hanfstaengl bade his guest a cordial farewell. But his son did not show up the next day, or the next. On the third day he heard from his go-between, his sister in Munich, who called him periodically from a public telephone in case her own was tapped. There had been further delays, she told him, but it was finally set now and the boy would arrive at the Zurich train station within the next forty-eight hours. She also told him that the order for his arrest had been withdrawn, so it was no surprise when Bodenschatz, who rang soon after, informed him that Göring had seen Heydrich and had the order rescinded. "As for the other matter, he says he'll keep the scorpion out of your pants, don't worry. But we'll discuss it all when I see you. I'll be back down in a couple of days."

"Don't break your neck getting here," he said with exasperation when the colonel had rung off. This damned persistence of Hermann's. Why does he have to feel so strongly about making things up to me? Of course, it was not Göring alone who wanted him back. His defection had put them all in a very uncomfortable position. Questions about his disappearance must be rife in diplomatic and foreign press circles; what were they to answer? And what if their filthy treatment of him came to light? Much simpler to have him back than risk damage to their prestige. There was little doubt that Göring was again acting on Adolf's orders, and if they coincided with Göring's own ebullient urge to make amends, so much the better from the fat one's point of view. But from Hanfstaengl's point of view, so much the worse to be the focal point of that tremendous energy. Bodenschatz's constant coming and going, this imminent sense of interruption and petition, when all he wanted was to anticipate the moment his arms would go around the boy at last, the moment they would climb aboard the first Paris-bound train.

That evening he sent his luggage on to the station to expedite matters for the next day's departure. He was determined that the boy would arrive tomorrow, and the colonel the following day, after they had gone. But the next day passed without any sign of his son. And the following day was the same: morning and afternoon dragged by as he paced in his room, the forty-eight-hour period coming to an end. He risked a telephone call to his sister's house in Munich, but there was no answer. He returned to his pacing, wondering why Bodenschatz had not turned up either, and feeling a new dimension to his foreboding. Something had gone terribly wrong. With a growing constriction of fear and helplessness, he tried again and again to get through to his sister until the hotel switchboard closed at midnight.

He tried to see everything in a reasonable light. It was just another delay, the boy would arrive tomorrow. His sister didn't answer because she was out somewhere. Bodenschatz had said he would come in a day or two, that could mean three. But it was the worst thing that he saw now: the boy arrested at the frontier, pulled off the train and shoved into a car. Or he had never left at all, but been arrested there, along with his sister. The plan had been known from the start. What did they have Himmler and Heydrich for? The ones who go through keyholes, through sealed envelopes, through telephone wires. But he was being irrational. There were limits, after all, to what they could manage. All these thoughts were absurd, extreme, they could not possibly know anything . . . and yet they always knew everything. And Bodenschatz— was his job finished now that he had kept the defector baited long enough for family hostages to be taken on grounds of conspiracy? In the Germany of today no sparrow went unobserved, unacted upon, and he was no sparrow, he was the foreign press chief, and he had fled the Reich, and he carried with him not only the fact of a vile prank but fifteen years' worth of gossip and scandal. What he didn't know about the National Socialist dramatis personae wasn't worth knowing. They had gotten rid of Röhm and Strasser without an eyeblink; why should they balk at him?

And still pacing, the sky having gone from black to gray to tints of pink, he felt that it was unbelievable that he had ever lost sight of the fact that there were no limits. He had known it in that moment of sheer icy horror up in the plane, and he had known it once before, that time in the forest, but it was a truth which he had somehow been unable to keep before him. It was not in the human soul to realize that the ordinary daylight hours were the illusion, and the hallucination, the dream, the nightmare that was reality.

He sank into a chair and closed his eyes. When he opened them the sky was a clear morning blue. Getting hurriedly to his feet, he headed for the phone to try his sister again, but it began ringing before he got there.

"Papa? Hier bin ich endlich!" came a cheerful young voice.

"Ach, du lieber! Egon!"

A few minutes later, having hastily shaved, thrown on his overcoat and grabbed his overnight case, he had hurried downstairs and was settling his bill at the desk. And as he stood there in the foyer with its thick carpets and tall potted palms and marble pillars, with its tranquil air of leisurely comings and goings, he realized that not once had he thought of taking refuge in some down-at-the-heels pension smelling of cabbage soup, where no one in a thousand years would have recognized him. Even in the extremity of his escape, he had kept mechanically to the dictates of habit and taste. How binding was the familiarity of certain textures, scents, intonations, all the things that created one's natural surroundings. And how right those things were, as if sanctified by God, so that one felt a deep, unconscious sense of benignity and indestructibility, simply to sleep between fine-woven sheets, to eat from good plate, to move among subdued and mannerly voices, simply to exist in the always-known, as if that were somehow an obviation of the unknown. Even as he concluded his little negotiation with mutual smiles and courteous phrases and walked out into the sparkling sunlight of the crisp cold morning, a gold-braided doorman zestfully tooting for a cab while well-dressed figures strolled by, he felt only the rightness and goodness and holy ordinariness of all this, its quality of sanctified permanence heightened by the joy of his imminent reunion with his son. Which joy was sending him in two eager strides to the cab that had just pulled up, and from whose door—swung open by the doorman as he bent down to climb in—he was startled to see, with a stab of embarrassment, Colonel Bodenschatz climbing out.

The colonel's own face reflected his startledness and embarrassment, for the situation was awkward to the point of comicalness—the seeker arriving, the sought decamping, their faces abruptly caught only centimeters apart.

"Off on a little trip?" asked the colonel as they both straightened up.

"Ah well, opportunity, you know. Just a little overnight rendezvous, seeing as I never did get to the Hispanic damsels." he replied, flushing at the idiocy of his words. But he was as good as gone, nothing could keep him, and both knew it. Since some word had to pass between them as civilized beings, it had to be a lie off the top of his head, and they both knew that too. And the ordinariness and civility of their mutual embarrassment, despite his burning face—Hispanic damsels!—was a pleasing thing to him as he climbed on inside, the doorman shutting the door behind him. "Hauptbahnhof," he told the driver, and rolled down his window. "Well then, Colonel, auf Wiedersehen. We'll talk tomorrow, of course."

"Of course."

He waited to be whisked away, but the driver, not to be hurried, was lighting a cigarette. He felt more embarrassed than ever to be stalled in last-minute silence. It was an anticlimax of normality, as was the colonel's long well-bred face stern with surprise and disconcertment, a face whose innocence Hanfstaengl felt an overwhelming need to splinter as the cab pulled away. He thrust his head out the window. "This isn't it, Bodenschatz!" he called back, sweeping his arm at the sunlit scene. "Don't you know that? Doesn't even he know that? Listen to me—when you hear a truckload of singing workers, that's not what you're hearing! That's not it at all!"

A day and a half later, Hanfstaengl and his son arrived in London, and Colonel Bodenschatz was back in Berlin at the Air Ministry, delivering the news of his failed mission to his chief.

"He checked out of the hotel the day I came. In fact, he was leaving as I got there. He was in a great rush."

"Well, did you talk with him at all?"

"A few words. Said he'd be back the next day, some ridiculous story. And something about singing, I don't know what he meant. He called back as he drove off—singing workers, I think that was it."

"Ah well, that's Putzi for you. He was bound to say something musical."

Chapter 41

ON weekends Kropp—or Robert, as he was now familiarly called by the Minister President—would have liked to sleep late, but there was no changing his employer's habit of rising early. Every day of the week he was up at half past six, in need of his coffee and his record music, and at about seven Robert began preparing him to meet the day. It was here that the Minister President's habits had changed. He no longer ran his own bath, shaved himself, or dressed with lightning speed or otherwise, but preferred to be set by others onto the hard rails of the morning, like a locomotive to be industriously stoked, oiled, polished, and heaved on its way. This was fine with Robert, who was, after all, a gentleman's gentleman; with no regret had he relinquished his duties as chauffeur to practice his profession on a full-time basis.

By now the routine was automatic. First came the steaming bath, into which the Chief sank with a great displacement of water, to lie soaking for a good long while. Eventually he would wash, and Robert would scrub the broad expanse of his back. Then he would rise from the tub with an enormous whoosh and step onto the mat, and Robert would briskly towel him dry. The scar tissue one had long since grown used to, yet one could not get over its impressive unsightliness. Covering hip, thigh, and part of the belly, it was red, like the inside of one's mouth, but rough and creased like a rhinoceros hide. It was tender and sometimes painful. This the Chief blotted dry himself. One then got him into his terry-cloth robe, and they returned to the bedroom, where the resident barber stood waiting. One still had difficulty lassoing the Chief for hair-cutting sessions, but he didn't mind being shaved and would sink back into the chair, closing his eyes. His face, always haggard in the morning, with heavy pouches under the eyes, was first steamed under a hot damp towel, then spread with lather, scraped clean by the razor, given a stimulating finger massage, refreshed with astringent cologne, and finally dusted with talcum. Often while he was shaved he had his nails done, a manicurist at either hand. Sometimes the pedicurist was also at work.

When these people had packed their equipment and gone, the dressing began. If it was a weekend the Chief might simply step into one of his big roomy dressing gowns, and that would be that. Such was never the case on weekdays. If he was to preside over the Reichstag, he would wear the brown Party uniform. If he was to work at the Air Ministry, then the gray-blue Luftwaffe uniform. If he was to attend some outdoor ceremony as Reichsmeister of the Hunt, then a modified hunting costume. If he was to work at his Prime Minister's office or his Four-Year Plan office, then a civilian suit. Later activities in the day might require other outfits, but even if not, one always accompanied him to Berlin for further changes necessitated by his copious sweating. The Chief was repelled by his sweat, and bathed and changed as often as four times a day.

Having selected the appropriate uniform—it was usually a uniform—Robert would first work his master into his special sweat-absorbent underwear, afterward spraying him up and down with cologne; then he would encase the body before him in shirt, tie, trousers and belt, and finally, as the Chief sat down and stretched out his legs, in hosiery and boots or shoes. They usually talked of one thing and another as Robert worked, his fingers nimble, smooth and deft. When the Chief rose again, Robert got him into his jacket, buttoning and belting it, after which the decorations went on. In this task Robert's fingers were also nimble; even if a special ceremony required that all the decorations be displayed, he had them pinned in place in a minute flat. But usually only three or four went on. Afterward he would bring over and open a jewelry box, from which the Chief would choose his ring of the day. He favored a great ruby, but was also fond of the emerald and the sapphire, and sometimes he chose more than one. Depending on his master's current weight, Robert would with ease or difficulty twist them onto his fingers.

Finally the Chief, stepping over to the cheval glass, would himself smooth his hair with two silver-backed brushes, turn to receive the cap and gloves Robert held out, and with a jovial word, now looking fresh, fit and resplendent, stride briskly down to breakfast, after which he would be driven to Berlin—bodyguard and adjutants following in two cars, Robert among them—to confront the demands of the day.

Outside the Air Ministry, a new and starkly modern building magnificent in size, Generalmajor Ernst Udet parked his car, which was not much bigger than himself, and went inside to collect his briefcase from his office and meet with the Commander in Chief. He had rolled out of bed only half an hour before, bleary-eyed, nostrils filled with his favorite bouquet of perfume, sloshed liquor, sweat, and the pungent tang of sex juices. As he passed through the main hall, which featured enormous murals depicting the history of German aviation from balloons to bombers, he glanced at the cheap tin watch he had worn in his combat days and every day these twenty years since. Dented, scratched, it still kept good time. He was late as usual; but then, the Chief was usually late. Upstairs by the reception desk he sat down and lit a cigar, a short well-padded man with a handsome, snub-nosed, ruddy face, a ruddy pate bordered by a respectable remainder of seal-brown hair, not particularly well trimmed, and eyes that looked out in a perpetual easy squint, the combined result of high rushing wind, wreaths of cigar smoke, and anticipated amusement.

At the sound of an echoing clatter down the hall, he rose, exchanged a friendly greeting with the rapidly approaching Göring, who did not break his stride, and fell in alongside him as aides hurried ahead to swing open the doors of his office, a room so vast that it resembled the stage of a theater. Accompanying him down the great length of the room, their footsteps resounding in a steady din, Udet was reminded of those endless pavement-pounding walks they had used to take in Munich. Short-legged, no bustler by nature, he was still hurrying to keep up as his companion strode rapidly along. But there was one difference: in the old days they had pounded around in circles, here at least they had a goal.

"Why don't you put this thing closer to the door?" he asked as they reached the desk, their din ceasing. "Ever thought of that, Hermann? Save a lot of fallen arches."

"What! Good exercise for everyone. You want to get fat?"

"Get?" he said as they sat down, the great polished expanse between them. "I already am."

"Nonsense," Hermann scoffed, lighting a cigar and pushing forward an ashtray to share. "Well, what have you got there in your suitcase? Let's have a look."

Portly, Udet said to himself as the Chief began to read. Let's face it, I'm portly. How in the name of a baboon's ass did I ever wind up with a desk job!

It had come about through passion at its purest. In 1933, stunt-flying in the United States, he had been invited to fly one of the Navy's dive-bomber prototypes, a plane that had thrilled his soul and a plane the German air arm should experiment with. He informed Hermann, the Curtiss Wright plant sold and shipped off to Germany two Curtiss Hawks, and for two years—until the official unveiling of the Luftwaffe—he had worked as a civilian with the air arm to perfect his beloved dive-bomber. But if he was to continue to oversee its development and champion its importance, he must have an official Luftwaffe post. Hermann had made him Inspector of Fighter and Dive-Bomber Forces, and he had been in his element as a connoisseur of small planes. When he wasn't test-piloting, he was flying from one factory to another in his little Siebel Beetle, scarcely ever sitting down in his office. But then somehow he had allowed Hermann to promote him to Chief of the Technical Office, a desk job loaded with responsibility. And he had accepted with reluctance.

Yet he was not entirely averse to occupying this sphere of greater influence. He had pushed the claims of the Stuka and its two variants, had guided the development of the Me-109 fighter that was proving so effective in Spain, and was solidly behind the work being done on the medium bombers. In the controversy following the air-crash death of Chief of Staff Wever, he had sided with Göring, Milch and Kesselring in the opinion that Wever's pet project should be abandoned: there would be no practical use for long-range bombers. All effort and funds pouring into this unnecessary prototype must be redirected to the increased manufacture of fighters and medium bombers. The stress must be on small machines capable of lightning attacks. Here on the desk between them were reports on the progress of one of Udet's favorites, the He-118.

Still, he would rather be flying an He-118 than bringing in reports on it. Although he continued to do some test-flying, it wasn't nearly enough to slake his thirst. How must Hermann feel, unable to squeeze into a fighter cockpit if he tried? Unbelievably oversized, and everything about him oversized: the heavy gold watch encrusted with diamonds; the enormous batonlike pencil, with which he made an occasional swift checkmark on the reports. And Carinhall—who needed a place like that? Too many rooms, too many objects, too many servants. He always enjoyed getting back from Carinhall to his small messy bachelor flat, and to his lovebird, Bubi, who rode around on his shoulder, and to his own set of friends, film actresses, journalists, race drivers, jockeys . . . his and Hermann's paths had diverged immeasurably since their youth. It was only their youth, their shared combat days, that provided a meeting ground. But there they met well. Their conferences always turned into long nostalgic chats.

The papers were pushed back across the desk and a discussion ensued, ending with Hermann's advice to inform him if there was any problem with the request for funds—although this problem seldom arose, Hermann being in charge of the German economy—after which they settled into their reminiscences. Presently they were interrupted by the telephone buzzer.

"Tell him to wait," Hermann said, glancing at his watch. "I said ten forty-five. Not ten-forty." And he set the receiver down hard. That would be Milch, Udet said to himself. Milch's time had come. Even to be demoted, he arrived early.

A few minutes later, as he began his long racketing trek down the room, briefcase in hand, Udet saw the distant doors open to admit Milch and his eternal ashtray. Always carried an ashtray. Compulsively tidy, wouldn't think of dropping an ash on the floor. The face grew steadily nearer: round cherubic features, ice-water eyes. Made you think of a virtuous calculating machine, although he was neither virtuous nor a machine; no machine turned crimson at the smallest word of criticism—if only for an instant before the heat was pulled back with a hiss into the ice. Tough, controlled, driven; and driven to no purpose as far as Udet could see: Milch worked hard in order to work harder, was efficient in order to be more efficient. He administered the Luftwaffe, but it might as well be a dry-goods store or a sausage factory. Still, different as they were, they had been on good terms until recently. Milch's increasing control over the ministry, his penchant for filling offices with his own appointees, was beginning to interfere with the running of Udet's own department. Udet acknowledged his debt of gratitude to the man's technical expertise, but he felt a definite coolness toward the figure whose echoing path now crossed his own.

Milch curtly returned Udet's nod. He knew why he had been called in, and was deeply angry. The pretext would be his increasing friction with the General Staff, who resented his position, but no one resented his position more than Göring himself. Jealous, hostile, rude. Sometimes his voice rose in a shout—that was hateful, like a physical assault. And could he help it if people said he ran the Luftwaffe? Could he help Goebbels's latest quip? "What is the definition of a Milch? A Milch is a Göring who works." It happened to be true. He showed up, Göring didn't. He put time in, Göring didn't. He knew what he was doing, Göring didn't. What did Göring know about the technology of modern aviation? He, Milch, had been head of Lufthansa, whereas Göring had lost all contact with planes after the war, hadn't kept up with technical advances, and anyway wasn't interested in that side—the practical, dull side—of aviation. In that respect he and Udet were a perfectly matched pair of ignoramuses. Without him neither would have the slightest grasp of bomber engines, the complexities of manufacturing, the meaning of production figures. Above all, without him there would be no supremely organized ministry. Göring owed him everything, and now he would reap Göring's gratitude.

He had arrived at the desk. He set down his ashtray, seated himself, and was immediately attacked.

"I've had one complaint too many from the General Staff. Stumpff tears his hair out over you. He came to me yesterday. It can't go on. The changes that have been under discussion must be put into effect."

Milch felt a stab of facial heat, but replied coolly, "If those changes go into effect, you will find that nothing can go on."

"Don't tell me what I'll find! It's not only the General Staff, it's every department in the ministry! Don't you think I've got eyes in my head? You're my deputy, but you're no more than that. I put you where you are, and I won't tolerate your usurping my authority!"

The loud angry voice sent another, more scalding flush across Milch's face, leaving a frosty sensation around his lips. He answered yet more coldly: "Someone must be in charge of everything. If I don't do it, you will have to. But you won't."

"Don't tell me what I will or won't!"

Milch moved his eyes, with eloquent obviousness, to a framed picture standing with other objects on the broad desktop. A sketch that Udet had done in 1934, it showed Göring in rolled-up sleeves hard at work over a lathe, drops of sweat flying from his face; covering the work table and floor were multitudes of little wooden planes; at the bottom was written: *And look, as morning dawns afar, our man has built the Luftwaffe!* There was no question that he had worked like a maniac laying the foundation of the Luftwaffe, or that his energy and zeal had inspired everyone around him to great heights; he had been a tremendous driving force, a man of huge impulses, which had been translated by himself, Milch, into practical actuality. But then he had begun sloughing off, maybe the sort to lose interest once he had breathed something into life, maybe too many other offices; whatever the reason, he had never put his hand back to the lathe. The drops of sweat never flew again.

He lifted his eyes from the sketch, as did Göring, whose face still expressed anger, if anger now under control.

"Naturally I'll put more time in," he said shortly. "I'll make the time."

"It won't be enough," Milch replied, giving his cigar a sharp tap over the ashtray. "You mean to put me on the same level as the other departments. They will no longer work with me, but will consult with you directly. Well then, you must be available to them, but you won't be. I warn you, if you demote me you'll ruin the continuity of ministerial work. There must be a single, central authority. And if you won't be, then I must be."

"You have the gift of repetition, Milch. That gift comes from an inability to hear. My decision is *made.*"

"Then there's no point in our talking further," Milch said, getting up. "We only waste valuable time. I, at any rate, have work to do."

"Gut. Go do it," Göring told him dismissively. "And take your damned ashtray with you."

Flushing anew, he started the long walk to the door. One thing he would say for Göring, his manners were a first-class imitation of a sow's. But Göring needed him. Think of the trouble he had taken to get him, and then to keep him when it became known he was half Jewish. "I will decide who's a Jew and who isn't! We'll find a loophole for you, Milch, depend on it." Actually, Milch had found his own loophole. His mother being Aryan, his dead father Jewish, he would simply ask her to state that she had deceived her husband with some non-Jew, the result being himself. A simple plan, but she could not understand, had carried on, had wept into her handkerchief. It took him three visits to make clear to her that his career was ruined if she didn't comply. Göring supplied the affidavits, and suggested he make his new father a baron. "Why not do it up well as long as you're doing it? But tell me—your mother is really willing to sign this thing?"

"Of course she is. She has only one wish, and that is to help her son in any way she can."

And Göring had answered, with a sardonic smile, "Well, your choice in mothers can't be improved on, at any rate."

Caustic bastard. But he needed his deputy, and would protect him. No one would attack Milch on racial grounds. And Milch had improved on Göring's protection by taking up a strong anti-Semitic line. His position was in most ways secure. He was on excellent terms with the Führer. His frequent dinner guests were Goebbels, Himmler and Hess, who clearly saw in him a future Air Minister. Above all, Göring needed him. Today he had had his wings clipped, but they would grow again. When one was indispensable, one regenerated. Even so, his anger was enormous as he went out the double doors, holding his cigar over his ashtray, and headed down the hall with a nod at Colonel Bodenschatz coming around the corner—the original Göring man, the worthy shadow, the bright-eyed listener. Bodenschatz was the first, but there were too many Göring lovers. Flocks, especially the younger officers. A whole new generation of hero worshipers.

"Angry," Bodenschatz commented to himself. The only way you ever knew was by a white line around the lips. No frown, no flash of the eyes, a face perfectly composed except for the white line, which was very white indeed. He went on to the reception desk, and a few minutes later was sitting down opposite Göring. "A little contretemps?" he asked, indicating the door with his hand.

"What is Milch? A fart out of my asshole! Never mind, so you're back. How did it go?"

"Very well indeed. They're fine fellows, those RAF men. Couldn't do enough to make my stay pleasant. I have regards from those who visited us last spring. They want to return our hospitality and have Udet and his staff come over for their air show in Hendon. Oh yes, and I talked with Hanfstaengl. Said he wouldn't come back under any conditions. So I got tough as you suggested, told him things might become unpleasant for his family. But he said if he heard the slightest thing against them he'd publish everything he knew. He made special mention of his joyride."

"Well, that's good enough. Just so he doesn't run around blabbering. As long as he thinks he's over a barrel he'll be the soul of discretion. How was he, by the way?"

"Seems to be thriving. Nice flat in the West End. Piano, of course."

"No musical message?"

"No message at all."

"Well. Well, tell me what they thought of their tour of the Messerschmitt factory when they were here. It should have scared the pants off them."

"Their pants are back on, but they express a very healthy respect for German air power. Here, I have everything down in notes," said Bodenschatz, bringing them out.

At the Leipziger Platz Palace, Robert expected the Minister President back at about one o'clock, for he was to attend a formal reception at the Italian embassy at half past. From the closet, which contained a duplicate wardrobe of the one at Carinhall, he had already taken out the special cutaway uniform appropriate for the occasion. He stood rubbing up the buttons as he heard from the courtyard below the clicking of heels, slamming of car doors, and multiple clatter of footsteps. However, his master did not come up the stairs to change, and it was already ten past one.

At a quarter past one, Feldmarschall von Blomberg was shown into the palace study, where General Göring awaited him. "I apologize for descending on you like this," he said as they shook hands, for he had telephoned the general only an hour earlier to ask if he could speak to him privately as soon as possible.

"There is no need to apologize. I am glad to see you, Herr Feldmarschall. Bitte, sit down."

They sat down, but Blomberg did not begin at once. The walls were lined with beautifully bound old books that imparted a gold ambience, a mellow aura. It was a restful room, and he hoped that his problem would find rest here. Finally, he said, "I would like to ask your help in a private matter. I'm not sure that I should trouble you with it. But I . . . as you know, I've been a widower for some years. The fact is, I intend to remarry."

"But that's fine news. Congratulations!"

Blomberg nodded. Surely he was to be congratulated on being reborn. He felt awakened to life's poetry, dazzled by flowers, butterflies, flaming sunsets. But he was past sixty, and he knew how foolish must seem a man his age who has fallen in love. His face grew severe as it gathered even more dignity than that which characterized it.

"It is not a simple thing, I'm afraid."

"What's the difficulty? The lady has a husband? We'll get her a divorce, that's simple enough."

"The lady is not married, that's not the problem. I should tell you at once, General, that she is much younger than I. Thirty years. But our relationship is not what it might seem from the outside. It is based on deepest love and deepest mutual respect."

"But forgive me, Herr Feldmarschall. Surely this is a matter that concerns only you and her."

"But you see, there is this too. Here we come to the problem. My fiancée is—how shall I put it—of a very modest standing socially. To be frank, her mother is a laundress. She herself works in a restaurant. For some weeks I've wished to make our engagement public, but I've held back. Today I told myself I could not go on like this any longer." And as he said this, he was painfully reminded of the nickname Gummilöwe, and felt his face grow stonier yet with dignity. "The subject must be broached to the Führer. Naturally my private life is my own affair, but as Germany's senior officer, as Feldmarschall and Minister of War . . . as a brother officer you understand what I'm saying. Such a marriage is not within the tradition of the officer corps. It may provoke reaction. Nothing will deter me from marrying, but I have a responsibility to my position, and I could well understand if the Führer were . . . were not happy with my news."

"You're making too much of this. It is a *mésalliance,* but not a disaster. A disaster would be if you married the crocodile woman in the circus. I think you may provoke a few raised brows among our colleagues, but nothing worse. But if you wish me to tell the Führer on your behalf, to pave the way, so to speak—this is what you're asking?— I will do so gladly."

"I would be most grateful."

"I think the Führer will consider it a step in the direction of a true classless society. For his most senior officer to marry a daughter of the people—that can only impress him as an act exemplifying the ideals of national unity. But on a more practical level, you might consider lowering some of those brows by giving a different professional status to your friend, temporarily, until the wedding."

"That was something else I wished to bring up."

"No difficulty. Let me think . . . something in the Four-Year Plan, perhaps. The River Purification Authority? Perhaps the Crop Coordination Office? What about the State Beef Unit? Nein, the State Egg Marketing Board. They're understaffed just now. I shall see to it."

"I hardly know how to ask you something else. There is a man, a good deal younger than I. An ex-suitor of the persevering type, and not very pleasant. If he could perhaps be—"

"No difficulty. We'll give him a check and a ticket for South America. Just give me the information, and I'll go ahead with it all. And of course I will attend the wedding myself, as a gesture of confidence. I am certain the Führer will do the same."

The two men rose.

"I can never thank you sufficiently, Herr General, on behalf of both Fräulein Gruhn and myself."

"No thanks are in order, Herr Feldmarschall. I am glad to do it, and I do it from the heart. For I too am a romantic."

March music, drums, the thud of the Stechschritt: the changing of the guard came echoing down the street from the Air Ministry. Two o'clock, and the Minister President had not yet come upstairs to change for the embassy reception. Robert sat leafing through an issue of *Der Adler*, the official Luftwaffe magazine. It was one of those which was printed in English, for American and British distribution, and he could not read it. He looked at the pictures instead, glancing from time to time at his watch. He was a thin wiry man with glossy black hair, dressed in impeccable gray pinstripe trousers, dark suit jacket and vest, and a silk tie from which gleamed a discreet pearl stickpin. He got crisply to his feet as the Chief finally came hurrying through the door, already unbuttoning the jacket of his uniform.

"I'm late," he said, as Robert took over the buttons.

"Very, Excellency." He stripped off the jacket and began on the shirt.

"I must see Schacht afterward, I won't have time to come back and change. Get an afternoon suit out."

"That will not be appropriate for an embassy reception, sir."

"Ja, well, I'll set a new style." He stepped free of his sweaty clothes on the floor and headed toward the bathroom to shower. "The pongee," he threw over his shoulder.

"The pongee? Impossible. One cannot wear silk after September."

"But I like my pongee suit," protested the Minister President, turning around in the doorway. "It's my very favorite."

Robert's brow knotted with this crisis. The officer class knew exactly what it was about when the matter was uniforms, but not one of them had an inkling of what was customary in civilian clothes. It was lack of training. One saw them in white linen on a foggy day, in brown tweed in July; what's more, the cut was usually deplorable. No one could look dowdier than an officer in mufti. Robert was proud that he had done such wonders with the Minister President, but on occasion the valet's wisdom and taste went for nothing.

"Pongee is out of the question," he said firmly. "It is forbidden after the summer months."

"I see. I shall be executed."

"Ja. By me."

"Then do as you will, Robert. I leave it to you." He disappeared through the door.

Chapter 42

Before a palatial stone building on Matthäikirchstrasse, the spectacle of diplomatic top hats and emblazoned uniforms had dwindled away; with no further guests arriving, the crowd of onlookers began drifting down the street. Inside, the liveried pages who lined the stairway were leaving their posts, while upstairs the reception line had dissolved and become part of the general socializing. The Italian embassy, second only to the French in opulence, boasted an ambassador's wife as elegantly beautiful as her surroundings; thus all the more startling was her absence of decorum, for Madame Attolico would embrace and kiss the women she knew, would swing a man's hand coquettishly or lightly slap his face, would talk freely about her children's antics or the cost of her servants. This behavior had at first rumbled like a shockwave through the rigid Prussian formality of diplomatic gatherings, but no one could hold out against her, she was too captivating; and her husband's receptions had become the most popular in Berlin. He was a squat man with cropped gray hair, his face glum and gruff behind thick pince-nez. "Isn't he more German than you Germans?" she would ask in her low, thrilling, Garbo-like voice, pausing at his side for a moment before gliding off to someone else; and the Germans, not knowing if she had insulted them, or him, or both, or no one, would lift a brow and continue the conversation, for she was after all captivating, and her parties possessed a verve and originality that were unquestionably refreshing.

Frau Ambassador von Papen, standing with Frau Minister Goebbels, observed their hostess leaning down to adjust the strap of her silver slipper.

"Everything she does is so unusual. Wouldn't one have taken care of that in private?"

"It is all done for effect," said Frau Goebbels, not sipping her champagne for fear of nausea, being in the early stages of her fifth pregnancy. "Her only desire is to be different. See whom she invites."

"Surely the embassy staff does the inviting."

"Surely she has her way."

They were both looking at the Russians standing in a group across the room. As if certain of being snubbed, the group refrained from mingling, while with good-humored naturalness they received the overtures of those guests who chose to socialize with them.

"Fifty thousand, I have heard," said Frau von Papen.

"Perhaps a million."

Stalin's purge of his officer corps and of former Bolshevik comrades had reaped worldwide notoriety. Improved relations with Britain had taken a sharp nosedive as the Soviet leader revealed himself to be an Asiatic savage. What's more, by directing his savagery at his army officers he had stupidly torn his own forces to bits; not only spiritually but practically, Russia had disqualified herself as a possible ally. As for Germany's moral outrage, it was best seen in the fact that not one German was among the modest number of guests conversing with the savage clot. This was a matter of quiet amusement to the pariahs themselves, who had been the object of National Socialist scorn and insult for so long that they could only consider Stalin's purge to be, for the Germans, a welcome icing on the cake.

"So original to have them here," remarked the Minister of Culture, joining the two ladies.

"Everything is so original," Frau Goebbels agreed. "Especially the hour."

"I am told it's because he leaves early this evening," said the Minister, referring to the Italian Foreign Minister, the guest of honor.

"I am told he was not eager to come at all," said Frau von Papen.

"Ciano?" The Minister smiled. "Forgo a reception?"

"But there's bad blood between them," added a young attaché. "Look at the face."

"Attolico's? When isn't it like that?" added yet another male newcomer, for Frau Goebbels was having her usual magnetic effect. And she was enjoying it, although she had not used to. Her social success made Josef suffer. After parties he was woundingly sarcastic, and not from jealousy—that she might have welcomed—but from envy. And

this knowledge had once made her suffer more than he: to know that
when he looked at her from across the room it was not she whom he
wanted for himself, but those around her. Now she didn't care. She
was attracted to another man, and this filled her with a happiness that
nothing could disturb, not even Madame Attolico, whom she considered a calculating hostess parading as a child of spring. See her gliding over to Josef and taking hold of his hand, and he of course
charmed and charming, grinning from ear to ear—Gott, so many teeth
he had—and see the vapors of flirtation rising, a thing that once would
have distressed her even though his taste was not for ambassadors'
wives but for vulgar starlets. The scene could not touch her happiness.
What could? she wondered. Perhaps the presence of the so-called First
Lady of the Reich . . . but no, not even that could bother her, although
the Görings' absence certainly took nothing from her enjoyment.

"My dear, you're looking radiant," Frau von Papen said, pressing
her hand in leaving. "I must go rescue my husband from that Japanese
gentleman who talks so much."

"Does he need rescuing?" Magda asked with a smile, Papen being
an eel, a magician. Think how he had barely escaped with his life during the crisis of 1934—two assistants shot out from under him, so to
speak—and had given such a smart midair twist that he landed neat as
a cat and was soon flourishing again, at present as ambassador to
Vienna.

"Ach ja, he is too courteous. The Japanese gentleman talks
ceaselessly in impossible German."

And she moved off, glancing at a press correspondent crossing her
path. Journalists were another original touch. One could pick them out
by their tacky suits, as well as their gypsylike way of wandering about.

A newcomer to Germany might in fact have judged who was of
current importance by observing the wanderings of the journalists. For
instance, they spent no time at all near the Deputy of the Führer of the
National Socialist Party for the Entire Spiritual and Ideological Training and Education of the National Socialist Party, who under this staggering title carried out a few vague duties but nevertheless harbored
strong hopes of becoming Foreign Minister. He was also known as "Almost" Rosenberg, dubbed so by Goebbels because he had almost managed to become a scholar, a journalist, a politician, but only almost.
And Rosenberg was cut to the quick by this name, though not for its
literal meaning. Goebbels was an almost, but Rosenberg himself was a
totality. "Total" Rosenberg should be his name. Goebbels utilized bits
and pieces of ideology to build power for the regime, whatever was
useful, and if it didn't prove effective, why, then grab a different bit—
all hit or miss, impromptu, without core; Goebbels had even said National Socialism was indefinable, for it was subject to continual change
and transformation. Such a statement was beyond comprehension. The

movement meant nothing, and could result in nothing, unless it con-
formed to the letter of its ideology. The sight of Goebbels pegging by
had sparked these continually smoldering thoughts, but now Rosenberg turned back to the more pleasant activity of bowing as someone
yet again paused at his side to congratulate him.

"My best wishes, Herr Rosenberg. A great honor."

"Danke. Most kind."

At Nuremberg this year the Führer had presented him with the
first German National Art and Science Award, the regime's equivalent
of the Nobel Prize. It had done much to lift his spirits. Time and again
the Führer had passed him over for an important post, but now at last
it seemed that he had been given an augury of greater things.

His wife came over to him smilingly, with a new joke about Goebbels, thinking to please him. "Why does Goebbels have such a big heel
on his shoe?" she asked in a whisper. "It's where he keeps his battery."

He did not smile back—it was low to attack someone for a physical
disability—and she went off with a shrug. He stood looking at Foreign
Minister von Neurath, whose place he hoped to fill. The Baron was of
the old school, he lacked understanding of the movement's ideology.
And it was in the field of foreign affairs that National Socialist ideology
was meant to fulfill itself. It was a philosophy that went outward. Eastward. Its boundaries were not domestic.

Rosenberg's face was solemn. Years of disappointment had removed what little lightness it had ever possessed. His black formal attire of this afternoon suited the gravity of his countenance, but even his
ordinary clothes were dark and sober, so far a cry from his youthful
outfits that one of Hanfstaengl's last witticisms, before he had disappeared, was that the Costermonger's Donkey had turned into a hearse.
And this thought did cause a small smile to form on Rosenberg's lips.
Hearse indeed. It was Hanfstaengl who was gone, perhaps under a
black plume. It was he himself who was alive and forward-looking, and
again he looked at Neurath, and in his mind the philosophy of his
mission burned with a thousand flames.

The urbane von Neurath, portly and silver-haired, also held little
attraction for the journalists, but this was not true of his underling,
Ambassador to Britain von Ribbentrop, who stood talking with French
Ambassador François-Poncet. Von Ribbentrop possessed a monumental dignity at once arrogant and sleepy-looking. In it was no recognition
that he had acquired his von from a childless aunt, or his fortune
through marriage to the Henckel wine heiress. He knew these facts
were without meaning, for they were without pertinence to the inner
man. The inner man consisted of statesmanship genius. On this he
stood—tall, slender, straight, yet with the merest suggestion of an English upper-class slouch. He had impressive good looks, a smile that
could sometimes surprise by its warmth, and hair that prematurely,

with a sense of the proper thing, had gone a magisterial gray at the temples. He was deep in conversation with François-Poncet, who stroked and twisted his black waxed mustache as they talked. Connected with powerful munitions interests in France, Poncet owned a mind to match, although its power was expressed in the most elegant of wordplays, epigrams and innuendos. Conversation was to him an exhilarating duel, or should be. He, the most mannerly of men, was apt to cut himself off in midsentence and depart with a nod—as he did now, giving his mustache a final twist—when he found dull minds too excruciating to bear. Ribbentrop, whose experiences with Poncet were always of this order, had long since concluded that the man was an eccentric, and was not offended by his abrupt departure. He turned his head a trifle, scarcely looking around or having to, for others were stepping eagerly toward him.

Another cynosure was the guest of honor, Count Ciano, Italy's Foreign Minister. Italian career diplomats considered him a spoiled child of fortune, a handsome and ridiculously young Fascist interloper with Mussolini as a father-in-law. Handsome he was, glossily black-haired, with a tawny smoothness of even features, but nature had sabotaged his beauty with a slack excess of flesh beneath his chin, and in order to minimize this he held his head extremely high, higher than his father-in-law's. The effect was astonishingly arrogant, many degrees more so than his sprightly swagger or his cheerfully disdainful smile, which consisted of one side of his mouth pulled down lower than the other, a smirk, actually.

His glory of pride lay in being the representative of a young new Fascist generation, and in his overhauling of foreign policy, and he spoke boldly and gladly on these subjects.

"In Italy, the most Fascist ministry is that of foreign affairs," he was telling his listeners. "But of course that was not so until last year." Until his arrival, to be exact. He had filled the ministry with his own youthful appointees, and felt deepest contempt for the old professional diplomats whom he had removed, and for those like Attolico who still headed the great embassies abroad. They belonged to the tradition of decadent Western democracy, they lacked fire and faith, they betrayed the heroic spirit of the new regime. His predecessor, Foreign Minister Grandi, supposedly a Fascist idealist, had been tamed by these old hens in striped trousers. Someone brought up Grandi's name, and he replied absently, moving on to another group awaiting his company, "He is quite uninteresting, and has the intelligence of a mosquito."

He is speaking of me? How dare he! thought nearby Ambassador Attolico for one fantastic, outraged moment before realizing that not even Ciano would publicly insult his host. With his face so gloweringly gruff by nature that neither his momentary anger nor his resumed enjoyment made any difference to it, he continued his conversation

with Count Ciano's wife, who charmed him very much. Daughter of a
peasant she might be, but she was chic, bright, and cultivated, and even
more winningly, she was thoughtful enough to remain at his side for
more than the few obligatory moments he usually received. But, stag-
geringly charmless himself, he was soon having to bow at the departure
of even this kindly creature and to sip his wine in order to be doing
something, his eyes resting again on the thrown-back head of Ciano.

The journalists were aware of the coolness between the Italian Foreign Minister and his ambassador. They were aware of many
coolnesses, many frigid drafts crisscrossing the room, creating a mesh-
work almost impossible to sort out, so that one was always straining to
hear some clear, concrete remark, such as the one the British Ambassador, Sir Nevile Henderson, had reputedly let drop at a recent Carinhall dinner party, commenting to Göring as if referring to a plate of
radishes, "You can have Austria as far as I'm concerned." But gems like
that were rare. This particular gem got bruited about, the Austrian
Ambassador learned of it and was outraged, and Ambassador Henderson was pulled back to London. But not to be replaced, obviously, for
here he was back again, cheerful and outgoing as ever.

He was a round man, the Austrian Ambassador, with a plump and
childlike face. A mildly comical little figure, representing a helpless
rump state, he was returning from the buffet table with a plate held
before his roundness. Small tables had been set up throughout the
room; he sat down at the one nearest the buffet, for he would want
seconds. The table was occupied by Dr. Schmidt, Hitler's personal interpreter and an official of the Foreign Ministry staff, who was on hand
for translating at most diplomatic functions. The two men knew each
other, and there was an exchange of pleasantries. Then silence fell, for
the Austrian Ambassador ate with the seriousness of a child.

"I had a dog once, a whippet," he said at length, sitting back to pat
his lips with his napkin. "Very beautiful, only its head was so narrow
there was no room for a brain."

"Interesting," replied Dr. Schmidt, with the shadow of a smile.
The Ambassador was known for his non sequiturs, like those of an
absentminded professor. They hung in midair for a moment, then dissolved into eternal mystery.

Ja, interesting, the Ambassador said to himself, a curious breed of
dog, the Hendersons. And he saw in his mind's eye, superimposed on
the piece of food his fork was spearing, the figure of the British Ambassador, narrow from head to foot, a perfect caricature of the upper-
class Englishman. Nothing had enraged him more than that "go ahead,
take her" remark, its insulting stupidity. Britain's attitude, embodied by
Sir Nevile over there, back from London with his wrist lightly slapped,
was that Austria was a passive entity. A chunk of meat—rump steak—
best fit to fill the German belly. Let Germany do whatever she wants

for a while, let her have her way and so regain her self-respect, then she will be satisfied and settle down. But it was a British concept entirely, the gobbling-up of Austria. Why should Hitler bother with that? Certainly he wanted Austria to go National Socialist, but he would see to that by continuing to back the Austrian National Socialists; it was what he meant by a "natural, evolutionary process toward unity." And it was inevitable. Here the Ambassador differed with Chancellor Schuschnigg, who loathed the idea of releasing National Socialists from the Vienna jails and allowing them a voice in his government. Schuschnigg was willing to accept all the benefits of Austro-German closeness as long as his own government remained intact. But it would not happen. Austria would become a National Socialist state. But an *Austrian* National Socialist state. And it was this—Austrian self-determination, Austrian autonomy—that the British so obscenely insulted with their sanguine, cretinous attitude: do with her as you want, fill your belly, be content.

Others were sitting down with them. The small tables were gradually filling. Having finished eating, Dr. Schmidt rose with a polite word and began wandering about. Like the journalists, he did a lot of this. But they did it to learn more. He, who was present at almost every conference between German and foreign leaders, even the most private, did it through boredom, already knowing more than anyone else in the room. What would the journalists like to know? That, for instance, of all the diplomats he had worked with the most talented was not an official diplomat at all but Göring? Blunt Göring was actually the most cunning of men, with a lightning finesse of thought that was not apparent until afterward, when one realized that his seemingly forthright, ingenuous conversation had with immense subtlety gained his ends. Dr. Schmidt had accompanied him to Poland, Yugoslavia and Italy, and had been consistently impressed with his work in carving yet a new sphere for himself, in the diplomatic field.

Yet Dr. Schmidt was not impressed with diplomacy as such. Perhaps he was too objective. Politesse surrounded him as he walked along: mannerly voices, courtly nods and bows, an elegance of deportment like a behavioral twin to the beauty of the room with its marble pillars, its gorgeous floral arrangements, its long mirrors reflecting the brilliant chandeliers and brilliant crowd—all those glossy, well-groomed heads, not a hair out of place. If every jugular vein in the room were cut, and it might not be a bad idea, the blood would rise along these gilt-arabesqued walls to a level of probably ten, twelve centimeters, he guessed . . . but blood, the merest speck, was as unthinkable here as vomit or excrement. Unthinkable unless you happened to think of it. And you thought of it if you happened to think, for instance, of the Austrian Ambassador back there at the little table, whose government under Dollfuss had shelled to death some hundred men, women and children in the Vienna workers' housing project. If you thought of Ciano, and of Abyssinian corpses rotting by the thousands in the sun. If you thought of Neurath and of German aid to the Spanish rebels, of bombers disemboweling old people and infants among others. If you thought of Sir Nevile and of England's nonintervention in Abyssinia and Spain, of her pale, well-manicured hands resting motionless in her lap. If you thought of the Russians over there, of thirty or fifty or eighty thousand bodies falling before the firing squads. Ironic that the Russians were ostracized for doing things on a grand scale. What was the real difference, after all? And it seemed to him as he paused to take a glass of wine, sipping from the etched Venetian crystal, that he was in a tank of sharks, or inside a lunatic asylum, and again he envisioned bright blood gushing, pooling, rising up these creamy gilt-arabesqued walls.

"Dr. Schmidt, if you will be so good," someone said, coming up to his side. Carrying his glass, he followed, passing Madame Attolico's beauteous back as it rippled with her Garboesque laughter; and farther on the resplendent green-gold-and-white uniform of the guest of honor; and here came Herr and Frau Almost Rosenberg, plates in hand, sitting down at the radiant Frau Goebbels's table; and here at another table sat Mahatma Propagandhi, something of an Almost himself—or more accurately, a Got There but Now Slipping—his food ignored as he held forth to his tablemates; and here by a pillar the lonely Attolico, but not so lonely, no, being talked to nonstop by a small Japanese gentleman; and here—they had arrived—was the Polish Ambassador in need of lingual assistance in his conversation with an Argentinian attaché. *"Jestem gótow tilumaczyc, panow,"* said Dr. Schmidt, bowing, and at once became absorbed in his task.

Suddenly through the door charged a latecomer, someone in an ordinary gray suit who made his way straight through the crowd toward the buffet table. A murmur arose as Göring was recognized, clearly in one of his don't-give-a-damn moods, plowing forward without a word of greeting to anyone. Hungry. This directness was part of his popularity, and the murmurs were mostly admiring, especially among the women. He could be the exact opposite, too, the soul of urbane charm—his moods fluctuated so drastically, along with his weight, that rumors were thick that he had relapsed to his morphine habit, for everyone knew of his former addiction, although he had gone so far as to have the records in Sweden destroyed. Madame Attolico was not at all put out by the Prussian Prime Minister's lateness, nor his business suit, nor his single-minded disregard of the felicities, but thought him the most original of all original touches to the party and, well pleased, watched a score of excited ladies follow hurriedly in his wake.

At the buffet table he grabbed a plate and, firmly elbowing aside the ladies who had rushed up and were pressing around his great girth, loaded up with salmon mousse and asparagus tips wrapped in endive leaves. He ate standing, oblivious of the chatter around him. When he was done he took a second, more varied helping, and turning around from the table talked with the ladies between mouthfuls. Eventually, with a glass of Moselle in his hand, he began making a round of visits throughout the room. First to Attolico, his host, then to his hostess. A little chat with Count Ciano and his charming wife. A sociable pause at Frau Goebbels's table, another at the von Papens'. Then over to his friend Henderson. After that a few words with François-Poncet, and Neurath, and the Polish Ambassador. Then back to his host to thank him; and twenty minutes after his arrival he was striding back out through the door.

"So original," commented Frau Goebbels, with her radiant smile.

"Aboriginal," said the grave Rosenberg.

Göring arrived on the dot of three at his Four-Year Plan office, and a few minutes later Herr Schacht was shown in.

A year earlier the *Völkischer Beobachter* had stated: "By summoning Göring, the Führer placed behind the Four-Year Plan the man with the strongest will and the greatest energy in the National Socialist Movement. Party Comrade Göring has received power to do everything that is necessary to carry through the Four-Year Plan. There will be no struggle between departments, no question of jurisdiction. There will be only one ultimate authority in all economic questions: Party Comrade Göring."

Herr Schacht had not expected so literal a fulfillment of this statement as had come to pass. Prior to the Four-Year Plan he had, as Economics Minister, enjoyed as much freedom and independence as he enjoyed as Reichsbank President, for Herr Hitler was not greatly interested in economics; as long as Schacht maintained a balance of trade the Chancellor did not care how he managed it. But last year the Chancellor had declared a new economy and set Göring at its head, and Schacht had found both his independence and his policies growing increasingly ghostlike.

He crossed the room to the desk, in appearance anything but ghostlike, a sixtyish man with a vital, elastic walk and a long wrinkled neck rising from a high collar, so long a neck, such an expanse of nakedness, that it gave his face the chill aspect of a periscope that has slid up from the depths with metallic, all-seeing acuity. He sat down with a barely cordial greeting. His host, on the other hand, was in a warm and benevolent mood, as well he might be. Hitler had implored them to have one last talk, but both knew it would be useless.

"It comes down to this, Herr Göring. As long as you persist in making decisions without me, I cannot work with you."

"But as long as you disapprove of my decisions, Herr Schacht, I *must* make them without you."

It was said with such simple candor that for the flick of a moment Schacht involuntarily saw the other's point and agreed with its logic. Then he answered, dryly, "Apparently. Well, I'll never approve of chopping off foreign markets, expanding rearmament beyond the capacity of our financial capacities, or pouring millions into synthetic raw materials. I needn't repeat that production is justified only when it can pay its way."

"You want profit," Göring replied. "I only want production. My task is to make Germany self-sufficient. You criticize the uneconomical working of iron ore mines, for example, but I look at them differently. Our iron ore mines must be maintained even at a loss, because in the event of an emergency we might otherwise be totally cut off from iron supplies. That is one of the main purposes of autarky: to build up a reserve of raw materials and foodstuffs in case of emergency, whether that be war or crop failure."

"Thank you for explaining the term to me."

"I am not being overbearing. Do I not recognize you as Germany's greatest economics expert? I stress the purposes of autarky only because you continually dismiss them. Self-sufficiency is essential to Germany's well-being. And I would like to ask if you can deny that the working of even uneconomic mines is giving steady wages to thousands of the unemployed who would otherwise be supported by the state?"

Herr Schacht turned his head away on his long neck, as if from a bad smell. Iron ore was a sore spot with him, having always been under his jurisdiction until Göring moved in. The National Hermann Göring Iron Works represented everything about the new economy that repelled him most. A state-owned concern, it had been set up in large part by forcing private concerns, such as Krupp's, to invest in it a total of more than 130 million marks. In short, private industry was having to finance government projects in competition with itself. It was tribute exacted under duress. It was piracy.

"I admit I'm not an economics expert like yourself," Göring was going on, "but—"

"Expert?" Schacht broke in. "The rankest layman!"

"Absolutely true. What do I know about agriculture, for instance? I've never grown more than a geranium in a pot. But I think I have a grasp of the overall picture, and I think we are doing very well."

"All which is being successfully achieved under your plan is nothing but the continuation of measures I have introduced."

"Then what are you complaining about?"

"Because what I began in moderation you've turned into a steam-roller. You're riding high now, but take care you don't come to a bad crash. I see rearmaments straining the national purse, government infringement everywhere, and if I see increased employment I also see a drastic shortage of consumer goods. Drastic. In my time it was merely acute."

"It's necessary. We must conserve raw materials."

"It wouldn't be necessary if you reinstituted my bilateral trade agreements."

"That would be against the interests of self-sufficiency. Certainly the people grumble over shortages, that's only natural. But they understand the reasons and they're with us."

It was true, thought Herr Schacht reprovingly. Göring had gotten up before a crowd of thousands in Hamburg, where complaints about food restrictions were loudest, and had concluded his speech by saying, "I do not want to rearm for militaristic reasons or to oppress other people, but solely for the cause of Germany's freedom. Comrades and friends, we have no butter, but I ask you: would you rather have butter or guns? Shall we bring in lard or iron ore? I tell you, preparedness makes us powerful, butter only makes us fat!"—with a clap to his big belly. The brazenness of the man! Yet the people jumped to their feet as one, applauding, cheering, and acclaiming him, and Hitler sent him a telegram of congratulations. He was now going on about synthetic gasoline, but Schacht broke in, rising from his chair.

"There's no point in our talking further."

"How true," said Göring pleasantly. "What a pity we get nowhere. If only we could work together, that would be the ideal solution. But I must be able to give you instructions."

"Not to me—to my successor," snapped Herr Schacht, relieved to be done with the whole thing. With a curt nod he turned from the beaming Göring and took his leave.

Sculpted, gold-rimmed clouds had passed above all day with majestic slowness. As dusk fell and evening deepened, they seemed a chain of pale mountains moving through the darkness. Lights shone from the windows of the Four-Year Plan office, where Göring was working late. At seven o'clock the lights went out.

"Will you have supper here, sir?" Robert asked a while later at the Leipziger Platz Palace, helping his master from his sweaty clothes.

"No need, I had a sandwich. Anyway, I must get over to the ministry."

He went off to shower as Robert laid out a fresh set of underwear and a fresh civilian suit. "The ministry," as distinct from the Ministry of This or of That, referred to the Prussian Prime Minister's office. Paperwork, or perhaps a late conference. He brought out a coat and fedora, the autumn evening being cold.

"You may as well come along with me now—I'll go home from there," the Chief said as Robert buttoned up the ankle-length camel's-hair coat, and a few minutes later, carrying the case in which the medals were kept—for he had always to bring these back and forth—Robert climbed into the second of the two Mercedes-Benzes. Leaving behind the palace, the Air Ministry, and the House of Aviators—people called the area Göring City—the two cars drove up a while later before the ministry, where the Chief went inside. Half an hour later a janitor came out to the cars. "The Minister President says you shouldn't sit here in the cold." They followed him, adjutants, aides, Robert, bodyguard, chauffeur, to a small reception room, where the janitor disappeared. Presently he returned with a bottle of schnapps and glasses. "The Minister President says I'm to have a glass, too." It was half past nine before they were on their way again, driving across the Spree, through Alexanderplatz, through the tenements of the northern part of the city, and into open country. They sped through darkness, pale mountainous clouds above; then eventually came the tunneled blackness of the forest, clearings strung with the dark jigsaw pieces of little lakes, and forest again, the swift alternating pattern ending in a blaze of courtyard lights and the slamming of car doors.

The Chief took his final shower of the day. Robert slipped him into one of his roomy housecoats, of cranberry-red satin. It was past eleven by now, and the Frau Minister President would have been asleep for several hours. Of late she had spent the better part of her days in bed. Dr. von Ondarza, the resident physician, was often with her. No one on the house staff knew what was wrong, though there was talk that she suffered from the same ailment as the first Frau Göring. Cilly said no, the present Frau Göring was a much more robust type; Robert could add nothing, for the Chief did not discuss the matter with him.

Before attending to more paperwork in his den, Göring stepped softly into his wife's bedroom. She was dozing lightly, and opened her eyes as he came over to her.

"Are you awake, Emmy?" he whispered.

"I should think so." She smiled. "I've done nothing but sleep all day."

He sat down on the side of the bed and kissed her cheek, her brow. "How are you feeling?"

"Fine. I always feel fine. Ondarza is a terrible fussbudget."

"But you must do as he says, you know. Plenty of rest the first few months, just to be on the safe side."

"Oh, I know. It's not as if I were twenty, I suppose. But I feel just fine."

"I'm so happy for us, Emmy," he whispered, smoothing back her hair.

"I've thought of more names," she told him, taking his hand and beginning to lift his fingers, one by one, as she said them; but already she was slipping into sleep again, drowsiness being the one effect of pregnancy that laid siege to her. He sat for a while beside her as she slept, then, having gently smoothed the covers around her, he went quietly from the room and down to the den.

Robert knocked on the door, speaking through it. "I'll be leaving you now, sir. Is there anything else?"

"Has Lotte done her work?"

Lotte was the cook in charge of seeing that the Minister President's private refrigerator was stocked each night with foods sufficient for more than a hearty snack. At midnight he could usually be found sitting alone in the vast, brightly lit kitchen, eating what amounted to an entire supper.

"I've checked. A very nice selection."

"Gut. Then good night, Robert, thank you."

"Goodnight, sir."

After the Chief's snack, he would work until one or two o'clock. He held so many offices that he could probably work twenty-four hours a day and still not get everything done. And sometimes he did not work at all. Sometimes he was extremely lazy, then afterward he had to catch up. Much better to have a lower horizon, a narrower course, thought Robert as he went along the hallways to his suite in the east wing.

His bedroom windows overlooked the courtyard, in which the lights had now been turned off. You could just make out the scaffolding on the west wing, which was being extended. Work was always being done on Carinhall, it was continually being enlarged or improved. Last year a swimming pool, all in blue tile, had been built in the basement. Now a complete gymnasium was being constructed there. And the outlying buildings proliferated. The sound of hammering hung forever in the air.

He wound his clock, and set the alarm for six.

Chapter 43

"Y OU must come in, Herr Göring!"

"No, he won't," said Emmy, her head in its white bathing cap held carefully above the water as she swam along with her slow breaststroke, "he's off to the sauna."

"Oh, but it's so nice," Rose cried, striking off with her strong Australian crawl. She wore a plain black tank suit and no cap, her coppery hair, darkened by the water, pulled back in a knot. She swam in a circle that brought her back around to her friend in her flowered suit, whose skirt billowed in the temperate blue-green water. "To think it's snowing outside, it makes it so delicious. Tropical! Jump in, jump in!" she cried again to Göring, who had paused at the far end of the pool in a white terry-cloth robe, arms akimbo.

"I may later," he called back. "See that she puts in her half hour, Fräulein Korwan. Our Emmy is known to cheat."

Emmy, who could neither wave nor call out while at the same time swimming, sent a smiling shake of her head in his direction. For she was actually very good about following this particular order of Ondarza's, although she ignored the other little exercises, which she found boring. Well into her fourth month, she was radiant with health and uncomplicated anticipation.

"He's doing it backward," Rose commented as her host went on through the gymnasium door. "Doesn't one swim first and have a sauna afterward?"

"Weiss nicht," murmured Emmy, knowing that Hermann would not swim as long as Rose or anyone else, except herself, was present, for when at his peak weight he felt pained to show himself in a bathing suit. She was too loyal to him to explain this to Rose. "I suppose there's plenty of talk already," she said, progressing with her slow, stately stroke to the side of the pool as Rose dove under and emerged beside her.

"About your pregnancy, you mean? But you haven't announced it yet, so how can there be talk?"

"You don't travel in the right circles, my dear."

They hung floating from the blue-tiled edge, the water dancing around them in bright chips. Rose shrugged. "What could they say?"

"Oh, I don't know, but they'll find something. Do you remember when we became engaged? Next thing I knew, Hermann had banished all my illegitimate children from the country. Packed them off to darkest Africa, or was it the North Pole? I forget which. Poor little phantoms, in any case."

"You can't let gossip get under your skin. You must ignore it."

"I can't get used to it, Rose. I wasn't brought up that way. I suppose it sounds childish, but it's true."

"Why think about it? Don't let idiots hurt you." She pushed away from the side with a graceful backstroke, rolled over and dove under, emerging with a whoosh and a flashing smile of her beautiful white teeth. "Come, you must swim the length. Ondarza's orders!"

Göring sat with eyes closed in the steaming heat of the sauna. He was never comfortable when clothed, not even in his loose dressing gowns, for there was always the material's remindful touch along extraordinary swells of flesh that seemed to have been attached to him without his permission, surfaces so far removed from his bones, so far from his center, that he felt shackled on all sides by an alien load. Only when he was naked, motionless, with eyes closed, did he feel the inner body—that of the hard, lithe young officer he was—take full sovereignty. Then, without clothing or movement or sight to avouch the alien rind, he was in some timeless, quiescent way at one with himself.

After a while, the wooden bench beginning to sear, he took the wobbling rind up and down the floorboards of the enclosure, wiping the sweat from his eyes and running his hands through his dripping hair. Pausing for a moment in his clogs, he looked down at himself, unable to see beyond his belly, that gargantuan protuberance preceded by several sausage-shaped rolls on either side of which the fat of his great upper arms was dimpled and puckered. He turned the monstrosity around and replaced it on the bench, accepting the blazing contact with no grimace: better to feel pain and know something was happening, the start of another weight-loss regimen. He concentrated on the feel of his running sweat, the poisonous effluvium of the dissolving rind . . . and whenever he lost weight they said it was morphine, and whenever he gained they said it was morphine, and he had never gone back on the needle! "That vow has been kept!" he muttered aloud. "Wagging tongues . . . why should I care? The Reichstag fire too, still wagging on about that. What difference should it make? But to be accused of what I haven't done . . . I am no arsonist. I am no addict. Scheisskӧpfe—let them talk if they want."

He stood up again and walked back and forth in the intense heat of the white steam, thinking practical thoughts as the floor creaked beneath him. The revamping of the Air Ministry was well under way, with Milch cut down to size. And now that quibbling Schacht was out of the picture, the economy was entirely in his own hands. The year was winding up very satisfactorily. And what would the new year of 1938 bring?

At that conference the Führer called a few weeks back for the Wehrmacht chiefs and von Neurath, the Führer said that if France has a civil war, Germany will be free to deal with Czechia and Austria. If France doesn't have a civil war . . . well, that was left up in the air. But a feeling of crisis was definitely conveyed, mainly for the benefit of Fritsch. Set a fire under Fritsch. Not carrying out a large enough arms program for the Army. Arms is what they wanted, but now the military show all the cautiousness of the old conservatives. Well, the fire set under them was a good hot one; great consternation, it was in their faces as they listened, and in their questions and arguments afterward. Sitting there watching them, one saw that the last crack has not yet been closed. They came around, of course, but their makeup can't change.

As for the Führer's dissertation, who knows if he meant what he said, or if it was just to shake them up? He's not one to plan ahead. Always altering his plans. Consistency isn't his strong point. I know him, they don't. Look at Blomberg, how relieved he was when I told him the Führer would attend his wedding. But I know him and knew he would want to.

Again settling heavily on the bench, he wiped his dripping face with a towel. He thought how much younger Blomberg looked since this romance of his. Everyone should know true love and a happy marriage, and he was filled with tenderness for Emmy, and for this coming event they had both longed for. Tears of love filled his eyes, tears that lingered and brimmed as he thought of Carin in that way that sometimes came like a crystallization of what was always with him: her voice, her eyes, her walk, all suddenly so clear and real that it seemed they could almost touch each other . . . and if it was happiness it was pain, and if it was pain it was happiness.

Six years ago. In one way they seemed long, so much had happened since. In another, her death was as acute as if it had been yesterday—the black armband, black loneliness, having to appear normal and outgoing at social affairs, dinner-party chitchat, summer heat . . . the silver flick of a trout. He swiped back his hair and stood up.

Is it too simple to say you can't make an omelette without breaking eggs? Then call me a simple man. I follow the leadership of no one but Adolf Hitler and der liebe Gott. We're not running a girls' finishing school, we're resurrecting a nation—and I must check with Bodenschatz tomorrow about the inspection at Rechlin. And talk with Lipski. Another trip to Poland would be a good idea. Because pretty soon Ribbentrop will be sticking his nose in everywhere, it's in the cards. And think, when he was presented to the King of England he gave the National Socialist salute and said Heil Hitler. Does he think that creates warm feelings? Arrogant pinhead. I told the Führer a long time ago that Ribbentrop had no diplomatic finesse. Oh, but Ribbentrop knows so many people, he knows Lord So and Viscount So and Minister So, Ribbentrop knows them all. Ja, I said, but the difficulty is that they know Ribbentrop. What good does it do? The Führer is crazy about him. . . .

There was a rap on the sauna door. "Telephone, sir. It's Obersalzberg. The Führer is on the line."

Streaming with sweat, he hastily draped a towel around his middle, and for two hours sat talking in a drafty corner of the gymnasium, no one approaching him with his robe because no one was allowed within hearing distance when he talked with the Führer.

The next morning he arrived in Berlin with a raging toothache. The dentist was called and came hurriedly to the Leipziger Platz Palace.

Professor Blaschke had small patience with people who feared dentists. It seemed unintelligent of them to tremble and jump when they were being done good to. Yet even great men, even Bismarck himself—the man had let his teeth rot before summoning the courage to come creeping into his dentist's office—had this absurd attitude. Göring's eyes were rolling; he seemed ready to scream the place down before he was even touched.

"Try to be calm, Herr Minister President. I cannot help you if you intend to leap into the air."

"Go ahead!"

He was in a highly nervous state. Even at the best of times there was a certain tenseness in him . . . and an insomniac by his own admission; no, people would not expect it of unser Hermann, that jolly, easy-going figure. . . .

The examination disclosed that the problem was not a toothache but inflammation of the nerves due to exposure. The pain would go away by itself, but until then he should take a sedative every two hours.

"I have with me samples of a new sedative not yet on the market. They should last a couple of days, enough to see you through. They're a paracodeine pill."

"Codeine?" the patient asked, his hand pressed to his throbbing jaw. "A morphine derivative, isn't it?"

"Not codeine. Paracodeine. It's quite new."

"The same basis, I should think."

"The tiniest amount. Very mild. But an excellent sedative, I'm told."

The patient gave a negative shake of his head, closing his eyes with pain.

"Very well, I'll prescribe something else."

"Haven't you anything else with you?"

"I'm afraid not, only this."

"No, I don't want it."

"Very well, I'll write you a—"

"No, never mind. Give me this, I don't want to wait."

All this quibbling over a pill, thought Dr. Blaschke. Bismarck himself could not have been more trying. He set out the sample bottle, and with a bow left the Minister President in his sweat-drenched shirt.

Two days later he had a telephone call from the Minister President, saying that the inflammation was gone and where could he get more pills. Professor Blaschke told him it was not wise to continue taking them after they had served their purpose, and in any event they were not yet on the market.

But by the end of the year, since it had not been difficult to track down the source of the pills, Göring was taking ten of them a day.

Chapter 44

11 January, Tuesday. Amsterdam. Waiting for train to start. Black, freezing early morning, compartment not heated yet. Wheels finally beginning to turn, slow as sleep.

Icy scattered lights of Amsterdam receding. Glasgow, London, Brussels, Amsterdam, next Hamburg ... what an irony that I who detest commerce should have a gift for it. North Europe representative in only three years. Would there were a grain of satisfaction in it. Should go over the reports for the Hamburg meeting, don't feel like it. Unrelieved blackness beyond the window.

Better frame of mind after dining car opened. Breakfast, good cigar, and table shared by rather pleasant girl unfortunately getting off next stop. What a difference a couple of affairs make; one is so much surer, no longer spends twenty minutes clearing one's throat only to ask for the salt. Gave her my card in case she was ever in Stockholm.

Nordhorn. Customs inspection. Train gives a jolt, moves on into Hermann's personal fief, also known as Prussia. Daylight now. Gray heavy sky, dark fields marbled by frozen drifts, bare, sodden-looking black trees. Must go over the reports. Don't keep putting it off, the meeting is at three.

Have been thinking all morning that it's Hermann's birthday tomorrow. What if I said the hell with the meeting, and went to Berlin instead?

"You couldn't have made me happier, popping up like this for my birthday. And you can stay on for a while?"

"No, I've got to get back to Stockholm. A certain pressing matter I must attend to."

"Well, I must say you're looking good, Thomas. And . . . a little different, somehow."

Thomas made no reply; merely smiled, blowing out a plume of cigar smoke.

Göring smiled too, surprised and pleased by the change in his solemn stepson since his visit the previous summer. Buoyant, jaunty, even a bit superior. Happy and muscle-flexing within some new center of independence.

"You're looking all right yourself, Hermann."

"Ought to. There ought to be some result when you're beaten by masseurs, boiled in saunas, and starved to boot. But bring me up to date—how is everything? How is the work going?"

"The work?" Thomas said, with a gratified shrug. "I'm chucking it."

"Chucking it? You mean you've been offered a job with another firm?"

"No, I mean I'm washing my hands of the whole thing."

"But I don't understand. You've done so well, you've gone right up the ladder. Your mother would have been very proud of you, Thomas, as I am."

"That may be. I'm chucking it. I decided this morning."

"Well. Perhaps after supper we should have a little talk."

"I would like to have a talk, Hermann. I meant to have a talk. But not about my career."

The actual birthday party, attended by two thousand, had taken place the previous Saturday night at the Prussian State Opera House. A more intimate celebration in the form of a luncheon would be held tomorrow. But tonight's supper was an ordinary occasion, with some dozen houseguests present and the host comfortably garbed in one of his big loose satin robes. He had been obese when Thomas had last seen him, now he was merely husky and took little on his plate of the food he so adored.

Thomas felt dartings down his arms and spine, like electric currents, as he and Hermann left the dining room. In the den, the lamps had been turned on, a fire lit in the fireplace, a carafe and two snifters set out between two leather armchairs facing the blaze—everything prepared for the confrontation that was burning in his blood. There was a creaking of leather as they sat down, another as Hermann leaned over to the small table and unstoppered the carafe.

Once, Thomas thought, he had tried to write in this room, and had only been able to write descriptions of what was in it. Everything in this room had possessed him, chained him. He took a cigar from his breast pocket, bit off the end, lit it with slightly trembling fingers.

"A very nice cognac, this," Göring said, handing him a snifter. "You must tell me how you like it."

Thomas took the glass, sitting back with it.

"There's something I want to discuss with you, Hermann. It's of the greatest importance. I—"

Suddenly he broke off. It was as if his eyes had locked: the dark gold satin robe magnificently illumined in the firelight, the face above it cast like a Roman medallion in hard, pitiless, knifelike edges.

"I know." Göring nodded, his face—as Thomas saw, eyes unlocking—holding only affection and concern. "It's a big step to leave one's job."

"It's not that," Thomas said with a shake of his head. "That's simple enough: when I get back to Stockholm I'm clearing out the office. I've made up my mind, there's no point discussing it. I hate business. I've hated it from the first day."

"You've never said anything about this."

"I've never said anything about anything."

The significance of these words made his heart thud in his chest. He took a sip of his cognac, and procrastinated a little.

"Well, that's how it is. I'm chucking it. I don't know what my plans are. Maybe I'll cross the Sahara on a camel. Stow away aboard a Trans-Siberian freight train. But that's not what I want to talk about. What I want to talk about—what I want to talk about is the likelihood of war."

"Well," Göring answered, with a genial nod, "you know how I stand on the subject of war. We have that in common, nicht?"

"Absolutely. Spiritual twins. Both passionate antimilitarists."

"Nein, I may be a soldier, but I'm a soldier who doesn't want war."

"This is what I know. Very many people know this. And they talk about it. They admire your desire for peace. They even say you intend to take the reins from Hitler—"

A glare suddenly shot out at him like a lightning bolt, coring his brain, shriveling every thought to a crisp.

Göring dropped his eyes from the startled, mute face, trying to subdue the great annoyance he felt whenever he was reminded of these imbecile rumors that impugned his loyalty to the Führer. Looking up again after a moment, he said in mild tones, penitentially, "I know of this talk, it's spread all over the place. Heard it in Sweden, did you?" But the damage was done: there was no response. How precarious was the flight of this bold new Thomas, how easily those new wings faltered and drooped. He said again, encouragingly, "So you heard it in Sweden?"

There was a faint, tentative nod. "From friends of Uncle Erik's, in the diplomatic corps."

"There you are. I tell you, there's no need for the fantasies of the cinema screen as long as we've got our diplomats." He gave a good-natured laugh, and watched a small smile begin to thaw on the face opposite. The boy was getting his wings back in order; all he needed now was a good strong updraft. "Go on. Go on, Thomas, this gossip clearly interests you."

Another nod, this time somewhat sturdier. "It does. I knew, of course, that it was gossip—"

"Gossip, ja. Horse manure."

The boy's eyes were once again growing keen; he was getting off the ground, zooming into action.

"A fertilizing agent, manure—well, I wish these rumors would bear fruit, Hermann. I wish they were true. I think I've wished that for a long time, maybe for years. I have things to say, and I must say them. Others can't. The vast majority everywhere have no voice, and it's on the behalf of the people that I tell you I would like to believe these rumors. Everyone speaks of the people, but who is really thinking of them? Who really feels responsible for them? I know we both appreciate the early Middle Ages for its concept of honor, which rests upon loyalty not only upward but downward. The knight was bound by unconditional obedience to his lord and flag, but he was equally bound to protect those beneath him. The chivalric code was meaningless if it didn't work both ways. When the perfection of order of the early Holy Roman Empire is spoken of, it's not simply the social structure that's meant, but this deeper order of pledges, of which the knight was the purest embodiment. Times may have changed, but the knight still stands in the world's regard as the upholder of all—"

"You must do me a favor, Thomas," Göring interrupted, keeping an edge from his voice. "Speak plainly. You know I have an elementary mind," he said with a smile. "Kindly don't belabor it with allusions and nuances, but come to your point."

"Hitler has turned Germany into an armed camp that's very soon going to be an armed camp on the move. Everything points to it. He calls it rearming for peace. So do you, and I should tell you I object strongly to this arms buildup in the name of defense. Defense? Didn't the Great War tell us anything about the amassing of arms? That it can only end in catastrophe? And I believe he will precipitate such a catastrophe. And what I ask you is . . . what I ask you is, do you owe him more loyalty than you owe Germany? What has he made of Germany?

A nightmare of total mental conformity. *And* physical. When I think of the emphasis on physical fitness here in Germany, it's like . . . I don't know, it's as if those who don't measure up are no better than diseased cattle, useless stock, and that includes weak lungs and bad hearts. I mean, hasn't it struck you that in today's Germany Mother would be one kind of diseased organism, and I another? She with the wrong health, I with the wrong thoughts? If I were a German living in Germany today, I would have to stifle every thought I had, every belief, I would have to live like a mental beetle for fear of being carted off to Dachau. Well, those are wrong thoughts—what of wrong blood? Wrong this, wrong that—it's as if human beings are looked upon as objects; useful objects in one pile, the rest a garbage heap. Where is the greatness in this? Where is the greatness in telling some old shop-keeper who happens to be Jewish that he can't vote, he can't hang the German flag from his window?—if he's still got a window, if he's got anything at all left to his name. Where is the greatness in any of this? You can't tell me this is the heritage of the Holy Roman Empire. You can't tell me this is what you had in mind down in that little cellar room in Obermenzing, that—that plotters' corner Mother used to write about in her letters, where the great Germany of old was being reborn. Don't you ever wonder what Mother would say if she were to come back now? What happened to the Germany the two of you struggled for? It makes no sense to hang on to Nibelungentreue when you look around and see how things are. When all the values and traditions one believes in are being trampled down—I mean, how can one believe in them while at the same time supporting a regime that works for their destruction? And now he'll push outward to greater destruction, as if the Great War had never been, as if armies could step over that huge filthy annihilation and carry forward the grand contests of the past. But if Europe goes to war again it will be so horrible, so final, it will beggar all wars that have ever gone before. He's got to be deposed. Forced out. And I know this as clearly as I know anything, and you know it too."

He sat back in abrupt silence, his heart thudding on like a riderless horse. He flung an ankle across a knee, where it slid, where he had to hold it fast with his hand, tremblingly, astounded that he had actually said what he had said. But Hermann had listened intently, not even moving except to put in his mouth one of the small white tablets he took for the pain in his hip, and to chew soberly as the speech had gone on, the line between his eyebrows deepening to a furrow. Now, in the silence, he gave a slow nod of his head.

"You are free to speak in particulars, of course, but I can only answer in generalities. Whether in Germany or anywhere else, a state official cannot discuss state matters with an outsider. At least not a matter of the sort you have just propounded. I know you understand that. I know you will also understand when I say that those on the outside always seem to know more than we on the inside. Your absolute certainty of war is not one that I myself can claim. But you may be right. And some of the things you have said . . . these I can't dispute. I can only tell you that you have expressed yourself forcefully and that you were heard. I think we should drink to the admirable brutality of your words. And I will assure you of this, Thomas: with every atom of my being, I mean to uphold and preserve the peace of Europe."

Releasing his foot to the floor, triumphant, if spent, Thomas raised his glass.

"Has he got a sweetheart?" Emmy asked with curiosity.

"A what?"

"A sweetheart. That's what you should have asked, Hermann. It's clear that he's found a sweetheart, it's what has made him so happy."

"Well, if it's clear, we don't need to ask," Göring said, climbing into bed next to his wife.

"Did you find out why he's suddenly decided to leave his job?"

"Doesn't like it. Never has."

"It seems such a rash move."

"It's rash, but he wants to be rash. Let him, he's young; let him act like someone young. I'm glad to see it."

"Oh, I am too, I'm so glad that he's found someone at last. Haven't I said all along that that was what he needed? I think tomorrow, very tactfully, of course, I may just ask . . ."

"I think you'd better, Liebchen. Otherwise you may explode."

Sometime later, waking and turning, she saw that he lay sleepless. Very often—it was why they kept separate bedrooms—he was forced by insomnia to turn on the bed lamp and read, or to call Robert for a snack, or to pace the floor. It was to be one of those nights, she thought sleepily, her eyes resting on his profile, open-eyed, the prominent round chin moving just discernibly. It was by the ear that the real activity took place. There you could see the jawbone working away. She couldn't imagine chewing those pills like that, they were bitter, she had tried one. Nor could she imagine that his old wounds, or other assorted aches and pains, could really be the cause for this growing habit. A few times she had suggested that he was taking too many, but had gotten nowhere. "They're harmless, Emmy. I've told you that. They're no stronger than aspirin." "Then why not take aspirin?" "Because I'm taking these." And finally he had gotten annoyed, saying that the subject was closed. She saw drowsily that he had stopped his chewing. But only to bring his palm to his mouth, at which the bones by his ear began working again.

*   *   *

The birthday luncheon was a great success, if complacently eccentric in its earliness. At half past nine—for they were to sit down at ten—guests from Berlin began driving into the courtyard. Their host, his insomnia-racked night notwithstanding, was in excellent spirits. He loved birthdays for their warmth and goodwill and largess, and especially he loved his own. Though he was forty-five today, his happiness was little different from that which had filled him bubbling to the brim as a birthday child forty years ago. Exuberantly he took his guests into the room which held the gifts that had been arriving for some two weeks and, bustling and beaming, led them from one laden table to the next.

There were numberless bottles of fine wines, scores of wicker hampers filled with foil-wrapped delicacies; from the Führer had come a charming painting of a lion cub, from the city of Dresden a Cranach portrait, and from an old air comrade—this seemed to please him most—a large canvas showing the Luftwaffe commander's old Jasta 27 climbing into a red-streaked morning sky. There were model aircraft in cedarwood, in gingerbread, in gold; there was a set of fifty beer tankards, and a great deal of fine porcelain, including an exquisite Sèvres centerpiece from all the workers in the Four-Year Plan, who, at Göring's behest, and most cheerfully he was sure, had received their last month's salaries deducted of 5 percent for the purchase of the gift. I.G. Farben had sent some magnificent specimens of synthetic gems, there was an ornate birdcage with a pair of exotic songsters warbling away inside, and handcrafted gifts from ordinary people all over Germany—pipes and alpenstocks, home-knitted woolen scarves, and from one Hausfrau even a heart-shaped chocolate cake decorated in sky-blue icing with the words *Unser Hermann*. Exclamations followed him throughout the room, everyone was happy in the Minister President's happiness, and happy to see his or her individual gift set adazzle by the great gratitude and pleasure that streamed as if in waves from his rosy, smiling countenance. "Really, I'm quite overwhelmed by all these splendid presents!" Every year he said this, and every year it was no less true.

Uniformed and bemedaled, his step brisk and springy, he took them off to the old banquet hall—a new one was being built, but was not yet ready for use—where the long table had been set with places for fifty. Among flowers and silver coffee urns stood hams from Lübeck poached in champagne, platters of veal lost in truffled potatoes and tender baby carrots, bowls of crab-stuffed mushroom caps, trays of salmon, of caviar, of asparagus, and mounds of salmon mousse smothered in whipped cream; there were sculptured butter roses, Hansel and Gretel gingerbread houses, fruit cakes, layer cakes, and puff pastries filled with sherry-marinated strawberries—almost all of which the host sampled, but in heroically small portions.

"You must eat for me," he joked with his stepson, who was indeed putting it away. Those guests who knew the somber young Kantzow were surprised by his animation, which was hardly less than that of the birthday honoree. They could not know that in a sense it was his birthday too: not only had he secured the peace of Europe, but with it had claimed his *vita nuova*. He felt free, new, radiant. The Frau Minister President, radiant too, partly due to the festivities and partly to her approaching motherhood, which so far lent only a slight convexity to the fall of her rose-colored gown, had received from Thomas in answer to her question only a flashing smile—what handsome teeth, one had never really seen them before—and she promised herself to ask more later.

But there was no later. As the luncheon progressed with many toasts toward half past eleven—by which time her husband must depart to attend Feldmarschall von Blomberg's wedding—he stood up, thanked everyone heartily, and to a tribute of a hundred clapping hands, took his leave with Thomas.

"I must be going too," Thomas said, stopping by her chair. "Hermann's giving me a lift to Berlin. I've got to catch the train. An important engagement."

"Oh, I know these engagements," she laughed, pressing his hand. A beaming kiss to her cheek, and he was gone.

The other people in the train compartment, an elderly couple gazing out at the passing iron-gray landscape, a naval officer turning the sepia-illustrated pages of a magazine, might have noticed, if they had been inclined to notice, that the young man in their midst sat with an open notebook on his lap, fountain pen between his fingers, and that he had been sitting that way for a long while, and that he had written nothing.

All sense of light, warmth, excitement, of meaning and purpose, had faded relentlessly with each clacking turn of the wheels. A chill gray reflectiveness had set in, a gray clarity in which he saw the past twenty-four hours as a chimera wrought of the most extreme self-dramatization. His great speech, that perilous confrontation which had beaten so urgently through his blood . . . he saw now that he had been helped along with tact and kindness, that he had been indulged, and that he had spoken from a position of perfect security, and that Hermann's promise at the end was no more than what he had said at the beginning. And that flashing smile at Emmy—it had been meant to convey the essence of his rich love life, which in fact, in the light of cold objectivity, consisted of a couple of prosaic liaisons; of passion—of wild, melting passion—there had been nothing. Even his decision to wash his hands of the shit-souled world of commerce, even that had been false; for somewhere deep inside him he knew he would get off the train at Hamburg, instead of traveling straight on to Stockholm to turn in his resignation; he would get off at Hamburg, give some reasonable excuse for his tardiness, and have his meeting.

Chapter 45

SOON after Feldmarschall von Blomberg's small civil wedding, from which the couple had departed for an Italian honeymoon, the Army General Staff began receiving strange and outrageous telephone calls—giggling female voices congratulating them and offering their services. Rumors began circulating, and the name Gruhn began pecking at memories in the Morality Crimes Department of the Criminal Police. A check was made, a file produced: the Feldmarschall's bride, née Gruhn, was a registered prostitute, a convicted model for pornographic photographs, and the daughter of a former brothel proprietress. The Police President himself hastened with the file to the senior ranking general, Göring, who read through the typed sheets with an expression of growing amazement.

"Lieber Gott!" he murmured. "He *did* marry the crocodile woman in the circus."

When the elderly bridegroom returned from his honeymoon, Göring went to him and informed him of the dossier. The Feldmarschall's face paled beneath its slight tan, bestowed by the wintry Italian sun.

"I realize it is a great shock, Herr Feldmarschall. I am sorry to be the one to bring you this news."

But it was not the news itself that shocked Blomberg. He had known of his beloved's past from the very beginning, she herself had told him. The shock lay in this moment, which he had persistently, blindly, in the power of his happiness, persuaded himself would never come to be.

"Under these circumstances—you will understand, Herr Feld-marschall—the marriage violates the officers' code. Your generals have stated that they refuse to serve under you."

A single eye-twitch broke in Blomberg's tightly controlled face. With rigid fingers he readjusted his monocle.

"The Führer has asked me to tell you, however, that if you have the marriage annulled, he will not request your resignation. The of-ficer corps agrees to this."

"I refuse to annul my marriage! I would rather put a bullet through my head!"

Göring sat looking at him. Commander in Chief of the Armed Forces, Minister of War—finished. He felt sympathy for the man, and he felt surprise, too, that the Rubber Lion was capable, in a crisis of the heart, of acting like a real lion—swift, strong, resolute. How strange human beings were, how inconsistent, and in this case, how self-de-structive. All these things he felt as he got to his feet, but mostly he felt happiness rising like a great tide within him.

Much had taken place in the few days between the discovery of the Gruhn dossier and Blomberg's return. Another dossier had come to light, this one concerning Commander in Chief of the Army von Fritsch, who, stunned to the point of paralysis, had already been fired and put under house arrest.

It had happened that some three years earlier, SS Reichsführer Himmler had set before Hitler a dossier and watched him read it, only to be rudely ordered to burn the filthy muck. Hurt and disappointed, Himmler had obediently, though first taking extracts, destroyed these important findings that showed the Army Commander in Chief to be a public-lavatory pervert in the hands of a blackmailer. Now, three years later, after the Blomberg scandal broke—unexpectedly, fortuitously, like a wild rose cracking full-blown through pavement—Himmler and Heydrich immediately reconstructed the Fritsch dossier and submitted it to Göring as senior ranking general, and he, in turn, wasting not a minute, submitted it to Hitler.

At the end of that day Hitler was still ashen. On this reading of the Fritsch file, he had not been so impulsively skeptical as he had been three years before. His pain was in fact massive. His faith in mankind was shaken. He confessed this to his political aide. "To have experi-enced within hours first the shock of the Gruhn file and then that of Fritsch! When a German field marshal marries a whore, then anything is possible!"

Presumably, thought the aide, even a flintily upright von Fritsch carrying on in public toilets.

"The thing must be cleared up at once," the Führer went on distractedly. "If Blomberg resigns, Fritsch is his natural successor. If there is any truth to these charges, if the inheritor of the most important military post in the nation is a pederast, it must be found out immediately."

Von Fritsch was called at once to the Chancellery, where the Führer informed him without preamble that a witness had testified to his having engaged in unnatural acts with two Hitler Youths. The Führer watched his face closely for its reaction. The severe, rocklike countenance, with its gray toothbrush mustache, turned crimson with outrage.

"That's a filthy lie! It's entirely innocent! I invite them to dinner once a week and give them map-reading lessons. If one is not attentive, I may give him a tap on the rear with my ruler—but what you have just implied—!"

But Hitler's face was also crimson, his eyes bulged from their sockets. Hardly able to speak, he fired the general on the spot.

Afterward, telling his aide of the scene, he cried, "I didn't even *know* about these two! That makes *four* he's mixed up with! And God knows how many others—in public lavatories, in his home—"

"If I may say so, mein Führer, I feel certain that the General conducts his lessons with perfect propriety. As for these charges of public indecency, they sound preposterous. They must be founded on some mistake."

"You're right," replied the agitated Chancellor. "I must have the witness's statement checked. I must ask for a report."

The witness, who was also the blackmailer, stuck to his story.

Once again Hitler called General von Fritsch to him. This time General Göring, Colonel Jodl, and several adjutants were present. Fritsch standing among them, the room crackling with tension, Hitler went to a door and had the Gestapo bring in the blackmailer.

The man's eyes swept the faces before him and stopped at von Fritsch's. He swung out his arm and pointed.

"That's him!"

"I do not know this gentleman," replied von Fritsch, a study in ice. And Göring, in a state of extreme excitement, suddenly rushed from the room, pounded down the hall, and burst into a small dining room where some other adjutants sat waiting. "It was him! It was him!" he cried to them, throwing himself onto a sofa and rocking back and forth, his face clutched in his hands. "It was him! It was him!"

Meanwhile Hitler listened to Fritsch state once again that he had never met the man who was accusing him. "It will go badly with you if you are lying!" Hitler sharply warned the blackmailer, a sleazy little fifth-rate criminal, round-eyed to be in such company. And to the icily departing Fritsch: "I promise you that the charges will be thoroughly investigated, Herr General."

And to Hitler's aide it all seemed crazily backward, first to fire a man and put him under house arrest, then to confront him with his accusor, and finally to investigate. The Führer had been conducting himself like a chicken with its head cut off, although he seemed finally to be calming. Not so Göring, who had rushed off like a maniac, purple-faced as if about to have a stroke, and who could now be heard pounding back along the hall.

For Hitler, everything was beginning to settle and take shape. When the following day Göring went to Blomberg and returned with Blomberg's decision to resign, Hitler realized that inside himself he had definitely decided against Fritsch as Blomberg's successor, though Fritsch had yet to be proved guilty. The trouble with scandal was that it left a mark. It was just as well that Blomberg had decided not to undo his disastrous union, for the officer corps might have accepted him back, but would they have been able to respect him again? He was tainted. It was the same with Fritsch. Whether innocent or guilty, Fritsch was tainted. The harm had been done. Kaputt. Who then?

He discussed the matter with his political aide, who considered the logical choice to be Göring, as senior ranking general.

"Göring? That fellow doesn't even know how to hold a Luftwaffe inspection. I know more about it than he does. He is out of the question."

General Keitel's choice was the same.

"Göring? Impossible. He must retain the Luftwaffe, for no better man can be found. Also, he must play his role in state business."

And when he spoke with Blomberg himself, he too recommended Göring.

"Göring? He has already got control of Prussia and the economy— I should give him the Wehrmacht too? Anyway, he's too impatient and lazy."

It was Hitler himself who assumed command of the Wehrmacht. He immediately swept out the last conservative elements by dismissing sixteen high-ranking generals and appointing the compliant General Brauchitsch to von Fritsch's post; at the same time he dismissed Foreign Minister von Neurath and replaced him with von Ribbentrop; he also replaced the German envoys in London, Rome, Vienna and Tokyo. And to placate the deeply disappointed Göring, he elevated him to the rank of Feldmarschall. Finally, he dismissed his political aide, as having expressed too many unnecessary opinions. From every streetcorner blazed the *Völkischer Beobachter*'s triumphant headline: "Strongest Concentration of All Power in the Führer's Hands!" Exhausted, he took himself off to the mountain purity of the Ober-salzberg, having first set in motion a military investigation of the Fritsch case, along with a parallel Gestapo investigation, in order to make both sides happy.

The Fritsch trial began on March 10, with Feldmarschall Göring presiding. But hardly an hour had passed before he was suddenly called away and the proceedings were suspended.

In the housecleaning of the previous month, von Papen, ambassador to Vienna, had been one of those swept out. Only momentarily stunned, he hurried off to the Obersalzberg and reminded Hitler of the rapport which he, Papen, had established with Chancellor von Schuschnigg, underlining this with the fact that Schuschnigg had expressed his wish to meet with the Führer and discuss the German-Austrian situation. Hitler was pleased. He asked Papen to return to Schuschnigg and arrange a meeting. "As ambassador?" von Papen asked hopefully. But he left, as he had arrived, an ex-ambassador.

The upshot of the meeting was the Obersalzberg Agreements, arrived at by way of the German Chancellor bullying, bellowing at, and pushing the Austrian Chancellor into making concessions. The snow-laden heights were blue-gray with dusk as Chancellor Schuschnigg descended the broad steps of the Berghof, and dusk too, he felt, was fast falling on Austrian independence. While inside the Berghof, standing at his picture window, the German Chancellor was satisfied that another step had been taken in the direction of evolutionary unification.

Others besides Schuschnigg were unhappy with the Obersalzberg Agreements. In Italy, although Mussolini habitually deferred to Hitler's successes, Count Ciano took it upon himself to turn to England. He found no support forthcoming. The Count wrote in his diary: "What can we do, start a war with Germany? At the first shot we fired, every Austrian without exception would fall in behind the Germans against us."

At this point Chancellor von Schuschnigg decided that his country's crumbling independence could be halted only by a national plebiscite. It would be a rash move, for it defied the Obersalzberg Agreements. But if the plebiscite succeeded—and it would, for it would be arranged to succeed—then Germany would dare not make further encroachments on a country which before the world had declared its desire for independence.

When, with other military leaders, Göring was called away from the Fritsch trial, Hitler had just learned of the projected plebiscite. The Führer was in a state of near hysteria. If Schuschnigg refused to change his plans, he must be threatened with invasion. The general conduct of affairs was given over to Göring, who immediately got on the Chancellery priority line to the German embassy in Vienna.

Five weeks earlier, his blood beating with the premature joy of being appointed Commander of the Armed Forces, he had come down with a crash. He had taken to his bed racked with physical ills, literally sick with disappointment. But common sense had eventually dragged him out from under the blankets. Life was too short to waste on regrets. And the marshal's baton also helped: as the only field marshal on the active list, he was now highest-ranking officer in all Germany. It was with vigorous spirits that he sat down and took up the telephone.

That night, his voice hoarse from ten hours of telephone talk, the Feldmarschall strode through the anterooms of the Haus der Flieger, everything designed by himself, everything simple, modern, luxurious. He was on his way to the great hall where one of his receptions was being held, to be highlighted by a ballet performance by his State Opera Company. He was very late. Suddenly he was approached by someone whom he saw to be the Czech Minister, his face desperately anxious.

"Herr Mastny, I am glad to see you here!" he said hoarsely, and took him aside. "I want to declare to you on my word of honor, Herr Mastny, that the entry of Reich troops into Austria should give you no reason for alarm. Your frontier is safe. We have no hostile intentions of any kind toward Czechoslovakia. On the contrary, we wish to continue working toward a *rapprochement*. Now, I hope you will be able to enjoy the evening without worry! Come, let us go in."

The thousand-voiced din was not gala, but anxious. All eyes followed Göring to the long central table where, among others, the British Ambassador sat. Sir Nevile coldly shook hands with Göring, with whom, under normal circumstances, he enjoyed a warm social relationship. As soon as Göring sat down, he gave a gesture for the ballet to begin and then tore off the blank half of his program and scribbled something across it. This he handed to Sir Nevile, who read: "As soon as the music is over I should like to talk with you, *and will explain everything to you.*"

Sir Nevile sat through the ballet with intolerable impatience. For Göring too, the music seemed untimely, out of place, yet he found its magic working on him—the glowing, romantic melodies of Schumann, the captivating antics of Harlequin and Columbine—and for minutes at a time he was totally immersed, nothing else existed.

At the music's end he scraped his chair back and left the room, all eyes following. After a discreet interval, Sir Nevile also got up and went out, all eyes following a second time.

*   *   *

"Schuschnigg is an underhanded scoundrel!" Göring began at once. "He has flown in the face of the Obersalzberg Agreements! He is a—"

"Is this the explanation you promised?" Sir Nevile broke in.

"It is! Don't you see that we could take no other course than invasion? He has forced us!"

"I do not see that, Herr Feldmarschall! Even if he has acted with precipitate foolishness, it is no excuse for Germany to act as a bully!"

"A bully? We are not going to overpower the Austrian people! We are going to free them from an unrepresentative government! You will see, Sir Nevile, that we have acted with a clear conscience. And anyway, what state in the whole world will get hurt by our union? Do we take anything away from any other state? This is purely and simply a German family matter."

That was not the issue, Sir Nevile said to himself with a sigh, taking a few steps away. The issue was the use of force. If everything had gone peacefully, he would have made no objection, but British policy could not sanction the use of force. On the other hand, if Britain formally protested and resorted to war, probably the whole of Austrian youth would fight on Germany's side. It was an impossible situation.

"Then I can only urge you," he said, turning, "and I urge you most strongly, Herr Feldmarschall, to do your utmost to see that the anti–National Socialist Austrians are treated with decency."

"Gewiss! You may be assured that I will see to that."

After further talk they returned to the hall, and to the thousand pairs of worried eyes. The Ambassador, who was neither a hypocrite nor a coward, nor the simple socialite that some Germans mistook him for, but perhaps even more than his Prime Minister a man who felt a burning mission to contribute to the salvation of mankind, sat down with the feeling that if the means of Austro-German unity were not as they might be, the unity itself was a step in the direction of fairness and world peace. It was a correction of the Versailles Treaty, and as such would be a balm to the nerve-racking ferment that had marked Germany since the end of the war.

The invasion had been so hastily organized that the proprietors of Austrian gasoline stations were astounded to see German Army trucks driving up to purchase fuel. Less fortunate vehicles ran out of gas in the middle of nowhere, or broke down because of mechanical failure and were left abandoned by the wayside. Their absence made no difference, for there was no resistance anywhere, no chaos except the chaos of welcome that grew throughout the day. People lined the roads laughing, cheering, dancing with one another, waving makeshift National Socialist flags, reaching out to grab the hands of the passing troops; while in towns and cities, the squares resounded with huge crowds roaring their ecstasy. All of Austria was *en fête*.

The Fritsch trial resumed a week after it had been interrupted. Although in a nearby building Reichsführer Himmler and a dozen of his men sat in a circle, with eyes closed, holding hands, endeavoring to bring a psychic influence to bear upon the proceedings by concentrating on a guilty verdict, things went disastrously wrong for them in the courtroom. Confronted with evidence in conflict with his testimony, the blackmailer tenaciously clung to his story until Göring lost his temper and shattered him with a blast: "You are the greatest liar I have ever heard! How long do you think you can go on lying to us?" The sleazy little criminal, with his dirty fingernails and haggard face, broke down and confessed that the Fritsch he had had dealings with was some other, obscure Fritsch, but that he had been coerced by the Gestapo.

"In what way coerced?"

"I was told that if I did not say what they wanted me to say . . . I would go to heaven."

The verdict was one of innocence. Though General von Fritsch was exonerated, he was not restored to his post but given a lesser command. He made no protest. The whole filthy business had been beyond his grasp from the start; he had felt dazed, paralyzed. Now he was cleared, but his good name had been dragged through the slime and he felt his life was finished. He asked only one thing, that Himmler be punished, but this the Führer refused to do. Fritsch then challenged Himmler to a duel, but there was no response. After that there was nothing left but to live out a meaningless existence.

Himmler's fear of Army retaliation was unrealized. After its courtroom triumph, the Army did not strike against SS headquarters; no troops marched from the Potsdam garrison. Much relieved, Himmler was nevertheless cast down by the whole affair and extremely sensitive about it. Only his demanding new duties in Austria took his mind off the humiliating episode. As for the little blackmailer, he had him thrown into a concentration camp and subsequently shot.

Chapter 46

S$_{\text{IR}}$ Nevile drove out to Carinhall one day in late April to see Göring, who, apparently in one of his lazy phases, had taken a week off from his duties. The Rolls-Royce hummed through a landscape so long locked into iron winter that its transformation seemed miraculous—frozen fields suddenly delicate gold and green, dark skeletal trees shimmering with new foliage in the mild air, wildflowers everywhere.

The Minister President was not in. He was out in the woods, but would soon return. In the salon Sir Nevile greeted several houseguests with whom he was acquainted, and as a sincere lover of continental royalty, which in no way disturbed his equally sincere belief that all foreigners from high to low were basically uncivilized, he was especially pleased to greet Prince Paul, Regent of Yugoslavia, whose first stay at Carinhall it turned out to be.

"*Mais ça n'existait même chez les Tsars!*" the prince exclaimed as they strolled through the room's opulence to the enormous, partly opened windows with their view of gardens and bronze statues and the forests beyond.

"*Vous ne chassez pas avec notre hôte, votre Excellence?*" asked Sir Nevile.

"*Non, aujourd'hui, il jette des lances; personnellement, je trouve ça un peu trop germanique.*"

Not far from where Putzi Hanfstaengl had stumbled in circles, the Reichsmeister of the Hunt was tramping along with a spear in his fist.

It was an authentic, very old Norse spear more than two meters in length, its wood beautifully engraved, a recent gift sent from Sweden by his former brother-in-law, Count von Rosen. The Reichsmeister of the Hunt not only was proficient in the old hunting art of the bow and arrow, but had also mastered that of spear-throwing. Today he was taking his new gift out to do some practicing, as guests and weapons carriers followed. For shoots Göring wore a medieval outfit like his late godfather's: green peaked hat, snowy blouse under black leather jerkin, chamois trousers stuffed into sturdy boots, and at his belt a hunting dagger in a scabbard of solid gold. But for stalking with a spear he was dressed less formally, in Lederhosen and open-necked shirt. Around his head was tied a cloth band to keep both sweat and hair from falling in his eyes. Having just completed one of his tortured weight-losing regimens, he was in brief good shape.

From time to time he would stop and draw the great spear back behind his head, his whole body arching, and hurl it powerfully, with a razored, rushing sound, through the green air. A moment later its bronze point would drive deep into the trunk of a tree, its long shaft quivering in a clean horizontal line. A pair of weapons carriers would run ahead and work it free, returning it to their master, who, with an exuberant step, tramped on with his guests in the direction of a field where the bison sometimes came. The guests wanted a look at the beasts.

The trees began to thin. Overhead crows circled and cawed, while from all around came other, more melodious birdcalls, an intoxicated concert of spring. The air was cool as water, but everyone was hot from the long walk. Göring stepped, sweating, into a sunlit open field, and stood looking around. Silently, he gestured to one of the weapons carriers and was handed a heavy ox horn. With both hands he lifted it to his lips, throwing his head back, and there issued through the sunny air a long, eerie, primordial call.

Then silence fell. For several minutes nothing happened; then there came a faint tremble of hoofbeats; they grew stronger, the ground began vibrating, and to a sound of thunder some ten or twelve huge, dark, shaggy creatures, thick-horned and broad-snouted, their massive shoulders rising above their great blunt heads—astounding great beasts whose likes Julius Caesar had beheld in the western reaches, some of which had been captured and exhibited alive in the Roman amphitheaters—came charging into the clearing to the sound of the mating call, for a few moments trotting about stiff-legged, pawing the ground, grunting, snorting, then thundering off again through the trees, taking with them a strong, bestial odor.

"Did you get a good look?" Göring yelled to his guests, who had stayed some distance behind him. "How could you see anything from back there? You should have come closer! What do you think—aren't they magnificent? Extinct all over Europe! Only in my forests will you find them!" And in an excess of enthusiasm he grabbed his spear from the carrier, stepped back and again let it fly, sending it quiveringly into the trunk of a pine.

"It is a tonic," he said to Sir Nevile a while later, as they walked together to the far end of the terrace. "I tell you, nothing lifts me like having a full week here. Especially this time of year. The air, just fill your lungs! And you will stay for supper? Gut! I'm sorry Frau Göring won't be present, but she is keeping to her room these days."

"The time must be growing near," said Sir Nevile, as they sat down at a white wicker table overlooking the little lake.

"It grows near," his host nodded happily, his face sunburned beneath his shower-dampened, smoothed-back longish hair, his body giving off a fragrant scent of cologne. He was in a pair of cream-colored riding breeches worn with wine-red boots. His blouse, with full sleeves gathered at the wrists, was of silk. From a gold chain around his neck hung a magnificent emerald the size of a pigeon's egg. His several rings flashed in the sun as he took out his container of pills—one had grown used to seeing him do this—and shook two or three into his broad palm. He sat back chewing, gazing with pleasure at the shimmering water.

"He remains there, Chancellor von Schuschnigg. It is a shocking thing that he sits in a concentration camp."

The eyes moved reluctantly from the lake. Then there was an amused shrug of the great shoulders. "Well, he sits in one of his own."

"I don't see that that is relevant, Herr Feldmarschall. And it is not only he and the members of his government, but thousands of other—"

"I am *aware*," Göring broke in. "I spent my whole time in Vienna ordering people's release, my own brother's included—thousands of people. And what happened when I left? Himmler had almost all of them rearrested."

"And I am aware of *that*. I am not implying that you didn't try to encourage moderation, but aren't there further steps you can take? And what about the Jews?" Here the Ambassador's eyebrows went up pointedly. "The Jews are committing suicide every day, by the score."

"I can't help it if the Jews do away with themselves. I can't put a policeman behind every Jew to prevent suicide."

"But you yourself ordered them to leave Austria," Sir Nevile persisted. "Your speech in Vienna, as I read it in the newspaper, was very clear on that point."

"I did not order them to leave. I do not make policy. When a decision has to be taken, none of us counts for more than the stones we are standing on. It is the Führer alone who decides. He has decided on a policy of wholesale emigration of Austrian Jews; what I said in Vienna was an elucidation of that fact."

"That they must all get out. Simply get out."

Göring was silent for a moment. "It's better for them that they don't stay, isn't it?" he asked philosophically. "Austrian anti-Semitism has never been a very pleasant thing, as we both know, but it is much worse now with Himmler organizing the native talent."

"And you didn't foresee this when you brought about annexation?"

"And it didn't cross the minds at Whitehall either?"

"That's going a bit far. We believed in the moral justness of unification, but we did not endorse the threat of invasion, and we do not endorse the expulsion of Jews or the arrest of thousands of political—"

"You British drive me mad with rage! You're always standing in Germany's path! We must do what we must do!" He sat back in his chair with an explosive sigh of impatience. "The Anschluss was a great historic act which was achieved without one drop of spilled blood. We came as a liberating force and were welcomed with tears of joy."

Sir Nevile, in his turn, sighed deeply. "That is not the point I'm making."

"But it's my point. The Versailles injustices must be corrected, and England agrees, oh, ja, ja, she says, but then when it is done she sets up a big fuss. Well, now that the Anschluss has inspired the Sudetens to clamor for self-determination, is England again going to say ja, ja, and then criticize afterward?"

The introduction of the Sudeten problem was so swift and subtly phrased that Sir Nevile did not answer at once. After a few moments, he said, "It is very early to presume anything."

"Because it's going to happen, you know. They are a German minority, they want union with the Reich, and we want it too. That, incidentally, is all we want. We are not interested in the rest of Czechoslovakia. We will be fully satisfied with the settlement of the Sudeten question."

That was to have been Sir Nevile's query. He absorbed the information with a nod. "And we will be fully satisfied if a peaceful future for Europe can be secured."

"Which is my own deepest wish, as you know."

Feeling the talk coming to an end, Sir Nevile asked again about Schuschnigg—but it was too late. With a handclap to the thighs and a scraping back of chair legs, the large figure rose, inhaling deeply. "Come, my friend, we should enjoy this outbreak of spring!"

Just then something came bounding up, a manservant rushing after it, and Göring was leaped upon as if by an enormous dog that threw its paws over his shoulders.

"Forgive me, Excellency, I can't keep up with him today, he's running all over the place—"

"Macht nichts," Göring laughed. "It's the spring weather, isn't it,

Caesar?" And he patted and stroked the big, amber-eyed face as Sir Nevile looked on smilingly. The Ambassador was not ruffled by the oversized pet; it was one of Göring's idiosyncrasies that he always had a lion in residence, that when it grew too big he returned it to the Berlin zoo and took a cub in its place, that he called each one Caesar, whether male or female, and that he often went back for emotional visits with his former Caesars. That's how he was, a bit odd, but a warm, charming, picturesque fellow, leaning over now, the great emerald swinging from its chain, to give a vigorous pat to the tawny flank of the lion, who then loped ahead of them as they strolled on across the terrace.

All over Germany the spring light was radiant, from the northern forests of Prussia where the two men descended the broad steps of the terrace, to the southernmost tip of Bavaria where Hitler, in his study at the Berghof, was sitting at a table deep in gratified concentration. Spread before him were samples of leather in shades varying from green to blue, brought him by a Munich bookbinder who sat with him awaiting his selection. An elderly soul dressed in his good dark suit for the occasion, chauffered from Munich in one of the Führer's open Mercedes-Benzes, and ushered up the Berghof steps before a crowd of staring sightseers who doubtlessly took him for a Cabinet minister, the old bookbinder now and then allowed his bespectacled eyes to roam around the large study, flooded with lofty mountain sunlight. The Führer, a pleasant and simple-mannered man who put one quite at ease, was deeply immersed in the many squares of leather; he would study the color of each, rub it, hold it to his skin, sniff it. He wanted to have specially bound the entire works of Nietzsche.

Hitler, holding up a sample before him in the sunlight, had been charged with gratitude for Mussolini's noninterference during the Anschluss. "I shall never forget this," he had told the message bearer. "Never, never, come what may. Tell him I thank him most heartily, tell him whenever he should be in need or danger I shall stick by him, rain or shine—even if the whole world would rise against him—I will, I shall—I shall never forget him!" Now he wished to send the Duce a gift, and had decided on a beautifully bound edition of Nietzsche's works. He took up yet another sample, gazed at it contemplatively.

"Es muss Zarathustra grün sein . . ." he murmured, meaning the high blue-green of the great glaciers from which Zarathustra had contemplated the world. "Ja . . . diese . . ." And his eyes seemed to the old man to be far, far away, entirely in some other world, a strange, unsettling gaze. In silence, the old man was handed the blue-green square. The old man wrote down the number of the sample in his notebook, and when he raised his eyes, he saw that the Führer was once more his cordial, businesslike self. The color having been decided on, they proceeded to the matter of the lettering.

In Nuremberg, another old man was discussing the matter of lettering. "'Tis as good as I could have done," Herr Schmidt nodded approvingly, leaning on his cane as he looked up at the Haus Sonnenblume sign, which his wife, climbing down the stepladder with a bucket of paint, had just renewed. The letters faded every few years and had to be touched up. This was the first year he had been unable to do it himself.

Nikki put the bucket down. "Well, I don't know why I'm doing it. It's just to humor you."

He hobbled away into the garden, unwilling to listen to what he knew would come. Nikki wiped her hands on a rag and followed, her eternal argument ready to flow from her lips: the garden was choking on itself, the house sinking into its foundations, falling apart, they hadn't even been able to keep warm last winter, he had gotten bronchitis—what would it be this coming winter, pneumonia?—and it was terrible for his arthritis; they could afford an apartment, they must move. It had become for both of them the Subject. She spoke it, he clamped his teeth together. But today, watching him somehow contrive to get down on his knees and begin weeding with his painfully crippled, clawlike fingers—he could no longer get them into gardening gloves—and seeing on his face a growing expression of contentment, she forbore bringing up the hateful Subject. Instead, she kneeled at his side in the chaos of greenery and began to help him, useless as it was.

". . . and I said to her, Frau Kloppmann, just because I'm an intimate friend of Feldmarschall Göring doesn't mean my larder is stocked with bacon and butter. The Feldmarschall himself ordered our rationing, and I for one am perfectly happy to make do with what I am allowed—"

"Because you eat like a bird. 'Tis no sacrifice for you."

"And you, Hans. Do you find it a sacrifice?"

"Nay, for I'm the same as you. But her, she's an eater."

"She's an absolute tub. The best thing that ever happened to her was rationing—she may actually wind up with a figure. I tell you, I can't stand these little Party people that are always grumbling. Not openly, of course, but it's there and you can tell—her hinting like that, well, I said, you're happy enough to come to the rallies with me and scream yourself purple in the face, but to give up a little butter, or to take the time to collect the little things of metal and rubber around the house you have no use for, oh, that's too much work, and she said, I *most* certainly do, and I said to her I am not even a member of the Party, I am only a member of the Fatherland, and *I* do these things with pride because they make the Fatherland strong, and she said, you are very mistaken Frau Schmidt if you think you are the only one who . . . oh, and she blabbered on, the woman is impossible."

"Why always be talking with her then?"

"Because we're neighbors," replied Nikki with a logic that was lost on her husband. He leaned back, pain throbbing in every bone, and looked around at the immense amount of work that was needed. Last year, Nikki had suggested he have a gardener in. That had annoyed him most deeply. For a gardener to call in a gardener!

". . . and of course now she's an authority on Austria because her nephew was sent in with his regiment, as if being in a place three days was worth mentioning. Whereas I've been there countless times, entire summers, at Schloss Mauterndorf, but she says, oh that was long ago—as if that made any difference!—but you can't talk with an idiot . . ."

Yet it was indeed long ago, and thinking of those vanished days, Nikki felt a sadness overcome her. Then a pleasant thought broke through: "I wish Epenstein were alive today, to see himself incorporated into the Reich. That would take him down a peg or two!" Even though she knew very well that the old rhinoceros had been pro-Anschluss and for that matter wasn't Austrian at all but Prussian, she enjoyed the thought.

Hans was pleased that Nikki still had the spirit to get after von Epenstein. It made everything seem more normal, as if their life would never change. But in his heart, he knew they would have to leave the house. They couldn't manage the place any longer. And she, falling silent, thought as she sat pulling up the weeds that soon she would be pulling up her roots. She had been happy here, in this unlikely place. They had been very happy, and now it was coming to an end. And like her husband, she tried to lose herself in the moment, in the warmth and fragrance of the fresh April air.

Which in the woods near Weimar was causing a phrase of Hölderlin's to come to the lips of Rose Korwan's companion, "Glänzende Götterlüfte rühren leicht . . ." Luminous, divine breezes touch you gently . . . and she, almost asleep, smiled and drowsily moved her hand to his. They lay with the remains of a picnic lunch in a small clearing, the actress of forty-two and the young man of twenty-three. She liked them young. Younger and younger. But one sometimes made a mistake, or rather nature did, putting a dry elderly soul into a magnificent young body: how pleasant it was when he stopped his endless lecturing and simply lay silent on the grass beside her, or invoked a line of poetry. Luminous, divine breezes . . . and she began drifting off, hair loosened, lips slightly parted, disclosing the gleam of her flawless teeth. She had pulled off her shoes and stockings and hiked her dress up above the knees of her bare legs; the cool grass, the caressing warm air, the sun bursting through the green leaves like hundreds of little suns, all this had created a feeling of perfect happiness within her. ". . . let's be honest, we're anti-Semitic ourselves. We hate Eastern Jews because we're identified with them. It's logical. Fear has its own logic. Fear, in fact, is the most logical of all emotions. Nicht wahr? The most primitive, thus the most simply structured. Like tropism. The basic logic of stimulus and response . . ."

Oh Gott, why doesn't he shut up? Or go back to Hölderin, to Glänzende Götterlüfte, that was so beautiful; and yet no, she didn't really care for this poem, she knew the rest . . . es schwinden, es fallen die leidenden Menschen, suffering mankind cast like water from cliff to cliff, down, down into the unknown. She was galvanized by a terrible noise.

Three screaming children raced past with a barking dog, disappearing into the trees that ringed the glade. "There ought to be a sign, 'Kinder und Hunde Verboten,'" said Walther, scowling after them. "And what about 'Juden Willkommen,' just for a change?"

"I go anywhere. I pay no attention to the signs. And you needn't either." He being as fair and straight-featured as anyone could be. But she wished no discussion. "Aren't you sleepy?" she asked, lying back again and closing her eyes.

"Nein. I keep normal hours."

A sigh drilled through her nostrils. He was so well regulated and so self-righteous, droning on again now, analyzing her dental trips. ". . . you say yourself that you have them checked for no reason, they're indestructible, and that you started going only five years ago. Why then? Why 1933? Consider that date. It's a classic case of displaced anxiety. Your fears were sublimated right into your teeth. All at once you began to doubt their indestructibility and had to seek repeated assurance. It makes perfect symbolic sense. Nicht wahr?"

Gott, how he wearies me, how he wearies me! she thought, and said without opening her eyes, "Why don't you go, Walther? I mean it—hinaus! Take the basket. Leave the wine."

There was no answer. Instead, she felt on her cheek the warm breath through his nostrils, and then his moist warm lips on hers, and the exasperating moments dissolved in pleasure, as the sun fell in moving dapples on their two embraced bodies. It fell on other picknickers and strollers, whose voices, mixed with the warbling of birds, drifted into the glade; it fell on the yard of Buchenwald concentration camp a few kilometers away, where, in the blackness of a box too low to stand in and too narrow to sit in, crushed on all sides in a paralyzed crouch, an inmate could see through two bored holes the glint of sunlight on gravel; and it fell on the brook that gurgled its way through the trees, and on the three children and the dog splashing in it, presently causing an explosion of parental scolding to invade the little clearing. The lovers stretched, and poured themselves more wine. He had finally entered a nonlecturing mood, Rose saw, flushed, smiling, lean and muscular in his grass-stained white shirt; and they lay back with their wine, in the warbling stillness.

* * *

On the balcony of her Berlin residence, Frau Goebbels, greatly pregnant, was also listening to the singing of birds. The wild back gardens, stretching to Hermann-Göring-Strasse, were splashed everywhere with flowers. Now and then she heard the clear high voices of her four small children playing below.

She had told the maid to go inside, she hated being hovered over. Josef had instructed the maid to be with her every moment. This might be interpreted as thoughtfulness, except that he himself would be doing no hovering. While she was in labor, he would be off on a trip with one of his actresses. He said it was an official trip, of course. And no, he could not postpone it.

But everything that had tormented Frau Goebbels in the past she had now become resigned to. For a while last year she had lived in a golden fantasy, building up in her mind a great romance with a playwright whom she knew slightly. She had planned that she would take the children and run away with this man whom she so passionately loved . . . but when one day the playwright declared himself, she was shocked and disappointed. The fact was, she did not love him at all. And the fantasy that had sustained her fell in ruins.

At first she had been desolated; then she felt a growing philosophical attitude. If she could not break out of this situation, she must accept it. And with her acceptance she saw that she understood things with greater clarity than before. The enormous number of Josef's infidelities, for instance. That had always seemed the worst thing of all, but she saw now that it was much better that mistresses went endlessly through his turnstile than if he had only one. One would be a matter of the heart, many was only flesh. And his endless lying about it . . . if in fact he was lying, because when she came right down to it, what she knew she knew only through gossip, rumor, there was no concrete evidence at all—but if he was in fact lying, wasn't that an indication that he loved her and desperately wanted to keep her? . . . Keep her for what, to practice his sarcasm on? Yet she understood that too; his need to be the only one, the shining one, the one to whom all things came and all things bowed, and perhaps she shone too much in her own right. But he had not always been so sarcastic and bitter toward her. During the last few years it was as if a dark shadow of doubt and worry had fallen over him; he felt he no longer held his special place in the Führer's favor, he had slipped, lost ground. And that was a terrible feeling; she knew because she was in a similar position. She had always been open with the Führer, but last year when she had mentioned a cartoon in Streicher's *Stürmer* and called it a disgrace, she sensed annoyance behind his reply, "It is only Streicher's hobby. I wish him joy in it." And when later she had criticized the lack of religious training in the League of German Maidens, he had not bothered to disguise his irritation. Soon after, at the Nuremberg rallies, she had caught sight of Fräulein Braun characteristically hidden away on a back bench; she had glimpsed this Braun woman once or twice at the Berghof, a rather dowdy type, and she could not help remarking to a woman friend, "Fräulein Braun looks frightfully insignificant as usual." The remark had apparently reached the Führer's ears, because since then she had felt he was cool toward her at gatherings, he did not seek her out. It was very sad, very hard, to look at those eyes and not see approval in them, favor; those eyes that had suffused one with such life, such gratitude. It was perhaps the hardest thing of all, to have lost the light of those eyes. . . .

Yet she did have the sunlight. She could enjoy this extraordinarily beautiful spring day. And she had her children, and was so fortunate that they were healthy and lively and bright, and beautiful; they possessed an almost unearthly beauty. Her love for her children was like a sweet achingness, so deep, so deep, and now in a few days there would be another child . . . another, and her thoughts strayed here and there in the realm of motherhood, settling for a moment on Emmy Göring, also expecting at any time . . . the *soi-disant* First Lady of the Reich finally producing, at the age of forty-five, some late-life, wan creature.

But Emmy Göring did not give birth that week, or the next either. It seemed that the pregnancy would go on forever. Yet she was cheerful, and entertained no doubts that all would go well. There was a constant flutter around her as the days wore on toward June. Her sister and niece were with her, her two sisters-in-law, Olga and Paula, and two close women friends from the theater. Rose was not there, but she had sent an exquisite little sleeping gown, all silk and lace and satin ribbons, quite impractical but touchingly romantic and extravagant, like Rose herself. The room was crowded with people coming and going, as if it were a state occasion, which in a way it was. Finally the sensible Cilly took over.

"I don't care if this child will inherit a thousand-year Reich or the whole world, it must be born first, and to that end the mother needs peace!"

After that it was quieter, her visitors came one at a time; and of course Hermann came every morning before he left the house, and every night when he returned. It was at night that the pains at last began; Dr. Ondarza was hurriedly summoned, and Hermann banished from the room, his eyes expressing badly concealed anxiety. But once begun, the birth went quickly and easily, as she had known it would. A little after midnight she was delivered of a lustily crying baby girl. She felt terribly weak, but terribly happy, and asked at once for Hermann.

Moments later he was covering her face with kisses, crying almost as loudly as the child. With the tears streaming down his face, he went over and peered at the small bundle, and came back to her bedside still weeping; he could not stop.

Then the room became quiet again, and she felt herself drifting into sleep, covered with his salt tears.

Chapter 47

"How Carin would have loved it here."

Emmy was silent as they stood looking out over the water. He always expressed this sentiment at least once during their stays at Sylt, usually on the first day, when the beauty all around was so new and fresh; then out it came, like a sigh or smile. As spontaneously, but also as passingly. One waited a few moments, as one did with all his Carin remarks, until the present inevitably returned.

They pointed simultaneously—it had returned—her hand and his both lifting to a sea eagle in slow, majestic flight. The sky was cloudless. It was a sky she knew from childhood, for she had spent her young summers here. She loved the white sand cliffs, and the white beaches with their great expanse of white foaming surf, which only far out graded into blue. And when you turned, there were fields of heather and the blue sea again, and the pale coast of Denmark.

In her childhood that pale coastline had been part of Germany, of northern Schleswig; but after the Great War it had been restored to Denmark by plebiscite. She found no fault with that. The people there had wanted to be Danish again, they had voted for it. If Germany was consequently a little smaller, what difference? If Czechoslovakia became a little smaller for giving up the Sudetenland, what difference? Why would Czechoslovakia not agree to a Sudeten plebiscite? Why were the Czechs willing to plunge Europe into war over such a thing? Did one bring a child into the world only for it to face war?

The calm was broken by a sound of squalling. The couple walked back to the cottage porch, where the nursemaid sat with the crying little Edda. Dotingly they lifted her, patted and soothed her, happily unaware that rumor had her the product of artificial insemination, Göring being impotent—shot in the testicles, as everyone knew—as well as a face-powdering homosexual and decrepit morphinist; whoever had started the rumor had dredged up every possible reason for nonpaternity. The theme was even at this moment on tongues everywhere in Party circles. Nein, he's got wop horns; nein, it's a test-tube baby; but has science really invented such a method? Gewiss, he forced science to invent it, after all he can force anything, can't he? except his Schwanz to stand up; I still say Mussolini banged her under the stairs; Quatsch, it's a test-tube baby.

Thomas was glad for the earsplitting noise as he came up the porch steps, his rucksack on his back; it made his entrance easier for him to bear. Greetings, embraces, introductions to the screaming infant . . . and so the moment of his arrival was over, mercifully diffused by commotion. It was the first time he had seen Hermann since his Carinhall visit of last January. He disliked remembering that brief sojourn and his own inflatedness.

The three of them sat down, talking, as the baby's squalls disappeared inside with the nursemaid, and it was as if everything were the same as before. He mentioned his job in passing. They had accepted what he had written from Stockholm, that he had decided to stay on after all.

Of war he said nothing.

The days went by filled with sea bathing and long walks, and he said nothing. It was only in his mind that he asked: Are you going to let Hitler invade? Are you going to let this thing turn into a war with the Western powers? Are you planning a coup? Are you going to get rid of him?

Thomas was not the only one contemplating Göring's role in the growing crisis. A plan to overthrow Hitler was taking root among the generals, who knew that war at this time would be suicidal. They had no love for the captain who had shot like a cannonball to the rank of Feldmarschall; this arrogant, medal-dripping senior officer of all Germany was to them a National Socialist upstart. Still, he was the only sensible man in Hitler's highest circle. Above all, he was adored by the people. He was the only man whom the people would accept in Hitler's place. The people did not want war. That was the strongest card the generals held. They must act, and act soon.

The generals' secretive talks went on as Thomas walked each day with his stepfather along the cliffs, the sparkling sea below.

"Tell me, Thomas, is it what you really wanted, to stay on in your work?"

"Certainly. I wouldn't have done it otherwise. There's always time later if I should change my mind."

Thomas knew his succinctness would preclude further probing, as it had when Emmy made her delicately phrased inquiry about his love life. "There was someone. There isn't now. But there are plenty of girls in the world."

Thomas of old, Göring thought as they walked along. Those soaring wings hadn't held up; he had crashed to the ground, all intoxication, all youthful happiness gone. Although he didn't seem unhappy either; but then, he had never seemed unhappy. Just dry, formal, observant. A solemn bystander.

The days began running out.

Thomas flirted a little with the nursemaid, grew fond of the infant. He and Emmy had the entire beach to themselves, for other vacationers were prohibited within a kilometer's radius around the cottage: Hermann was at his peak weight, and preferred no onlookers. Enormous as he was, and unwell with swollen and painful lymph glands, he tramped off every morning for his plunge, a robed and vigorous figure disappearing down the sandy path. Afternoons he was lazy, napped on the porch, an Agatha Christie novel lying open on his lap. The life was quiet, adjutants and bodyguards housed in a nearby village. One heard only the sound of birds, and the long, soft sighing of the surf.

A week after Thomas had returned to Stockholm and his job, the Görings set off on a cruise. Göring's yacht, the *Carin,* had recently been replaced with a newer and larger one, *Carin II,* with a rosewood interior and solid-gold bathroom fixtures. Its sleek white hull reflecting the summer sun, it cleaved slowly along the coast of Denmark, its destination Helsingor, where Göring's Prussian State Theater was to perform *Hamlet* in the legendary castle of the tragic prince. In Nyborg the yacht discharged two Mercedes-Benz limousines, which followed it along the coasts of Fyn and Sjaelland, the cars' passengers being intelligence officers who examined sea and land fortifications as they drove along. In the event a war did come, soon or late, Göring meant to use Denmark as the German "war kitchen"; it would be essential, and it must be planned for. If it turned out to be unnecessary, so much the better.

After the performance at Helsingor, the Görings sailed back to Sylt, where the Feldmarschall left his wife and infant to continue their holiday, and himself returned to Berlin.

"Why doesn't Ribbentrop go back to peddling his pisswater? I tell you, Bruno, the biggest mistake the Führer ever made was to make that wine salesman foreign minister—"

"It could be worse—what if he'd made him wine minister?" General Loerzer yelled back through the wind.

"True," Göring laughed. "But his handling of the British—whatever rapport exists between us he undermines."

"He's developing a twitch for his pains."

"He's always had that—it's the poker up his ass."

They were driving from Berlin to Carinhall in Göring's cinnamon-red open two-seater. He was stuffed behind the wheel, his great thigh mashed against Loerzer's, who himself had grown thicker with the years. The wind rushed deafeningly against them; their clothes flapped like flags, their hair flew, their eyes were slits. Now and then Loerzer curled his toes. He had never gotten used to Hermann's driving.

"I want him given the full works!"

"Who?" asked Loerzer. "Ah, Vuillemin!" The French Air Chief was to arrive for a visit next week.

"Tours through the aircraft factories first, then up to the Baltic, make it a whole afternoon at the Tactical Experimental Center. I want him to see at least three solid hours—both high-altitude bombing and dive-bombing. We'll want to make sure the Stukas are equipped with this new whistle device of Udet's. It's really something—the fellow's a genius!"

"Vuillemin will appreciate it!" Loerzer shouted, for the French Air Chief's squeamishness about bombers was no secret. During the Great War he had led a bomber squadron over occupied Alsace and had accidentally hit a circus tent, killing numerous children. In flying circles it was known that he had never gotten over this.

"He's a humane man, and I respect him for that—I am humane too!" Hermann shouted back. "But a man shouldn't command an air force if he doesn't have strong nerves."

They swung off the highway and roared on through the green bower of trees, presently coming to a skidding stop in the courtyard. "Smell the air, Bruno!" Hermann commanded, filling his lungs, and in an expansive and energetic mood, took his guest inside.

There was to be a meeting later on, but first, having changed into one of his flowing velvet robes, he relaxed upstairs with his model trains. Loerzer was also a model-train lover; in fact, few people could resist Hermann's miniature railway under the rafters of the attic. There were villages and green fields, lakes and rivers of silvered glass, a mountain, tall as a man, crowned with a castle; and throughout, a network of gleaming little tracks along which clacked the bright, variously colored trains; everything perfect down to the tiny flowerpots on the station platforms. Everything went perfectly, according to command. Loerzer watched Hermann push this button and that of the elaborate control board, at which a drawbridge went up or came down, lights turned red or green, trains stopped or trains started, all at his will. What went on behind the control panel was not Hermann's concern; if something misfunctioned, an electrician could be called in. He himself just pushed the buttons and watched the results, apart from Hitler the only man in Germany to make his own decisions. Unquestioned power, immediate obedience.

The following week Göring hosted a garden reception for General Vuillemin, who had been duly subjected to a solid afternoon of Luftwaffe savagery. The German Air Chief, in his big white summer uniform, puffing on a slim Virginia cigar, lost no time confronting the French Air Chief with a blunt but amiably spoken question.

"Monsieur le Général, what will you do if we are forced to start a war with Czechoslovakia?"

Vuillemin, whose ambassador, François-Poncet, was standing with him, hesitated a fraction. Then he replied firmly, "France will remain true to her word."

"I see," Göring said mildly, and turned the conversation to other things. The moment's hesitation had spoken volumes, he was satisfied.

Yet what good was it? he asked himself later. So Vuillemin went to his Prime Minister, Daladier, with tales of doom for the French Air Force—what if Daladier didn't listen? One knew only too well that heads of state did not always listen to the right person. Ribbentrop was glued to the Führer. He, Göring, who had done so much to achieve the present rapport with Poland and Italy, was being left behind in the diplomatic backwaters. Regent Horthy of Hungary had been to see him, and Marshal Balbo of Italy, wanting to know what was going to happen. What could he tell them? He only knew that the likelihood of another Great War loomed ever larger.

A few days later, when Sir Nevile drove out to see the Feldmarschall, he found him looking ill, worn, tense. When asked conversationally if his wife and child had returned from Sylt, he answered that they would be back tomorrow, at which a black mood seemed to seize him—his very long mouth tightened, and the chair he was pulling back on the terrace made a violent scraping noise. "I may deserve many things, but I don't deserve this!" was echoing through his mind, the ring of his angry voice in the Führer's study. "I've just heard this talk about me and my wife and child, and I want it stopped! It's a filthy paternity attack, and it's Streicher behind it—it's his brand of venom! I want it stopped, I want him punished!"

Concern and sympathy had been forthcoming, but nothing more. "It's true that Streicher has generally been getting a bit out of hand lately, but let us be practical, Göring, unless you have proof of what you say, it is difficult to do anything. That's the problem with rumors, they're really impossible to trace."

And it had laid him low, he had taken to his bed for two days, had lain ill and gargantually heavy beneath the blankets, the curtains of the canopied bed drawn around him, a dark and muffled solitude in which tears of fury burned in his eyes.

"So, things aren't going very well, are they?" he asked Sir Nevile, and sat back in his white wicker chair. "It's beginning to feel like the summer of 1914 rather than the summer of 1938."

Sir Nevile nodded, hearing the Feldmarschall's quietly spoken words with a feeling of exasperation for his radio speeches: "The German Air Force will be the terror of its enemies! When the Führer says that we can no longer tolerate the suppression of German comrades beyond our borders, then the soldiers of the Air Force know that if it must be, they must back these words to the hilt! We are burning to prove our invincibility!" This man who did not want war was certainly not reducing the war tension with his belligerent threats.

"Peaceful negotiations are difficult," Sir Nevile said, "when the atmosphere resounds with threats of force."

"Who mobilized first, the Czechs or we? We are mobilizing in response. And if I state publicly that we're strong and cannot be pushed around, and if that sounds threatening, then that's how it must be. I don't want war with Czechoslovakia, but I want to make clear that if war is thrust upon us, we will be a formidable foe. I want to make clear that it is better if war is avoided."

"And if war with Czechoslovakia cannot be avoided? Then it is imperative that your government realize now that if France acts, Britain will also act."

"It is my own greatest wish that the Führer not take British nonintervention for granted. Unfortunately, Ribbentrop tells him you people will not make a move."

"And so," sighed Sir Nevile, "where are we?"

In September of that year, late in the afternoon, the diplomatic train from Berlin drew into the outskirts of Nuremberg, its wheels clacking past warehouses and factory buildings interspersed with the sheds and vegetable rows of allotments, in one of which Frau Schmidt was being pushed over the edge of her small self-restraint by the familiar, passing train whistle. Tearfully, she groped for a handkerchief. Haus Sonnenblume stood disemboweled. A taxi had been called, but it hadn't arrived and probably wouldn't; they would have to go by tram to their new apartment, if they could even squeeze aboard; and suddenly it was overwhelming, leaving their home, and so lacking in sense as to move during the rally when the streets were congested and war about to begin. "But if *we're* the strong ones, and *we* want peace . . ." she said through her nose-blowing to the intolerable Frau Kloppmann, that round, know-nothing upstart whom she was finding it so hard to part with, and whose eyes were also moist. Her husband, with a last look at his rampant garden and sunken little house, had placed his hat on his head. Exchanging an embrace with Frau Kloppmann, Frau Schmidt put her arm through his and prepared to meet the chaos of the streets and of approaching war.

Ambassador François-Poncet, of the black waxed mustache, who sat gazing out his window at the passing outskirts, was thinking of Hitler's Berghof, the peaks all around looming grand, savage, hallucinant . . . all Europe on the edge of a volcano, the Maginot and Siegfried lines being manned this very moment; and he went over in his mind the carefully thought-out words he would address to the Führer tomorrow at the diplomatic reception. In another compartment, the dour but able Ambassador Attolico sat with his eyes closed, worn out from trying to bring about an understanding between Britain and Mussolini, his vivacious and original wife sitting gravely beside him, just returned from Rome, where she had gone for the express purpose of praying for peace at the family shrine. And in another compartment, Ambassador Henderson was planning to talk with as many National Socialist leaders as he could, in order to impress upon them the inevitability of British intervention if Germany attacked Czechoslovakia. He hoped this might prevent their supreme leader, in his political speech at the end of the rally, from giving vent to words he might feel he could not back down from later. The entire world was waiting to hear what would be said in that speech. But Sir Nevile wondered if he himself had the physical strength to do much talking. He had felt unwell lately, was losing weight, and was easily fatigued. He closed his eyes, but a few minutes later the train jolted to a stop before the station platform, where a red carpet was being unrolled with dispatch by black-uniformed, white-gloved SS guards.

The annual festivity this year was raised to new heights for having become, through the incorporation of Austria, the First Party Congress of Greater Germany. There was an extraordinary and awesome ceremony, at its center the crown of the Holy Roman Empire. Made of gold, set with great uncut gems above which rose the jewel-encrusted cross of the universal church, the diadem which had been placed on Otto the Great's head a thousand years before had now been brought from Vienna, where it had resided since Napoleon's crushing of the Holy Roman Empire; it was to be ensconced in Nuremberg, spiritual home of both medieval Germany and National Socialism. Here in Nuremberg, the Führer solemnly vowed in his speech of presentation, the symbol of the First Reich would remain forever.

The Führer's last-day speech was apprehensively awaited throughout Europe, but before the Führer's speech came Göring's. On that day Frau Schmidt made a point of listening to the radio. The apartment was a jumble of half-unpacked belongings, through which she had to thread her way to where the radio stood. She twisted the knob with her red, bony fingers, and a squawk of static filled the room, followed by a roar which was the roar of tens of thousands of voices, followed by the single, familiar, metallic voice.

". . . a trifling piece of Europe is making life unbearable for mankind! The Czechs, that vile race of pygmies without any culture—nobody even knows where they came from—are oppressing a civilized people! And behind them, together with Moscow, can be seen the everlasting face of the Jewish fiend! It would be well for the world to realize that our defenses are impregnable! And it ill becomes British statesmen to speak against German claims and German forces, when the whole British Empire has been held together only with the lash! . . ."

"Ach, du lieber," Hans murmured when the speech was over.

"He won't allow war. Hermann is for peace," Nikki said tensely, clicking off the radio.

"Why doesn't he talk peaceable then?"

"Why? Why? I'll tell you why! Because Hermann always has to say the unpopular things. No one loves Hitler as they love Hermann. When Hermann gives a speech that people don't like, they like it anyway because they like him. That's why Hitler has him do it."

"Mayhap . . ."

"That's how it is in politics, Hans. I told Hermann years ago that he shouldn't get involved. It's no good getting mixed up with that low nobody, I told him, you are one of our great heroes and he is just another cheap politician."

"You told him that?" asked Hans, raising an eyebrow.

"Certainly I did."

This Hans doubted, or she would have regaled him with it long ago. But he nodded, because it was so purely Nikki, so familiar and homey in this strange place, this disordered, curtainless room whose bare windows looked out on brick apartment buildings without a speck of green.

"Certainly I did. But I was not listened to. But maybe he will now step on him at last—oh, he's got to get rid of this upstart who wants war! Ach, I feel as if everything were going to explode around us!"

"'Twas that speech of his . . ."

"Why do you keep harping on that! I've told you how it is in politics. If one is in politics, one has always got to play on two pianos."

And she felt indeed as if she could hear two pianos, ten, a hundred, all pounding through the chaotic, uncurtained, unfamiliar room.

Millions of radios were clicked off the next evening to the accompaniment of millions of relieved sighs. Hitler's speech had been a passionate recounting of Sudeten grievances, but it had not culminated in a threat of war. The dreaded ultimatum had not been given. From a peak of tension, spirits everywhere began to relax.

The next day anxiety shot higher than before as the Sudeten Germans broke into new bloody protests against Czechoslovakian President Beneš and were put down at once: now surely Hitler would march. Instead, hope soared as headlines everywhere blazed with the news that the British Prime Minister, Neville Chamberlain, was flying to meet for a talk with the German Chancellor. Hope soared higher yet when the Prime Minister returned to London to inform the world that Herr Hitler was asking for a Sudeten plebiscite, and that Britain and France would propose this to Czechoslovakia. After a crushed President Beneš announced his acceptance of this proposal from his allies, there remained only the practicalities of self-determination to iron out. As Europe sank back with relief, the Prime Minister once again flew to meet with Hitler, only to be told that the agreement was no longer enough: five days hence the Sudetenland must be evacuated of its non-German population and the area occupied by German troops. British and German warships were put on the alert, gas masks were passed out in London, France mobilized half a million men.

At dusk on September 27, motorized divisions rumbled through the Berlin streets on their way to the Czech frontier. Two o'clock the following afternoon was the hour that Hitler's ultimatum would expire and the invasion commence. Early that morning Ambassador Henderson telephoned Göring to tell him that François-Poncet had vainly requested a meeting with Hitler, that it was a matter of fresh proposals, and that peace or war depended upon it.

"You needn't say a word more—I shall go immediately to the Führer."

It seemed ironic to the Führer's interpreter, Dr. Schmidt, that his services on this day of ultimate crisis were not to be used. There was apparently to be no discussion between the Führer and any foreigner. Or for that matter, between the Führer and anyone at all. The Chancellery halls and anterooms were filled with a hectic tension emanating from a swarm of generals, aides-de-camp, department heads and ministers, while the Führer remained isolated in the winter garden. Herr von Ribbentrop, hovering by the winter garden door, clearly wishing to be at his Führer's elbow as usual, suddenly scowled. Dr. Schmidt saw Göring, with Baron von Neurath, walk hurriedly to the door and disappear inside.

"Mein Führer," von Neurath began at once, "do you want to start a war under any circumstances? I can't believe that you do—"

"We are in no position to undertake a war," said Göring. "Mein Führer, you saw yourself what happened in Austria. And now this same ill-equipped, half-trained army is supposed to take on France,

Britain and possibly Russia? Even war with Czechia alone would result in huge German losses. We have had an armed forces for only two short years; the Czechs have had theirs for twenty. For twenty years they have been arming and training, while we are still striving to build and perfect our forces. Why send our men off when the result will only be needless slaughter? And if the Great Powers join in? I tell you, if we go to war now it will be the end of Germany! And the whole thing is completely unnecessary, for we can surely achieve our aims through peaceful negotiations. Of that I am absolutely certain. Even at this eleventh hour it is not too late—"

"There is still time," von Neurath broke in. "But if these few hours are allowed to slip by without heeding any French or British overtures . . ."

They received no reply to their arguments. They went out again. Dr. Schmidt saw Göring turn to von Ribbentrop.

"If war should break out, Herr Ribbentrop, I will be the first one to tell the people that you pushed things to this end. I know what war is!"

"I know what war is too. I was an officer at the front—do you forget that?"

"It's you who have obviously forgotten!"

"I have not forgotten! But the difference between us, Herr Göring, is that I am not afraid of combat. Apparently you are!"

"Let me tell you this! If the Führer says march, I will take off in the leading airplane, but only on the condition that you're sitting in the seat beside me!" He stomped off, turning to hurl a final epithet over his shoulder. "Criminal fool!"

Quiet descended as the flushed, heavily stamping Feldmarschall disappeared from the room, and the smoldering, white-faced Foreign Minister resumed his wait by the door. Dr. Schmidt began walking around, hands clasped tightly behind his back, involuntarily glimpsing all these striped trousers and mouse-gray spats and polished military boots standing in a wall-to-wall pool of clotting red. He looked at the clock on the wall. Three hours remained.

As Göring boarded his private train for Munich that night, he wondered what had changed the Führer's mind and caused him to see François-Poncet after all. Was it an accumulation of things? Realization that the people weren't behind him? The antiwar counsel he had been receiving endlessly from his generals? His, Göring's, own intervention this morning? Or perhaps the Führer's mind had not required changing at all. Perhaps he had never meant to march, only to twist the international screws until the very last possible moment. Had the man meant to invade at two o'clock, or had he not? How could one know? In any case, the Feldmarschall mused as he sat down in his salon car, it was all well now. There would be no war. And the negotiations in Munich tomorrow would bring them what they wanted. Self-determination of the Sudetens was the least of it, only a means. It was the Sudetenland itself that was important; by allowing it to secede, Czechia would be relinquishing her impregnable mountain fortifications, her military bastion, removing herself from her threatening geographical position. He foresaw a simple cut-and-dried affair tomorrow, and was in good spirits as the train carried him through the night toward this excellent conclusion.

The conference was indeed a cut-and-dried affair insofar as it concerned the dismemberment of Czechoslovakia, which was agreed upon in the first hour. Then followed thirty-six hours of discussion over details, interminable talks hampered by the necessity of constant translation, while ambassadors, delegates, and secretaries wandered around the room. Everyone but French Premier Daladier was in good spirits. He, who was breaking a treaty, abandoning an ally, dishonoring his country, seemed several times on the verge of tears.

At half past two in the morning, the leaders of the four Great Powers—Britain, France, Germany and Italy—put their names to the agreement. Then, as an afterthought, the two Czech emissaries who sat waiting in an outer room—Czechoslovakia had not been invited to participate—were informed that the Sudetenland was now ceded and would be occupied by German troops in ten days' time.

Relief was felt throughout the world. Prime Minister Chamberlain was greeted with mass demonstrations of joy on his return to London. Premier Daladier, too, found himself cheered wildly by his people, which helped lift his spirits. Mussolini's train trip back to Rome was punctuated by crowds waving with passionate admiration. And Hitler returned to an ecstasy of worship, the hero of another bloodless victory.

As for the generals—who for their coup had depended on the backing of public disapproval once war was declared—now that Hitler had triumphed without jeopardizing one soldier's life and was more wildly acclaimed than ever, they felt themselves at a loss, without any choice but to make their military most of this gratuitous triumph.

Chapter 48

THE slanderous talk about Göring had buzzed in Party circles all summer, but it was parochial compared to the talk set off by Goebbels's affair with Lida Baarova. The higher the war tension had mounted, the faster the Baarova scandal had spread and crackled, like a bright diversionary wildfire, until all Berlin was gossiping.

How many actresses the Propaganda Minister had slept with since taking control of the German cinema five years before he could not have begun to count, for despite a strong romantic component he was efficient in the extreme. He had a small bachelor apartment connected by a door to his ministry office, and a special button on his office desk by which he could signal his staff not to disturb him under any conditions. He would summon the young lady thespian to discuss some film matter, and presently suggest they retire to his private quarters; he was seldom refused, since the price of refusal was a matter of record in cinema circles—an impeded or even destroyed career, while incurring the torment of being shadowed by the Secret Police—and within minutes he would be closing the door of the little bedroom. Many of the faces were distressed, but many were agreeable; nor did it matter to him if the agreeableness stemmed from his sexual magnetism or from the hope that his patronage might be secured. Half an hour later he was back at his desk, and if the lady was bliss-besotted—for his usage was of a high order: potent, hot-blooded, yet sensitive, deeply knowing—and hung about reluctant to depart, he had another desk button which, covertly pressed, brought his staff barging in to inundate him with official matters. There were times, however, when he felt himself fascinated and would enter upon an affair. Inspired, ardent, he was a lover who sent flowers and lines of poetry, for whom no attentive gesture was too much, a wholly entrancing cavalier for two or three weeks, after which he invariably felt staleness setting in and abruptly brought down the curtain on his startled paramour. In addition, liaisons of any duration could never be kept discreet, and he had no wish to upset his Führer.

Thus he went his way year after year, nimbly juggling his extramarital activities with his domestic and official life, until Baarova.

The birth of Frau Goebbels's last child had been difficult and had undermined her health. At Schwanenwerder, the Goebbelses' lakeside estate near Berlin, she spent a quiet, recuperative summer, neither entertaining nor going out, with the result that she knew nothing of the great affair. This seemed a preposterous situation to her close women friends, but they hesitated to speak. Magda's married life had always been a closed book; she never said an intimate word about her husband, and her entire attitude prohibited frankness. They knew that she was usually unhappy, and that sometimes she managed not to be, that was all. They knew that she was in one of her less unhappy phases just now, and they saw Goebbels's solicitous touch in the exquisite Maréchal Nil roses and thoughtful little gifts that surrounded her. All the more difficult to break it to her that she was being subjected to public humiliation, that he was involved in an ongoing, flagrant affair utterly unlike his others. Even Magda's closest friend, her former sister-in-law, Ello Quandt, could not speak this truth. Often she was on the brink, but the fragile, shatterable look of the invalid held her back.

Frau Quandt had always tried to understand her friend's extraordinary step in mating with Goebbels. That he was physically a poor scrap with one foot encased in a thick heavy thing that looked like an old-fashioned clothes iron she was above thinking about. She found disgusting the nicknames wrought from his affliction—the shrunken Teuton, Wotan's Mickey Mouse. One did not have to stoop to that; his personality and actions provided more than enough grounds for obloquy—because, try as she might, and despite the surface cordiality that had always existed between them, she could never free herself, even when he was at his most charming and companionable, of a feeling of something dark, shriveled, bitter as gall. He seemed a strange fate for Magda, who, until her infatuated plunge into National Socialism, had been entirely unpolitical; true, many people of their class had taken up National Socialism, but to do it with such totality, to live and breathe within its very heart, coupled to Dr. Goebbels—this was a mystery. Per-

haps she had simply sought excitement? And was it exciting to suffer?
Very clearly it was not. The years with Goebbels had worn her down;
she seemed a lost creature, thought Frau Quandt. Why did she hang
on to this empty, tormenting marriage? Why did she allow herself to be
patted into eternal compliance? Why did she not feel hatred?

Frau Quandt drove out to Schwanenwerder one afternoon with
the express purpose of breaking the truth to Magda. Nervously and
grimly, for she knew the shock and emotional turmoil she would cause,
she went out to the garden where Magda was sitting.

"Josef brought his mistress to see me. Lida Baarova."

The words caused Frau Quandt, just seating herself in a striped
lawn chair, to drop the rest of the way like a stone.

"I had no idea Josef had a mistress," the calm, quiet voice went on.
"I mean, a mistress of some duration. A true love. I suppose I'm the
only one who didn't know."

Through Frau Quandt's astonishment she felt a painful stab of
guilt; tears of self-recrimination leaped to her eyes.

"It's not your fault, Ello. I've never made it easy for you to be
honest with me. You mustn't cry; I'm not crying, am I? I did earlier,
but then it passed. I washed my face, I came out here. It's always nice
out here."

The lawn was green, the lake blue, the air sunny. Frau Quandt
tried to gain clarity from these indisputable facts, and discovered that
her mouth was open. She closed it. Magda was lighting a cigarette; her
slender, beautifully manicured fingers were steady, the flame was unwavering, serene. Her recently washed face was without lipstick, but
gave no impression of pallor; rather did it seem to possess a glow, as if
the blood beneath the skin had been stirred to new life. The eyelids
were reddened, but the eyes themselves were clear, and held a light of
some sort in their blue depths.

"I don't understand, Magda. What in the world are you saying?"

"He simply appeared with her, it was about noon. He said they
were in love. He wants her to live here in the house with us . . . we
would be some kind of happy trio, apparently. He was terribly happy,
and she too. He called her his second wife. And I am the old wife. You
are and will always be my good old wife, that was what he said. He
embraced and kissed me, and called me his dearest Magda, his calm,
understanding, reliable Magda . . . well, that was because I didn't say
anything. I was speechless. Stunned. I left the two of them holding
hands and beaming at each other, and went up to my room. And presently I heard them drive off."

"But he's become unhinged!" exclaimed Frau Quandt, shaking her
head with disbelief. Yet from the very beginning the affair had been
extreme. He had lost every vestige of discretion, flapping his blackened

marriage vows in the public's face as if he'd forgotten that he was minister of National Socialist morals, as if he didn't see that he was heading for a great fall. "I've thought so all along. He's taken complete leave of his senses."

"So it would seem," Magda replied, exhaling a slow stream of smoke. "It's clear that he's absolutely mad about her. And of course that's not hard to understand."

"What, Baarova? Why, she's not even pretty!" Frau Quandt responded in a burst of loyalty and indignation. "She has a flat face like a—like a plate with features drawn on it. Her face is too big for her body. She's very tiny, and she has this big head—"

"Dear Ello, you're trying to be kind," Magda said soothingly. "You needn't."

"But it's true! She's not at all attractive, and neither is that Czech drawl of hers. And what's more, she's a fifth-rate actress."

"She's one of the most popular young actresses in Germany. People flock to see her films. And she is very pretty."

"But how can you stand up for her! I couldn't be so noble!"

"I'm not being noble at all. I think she's tailor-made for him. So tiny, for one thing. That in itself must be a great relief for Josef. Think how few women Josef can talk to without getting a stiff neck."

"Ach, Magda," Frau Quandt murmured, somehow shocked.

"And then, she is quite young. Her mind, always supposing she has one, is unformed. Josef can shape it as he likes. That will appeal to him. And then, she's a Slav; the foot can be at peace. Nicht wahr? A clubfoot can't be shamed by a subhuman."

This time, Frau Quandt could not even come out with a murmur.

"Not that Josef believes in the racial garbage he spreads. Josef doesn't believe in anything. Except usefulness, perhaps. I don't mean to suggest for a moment that he consciously sees his treasure as a Slav cockroach—"

Frau Quandt lowered her eyes.

"—but only that he seems so, how shall I put it, so poignantly at home with this dark little creature. She's someone with whom he can take off his suspenders, if you see what I mean. Perhaps even his stocking . . . he makes love with it on, you know. But with her, I think he's stump-naked."

The voice fell mercifully silent. Then it resumed.

"Poor Ello, first you cry, then you close your eyes. I'm afraid this has been a great shock for you. But for me, it has been a very, very good thing. I feel free for the first time in years."

Frau Quandt, lifting her gaze, saw that Magda was pressing her cigarette out in the ashtray, sharply, purposefully. The light in her eyes was clear and steady.

"I mean to divorce him, Ello. I shall start proceedings at once. No doubt it will break his neck politically, which is all to the good."

A week or so later Frau Quandt attended a film premier at the Gloria Palast; and as she and her friends came out of the cinema afterward into the lights and late-evening crowds of the Kurfürstendamm, two men materialized on either side of her like bookends, requesting that she accompany them and swiftly conveying her into the backseat of a car that pulled out into the traffic. The suddenness was such that she felt she was still standing in the lights and crowds conversing with her friends, but she was not. Unbelievably, but undeniably, in her white satin cloak, her cinema program in her hand, she sat crushed between two mute Gestapo men in the backseat of a fast-traveling car.

Somewhere in the suburbs she was taken out, her legs so weakened by fear she felt she would stumble, and conducted into a relatively large brick house, where she was left alone in a room, an ordinary parlor, whose side door was opened by Goebbels.

"It's my sister's home," he explained cordially as he came in, gesturing for her to sit down. "I wanted to have a word in private with you, Ello."

She lowered herself into a chair, her heart racing with astonishment and outrage. She saw that abducting people off the streets was routine with him, that it was effective in opening up the mind for discussion, and she was determined to keep her mind cool, nimble. Smoothing her cinema program on her lap, she said crisply, "I'm sure I know what it's about."

Sitting down, he took a silver cigarette case from the pocket of his gray pinstripe suit. "To be frank," he said conversationally, "it stunned me."

"So I understand." Although "stunned" was not quite the word. When Magda had informed him that she was going to sue for divorce, his rage had shaken the pictures on the walls. Frau Quandt watched as he lit a cigarette, then turned his eyes on her with a mild look of incredulity.

"But when she said you were standing by her, Ello, that stunned me even more. Magda is hysterical, but you're not. Don't you realize you're encouraging her to take a step that will destroy her? Magda's life is that of a wife, a mother, the life spirit of a home. If she is deprived of that, what will she have left? Ask yourself that, Ello. What will be left for her?"

His quietly compassionate voice conjured up a picture of Magda in a cold, drab attic room, hunched gray-faced over a scrap of knitting. Frau Quandt allowed her eyebrow a slight humorous lift, which she saw register in his eyes. His voice became practical.

"In any case, she's going to have to obtain evidence of adultery, which will be impossible. She's going to damage her health irreparably by undertaking this lawsuit. Think, Ello, do you really want her to succumb to the strain of a case she can't possibly win?"

Frau Quandt gave an honest shake of her head, while telling him silently: But things aren't quite as you presume, Doctor. Your State Secretary is being most helpful. Yes, the shy Herr Hanke. Had you no idea he was in love with Magda? It's always been so apparent in those tender, hopeless eyes. We turned to him, we risked it, and we weren't disappointed. Herr Hanke glowed with gratitude. He clicked his heels. He kissed Magda's hand. He said: I am willing to testify against the Minister in court. I will bring you a list of women's names along with conclusive proof that the Minister has had relations with every one of them. I will also provide you with photocopies of his letters to Frau Baarova, since his correspondence with her passes exclusively through my hands. And if this would seem a gross betrayal of my chief, may I say, gnädige Frau, that it is only to avenge his gross betrayal of you. I act from a sense of honor and with a clear conscience. . . . Those were his words, Doctor, didn't you feel a shadow cross over your grave? Aloud, she said:

"But you really shouldn't worry yourself so much over Magda's health. Actually, she's looking better than ever."

"Nonsense, and she'll have a serious relapse if she pursues this stupid business." He spoke sharply, and she saw with surprise that his fingers holding the cigarette were trembling slightly. "Now I learn that she's scheduled an appointment with the Führer. To what purpose? Why drag the Führer in? What have I done to *deserve* this!" he suddenly cried, surging to his feet and pacing, his voice filled with the pain of a hounded creature. "I'm only doing what every other man does! Only I was honest—that was my mistake! I thought she would rejoice in our happiness—instead she does this!"

He *is* unhinged, thought Frau Quandt, staring at him as he paced with long plunging steps, grotesquely underlining his limp. Abruptly he drew himself up, his narrow pinstriped back stiffening with self-consciousness. Turning, he walked back and sat down, his hand, she saw as he put out his cigarette, still trembling slightly. When he spoke, it was in his earlier, mild tone.

"You should really try to persuade her to cancel this appointment with the Führer, Ello. You must do all you can to calm her. Don't you see, it's for her own sake."

And for twenty minutes, he quietly urged her to nurse Magda back from her hysterical and self-destructive idea of suing for divorce. It was past midnight when Frau Quandt was deposited by the Gestapo car before her building. With disgust and anger she watched it drive off. Yet she was gratified to know her abductor's state of mind. Already he was at his wits' end, and he was not even aware of the worst. This she was eager to tell Magda.

The next morning, in the bedroom of his newly built city palace, Goebbels awoke with a headache. His hand lay loosely curled on the pillow beside him, causing him to think how ironic it was that it had broken into unwanted trembling last night. He was unable to make his hands tremble when he wanted them to, before the microphone; his voice, his face, almost his every gesture could convey the utmost in spontaneous feeling, and so expertly that he easily kept track of the time by covert glances at his watch, but in spite of this high accomplishment he had never mastered the finishing touch of a trembling body. It was only a point of private artistic pride, since he considered his audiences too bovinely gullible to notice if he trembled or not; but still, it was ironic that last night when he had wanted to appear easeful and reasonable, he should have trembled, lost control of his words, burst into pacing. He never paced before others. He was coming apart. What could have possessed him to talk with Ello in the first place? How could he have thought to persuade her, who was Magda's closest friend? It was totally unrealistic, a fantasy of the same kind that had made him believe all along that Magda knew of the affair and with every smile was conferring her blessings. It had been a sinking into Schlaraffenland, the fool's paradise, a deep, sweet sinking . . . blown to pieces by her divorce confrontation. Yet even last night he had still held on to the shreds of illusion, imagining that a Gestapo ride combined with his golden gift of words would fix everything.

No illusions were left this morning. He saw before him his ruination. And had he not seen it all along? In some clear pocket of his fantasizing mind, in some rational corner, had he not expected from day to day that the sword would fall? What matter if Magda precipitated it? He himself had made it inevitable.

Getting out of bed, he bathed, shaved, took two aspirin for the throbbing of his head. The usual ministry duties awaited him, but of what importance to him was the Czech crisis? All summer he had conducted a newspaper campaign in keeping with the Führer's wishes, inventing or grossly exaggerating stories of atrocities committed against the Sudeten Germans, thus whipping higher and higher a war atmosphere; but it had not gripped him, not only because he privately disapproved of plunging into war but because his love affair reduced everything around it to insignificance.

Returning from the bathroom to the bedroom, where his valet had laid out his clothes before discreetly retiring, he began dressing. His life of the past few months seemed to him extraordinary and mad— how could he have thrust into jeopardy his career, his life's work? Again and again, to the pulsating pain of his head, he asked himself that as he got his clothes on. Dressed except for his shoes, he sat down and slipped on the left one, then with practiced deftness, eyes averted, he strapped on his leather-and-metal prosthesis and eased over it the thick-soled, ankle-high boot, heavy, in shape a kind of exaggerated hoof, and laced it up with small punitive jerks ending in a swiftly tied knot, after which he stood up and felt the merciful sliding down of his trouser cuffs. He went to the mirror. Black trousers, brown jacket with red Hakenkreuz armband, visored cap with gold braid. All that would go.

But even as he left the room, head aching, stomach in a knot, his overriding thought was that after a few inescapable hours at the ministry he would once again be with his Liduschka.

They took a drive into the country. They bumped along in her little ramshackle car. She was fond of it and would not give it up, though she could easily afford better. That always touched him, as did the way she drove, like an earnest child propped up on an encyclopedia. Now and then she peered, nearsightedly, at the passing scenery. Anything outside the city bored her, but her initial pout had soon dissolved into adoring compliance. This touched him most deeply of all, her eagerness to see with his eyes, feel with his feelings.

Usually they were talkative and lighthearted; but since Magda's bombshell, a quietness had fallen over them. The rattletrap bumped along with hardly a word between them. He had changed into a white linen suit, and now and then his hand on his knee would move its thumb back and forth across the civilian material. Forever, then? This always: warm afternoon, her profile sunlit. The dark ringlets sunlit, sunlit the so young cheek. Poetry. A formula song? Song of the middle years? A man grows tired, stale, he seeks resurrection. She says nothing. Her small hands on the wheel have a pathetic look; there is a nervousness about her, a timidity unlike her. She wonders where we're going. Where are we going? Trees, water, so much water around Berlin and in it. A poor man's Venice. I should like to see the real Venice. I have traveled nowhere. We could go there. We could travel around the world. The Orient. I've always wanted to visit the Orient. Forever, then, this? A private individual, stripped of all I worked for? Years, years . . .

"I want to stop."

"Stop? Stop what?" she asked in a fearful voice.

"I want to get out. My head's splitting."

She looked over at him. In her eyes was relief that it was only the car he meant, and concern for his splitting head, and hurt for the sharpness of his tone; her eyes were very large, very dark, utterly beautiful. He closed his own eyes until she had brought the rattletrap onto the side of the road.

They walked through the meadow grass toward a small green pond, its surface smooth as glass, and stood looking down at it. In the still green water was reflected the white limbs of birches; the air was warm, filled with the sweet smell of grass. He felt a calming sense of beauty; he felt his eyes grow moist. "'Er liegt so still im Morgenlicht, so friedlich, wie ein frommes Gewissen . . .'" he intoned softly. It lies so still in the light of dawn, as peaceful as a pious conscience . . .

"How pretty that is. Did you write it?"

"I?" He turned and looked at her. "Annette von Droste-Hülshoff." There was no flicker of recognition. Cultureless. *Canaille* . . .

"A woman?" she asked, with her little pout.

"A woman with whom I was very deeply in love," he found himself saying, pointedly, and watched the large dark eyes move away. Slowly, he drew his finger down her cheek. "She died a hundred years ago."

"Oh, that is good." Lida smiled.

"When I was a student, I made a pilgrimage to her grave," he said reminiscingly. "I brought flowers, and laid them over her heart."

"Was she beautiful?"

"Ugly," he snapped. "Ugly and sickly. Her life was unhappy, but from it she created some of the greatest lyric poems in the German language. If that's what you mean by beautiful."

Her eyes were again pained by the sharpness of his tone, hurt and puzzled, yet at the same time she was listening carefully, always his good little pupil, eager to absorb and parrot back his knowledge. Now she would kneel and pick the small white flowers that grew on the bank, because it made a pretty picture, because she had done it in one of her films. Hollow, marrowless . . . for this, to be stripped of everything? Years, years . . .

They walked on. She picked no flowers. She kept her eyes averted, she sulked.

To be stripped of everything, to be dismissed, replaced, forgotten . . . but what will I be stripped of, except a dead skin? Sick to death of it. A cog, I with my genius. He has forgotten my genius. What is the point in this kind of existence? A dead skin. I want it stricken off, I want to live as a free man. Isn't that what I want?

Suddenly she turned and looked at him. Tears stood in her eyes. She pushed him.

"You can stay here with your—your puddle and your poetess, I'm going home! If you don't want to talk to me, then talk to yourself!"

He grabbed her wrist as she flung away, and pulled her back.

"Is it over?" she demanded. "Tell me!" And her face was a radiance of spilling tears, of untrammeled hope and love, a radiance that swept out the last of his qualms, as the sun casts out shadows.

"It isn't over, it will never be over," he said in a voice that broke with emotion as he drew her to him. "My darling Liduschka, this is the beginning." The old withered skin shed, his whole being infused with her intoxicating freshness. How he loved her every word and gesture, her sparkle and gaiety, her dark beauty, with its faintly Slavic cast, the touch of the exotic mixed with an incredible familiarity, a closeness such as he had never known before, in her step no polite conformity with his, never, but an instinctive falling-in with the pace that was his, with all that was him, a oneness that he had never known with Magda or with any other woman. His Liduschka, who from the first had spoken to his depths, and he to hers. "Let my wife do as she will. Let the Führer do as he will. I'm finished with it all."

Chapter 49

THREE weeks later a family portrait of the Goebbelses appeared on the front page of all leading German newspapers. It had been taken on the sunny terrace of the Berghof, with Hitler standing just beyond the range of the camera. Surrounded by their offspring, the parents sat intimately close, both wearing smiles, which vanished as soon as Herr Hoffmann's shutter clicked. But marital solidity had been reestablished for all the world to see. The Baarova scandal was kaputt.

The Czech crisis had passed, and now this mess was settled; the Führer was in good humor even if the Doctor and Frau Magda were not. Getting to their feet among their little ones, they looked like little ones themselves, like two sullen, obedient schoolchildren forced to stand side by side.

Yet the sullenness was only for each other, not for the Führer. In spite of their wrenching disappointment at being relinked, both felt an inner sense of triumph. Of the two, Frau Goebbels would certainly have seemed to have the greater reason. When she had gone to the Führer, shown him the evidence against her husband, and asked for approval to proceed with a divorce, the Führer had expressed the deepest repugnance for what he had just read—especially the declarations of a dozen actresses who described the threats used by the Propaganda Minister in forcing them into his bedroom—and he had expressed his deepest sympathy for her. However, he could not sanction a divorce for reasons of state, and asked that in the interests of Germany and the Party she drop the idea for the moment; but if in a year's time she still wanted a divorce, he would not stand in her way. Meanwhile she could make any conditions she wished. That was supremely appealing.

As for Goebbels, when he was called before the Führer he stated his case even before the Führer could speak. "I will not contest a divorce. My wife wants it and I want it too. I want to be free to marry Frau Baarova. I am willing to give up my home, my children, even my career in order to live with her legally. I will resign from the government, mein Führer, and I am not only willing—it is the only thing in life I want."

The Führer's reply was sharp: "I have already told your wife that I will not permit a divorce. As for your resigning, that is out of the question."

The Doctor argued and pleaded, but the Führer would not be moved. "Then at least give me a post somewhere else, let me live with Frau Baarova abroad. Appoint me Ambassador to Tokyo—"

The Führer refused. His eyes were hard, unyielding. When Goebbels finally took his leave he felt torn to pieces, yet in this terrible pain was a strange quality of bearability, even of welcome and exultation.

The following night Frau Baarova, who had not heard from her lover for two days, hurried in her filmy, salmon-colored peignoir to the door at the sound of the bell. But instead of the Doctor, it was Hitler's personal adjutant. He asked if he could come in, then informed her that by order of the Führer she must get out of Germany in twenty-four hours. Frau Baarova became hysterical, she screamed, wept, beat her small fists upon the adjutant's chest and finally fainted, and he, rushing into her bathroom for eau de cologne, grabbed up by mistake a bottle of hair oil, which, in his haste to aid her, he poured too freely—greasy liquid ran down her face into her eyes, into her ears, made dark blotches on her filmy robe; she regained consciousness sticky, dripping, half blind, and grew even more hysterical, so that the adjutant had to telephone for a doctor. Then at last, a mess of hair oil and tears, she was injected with a sedative and went out like a light.

All the next day Frau Baarova spent desperately trying to get hold of her lover, first by phone, then in person. She drove to the Propaganda Ministry, and to the Minister's palace, only to be told that the Minister was out of town on business. But then as she was driving along the Kurfürstendamm, weeping over the steering wheel, she saw with a shock of joy that the car alongside her was Josef's black Mercedes.

In the backseat of the Mercedes, Goebbels glanced to his left at a sound of honking and felt a jolt through his whole being: Liduschka's ramshackle car was driving alongside. He saw her at the wheel straining both to steer and to signal to him, one familiar small hand waving frantically. For a few seconds the two cars kept apace, then, abruptly sitting back from the window, he ordered his chauffeur to turn at the next corner. The Mercedes turned, the little rattletrap was carried on in the flow of traffic.

That night, accompanied by the Führer's adjutant, with two suit-cases hastily packed and the rest of her belongings to follow, Frau Baarova boarded the train for Prague. In one arm she held a bouquet of red roses, presented to her by the adjutant; for he was not an un-feeling man, and he regretted both the squalid episode of the hair oil and the tragic briefness of her film career. She seemed to take some comfort from the flowers, as a despairing child might clutch a stuffed bear or a doll. Perhaps, he thought afterward, she believed that he had been instructed by Goebbels to give them to her. Very wisely, she had not asked.

Frau Baarova's immediate expulsion from Germany and the recall and banning of all her films were among the conditions Frau Goebbels had made. The other conditions were that she and her husband live separately, he in Berlin, she at Schwanenwerder. If he wished to visit his children, he must first secure her permission. Meanwhile, she would appear with him at all important functions. If at the end of a year she still wanted a divorce, she could proceed with it. If, however, she decided against a divorce but her husband still wanted one, there would be no divorce. Frau Goebbels had lost weight during her illness and looked svelte in her new fall wardrobe. She had her hair restyled. She began entertaining again. She took up horseback riding. She saw a great deal of State Secretary Hanke.

Goebbels had not lifted a finger against Hanke when he discovered the man's treachery, for he was in no position to lift a finger against anyone. He dared not make the smallest wave. He was very weak. He attended to his duties, he mourned his Liduschka. He had no other women. "It would behoove you to live as a monk from now on," the Führer had warned him, and so he did. His life was quiet. He was not invited to the Führer's evening parties and found himself unwelcome at the Führer's luncheons at the Chancellery. He had been expelled from the Führer's circle. At official social gatherings the Führer did not speak to him. The gray-blue eyes were hard and punishing. The Doc-tor was very weak, he had never been weaker, yet in a strange way he felt strong, vital, purposeful, as he had not felt for years. To be pun-ished was a thousand times more bearable than to be ignored. To see coldness and hardness in those eyes was a thousand times more inspir-ing than to see indifference in them. To be told *I will not let you go*— how infinitely relieving it was to know that. His passion for Liduschka had forced the issue. Perhaps he had sensed all along that this would happen; he was shattered by her loss, but in some greater way he felt whole again. The Führer would not let him go. The Führer's coldness was the coldness of caring, his punishment the severity of testing. The Doctor felt himself pincered between his vengeful wife and his harsh Führer, but he also felt himself cleansed, clear-minded, regenerated.

Frau Quandt never saw Goebbels at Schwanenwerder. If he happened to be there visiting the children—which was seldom, for Magda was not lavish with her permission—he was not invited to socialize afterward; he was like a reprobate in his own house. But she did see him occasionally at social functions with Magda, and she was always struck by the excellent front they showed the world. There was a kind of light and vitality in them, a quality of rebirth, so that if one did not know them, if one did not know that the reconciliation was all on the surface and that they were bitterly hateful of each other, one might think they were on a second honeymoon. In fact, they were; undeniably, they were. Only it was not with each other. It was for the Führer their eyes shone, of that Frau Quandt was certain; and she felt that both of them, in their own separate ways, were lodged deeper than ever in the core of the mythos.

Chapter 50

Young Walther, Rose's current and perplexing lover, the most boring man she had ever known if also the most physically enthralling, lay at her side, talking, as usual. Always after lovemaking, they would lie entwined in spent, dazed silence, and in those moments she felt she loved him very much; then invariably his voice would pick up where it had left off . . . it was like a sickness. Fortunately, good sex always had a soporific effect on her; in five minutes she would be fast asleep whether he was talking or not.

"Gute Nacht, Herr Kopf," she interrupted his flow of words, turning on her side.

"Herr Kopf, is it? I could take that as a verbal caress, you know, since you make no distinction as to which Kopf you refer to. A man has both an upper and a nether, and though you deplore my cerebrum, the same can't be said for my *corona glandis*. Therefore, I'll take it as the latter, a compliment. Probably the highest you're capable of. But dispensing with wordplay, I realize you're attacking me as usual as a thinker. I have no comeback. If you look at the triptych of quintessential Jews so vividly painted by the regime, you'll find me splat in the center. On one side we see the louse-infested rag-and-bone dealer slitting the throat of an Aryan infant on the altar of Jehovah. On the other side we see the merchant, the ultimate materialist, a bloated specimen of greed, rubbing together, with ravenous obsequiousness, his expensively manicured if not quite clean hands. But it's there in the center that we see Walther—Walther with his big poisonous brain: the bloodless, life-killing intellectual, the cosmopolite and internationalist who putrefies with rationality all that's pure, joyous, unified—all that's völkisch, in a word. Ja, there is Walther with his virulent, overgrown brain—except he'd never really do as a model; don't you think it amusing that I could pose for an SS recruiting poster? I think it very amusing, and I stress this because you don't credit me with a sense of humor. You consider me a pedant through and through, dry as dust. But I have feelings, which fact is borne out by my infatuation with you. It may even be more than infatuation, since infatuation implies blindness, whereas I see your drawbacks clearly. Incidentally, I don't see your advanced age as a drawback, since it's nowhere in evidence either physically or mentally. What's more, you must be classified as beautiful, although appearances are of no importance to me. Whereas in your case, you're entirely attracted to my appearance. That's a tremendous shortcoming in you, Rose. I'm not sure if you're a case of arrested development—an eternal juvenile whose idea of love has never gone beyond kissing, coupling, whispering romantic poetry—or if you have the mentality of an old roué slobbering for young flesh and the immortality it represents. One thing's certain, you lack integration, maturity. But oddly enough, that's what appeals to me. Don't misunderstand: I lament your refusal to look inside yourself or around you, I lament your need to exist on an unconscious level, which may in part be caused by living in the dreamworld of the theater—actually, you'd make a good National Socialist—but the other side of this lamentable coin of your character is a child's ecstasy in life."

He drew the eiderdown around his shoulders, listening to Rose's smooth, deep breathing. She had moved from her rooming house a few months before, a step she had long meant to take, but like all her plans, it had been postponed in the disorderliness of her daily round of life. The apartment was small and messy. Walther was forever straightening things when he came, which was three or four times a week. His height was such that he didn't fit very well into the bed. His feet always stuck out from under the quilt. Tonight he drowsily drew them in. It was early November, damp and chilly.

Rose was awakened by a sound of crackling. The room danced with reflections of orange. Tearing out of bed, she ran over to Walther, who was throwing open the window. She saw that a house across from them was burning, and simultaneously heard from farther down the street a sound of shattering, as of plate glass. People were running below, some carrying clubs.

Shouts of *Jude!* came through the thud of running feet and the shattering of more glass. He began hurriedly getting into his clothes.

"I've got to get down to the store. You stay, Rose, don't go out. I'll be back as soon as I can."

He ran the four or five blocks to his father's import firm, where, in the display windows, of which only a few pieces of glass remained around the edges, people were busy heaving things out onto the pavement. He watched as the marble statue of a fawn flew through the air and broke in pieces on the concrete. It lay among splintered porcelain, broken antique furniture, Persian carpets. People crunched around on the shattered glass grabbing up what was salvageable, the priceless carpets were fast being dragged off; other people were coming out from the door, staggering under their loot; while those in the display windows kept grunting, lifting, heaving, as with superhuman vigor, as if irradiated by an ecstasy of destruction. They were all civilians, not one SA or SS uniform among them: a spontaneous uprising—the ordinary, law-abiding Weimar citizens he passed every day on the streets. This more than anything frightened him. He swung around as a club-swinging, *Jude!*-chanting mob of people came along the street in rapid approach; but they took no notice of him, gave him not a second glance as they swarmed by. It was his looks. His looks were his protection. Suddenly he began running again, in the direction of his house, certain that it had been set fire to like the house across from Rose, like the house he passed now, which was surrounded by a mob, some of whom were dragging off the bathrobed occupants while others flung gasoline on the flames. When he arrived at his own street, dead for breath, he saw that there was a mob here too, but that his house was not on fire. Instead, it seemed that every light was on inside, as if a party were being given. Hurrying up the stairs, he felt a jolt as he saw that the door stood battered and half open. Another jolt went through him as he stepped inside to be confronted by two SS men with revolvers.

"Out! No one may enter."

"But I live here," he said slowly, feeling very frightened, for the house held an abnormal silence.

"Papers," said one, and when he was satisfied, he gestured with his revolver. "You'll find your father in the study."

Walther walked through the silent, brightly lit rooms. Chairs and tables were overturned. Potted plants lay on the floors, their black dirt spilled out across the rugs, along with toppled lamps and vases. The grand piano seemed to have been mutilated with an ax. From the drawing room, blood in large splattered dots led down the hall to the study. At the study door, he stood for a moment with his eyes closed before turning the handle.

"Ah, the young gentleman of the house. Come in, bitte."

He was being addressed by a man of about thirty-five, in a gray topcoat and white silk scarf, whom he recognized as a National Socialist lawyer who on three occasions had been to the house. He wanted to buy it. Standing by the lawyer were two SS men, who politely stepped apart, revealing to Walther his father seated in his leather armchair, in his pajamas and robe, his face and head literally blazing with blood.

"Papa! What have they done to you?" he cried, barging over and crouching before him.

"What have we done?" asked the lawyer. "We have saved your papa's life. We have liberated your papa from the mob."

Walther's father, as if very tiredly, nodded his bloody head at his son.

"They smashed open the door and stampeded through the place ransacking and looting," the lawyer went on. "Just like the French Revolution, nicht wahr? Locked up the servants in one room, your mother and sisters in another, and dragged your poor papa downstairs, where they proceeded to beat him up. Fortunately, we arrived just then. We drove them out."

Walther was dragging a handkerchief from his pocket with shaking fingers. He began blotting the red with it. "My father is badly hurt."

"On the contrary. Superficial wounds bleed profusely, deep ones hardly at all. You might say the more blood the better. No, your papa is not badly hurt, just rattled. We're waiting for him to become unrattled. But time is short."

"How do you mean?" asked Walther, looking up.

"I mean I would like your papa to sign this before it's too late." The lawyer gestured at a table on which lay a sheet of paper with a fountain pen beside it. Getting up, Walther went over and looked at it. It was a bill of sale.

"Three times you've asked my father to sell. Three times he's told you he doesn't want to sell. His answer is still the same."

"My offer, however, is not the same," said the lawyer. "As I have informed your papa, whereas I originally offered one half the value of the house, I am now offering one fiftieth."

"One fiftieth?" Not only Walther's hands, but his whole body began to shake. "Are you insane? This home is *ours*, we eat here and sleep here, my father was *born* here. Don't you understand that it belongs to *us*, just as our—our ears and toes?"

"Walther, please stop talking," his father said wearily.

"Your papa should sign this now," the lawyer went on. "Your womenfolk are safe for the present. Locked up, as I have told you. But when the mob comes back, and they will, I can't guarantee their safety. I've already heard reports of some very brutal rapes. Some deaths as well. I fear that if they return, they'll finish off your papa."

"I understand," Walther muttered.

"You see, to repulse a mob once—well, that's one thing. But to repulse it twice—for that one requires a special incentive."

"I told you I understand!"

He took the paper and pen over to his father, who with effort, having wiped his smeared hands on the lap of his robe, slowly wrote out his signature. He leaned back and looked at his son.

"I am not rattled, Walther. Tell this gentleman I am not rattled. And tell him not to refer to me as Papa. And tell him I hope my house falls down on him and buries him alive."

The transaction completed, an arrest was made. The two SS men at the door remaining to guard the residence, the other two took father and son to the Weimar jailhouse, where they were shoved into different cells, both packed. The next day the inmates were transferred to Sachsenhausen concentration camp—Buchenwald was nearer, but overcrowded with Austrian political prisoners—where young Walther received a swift and seemingly gratuitous rifle butt jab to the belly, a jab in passing as it were, perhaps provoked by the insolent illogicality of his Viking looks. The jab, with a certain illogicality of its own, landed him in the caring hands of the infirmary doctors when he complained of pains; despite their efforts, however, he succumbed to a ruptured spleen.

In Paris, a seventeen-year-old Polish Jew from Germany, trying to find work in the French capital and half demented by news from his parents that they were to be expelled from the Reich though they had lived in Hamburg for thirty years—that all Polish Jews were being sent back to Poland, that Poland would not have them, that they were being dumped in a no-man's-land between the two borders without food or shelter—had stuck a revolver in the coat of his shabby raincoat and gone to the German embassy in the Rue de Lille, shooting the first official he came upon: a third secretary, who, ironically enough, was being investigated by the Gestapo for sentiments antipathetic to National Socialist policy.

The wounded man had died two days later, the news reaching Hitler in Munich's Bürgerbräukeller, where the annual celebration of the 1923 Putsch was in full swing: songs, frothing beer steins, a mass of *Alte Kämpfer*, Old Fighters, in the midst of whom the Führer was handed a slip of paper. He exclaimed something, rose and looked around him, and gestured to Goebbels, who hurried after him into a side room.

The seeking eyes, the gesturing hand—resurrection had shot through the Doctor, who shortly returned to the din and cried out for attention.

"Members of the old guard! Third Secretary vom Rath has died of his wounds! This good German, this staunch and loyal servant of the Reich, lies dead tonight, cut down by a creeping, cunning, unscrupulous Jew. Who gave this Jew orders? Who paid him? We know, do we not? We cannot allow this attack by international Jewry to go unchallenged. It must be repudiated! Our people must be told, and their answer must be forthright, ruthless, salutary! You must listen to me, and together we must plan what is to be our answer to Jewish murder and the threat of international Jewry to our great and glorious Reich!"

Göring, who had found himself out of favor with the Führer since his antiwar intercession in the winter garden, had felt it circumspect to attend the beer-sloshing event, though in the past he had usually sent cavalier regrets on the grounds of sudden ill health. This time he dared not. But having put in an appearance, with much ostentatious backslapping for the edification of the Führer, he departed early, boarding his private train with General Bodenschatz and settling down for a late supper in the quiet of the dining car, with its beautifully carved cherrywood walls, its fresh flowers, mellow lamplight, and scrupulously polished windows, outside which the dark landscape and misted stars went by.

Much later he and the general were puzzled to see distant conflagrations, like passing red-gold roses in the night. Only when they reached Berlin did they learn that the Paris embassy official had died, unleashing fires among much else.

Throughout the day Goebbels broadcast violently anti-Semitic speeches, and it was with little surprise that Göring read in a report from his private intelligence agency, the Forschungsamt, that the Doctor had returned from Munich posthaste by air to Berlin, where, with Heydrich, he had instigated the uprising. Himmler, the soul of orderliness, had not been in favor of it. Orders had been sent out to the SS, SA and Hitler Youth to dress in civilian clothing and act as mobs, inciting riots and destruction. The result in rough figures: forty murdered Jews, twenty thousand in jails and concentration camps, seven thousand Jewish shops destroyed, two hundred synagogues and two hundred homes gutted by fire.

He flung down the report. As soon as the Führer had returned from Munich, the Feldmarschall took himself to the Chancellery.

"Here I've been working my guts out trying to reach a peak of effort for the Four-Year Plan, asking people to save every old toothpaste tube for me, every rusty nail, every bit of scrap metal, so that it can be collected and used—and in one night Goebbels destroys property worth millions of marks! Not only that, with one stroke he has set half the world against us. Even some of our closest sympathizers abroad have been antagonized. Some countries are even talking of boycotting German goods! That's all that has been achieved by this repulsive violence—untold destruction of valuable goods and an avalanche of criticism from abroad!"

He was relieved to see the Führer nod his head in agreement.

"It's a bad business. A shocking business. Still, you mustn't be too hard on Goebbels. He can't keep calm when these Jews emerge from their hiding places and attack us."

"But for one Jew in Paris, to mobilize a whole nation?"

"Mobilize?" asked the Führer. "What do you mean by that? Goebbels made a strong speech at the Bürgerbräukeller, and he has carried on the same way in his broadcasts, but he is only reflecting the feelings of the German people. This has been a spontaneous uprising."

Göring was silent; he did not contradict his Führer. He realized that he should have foreseen, considering the indefensible savagery of the night, that the Führer would wish to appear uninvolved.

"Well, in any case, mein Führer, we agree that it has been a bad business. I hope by now it has been brought to a halt."

"You know what popular uprisings are like. They burn high and hot, but not for long. I believe it is essentially over. In fact, the Jews are probably already lining up before your wife's door. She will be keeping you busy."

No smile accompanied the remark, no sense of indulgent exasperation, as in the past.

"You should be more careful, Göring. Too many people know of your pro-Jewish attitude."

As Göring tried to interrupt, the Führer gave an impatient shake of his head.

"Pressing matters must be dealt with as soon as possible. A conference must be held to determine the property damage incurred last night, and to decide what steps must be taken. Dr. Goebbels has already made a suggestion that sounds reasonable to me: for having provoked the German people to demonstrate against them, the Jews should be fined to the hilt. This and all other aspects of last night's events must be dealt with. The Jewish economic position—the Jewish problem altogether—must be clarified once and for all."

Göring gave a nod of his head. "Then may I suggest that as chief coordinator of the economy, I call a meeting of the department heads with jurisdiction over such matters as Jews, property, citizens' rights, and so forth."

"Good. Excellent. And let me add that I specifically want Goebbels to be there."

Göring was not the only one dismayed by the Propaganda Chief's rebound. Everyone thought the Baarova scandal had finished him off. True, the Führer had not dismissed him, but he had turned him into a pariah, refusing even to speak with him at official functions. It was known that the Führer truly despised him, that he had been shocked to his depths by the written testimony of actresses whom Goebbels had bullied into his bed. This the Führer could not get over. When someone mentioned to him that Goebbels cherished the hope of writing the Führer's biography, he had responded with outrage: "Is he crazy? I would never allow a man of such low character to write about me." Yet now, overnight, Goebbels had regained in one swoop all the ground he had ever lost.

The Führer's watchdog, Göring thought acidly as the small figure, intense and keen-eyed, with a kind of monolithic assuredness, took his place at the conference table to discuss Kristallnacht.

The poetic term had been coined by Dr. Walther Funk, Schacht's replacement as Minister of Economics, a paunchy, bleary-eyed closet homosexual whose flaw was tolerantly ignored by the Party, along with his wit, culture and giftedness as a classical pianist. "See how it sparkles, like crystal," Funk had said of the broken glass that littered the streets, and the image had caught on. It was to discuss the broken glass, among other things, that Minister Funk and twenty other government representatives had gathered in the great conference room of the Air Ministry, where Chairman Minister President General Feldmarschall Göring now banged his gavel on the long table.

"Gentlemen. Today's meeting is one of a decisive nature. Since the problem is mainly an economic one, it is from an economic point of view that it will have to be tackled."

He went on to complain angrily that the destruction of Jewish goods had hurt him more than it had hurt the Jews.

"Whole bales of clothing in warehouses have been burned, and the nation is very short on clothing. I might just as well burn everything even before it reaches me! What's more, who is going to pay for all this destruction? Our insurance companies. It's not the Jews but the German insurance companies that must carry the loss! It has been suggested that the Jewish community be forced to pay a fine of a billion marks—"

At this, exclamations of surprise, some of them greatly gratified, even to the point of laughter, went up around the table.

"—but this still does not solve the problem of the insurance companies."

The problem did not much interest Goebbels, who contributed little to the discussion during the following two hours. At one point he suggested that the insurance companies simply be exempted from paying, but was told by the National Insurance Commissioner that this would ruin the integrity of the German insurance industry, and he lapsed back into patient, observant silence.

At another point, the high-pitched, thin voice of SS representative Heydrich broke in. "What about this? The insurance will be paid to the Jews, but as soon as it's paid, it will be taken back. That way, the insurance industry will save face."

"I am inclined to agree with what General Heydrich has suggested," said the Insurance Commissioner.

"No doubt," said Göring. "But if the money is confiscated, it will be confiscated for the Finance Ministry. The money belongs to the state. However, you won't have to pay for all damages, since I am informed that foreign insurance companies are also involved. I congratulate you on making a profit."

"How is that?" asked the commissioner. "The fact that we won't have to pay for all the damages is called a profit?"

"If you believe you are under obligation to pay five million, and all of a sudden there appears an angel in my somewhat corpulent form and tells you that you can keep a million—is that not making a profit? I can see it looking at you, your whole body is grinning! You made a big profit!"

But the chairman's jokes dissolved immediately afterward, when the subject arose of replacing the broken glass of the seven thousand shops.

"Nearly all Germany's glass is imported from Holland and Belgium," the Insurance Commissioner told him, "which means that the windows will naturally have to be replaced from there."

"With our foreign currency reserves!" Göring struck the table with his fist, turning furiously to Heydrich. "I wish you'd killed two hundred Jews instead of breaking so much glass!" Turning back, he got his temper under control and heaved an exasperated sigh. "The entire thing is a mess. The Jewish position in the economy has been nothing but a fluctuating confusion. The Führer wants it settled once and for all. Total Aryanization must take place."

He was in inner agreement with what he stated. The Jewish problem was the problem of wealth concentrated in too few hands: the rich Jews must be struck through their pocketbooks. They would, of course, be compensated by the state for their establishments, for those palatial department stores, those important industries. But ordinary small shops and businesses would also have to be sold, for once you began trying to set boundaries, to make exceptions, you would have the same complications and confusion as before. Total Aryanization of Jewish enterprises was the only answer. The answer to plenty of private prayers, for that matter: very many people had profited through the Aryanization of Austrian businesses and factories; he himself was one, and he was not averse to making similar gains here in Germany. It would be a great absurdity if he alone did not put to advantage an unavoidable situation. But the rules must be kept to.

"The Jews," he went on, "will receive compensation for their establishments in the form of a set percentage of the establishment's value. The value will be determined by agents of the state, and will be determined accurately. They must report the true value. They will then turn the establishment over to the Aryan proprietor. Here the difficulty begins, because there will be cases where the value will be misrepresented as infinitely lower than it actually is, for the benefit of Party comrade buyers. I've seen little chauffeurs of Gauleiters who have profited so much by these transactions that they're now worth half a million. If such tricks are played again, I will not hesitate to act ruthlessly. If the individual is prominent, I shall report him to the Führer."

There were some exchanged glances and badly suppressed smiles at this righteous threat: would Göring report himself to the Führer? But Minister Funk, smoking a bent cigarette, knew that the Feldmarschall kept within the rules, such as they were. The two of them were on fairly close terms; if Göring made a lot of noise about legality, it pleased him to abide by the rules. It was necessary for him. It was a point of honor. He was much concerned with his honor, and his word of honor. One evening, after the troops had entered the Sudetenland, he had gone on and on about his word of honor given to Czech Minister Mastny during the Anschluss that Germany had no intention of also crossing the Czech frontier. "I didn't promise him that we'd *never* cross it. How could anyone say what would happen in a year, or twenty years, or a hundred years? I was speaking only for that particular moment during the Anschluss. And that was clear as day. To put any other construction on it would have been completely unrealistic." Minister Funk scraped his chair back as the gavel came down on the table. The committee was being adjourned for lunch.

Passing along the corridor, General Udet saw emerging from the conference room a host of civilians sprinkled with SS; he frowned with annoyance. Hermann had his fingers in so many pies that he was always involved with these types. But why bring them into the Air Ministry? Maybe because the conference room here was bigger, more impressive than those in his other offices. Maybe there was some special need today to impress. It would be better, he thought, going on down the corridor, if Hermann limited himself to impressing the Air Ministry with his daily presence.

When the committee reconvened, Dr. Goebbels took the lead. He had scarcely participated during the discussion of economics, but now, as the general position of the Jews was to be considered, he sat forward, a very small figure at the massive table in the huge, imposing room.

"The Jews at present are enjoying an intolerable degree of freedom. For instance, there is no ban on their frequenting forests and parks. I propose a law be passed forbidding them access to all German woodlands. Why, whole herds of Jews are running around the Grunewald! This is extremely provocative! This must—"

"All right, then," Göring interrupted him, "we'll set aside a special part of the forest for these great herds, and we'll see that the various

beasts that looked damned like them—the elk has the same nose—get
there too and settle down with them."

"This is no joking matter, Herr Göring! A law must be passed to
keep them out. The social freedom of Jews in Germany must end.
Consider railway travel. Do you realize it's still possible today for a Jew
to share a compartment in a sleeping car with a German? This is intolerable! A law must be issued allotting Jews a special compartment for
themselves, and stating that if the compartment becomes full, the extra
Jews cannot go into a German compartment but must stand in the
corridor."

"Wouldn't it be more sensible to give them enough compartments
so that this wouldn't happen?" Göring asked.

"But suppose there were only very few Jews aboard, and suppose
there was an overcrowdedness of Germans?"

"So?"

"Why, then we have the intolerable situation where a few Jews are
enjoying a whole set of Jewish compartments while Germans have to
stand."

"Then put those few Jews in one compartment, and let the Germans use the others."

"Nein—Germans should sit in Jewish compartments? There is
only one way around the problem: the law must give the Jews only one
compartment."

"All right, give them one!" Göring said impatiently. "And if it's
overcrowded, I don't need to issue any damn law—they'll be kicked
into the corridor, or they can sit on the toilet the whole way."

"I don't agree! I don't believe in this. There must be a law. I also
deem it necessary that a law be issued forbidding Jews to enter German
theaters, cinema houses and concert halls. Their presence in these
places is a moral and physical offense. I also see great danger in Jews
sitting about on public benches with Germans, where it's very easy for
them to complain and pick things apart. We must have benches
marked 'For Jews Only.' In addition, there must be total expulsion of
Jewish students from schools and universities. I also believe that we
now have the opportunity to dissolve all the synagogues in Germany.
More than a hundred have already been destroyed by fire; those remaining should now be razed. By the Jews themselves. We will make
them tear down their own synagogues. We must make the Jews suffer!"

"A billion-mark fine should make them suffer enough," Göring
said.

"None of this gets to the core of the problem," Heydrich complained. "The problem is to get them *out*."

"Natürlich, but it cannot be done overnight," returned Goebbels.
"Only eight or nine thousand a year can emigrate, as long as foreign
countries refuse to increase their quota for Jews. The Führer has told

me he is going to approach the countries most agitated by the Jewish question, the United States, for instance. He is going to say, 'Why are you still chattering on about the Jews? Take them! They're yours!' But of course they don't want them. No one wants them. The point is this: until full emigration can be achieved, we must see to it that the Jews cannot enter into the normal German routine of life."

Heydrich nodded. "They must be entirely isolated, then. There must be total segregation."

"But my dear Heydrich," said Göring, "you won't be able to avoid the creation of ghettos on a very large scale, in all the cities."

"That could be done. They would be self-sufficient communities. Jews could conduct business among themselves, but not with Germans."

"But that's unfeasible. For one thing, they'll have no shops of their own if all their shops have been Aryanized. And they must have their own shops or they'll have to buy from Germans."

"No German will be allowed to serve a Jew."

"You cannot let them starve."

Goebbels sat listening, rubbing his forehead. "It's true. Ghettos would be stinking sores in our midst. The only answer is to isolate Jews as individuals, to restrict and punish them as severely as possible. I have already cited steps which I believe should be taken."

At the end of the conference, late in the afternoon, Göring once again banged his gavel on the table.

"So we are agreed, gentlemen. I shall close the meeting with these words: as punishment for their abominable crimes, et cetera, et cetera, German Jewry shall make a contribution of one billion marks. That should work—the swine won't commit another murder! From now on, I wouldn't like to be a Jew in Germany!"

Chapter 51

9 December, 1938
Vienna

Dear Paula,

This is just a brief note to let you know I am back in Vienna after a month's stay in Berlin, where I arrived on the very eve of the terrible events now called Kristallnacht. Throughout my stay I was besieged on all sides by petitions to influence our brother. Emmy too was besieged, in most part by relatives of Jews in need of help. Emmy conducted herself splendidly the whole time, and did much good. Hermann told us this was the last filthy business to which he would lend his name, and he condemned the pogrom most sharply and openly before a great meeting before all ministers and Gauleiters. Hermann's Prussian Minister of Finance tendered his resignation to him in protest of the pogrom. This is what they should all do, Hermann too—resign. But what is simple in theory is perhaps not simple in practice. I don't know, I only know I am left in despair over these terrible happenings. I will write again after I have settled in.

Your affectionate sister,
Olga

9 December, 1938
Munich

Herr Minister President General Feldmarschall Göring, Your Excellency:

We heartfully thank you for the visit of your representative, General Bodenschatz, to this house where you were brought wounded fifteen years ago.

We are grateful for your wish to help us in these difficult times which have recently arisen. Herr Bodenschatz informs us that in the event that my late husband's furniture business has been Aryanized, which it has, you yourself will recompense us with its full value; that further, you will personally oversee our emigration to Argentina if we so desire, and that you will arrange that we may take that payment and all other assets with us out of Germany.

I have already expressed my thanks to Herr Bodenschatz, but shall ask him to bear this letter to you so that I may express the surprise and gratitude that have filled these rooms since yesterday. I only wish that others might be as fortunate as we. I wish, even more deeply, that there were no need for any of us to have to be fortunate.

My sister and daughter join me in thanking you for returning a kindness done many years ago.

Yours sincerely,
Frau Ilse Ballin

9 December, 1938
Weimar

Dearest Emmy,

The names I sent you through my cousin Max—they're almost all out now, thanks to you. But the one you couldn't find out about, Walther Schneider—3 days ago his remains were returned in a small cardboard box. These are the details: the box was originally sent to his home but it isn't occupied—the new owner, no need to elaborate, hadn't moved in yet, so there the box sat for maybe two weeks before being forwarded & the family frantic not knowing anything. The box contained ashes, also a statement that he had been unsuccessfully treated at Sachsenhausen for an injury sustained here in Weimar, which isn't so because his father says he was all right that night, though it can make no difference now. His father as you gather is out, again thanks to you. They didn't take kindly to me because he was so much younger, but they were grateful for my help and had me to the service this morning. When I saw him last he was running down the stairs. He forgot his watch, I didn't return it to them. I mean to come to Berlin soon & we can visit somewhere, maybe at some friend's house, I don't want to make things harder for you. It would be after Iphigenie, we're doing that now. Your suggestion, brought to me through Max, that I emigrate and you and H would see to it—thank you but I said I never would and I never will. I could also go with my cousin Otto, he's got holdings in America so no problem getting in, he's leaving as soon as possible. Cousin Otto was right, and Cousin Max and I were wrong, but we'll stay. With Max it's his shrapnel, I think it's like a kind of anchor he can't pull up. With me it's—I don't know what it is, I don't know anything. This note is making little sense, a box of gray ashes is all I see. I've been crying for 3 days, I cannot stop.

Rose

9 December, 1938
Berlin

Esteemed Parents,

I am taking a moment from my work to write a long-overdue greeting. Since I expect to be promoted to the position of Chief of the General Staff in the near future, I'll doubtlessly be kept busier than even before.

I'll tell you something amusing. I am referred to as "the Youngster," since a potential Chief of Staff not yet out of his thirties is unusual. But that is the spirit of our Luftwaffe. Its accent is on youth. Strong, vigorous, soaring youth.

I need not tell you that my habits will remain unaltered by my new status. Since my habits have not changed since my cadet days, they are scarcely likely to do so now. My breakfast still consists of cereal, coffee, Army bread and issue jam. My relaxation is still that of taking long silent marches through the woods. That has always restored me. My health is excellent, my work demanding and challenging, and will become more so.

Dear parents, I thank you sincerely for your last letter. I was gratified to know that you are in good health and that God looks after you well. Your pride in my achievements touches me deeply. I shall always try to live up to it, and to strive to fulfill my new duties in a manner to bring the utmost credit to the Luftwaffe and to Germany.

Your respectful son,
Colonel Hans Jeschonnek

Chapter 52

Iɴ March of the new year of 1939, snow was falling heavily. Driven by
a fierce wind, the white flakes obscured everything outside the windows
of General Udet's office; a new office, for he had been promoted to
Chief of Supply and Procurement. He was awaiting Milch, who was off
on his winter holiday—his one and only annual break from work—in
the Austrian Alps. He was due back today at the behest of a courier-
sent message: *The Czechoslovakian state is breaking up. It may become necessary for the Wehrmacht to intervene within the next days. The Führer requests
your immediate return to Berlin.*

Göring was also away—had in fact been away for six weeks, recovering from various ailments in the salubrious sun of the Italian
Riviera. He too would be arriving back today or tonight. Meanwhile,
Udet had been working with Luftflotten commanders Kesselring and
Stumpff, and with Chief of Staff Jeschonnek, to mobilize hurriedly in
case attack became necessary. He got along well with General Kesselring, whose face when he laughed disclosed seemingly numberless
big teeth, and with General Stumpff as well, a less toothy and more
retiring type. Both were former Chiefs of Staff, both had requested
reassignment because of bitter resentment toward Milch. Now here was
the latest Chief of Staff. "The Youngster" also resented Milch's interference, but Udet had a feeling Jeschonnek would stick, because
Jeschonnek possessed Milch's own coldness and remoteness; he would

not be driven to pull out his hair in despairing clumps. Udet did not get along well with him. He was offended by a remark of Jeschonnek's to the effect that he, Udet, was concerned only with the aerobatic quality of planes; he did not like his personality; he even disliked his face, which, although the opposite of Milch's—Jeschonnek's being long, heavy-featured, with large rubbery lips—was the same in its granite immobility.

An adjutant stepped into the office to say that General Milch had just arrived.

"You should really have a haircut before you see anyone," Robert advised the Minister President as he finished dressing him. It was morning, they were on their way from Italy to Berlin, snow flew alongside the train windows. There was no response to the unwelcome suggestion. Robert persisted.

"I do not exaggerate, sir, when I say it is hanging almost to the floor."

At this, Göring turned reluctantly to the gold-framed mirror and gave a squint at his hair. It was indeed a good deal longer than usual. Italian long, holiday long. He nodded.

"But you do exaggerate."

"I must, sir, if I am to have results."

"You have learned that from me," he said, with a clap to his valet's shoulder. "Now you too can go into politics."

Robert smiled at the first joke the Minister President had made since leaving San Remo. It was obvious that he hated to leave. Robert himself would have liked to stay on in the sunny resort town, far from the miserable weather they were now entering. He began straightening the bedroom as Göring lumbered down the swaying passageway to the dining car.

Usually the Feldmarschall was surrounded by his retinue wherever he was; but this morning, except for the carved Gothic figures along the cherrywood walls, he ate in solitude. The holiday had been strictly private—only he and Emmy and the baby, the nursemaid and Robert. And so, leaving Emmy to continue her holiday, he was returning alone, abruptly summoned.

Or not so abruptly summoned. He had been expecting it. Seven days ago a courier had arrived with a letter from the Führer, which had hung like a dark cloud over the past week. The Führer felt he had made a mistake in not occupying the whole of Czechoslovakia the previous September. He had allowed himself to be satisfied with the Sudetenland, and now see: granted the government that had followed Beneš's retirement was a groveling and compliant lot, great problems still existed. Czech newspapers made attacks on the Reich, Communism had not yet been declared illegal, and Slovakia was demanding inde-

pendence. The Czechs were obviously unable to handle their own difficulties. It was possible that Germany would have to act.

Göring had written a careful letter for the courier to take back to
the Führer. Occupying Prague at this time, he said, might create turbulence just when the skies were clearing for Germany. It might also
mean a serious loss of prestige for Herr Chamberlain. What if he was
forced to leave office? Then Herr Churchill would come to power, and
one knew Churchill's malevolent attitude toward Germany. Surely,
control over Czechia could be achieved in a way which would not excite
either the Czechs or other nations. It would take time, but by strong
economic ties, a German-Czech customs union could be formed which
would serve the interests of both countries. Then Czechia would be so
politically bound to Germany, and to Germany's interests, that there
would be no further problems with her.

From day to day he had waited for an answer, but none had come
until yesterday's telegram: Return at once.

Anyway, it had been a good holiday. He had needed for months to
get away, his whole body having given rise to maladies as to an out-
cropping of pus-filled boils. That was the picture he saw, although he
had no boils, only high blood pressure, heart palpitations, headaches,
inflamed gums, severe hip pain, swollen glands. The change of scenery
had worked wonders; blue sky, green Mediterranean, and the air clear,
sunny, warm. Gradually the ills had evaporated. He played with little
Edda, took walks with Emmy, they gambled at the casino. He put all
but the present out of his mind, all except for Streicher, on whose
downfall he often mused with relish. Rumors had arisen that Streicher
had extorted shares worth some quarter of a million from an arrested
Jewish banker, at which he, Göring, and Hess had persuaded the
Führer to order an investigation. The investigation, concluding in a
trial before the Supreme Party Court, established that the Gauleiter of
Franconia had been practicing for years every kind of fraud in the
book, along with sexual quirks not even found in the books. He had
been expelled from the Party and banished to his farm near Nuremberg. That he was still permitted to publish his *Stürmer* was an uncon-
scionable indulgence, but in the main he had been well punished.
Altogether, it had been a very fine holiday. A pity it was ending in the
way it was.

After squirming through a haircut at the Leipziger Platz Palace,
the Feldmarschall called a hurried conference at the Air Ministry. It
was evening when he strode through the new Reichskanzlei to meet
with the Führer.

Herr Speer had only recently completed the new Chancellery
building. Its four hundred rooms housed the Civil Service, the Party
Organization, and the State Chambers, these last being on the ground

floor. Here the corridors, with their polished marble floors, continually increased in grandeur until they culminated in a huge magnificent room with red marble pillars, between two of which was the door of the Führer's study, a vast room adorned by glittering chandeliers. The disappointing thing to Herr Speer was that the Führer seldom entered his splendiferous new building, but kept his private residence in the old, adjoining Chancellery, "fit for a soap company," and worked there in his old study. A creature of habit, not someone to be pried from a routine once it was part of him.

On this occasion Hitler was neither in the new Chancellery nor the old, but in the room that linked the two buildings, the dining room. Here Göring to his surprise found himself in the midst of a party— Ribbentrop, Himmler, the lovely Frau Magda with her good friend Hanke, a dozen courtiers, young women in evening gowns. The Führer was just escorting them toward the cinema room. Seeing Göring, he took him aside.

"I have just had excellent news. President Hácha has requested a meeting with me. He arrives by train from Prague tonight."

"But if that is so, shouldn't the invasion plans be called off?"

"What for? I'll let the old man come and talk with me, but it's not going to change anything. Except perhaps in our favor. We shall see."

"But in any case, the weather—"

The Führer shrugged. They went on into the cinema room, where everyone sat down. The lights went out, the projector hummed, the blank screen leaped to silvery life accompanied by a sweep of silvery music, and a romantic comedy got under way.

Presently General Keitel, Chief of Staff of the Wehrmacht, came in and bent over his Führer.

"Don't worry," Hitler whispered back, "the old man isn't due until ten o'clock. I'll let him rest at his hotel for two hours, then receive him at midnight. What are you fretting about? Sit down, Keitel, enjoy the film."

The general did not wish to sit down, but he did. He squirmed impatiently throughout the romance, as did the Feldmarschall. Both knew the invasion was set for six o'clock the next morning, that within ten hours the first shots would be exchanged. Both also knew the weather was badly against them. In Göring's case, his Air Force was totally grounded.

The gnomelike Hácha and his Foreign Minister were received in the Führer's imposing new study. Thick black eyebrows left over from his youth were the only distinctive feature in the Czech President's bony, drawn face. Worn down by the strain of weeks, fatigued by his train journey, and sapped by the bitter cold, he had almost no voice as he shook hands with the Führer.

"Your Excellency," he uttered in a hoarse croak, "I greatly appreciate this personal meeting with the most powerful statesman of our time," after which he was introduced to Feldmarschall Göring, Foreign Minister von Ribbentrop, General Keitel, and State Secretary Meissner. The group sat down in a semicircle of armchairs, and the visitor began explaining his reasons for coming.

"My ties with your nation have always been strong. As a youth I spent my summers in the Bavarian Alps, where I understand, Your Excellency, that you have your summer residence—what a felicitous location. Although we have beautiful scenery in Czechoslovakia, we have none to match yours. Indeed, who can match anything in Germany? May I say that I consider this interview the very high point of my career. My career began in the Austrian civil service many years before the breakup of the empire and the formation of Czechoslovakia. I practiced law in Prague for some two decades . . ."

On he went, in his strained, hoarse voice, which, combined with a thick Czech accent, gave rise to a small smile on the Führer's lips.

He gave Keitel a nudge. "The old fellow sounds like a drunken sot."

The stiff and proper Keitel did not reply, although he felt obliged to lift one corner of his lips.

"Herr President," the Führer broke in, "the hour is late. Perhaps you could come to the point."

"Forgive me, I have rambled. Of course I will come to the point, which of course you already surmise. I have come for help against the forces of disintegration in my country. I am in desperate need of your advice."

The Führer dismissed Göring, Keitel and Meissner. The heads of the two nations, each with his Foreign Minister, remained in the study.

"The old gentleman in very naïve," Göring said to Keitel as they sat down in an anteroom. "The high point of his career? Doesn't he realize what happened to Schuschnigg when he asked for an interview with the Führer?"

General Keitel—or Lakeitel, "the lackey," as he was known in some circles—a tall, broad-chested man with the erect bearing of a Prussian officer prototype, gave a sigh of agreement. Both knew the Führer would launch into an enraged harangue that would shake the old man to bits. Both knew that the Führer's harangues, once begun, usually lasted hours. Both looked at their watches.

At half past two in the morning, a highly agitated Keitel took it upon himself to interrupt the discussion. A roar of invective shattered his ears as he entered the study. It broke off as Hitler got up and came over to him.

"What is it?"

"Mein Führer," Keitel whispered, "I must inform you that the Army asks for a final decision on whether they are to march or not!"

"There is plenty of time," the Führer muttered. "Don't bother me again." With an abrupt gesture he dismissed the general, whose glimpse of the two Czechs—both had jumped to their feet when Hitler rose, as if in obeisance—was of two confused and whipped creatures.

Over an hour later, Keitel and Göring were called back into the study, where they were informed by the Führer that President Hácha had been apprised of the impending invasion and had agreed to non-resistance by the Czech Army. The old man had been weeping; his handkerchief was still clutched in trembling fingers. "But how can this be done?" he suddenly cried, frantic. "If the invasion is to begin in only a couple of hours?"

"Could you not telephone Prague, Herr President?" General Keitel suggested tensely. "You could have orders issued to the Army at once."

"Good. Prima," said the Führer, gesturing to Ribbentrop and Göring. "If you will go with these gentlemen, Herr President, they will help you make arrangements."

The old man could scarcely walk, Göring supporting the frail tottering body as they went from the room. In a smaller study, he led the old man to a chair as Ribbentrop and the Czech Foreign Minister conferred over a paper Hácha was to sign. The Feldmarschall was sweating heavily under his uniform. He was dead set against the whole operation, but relieved that outright war could at least be avoided. *If* it could be—*if* the Czech government accepted Hácha's order. If not, the outcome might well be disastrous for Germany. The troops would be severely hindered by ice and snow, and they would get no help whatsoever from the Luftwaffe. All night he had kept in touch with the Air Ministry. The planes were still grounded, and the hour of attack was growing dangerously near. Now Ribbentrop shoved the sheet of paper under the nose of the President, who took it with his trembling hands and blankly stared at it. His Foreign Minister reached into the President's pocket and withdrew his pince-nez, which he adjusted on the old man's nose; then together they began poring over the paper. Suddenly Hácha began exclaiming in Czech and shaking his head.

"What is it?" asked Göring.

"This is the draft of a proclamation," explained the Czech Minister, "announcing the acquisition of Czechoslovakia by Germany, with Czechoslovakian consent—"

"What's wrong with it?" Ribbentrop broke in. "He's already agreed."

"But you don't understand," Hácha cried. "It says I should sign in my own name and the name of my government . . . but that I can't do! It's not fitting! I am not empowered to make a statement in the name of the government . . . I cannot . . ."

"So, just sign for yourself then."

"No, it must be legal," said Göring. "President Hácha must sign for the government as well as for himself."

"But it's almost four o'clock," Ribbentrop told him in an undertone: "We haven't much time!"

"Don't you think I know that?" Göring turned back to the old man and said to him quietly, "Excellency, why don't you sign for your government? It is only a formality. It will save so much time."

White-faced with fatigue and strain, the old gentleman kept shaking his head. Was he purposely stalling, Göring wondered, or was he just confused?

"Excellency, please do sign," he said again. "For the sake of your own country, please do sign."

There was no response. The only sound in the room was that of the clock on the wall ticking the minutes away. Suddenly the Feldmarschall felt himself explode.

"Then I must tell you something! My job is not the easiest one. Prague, your capital, I should be sorry if I were compelled to destroy this beautiful city, but I should have to! I should have to destroy it in order to show the English and French that my Luftwaffe can do all that it claims! Because they still don't want to believe it, and I would have to use this opportunity of giving them proof! Absolute proof! A flattened Prague! At this minute, hundreds of my bombers are only waiting for the order to take off!"

The old man slumped sideways in his chair.

"Mein Gott, he's had a heart attack!" Göring cried. "Get Morell!"

Minutes later the Führer's personal physician came hurrying in, pushed aside the three men clustered around the limp form, and after a cursory examination declared that the old man had only fainted. He was already coming round, mumbling and fretting, feebly protesting against an injection the doctor was preparing. From under his black eyebrows, his pince-nez askew on his bony nose, he lifted his gaze to the figures of the Feldmarschall and the German Foreign Minister, both glowering down at him.

"Take the injection!" snapped Ribbentrop. "Sign!"

"Think of Prague!" bellowed Göring.

The injection, a mixture of dextrose and vitamins, brought his strength back sufficiently for him to sign the proclamation. He was then given a telephone, along with a cup of coffee and a ham sandwich. After disposing of the food and drink, he telephoned both General Syrový and the Czech Premier. There was a half-hour wait before he was telephoned back: the orders for nonresistance would be complied with. After which he was led by Dr. Morell from the room, the Feldmarschall's eyes following him with relief.

                          *   *   *

"Ja, I actually made him faint with terror," he told Udet when he had returned to the Air Ministry. They sat with brandy, both with bristled jaws and beneath their eyes the bagginess of a sleepless night. "You know I'm not a cruel man, Ernst, I don't get any pleasure out of bullying old people. But why did the Czechs choose such a man of straw in the first place? And anyway, we've avoided war. What's a fainting fit beside that?"

At the Reichskanzlei, General Keitel had just finished issuing orders to the Army not to open fire, in keeping with the instructions issued to the Czech Army. While in his study, the Führer sat at his desk, alone. Suddenly he rose and went through the door of a small office where his two women secretaries, half asleep, had been waiting all night for the conference to end. The Führer's eyes were shining. "Well, meine Kinder, now you must put one here and one here!" Beamingly, he tapped his cheeks. "One kiss each!" The astonished secretaries bent to him and did so. "This is the most wonderful day of my life!" He clasped his hands to his breast. "Do you realize I have now accomplished what others have striven in vain for centuries to do? Bohemia and Moravia, which for a thousand years belonged to the Holy Roman Empire, have been returned to the Reich! I shall go down in history as the greatest German!"

While in his suite at the Hotel Adlon, President Hácha was being helped out of his snow-powdered overcoat by his daughter, who had accompanied him on the trip.

"Did it go well, Father? Is the Führer going to help us?"

Her tiny father gave her a searching look and shook his head, walking over to one of the windows, where he stood looking out.

"That man is going to take everything. Everything in Europe."

Chapter 53

THE young girl, radiantly blond and blue-eyed, in a smart brown leather jacket over a light summer dress, rapped vigorously on apartment door 4-III, her other hand holding a white bakery box. The door was opened by an elderly woman, sharp-nosed, ruddy-faced, gray hair twisted in a bun smack on top of her head. She wore small garnet earrings and a rather handsome dress, good material if old-fashioned. The girl was observant both by nature and by training.

"Frau Schmidt? Heil Hitler! I've come with your Mohrenkopf."

"Our Mohrenkopf? How is that?" queried Nikki.

"Because my father is Herr Baker Bang next door. He had this one put aside, and he said you were coming in for it later and that you had to climb a lot of stairs down and back. I wished to save you the trouble."

Nikki felt she took the stairs with great agility; nevertheless, she was impressed by the child's thoughtfulness. "Danke, that was kind of you, Fräulein Bang," she said. "Won't you come in for a moment?"

"Ja, I will."

The girl stepped in with alacrity. She was filled with such life and enthusiasm that she could turn down no invitation, not even one as dreary as this. Old people were not her style. There was another one, all mustache, sunk in the corner of a sofa.

"How is it that I've never seen you in the bakery?" Nikki asked, taking her over to be introduced to Hans.

"Vati says I'm too good to help out," the girl replied cheerfully, shaking hands with Herr Schmidt, who except for his fantastically big drooping mustache, like the tusks of an elephant, looked exactly like his wife.

"Indeed," murmured Nikki, then said to Hans, "Fräulein Bang has been kind enough to bring us our Mohrenkopf."

"It is my good deed for the day. Every day I perform a good deed."

This decreased Nikki's feelings of hospitality, to be the object of a mechanical act. Still, she and Hans had so few visitors that she found herself replying cordially, "A commendable habit."

"Ja," the girl said happily, looking around her. The place had a stuffy, decadent, bourgeois feeling. Old-fashioned dark furniture, lace antimacassars, fussiness, a sense of being closed in. Her own ideal of a home was one that would have rustic furniture, handwoven wool rugs on unvarnished floors, earthenware jugs standing on the sideboard, and on the sand-and-water-scrubbed table a pair of simple Germanic candelabras of wrought iron. Everything simple, clean, not machine-stamped. Her own flat, where she lived with her parents, was not a cluttered bourgeois cave like this, but in a way it was worse: cheap modern furniture right off the factory belt, gaudy linoleum, sleazy oilcloth on the tables. Her mother was pleased with it all.

"Won't you sit down?" asked Nikki, indicating a chair.

But with her radiant yet somehow efficient expression, Fräulein Bang began walking around the room. Nikki wondered if all children nowadays were so rude; and yet it was not exactly rudeness, but a kind of energy and openness, part of the brightness that streamed from the child's clear blue eyes and flaxen hair. She was like the beautiful summer weather outside. Still, to have one's home taken over by someone just out of diapers—that was so unheard-of that she shot a glance at Hans to share her surprise. But his eyes had closed. He was sleeping away what was left of his life. Granted, it was not much of a life; no garden, and even if there were one, he couldn't take the stairs; and no neighbors to visit with, for the people in the building were not friendly either with each other or with her and Hans. Yet she made the most of each day, always dressed with care, saw that Hans was neat as a pin, always had flowers to brighten the room. She took pride in these things, but as the dazzling, nosy girl wandered around, she felt reduced, shriveled, angry.

"Fräulein Bang, will you kindly sit down!"

"Minna. Fräulein Bang is so stuffy," the girl replied, pausing at the small table where Nikki's framed photographs stood in a group. Nikki observed her eyes go out on stalks as she picked up the largest one in its elaborate silver frame.

The girl stared at Feldmarschall Göring, uniformed, bemedaled, his baton clenched in his fist, the bottom of the photograph inscribed in a dashing hand: *To my dear Nikki—from your Hermann.*

"Hermann . . ." she murmured, the intimacy of the first name almost too much for her to take in. "Who is this Nikki?" she demanded excitedly.

"Who do you suppose?" said Nikki quietly, coming over to the girl's side. She felt her ill humor drop away like a dead skin. She took the picture gently from the girl's hands and regarded it with calm familiarity.

"You?" asked the girl with wonderfully round eyes, upon which Nikki smiled benevolently.

"We are very old friends." She replaced the photograph and took up another. "This is the Feldmarschall's mother. A handsome woman. You will see the strong family resemblance."

The girl nodded, enraptured.

"This is the Feldmarschall's father, Dr. Göring, first governor of Southwest Africa. A man of great achievements. Here are the Feldmarschall's sisters and brothers. The elder brother, Karl, was a young man of promise. He was killed in the Great War." And she added, bestowing upon the child an almost maternal smile, "That was before you were born."

"Ja, but I know all about the heroic struggle of the Great War."

"Then you will recognize this gentleman," Nikki said to her, graciously indicating yet another photograph.

"General Ludendorff died two years ago with great military honors," the girl rattled off. "You knew him too?"

"I knew them all," Nikki said with a modest shrug.

"And the Führer? The Führer too?"

"Natürlich. But you will see no picture of the Chancellor here."

"Chancellor?" repeated the girl. She had never heard anyone refer to the Führer as plain Chancellor.

"Our picture of our beloved Führer hangs in the bedroom," Hans said from the sofa, where, despite his closed eyes, open now, he had been listening. "He hangs above our bed. Protects us through the night."

As he spoke, he kept his eyes on Nikki, who compressed her lips sourly but said nothing. That was a relief. It was amazing that for all Nikki's conversations with Frau Kloppmann, she had never absorbed anything Frau Kloppmann told her. Like how the young people went about denouncing friends and neighbors, even their own parents, for the smallest thing. That this lovely child, who was like a breath of sun and wind and did good deeds—that she was the sort to bring trouble and misery down on the heads of two old people didn't seem likely. But still, she was in brown.

The intrusion of Hitler had soured Nikki's majestic spirits, but only momentarily. Hospitality beat high inside her. "The Mohrenkopf is for Herr Schmidt's birthday tomorrow, but it is so large why shouldn't we have a piece of it now? Say you will join us, Fräulein Bang." She was already on her way to the kitchen.

"Ja, I will," murmured the girl, staring again at the picture of Göring. You just never knew about people. These two ancient gnomes having such high connections. Suddenly she turned to Herr Schmidt.

"Did you fight with General Ludendorff?"

"Me? Nein. Too old to be in the war."

"That's true, you're very old."

How awfully bad-mannered the girl was, yet in such an open, happy way, you could hardly be offended. Now she went over to Nikki's needlework, and took it up to examine. Next thing, she would probably open the bedroom door and peer in.

"Bring it over here, child. I want to see how far she's got."

"I approve of needlework," the girl stated, coming over with it. "It's bourgeois, but at least it's done with one's hands. That's the main thing."

"'Tis my own feeling." Hans nodded. "I used to be a gardener, you see. But—" He gave a shrug at his clawlike hands.

"Ach, you're really all crippled up, aren't you? What a shame! But don't worry, we'll carry on for you. We love the soil."

Her marvelous blue eyes shone, and in an excess of high spirits she leaped forward to help Nikki coming in with the tray. Hans saw that his wife had used her best china, the set that had been given her after her mistress's death. It had been in the flat in Munich. It had been at Burg Veldenstein. The girl grabbed the tray with her strong young leather-clad arms and set it down on the low table by the sofa, while bubbling on. "We love the outdoors. We do everything in the outdoors."

"I must congratulate you on the fact that your father makes the best Mohrenkopf in Nuremberg," Nikki said as the girl helped her set the things out. "Neither Herr Schmidt nor I are great cake fanciers, but we do love our Mohrenkopf for our occasional little fêtes."

Hans could tell by her enunciation, her vocabulary and the light in her eyes that sagas from Burg Veldenstein would be flowing the moment she sat down. But she might have a time of it with this exuberant guest, who, already cutting the cake as Nikki went back for the coffee—cutting it efficiently and slapping the wedges down on the delicate little plates—was continuing her description of her life.

"I am the Sports Group Organizer in our section, I'm very good at sports. I've received the Reich Sports Badge, my picture has appeared on the title page of *Das Deutsches Mädel*. I'm also good in school, my marks are all high, except not so high in math but that doesn't matter. The analytical spirit of mathematics is essentially Jewish, and therefore opposed to the Nordic system of thinking, which is that of synthesis. In fact our teacher winks at our poor performance in math. But in everything else I'm tops."

"A very unusual young lady," Hans commented wearily.

"Nein, nein, I'm not unusual at all! We in the Youth Movement are all the same. No one is better than anyone else. We're all for one and one for all. We are bound by loyalty and honor. We are bound by our love of the Fatherland. We are bound by our love of the Führer."

And to Hans's amazement, just as Nikki came in with the silver coffeepot, the child began to sing.

"For Hitler we march through night and death, with the flag of youth and freedom and bread; our flag flies above us, our flag is the new age, our flag leads us to eternity; ja! the flag is more than death . . ."

Nikki had sat down. This was not at all what she had had in mind. This was quite unbelievable. But straight from her song into her cake the girl had plunged. There was sudden, shimmering silence.

"These cups, you may be interested to know, Fräulein Bang, are from—"

"I shall take off my jacket. It's become too warm."

She stood, stripped it off, and laid it carefully over the back of her chair. She wore a polka-dotted blue summer dress that made her appear even younger than before. "It's the BDM jacket," she stated with pleasure, reseating herself. "It's very smart, don't you think?"

"Ja, smartest over the back of a chair," Nikki retorted. "People do not customarily take refreshments bundled up in leather."

The girl, with her unfailing cheer, was not rebuked. Returning to her cake, she said through a mouthful, "I think there will be war with Poland. Have you talked about it with Göring? What does he say?"

"As a matter of fact," replied Nikki, her annoyance somewhat ebbing, "I have not, for our meetings are on a social plane. But for myself, and for my husband too"—she bowed at Hans, who seemed much more alert than usual, his eyes narrowed at her from over his coffee cup—"we hope most deeply that there will be no war."

"My parents are the same. They say, Minna, you don't know what war is. They say how the Great War was, and how things were afterward; and now everything is good, and Mutti's got oilcloth on the table and linoleum on the floor, that's all she really wants is my opinion. Sometimes I think everybody over thirty is just a materialist at heart. That's my own opinion. I hope when I reach that age I won't turn into a materialist. But I won't, it's not in me. Vati understands me better than Mutti, his heart is purer. But Mutti isn't a complete materialist, I could never say that. I have a lot of hope for Mutti. During the rally last year, she and a bunch of other ladies squeezed into the Deutscher Hof and each paid the cloakroom attendant three marks to sniff the bouquet that had been presented to the Führer. So I have hope for Mutti, but it still seems to me that only we young people really understand the Führer and belong to him. We are Germany's most precious asset, the guarantee of the future. We are the New Youth, and everyone else is just going to have to learn to think the new way. They're going to have to become pure in spirit, dedicated and noble. Be good and noble, German girl! That's the BDM motto. Don't think I'm naïve; I know there are jokes about our initials standing for Bund Deutscher Matratzen; certainly there are girls who behave shamelessly with the Hitler Youth, but I'm not one. I am pure in body and pure in mind. I belong to no one but the Führer, even if boys run after me because I'm so attractive. At the great Reich Youth meeting, the Gau leader herself picked me from hundreds of girls and said I must step out in front of the others, and she said: 'This is a glorious example of young Nordic womanhood.' That was a wonderful moment. All the girls clapped. There's no spirit of meanness in the BDM. We're all for one and one for all. We're the Führer's children and the Führer's hope. We're the new, better Germany—"

Mein Gott, will she never stop? thought Hans, who had sunk back into the corner of his sofa; and he knew that only his constant little frowns at Nikki, who was positively trembling, prevented her from turning on the girl like a fury.

"—We don't want war, but it is right that we want Danzig back since it was taken away by the Versailles Diktat. And then the German minority in Poland is treated in such a beastly way, just as they were treated in Austria and Czechoslovakia, that it makes your blood boil to know your German brethren are so horribly oppressed and degraded. We young people don't want war, but we want what is right for the Fatherland. And if Poland won't stop abusing our German brethren, and if they won't give us back the land that is rightfully ours—if Poland forces war on us, we will throw ourselves into the fight heart and soul! We of the new Germany will lead the rest of you. Purity, justice, glory—that's what we stand for! That's what we'll die for!"

The child broke off as if overcome by her own words, her cornflower-blue eyes streaming with light. Then she expelled a deep sigh and drank the rest of her coffee. The two old people were silent.

"I must go now." She set her cup down with a resounding clink. "I've enjoyed myself. That's the truth, a German girl never lies. I didn't think I would, but I have." She got to her feet and put on her smart jacket.

Quivering with rage, Nikki did not rise to accompany her guest to the door.

"Frau Schmidt, I compliment you on your coffee. Herr Schmidt, I congratulate you on your birthday tomorrow. Heil Hitler!"

The arm shot out, then off she strode, pausing at the table of photographs to drink in once more the picture of Göring—you could fairly see in the bend of her neck that she claimed the photo as her own, the small leader communing directly with the big leader—then on to the door where she turned with her radiant smile. "I hope I have gladdened your day. Auf Wiedersehen!" The door slammed. They listened to her footsteps descending the stairs.

"I tell you, if you hadn't kept making faces at me I would have given it to her!"

"All I know, 'tis best to be careful."

"A Fanatiker! And *rude*? Poking about, and butting in, and holding forth! And the self-dramatization—ach, I belong only to the Führer, ach, I was picked by the Gau leader herself, ach, it is we who will lead you all. Oh, I could have vomited!"

"That's how the young ones are. Think Germany belongs to them. Them and him. Him who hangs over our bed."

"Ah! That *really* made me sick!"

"A body's got to be careful, saves trouble all around."

"I don't want to be careful. It's degrading. I never agreed with a word Frau Kloppmann said, but at least we trusted each other. But here you daren't trust anyone. A slip of a girl comes in with a bakery box, and two minutes later she's making speeches and bursting into war songs. War songs, hah! Where has this pinhead of a child been? Doesn't she know the German woman in this regime is no more than a brainless cow, a breeding machine? Marching through night and death, indeed!"

"Well," Hans said, picking up the embroidery beside him, "she approves of needlework. Said so."

"What, was she poking about in my needlework too? Approves, does she? The patronizing little slut."

"Nein, a slut she's not. Married to the Führer. Pure as pure can be."

"You're right, I take it back. Pure body, pure heart, pure blood, pure everything—all this emphasis on purity, it's all you ever hear or read, and it's all such Quatsch. How can it be anything but Quatsch, coming from that low nobody with his flattened T's? That cheap vulgarian. All he's managed to do in six years is to turn out these puffed-up juveniles by the millions!"

"And military power," Hans put in.

"Ja, so he can get us into war!" she said with agitation.

Hans nodded, but he could not help thinking back to that drizzly day in 1934 when he and Nikki, sitting in the distinguished visitors' section of the stadium, had watched the first military exercises to be shown the world since the black, shattering year of 1918. How Nikki's foot had stamped in ecstasy, how the tears of joy and pride had coursed down his own face. . . .

"We never minded it, you know. The Army, I mean. Do you remark that day at the rally, how we—"

"I know, I know," she said impatiently. "Herrgott, it was wonderful! It was like being alive again. They took our Army from us . . . it was like taking our religion, our symbol, something so deep! They might as well have taken the German forests. And they took it! No, I'll never regret that day we got our Army back. That day is forever a glory in my memory."

"Mine too, but it was him who did it . . . you can't get away from it, Nikki. It was him who did it. And now he wants to use it."

If only Hermann would get rid of him! Nikki thought, smoothing the fine heavy material of her dress across her sharp knees. Him and all the other brown-clad upstarts, and the loudspeakers on the corners, and these horrible war clouds—sweep it all out!

She saw that Hans's eyes were closing. He had talked more these last few minutes than in days put together; at least the girl's visit had stirred things up. She hated to see him slip back into sleep. She tried to stimulate him anew by bringing up Streicher, whose recent downfall had gratified him considerably.

"He went much too far last November, Streicher did. I'll say again what I have often said before, that I have never been a great lover of Jews—but *that* business, it almost makes you want to do something for them. I, for instance, will refuse to ostracize that family on the second floor. Do you recall I told you about that piece of paper the landlord put under the door last week? An official notice slipped under every door that we're not to speak with Jewish tenants. Well, how dare they order one about? I shall speak with anyone I please."

But Hans had fallen asleep. The clock ticked from the corner. The afternoon light struck gleams from the beautiful old china on the table before her. She kept sitting, thinking that the two of them were growing apart, here in this strange new life. She retreated more and more into her past; she had her shrine of photographs, her memories. And he? Did he always sleep, or did he sit there with his own thoughts beneath his closed lids? Was he, too, living in his past? Did he live with his first wife, and his two young sons, and his young daughter? All dead, all dead in the war.

Chapter 54

17 July, Monday. London. The city has begun preparing. Just as when I was here last September during the Sudeten crisis: sandbags, yellow signs pointing to air raid shelters. England has promised aid to Poland if she requires it. There is plenty of criticism. Remarks overheard on my walk around Trafalgar Square: "Never before have we allowed one of the lesser nations to decide whether or not Great Britain goes to war," and "Do you realize that our frontier is now on the Vistula?" and "Poland is the least moral country in all Europe," their eyes going resentfully to the sandbags and yellow signs. Britain doesn't want to go to war for Poland, or for anyone, but it's going to happen. It's going to be the Great War all over again.

Evening. The most extraordinary series of events! My employer, Herr Dahlerus, seldom discusses anything but business with me, so I was surprised when at dinner tonight he said with emotion: I lie awake nights, thinking, didn't they get enough last time? And it will be much worse this time, Herr K. Think of the technological advances. And just because the damned leaders won't talk. If they would just sit down at the conference table, surely Danzig and the Corridor could be negotiated. But Poland won't talk with Hitler, Hitler won't talk with England, and if you ask me, England is making no serious attempt to talk with either of them. I don't know what His Majesty's government thinks it's doing. They go ahead and make a pact with Poland, then sit back and act as if they hadn't. I understand they sent Ambassador Henderson back to Germany after his sick leave, and that Hitler refuses to see him. But do they send anyone else? No. Do they try to make contact? No. What is to be done, Herr von K? Is Europe to be swept into war for lack of communication? What does Herr Göring think of all this?

We began to talk. What if a meeting were set up, without Hitler's knowledge, between Hermann and some private citizens sanctioned by His Majesty's government? Dahlerus has connections in the highest circles of British commerce. If they and Hermann were to meet secretly somewhere, communication would be restored between Britain and Germany, and with it hope for peace. And my own special hope being that Hermann would finally take things into his own hands and send Hitler sprawling. This is the time if ever there was a time. There must be a whole network of anti-Hitler conspirators who would back him. War would be averted and the regime ended in one swoop. My heart races as I write this. I cabled Hermann immediately after dinner and said I would be arriving in Berlin tomorrow with Herr Dahlerus. That's how fast it has gone!

Naturally the ironic element is not missing. If this should all go through, and peace be saved, it wouldn't be thanks to the diplomats or churchmen or idealists, but to some representatives of the squalid shit-souled world of commerce. To think I was once going to deliver that phrase in Dahlerus's face. I still feel the same about that world, I will never like it or feel at home in it, but it's my niche for better or worse.

When we got up from the dinner table, Herr D's face bore the glow of a man who sees himself as a holy crusader. I know that he has property in Germany which he wouldn't care to lose in the event of war. Still, he's wealthy enough so that I doubt it would matter much. As for the glow, do we ever do anything without our self-image being involved? Genuine as my feelings are, I know I'm thinking: To bring peace about, to do that! I could go to my grave knowing I had served a purpose in life. Of course, it all depends on Hermann. He may turn the idea down flat. But I feel, for once, that I can bring great influence to bear on him.

18 July, Tuesday. Berlin, L Palace. He was interested from the first moment. Doesn't look in the best of health, chewing one after another of those pills, but in good spirits, eager to discuss everything. "Let it take place at Rockelstadt. Think of it, Thomas, peace talks in the place where I met your beloved mother. They could not help but be fruitful." He is very optimistic. Both Herr D and I are stunned by the success of our suggestion. Only one disappointment: Hermann won't go behind Hitler's back. He will put the idea to Hitler. Meanwhile we are to return to London and await his cablegram: yes or no. If yes, Herr D is to go straight to Whitehall and get things rolling. If he can. It's really so farfetched when you think of it, an unknown foreigner simply presenting himself to the government with a plan like this.

19 July, Wednesday. London. Before we left this morning, Hermann suggested that if the answer is yes, I go with Herr D to Whitehall. You will be the stamp of authenticity, he said to me. If they have any doubts as to what you propose, Herr Dahlerus, they will say to themselves, but he must be what he says he is, he has brought Göring's stepson along to prove it. If you would do that, Thomas, I would be grateful. You will stand in my place.

I think of these words again and again.

31 July, Monday. Stockholm. It has all gone perfectly. His Majesty's government will brief seven English industrial magnates, friends of Herr D's. The time is set for 7 August. The place won't be here in Sweden because the place must be kept secret, and Hermann's appearance in a foreign country is always too conspicuous. So it is to be in Germany, but as close to Sweden as possible. Dahlerus insisted, he wants the spirit of neutrality to prevail. So it will be in Schleswig, practically on the Danish border.

And I am to be present. I had no expectation whatever of that. But Hermann says he wants me to be there.

7 August, Monday. Schleswig. The meeting took place here in this summer house belonging to Herr D. He arranged for a real English breakfast this morning. Then he drove off to meet Hermann's private train at Bredstedt. At noon they were back. Hermann was in a pale gray pongee suit, sweating like anything, still not looking well but in good spirits.

The talks began at noon and lasted until seven this evening.

Hermann always spoke in a quiet, friendly manner, and never got angry, no matter what was said. He listened to everything, and never tried to interrupt or score points. It was terribly hot, he was constantly wiping his face with his handkerchief. He had circles under his eyes, but the eyes themselves were clear and unwavering. He was frank and to the point.

"You want decency and order in Europe and in the world," he said, "but it is the fault of the British govenment that there is none. Why do you not have the strength to make clear exactly how you stand?"

To this the British spokesman said: "The hesitations of the British government are over. It has definitely decided that it will stomach no further aggressions in Europe. If Germany tries to take Danzig forcibly, Britain will fulfill her obligations to Warsaw."

"Then the only hope for peace lies in talks between our two nations," Hermann answered. "Because the Poles won't talk. They refuse to talk. Poland's Marshal proclaims: 'Anyone who attempts to take Danzig from us will be repelled by force. Polish guns will speak!' That is the only kind of talk we get from Poland concerning a city that is ninety-nine percent German and unanimously in favor of rejoining its homeland. Only over a conference table can the question of Danzig and the Corridor be settled peacefully. And may I add that the settlement of these two areas will not be followed by demands of territories elsewhere. On that point, gentlemen, I give you my sacred assurance as a statesman and an officer."

At the end of the talks, the Englishmen conferred. They then stated that they were now strongly in favor of a four-power conference—Britain, Germany, France, Italy—to be held as soon as possible in neutral Sweden, under the auspices of the Swedish Premier.

Dahlerus's eyes were filled with tears of joy. Mine were too. Afterward, I was completely wrung out, like someone at the end of a victorious battle. Of course, it's not won yet; both Hitler and the British government have got to agree. But the first big step has been taken, and again my feeling is that it is going to happen, it is going to work!

11 August, Friday. Stockholm. I talked on the telephone with Herr D in Berlin. He says things have got stalled. Hermann obtained Hitler's permission for the conference, but nothing is happening across the channel. Parliament has adjourned, and all the important people are away on holiday. As if the fate of Europe weren't hanging by a thread!

Chapter 55

FOREIGN Minister von Ribbentrop and Foreign Minister Ciano were eating lunch at Ribbentrop's recently acquired castle near Salzburg. Each detested the other to such a degree that neither enjoyed the food, which, since they both had a manner of holding their heads extremely high, was lifted long majestic distances to their respective mouths.

The younger man, tight and nervous inside, finally broke the silence which his host seemed prepared to maintain indefinitely.

"Well, Herr Ribbentrop, what do you want? Danzig or the Corridor?"

The German Minister, not raising his drooping eyelids, replied sharply: "They are no longer the point. We want war."

Count Ciano felt an iciness drop down his spine. He tried to speak calmly.

"You may be rash in presuming Britain and France won't intervene."

A glance flicked across at him from under the eyelids. "Would you care to make a wager?"

Another long silence ensued, during which only the clicking of their forks on their plates could be heard.

"So it is quite certain," Ciano finally said. "You mean to march. When? The plans have been made?"

Ribbentrop flicked him another glance. "All decisions are still locked in the impenetrable bosom of the Führer."

Santo Cielo, thought the Count. I shall vomit.

As everyone knew, it was impossible for Chamberlain to fly again to Germany with his umbrella; the occupation of Czechoslovakia in March had been the last straw. Now in the burning August heat his ambassador tried in vain to set up appointments with Hitler and with Ribbentrop. Herr Dahlerus, rushing back and forth by plane from Berlin to London, was getting nowhere. "Foreign Secretary Halifax is sick of my face," he told Göring, "but he's going to get a lot sicker of it."

The Feldmarschall shook his head with impatience. "I'm going to try something radically different, Herr Dahlerus. I think it's the only way to break the deadlock."

Within the hour, Ambassador Henderson was sending a cipher message to London at Göring's behest: "Field Marshal Göring believes that the present tension can be alleviated by a personal talk between himself and the Prime Minister. He is prepared to fly to London two days hence, 23 August." The message was read by Lord Halifax, who showed it to the Prime Minister, a man who had aged greatly in the last weeks. That evening Henderson received a cipher message back: "Our Air Ministry has been informed, and has been asked to arrange for Göring's reception. We await confirmation from Germany."

Göring was at that moment at the Obersalzberg, where, summoned abruptly by the Führer, he had flown earlier in the day. All high military leaders had been summoned.

"I feel the need to strengthen your confidence, gentlemen. I carried the point with the Sudetenland, but you lost your nerve. I don't want this to happen again. A conflict with Poland has to come about sooner or later, and it is better that it be now than later. We need not fear the Western powers—they will do nothing. They hoped that Russia would become our enemy in the event that we attacked Poland. And so they tried to woo Russia, but they are worms, I saw them at Munich. I knew Stalin would never accept an English offer. It was then that I began exercising my great genius for resolution. I proposed to Russia a commercial treaty, and this worked into conversation involving a proposal for a nonaggression pact."

A wave of astonishment went through the audience at this turnabout of the raving anti-Bolshevik. How would he explain such a pact to his Party, after the buckets of passionate filth he and they had thrown on Russia for years? Even the Soviet embassy in Berlin was treated like a leper colony.

"Four days ago I learned that Russia is ready to sign. Today von

Ribbentrop has left for Moscow, the day after tomorrow he will conclude the treaty. Now Poland is in the position in which I want her: Russia is neutralized. The political arm is ready, the way is open for the soldier."

At this point Feldmarschall Göring, his face very white and running with sweat, got to his feet and led a round of applause.

"As for our conduct of the war," Hitler went on, "have no pity. Attack and achieve brutally. I have the strongest faith in the German fighting man. The Wehrmacht cannot fail. Nothing can fail if the nerves of Germany's leader stay firm! The complete destruction of Poland is my aim. I will probably order the start of operations on Saturday morning, the twenty-sixth."

He turned and went out, as his shaken audience looked around at one another. First it was to have been the 20th of August, then the 1st of September, now the 26th of August. Had there ever been another Commander in Chief who leaped from one date to another without even conferring with his General Staff? But perhaps it was all hopscotch; perhaps, as in the Sudeten crisis, he would not attack at all; perhaps he meant again, when he had got his way, to recoil at the last moment.

Before returning to Berlin, Göring took Hitler aside. "I've just telephoned Ambassador Henderson. I've been successful in setting up a personal meeting with Chamberlain in England."

"There is no need. Our pact with Russia will panic the democracies. The British government will fall within days, and be replaced by a pro-German administration that will at once accommodate itself to our needs."

"I don't believe that will happen."

"Your trip is unnecessary. Cancel it."

The following day, Ambassador Henderson flew from Berlin to Berchtesgaden with a message from his government: for once Hitler could not refuse to see him. In fact, Hitler had already read the message, thanks to the German code-breaking department, and was indifferent to its content: that Britain would fulfill her obligation to Poland, but if any negotiations were still possible, Britain was willing to discuss them. He felt, however, that it would be a good opportunity to express himself powerfully, and began shouting at the Ambassador as soon as he sat down. "We could have had a peaceful settlement with Poland, but Britain has put the sword in their hands! And all the while, this very minute, they're raping defenseless German women! Emasculating German men! Castrating them! We will not tolerate it!" Sir Nevile hated the Führer's outbursts, but his illness, which deprived him of much energy, gave him in turn a kind of calm. He let the furious words pound against his ears. At length he was told to eat lunch in

Salzburg; when he returned he would be given an answer to his government's message. Coming back from Salzburg, he was handed the text. It was very short. Its gist was that England would find Germany prepared. The Ambassador felt tears come to his eyes. "I so much regret all this . . ."

"It is in Chamberlain's hands, he can decide if there is to be war!"

"Chamberlain is a friend of Germany. He will go on being a friend."

"Then let him take a step toward us!"

"But that is exactly what he has done in his message."

The Führer shrugged and dismissed him.

The day after, Hitler returned to Berlin to greet Ribbentrop, just back from Moscow. They fell on each other's necks like brothers, then Hitler stood back with arms outspread. "Herr von Ribbentrop, you are the new Bismarck!"

And the tall, distinguished-looking, youthfully gray-haired figure, he of the cold, haughty mien, was transformed by the radiance of his Führer's smile; his eyes shone, he clapped his hands together, his happiness made him seem like a boy, he laughed, he almost wept. It was the greatest moment he had ever known.

Polish Ambassador Lipski's hands had begun exhibiting a tremor in the last few days. He was very much aware of this as he held the telephone receiver to his ear. For almost an hour, Ambassador Henderson had been badgering him to ask for a meeting with Hitler as a sign of goodwill. "It will not be taken as a sign of goodwill, but of weakness," Lipski had repeated so often that Henderson finally hung up. And now Göring came through the door—he always came through a door like five men; Lipski was tired, nervous, he was not up to the Feldmarschall's vigor today. He gestured silently to a chair.

"I am sorry that my policy of maintaining friendly relations with Poland has come to nothing. But I no longer have the influence to do anything, Herr Lipski. It is out of my hands. It is up to you now, my friend. You can't go on like this. The channels of communication must be opened up."

The talk was fruitless. Göring hurried back to the Air Ministry to confer with his staff. Unless a miracle took place, the Luftwaffe would be flying over Poland in less than forty-eight hours.

The following day, the British government not yet having fallen, Hitler began having second thoughts. Summoning Ambassador Henderson, he offered a mutual nonaggression pact with England and gave the Ambassador the use of his private plane to get to London as soon as possible. But that evening he underwent two shattering blows. One was a report that the Anglo-Polish agreement, which had been sitting on a shelf since April, had finally been formalized that very day. The other was a message from Mussolini confessing that his armed forces were so weak that he could give Germany no assistance in the event of war.

The Western powers had stood fast, Italy had reneged, Germany was on her own. "Get me Keitel!" he barked, and sat gnawing his knuckles until the general was shown in. "Can the troops be stopped?" he asked.

Keitel looked at him with a sharp, questioning frown. "They are already marching toward the Polish frontier."

"I know that! Can they be stopped?"

"I shall have to consult the timetable, mein Führer."

"Then send for it!"

A short while later, General Keitel looked up from the timetable. "It can be done, provided the order goes out immediately."

"Then send it!"

When Keitel was gone, the Führer telephoned Göring to halt Luftwaffe proceedings. "We're going to negotiate with Poland?" came Göring's voice over the wire.

"Nein. I need time to eliminate British intervention."

In London the indefatigable Herr Dahlerus, learning from Lord Halifax that Ambassador Henderson was being sent back to Berlin with a message making clear to Hitler that the formal signing of the Anglo-Polish Pact was not to be interpreted as a challenge, gave a shake of his head. "I don't know, but it seems to me nothing remains clear when it goes through official channels. May I suggest that I deliver to Göring a personal letter from you, Lord Halifax, in which you express in absolutely clear, unambiguous language England's genuine desire to reach a peaceful settlement?"

Within two hours, the letter in his possession, Herr Dahlerus was on a special plane back to Berlin. By midnight he had put the letter in Göring's hand, and a few minutes later the Feldmarschall swept him off to the Chancellery, where the Führer was roused from bed. Herr Dahlerus beheld him in the flesh for the first time. He looked unpleasant, and annoyed to have been wakened. His dark hair was hastily brushed, his brown jacket awry. As soon as the three of them had sat down in the Führer's great study, the Führer launched into a history of the National Socialist Party. This seemed surpassingly strange to Herr Dahlerus, and stranger yet as the monologue went on and on, the speaker's face darkening and brightening by turn as he described his Party's setbacks and triumphs, year by year. Twenty minutes, half an hour went by. Göring, who was perched on the arm of the sofa where Dahlerus sat, was highly impatient, constantly tapping his thick beringed fingers on the side of the armrest. But his face expressed only the deepest absorption. Suddenly the voice rose in volume and grew harsh. Herr Dahlerus heard the British people attacked as low and cowardly, and with some nervousness he ventured to interpose his own opinion. Learning that his guest had once worked as a common laborer in England, Hitler was now all ears. He wanted to know everything about the British workingman, and as Göring gave covert glances at his watch, the conversation drew out into the small hours. "Well, I'm glad to know about the working people," Hitler said, "but the trouble with England is her plutocrats." Suddenly, in the space of a moment, he was in a rage. "Yesterday I sent Henderson to Chamberlain with a magnanimous offer! This is my last magnanimous offer to England!" He had jumped from his chair and was pacing rapidly as he shouted. "If there should be war I will build U-boats! U-boats! I will build airplanes! Airplanes! I will disintegrate my enemies! I will disintegrate them!" The astonished Dahlerus stared at the enraged, pacing Führer, who gradually calmed. "The Feldmarschall has shown me what Lord Halifax has written," Hitler said quietly. "It appears to me a show of goodwill. I am willing to respond directly. You must return to England at once, and tell them that I sincerely want to bring about an understanding."

"I will, gladly. But what are the terms? Otherwise I shall just have to fly back again and find out."

At this, the enormous Feldmarschall leaped with agility to his feet. Going over to an atlas, he opened it and with a red pencil drew some swift lines. "This is the passage we want through the Polish Corridor," he said, ripping the page out of the book as Hitler gave a sour wince.

"And Danzig?" asked Dahlerus, taking a pencil and notepad from his pocket.

"Danzig must be returned to the Reich," Hitler told him. "But Poland will have a free harbor, a corridor to her port of Gdynia, and territory around it. Germany will guarantee Poland's boundaries."

A few hours later, Herr Dahlerus was the sole passenger aboard a Luftwaffe transport plane. Permission had been obtained from the Dutch government to fly over their territory, and from the British government to land in England. By now there was no air traffic over the frontiers of Western Europe. His craft was the only one in the blue morning sky, as he sat with his hand in his pocket, fingers around a torn atlas page and a scribbled notepad.

In German diplomatic circles, there was no knowledge of Dahlerus's comings and goings. The diplomats placed their hopes on Henderson's returning from London with a report that the British wished a peaceful settlement. They said to one another that it might still be possible for Hitler to achieve a success that he could represent to the nation as the fruit of a policy pursued "with fixed determination up to the very verge of war." They also said: But who knows? We may be hurled into the abyss just because of those two madmen, Hitler and Ribbentrop. And yet, one could never be sure with Hitler; he might have planned all along to step back at the last minute. Meanwhile, the people were in the throes of unrest and anxiety. There were now bread cards, trial blackouts, war weddings for weeping couples—all this even before war was certain.

When Ambassador Henderson arrived back in Berlin he drove immediately to the Chancellery, where for once everything went smoothly and quietly. The British note stipulated that any settlement with Poland must be the subject of an international guarantee. The Poles had already been advised to establish contact with the Germans immediately and begin negotiations. Hitler seemed pleased, even happy. He shook the Ambassador's hand with warm cordiality, and promised to have a reply for him the next day.

Herr Dahlerus had also returned to Berlin, going straight to Göring's Leipziger Platz Palace. He found himself rushed at, his hands grabbed and squeezed with affection. "God save the Swedes! A wonderful people! We shall have peace, Dahlerus!"

> **29 August, Tuesday.** Stockholm. Both Hermann and Herr D called from Berlin. Peace is assured! The Poles will negotiate! There will be no war!

At ten o'clock that night, Herr Dahlerus was summoned from his hotel by Göring. The Feldmarschall, in a royal-blue satin robe fastened around his middle with a jeweled buckle, was in a colossal rage. He clutched a copy of the reply which the Führer had given Sir Nevile.

"This reply of the Führer's is as concilliatory as can be. Yet Henderson calls it an ultimatum! So what if it demands an immediate talk with the Poles? We hope military action between the Poles and ourselves won't become necessary, but in view of the critical situation we must insist that a settlement be reached without delay. That they send an emissary by tomorrow, the thirtieth. The Poles are mad, I tell you they are shameless and insolent, Dahlerus! Their propaganda is beyond belief. Today the Polish radio reported that the German Army is miserably equipped and that their uniforms are held together by string! Can you believe such an insult? String!"

As if that were the ultimate affront, he collapsed into a chair, where he sat mute, his fingers spread across his face. Presently he removed them. He seemed calmer. "I realize that Henderson is ill, poor fellow, but of all times to show such poor judgment . . ."

Then he was out of his chair again, hurriedly striding over to an atlas, which he opened and tore a page from. He seemed always to be tearing pages out of atlases, Dahlerus thought, watching him make hasty marks on the map with an oversized pencil. "Here, I'll write the whole thing down in outline form. It will be clear as a diamond. Absolutely clear! So—take this and the map to London and show them to Chamberlain. This is what the Führer is offering!"

Two hours later Dahlerus was again airborne, while at the same time in Berlin Ambassador Henderson was on his way to the Foreign Ministry—all ministries were working around the clock—to keep an appointment with Ribbentrop he had just telephoned to make. In his briefcase was a message he had received from his government only an hour ago in reply to the negative report he had sent twelve hours earlier. The government stated that it still approved of direct negotiations between Berlin and Warsaw, but that it was impracticable for the Poles to establish contact as early as today. "Today?" he said to himself as the car drew up before the ministry and he hurriedly got out. "Tomorrow has already become today. Why were they so slow in answering?" He regretted the suspiciousness of his report, he was relieved that his government had nonetheless replied positively, but to have dawdled the whole day away like that—it was as if they were in the grip of a death wish.

Dr. Schmidt was on hand to interpret. Although Ribbentrop spoke fluent English, he refused to speak anything but German with Ambassador Henderson, whose command of the German language was not the best. At a time of such crisis, thought Dr. Schmidt, language barriers should be reduced as far as possible, but that was not Herr von Ribbentrop's way. The Ambassador, who looked very poorly, at once took out his government's message concerning the meeting between the Germans and the Poles and began reading it aloud in English. Ribbentrop listened impatiently. "Ist das alles?" he broke in. "No, that is not all." Sir Nevile continued reading as Ribbentrop sat scowling and fidgeting. "Ist das alles?" he broke in again. "No, that is not all! Stop interrupting!" The face of the German Minister twitched violently. He leaped to his feet. "So spricht man nicht mit mir!" Suddenly the room erupted with two furious streams of words, one in English and one in German. The two voices obliterated each other, there was an actual threat of physical violence, it was the stormiest scene the interpreter had ever witnessed in his years among the diplomats; and with his particular imaginative inclination, he saw the room filling with liquid red, except that this time—because all was finally lost—it was rising up the walls with tremendous rapidity, like a channeled river torrent.

The voices broke off. Breathing heavily, the two men glared at each other. "My purpose in coming here is not to trade insults, Herr von Ribbentrop. I have read you my government's statement. I now wish to know what proposals the German government has for a settlement of its dispute with Poland."

"Es ist sowieso zu spät! Wir baten um den polnischen Gesandten für den dreissigsten August . . ."

Dr. Schmidt began translating: "It is too late in any case. We asked for a Polish envoy to arrive on the thirtieth of August. It is now past midnight, and therefore too late. But I will read our proposals to you."

Picking up a sheaf of papers from his desk, Ribbentrop began reading aloud in rapid German. When he had finally finished, the Ambassador asked to see the document, but it was flung down on the desk. "Nein. Das hat sich erledigt . . ."

"The Minister says that since no Polish emissary has arrived, the document is out of date and therefore worthless."

At nine o'clock that morning an exhausted Sir Nevile telephoned the Polish embassy but could not get through to Ambassador Lipski. Unable to go there himself, for he had another appointment at the German Foreign Ministry, he asked his chargé d'affaires to get hold of this Dahlerus person, of whom he had just heard, and to go together with him to find out what was happening with Lipski. He gave his chargé the text of the German proposals, which he had finally received from Ribbentrop's undersecretary.

The two men drove through the already sweltering streets in the chargé's little open two-seater. At the Polish embassy, where they hastened inside, Dahlerus felt a plummeting of his heart. The hallways were filled with packing cases, and servants and staff were rushing about. Ambassador Lipski's large office, ornately and beautifully paneled, was carpetless, emptied of all furniture except a table and chair. The Ambassador was sitting at the table, involved in some work. What he was doing, Dahlerus saw as they approached him, was carefully tearing up pieces of paper and twisting them into little balls the size of marbles. The man's fingers were shaking. He was a stout, youngish man whose face showed a sickly green pallor. He was clearly on the verge of a mental breakdown.

The chargé, hastily writing out the main thrusts of the German proposal, gave the sheet of paper to Lipski, who raised his eyes from it helplessly. "I'm sorry, I can't read it." Herr Dahlerus rushed from the room with the scrawled sheet, found a secretary, and had it typed up. Rushing back, he gave the typed sheet to the Ambassador, whose shaking fingers laid it down among the twisted balls of paper. He did not look at it. After a few moments, the two men left the room.

"Do you know what Lipski said while you were out of the room?" the chargé asked. "He said he had no interest in any proposals from the Germans. He said if there is a war, there will be uprisings and rebellions in Germany, and the Polish Army will march in triumph into Berlin. Well, he may as well take that attitude, since he knows anything he does will be useless. It's all useless. The Germans made sure there wouldn't be time enough for negotiations. An emissary to arrive in one day—no, it was an empty gesture from the start."

"Was it?"

"I don't know. Who can know? But it's my feeling."

"Warsaw could have given Lipski plenipotentiary powers, couldn't they?"

"I suppose. But they didn't."

"I wonder what we came here for," Dahlerus said, looking around him in a sorrowful daze.

"I don't know. I really don't know. It's all too late."

At two o'clock that afternoon, Hitler ordered the invasion of Poland. It would begin at dawn the following morning. "Now you've got your damned war!" Göring shouted over the phone at Ribbentrop, and slammed the receiver down.

Gruppenführer Heydrich was also on the phone, talking to a group of SS who had been waiting for days in a small German town on the Polish border. "Operation Konserven is now to go into effect," he told them.

That evening Operation Canned Goods got under way. A small German radio station near the town was entered, a Polish-speaking SS man made an impassioned broadcast to the effect that the Polish Army had crossed the frontier and urged all Poles in the area to rise up against the Germans. Bullets were fired into the walls to show that a fight had taken place, and finally a man in a Polish uniform, previously drugged and now shot through the head, was left behind. He was a scrawny specimen, one of a dozen German inmates brought along from the Oranienburg concentration camp, the canned goods. Eleven of his fellow inmates, also drugged and in Polish uniforms, were hastily spread around the woods outside. Then they too were shot, and the SS departed into the night.

"Last night for the first time, Polish regular soldiers fired on our territory. Since five forty-five this morning we have been returning the fire, and from now on bombs will be met by bombs. . . ."

Nikki put her hands to her face as she heard Hitler's voice. "It's come, then," she exclaimed, turning to Hans beside her on the sofa.

". . . In my talks with Polish statesmen I formulated the German proposals, and there was nothing more modest than these proposals. These proposals have been refused. . . ."

Her eyes were filling with tears, the radio becoming a dark blur as the voice went on.

". . . I am asking of no German man more than I myself was ready throughout four years to do. I am from now on just the first soldier of the Reich. I have once more put on my old soldier's uniform, that field-gray coat which was to me the dearest and most sacred of all. I will not take it off again until victory is secured. . . ."

"When?" Nikki wept. "When?"

". . . If I should fall, Feldmarschall Göring shall succeed me. . . ."

Her agony was shot through with a spasm of joy. "Did you hear, Hans? Then fall! Fall now, you fool!" she cried at the radio, scrambling to her feet.

"If Göring shall fall, then Deputy Hess shall succeed him. If Hess shall fall, then the Senate will choose from its midst the most worthy successor. We shall carry on, no matter what. From this moment, my life shall belong more than ever to my people. Together we shall secure victory. Victory will come! There will never be another 1918!"

The old man, badly upset, but not so upset as his wife, whose emotions always went the limit, creakily rose with his cane and hobbled over to the window, where she stood with heaving shoulders, her trembling hand holding aside the lace curtain. What did she expect to see down there in the street?

"'Tis in Poland, not here," he told her soothingly.

But she wept on anyway.

1 September, Friday. Stockholm. Poland was invaded this morning.

Chapter 56

Aᴛ dawn of the third day, Poland's Pomorska Brigade gathered in the forest beyond which spread the Tuchel Plain, shrouded in mist. In the darkness the dripping trees made a delicate tapping on the cavalrymen's old French-style helmets, their scabbards, their long wooden lances. The magnificent horses, white and pale dappled gray, breathed out clouds of steam, their hooves occasionally stamping the damp ground impatiently. Gradually, the mist across the plain burned off, the morning grew full and bright. At about noon, the enemy came into view: a horizontal line of armored patrol cars flanked by infantrymen.

The brigade in its hundreds moved out from the trees, the riders tautly holding back their eager horses as they maneuvered them into position; then the long lines proceeded forward at a disciplined walking pace until the order was heard:

"Unsheathe!"

As one they whipped sabers from scabbards, causing a single, keen *whoosh* to carry across the plain like the sweep of a giant scythe. Simultaneously they released their mounts into a canter, then into a gallop as from the surrounding woods small field guns fired ahead of them into the enemy. The Germans dispersed, the Poles galloped after them with fierce cries, firing revolvers, slashing with their sabers, thundering along before seeing an astounding formation of slowly approaching gray tanks with long-barreled guns. Within forty minutes the brigade lay demolished across the plain.

At that very hour in London, Mr. Chamberlain was declaring a state of war between Britain and Germany.

Sitting at his desk in his Chancellery study, with only Ribbentrop present, the Führer stared scowlingly into space. Suddenly he turned. "What now?" he asked accusingly.

"What now," repeated the unhappy Minister. "Now France will do the same. . . ."

While in the anteroom, filled with ministers and military men, there was a continual low, shocked murmuring of voices. Above the murmuring, Göring's voice could be heard. "If we lose this war, then God have mercy on us!"

Late that afternoon, Ambassador Henderson took a last walk down Unter den Linden. There were few people on the streets; a sense of desolation and gloom hung in the sullen heat, a feeling as heavy as his sense of personal failure. He had believed that the absorption of German minorities into the Reich was the final goal of German foreign policy, and that with the achievement of this goal Germany's ferment would disappear . . . but that was perhaps the problem, he thought, walking along while watching for a pharmacy open on Sunday, for he had run out of pain pills. That was perhaps the problem . . . millions of Germans had grown sick of repeated crises; they longed for a placid existence; guns before butter had grown increasingly unpopular except with the younger generation. And perhaps Hitler had wondered what would happen to his National Socialist revolution if its momentum was allowed to cease. Most of his people, like people everywhere, would sit back and enjoy their petty gains, would happily express their small materialistic souls in the shops and department stores, would become a nation of complaisant purchasers, of cinema-goers and beer drinkers, and was it for this he had fought and struggled for twenty years? No, onward, onward, anything but that they should sink back into their trivial natures. Was this Hitler's thinking? That the momentum could not be allowed to stop? Power, superiority, grandiosity—these things could not survive in a settled environment, for people were the same whoever or wherever they were: they adored comfort, convenience, entertainment. Since the Middle Ages this had been so, as God and the ruling classes had declined together. . . .

He turned into a pharmacy, but was told by the pharmacist, whose face was as glum as the entire atmosphere of Berlin, that the pills could not be sold without a doctor's prescription.

"Would it help if I told you I am the British Ambassador?"

There was an adamant headshake. "I am very sorry, sir, but the regulations on these pills are quite definite."

"But you don't understand," Sir Nevile went on, smiling and feeling himself come apart in some lugubrious, fantastic way. "I am the British Ambassador. If you poison me with your drug, you will get a high decoration from your Dr. Goebbels." And he began to laugh.

The pharmacist's gloomy face grew sharply quizzical. Then he also began to laugh. They both stood laughing at the stupid grisly joke, and when the Ambassador left with his bottle of pills, his haggard face still bore a lost smile.

That he had come under the sway of National Socialism he knew . . . yes, for it had seemed to hark back to an older, a greater world. And that he had wanted to contribute to the salvation of mankind he also knew; that had been his sole quest as a diplomat—the preservation of world peace. God knew he had wanted peace. But he had also wanted something old, something great and absolute, he had wanted to go back into the mists of time. A diplomat had no right to envelop himself in any kind of mist. . . .

"The gods remember everlastingly, and strike remorselessly," he said to himself as he walked along in the pounding heat. "By their long memories are the gods known."

At his chaotic embassy, he took three pills to subdue the pain. The next morning he and his family and staff climbed into eight limousines, and, followed by a line of trucks filled with furniture, drove from the embassy to Charlottenburg train station.

The Poles were waiting for the promised military help from Britain and France. None came. No French troops attacked Germany on her western front, or only in the feeblest manner, advancing a little from the Maginot Line and sitting down well within France. No RAF bombers wreaked havoc on Germany. A few RAF planes did fly over some west German cities, but only to drop leaflets suggesting the Polish war be stopped. There was no substance to the pact of assistance; the promise had been empty words.

Her troops poorly deployed, her capital bombed continually from the air and by heavy ground artillery, her eastern parts moved in on by Russia, Poland surrendered on September 29, having suffered tremendous losses. German losses by comparison were light, ten thousand men, among whom was former Army Commander in Chief von Fritsch, who had thrown himself into battle with suicidal intent and had been killed within days.

And so the war was over. It had been swift and victorious, largely due to the effectiveness of the Luftwaffe. Göring was the man of the hour. He had not wanted the war, but once it began he had done all he could to help win it. He stood immensely high in the eyes of his men, in the eyes of Germany, and in the eyes of his Führer. Commander of the greatest air force in the world, heir presumptive to the Führer, higest-ranking officer in the nation—flushed with triumph, he disappeared from Berlin the day after the war was won. He boarded his private train with only a few aides-de-camp in attendance and headed south. At Creussen, the train came to a standstill on a siding, an ordinary civilian coupe was driven down a ramp from one of the flatcars, and the Feldmarschall, having climbed in behind the wheel, drove off through the woods.

The car was often at the bottom of the world, on either side the high jagged gray of precipices, of rock formations like fists or thick upthrust fingers amid a towering leafiness, the road below winding deep through shadowy coolness, alongside a rocky gorge of rushing crystalline water. Then the sun would burst overhead as the road emerged into meadowland beneath open skies. The day was very fine: warm, hazed gold as if with pollen. After not too many kilometers, there could be seen in the distance, high, a dot of red.

Dust rose behind the car as it ascended the old dirt road. Before the gate, the driver climbed out and went over to the frayed bell rope, giving it a series of yanks that set up a rusty clangor.

Silence. He waited. Again he yanked the rope; again the reverberations faded to silence. Then someone shouted from the other side: "Keep your shirt on!"

A few moments later came the sound of the iron bar being pushed scrapingly along its holdings, the rattle of the old handles turning, the heavy, slow, familiar creak as the gate was drawn back. He was half aware of a squinting leathery face as he stepped through with one hungry, sweeping glance all around. He turned on his heel. "You're the caretaker?"

"I—I be that," the fellow stammered in Franconian dialect. His eyes had grown wide. He took off his cloth cap. "Is there—something I can do for you, sir?"

"Just drive my car inside." He was already walking on with long strides. The man stared after him, then hastily turned to do as he was told.

Göring was realizing the truth of the old saying that one's home is always undersized upon return. Surely it had been much bigger, much grander. Here was only a ruined fortress, crude, crumbled, of no extraordinary dimensions. And yet he felt his heart would break with happiness as he took in the walls, the tower, the manor house.

Inside the house, walking through the rooms, he breathed in the stony dampness from his youth. The rooms were bare, his footsteps echoed in the emptiness, but there rose all around him sights, sounds, movement: Vati in his black quilted morning coat, with his scent of talcum and cigar smoke, cracklingly turning the pages of his newspaper; and Mutti, her dark gold hair upswept, going briskly to the kitchen to discuss something with the cook; and Olga and Paula, and Karl bent over a book, one finger abstractedly pushing his sliding spectacles back up his nose . . . and here on the curved oaken staircase, exactly where he placed his foot, here on Christmas Eve they would wait for Nikki, all decked out in her holiday finest, to summon them to the dining room where the giant dark fir stood, blazing with hundreds of candles. . . .

Upstairs he entered his old room. Going over to the leaded, diamond-paned windows, he opened one of them out and stood with his hands spread on the sill, gazing down the rough ancient stonework of his east wall, and down his yet more ancient cliff, down the face of that immense, sheer, jagged drop.

He came back out into the courtyard and the warm afternoon.

The latest tenants had moved some time ago, but the Baronin Lili had not got new ones. For the Baronin Lili—of all strange ironies, a woman not even old, his own age—had died at Mauterndorf on September 1, had slumped over with a fatal heart attack while listening to the news of the Polish invasion. Thus from that war, which he had not wanted, he had gotten back Veldenstein, which he had never stopped wanting. For it transpired that Pate had left him everything in the event of the Baronin's death. From the grave, Pate had restored to him what was his.

He walked through the long grass of the courtyard, much too long, hanging over in clumps, and took a path down through the gardens toward the north wall, where he walked along in the sunlight, pausing once or twice to rub his hand against the warm, time-eaten stone. From a crumbled archway, he brushed back the ivy.

Master builder Erhart has made these walls, towers and doors. May God and the heavenly hosts protect them. Amen.

After a few moments he walked on, seeing the small round stone building that had originally been the burg's powder magazine and in his youth had been used to store potatoes and turnips. He went inside, coming out with a soil-covered turnip in his hand and walking back up to the grassy courtyard. Among the golden autumn trees, the dark work clothes of the caretaker could be made out. He stood up from his work as he was approached.

He could still not understand what Göring was doing here. Of course, Göring and his family had used to live here, he even remembered seeing him in the village as a boy and then as a young cadet. But that was years and years ago. Now he was Feldmarschall, Luftwaffe Commander, Prime Minister of Prussia, second man in Germany. Everyone hereabouts was swollen with pride over him, and he did look magnificent, did unser Hermann . . . not overheavy as in some pictures, just husky, solid, strong. He was in a plain feldgrau uniform. No medals at all but a blue one at his throat. It was a bit disappointing.

You would think he would come in a line of open cars, with pennants flying, him in dress uniform, medals, everything. Instead he came walking up with a turnip in his hand.

"What is your name?"

"Schelling, sir."

"I hope you realize, Schelling, that the lawn and gardens are a total mess."

"The Naumanns didn't keep a steady gardener, sir, only a fellow come up from down below once in a while. They didn't keep a work staff, you see. Only me, I was handyman. 'Tis a big place to keep up alone."

Göring was smiling at him.

"You're not from Neuhaus, are you?"

"Sackdilling, sir."

"I could tell." Sackdilling was a hamlet in the woods. The people there spoke differently from the villagers. "Good hunting around Sackdilling. Used to be. Is it still?"

"Ach ja, nothing ever changes in these parts."

"Tell me, though, didn't the Baronin von Epenstein object to the way things were kept here?"

"She never come, sir."

"What of Epenstein? Did you know him?"

"Nein, I only been working here four years. He were before my time."

"I can tell you he wouldn't have liked to see the place run-down like this—grass up to your knees, the gardens all gone to seed."

"The Naumanns just wouldn't keep no workers but me. They had plenty of money, but tightwads?" He pinched his gnarled thumb and forefinger together. "So tight they squeaked."

Göring laughed, as the caretaker stood beaming.

"Well, we won't be having that problem. Veldenstein is now mine, and I mean to bring in a staff of workers. I want things put back in shape and kept that way. We'll discuss all this when I return. I'll be back in a few weeks. I'll want the villagers invited, I'll have a celebration in the courtyard, a band, plenty of food. If it rains we'll put up a tent. But it won't rain."

He tossed the turnip into the air, caught it, and set it down on a tree stump.

"I want to walk around some more. When I leave I'll open the gate myself and drive out. It's been a pleasure, Schelling. I look forward to working with you."

"And you, sir, a pleasure!" said the caretaker as they shook hands. He felt as if he stood watching an old friend go off.

The Feldmarschall continued his tour, walking through a drift of golden leaves to the watchtower. There he pushed open the door, hearing the same heavy wooden creaking that he had heard forty years before, when he had pushed it open the first time. He walked around the semidark interior, and on impulse felt for the ladder. Putting his foot on the first rung, he began pulling himself up. The ladder was much narrower than he remembered, and much steeper. Yet how could it be anything but steep, built as it was flush into the wall? It was just that he was pulling up a great deal more this time.

At each landing he stood a few moments to regain his breath, then climbed on. The enveloping blackness never changed, nor the close, stale, chilly air. Under his uniform his flesh grew clammy with sweat. He lost track of the landings. He knew there were six, but it seemed he already had a dozen behind him. Straining fist over fist, breathing like a bellows, he felt he would never gain the top, the ladder would go on forever . . . then suddenly he discerned a gleam above him, and with renewed vigor climbed on to the final landing.

Blazing sunlight poured through the four window slots. The winds whirled and keened and whipped his uniform as he walked over to the east slot, where he put his head out over that always startling vastness. The tremendously high wind battered his face, whipped his hair, swept up the gold-edged blue medal at his throat, while below him spread the great reaches of forests and fields, lit in the golden haze.

Chapter 57

THROUGHOUT Europe the closing months of 1939 were the coldest in recent history; but though miserable for many, and even fatal for those unfortunates unable to keep their hovels warm, it was as if the fierce frozenness had locked itself as an ally, a sweetheart, into the arms of peace. Since the fall of Poland nothing had happened; and with the land overlaid with snow as hard as rock, and the trees so rigidly encased that no wind could stir them, not even the gales that swept across the Prussian plains, it was as if the land's immobility suggested some higher power that said stillness would prevail.

In the courtyard at Carinhall, the newly completed lily pond was frozen solid; its goldfish, an exotic rose-gold species longer than a man's foot, had been scooped out with a net and transferred to an aquarium inside, but the lily pads were embedded like metal in the ice, from which rose a bronze equestrian statue of a naked Indian brave about to let fly with his spear; icicles hung in profusion from the horse's underside, smaller icicles like elongated eyeteeth lined the drawn-back, naked arm and the slender, perfectly balanced spear. The wind beat against the statue without effect. It beat against the icicles that hung so thickly from the eaves that they resembled a hanging fence of jagged iron. It beat against the heads of the boars and antlered bucks that were nailed to the walls staring before them with their dark eyes made of glass, heads frost-whitened and contracted by the cold, giving them a pinched, shriveled look.

In the newly completed banquet hall, where Christmas Eve dinner was about to begin, the host was taking his guests around the room and pointing out the six enormous tapestries which he had commissioned, and for which he had provided the designs himself. Each was a quasi-Botticelli scene of undraped maidens in forest glades, and to each he had given a title: Faith. Purity. Simplicity. Goodness. Grace. Mercy.

"I see you've developed the virtues of a saint," Herr Albert Göring remarked to his brother, who turned beamingly from his tour-conducting.

"Come, Albert, you can't ask patrons of art to be saints as well. That's not how it works. Otherwise you would have a—Saint Sforza of the Sparrows. A Saint Medici of the Mendicant Monks."

Pleased with his lyrical improvisations, his arm linked with that of his wife, the Feldmarschall led his guests on through the vast new room, with its rosy marble floor and pillars, its dazzling chandeliers. Many were the comments on the room's magnificence, and he basked in them. At the immense table, covered with Belgian lace over white satin, sparkling with crystal and silver, and bright with decorations of red berries and fresh green fir, he cast a happy look at his sixty guests—family members and house servants—as everyone was seated.

The sixty footmen who seated the diners were no longer in sober blue-and-black livery, but in an eighteenth-century costume of high white suede boots, green velvet tailcoats and knee breeches trimmed in gold braid, and white lace jabots and cuffs. But they were not in the powdered wigs of the period, and their cropped heads and thick necks had a jarring effect atop such finery.

"Is it that the wigs didn't arrive in time?" Frau Emmy's old aunt asked Herr Kropp, the host's valet, who sat next to her. "What a shame," she whispered. "They look so undressed."

"They are not meant to be in wigs, madame. They are wearing the hunting costumes of the old court servants, and wigs were not used on the hunt."

"I see. Yet they do look odd," insisted the old lady in her politely hushed tone. "Be honest, Herr Kropp, don't you think so?"

Herr Kropp, silent for a moment, replied, "The Minister President is a lover of beauty. But he is also a realist."

The Minister President, shaking out his napkin, was greatly pleased with his footmen's appearance, and that anyone could possibly have felt otherwise would have surprised him very much. Chatting with the guests in his vicinity, and tucking one end of his napkin under his chin, he prepared to enjoy the feast to the fullest—there would be time to repent when the groaning tables of Christmas, New Year, and his birthday Opera Ball were behind him. And as the first course was served, he looked actually as if he were going to roll his sleeves up above his elbows in preparation for the attack.

But no, observed his brother, the sleeves remained in place. One was relieved. The napkin hanging down the front of his dinner jacket was bad enough. It was a new eccentricity. He was breaking out in eccentricities like boils. Such as the habit of carrying about a buckskin pouch filled with opals, tourmalines and amethysts, scooping them out and playing with them, letting them run through his fingers, explaining that precious stones discharged the static electricity of the body, that they acted as a sort of alchemical tranquilizer. Right out of the Dark Ages, was Herr Göring's judgment.

"I hear you are no longer living in Vienna," a nephew of Emmy's remarked conversationally over the soup. Herr Göring nodded, but it was not a subject he cared to discuss, and he was glad to be able to turn his attention to his sister Paula, who was exclaiming, "Roswitha, go back at once!"

Paula's small daughter, a little figure in a red velvet dress, had slipped from her place with the other children and darted to Emmy's side, where she stood pestering her.

"But Roswitha, Edda is still too small to eat at the table," Emmy told her with good-natured patience.

"But I would like to *see* her."

"You will, dear, afterward. At the tree."

"The tree!" cried the child, as her mother rolled her eyes in exasperation. From farther down the table, her father motioned sternly that she return to her seat. But she was carried away, her eyes shone, and she ran on alongside the statuelike footmen as guests frowned or smiled according to their nature, and someone singing out "Röslein, Röslein" extended a hand to touch the flying curls. Her goal was her Uncle Hermann; and arriving breathlessly at his side, she took hold of his large ear and whispered something into it that sent them both into a gale of laughter.

"Paula, your daughter tells me I should eat with Edda because I'm wearing a bib!"

There was laughter around the table, and the child, completely beside herself with the massed attention, began a kind of whirling dance, bumping against one of the footmen. It was too much. Hermann gave a loud snap of his fingers, and pointed at the row of seated children where she belonged.

Off she went as directed, and decorously took her place among her small companions, while Emmy, whose thoughts had gone from Roswitha to Röslein to Rose, reflected again upon the strangeness of being entirely out of touch with Rose, although she now lived in Berlin. She had left Weimar. She had quit the theater. They had had one meeting at a friend's house. Rose had looked quite the same, except for a man's big watch around her wrist; but she was not the same, for she had said . . . But Emmy was leaning toward the ear trumpet of her old uncle, who had asked about the festivity at Veldenstein. He had seen pictures in the magazines.

"It was very nice, Uncle Emil," she enunciated roundly into the trumpet. "There was eating, and dancing, and the whole village came."

. . . for Rose had said, I don't want to be protected any longer. I don't want the connection.

"Looked a chilly place to live in. Dampish."

. . . I want to be anonymous. Berlin is huge, and I intend to disappear in it. . . . But how will you live, Rose? Oh, my dear, if you intend to do this foolish thing, at least let us help you.

"Well, of course it is ancient," she said into the ear trumpet.

. . . No, I don't want the connection. You understand that it's not you, Emmy. It is just that I cannot accept the connection any longer. And please don't try to find me. You must give me your word.

"Is what, you say?"

"Ancient. A *ruin*."

"Ah. Like me," cackled Uncle Emil.

"From the picture, Emil, it looks in better condition than you," his old sister dryly teased.

"What does?"

"Veldenstein. *Veldenstein*, Emil."

The Feldmarschall would have preferred not to hear Veldenstein brought up. He had not discussed the disposal of Pate's estate with Albert, but he wondered if Albert might not feel overlooked. Yet despite their blood relationship, Pate and Albert had never been close. Nor had Albert once in his life made mention of that blood relationship. Nor had he ever spoken of Pate except to criticize him. Nein, if Albert felt the slightest rancor, it was unjustified. Anyway, everyone should be happy on Christmas Eve.

But Veldenstein and Mauterndorf did not rankle in Herr Göring's breast. He felt no claim to Epenstein's property. He had never acknowledged in his mind the occasional whisper of gossip, and what was more, he had disliked Epenstein, had always tried to avoid his blasting voice and crashing footfall. It was Hermann who liked him. Hermann was his spiritual heir. It was only right that Hermann should be his material heir as well. What bothered Herr Göring was that having lost his job in the Austrian film industry, which had become an extension of Goebbels's propaganda machine, he had accepted through Hermann's influence a position in one of the Skoda works in Czechoslovakia. He had his wife and children to think of. The security of one's family came first, those deep bonds of love and duty. And he was grateful to his brother. But the fact remained that he who had opposed the gobbling-up of Czechoslovakia was now making a living there, and off the Skoda works.

"A friend of mine, she took hold of her gate handle and her hand froze right to it—"

A plump girl in mauve satin was speaking. The guests, whether family members or servants, were all dressed the same, the women in long gowns, the men in evening clothes. Democracy, mystery, thought Herr Göring. Which of these hands, now raising heavy gilt spoons, mopped the floors and dusted the furniture? Mystery was sustained only as long as the tongue did not reveal its idiom. But democracy was made of stronger stuff, and he responded courteously to the servant girl.

"The cold is terrible, Fräulein. But who knows, it may have its advantages. It is so cold it is too cold for war."

"That's blessed true," she agreed.

"Not in Finland," someone else put in.

"But they're used to it up there," said the girl, who was not sure where Finland was, but pictured it filled with seals and polar bears, and knew it had been attacked by Russia. She also knew that Germany was all for Finland while at the same time being a great friend of Russia. This was confusing, and she might have asked for enlightenment, but the fish course was being served, and her footman also happening to be her sweetheart, she paused to send a discreetly flirtatious look into his bending, impassive face.

"Well, Albert," said Paula's husband, Dr. Hueber, who was to make a Christmas toast in honor of peace, "I shall put in my speech that if it's too cold for war, may it last like the Ice Age."

"It *is* the Ice Age. If the sun turned the whole Reich into Arabia, it would still be the Ice Age."

Farther down the table, Paula was asking Emmy how they would manage to live in all their residences. "You will have to go by caravan," she suggested, at which Emmy laughed, while counting to herself with disbelief the number of homes they now possessed: Carinhall, the Leipziger Platz Palace, the Obersalzberg home, the summer house on Sylt, and now Veldenstein and Mauterndorf, not to mention the official residence of the Reichstag President, or the hunting lodge on Rominten Heath.

"What is the old saying?" asked Hermann's other sister, Olga, in her robust, carrying voice. "Hans owns twenty riding horses, but he's only got one posterior?"

"That's all wrong," Hermann called over to her. "Spirit overcomes matter."

"What a picture!" Olga laughed. "Twenty horses each trotting along beneath a phantasmal backside. Is that Kantian or Platonic, or what?"

"One thing it is not is mathematically sound," put in her husband, Herr Rigele. "There would only be nineteen illusionary posteriors, because the actual one would also be there."

"Nein, nein," she protested, "that would not be spirit over matter. If one actual Hans is riding with the intangible Hanses, that destroys the whole idea."

"But then where is our actual Hans?" demanded her husband. "He must be somewhere!"

It was a good question, thought Albert Göring. Where is our actual Hans? Where is our actual Hermann? And he thought of the chat he had had with General Bodenschatz during the Sudeten crisis. "What is my brother up to, General? I can't figure him." "Well, you must understand that he's got too many responsibilities, Herr Göring. As Luftwaffe Chief it is his duty to bring his forces to their highest peak of power. And as Hitler's spokesman, he believes his belligerent speeches will help deter any interference with the plans of the Führer. But as economic chief he has grave doubts as to Germany's ability to wage a long war. And as a diplomat he regards it as his task to avoid war at all costs." "And he himself . . . ?"

Could they all be as cheerful as they sounded? he wondered. With a general war hanging above like the proverbial Sword of Damocles? Still, it was Christmas Eve. What would be the use of sitting like two rows of death's heads? And he turned to his neighbor on his left.

"Very attractive, the table decorations," he told Fräulein Cilly, the head housekeeper, a woman quite young but matronly in her air of stolid efficaciousness.

Fräulein Cilly blushed. She could not rid herself of her blushes, and she felt they were unworthy of a person of her responsibilities. She said with dignity: "We used five full branches of fir. We had to thaw them first. And the berries were few this year, the cold killed them. The men had to look far and wide. But as you see, we managed."

"And most imaginatively."

"I can't take credit for that," she replied, her blush deepening with adoration. "The Minister President always directs."

"But of course," Herr Göring agreed. "What does the Minister President not direct?"

On his other side, Herr Kropp was answering someone's question concerning the big goldfish in the aquarium. The valet said that they had had to be removed from the courtyard pond when it began to freeze.

"I noticed the new statue out there," Herr Göring said to him. "Very striking, but to my knowledge Indians used bows and arrows, not spears."

"Is that so?" asked Herr Kropp. "I don't rightly know, but I believe the Minister President said that in Karl May they used spears as well."

"Karl May. Karl May didn't know a damn thing about Indians. He wrote his Wild West sagas in a Saxon jail cell. They're nothing but a heap of fantasy."

To this rather rude statement Herr Kropp, quite properly, made no reply.

The main course was being served. All along the table the guests were getting into gustatory high gear, and the host took a roving, gratified look around, for he possessed to a high degree the gift of enjoying not only himself but the pleasure of others. There was no doubt, thought Herr Göring, that much of Hermann's delight in his enormous riches lay in the sharing of them. Greedy he might be, but stingy he was not.

"Why is it," he asked conversationally, "that the major flaws are always more acceptable than the minor, petty ones?"

Emmy's nephew took up the question with cerebral ardor.

"It seems an incontestable fact of human nature. One thinks of Talleyrand's remark that the world can accept pillage and disembowelment, but not cheating at cards."

"Or that case in Halle a while back," interposed Herr Rigele. "That hired killer who strangled the wealthy old husband at the wife's request? Do you recall? And on being caught was also charged with stealing the old man's wallet?"

"I remember," said the nephew, "and he protested with indignation, 'I am a killer, not a dirty little pickpocket.'"

"Ja, and the odd thing was that in reading the newspaper account, one saw his point. One protested along with him, and felt the shameful triviality of the police in even suggesting such a thing. It was only a momentary reaction, but it was the first, the instinctive one." Herr Rigele added with a sigh: "What a depressing admission."

"But an honest one," said the nephew. Then corrected himself. "Forgive my tautology. An admission is always honest."

"I thought he stabbed him," said the plump girl in mauve. "I followed it close. I could have sworn he stabbed him."

Herr Rigele gave a shake of his head. "Strangulation."

"How is young Kantzow these days?" Herr Göring asked Emmy across the table. "What do you hear from him?"

"Ach," she replied with a woeful shake of her head. "He has gone to Finland to volunteer."

"Volunteer? Kantzow?" And he remembered how he had said, with an ironic eyebrow raised, "I wish you well, Herr von Kantzow," when the boy had cavalierly assured him he wanted to return home by air—going to his doom as far as he knew, a dead sky voyager, but at least a sky voyager. So he was still at it, he had not escaped his sad little destiny. But taking a plane was one thing, bearing arms was another. He had been a pacifist. Even that, apparently, had shriveled up in the blaze of the man who sat there at the head of the table. I'm being melodramatic, Herr Göring reproached himself, taking a sip of his wine. "Seems a little out of character for him," he said to Emmy.

"I know. I can't think what has come over him."

"Strange."

"Nothing strange about it," Hermann said. "He's going like every volunteer who has ever gone to defend an unjustly attacked people. He's going because he doesn't want a Bolshevik takeover. He's going because Sweden and Finland are historically entwined. He's going in order to fight for a righteous cause. And he's going because he's young and wants to test his manhood. I don't think there's any mystery about it."

And he returned to his roast goose, as Herr Kropp said to himself: Now he is beginning to go red. It was a heat phenomenon caused by his weight. When the Minister President ate heavily, one saw it happen before one's eyes: his face became suffused with blood, particularly the cheeks. Indeed, his enemies circulated the story that he used rouge, and this malicious gossip angered Herr Kropp very much.

Göring's face was not only very red, it shone with sweat, which he frequently mopped with the end of his napkin. The more he ate, the hotter he became. But the variety of flavors and texture, the toothsome, luscious chomping, with its grinding and sucking of savory juices, the full-bodied swallowing, the buoyant coursing down of wine—all this blotted out the uncomfortable heat of his body, and sometimes even his surroundings. At such moments his pleasure was so intense, so absorbing, that he was capable only of a vague nod in response to conversation directed at him.

But one good thing about his master's feasting, thought Herr Kropp, at least it would make him sleep soundly. His insomnia had been acute for some time. Only the night before, Herr Kropp had been summoned in the small hours to find him walking back and forth in his nightshirt.

"Bring me something to eat, will you, Robert? I finally got to sleep but I dreamed of a trout." "You wish a plate of trout?" "Nein, that's not what I mean. It was just the flick of a fish but it woke me up." "If it was just a flick, how do you know it was a trout? Perhaps it was a salmon. Shall I bring salmon?" "If I say it was a trout, it was a trout." "But you don't want trout? Or salmon either? What about some herring?" "All I want, dammit, is a roast beef sandwich and some beer!"

At least tonight he would not wake up hungry and argumentative, Herr Kropp said to himself as Dr. Hueber got to his feet.

"Meine Damen und Herren!"

Holding one of the four wineglasses that stood before his plate, each representing a different period of French and German glassmaking, Dr. Hueber waited until the table grew subdued. He nodded to his host and to his hostess.

"How great a joy it is to gather here on Christmas Eve . . ."

How great a joy, thought the Feldmarschall. How welcome was the warmth and family cheer of the holiday season after these last three months of ceaseless activity. First the trip to Poland . . . what satisfaction in ruined Warsaw to see the effectiveness of his Luftwaffe. Especially since it must have made Britain shake in her boots. Yet it was possible that most of the destruction had been caused by artillery shelling. The stubbornness of the Warsaw commander was deplorable; encircled and besieged, the city would not surrender. When the Führer ordered Göring to end the siege with a supreme Luftwaffe effort, he had first had thousands of leaflets dropped, stating that the city would be bombed if it did not surrender; he had got word to the Warsaw commander that if he refused to raise the white flag, he had better evacuate the civilian population. But every damned Pole was determined to fight to the last breath; and so he had sent out his order: attack. Yet as he drove through the gray ruins, he wondered who could ever sort it out, shelling or bombing. It must forever remain a question mark. Then on to inspect Polish agricultural and industrial areas, then back to Berlin, where economic decisions were forced upon him at such a rate that each morning he could scarcely remember what he had signed the day before—

". . . we are united not only by the bonds of family, but by our hope that Germany, Europe, all the world, might be free of strife and war . . ."

—mostly details, those endless documents, but on the main point he was very clear. Germany must squeeze every ounce of usefulness from her victory. Raw materials must be seized, Jewish property confiscated, at least a million Polish laborers hired to work in the factories of the Reich. He had signed these broad directives knowing they were harsh measures that were absolutely necessary. An irreversible process had been entered upon, a circular, tail-biting process: the larger your forces grew, and the more arms they used, and the more territory they took over, the more of everything was needed to support it all—

". . . Christmas is always a time of rejoicing, but I know too that in the heart of each of us lies a graveness, for we cannot help but wonder if, when we gather on this Eve next year, it will be a time of war . . ."

—one thing was certain, Germany could not withstand a long war. She had not had time enough to prepare for one, she lacked the resources. The Polish campaign was one thing, but a protracted, general war would be disastrous. He was still seeking a peaceful solution through Dahlerus, and there were signs that Britain might come to some agreement if Germany withdrew from Poland, keeping only Danzig and the Corridor. But that was impossible; the Führer would never relinquish Poland now that he had conquered it. What's more, if the Army moved out, Russia would move in from her ample portion and take it all. Poland was lost, and Britain must forget about her. Britain must come to realize there was no point in going to war. Germany had no designs whatsoever on Britain; Germany had no other wish than to leave her alone. Thus why should the British make unnecessary problems for themselves? For everyone? Plunge Europe into war over lost Poland? For Poland was indeed lost. Part of Poland was to provide living space for German settlers, the rest to be governed as a conquered territory; she was to be destroyed as a national entity, meaning that the Polish intelligentsia must be prevented from throwing up another leader class, meaning that the professional classes would be annihilated . . . were being annihilated . . . many unprecedented things had been done, were being done—

". . . we hope that war will not come, and if our hope has meaning and viability, it is in great part due to the vigorous and continuing efforts of the Feldmarschall, our host, our Hermann. Damen und Herren, I propose a toast to the success of those efforts. May the New Year bring us reason to rejoice."

The toast was taken up wholeheartedly. "To peace!" The Feldmarschall drank, they all drank, the meal continued.

"You must ask him, my dear," replied Emmy to her nephew's fiancée, who had asked her which period of history the Feldmarschall favored, whether medieval, Renaissance, or eighteenth century, for it seemed that every era was represented at Carinhall.

But the girl, being shy, shook her head.

"Oh but do." Emmy smiled. "He doesn't bite, you know."

The girl gathered courage to speak. But just then Albert Göring stood up.

"I should like to add a few words to Dr. Hueber's speech. It was a good speech as far as it went, but it didn't go far enough. We should not only pray for peace, we should pray for a change of the regime."

What is this idiot saying? thought Göring, swiping his mouth with his napkin.

"Germany will not have peace, or freedom or honor, as long as he who is in command remains in command. Last month at the Bürgerbräukeller an attempt was made on his life . . ."

An inner groan went through Göring. It had been such a fine evening; now Albert was going to ruin it. Why was he bringing up the assassination attempt? Didn't he know that he, Göring, because illness had kept him from attending the Bürgerbräukeller commemoration this year, was actually suspected in some quarters of being involved? He took a deep swallow of wine, his eyes narrowed at his brother.

". . . an attempt made by an ordinary working-class citizen, it should be noted. The attempt failed, as we know, because the corporal cut short his speech by an hour and a half and left, thus escaping the explosion. That is his famous sixth sense, say his admirers. His extraordinary instinct. His mystical grasp of what is beyond the common ken. Others say that it is God who protects him. I say it was an attack of gastritis . . ."

In spite of himself, Göring felt an inner guffaw. Let him stay funny, and let him get finished.

". . . I don't believe in the corporal's mystical instinct, and I certainly don't believe he is protected by God. Because if he is protected by God, then God has forgotten Germany . . ."

For six years, Göring thought, he has been talking like this. It was not easy to have such a brother, always needing to be fished out of some difficulty with the Gestapo. But he was one's brother and one loved him, pain in the ass that he could be. One even admired his outspokenness.

". . . I believe that God wants the corporal put aside. May he and all that he stands for be supplanted by righteous forces. That is my Christmas wish, Damen und Herren. I thank you."

Everyone was looking at Göring. He was not pleased, but neither did he appear angry. He gave a shrug of his great shoulders, and smiled.

"At my table, one may say what he likes. Thank you for your interesting comments, Albert."

General conversation resumed. The plates of the main course were cleared away. The young fiancée, blushing deeply, got her question out to the Feldmarschall.

"I am always asked that question, Fräulein," he told her genially. "Which historical era do I favor? All. All."

Sipping his wine, Albert Göring was disappointed with the words he had spoken. He had not been harsh enough. He had slipped into humor, as if to take the edge off, when what he had wanted was the sharpest of all edges. And then to have it all flattened by Hermann's pleasant shrug, his dismissive remark. Yet what had he anticipated? An outburst of anger? A passionate statement of agreement? "Yes, and I am that righteous force." He did not know what he had anticipated, or if he had anticipated anything. And he sat looking at the tall windows, at the still, starry night above the frozen forest.

"Ach, ist es wunderbar!" a small voice suddenly cried, and little Roswitha noisily clapped her hands as the flaming desserts were brought in, multitudinous tongues of fire soaring gold and red from the silver platters.

Chapter 58

HELGA, Hilde and Helmut—the two youngest children, Holde and Hedda, ate with the nursemaid upstairs—sat in a steplike row at the table, and as always, their beauty was a marvel to Frau Quandt. All five were utterly, exquisitely beautiful. In coloring some resembled the mother, some the father, but they resembled only themselves in their almost poignant flawlessness. One could not help but rest one's eyes long, long on those small faces, as if on the loveliest of God's masterworks.

If Frau Quandt mused upon the children more than was her habit, if she mused upon all kinds of things, it was because her attention was not tied by the slightest thread of interest to what she was eating. It was a one-pot austerity meal, the pot itself standing in the middle of the beautifully arranged table. It was filled with stew, and it was not bad stew, but it was stew, and would probably be followed by vanilla pudding made from a powder packet. Frau Quandt had undergone similar meals at Schwanenwerder these last few months, but she had not expected the Goebbelses' fanatic sharing of the people's lot to extend to Christmas Eve dinner. Yet why not? If Magda was so patriotically dedicated to wartime austerity measures that she even conserved gasoline by taking the crowded S-bahn or U-bahn, like any ordinary Hausfrau, why should she not serve stew on Christmas Eve?

Frau Quandt always spent Christmas at her parental home in

Brandenburg, but this year the severe cold had precluded railway travel; thus she had gladly accepted Magda's invitation, and even if the food was dismal, it was very nice to be warm. In her flat she had to keep her coat and gloves on all the time. Here the big dining room, the whole house, was beautifully heated.

Goebbels was holding forth, as usual. The table talk had turned to a letter which had appeared today in the *Berliner Morgenpost:* "Rudolf Hess Addresses an Unmarried Mother." Frau Quandt had read Herr Hess's message. It was supposedly addressed to a pregnant girl whose fiancé had been killed in Poland, but she was only a theoretical girl upon which to hang words: "A pure-blooded soldier has fallen for his country, and has left behind him a child to carry on the German race. The highest law is the preservation of the race. Every law, custom and opinion had to adapt itself to this highest law . . ."

". . . such an unmarried mother may have a hard path," Goebbels was saying, "but she knows it is better to have a child under the most difficult conditions than not to have one at all. What's more, from now on such a child will not have the word 'illegitimate' stamped on its birth certificate, but the words 'War Father.'" And he quoted the final phrase of Hess's letter: "'Be happy, good woman, that you have been allowed to perform this highest duty for Germany.' The highest duty of a woman today is to continue the Fatherland's heritage; the onus must be removed from unmarried mothers . . ."

He talked on and on, as he did over the radio, and Frau Quandt was reminded of a brutal joke: when Goebbels dies, they're going to have to kill his mouth extra.

She looked around at the other stewpot guests: relatives of Magda, relatives of Goebbels. The Minister's small gray-haired mother was there, and his sister and brother-in-law . . . the same sister to whose house Frau Quandt had been brought in a state of collapse by the Gestapo. How strange that she and the sister should be seated here tonight, as if that evening had never happened. Stranger yet that this was also true of Frau Quandt and her host, that everything was just as before, that he and Magda were right back together again.

Yet Frau Quandt had seen it coming. Very slowly, Josef had wooed his wife back. How, exactly, he had done this, Frau Quandt did not know. She only knew that Magda's attitude toward State Secretary Hanke had gradually changed. "He is an honest, well-mannered, intelligent man, Ello, but in many ways his education is deficient . . ." "He feels himself a modern-day knight, he idealizes the ancient chivalric tradition, and that is wonderful, but somehow . . ." "He adores me, Ello, but he lacks spark; he's a hardworking, good man, but . . ." "I was terribly unhappy with Josef, I thought perhaps I could find some quiet happiness with a more ordinary kind of man, but . . ." "I cannot forgive his treachery toward Josef, how can one respect such a man? . . ."

"I have told him that it is over . . ." By this time the stipulated year had come to an end, Josef had moved back into the house, Magda was radiant. But Hanke's presence disturbed the reconciled couple. "He has been promoted, Ello. He is to be Gauleiter of Silesia and live in the Castle of Breslau. The son of an engine driver is now going to be chief official in his native province. I think that will make him very happy."

Who knew if Hanke was happy? But Magda surely was. Frau Quandt had given up trying to understand her. In some deep way Magda was bound to, needed, this small slope-browed man who was still talking as the stewpot was removed from the table. And he was faithful now. That terrible thorn had been removed from his wife's side. Not one whisper of romantic gossip had attached to him during the entire year of their separation, or in these several months that they had now been living together again. All was well with them. The Doctor once again enjoyed Hitler's favor, and worked night and day to keep wartime morale high, although in private it was clear that he did not want war. Nor did Magda. Nor, it seemed to Frau Quandt, did anyone. But if war came, the morale must be there. And it was there in both of them, in her large violet-blue eyes, and in his dark, liquid ones—a shining, glowing quality, a sense of unitedness, of dedication.

The patriotic pot was gone, the patriotic pudding had been brought in. Helga, Hilde and Helmut, who, in addition to their great beauty, were extremely well-mannered, betrayed no disappointment. And as Frau Quandt spooned up the grainy dessert, she wondered idly, as she sometimes did, why all five children had been given names beginning with H. She had once asked Magda, who had said she didn't really know, it had just turned out that way; but Frau Quandt had a feeling that whether Magda was aware of it or not, she had named them all for the Leader.

While Frau Quandt's thoughts wandered, long lines of bundled-up Berliners stood waiting for the S-bahn train on the blacked-out platform of the Friedrichstrasse station. It was true that Frau Minister Goebbels had taken to riding the S-bahn like any commoner, but she had lately given up this mode of travel. The once supremely punctual trains now followed no schedule whatever; it was all chance and hope. When switches were frozen and buried under snow, when the electric motors became clogged with ironlike ice, and when half the railway workers had been called into the Army or munitions factories, it could not be otherwise. With much foot-stamping and muffled beatings of gloved hands, but with no grumbling, the long lines on the dark freezing platform had been waiting for more than an hour. Now, as the train appeared at last, the queues broke into rushing mobs. Some of the train doors were frozen shut, but others could be worked moderately apart, and through these narrow openings the crowds pushed and squeezed.

The train emerged from the station onto the elevated tracks, below which the blacked-out city spread. The crammed coaches swayed. Now and then, because of the wheels' ice-coated electrical contacts touching the third rail, there was a dazzling flash of white sparks that made everyone inside look momentarily ghostlike.

Rose had been lucky enough to find a seat. With her beret pulled down over her achingly cold ears, she held on her lap, along with her purse, a net shopping bag containing a few small Christmas parcels. She was already half an hour late for Christmas Eve dinner at her Cousin Max's, but God willing the twelve-minute ride to Bellevue would pass without a breakdown. Another flash of white lit the coach through the glaciated windows, and she saw with an instinctive nostril flare that she sat next to a man in a heavy-duty SA overcoat. Simultaneously there was a heart-sickening loss of speed. Groans were followed by a crushed silence as the train came to a dead stop. It might stand here between signal posts for ten minutes, or thirty, or sixty, held up by frozen switches. Rose wanted to bang her purse furiously on her knees. Instead, she brought out a cigarette with her gloved fingers and lit it, although she was not in a smoking car.

Voices rang out: "Smoking verboten!"

Exhaling one deep puff, she sharply tapped out the ember and returned the cigarette to her pack. A slurred, drunken voice was suddenly heard, "Verboten, verboten . . . alles verboten! Scheisse . . . those posters, 'Nobody Shall Hunger or Freeze'—even *that's* verboten now! . . ."

The brownshirt was clambering past her knees. He pushed over to where the treasonous drunk sat, and in the darkness seized him by the shoulder. "What did you just say?" he demanded. But from the drunk came a confused, cringing silence, a mute fearfulness that one could almost smell through the icy cold. Keeping his grip on the drunk, the brownshirt turned to someone else. "I need you as a witness, sir. What did this traitor just say?"

"Did he say something? I was sitting here sound asleep, I just woke this minute."

"You, madame, will you please repeat what this man has just said?"

"Me? Do you think I listen to the babbling of drunks? I've no idea what he said."

After several more such responses, the SA man came barging back past Rose's legs and flung himself down in his seat. With angry movements, he lit a cigarette. No one snapped "Smoking verboten!" They had used up their boldness, they feared he might do something unpredictable.

What if he should demand to see everyone's identification? Rose thought. She never carried her identification. Because she always went places forbidden to Jews, and often broke the eight o'clock curfew imposed on Jews, she felt that the simplest thing was to leave her papers at home. If she was asked for them—never once had she been—she would simply say she had lost them, or they had been stolen from her purse. But how flimsy that story now seemed. Why hadn't she realized this before? Why, as always, had she neglected to think clearly? In the glow of his cigarette, the eyes of the SA man were wrathful.

In the past she had been protected by Göring. Now she had severed that connection. For almost a year she had been without it. She had also left the circle of her Berlin theater friends, wanting to be free of her reputation as a Göring pet. She had wanted to be entirely anonymous, entirely independent. She had not achieved this. When your papers identified you as a Jew, and when you were registered with the police as a Jew, you were not anonymous. And when you were beholden to Cousin Max and his gentile wife for getting you a room and a job, you were not independent. But she had come as close to a free life as was possible.

Her room was on Ziegelstrasse, just over the Spree from the Friedrichstrasse station. The owner of the building, a gentile, was a friend of Max and his wife. Thus she had escaped being assigned to a Jewish house. Jews new to the city, seeking a place to live, were assigned to apartment buildings already predominantly Jewish. She had not realized how many thousands of Jews had flocked to Berlin since Kristallnacht, pouring in from villages and towns and other cities to lose themselves in the hugeness of the capital. Just as she herself had done. But she had been fortunate; she had not wound up in an apartment house figuratively stamped with a J. If her room was dismal—she could afford no better—it at least had the smallness and remoteness that she associated with anonymity.

She had also been lucky in regard to work. Another friend of Max and his wife was a fashion designer, Jewish, whose dresses and patterns were a great boon to the garment industry, bringing into the Reich badly needed foreign currency. The fashion designer lived well, she had two Jewish assistants, both sheltered under her work permit, and when her cleaning woman retired she took Rose in her place, listing her as a third assistant. The wages of a cleaning woman were small, but they were enough to live on, and she was protected by her employer's work permit.

Now suddenly she might lose everything—her job, her room—yet even in her anxiety she saw how laughable it was to want so badly to go on mopping floors and living in a cubicle with stained wallpaper, freezing and starved for decent food—although cold and hunger were the lot of everyone just now. Too little fuel to combat the arctic temperature; and the austerity food program worsened by the absence of fruits and vegetables, all rotten and frozen black; and tinned goods verboten, doubtlessly being saved for the war. And so people ate bread and macaroni, and there was no great amount of these things either; and if you were a Jew you were allowed to shop only in the late afternoons when most everything was gone. It was perhaps not much of a life, but it was the life she had secured for herself.

And she went wherever she wished. Across Wilhelmplatz, down Wilhelmstrasse, along the north sidewalk of Unter den Linden from the university to the canal, all places specifically forbidden to Jews. She walked there because she always had, she felt the right; and the right was on her face; it was the worried brow and uneasy eye that gave a person away; it was the arrogance of naturalness that made for anonymity. No one questioned her. She went to cinemas and museums, bought cheap seats at the theater and concert hall, and because she had the right, and the right was on her face, no one questioned her. She ignored the eight-o'clock curfew, because night was hers as well as day.

But she had never sat crammed beside an angry representative of the enemy who at any moment might confront the person nearest him in a display of power. "No papers? It is forbidden to be without papers. You say you lost them? You say they were stolen? Make up your mind which lie it is!" And at the next station he would hustle her off for questioning, and her drab-walled little sanctuary would be taken from her along with her cleaning job, because she was depriving an Aryan of work she had no right to.

He had tossed down his cigarette and was grinding it out under his heel. She would be sent to a house filled with Jews hungering for anonymity and having none; she would be unemployed and dependent upon some Jewish charity organization; and even if she wanted to move in with Cousin Max and his wife and become a family parasite, which she did not want, that was also forbidden: no new Jew in any but a Jewish building. She must do something quickly, before he spoke— pretend a fit—something—

But the brownshirt was leaning back. He crossed his arms. He looked out the ice-covered window, and through his nostrils released a prosaic sigh. His wrath had wearied. He too only wanted to get wherever he was going for Christmas. Within herself, and throughout the coach, she felt a sense of untightening. And she wondered what he could actually have done. Any citizen could turn in a grumbler, that didn't take a uniform. What special thing could brownshirts do? Who, besides the Gestapo, was empowered to demand papers? She did not know, nor probably did anyone else in the coach. They only knew that the presence of a brown or black uniform opened up the unknown, where nothing could be predicted. But the tension was gone now; they had all returned to the concrete, miserable known. And it was heaven, she thought, heaven to sit here shivering, feet two lumps of ice, stomach growling for Christmas dinner, and only worry when the train would start. It was a worry akin to nothing, because her little sanctuary was still hers, and her life would go on as before.

An austere life. She seldom visited Max, and never anyone else, except Dr. Weinblatt.

"I'm afraid this must be my last visit," she had told him soon after her move to Berlin, sitting before the tall elegant windows with their upper panes of pale green and lilac stained glass.

"Natürlich," he said. "It was unwise for you to come at all."

And she realized that all this time he had taken her for Aryan, as was—as had been—the larger part of his clientele.

"No, it isn't that," she explained. "I am, how to put it, fully qualified to be here. It's only that I can no longer afford the fee. That is the embarrassing truth."

He had nevertheless set about examining her teeth, his eyebrows, which like his fringe of hair were now completely white, rising high in their usual fashion as he peered at the two strong, pearly, gleaming rows.

"For me it has been a privilege to look at these teeth, Fräulein Korwan. Whatever one's field, whatever one's overriding interest in life, one experiences a sense of wonder and gratification to behold perfection, to gaze upon the ideal. Nicht? There is no fee. Come as always. You say you now live nearby? Then come more frequently. Come once a month."

Thus once a month she visited Dr. Weinblatt. But she made no friends where she lived, nor had she a lover. No man shared her narrow bed with its lumpy mattress, or sat on her worn armchair afterward, pulling on his socks and shoes. If she was to be anonymous, she must be alone. When the cold let up, things would be better. But it would still be a lonely existence. That was how it must be if she was to endure, and she meant to endure. The regime must inevitably collapse, for it employed treacherous and brutal methods which could not achieve good ends, and thus could not long exist in the world. When it came crashing down, she meant to walk through its dirty debris and kick clear a space of clean German ground, and to stand there, just stand there, with Walther's watch around her wrist.

Beneath the elevated tracks where the S-bahn train stretched immobile, like a long metal serpent frozen in sleep, a small car with hooded dim-out lights sped between hillocks of snow, swerving and releasing yelps of alarm and laughter from the three roller skaters stuffed into the small interior. These were three American girls who were appearing at a Berlin variety hall. Two were squeezed in the backseat with a cumbersome pair of crutches, the third sat next to the driver, a short, thickset, middle-aged man with a cigar in the side of his mouth, who had greatly appreciated their story and was still exclaiming "Wonderful!" in English as he sped on toward the black Spree.

The three girls had been invited to a Christmas gathering, and had wanted to go by taxi. But because of the terrible cold, taxis were forbidden to all but government officials and people having to go to the hospital, so the trio had borrowed an appropriate prop and stood on the street corner, one girl draped piteously on the crutches, the other two solicitously holding her. But no taxi went by. They were half frozen when the little car skidded to a stop and they were offered a lift. "Wonderful!" the driver laughed again as they sped across the Spree. "Professional roller skaters mit crutches, it hits the funny bone. That's how you say it, funny bone? And where are you going, Kaiserallee you say? I'll take you there."

"You really drive like a bat out of hell," one screamed admiringly as they swerved onto the broad avenue of the Siegsallee. The frozen trees of the Tiergarten were zipping past. Now and then you glimpsed one of the heroic marble statues made crazy-looking by long icicles. "Hey, we heard a joke. Germany's new pals, the Russians, threw the cold in free with their friendship pact."

The driver gave another loud laugh at this. He was a cheerful fellow. Although there was a faint smell of liquor on his breath, he wasn't drunk. He drove fast, but well, and his voice was clear. He had on a heavy overcoat, a heavy scarf was wrapped around his neck, a fedora pulled down over his ears. The cigar, which had gone out, moved up and down whenever he laughed or talked. "How is it that you girls stay here in Berlin? Mostly all the Ausländer are gone—weg!"

"Who wants to stay? We're trying to get a booking in a variety hall in Amsterdam. Hey, what kind of work are you in?"

"Me? How to say? I'm connected with birds."

There was a triple scream of laughter. "You work on a chicken farm?"

"I work in a zoo," he said emphatically.

"A zoo? Really? That's fascinating."

"Ja, fascinating."

They had turned off the Siegsallee in the direction of the center of town. "It's really crazy along the Kurfürstendamm, all those store windows filled with everything and nobody can buy it. All those signs saying goods displayed in windows are not for sale. What's the point? The other day we saw a candy shop with the most gorgeous chocolate boxes in the window, and the sign said, 'Display is made of empty boxes.' We just stood there and laughed, we couldn't help it."

"It's for the look of things," the driver said with a shrug. "But now I invite you for a drink. You have your Christmas party, I also go to one. But first, I take you to a nice bar on Kurfürstendamm—"

"Thanks, but we really can't, we're already way late." It was clear to the three girls that the jaunty zoo worker had amorous designs; flirtation was rich in his voice. They were not late, and they had nothing against flirting, but he was of an age beyond their realm of imagination.

He left them off at the Kaiserallee address they had given him. They plunged out into the freezing night, laughing and waving the two crutches. "Thanks a million, you saved our lives! Merry Christmas—and good luck with your birds!"

"Thanks," he laughed, pulling the car door shut. He made a tight turn, and sped back down the dark street, thinking that it was too bad they were late for their party. Pleasant things might have developed.

But most of his thoughts, as always these days, centered on the problem of the Ju-88. It had started off as a high-speed bomber with long range, but the General Staff had required it to be a diver as well. As a diver it needed extra equipment, and being heavier it was slower, and being slower it needed more armaments, a vicious circle that had doubled the plane's weight and drastically reduced its range. In two years it had gone through 25,000 changes, and was still being worked on. Not only was the Ju-88 drastically behind schedule, all the Luftwaffe program goals had been slowed down by the raw material shortage. And it all falls on my shoulders, he thought. Udet has to give the production figures, Udet has to give the guided tours . . .

As the deskbound former air ace had come more and more to realize the labyrinthian complexities of the air armament functions and his own lack of a comprehensive view, he had come more and more to put things into the hands of his subordinates. The organizational genius, Milch, he did not seek advice from, for the Air Ministry now consisted of Milchians and Udetians, between whom there was no cooperation. Milch bitterly resented Udet's direct access to Göring; Udet guarded his privilege jealously; but this privilege made all the clearer to him his lack of efficacy, and thus he tended, when conferring with Göring, to put a rosy hue on things. And when he took Göring and Hitler on guided tours, he found himself giving overoptimistic information about the planes they looked at. Many times, in spite of himself, he indicated the readiness of a plane which in actuality could not be perfected for several years. But, he thought, Hermann knows that, he *must* realize it. The one thing he really fears is fine weather, he says so. He *knows* we're not ready. But he knows we won't be any readier in six months or even a year. We haven't enough airfields, no night bombers, no bombs over five hundred kilograms, no communication between bomber squadrons and fighter escorts; we lack fully trained commanders at every level, we lack a reserve force, we lack iron, steel, aluminum . . . it's all empty chocolate boxes. We won't be up to a general war until 1942 or '43. And is that my fault? Any service that's been in official existence for less than five years can't be expected to reach its peak in that time, it's impossible. Impossible . . .

And with the word "impossible," his mind went back again to the Ju-88 quandary, and then, with a sharp shake of his head, like that of a horse ridding itself of buzzing flies, he turned up Wielandstrasse.

Behind one of the dark facades an exuberant party was in progress. The hostess was a sculptress, fortunately well-to-do, since her work was forbidden to be exhibited anywhere except in her own living room. Large primitive stone forms of an African nature, many with hats and coats slung over them, stood about the dimly lit room, where people were dancing to American jazz. Mixed with the music from the phonograph was a din of mirth edged with strain. Everyone was trying too hard.

The din rose in welcome as Udet entered, stomping his cold feet and pulling off his heavy overthings, regaling everyone with some joke about roller skaters on crutches. "Fork over thirty marks, Ernst," his hostess demanded, planting a kiss on his icy cheek. "I had to bribe the boiler-room man to get some heat into the radiator tonight. So the whole damn building's heated, and all at my expense, so you've all got to chip in."

Udet dragged out some bills and stuck them in the low neckline of her gown. "Wait," he said. "Something's wrong here. Your neighbors should be contributing. Where's my hat? I'll take it from door to door."

"Don't be silly, my love, something's wrong everywhere. Have a drink."

"We'll form a conga line," he went on, strolling to the bar with his arm around her. "Everybody get your hats, we're doing a conga line through the whole building!"

Bursts of laughter went up; it seemed a fine idea. People retrieved their hats from the stone figures and formed a conga line. It pounded zestfully around and around the room, but it never did get out the door because it kept waiting for Udet, who, in the whiskey-rich bustle of the bar, had forgotten the enterprise.

"So beautiful," murmured Frau Schmidt, listening to the Christmas Eve church bells sounding from outside. "And yet I'll tell you," she said to her husband, sitting across from her at their small dinner table, festively laid, "I'll tell you they can never compare to that one little church bell in the village . . . oh, its sound has never stopped reverberating in my heart! And now you will know it too, Hans."

Frau Schmidt had undergone a great change in recent months. She was poetic, her step was again brisk, she often laughed. And Herr Schmidt, too, was recognizable as his former self. He had emerged from his senescent drowsiness, his body was not so badly bent over, he did not drag about so shufflingly. "And isn't it true what I always said?" she went on. "The air? The high, pure, beautiful air?"

"'Tis true." He nodded.

Göring had invited them to his homecoming festivity, sending a special chauffeured car. He had squashed Nikki in a bear hug. "So you see, Nikki, it has happened. Here we stand again." She could not speak for her tears, she could not say a word. "Well, clearly you must live here. You belong here. And you, Herr Schmidt, look at these wretched gardens. You must revive them. You must act as my head gardener."

Hans had felt ecstasy flowing through his old body, almost a sense of faintness. "I don't mean that you should labor and sweat," Göring had gone on. "Only supervise. Supervise, Herr Schmidt. Who in Franconia knows more about gardening than you?"

"'Twas like a dream," Hans said now, having for a moment forgotten to eat. He was to have a garden again. Tiers of gardens. And at Burg Veldenstein.

This unbelievable thing that had happened to the old couple was their single topic. And they need wait only a short while longer. Scores of workmen had been laboring around the clock to fit out the old place with central heating. When Göring wanted something done, it was done.

"We'll be much warmer there," Nikki said with an admonitory look at the green tiled stove, whose mild heat proceeded from some chunks of factory furniture wood.

"But you've got to admit it's nice of the child."

"As far as I'm concerned, Hans, we're just a receptacle for her good deeds. What's more, her uncle works there, he's always loading her up with wood scraps. It's no sacrifice for her to give us some. I disliked Minna the day she came with our cake, and I still dislike her."

"True, she's hard to figure. But then they all are, the young ones."

And for both of them, as they sat there, the reality of their daily lives—the restrictiveness of their city dwelling, the remoteness of their neighbors, the sack-of-wood visits from war-spouting Minna, the pressing threat of war, even the fierce cold outside—these things were already fading in the glow of their moving day.

Chapter 59

H E was from the Allier, and had never before laid eyes on the sea. Like other inlanders in his unit he was distrustful of so much water, had no wish to know it better. Stone jetties and wooden piers, and piers created from abandoned vehicles, stretched into the water, where small waiting boats rocked and bobbed like wine corks. Long columns filed out along these piers and jumped down into the bobbing corks. Other columns filed down the beach itself and waded out to other bobbing corks. *"Ce n'est pas naturel,"* he murmured, watching torsos and shoulders disappear under oily waves.

At first confusion had been great, everyone had run around like mad trying to escape the bombs. But there was nowhere to escape to, one spot was like another. So the running had ended. Also, the soldiers realized, the bombs were digging deep into the sand. The explosions remained an endless torment, but they weren't devastating in the way bombs were when they struck hard ground. So it had become like sitting in a cinema theater. There was no conversation, it was useless to shout against the Stukas' screaming. You just sat, watched. Sometimes you saw little because of the smoke billowing black from the town behind the beach, and from the oil tanks on the docks and the British destroyer keeled over on one side in the water. But usually the smoke was blown back by the sea wind, which stank of brine like pickled pigs' feet, and you could see the air battles above the late May sky, not the strong clear blue of the sky at home this time of year, but a washed-out chilly gray. The Stukas did not do too well against the British airplanes. They were slow, and they were shot down and plunged into the sea, where they exploded. But more always came.

At night there was artillery fire instead of the Luftwaffe. Shells burst over the beach and water in brilliant red flashes. The flames from the docks roared high into the dark. Everything was red, and was doubled by the black water's reflection.

By the third day it was clear that the French troops were going to be evacuated last. But he doubted it would make much difference, since the evacuation was getting nowhere under the constant bombardment.

The next morning a miracle moved in. It was not like any fog he knew. This sea fog was like clammy gray cotton wool, you couldn't make out the man next to you. There were no screaming Stukas, no bombs exploding in the sand; in the gray quiet all you could hear was the crackling of the town behind you.

The cotton wool clung to the beach all that day and all the next. When it lifted, he was among those being formed into a column facing the sea. The column stood motionless for hours at a time, moving only to fly apart under the Stukas, then regrouping. Whenever it did go forward, only a few paces were the result. But by nightfall the destination was reached. The town, as he looked back over his shoulder, was still burning into the sky. His boots were lapped by the shallow surf, and gradually he felt a sloping beneath his steps as his trousers were swamped by iciness smelling of brine and pickled pigs' feet. Bit by bit he was engulfed, thighs, hips, waist, torso, until all but his shoulders and helmeted head were engulfed by this black slurping beast. They did well enough without a sea where he came from. The men ahead were being pulled up over the side of a motorboat rocking in the red-shattered confusion. There were shouts in English: Inyugomate! What did it mean? Why couldn't they speak French? Why must he descend yet farther, his shoulders disappearing? In his mind he grabbed hold of boundaries: the line of elms behind his parents' house, the fieldstone wall, and hot, everything hot under the blazing sun, at which moment an explosion sent a wave crashing over his head, dislodging his feet, sweeping him under, and in his terror of the churning blackness he breathed in violently for air.

His was one of the bodies littering the beach when it was taken two days later. He lay half in the surf, half out, moving slightly with the rhythm of the waves. Only two or three hundred corpses could be seen; losses were extremely light. Thousands of prisoners, most of them French, were being led off through the gutted town; but the bulk of the troops that had been trapped here, over three hundred thousand men, had escaped.

They had left behind a whole city of belongings. Bicycles lay everywhere on the white sand, weapons, knapsacks, books and photographs
that fluttered in the breeze. Hundreds of vehicles stood about, many of
them bombed or shelled and still smoking. Hulks of a dozen ships lay
half submerged offshore. The sea was calm, the sky blue.

Hitler was unperturbed by the evacuation of Dunkirk that late
May and early June of 1940, counting it not as a German failure but as
yet another victory, if of a special sort.

The victories had been dizzying in their rapidity and scope, as if
part of the rampant surge of spring, of the natural, unstoppable force
that had swept frozen Europe into green regeneration. In less than
eight weeks: Denmark, Norway, Holland, Belgium, France—for
France was as good as through, after which England would sue for
peace. The Führer was in a state of bedazzlement.

This had not been his state for most of these eight weeks. He had
been displeased to invade Norway, a great waste of manpower necessitated by British moves to cut off the German iron-ore supply from
Sweden. The little stepping-stone of Denmark had fallen within hours,
but the rugged landmass of Norway was not such an easy nut to crack.
Nonetheless, a month had seen it done. Then Holland, Belgium, the
drive into France. The victories had come so fast and furiously that he
had begun to feel they were too good to be true. The day after the
French defense had collapsed behind the Meuse, the Army Chief of
Staff had noted in his diary: "The Führer is terribly nervous. Frightened by his own success." And eight days later: "The left wing, consisting of armored and motorized forces, is to be stopped in its tracks
upon direct orders of the Führer. Finishing off the encirclement of the
enemy is to be left to the Luftwaffe!"

The Luftwaffe Chief had indeed assured the Führer that his force
was best suited for the task.

"Leave it to me—only fishbait will reach the other side! I hope the
Tommies are good swimmers."

"Shooting off his big mouth again," General Jodl acidly remarked
to an adjutant. No love existed between the Army and the Air Force,
and it was clear that the Fat One wished to rob the generals of their
glory. "Halt the tanks indeed! Fishbait indeed!" Jodl added in a mutter,
although he himself as well as General Keitel were in agreement with
the Führer that armor could operate in the Flanders marshland only
with heavy losses. All three men felt this to be borne out by their personal experiences in the Great War. Moreover, General von Rundstedt,
commander of the invading army in France and a wary strategist, had
concurred with the Führer that the panzer forces must be conserved.
But that did not mean that the Fat One had any right to rush in and
take over.

General Milch was greatly annoyed. He objected to his Chief's enthusiasm, and that of Jeschonnek, because, as he warned them, the bombs would sink too deeply into the sand before exploding.

"Leave it to me," snapped Göring. "It's not your business."

The Luftwaffe's failure to capture or destroy the British Expeditionary Force was not borne in deeply on the Air Chief. Far from stomping about in a rage, the Führer welcomed him in exceptionally fine spirits. "It is always good," said he as they sat down, "to let a broken army return home, to show the civilian population what a beating they have had."

Heartened by these words, Göring felt he could now put forward his wish to attack Britain before she had had time to recover from her debacle. During the next few days there would be no possibility of British retaliation against a strong and determined attack, whereas in a few weeks it would be too late. The moment was ripe, it would not come again. But there were problems. He had only one paratroop division; he must be given four divisions from the Army, but so far had made no headway in his demands. The Führer, in any case, was going on in an amazing manner.

"We will soon conclude a reasonable peace with France, and then the way will be clear for an agreement with Britain. Our two peoples belong together racially and traditionally—this has always been my aim, even if my generals can't grasp it. Herr Churchill will at any rate grasp it. He will appreciate the sporting spirit which I have given proof of by not creating an irreparable breach between the British and ourselves."

It was almost as if he had planned to spare the Expeditionary Force, thought Göring. At least he seemed to look upon it as a masterstroke of good fortune that they had not suffered the ultimate humiliation. It was humiliation enough that they had been kicked out of France, beaten, trapped, smuggled back like sopping rats. They might have been utterly smashed on the beach, but they had not been. If it was chance, fate, fog, the escape was now sanctified by the Führer, and Göring saw there was no point in putting forward his plan for attack. Britain was to come to a wise, grateful, sportsmanlike agreement.

At the end of June, a few days after the terms of the armistice were dictated to the French delegation in the same railway coach at Compiègne where the German delegation had been dictated to twenty-two years before, Göring moved into a wing of the Hotel Ritz. There was a ducal apartment for himself, and suites for his extensive staff, all with windows overlooking the lovely Place Vendôme. Having bustlingly approved of the rooms, he was driven directly to the Salle de Jeu de Paume in the Tuileries Garden, a small Louvre-affiliated museum rapidly becoming Reich headquarters for art experts and painting brokers. The Feldmarschall had already been busy with works of art in Holland and Belgium, and now that he was at the epicenter of European art, he looked forward to being even busier.

It was almost evening when he left the Jeu de Paume. He had an urge to walk back to the hotel, and dismissed his car. His old comrade Loerzer was with him, and three bodyguards walked behind; yet he felt strangely separate. The streets were golden in the evening light, and extremely beautiful. Seeing that he was not in a mood to talk, Loerzer kept silent.

Later on, up in his grand apartment—for which he was sure he was being heavily overcharged—the Feldmarschall sat down at a Louis XVI marquetry escritoire and took up a creamy sheet of hotel stationery. His valet, coming in and seeing him writing, turned and went out again. "He is busy, he cannot be interrupted," he told Nurse Gormanns, who stood outside the door with a tray of medicines. She said she would try a little later. But Herr Kropp would have preferred that his master was never interrupted with these medicines, and considered it ridiculous that a registered nurse was now part of the Minister President's staff and traveled with him everywhere. It was quite enough that the Minister President chewed twenty or more of those little white paracodeine pills each day without his being stuffed with other pills and liquids as well. But Nurse Gormanns was under instructions from Dr. Ondarza, and the good doctor believed that Göring's aches and pains, his enlarged lymph glands, his swollen joints, his insomnia, his irregular heartbeats could all be treated medicinally, while Herr Kropp was of the opinion that his master's ills would be best treated by a relinquishment of at least half his demanding offices.

As Göring sat writing, he was unaware of his aches and pains. They were as far from his thoughts as the room he sat in, or the glorious experience at Compiègne, or the problem of silent Britain, or worries over the Luftwaffe, or even the succulent paintings he had discussed just an hour ago. The present had disappeared. He was walking from the Tuileries with Carin, she was pointing out all the things that she had described to him years before. She had lived in Paris when she was very young and first married, and she had loved the city. "Someday we will go there, Hermann," she had used to say, "and I will show you." And so it had come to pass, today. He was moved to write to Thomas, who by the grace of der liebe Gott had returned home safe from the Russo-Finnish War, and whose mother would have wept with joy.

. . . A while ago, in the hush of the early evening, I strolled along the beautiful streets of Paris, and I felt your dear Mother's hand was in mine. There was a beautiful feeling of peace, and I was reminded of the days in Kreuth when the three of us were together. How close we all were, how happy your Mother was because you had come. How fortunate we have both been, Thomas, to have known such love. That love is with us still. . . .

Chapter 60

T HE bodies on the Dunkirk beach were adequately buried. This had not been the lot of many elsewhere, who had been hastily sodded over in the pressured rush of defeat. At Dunkirk, in the relaxed aftermath of its capture, the fallen were properly, formally, deeply interred, and far enough away from the sea to have pleased the young Allier villager retrieved from its surf. Even so, the earth was sandy, moist, saline. He would not have called it dry land, he would have protested, *"Ce n'est pas naturel."* But above him were fields of familiar yellow wildflowers, the common far-flung dandelion, or pissenlit. Bursting up in April, they had grown thick by June, and by mid-July were at the height of their dense yellow brilliance.

All through the Low Countries and northern France there had been an increase of subterrestrial residents. In Rotterdam alone, because of an unfortunate error in Luftwaffe communications, the city's graveyard had been augmented by eight hundred plots. Numerous villages had been reduced to rubble by artillery shelling; and though most of the villagers had fled beforehand, there were those buried alive in their cellars. There were also the isolated graves of soldiers in the green silence of forests, and in open fields and by the sides of roads. Above all, there were the military cemeteries, both native and German, with their appearance of small cities. By mid-July it could be roughly estimated that in the space of eight weeks several hundred thousand beings—in addition to the standard toll of the sick, the aged, the still-born, the accident victims—had gone into the earth.

To the east, where French pissenlits became German Löwenzähne, all remained as before; the same was true farther east, where Löwenzähne turned into Czech *poupova;* but farther east yet, where *poupova* became Polish *mlecze,* there, where a figurative curtain had been hung almost a year before, who knew how increasingly enriched the soil might have grown?

In Berlin a shatter of gunfire electrified the Pariser Platz crowd, causing a panic of pushing and crying out until it was discovered that no one among them was firing a gun, only that some people standing on a crate had fallen through it with a splintering crash. Several people had already been carried off to the first-aid station, having fainted in the crush and the heat. The heat was flattening, the sky above Brandenburg Gate a dull burning gray. Despite this the crowds were in buoyant holiday sprits. All stores, offices and factories had been closed. On this day, for the first time since 1871, there was to be a victory parade through the Gate. Across the square, the reviewing stand had filled.

Rose was one of those who had arrived at the square early, though not as early as she had intended, because she never managed to arrive anywhere as early as she intended. Still, she was relatively in the forefront of the crowd, which had begun cheering. She felt no kinship with those around her, she had grown too solitary and suspicious; what she felt part of was glory, history—the columns of feldgrau now marching through the great arch, legs shooting straight out and slamming down in the resounding boom of the Stechschritt, officers alongside on glistening mounts that danced with excitement, the band breaking into the "Kaiser Friedrich March" and setting her whole body moving in rhythm—the crisp sunny tempo, the thrilling gaiety, something so pure and wonderful in the melodious trumpets and brisk drums, high warbling fifes and bright chiming of Glockenspiele. "Hoch!" she cried. "Hoch! Hoch!"

"Why don't they shut up?" Thomas von Kantzow muttered to himself. He had meant to stay on the fringes, but the fringes had coalesced, he had been sucked in. Only an hour ago he had arrived at the Friedrichstrasse station from Stockholm; he had sent his luggage on to the Leipziger Platz Palace, but wanted to wander around for a while. Now he had become caught up in a victory-parade mob and stood squashed on all sides, deafened by cheers. Victory, vindication, a defeated France—bravo! Belgium and Holland thrown in—bravo! Denmark, Norway—bravo! Now the Reich extended from the North Cape to the French Atlantic, and in the east almost to Russia—bravo! But it was enough. That was what he sensed: the delirium of triumph dancing on the anticipation of peace. Which depended on England, which sat isolated in the sea and would be reasonable. The crowd pressed against him, waving handkerchiefs and screaming "Hoch!" He hated their noise. He hated the cadenced stomping of the black boots. And he hated the music because he could feel its pull. In spite of everything, he was capable of giving way under that thrilling martial glory. Not much, God knew. But a bit. A bit. In every human being there must be a permanent, rotten little spot where the splendor of death could always take flame. He stood impatiently waiting for the thing to end.

From where he stood he could not see the reviewing stand across the Pariser Platz. He wondered if Hermann was there, but doubted it. The parade was strictly Army, no Luftwaffe. Hermann would never show up to be overshadowed by the Army. Even Hitler might not be there; he was an arbitrary character, nor did he like Berliners. It was horribly hot. In Finland he had thought if he could just be warm again, he would never want anything else.

Suddenly there was a commotion in the reviewing stand. The crowds on the other side of the square could not see what it was about, which was just as well, since it involved extreme humiliation for one of the dignitaries. Propaganda Minister Goebbels was sitting in the front row when all at once a horse reared, its officer unable to control it. It plunged, kicked, turned in circles, then backed straight into the railing with an earsplitting crash. It would have squashed the Minister had he not lunged clumsily aside, swinging his heavy right shoe behind him, and landed half in the lap of Minister Frick. Startled cries went up throughout the stand, then laughter as the horse was subdued. The small fallen Minister, face flaming, laughing too, with all his teeth bared, straightened up and brushed off his uniform with sharp, furious movements.

"How fortunate your wife was not with you," said Minister Frick, feeling that he should say something.

"Ja," muttered Goebbels, lifting his head and gathering back his dignity. Though the laughter had died away, it still rang in his ears. His body trembled more with insult than shock. An attendant had already set his chair back up; the police guards were hurriedly replacing the broken section of rail. He sat down again and resumed his observation of the marching troops as if nothing had happened, but his eyes were like flint. It was only toward the end of the parade that he relaxed enough to realize how fortunate indeed it was that Magda had stayed home because of the heat. Even if she had not been hurt by the plunging horse, the shock might have caused her to lose the child she was six months pregnant with, the child who was the fruit of their reconciliation.

The parade was over. The crowd began slowly untangling itself. From the Pariser Platz Rose intended to go for a long walk in the

Tiergarten. Since the end of the terrible winter she had taken up her walks again. They had become her symbol of freedom. She also believed that long walks and fresh air had a calming effect on one who was celibate, a condition she was still not used to.

During the long, freezing, indoor months her skin had turned pallid as a mushroom. And she had grown thin. Undernourishment had put bones in her face. Sometimes, giving herself a glance in the mirror, she would say, "You don't look forty-four at all, my dear. Not at all. More like ninety-four." She was not crushed by her drab reflection. Her teeth, at any rate, were what they had always been. As for the rest, it made the absence of a love life easier. No man looked at her twice. Temptation was removed. Fate was kind.

Then, unbelievably, spring came. The food crisis passed. On her little spirit stove she cooked big meals of onions and potatoes. She was not concerned with tastiness, only with enduring. Gradually, the leather strap of Walther's wristwatch grew tight. She had had to take it in a notch during the winter; now she let it back out. Her wrist was once more smoothly fleshed, as was her face. She went out and walked, stretching her spine in the warmth like an animal emerging from its cave. Her face grew golden from the sun. Men's glances again turned her way.

It was hard never to return a glance, but in order to endure she limited those who knew her to the smallest possible few. She pinned up her shining chestnut hair and clamped over it a navy-blue felt hat of the arc-shaped kind worn jauntily on one side of the head, with its front tip coming down almost to one eyebrow. It was piquant, yet eminently respectable. Under this hat, and with a wedding band on her finger, she had a wall between herself and whatever male looks came her way.

Some of the crowd were going over to the reviewing stand to look at the generals, perhaps to see what the commotion had been about. She went in the opposite direction. Part of the secret of enduring was to keep a wide space between oneself and any kind of officialdom. She would go around the south side of the Gate, and from there to the Tiergarten. She would have a good long walk. Then she would go home to her room. Sit on her windowsill, look down into the gray courtyard. Smoke a cigarette. Make time pass.

She never conversed with anyone. She no longer had her visits with Dr. Weinblatt. He had retired, closed his doors. No clients: no income. The stately old office had been snapped up by a National Socialist eye doctor. Once she had told Dr. Weinblatt about Walther. It was a bitterly cold day, the office was like an icehouse, they sat in coats and gloves, and all at once she had said that this large watch that she wore belonged to a man named Walther, and that he had died. Dr. Weinblatt had nodded sympathetically. "Es tut mir leid." He looked tired, there was no bounce left in him. She wanted to say something to cheer him, but instead went on about Walther.

"I did not love Walther, really, when he was alive. He was a person who was always explaining. I must confess that I often found him extremely tiresome. This is something that hurts me very much to remember. Because I love him now, very deeply. I think it takes something very big and sad to make me feel deeply. With Walther's death I felt this deepness. I want to help him, but I can't. It is all too late. But I can wear his watch, and I can endure for both of us. You see, Herr Doktor, it does feel like love . . . but I don't know. I am no thinker. He was the thinker. You can see that I don't make much sense. . . ."

So much she had said in one burst. It was because she was lonely, and never spoke with anyone. She waited with hope for Dr. Weinblatt's reply. He sighed, and patted her hand with kindness.

"Who can make sense of anything?"

He was no great thinker either. There they sat in silence, together watching the snow lash against the window with its stained-glass top of pale green and lilac.

"Entschuldigen," she murmured, bumping against someone as she came around the Gate, a young man lighting a cigarette. Very nice, she thought as she passed on: tall, well built, glossy dark hair and a glimpse of lifted blue eyes, reminding her of someone . . . Emmy's stepson, the little Kantzow, with his thin neck and proper, courteous air; but this one was entirely different, hard-faced, with a slouched arrogant bearing; no, it was just the coloring, dark hair and blue eyes, a very attractive combination, and she allowed herself an erotic fantasy as she went on toward the dusty trees of the Tiergarten, while he, blowing out smoke, remarked to himself that that was a good-looking woman, somewhat in the way of Emmy's great friend, the actress, what was her name . . . Rose. Rose, into whose bed he had lusted to climb. What had become of Rose? He hadn't seen her, thought of her for years. He thought of her flamboyance, her dramatic gestures, a high-flown sort of woman . . . this one was as different from Rose as stone from water. Serious, proper, off to have tea in the Tiergarten with some other proper Frau. And forgetting her as she disappeared among the trees, he wandered on down the Hermann-Göring-Strasse in the sullen heat.

"Wie geht's, Kropp," he said over the plashing of the fountain. "No, don't get up."

Herr Kropp, sitting on a bench in the back garden of the Leipziger Platz Palace, a neatly folded newspaper on his knee, sat back as young von Kantzow slouched down beside him.

"Hot enough for you?"

The banal phrase, the entire casualness of the greeting, confused

Herr Kropp, if only momentarily. Bowing, although seated, he said formally, "Welcome, Herr von Kantzow. May I say how happy I am that you are here once again for a visit."

"That I'm not dead, you mean. I accept your happiness."

Herr Kropp felt he had been replied to rudely, but for some reason he was not offended. The visitor sat looking around the garden without much interest. His face was greatly altered.

The jet spray of the fountain shot high from the mouth of a stone fish, and came splashing back down into the clear sun-dappled pool. Beyond the fountain a manservant was walking among the trees, followed by a clumsy, frolicking little lion cub.

"A new Caesar."

"Ja. The last one grew too big, as of course they always do. This one in fact is to remain here permanently. The Frau Minister President doesn't wish any lion roaming about Carinhall now that the child is toddling all over."

Herr Kropp essayed another look at the visitor, whose face had altered so greatly, and the strange thing was that it had not altered at all. One could not say what made it look different. It was an inexplicable impression, there being no physical basis for it. Herr Kropp returned his gaze to the garden. The lion cub was disappearing from view, bouncing through the green grass.

"Well, tell me. You were in France with Hermann. What's it like there now?"

"In France? Well, that's a large question, sir, but I'll try to answer it—"

"No, never mind," Kantzow sighed, taking a pack of cigarettes from his pocket. "Who cares about the big questions? I'll ask a small one instead. Would you like a cigarette?"

"Is that the question?" Herr Kropp asked uncertainly.

"That is the question."

"I don't smoke," answered the valet, thoroughly bemused.

"I interrupted your crossword puzzle," Kantzow said, lighting a cigarette. He took up the folded newspaper. "Crossword puzzles are the best kind, all the answers on the back page. You look, of course?"

"Certainly not," replied Herr Kropp, but he went unheard, for his seatmate was reading the advertisements aloud.

"'Alles Schönes festhalten mit der Leica . . . Darmol, die gute Abführ Schokolade . . . Pedicure Efasit.' Life goes on." He set down the paper only to take up Herr Kropp's pencil, casually turning it between his fingers. "Gold-plated. Attractive. A gift from Hermann, yes? And engraved, too. R.K. Very nice, quite nice." Setting down the pencil, he stretched his legs. "I walked a lot this afternoon."

"It can't have been pleasant in this crushing heat."

"Crushing? Yes, it was crushing," young Kantzow said with a

laugh. "I found it crushing. But one is perverse. Aren't you sometimes perverse?"

"I really don't know," replied Herr Kropp, thinking that the young man's laugh was as unmirthful as his rudeness was somehow unrude. As if it were all one and the same. Indifferent, empty. Yet there was an odd effect of command, a kind of slouched, uncaring authority.

"You know," said the visitor, getting up and going over to the fountain, "I once wished never to be cool again. Not just never cold again, but not even cool again."

"I can well believe that, sir. We heard much about the murderous winter up there."

To this there was a shoulder shrug, as if to imply that his experience had amounted to nothing. And that was right, thought Herr Kropp. It befitted a hero not to make much of what he had been through. Altogether he was impressed by this new Kantzow, even if he did make one feel uneasy. The fact was, he had become significant, a man of weight, despite the odd sense of emptiness he conveyed.

"Is Hermann inside?" he asked.

"He is. And he has been greatly looking forward to your visit."

"I'll go in in a while," he said, sitting down on the stone rim of the fountain.

The next night, Reichstag President Göring took his place at his dais in the Kroll Opera House. The foreign correspondents had never seen the house so crowded, or so many generals collected under one roof. Both Army and Luftwaffe, they filled an entire third of the first balcony. Part of the proceedings would have to do with the generals, but of greater importance to the journalists would be Hitler's speech. As the Führer got gravely under way, his audience as grave as himself, one of the journalists nudged a colleague. "Sounds like a peace offer."

"What's he got to lose?" the other whispered back. "A peace with him sitting astride the continent as its conqueror?"

". . . in this hour I feel it my duty before my own conscience to appeal once more to reason and common sense. I consider myself in a position to make this appeal, since I am not the vanquished begging favors, but the victor speaking in the name of reason. I can see no reason why this war should go on . . . I am grieved to think of the sacrifices it will claim. I should like to avert them, also for my own people . . ."

The correspondents were impressed; the speech was a masterpiece of calculation, a shrewd maneuver to rally the German people for the fight against Britain. The people would now say the Führer wants peace, if there is no peace it is Britain's fault.

From time to time applause broke out, but there was no cheering; throughout the packed house one felt the genuine wish for peace, one saw that faces were solemn, tense. The Reichstag President, however, was preoccupied with something he was writing. He sat scribbling away at his dais, sometimes pausing to chew on his overlarge pencil, before scribbling on like a schoolboy at work on a composition that must be finished by the end of class. But always he kept one ear cocked for his Führer's words, and at appropriate moments would throw down his big pencil and applaud.

There was a dramatic break in the middle of the speech: suddenly the Führer addressed himself to the generals in the balcony, and in the manner of Napoleon, as with the flick of a hand, created twelve field marshals. Göring looked on from his dais with a pleasure that could not contain itself when the naming came to three of his Luftwaffe generals, Kesselring, Sperrle and Milch; with all the happy naturalness of a child, beaming like a proud big brother, smiling his joy and approval up to them, he clapped his hands with gargantuan gestures, then pointed with both clasped paws at his new field marshals, like a boxer in the ring. Wreathed in smiles, he sat back as the naming continued. Then came another great moment for him.

"I hereby reward the Commander in Chief of the Luftwaffe, for his mighty contribution to victory, with the newly created rank of Marshal of the Greater German Reich."

And as Hitler turned and handed him up a small box, Göring's pride and satisfaction were so open and unguarded, so great, that the journalists felt touched, old murderer that he was—one didn't forget that in '34 it had been he who had dispatched so many to the firing squad during the Röhm Purge. It was hard to reconcile the ruthless Göring, Hitler's Fist, Hardboiled Hermann, the Iron Man, with this happy and terribly human fellow who, like a child on its birthday, could not deny himself little sneaking glances under the lid of the box as Hitler resumed his speech. One could understand why he was so popular with the people, for one could feel it oneself: a kind of streaming warmth, something as simple and contagious as the beneficence of a sunny summer morning.

The box contained two collar tabs, each a square of silver brocade on which crossed marshal batons were embroidered in gold. "Unique in their simplicity," said Göring afterward, standing in his bedroom in the Leipziger Platz Palace being divested of his uniform. He held one collar tab in either hand. "No gold leaf, no eagles, just the crossed batons. A unique symbol for a unique rank. But the Führer is not correct in saying that it is newly created." He bent forward, arms outstretched, as Robert pulled his sweat-soaked undershirt over his head. "The Führer never lies, but he sometimes says things in such a way as to give a certain impression. Such as that he has created the rank of Marshal of the Reich. Whereas it was created for Prince Eugen. Eugen is the only figure in history to have been made Reichsmarschall. Think of it, Robert, the title has not been resurrected until now, two hundred years later. For me."

"It is only what you deserve, sir," said Robert, holding up his master's white terry-cloth robe. "It would have been unthinkable for you to remain a Feldmarschall now that there are others."

"Exactly. And so many." With one arm in the bathrobe, he strode off to the heavy baroque table on which lay a full-scale color photograph of the new baton he was to receive. The baton presentation ceremony was not to take place until the following week, but somehow he had got a photograph smuggled out to him. He stood beaming down at it as his valet, having followed the dragging robe with rapid steps, managed to maneuver the other arm into its sleeve. The baton was truly dazzling, entirely of gold and thickly embedded with diamonds. By comparison, the gold-decorated ebony baton of a Feldmarschall paled to nothing.

"How much do you think it weighs?" Robert asked.

"You tell me. What's your guess? Keep in mind it's not solid gold. They'll have tried to save a few marks by making it hollow down the center."

"Or perhaps for practical reasons? If it were solid, it might be too heavy to lift."

Göring laughed. "By me?"

"Well, that is true, sir," Robert acquiesced. Although his master was not always in the best of health, he was physically powerful as a bull. Whenever he shed his layers of fat, it was all rock-hard muscles beneath. "Let me think a moment . . . possibly three kilos?"

"Sehr gut! My own guess exactly. Quite a respectable weight, actually." And off he strode again, barefoot and buoyant, before Robert could tie the sash of his robe or get him into his slippers. "By the way," he threw over his shoulder, "I hear Goebbels was sat on by a horse yesterday."

"Goebbels sat on a horse?"

"Was sat on *by* a horse."

"My word! Was there anything left of him?"

"Weiss nicht," Göring laughed, swinging open the bathroom door to take his shower.

"One moment, bitte." Robert held up a forefinger, smiling. "May I wish you a pleasant shower, Herr Reichsmarschall."

"Ah, a miracle!" his master exclaimed, disappearing through the door. For Robert, being a stubborn creature of habit, had always referred to his master as the Minister President, although the latter himself much preferred his military title. Even when he became Feldmarschall, Robert had refused to change his ways. But Reichsmarschall—that was so towering a rank that to use any other title henceforth was out of the question.

A while later, the Reichsmarschall came thumping briskly down the stairs for dinner. It was to be a small, intimate celebration: he and his wife, his stepson, the Loerzers, the Körners. As he passed the library he saw that his stepson stood over the low hexagonal table where the new art books from Paris were piled. There were so many that the tabletop, of dark red Florentine leather, could only be seen in chinks. Thomas looked up at the sound of an enthusiastic voice—"Beautiful, aren't they?"—and smiled in agreement as his stepfather came over to him in a white summer uniform, radiating a fresh scent of cologne, his face rosy and beaming. "I couldn't resist them. What have you there, Holbein?" One large plump hand, sparkling with gems, reached down and smoothed the page, as if absorbing the colors' richness through the skin. It was a reproduction of the *Adoration of the Shepherds*. "What chiaroscuro . . . magnificent. Ah, Photo Hanfstaengl, I see."

"I was thinking that name seems familiar."

"Ja, Putzi's family, they have a big art reproduction firm. You must have met old Putzi—huge tall fellow, very musical. Went off to play the pianos in England," he said, and flipped the page over to a portrait of Charles Saulier, Photo Alinari. "Time for dinner, come. And you must take any of these books you want, Thomas. After all, you're the only one in the family with artistic talent. Nein, let's have none of your modest protests."

"I could accuse you of modesty too, Hermann. You come in talking of art, and give me no opportunity to congratulate you."

"I am not modest in the least. Go right ahead."

"Then may I offer you my very best wishes. It is a tremendous honor."

"Danke, Thomas. Danke. And tell me, what did you think of the Führer's speech?" he asked as they walked from the room together.

"Well, I should like to think it would result in peace."

"So should I, but I doubt that it will. But tonight we shall bask in the possibility. There is always the possibility."

Had Herr Kropp been present as the two men went down the hall talking together, he would not have recognized the Kantzow he had seen yesterday in the garden. The rudeness, the inattentiveness, the casual inner authority were nowhere evident. They had dissolved as soon as he had gone inside to Göring.

It was why he had lingered there in the garden. Finally he had gotten up from the rim of the fountain and gone in. Perhaps it won't happen, he had thought. It has always happened, but perhaps this time it won't. After all, everything is essentially different now. But when it did happen, he was not deeply disappointed. He said to himself: It cannot be otherwise. I realize that. What does it matter?

As for Göring, he had been puzzled and frustrated by the reunion. Although the mutual warmth had been there as always, the elder man had wondered, ever since Thomas returned home from Finland, why in his letters he never mentioned his war experiences. One would not even have known of the Tank Killer's medals had Count von Rosen not spoken of them in a letter, and Rosen had not learned of them from Thomas but through official channels. It was Thomas's old close-mouthedness, but his stepfather believed that when they met face to face, the youth would open up like a blossom. It was inevitable. For so long he had burned to act meaningfully, outstandingly, and now he had done so: had finally gotten his wings off the ground and flown straight to the heights. For the first time they would be sitting down and talking as soldier to soldier, hero to hero, and Göring was happy that this was so. But the fellow was nothing but nods and courteous smiles. He would not even speak in generalities. "Tremendous Russian losses . . ." A nod. "An undesirable treaty for Finland . . ." A nod. "Marshal Mannerheim was a great rallying force for the Finns . . ." A nod. How long could one carry on a conversation alone? Finally he had given up, and talked of other things. But he had said to himself, Even so, Thomas, for all your diffidence, the thing is there in your eyes. The experience of battle is in them, and around them. You wanted to achieve manhood. Now you have.

The dinner was very gay, and everyone got a little tipsy. The three women were dressed in the latest fashions from Paris—bright colors in large stripes or floral patterns, tight waists, padded shoulders—and liberally doused with French perfume. "Liebchen!" declared the new Reichsmarschall, very red in the face from his eating and drinking, "You look just as good as you smell!" And he grabbed and hugged Emmy, planting a kiss on her cheek. There was vodka in varied colors from Poland, *pâté de fois gras* from Paris, roast salmon done in the Danzig style, served with Moselle from a private cellar the host had recently bought in Trier. Young Kantzow, never one to go light on the liquor, was perhaps the merriest of the lot.

"Prost!" he said, lifting his glass.

"To peace!" said Göring.

"To our new Reichsmarschall!" said Loerzer.

"To the Reichsmarschall!" they all chorused.

"To Germany!" said the Reichsmarschall.

On and on the toasts went, and the eating, and laughter.

"Prost, Emmy!"

"Prost, Thomas!"

She drank to him, smiling, her pink cheeks pinker yet from wine.

When she had greeted him yesterday, she had had a brief, terrible sensation she could not account for: he meant to die. Something about the eyes, slightly hollow, something . . . but the chilling impression was only momentary. He had just grown older. She gave a shake of her head to clear it. She was not used to all this vodka. But it was a very special celebration: the war was won, peace with Britain was around the corner, and Hermann had been made Marshal of the Reich.

Even State Secretary Körner was in vivacious spirits. Second-in-charge of the Four-Year Plan, he was a slightly built man with a flat face, round brown eyes, and quiet disposition. He was extremely deferential to his powerhouse of a chief, and had been from the very beginning, in the late 1920s, when he had chauffeured the ambitious would-be businessman around in his one and only asset, his Mercedes-Benz motorcar. Even before that, when they had been air comrades, he had looked up to Göring. This had never changed. He was loyalty itself, and Göring was absolutely loyal to him, as he was to all his old air comrades. Göring had a fetish about loyalty: he demanded it, he gave it. It was part of the officers' code, but in the Chief it went even deeper, it was something in his nature. Perhaps it was a kind of love, thought Körner; a need for love, and a need to give it. He was awash with sentimental thoughts about love, his flat cheeks aglow from countless toasts. He lifted his wineglass to his wife. "To love, Liebchen!"

"To love!" she exclaimed, delighted, for he was usually so quiet in company.

General Loerzer, Göring's oldest comrade, was knocking back the wine. He had always been a hard drinker, and though he held his liquor well, it had left its physical marks over the years, making him overweight, puffy, coarsening his features. The broad nose had broadened further, seeming to take up the entire center of his face, and possessed a perennial if unpronounced reddish-blue tinge. Of all Göring's old comrades, Loerzer and Udet were the most dedicated drinkers; but whereas Udet seemed to have grown increasingly nervous and irritable the more he drank, Loerzer was a picture of sturdy, cheerful complacency. With his broad smile, his gourmet's indulgence in each dish, his deep rumbling laughter, similar to that of his Chief, he seemed a lesser Göring, a smaller-scale twin. Even his hair had receded in exactly the same pattern. Both men were very red in the face.

"Prost, Hermann!"

"Prost, Bruno!"

And Thomas could see them in a dogfight over Flanders twenty-five years ago. Clench-jawed, goggled, zooming and diving, machine guns blazing, heroes of the sky . . . Yet what had they really been doing? Didn't it all start out as observation, with a couple of hand-dropped bombs that fell any old place and weren't much better than firecrackers? Then on both sides the planes got machine guns, and they could go after each other, and that became their object. The planes made their own importance, they shot each other down—zoom, bang, crash; they were obsessed with each other, they were a sideshow, a curiosity, a spectacle, they were an opera in the sky. Strange that no one had ever described it that way. He himself had never thought of it that way.

"A toast to the opera!" He clinked glasses with his neighbor, Frau Körner. "The opera isn't what it used to be. Now the firecrackers are the main thing, and they're big. But the old Heldentenors don't go along. No, they sing from their couches. They sing from their baths. They sing, and the others go. To the new opera—a toast to modern music!"

"Don't tell me you are a lover of *Wozzeck*?" inquired Frau Körner, confused and laughing.

"I am a lover of everything. Torten too." They were being served tiny light Viennese torten for dessert. *Pâté* from France, vodka from Poland, tortes from Austria—they should really have something from Czechoslovakia, and the Lowlands, and Denmark, and Norway, to make it complete. And I would swallow it all without a qualm, he thought. I have become part of the process.

"Meine Damen und Herren," Göring said, lifting his glass. "I propose a toast to my stepson, Thomas. I have held off because I know he doesn't want to be toasted. Forgive me for paining your modesty, Thomas, I will make it as short as possible. Damen und Herren—to a brave soldier!"

Thomas felt a spasm of joy as the table honored him; as Hermann sent him a look, over the rim of his wineglass, of deepest pride and love. A spasm, a kind of posthumous jerk, a nerve reflex, a ghost-jolt of happiness so brief it was gone before he knew it. He gave a smiling nod of thanks; then, in consideration of his modesty, he was released as the center of attention.

If it were modesty, I would be happy. Hermann thinks it is modesty, because he is incapable of imagining any other reason. Dear God, will I ever behold him in my soul as I behold him with my mind? He lifts his glass to me, and all I see are corpses frozen black in the snow, yet for a split second I know unsurpassed joy, because I have made him proud . . . and then I feel nothing at all, but I smile, I nod my thanks for the fact that I no longer exist. . . . Well, what are they toasting now? Peace? Again? Do they actually believe Britain will accept Hitler's peace offer? Yes, Hermann believes it. You can see it in his face. He believes it because he wants tonight to be unblemished. Tomorrow he will again become a realist.

Chapter 61

Eʀɴsᴛ Udet was also celebrating that night, at a larger and more uproarious party. The newly promoted Generaloberst, his newest woman friend at his side, was in highest spirits throughout the evening, but as they were driving home afterward in his small car, he grew silent.

"What did she call me? That one in the ruffles. What did she call me?"

His girlfriend, sighing through her nostrils, took a cigarette from her bag and tapped it on her polished thumbnail.

"Professor Canaros," he answered himself, driving too fast through the blacked-out streets.

"You'll get us killed, Ernst."

"Professor Canaros, she called me!"

"Well, why shouldn't she? And will you *please* slow down?"

He slowed without thinking, his mind filled with Professor Canaros of Vaduzia. "Why should she say that?" he demanded.

"Oh, for God's sake." She blew smoke out irritably. "It was one of your best-known feats." She felt frustrated, impatient. Whenever he got into one of these moods, she wished herself far away. But her words seemed to have calmed him.

A smile grew on his face as he remembered his barnstorming days billed as Mad Professor Canaros, in spectacles and top hat, an umbrella hooked over his arm, climbing into the cockpit backward. "What's this? Where is the steering wheel?" Squinting, searching, he would finally get himself turned around, flopping down to stare openmouthed at the control board. "Ah, well, any idiot can fly. Nothing to it, ladies and gentlemen!" And in a crazily bouncing takeoff, he would leave the ground for a full hour of extraordinary stunts. He would fly upside down and pretend he was falling out. He would right the plane and climb out on the wing with his umbrella, opening it as if to jump, only to leap with terror back into the cockpit. He would struggle to close the umbrella as the plane went seemingly out of control, spinning earthward faster and faster while he continued struggling with the umbrella, until at the very last moment, with only meters to spare, he would perform a miraculous aerobatic loop to the thrilled screams of the crowd. And at the end when he landed and jumped down, tripping over his umbrella, swinging off his top hat, grinning, the cheers were deafening, everyone came running to him.

"Wherever I went, I was appreciated. *They* knew what they were watching." His smile faded. "It's only in the Luftwaffe that they consider me a clown. That fat-assed civilian, Milch. And Jeschonnek—you realize Jeschonnek crashed into another pilot in training, killed him? That's how well Jeschonnek handles a plane! And Kesselring—one of those transferred Army types. Those groundhogs, those earthworms—and they dare think of me as a joke!"

"I don't want to come in," his girlfriend said. The car had drawn up before Udet's apartment building. She rolled down her window and threw out her cigarette with a gesture of finality.

He drove her to her flat, and drove back. For the first time in his life, despite his fame, his prestigious position, his great personal charm, Udet was having trouble keeping his women. But that was only one problem among many.

In his flat, he went over to the bar and poured a glass of brandy. Drinking from it, he walked around the room, looking at the walls. Framed photographs of the Richthofen Squadron, pieces of planes he had brought down in the Great War, a target that he used for rifle and pistol practice—it didn't endear him to his neighbors. On tables and shelves stood souvenirs from his moviemaking days in Africa and the Arctic, and stacks of picture albums from his stunt-flying career. He had had to make special shelves for the abundance of trophies he had won. He kept them polished to a high gleam. He stood looking at them for a while, then wandered over to the target. It was attached to a heavy piece of wood to protect the wall. No bullet holes marred the wood. The center of the target was riddled.

"I'm a better shot now than I was in the war," he said aloud. "At least that's one skill they can't keep me from practicing."

He looked at his old tin watch. It was almost four. He had an early-morning conference.

But in bed he lay sleepless. He tried to feel his earlier happiness. It seemed that promotion was his only source of happiness. In April he had been promoted to General der Flieger, today to Generaloberst. Two great leaps in three months—and again he felt a rush of warmth, a glow of confidence and strength that blotted out the nagging sense of sweeping things under the carpet. Then the glow went out.

Back in March he had said to the long-nosed, owl-eyed Heinkel, "I hope there won't be further trouble with the He-177. The Ju-88 has caused enough difficulties for my taste. The 177 has got to get into operation—we don't have any other large bomber that we can use against England. It has to fly, Dr. Heinkel!"

His voice had risen in frustration over this damned plane with its four engines welded together in two couples, causing them constantly to catch fire. And why were they welded together? To reduce drag, because like the Ju-88, this big bomber must be capable of diving. And why must it dive? Because Hitler had demanded it and Jeschonnek had agreed. Because for Jeschonnek there was no military mind greater than his Führer's, for Jeschonnek the Führer was God, for Jeschonnek the sun shone from his Führer's asshole. But who was responsible for the plane's success or failure? He, Udet.

And then three months later, it suddenly didn't matter at all. With the storm of rejoicing over the victorious French campaign, he had felt all his anxieties vanish.

"The war is over," he had told his aide exultantly. "Our aircraft plans aren't worth a damn, but we don't need them anymore!"

How extremely premature that had been. Britain had refused to come around; Hitler began making plans for its invasion. In the last week, Udet had been to two air conferences at Carinhall. The Luftwaffe was to cease its battle over the Dover Straits, where it had been centering its efforts on shipping, and begin attacking the airfields of England. The idea was to knock out the RAF so that a seaborne invasion could be made. But it was possible, Göring said, that the air attack alone might make Britain sue for peace. It was even possible, he had added, that there would be no Luftwaffe attack on England, because the Führer was going to make a final bid for peace in his Reichstag broadcast. But the Chief's voice had not expressed much faith in the outcome of this bid.

"So, what is it to be?" Udet asked aloud in the darkness, and answered himself with a sigh. "We know what it is to be."

An hour later, still unable to sleep, he got out of bed and went barefoot to the cage of his little lovebird.

"Willst du raus, Bubi?"

"Ja," Bubi chirped back.

Opening the cage door, he took the bird on his hand. Together they went into the living room, where he turned on the light. Lifting his hand where the bird was perched, he stroked the small yellow head. Bubi, who was very beautiful, yellow and jade-green, with cider-colored eyes of great clarity and understanding, fluttered up to his face and kissed him on the lips, on the bed-ruffled hair by his ear.

"Vergnüge Dich, kleiner Bubi." He smiled. Go enjoy yourself. Be happy.

"Ja," Bubi trilled, and began swooping around the room.

He went over to the bar and poured himself another drink.

"What do we care, Bubi? Here's to you."

In his pale blue silk pajamas, sipping his drink and rubbing his tired eyes from time to time, he watched Bubi flying around the room in free, clean, beautiful arcs.

Chapter 62

JULY of 1940 continued stifling, but August was beautiful; hot but fresh, as if the ground atmosphere were continually renewed by clear, buoyant particles from the highest reaches of the sky. In the mornings Rose came out of her building into a hum of heat, everything bright, quivering, alive. The heat burned against her skin and danced away. In her nostrils was an aroma of bread from the corner Bäckerei, and a scent of lake water, as if wafted all the way from the Wannsee.

She walked the long distance to her place of employment, and in the afternoon walked back. The heat was stronger but still buoyant. She felt like a sun-swimmer carried by the current, sunlight splashing from street traffic in crystal bursts. Her body beneath the light material of her dress felt as close to the burning, dancing sunlight as her naked arms. On her walks she felt suspended in time, a leaf floating in air, a fish gliding through sunlit water; yet she was never unaware of the metropolis around her; she had always loved Berlin, and for the very reasons most people disliked it: its immensity, noise, bustle. In the past she had been part of it; now she was an invisible onlooker.

When she reached the city's center, she always made a point of going along Voss Strasse and Wilhelmstrasse, because these streets were forbidden to her. She had no fear that she would be recognized by someone from the old days. Once she saw Bodenschatz in an open car, driving up to the Air Ministry. Another time she saw the familiar

face of a Göring adjutant as he came from the Chancellery. She was
not noticed, she was one pedestrian among many.

At the end of Wilhelmstrasse she turned down den Linden. Sometimes she took an outdoor table at Café Linden and ordered a glass of
lemonade. There was never any difficulty. If one looked surpassingly
Semitic there might be difficulty, or there might not be. Cafés were not
legally forbidden, as were theaters, cabarets, public beaches. Some
cafés bore placards: *Juden Unerwünscht*. That did not deter her; she
went to those cafés if she wished. There was never any difficulty. Here
at Café Linden there was no placard. Still, it was possible she would
have gone unserved if she had looked surpassingly Semitic. She once
saw such a couple wait and wait; finally they pushed back their chairs
and left. On the other hand, she had also seen surpassingly Teutonic
specimens sit unattended for a long while. On crowded days the waiter
could not reach everyone at once. The Jewish couple might have been
served if they had hung on a few minutes more. Or they might not
have been. One could not know.

She sipped her lemonade, served by the thin scholarly-looking old
waiter in black, his face severe, impassive, except for a tiny warmth at
the corners of his mouth testifying to the primal pleasure of serving a
lovely woman. "Danke," she said, her voice quiet, formal, as if she did
not realize the waves of sunlit sexuality that flowed from her.

The lemonade was sweet, tart, icy. She sipped it slowly, to prolong
her pleasure. She watched the traffic go by. Motorcars, bicycles, canary-
yellow buses with the advertisement *Creme Mouson* in maroon lettering.
People in summer clothes thronged the sidewalks. The buildings,
three- and four-storied, old-fashioned, of pale rose brick or gray stone,
many-windowed, with bright awnings at street level, were irradiated by
the sun, turning to pure gold. After she had sat a long while, her glass
standing empty at her elbow, she resumed her walk. But now it involved inescapable practicalities.

Along Friedrichstrasse, she turned in at her butcher shop. The
other customers present also had a red J stamped on their ration cards;
Jews were allowed to purchase food only late in the afternoon when
the best buys were gone. But this butcher saved good cuts for his Jewish customers, he would even sell you what was not listed on your severely restricted non-Aryan card, and he actually undercharged. In
short, he was a saint, and jolly into the bargain.

She bought sausages and went on to the greengrocer's. The greengrocer was not a saint. He dealt with you as if you were a number. But
no other grocer in the neighborhood was different, so she stuck with
this one. It was all the same when it came to grocers. For some reason,
butchers were better. As a rule, women shopkeepers were the worst.
Harder than the men, colder, and would shortchange you if they

could. And if the mistake was pointed out, the red J precluded all possibility of embarrassment in the cheater, much less apology.

Having bought half a head of cabbage, she turned down the street to her building. Passing a newspaper vendor, she glanced at the headlines. It had been the same thing for the last two weeks: British air bases being bombed. She hoped the British would soon give up. They could have peace if they wanted; then everyone would have peace.

Like a narrow upended box, her courtyard held at its bottom the dead unmoving part of the heat. All was in shadow, gray. Screaming half-dressed children chased each other around the rusty incinerator while their mothers, mopping their brows, gossiped listlessly from kitchen chairs placed by the sooty geranium plants. She opened the door and disappeared into darkness.

But her room was beautiful in the evening sun. Being on the top floor, it did not lack for light, and on a flaming evening like this the clutter and shabbiness was suffused by a rosy glow. After eating, she stood by the open window. The immense, glowing sky was still. Everything was still. Turning, she walked around the silent, luminous room, and her heart ached with loneliness as a tooth is said to ache, brutally, throbbingly.

Gradually, the sky emptied of color. The ache ebbed from her. She sat smoking as night fell. She did not feel like going anywhere, yet it was too early for bed. After a while she went to bed anyway.

Someone was blowing a whistle. It was a long flat silver whistle of the sort lifeguards use at the beach. "Listen to me," he said. He wore a bathing suit whose singlet was brick-red like the Café Linden awning, and whose black trunks fitted tightly around his muscular thighs. She wanted to ask him to come into the light, but he was talking too much to be interrupted. ". . . this room is as messy as your apartment was. See how one stumbles over everything, am I expected to swim through it? I used to put things in order for you. I explained everything to you. But you never listened. You treated me badly, Rose. You wounded me so deeply that my heart is still bleeding. I lose three liters of blood a day. Add that up. I have lost more than fifty liters of blood since we parted. The doctors say it is a miracle I'm still alive—"

"Oh Walther, you are really alive?" she cried, yet her words seemed to come from her lips as faintly as a kitten's mewl.

Even so he blew his whistle that she was not to interrupt him. "You thought I was in a tiny cardboard box, of the kind they make for cigarette ash. Do you think that's logical? There is no such box. Cigarette ashes are put in ashtrays. You must be logical. Logical."

She kept struggling to climb from bed and run to him, but it was as if she were underwater, her motions terribly heavy and slow.

"I have received a most upsetting communication. Your dentist has

written me a letter in which he states that you do not love me even
now. It is only pity. That is what your dentist writes: pity, sentimental
regret. A young lion shot in miderection. Ah! That makes you laugh.
You like that. That is the sort of thing you understand. Don't contradict me. Don't pretend you're blubbering or I shall blow my whistle
again! Dr. Weinblatt states that in your estimation I was, except when
performing in your bed, the most boring man you ever knew. Do you
deny it? Do you deny that you told him I talked too much? He has
witnesses. The waiter at the Café Linden has signed an affidavit. Also
your butcher. His sausages are made from the Sachsenhausen dead.
He took all my blood for a great blood sausage that he keeps in his
back room, coiled like a python. Ask him to show you. Ask him! Ask
him! Ask him!" Between each command Walther blasted shrilly on his
whistle, then abruptly she was sitting half out of bed, horrified and
weeping, with the air raid siren shrill in her ears.

Presently she released a spent, shaky sigh, wiping her eyes with the
heel of her hand. Her clothes lay where she had dropped them. A
coffee cup gleamed from the bureau top. On the bedside table, Walther's watch lay quietly ticking.

"They could do it earlier," she murmured, lying back on her pillow. "Why must they always wake people up?"

The siren rose high and stayed high for many seconds, keen, intense, then swung low as if for breath, and again climbed shrilly upward. Every few weeks one had to be awakened by this ear-piercing
practice drill. Closing her eyes, she tried to ignore the noise, which
eventually ceased. But, unable to sink back into sleep, she opened her
eyes with a frustrated sigh. There was a faint play of light across the
walls. That's something new, she thought, getting up from bed and
going with curiosity to the window.

Searchlights swung slowly through the night sky, many of them,
very long and straight, the color of ivory. She stood gazing up at them
in her nightdress. They were quite beautiful. She watched them inter-
sect gracefully, light passing through light, each continuing on its lan-
guid course. Now and then one would momentarily illuminate a small
night cloud, making it a polar bear, or a silver ship on black. There
were small bright stars out. The long, slow-wheeling beams were like a
celestial ballet, as lovely as anything she had ever seen.

The silence was jarred by a hollow thud, followed by more thuds,
causing her to stand back a little; but it was some moments before she
realized she was listening to antiaircraft artillery.

"That can't be," she said with disbelief.

The windowpane was vibrating. Suddenly it rattled hard. Every
flak unit in the city must be going off, far and near. She saw that the
searchlights were now moving rapidly back and forth, frantic, uncer-

tain, as if blindly trying to stab something. Against the dark sky she could see flak shooting up in chainlike accents of red.

Through the noise from outside she heard a pounding on her door. Pulling a kimono over her shoulders she opened the door into the dark little communal living room, from which the landlady and other roomers were disappearing. She followed them into the outer hallway, into a dark commotion pierced by flashlight beams. The porter, who was air raid warden for the building, was shouting, "Flieger alarm! Down to the cellar!" In the glancing beams of the flashlights she saw that he was in fire-fighting overalls of some dark rubbery material. A steel hat was held tight by a strap around his chin. He glared at the figures around him.

"Do as you wish, then, but turn off those flashlights!"

The tenants, in slippers and robes, looking suspicious and resentful, snapped off the lights and continued what seemed an argument with him.

"All this fuss of yours. It's only a new kind of practice."

"Ja?" snapped the porter. "There are planes out there."

"*Ours,*" said Rose's landlady.

"Of course they're ours!" someone else said.

Their voices were sharp in the darkness. The porter replied angrily, "That makes sense, doesn't it? Our guns are trying to bring down our own planes."

"But what else could they be?" came a man's voice. "No enemy planes can penetrate Berlin. *Berlin?* Central *Berlin?* Who are you trying to kid?"

"Impossible—"

"Göring promised us—"

"He said it could never happen—"

"Then go talk to him!" shouted the porter. "I only know I must carry out my orders, I must be obeyed. Come along, and no more arguing!"

"It's too stupid," insisted a woman.

"Pah!" he exploded. "Go back to your beds and be blown up!"

He stomped down the passageway, most of the tenants moving after him, nervously grumbling. It did not occur to Rose to go to the cellar, since her first thought was always to avoid intimacy. Returning to her room, she sank down into her lumpy armchair and mechanically lit a cigarette. From time to time, in the pounding and clattering of the guns, she gave a slow headshake of wonderment.

In the morning, when she went to work, children were excitedly running around the courtyard searching for and triumphantly holding up jagged pieces of antiaircraft shrapnel that had fallen, spent, from the sky. Along the streets she overheard snatches of conversation. Everyone was discussing the extraordinary night in grave voices edged with amazement. Near Bülowstrasse Bahnhof she passed a three-block area of apartment buildings that had been roped off. The buildings looked perfectly normal, and it puzzled her that they were behind a barrier. Then she realized that a building farther behind had probably been struck by a bomb, and that the entire area around it had been roped off to prevent curious pedestrians from gaining the smallest look.

Chapter 63

GÖRING was told the news that morning. He was in France aboard his private train, the *Asia*, which now served as his mobile headquarters and had thus been greatly augmented by operations rooms, a map room and command post, accommodations for the increased number of Luftwaffe staff, and open wagons at either end, mounted with anti-aircraft artillery, all of which were hauled by two of the heaviest loco-motives the German State Railways could provide. On this morning the train stood outside a tunnel near Beauvais, north of Paris. The birds had been noisily chattering for hours, but the Reichsmarschall heard nothing, for he had taken a sleeping powder the night before and lay snoring heavily in the shade-drawn bedroom of his private coach.

The snores, rising and falling, seeped out beneath the door, but at about nine o'clock they faded away and Nurse Gormanns, sitting on a jump seat in the passage, got up and knocked. The nurse's tall, solidly constructed physique was clothed in a flowered jersey dress, her em-ployer having requested at the start that she not convey a hospital at-mosphere by wearing her white uniform. In one strong hand she carried a blue lacquered tray on which stood a glass of freshly squeezed orange juice surrounded by bottles of pills.

The Reichsmarschall was sitting up in bed in the darkened room, heavily kneading his face. "Where is Robert?" he asked.

"I thought I would just look in on you first, Herr Reichsmarschall, to see how the new sleeping medicine worked."

"Ein bisschen zu wirksam . . . like a truck ran over me."

"That's the trouble with soporifics, they are either too mild or too strong." She set the tray down by his bed. "But when you've showered and eaten, you will feel much more yourself."

Nurse Gormanns had a brisk, soothing manner. Quiet-spoken, imperturbable, she was a figure to inspire confidence and respect. She went to the windows and sent the shades up. Sunlight brought everything to life: the thick auburn rug, the cream-colored flowers, the blue silk eiderdown beneath which the Reichsmarschall, in his white silk nightshirt with its long flowing sleeves, was slowly kneading his scalp. His hair stuck out in all directions. Sleep-swollen bags hung beneath his eyes.

Nurse Gormanns assessed him not only with professional acumen but personal concern, for she was devoted to him. But her job was not an easy one. He refused to relinquish his paracodeine supply and was now downing thirty tablets a day. Nor could she force him to follow her dietary rules. And since the air attacks against Britain had begun two weeks ago, his insomnia had shot to new heights. So had his blood pressure.

She shook out two blood-pressure pills along with various other pills and handed them to him with the glass of orange juice.

"Danke, Frau Gormanns."

Except for his paracodeine and dietary recalcitrance, the Reichsmarschall was a good patient: courteous, agreeable, easy to deal with. They often had pleasant chats. Even so, she drew in a deep breath before remarking conversationally, "I heard there were a couple of British planes over Berlin last night."

To this he made a slight grimace and muttered something. Having finished drinking down the pills, he handed her back the glass. "Dropping leaflets, I suppose."

"Ja, they dropped some leaflets . . ." the nurse assented, in an obscure tone that caused him to study her for a moment.

"Where?" he asked. "Over the outskirts, of course."

"Ja, over the outskirts . . . also over the center of the city. Also, they dropped a bomb or two."

The Reichsmarschall's eyes closed.

"But there was hardly a bit of damage, and no casualties. It was a very minor—"

"Did they bring the planes down?" interrupted the Reichsmarschall, his eyes still closed. His face had drained of color.

"I couldn't really say, sir. Although I'm afraid it was my impression that—"

"Your impression!" The eyes broke open. "Why am I hearing this from you, anyway? Why am I not informed by my staff! Where is Brauchitsch! Where is Bodenschatz!"

"Well, naturally they will not be conferring with you until you are up, Herr Reichsmarschall," the nurse said calmly, relieved that the thing had been gotten over with. In fact, it was the staff who had suggested she drop a hint along with her morning ministrations; she had such a way with the Chief; he would take her verbal pill along with her other pills; he would have time to digest it, and thus avoid the risk, in conference later, of having his blood pressure shoot through the top of his head; and in all truth, it was a minor incident. "When you've dressed and eaten, Herr Reichsmarschall, you will feel in a much better frame of mind to discuss the matter. Not that it is a very great matter. My impression was that it was very minor. Quite insignificant. One might say puny," she concluded, taking up the tray. When he did not answer, she gave a bow of her head and left the room.

The Reichsmarschall's eyes had closed again. Between them was a furrow cut so painfully deep it appeared black in the pallor of his face.

Although the raid gave shocking evidence that the capital was not safe from air attacks, the actual damage was small. But three nights later came another raid, killing ten people. A few nights later came another, and then another. At the Sportpalast the Führer gave a speech, his audience consisting of young nurses and social workers.

"I have waited these ten days without answering the British bombings in the hope that they would stop this mischief. But Herr Churchill has apparently seen this as a sign of weakness. You will understand that we will now answer. And when the British Royal Air Force drops two or three or four thousand kilograms of bombs on our capital, then we will drop two hundred or three hundred or four hundred thousand kilograms on theirs. When the British declare that they will increase their attacks on our cities, then we will raze their cities to the ground!"

His last words were drowned out by overwhelming applause. He waited until the young women had recovered themselves.

"We will stop the handiwork of these air pirates, so help us God!"

This time they leaped to their feet, screaming approval.

"The hour will come," he shouted, "when one of us will break, and it will not be National Socialist Germany!"

"Never! Never!" they cried.

He gave a sweep of his hand to subdue them, and with an expression of sly humor, crossed his arms. "In England they are filled with curiosity, and keep asking: 'Why doesn't he come?' Be calm, I say. Be calm. He's coming. He's coming."

Göring was at Carinhall when he received the Führer's order to bomb residential London. As always, he jumped to his feet as he took the phone and stood at full attention while listening. At the end, with a brisk nod, he stated to the Führer that his decision would be carried out. But afterward, he said dejectedly to his wife, "In Berlin the people have been shouting after me, 'What's going on, Hermann? Why aren't we bombing London?' But I held off, and for a good reason. I believed that if we didn't reply, the British would realize it's useless to drop bombs on cities just to drop bombs on cities. It's certainly no way to win a war."

"But why have they begun doing it in the first place?" she asked. "That is what I can't understand."

"Because of stupidity. Not theirs, *ours*. Some bombers were directed at sector stations at the outer edge of London, and a couple strayed off their course. They got caught in flak, dropped their loads, and turned back. Well, the fools had dropped their loads on central London."

"I didn't know that," said Emmy with surprise.

"How should you? It wasn't reported here in Germany." He began to pace as he spoke. "Do you think an error like that would be reported when our object is to carry out attacks solely against Fighter Command? For us to bomb nonmilitary objectives would be strategically stupid and wasteful. And Churchill knows it, he *knows* it was an error! But the very next night he retaliated, and he's been going at it for ten nights now. But I say we must stick to our policy and not retaliate against his retaliation. It's the worst thing we could do, it would be a fatal mistake. And that shrewd bastard knows it. He's chewing on his cigar in ecstasy! He is going to make us lose the battle against Britain through our having made one single stupid error! Do you realize that just one more week, just one more week of concentration on their ground installations, and we would have had them beaten?"

"But Hermann," ventured his wife, who knew nothing of sector stations and Fighter Command, who in fact never heard mention of military matters from her husband, but who did know one thing very clearly, "why didn't you say all this to the Führer?"

"How do you know I haven't! I told him three days ago that we were finally achieving the superior position we had been working toward, and that we would very likely lose this position if we funneled all our efforts into London. But the Führer feels he has lost face by these raids on Berlin." He suddenly plunged his fingers through his hair. "*He* has lost face—what about *me*? But the whole thing could be put right if we could just continue our airfield attacks as we have been doing, for just one more week!"

The next day, traveling back to France on the *Asia*, drinking coffee in the dining car, he had a conversation with Generaloberst Jeschonnek concerning the ordered mass attack on London.

"Do you think Germany would give up if Berlin were in ruins?"

"Certainly not," answered Jeschonnek.

"But you don't think the same of Britain?"

The youthful Chief of Staff, with his severe, rather glowering face, gave a shake of his head. "I believe the British civilian morale is not of the same strong fiber as the German."

Göring took a sip of his coffee and set the cup down on his saucer. "That is where you are wrong."

Nevertheless, on September 7, when the attack on London was to commence, the Reichsmarschall exhibited the most animated spirits. The *Asia* was brought from Beauvais to Pas de Calais, where he stepped down briskly, the salt breeze stirring his hair beneath the high-peaked visored cap, a pair of binoculars hanging around his neck, and with Kesselring and Loerzer walked to the top of a sand dune. Here he unsheathed his sword and planted it before him. He looked out at the glittering sea, up at the clear sky. He sniffed the air. He filled his lungs with it. He waited. Everyone waited. Gradually there came a roar from above and behind, it became more than a roar, a veritable exclusion of all but noise: sheer head-pounding, brain-blinding noise of the sort that makes the flesh contract, the eyes turn to slits as if in pain. In wave after wave, three hundred bombers escorted by six hundred fighters passed over the upsquinting, deafened faces. The blue of the sky was literally blotted out until the great winged armada had finally passed on.

The next day, Göring flew back to Berlin to deliver a broadcast to the German people. "In this historic hour, the German Air Force has for the first time delivered its blow right into the enemy's heart. London is in flames!" He also telephoned Hitler at the Obersalzberg: "It will be a matter of only a few days, mein Führer."

These words echoed the Reichsmarschall's declaration to his Luftwaffe commanders three long weeks ago, when the attack against Britain had been about to start. "From the information that you have given me, gentlemen, I reckon that the defense of southern England will last four days. And the Royal Air Force will last four weeks. We can guarantee invasion for the Führer within a month." To Hitler himself he had said the same: "The defense of southern England will last four days. Four days, then you will see, mein Führer!"

But even at that time they were badly behind schedule. The weather was their foe, having blanketed the Channel coast with fog for weeks. On August 12 it had finally lifted. But although the good weather held, the Luftwaffe's achievements had not been brilliant. It was almost as if the British could divine the exact route of the enemy planes and were prepared for them when they reached their objectives. This, although the Germans were unaware of it, was in fact true, British radar equipment being immensely more advanced and effective than that of their opponents. The radar sites were bombed as a matter of course, but the vertical masts made poor targets, and on August 15, Göring had called off the attacks.

"It is doubtful if there is any point in continuing," he said, "since not one of the radar sites attacked has so far been put out of commission. What is radar, anyway?" he added, with a contemptuous shrug. "A box with wires." He had neither interest in nor patience with the technological gimmicks of modern warfare, being still, intrinsically, the fire-eating young pilot in the open cockpit of his Fokker. As an associate had once said of him, without greatly exaggerating, "The Chief would love to fly through the air on a giant condor, his cape flowing, hurling a spear at enemy monsters."

The four days passed; a week; ten days. The Stukas were too slow and had to be withdrawn. The He-177, which had caused Udet to raise his voice in desperation at Professor Heinkel, did manage to fly without its locked engines catching fire, but because of a small wrinkle not yet ironed out, was unable to drop its bombs with accuracy. As for Udet's other headache, that huge flying barn door the Ju-88, it lacked the range expected of it. What was more, each bomber required three fighter escorts, cutting down the number of fighters able to engage in free combat. Not that there was as much free combat as the Germans wished, for the enemy was not sending its fighters up in great numbers. Knowing that the Germans' objective was to wipe out the fighters, the British simply, cannily, and as far as was possible refused to engage in air battles.

Nevertheless, German intelligence reports of enemy losses had been sanguine, even heartening. In actuality, they were grossly exaggerated; since the air battles took place over foreign soil, there existed no means of counting the wrecks of enemy planes. And since hard evidence was missing, and the tendency was to exaggerate rather than underrate, the reports handed to Göring at Carinhall had at first put him in excellent spirits. But rapidly he entered a state of ill humor.

"How is it that we are still suffering losses, when according to the official figures the British fighter force should no longer exist?" he demanded. His anger grew with each passing day. When on August 21 he had traveled to the Channel coast to check things out in person, he was in the foulest of tempers. "I am lied to by everyone," he growled to himself. "What do they think I am, some incurable invalid who can't be told the truth? Everyone from the engineers and technicians to the senior officers—they all lie to me!"

At advance headquarters of Luftflotte II, he strode in like an ogre, face flushed, hand pressing down on the pommel of his sword. "A few days would be enough! That is what I said because that is what *you* said at the start of the battle. Well, you had better start winning it! Look at you—all I see is a bunch of overdressed puppets who've gotten so attached to the easy life that you're afraid of losing it. What are you waiting for? There's England right in front of your faces!"

With a few snapped orders he strode out again. There was a slamming of car doors and he was gone.

At Cap Blanc-Nez the fighter pilots stood at attention in a light rain, battle-weary, eager for the sight of their Chief. He advanced on them like an enraged bull.

"Of all the cowardly, useless good-for-nothings! You've got the best fighter aircraft in the world! What more can you want? The Me-109 is peerless! But you have no fighting spirit, you have no belief in ultimate victory! You have failed miserably to protect the bombers! Don't you realize that close and rigid protection of the bombers is more important than record bag figures? And you're not making any records there either!"

For half an hour he strode up and down their ranks bellowing insults, after which, having gotten the fury out of his system, he grew somewhat more amiable, although his face remained severe. He asked for comments.

Captain Galland ventured to point out that the Me-109 was superior in the attack, but was not so suitable for defensive purposes as the Spitfire, which was slower but more maneuverable. The Reichsmarschall, stung by this criticism, again launched into a tirade. With his binoculars resting on his great paunch, his rain-wet face crimson, his eyes two glittering slits, he carried on for fully ten more minutes, flanked on one side by a grave and uneasy Kesselring, his toothy smile nowhere in evidence, on the other by Loerzer, who strove at times for a lighthearted expression, but failed. Finally the blasting voice subsided; once more the Chief became recognizably human. He turned to Captain Moelders, the Luftwaffe's most brilliant ace, and a great admirer of his Commander in Chief. He was asked what were the requirements of his squadron.

"I should like a series of Me-109s with more powerful engines, Herr Reichsmarschall."

"Request granted. And you?" he asked, turning to Galland.

"I should like an outfit of Spitfires."

Galland was shocked at himself even as he blurted out the words, since he much preferred his Me-109 to any Spitfire, but the injustice of the Chief's revilement, of his accusing these men of cowardice, had infuriated him. He stood not knowing what to expect—certainly not silence. But such brazenness struck even Göring speechless. The Reichsmarschall swung on his heel and stomped off in the drizzle, growling as he went.

But on the whole, returning to Beauvais, he had felt satisfied. He had put iron into the backbone of his men, infused them with the fighting spirit as he had done so often as a young squadron leader years ago. For the infusion of will, nothing could take the place of personal confrontation.

Even so, measures far more drastic had been needed.

The Luftwaffe must switch its targets farther inland. It must destroy the hornet's nest of airfields surrounding London, these being the fields from which the British fighters in the south were controlled. By doing this, they would not only strike at the heart of British defenses, but compel Fighter Command to meet their challenge with all remaining forces.

"The assault on these targets will go on by night and by day," declared Göring. "Massive numbers of bombers will destroy not only the RAF's ground installations, but also the oil tanks that supply their fuel and the factories that produce parts and replacements. The enemy is to be forced to use his fighters by means of ceaseless attacks. These damnably elusive fighters must be brought into the open!"

The new phase of Luftwaffe operations had begun on the morning of August 24. And despite everything—the wrongheaded decision to cease attacks on radar stations, the withdrawal of the Stukas, the shortcomings of the bombers, the fact that both bombers and fighters were now operating close to the limit of their range—the scales began tilting in favor of the Luftwaffe. Day by day, the British Fighter Command was being worn down. But it was during this time that the British had begun carrying on their pinprick raids against residential Berlin. And then had come Hitler's order to concentrate all air power on reprisal raids of London.

On September 16, with great parts of London in rubble or afire, but with no effective attrition of British fighters, their airfields and factories and oil supply now going unmolested, Göring received word from his Führer that the invasion of Britain was to be postponed until further notice. The London terror bombing was to be continued.

In the weeks that followed, the Luftwaffe Chief swung between euphoria and black depression. At times he believed, as he had not believed initially, that by pounding London to bits he could force Britain to sue for peace without one German soldier having had to fight his way up one English beach. At other times he knew without doubt that the moment of ripeness had passed and would never return.

On October 12, Hitler called off the invasion plan indefinitely. The air attacks on London were to be extended to ports and industrial cities. But this Göring left in his subordinates' hands, taking himself away on sick leave.

Chapter 64

F ROM the great Goudstikker collection in Holland, which was administered by the Enemy Property Control Office, Göring had bought for
four million marks, or the equivalent of a million and a half dollars,
Rubens's *Diana at the Bath*, once owned by Cardinal Richelieu, three other
nude Dianas by Rubens, Rembrandt's *Two Philosophers*, Hals's *Portrait of a
Young Man*, and four small exquisite altar panels by Memling. Since the
true value of these items was over five million dollars, the Reichsmarschall
had been well pleased with his bargain. "See to it, Brauchitsch," he told his
aide, and a day later the sum was paid out. The Reichsmarschall himself
never carried a pfennig, never saw money. It had become an abstract.
"See to it, Brauchitsch," and it was seen to.

The Goudstikker purchases, which had been made a week after
the collapse of Holland, were Göring's first big plunge into the foreign
art market. Afterward, gullible National Socialists began hurriedly pur-
chasing everything that bore the Goudstikker label—not realizing the
label was now being attached to inferior paintings—in order to be buy-
ing from the same collection as the Reichsmarschall. But the
Reichsmarschall's purchases were motivated by deeper feelings than
those of his imitators; he received passionate pleasure from every picture he chose, and his tastes were broad. Much as he loved Cranach's
tall, gold-glowing nudes in the severe late Gothic style, with their se-

rene, almond-eyed, piquant faces, with their jeweled necklaces and jaunty cartwheel hats imparting an eccentric tang to their nakedness, and with their austere Franconian backgrounds of cliffs and jagged peaks and castles—much as he loved these, he was enraptured by the billowy nudes of Rubens, by their white flesh so abundant and healthy, by the tumbled gorgeousness of cupids, roses, storm clouds, flashing armor, each huge and many-peopled canvas asprawl to the last centimeter with the flamboyant and grandiose. Rubens struck a lusty chord in him, Rembrandt a more somber chord; Hals brought a warm smile to his lips; but of these works which he acquired in his first big foreign plunge, it was the four tiny, intimate, lyrical musician angels of Memling that he fell in love with at once. These were part of Memling's shrine of St. Ursula, a reliquary adorned with panels depicting the life of the virgin martyr and culminating in a central panel, *The Slaughter of the Innocents,* showing her death and that of her myriad companions. This central panel, along with the others, had been removed from the reliquary by Enemy Property Control in order to be sold separately, but of all the panels, Göring had eyes only for the four tiny exquisite musician angels.

In the shape of a medallion, each panel depicted an angel playing a musical instrument—a violin, a lute, an ancient variety of zither, a kind of hand organ. The angels, against a dark vermilion background, and framed by their wings, stood curiously earthbound, like real people. They appeared to be twelve or thirteen years old, they might have been boys, they might have been girls, they had the pure, presexual look of early adolescence. They were slender, with long reddish-gold hair, and their faces wore a serious, tentative, faintly and buddingly pleased expression, as if they were just learning how to play their instruments. Every fold of their white robes was superbly rendered, as was every feather of their wings, as were the delicate hands and pure contours of the faces. Four hundred and fifty years old, they glowed with all that was young, just beginning, rapt with wonder. He took them away with him personally, in a box in his hands, they were that small—disks the size of coffee-cup saucers. He had circular gilt frames made for them, and when he returned to Carinhall he hung them not in his gallery but in his den.

Every day for as long as she could remember, the girl had been strapped into her wheelchair by a nurse. None of the other patients had lived in the nursing home as long as she; it had been her world forever. Her chin raw from the drooling she could not control, unable to speak except in guttural groans, she was quick-witted, cooperative, and grateful. The nurses endlessly wiped her chin, they bathed and fed her and exercised her deformed limbs. They understood the nuances of her groans, knew if she was making a clever sarcasm or delivering herself of a profound emotion. They joked with her when she was happy, soothed her when she was in pain, and read to her because they knew she liked that. They knew many of the things she liked, and they knew that everything outside her was sucked into her eyes and ears and nostrils, nothing escaped her. The only thing they did not know was how all this was arranged inside her head. This she could not communicate through her nuanced groans, or the laborious movements of her rigidly inturned hands. The interior arrangement was too complex, too highly calibrated, to be conveyed by such crude methods, for she lived in an immense drama peopled by nurses, doctors, patients, by literary and historical figures, and by herself, a drama illumined by sensuous colors and textures, permeated by musings on God, destiny, ultimate meaning, and all held subtly together by an artist's sure sense of design. None of this ever got past her brittle gray teeth, but she was not frustrated. This was how it was and had always been. This was she.

Yesterday the world had been overturned. "It's an old place, you know, and also we're crowded," the nurse had said, stroking her hair. "Of course it will be hard to change homes after so many years, but you'll like it there, I'm sure. We're told it's a very new, up-to-date hospital, with all kinds of opportunities for physical therapy that we can't provide here." At first the words were beyond her powers of comprehension, then tears went scalding down into her ear. Whenever she cried, which was not often, the tears did not go downward but sideways, running from one eye over the bridge of her nose to the other eye, and down her temple into her ear. This was because her head was held at an angle, as though fused to her collarbone. The nurse gently blotted the tears with her handkerchief.

This morning she and four others, all younger than she, had been wheeled out to a large white hospital van. It was early December, the sky was overcast but the air was not cold. Sunday church bells rang faintly from nearby Magdeburg. They were rolled up a ramp into the van, the wheelchairs were locked in place, the doors shut. She lifted her eyes to the van's window and watched the trees of the drive go by. She looked at the two hospital attendants sitting on a bench opposite the wheelchairs, a man and woman both in white. She could not move her head to see her four fellow patients, but she could hear them talking in her own manner, in groans or snorts, expressing their surprise and curiosity. The two attendants said not a word, nor did they move to wipe away saliva, or to check if everyone was arranged comfortably behind the wheelchair straps. The woman took out a pack of cigarettes and lit one.

About an hour later they passed through a gate bearing a sign: Bernburg Hospital. Trees lined the drive. The hospital came into view. They drove alongside it, but did not stop. They drove on past garages and outbuildings, past more trees, then turned and stopped. Some men in ordinary business suits came inside the van and helped the two attendants roll them out. The pair of hands that took hold of her wheelchair had the immediate feel of an amateur, and something began to flap inside her like a fish. With her head-locked, sideways look, as she was rolled down the van's ramp into the cool forenoon air, she saw that they were being taken to a wooden shed. The fish flapped wildly in her chest, her eyes widened to such roundness that the light pouring into them almost blinded her, but through the blinding light she could see an elderly gentleman in the white tunic of a doctor hurrying to them—

"Look here, if you're going to kill all these people, at least let us take the brains out afterward so that the material can be utilized."

"How many are you able to examine, Herr Doktor?"

"An unlimited number, the more the better!"

—and through the crazed sounds tearing from her throat, the wheelchairs now being crammed inside the shed and those who had wheeled them striding out and slamming the door shut, she heard something above start up in the darkness like a motor, then a sharp hissing took its place.

"And may I ask if the Reichsmarschall is in residence?" queried Frau Kloppmann as the car started up the steep, cobbled primary street of the village.

"Be he there, you mean?" said the chauffeur, who was peculiarly if picturesquely dressed in rough workman's jacket and coarse trousers stuffed into dirty brown boots. "Nein. Was, a bit ago. Stayed a fortnight."

Frau Kloppmann, who had come by train from Nuremburg, and at the village station had been met by this sleek, heavy, silvery-gray open motorcar, was disappointed only momentarily. It would have been too much to see him in person. As it was, she felt shivers of strangeness and excitement. And she had not meant to. She had hardened herself against being impressed. But it was useless. Even the weather thrilled and awed her.

"It is so mild for December. So springlike."

"Ja," Schelling nodded. "Not like last winter, thank God."

Frau Kloppmann drank in the mass of trees and the grayish-brown castle walls that rose above them. The car turned, and with its powerful purr ascended a narrow dirt road. They passed through the castle gate into a vision of battlements, pointed red roofs, tiered gardens. She was helped from the expensive smell of leather, the manor house was pointed out to her, and with a gracious smile she proceeded up the walk. She wore her best shoes, the silk stockings her nephew had brought back from France, a smart tweed cape borrowed for the occasion, and a newly bought velveteen beret set off by a long curved feather. Her shoes pinched at every step, but her buoyancy carried her. How pure was the air up here. Sweet, like spring water. Overhead the forenoon sky was grayish-pink, with long glowing clouds stretched across it in rippling bars. Everything was hushed; it was like another world. A faint clangor of Sunday church bells came drifting up from the village, the only sound other than the chirping of birds. The gardens, spreading out on either side of the rough-paved walk, glowed in the cool gray air. She crossed a big yard like a meadow and went up to the manor house, a long white building with red geraniums in the windows. Pulling the bell, she waited, nervously smoothing her cape. No liveried servant appeared, only a woman in ordinary housedress, unbuttoned cardigan with sleeves pushed up to the elbows, and large plaid carpet slippers on her feet. Frau Kloppman decided that she too, like the chauffeur, was picturesque. She followed her down a piercingly cold hallway to a heavy door, upon which the woman rapped, turning then with a bob and leaving the visitor.

"Frau Kloppmann!"

"Frau Schmidt!"

The two former neighbors fell into each other's arms, each exclaiming how well the other looked. Eyes were dabbed, the voluminous cape and fine hat were removed. "What a lovely room—so cozy! And so warm!"

"After the hallway, you mean. I know, it's like ice."

"Nein, nein, not at all," the visitor protested, "just a little chilly. Bracing, actually."

"Nein, nein, like ice," insisted Frau Schmidt, briskly and smilingly hanging up the guest's things. "Even with the heating system, the halls never get really warm. And right now they're not heated at all. They're like ice, all right, it's just as when I was young. It's because we're so high, you see, we're built right into the east wall above the cliff. It is the nature of the place. It has been so from the beginning."

"Ja, it is ancient," agreed Frau Kloppmann happily, her several bracelets clinking as she smoothed her tightly permanented brown hair. Her short and extremely round figure was encased in a vivid blue dress with flounces and scalloped neck. Three strings of blue glass beads sparkled beneath her chins. "It's just as you told me in the old days, absolutely another world. And this lovely apartment—oh, I must see the other rooms!"

Frau Schmidt, who was dressed with her usual taste and neatness, and whose red bony face bore an expression of mellow pleasure, took her guest through the rest of the little apartment. From the bedroom window she pointed out the spectacular east view of the great valley spread below. Frau Kloppmann drew in her breath. Then came the view from the dining room, of trees and of the watchtower. Back in the sitting room, the windows looked out on the lush green of the court-yard.

"I'm so happy for you, Frau Schmidt. Really, it's like a dream come true."

"That it is. And you should see Hans. Why, twenty years have rolled off him."

"He is out in die Natur?" asked Frau Kloppmann approvingly.

"Ach, he is more out than in. And I too. I take a walk around the grounds three and four times a day. We will take a stroll later."

"I would enjoy that," said Frau Kloppmann, who was dying to see everything, and added hintingly: "And the rest of the house, is it similar to your apartment?"

"Come, I'll show you. But put your cloak back on," Frau Schmidt told her, taking a knitted shawl from a peg and draping it around her sharp shoulders.

They went along several hallways and entered a large room, heavy with medieval atmosphere. The furniture was massive, dark, elaborately carved. Tapestries and ancient weapons hung on the walls. Full suits of armor stood in corners.

"All as it was," said Frau Schmidt, folding her hands before her.

"All as it was," echoed Frau Kloppmann in hushed tones.

She was shown the study. The dining room. The drawing room. With round eyes, she accompanied her hostess up the staircase. The upper floor was more rustic than downstairs. The hallway was slightly crooked, the floor slightly uneven.

"These are the bedrooms," her hostess informed her.

"And may I ask, Frau Schmidt, which is the Reichsmarschall's?"

Frau Schmidt indicated one of the doors as they walked along. "This. The master bedroom."

Frau Kloppmann would have dearly loved to see the room, but she knew it was too much to ask. With her buoyant sense of strangeness and happiness, her tight shoes pinching her small fat feet, the chill of the hallway piercing her marrow, she walked glowingly at her hostess's side.

"I understand from the driver that the Reichsmarschall was here only recently."

"Ja, with his wife and the child. They were here in late November. He was here in October also, and in September."

They turned at the end of the hallway and retraced their steps. The old floorboards creaked beneath their feet.

"It must be a great pleasure for the Reichsmarschall to come and stay at his family castle."

"Ja, it is. Only it is not a castle, you know, Frau Kloppmann. It is a burg. More of a burg than a castle. We always called it the burg."

"The burg," repeated Frau Kloppmann, like a student, as they went down the stairs.

Herr Schmidt was just coming in the front door from the outside. Dressed for Sunday in his old-fashioned black suit, with waistcoat and looped watch chain, he shuffled along bent over his cane, but there was life in the shuffling steps. "It's true, Herr Schmidt, twenty years have rolled off you!" he heard someone call from the staircase, and he greeted his round little ex-neighbor, who was half lost in an enormous cloak, as she descended with Nikki.

"I am in another world, another world!" she exclaimed, coming up to him as if on wheels, so long was the cloak, and kissing him emotionally on both cheeks, which caused him to blush. "When I came up through the gardens I was absolutely struck," she continued, as they went on down the hallway. "Why, they're like the hanging gardens of Babylon, Herr Schmidt! And the house here—Frau Schmidt has just given me a tour—oh, it is wonderful!" And there was joy in her, Hans said to himself, real true joy, that you could feel like waves of heat.

It was odd, he thought as they sat visiting, not to hear the old competition grinding away between the two. Nikki was quiet, Nikki was strong, at peace, she could even be humble—"We lead a very plain life, very ordinary"—because every stone of the burg spoke for her. And the little Kloppmann, all got up for battle in her blinding blue dress and bangles and beads, she couldn't fight that. She couldn't fight being here at Veldenstein, it was too much for her, she had sunk down under it like somebody baptized in a river, coming up streaming with light. Not a shrug or scoffing word left in her, all shining eyes, quivering ears. Hardly a thing to say about herself, she was that taken. Even the soldier nephew who had always been so big in her talk, who knew all there was to know about Austria because he'd been there three days, got brushed aside when Nikki inquired after him. "Kurt? Oh, he's with the occupying force in France." That was all; as if to say, of what interest is my nephew, what can he know about anything, so low in the ranks? And when Nikki asked about Frau Kloppmann's summer holiday with relatives who lived in the Bavarian Alps, the round one gave a happy, contemptuous swipe of her hand. "It was nice, but the air was *nothing* like you've got up here."

It was embarrassing, but Nikki continued graciously. "Really, you must tell us about your stay there."

"But it's not *me* we should be catching up with, it's *you*. I want to know *everything* that's happened since you moved in."

"Well, nothing much happens here. As you see, our life is very quiet."

"But when the Reichsmarschall comes?"

"Then . . . not so quiet." Nikki smiled.

The other looked at her with shining eyes. Suddenly the kettle began whistling from the kitchen. "You stay where you are," Nikki protested as the round one bounced to her feet; there was, however, no keeping her back. She followed on her hostess' heels, begging to help, her voice ringing with joy.

Hans understood her. He remembered his own sense of streaming light when a half-dozen open cars, heavy and sleek, the Reichsmarschall's in the lead, the others full of adjutants and servants and bodyguards, came purring in through the gate and stopped down below the gardens. There was a bustle, a slamming of car doors, and the paved walk was full of figures coming toward him where he stood: uniforms, swinging briefcases, the sound of voices and clattering footsteps; and the Reichsmarschall in the flesh, you could see his face, hear his voice, this striding big man who was the fate of nations—and it was not that Hans felt impressed, it was more like being all at once inside a big pulsing heart. Or on the high crest of a wave that could never crash. Or at the center of a storm, a great storm spreading all across Europe with its millions and millions of people who felt the strong wind in their faces; but the eye of a storm was calm, strangely calm, for all its bustle and clattering footsteps; and that was how you felt: a deep, deep calm, and a brightness of light, and happiness, because the pulse of power was like the deathless heartbeat of God, and you were in it, and of it.

For a bit. When they came near he would doff his cap, the Reichsmarschall might say a few words to him in greeting, the dazzling figure becoming a good-natured fellow passing on with a wave. The strange, happy, immortal moment receded, but not completely. Something of the man's light was embedded in the stones of the burg and mixed in with the colors of the flowers. It was a peculiar fancy. You knew it couldn't be so, but you felt it to be so.

Frau Kloppmann was a different case. She was more like the regular person always looking to be joined with something big and high. But she wanted it straight, not through Nikki. Nikki's powerful connection was Nikki's alone; what's more, it had never shown itself except in a yearly ticket to the rallies. Frau Kloppmann went wild at the rallies, but afterward she had nothing again. She had to listen to Nikki's big talk, which did Frau Kloppmann no good, and she beat Nikki over the head with her nephew and the small-time Party officials she knew, so as to keep her dignity. But now all that was changed. She was in the powerful man's house. She walked on his floors. She had been driven in his car. She had a piece of him, she had swallowed his light, she shone with it like the sun. And Nikki was his lieutenant.

"I confess we don't keep up with things," came Nikki's voice as the two of them returned from the kitchen. "You're probably better informed than we, Frau Kloppmann. Nicht wahr, Hans?"

"Aye," he agreed, but Frau Kloppmann, setting down a pitcher of cream, shook a coy finger at them. "Not likely."

"Nein, 'tis true," he said. "Up here we get to forgetting about things on the outside. Well, so much the better, we've no truck with the war."

"God willing, it will soon be over," said Nikki, taking the things from the tray as the round one sank deep into her armchair, nodding in vigorous agreement.

"In the spring," Frau Kloppmann said, "then with the good weather the Luftwaffe will again start bombing Britain in force, and will bring her to her knees. Not that my opinion is worth anything, of course. But it's what everyone is saying."

"That is how we view it too," said Nikki, pouring the coffee.

Neither of them mentioned the bombings of Berlin and other cities; Nikki didn't like that mentioned, for Göring's sake. Not that they were worth mentioning, pinpricks; but he had assured the public, "If one enemy plane drops one bomb on German soil, my name is no longer Göring, you may call me Meier."

The round one had poured thick cream into her real, non-ersatz coffee, and was sipping with deep pleasure. Earlier, Nikki had said to Hans: "It would be hypocritical of me to serve anything but what we ourselves always have. Everyone knows that at Veldenstein we're not subject to rationing, that it is the same here as at Carinhall. Frau Kloppmann shall have real coffee with cream, and the dinner will be our regular Sunday meal." Which, in true Franconian style, was always beef soup with dumplings, red cabbage, roast veal, dark beer, and prune compote with whipped cream. Nikki was still not much of a cook, and things were usually overdone or underdone, but it all tasted good to him. Neither of them was a big eater, so the portions were small; but today the meal was to be on the big side, for the sake of the guest, who, with dainty gestures, was covering a split roll with real butter and orange marmalade. "Such a beautiful set of china, Frau Schmidt. I used always to think so in the old days, but now that it is back in its proper surroundings, it looks more beautiful yet."

It was embarrassing, but the light streamed from her; she looked almost beautiful herself. He sipped his coffee, lifting his big white drooping mustaches away from the cup with his twisted, incurved fingers, then smoothing out the two white wings as he sat back in his chair, contentedly listening as the two of them talked on.

Chapter 65

Göring was on sick leave from October till the end of January. His ailments subsided as he busied himself at Carinhall, breeding his animals, sorting the art treasures that continually arrived in packing crates from France, Holland and Belgium, and working on architectural plans for the museum that would eventually house his collection. He had welcome time for his wife and little daughter, and took them on a holiday to Veldenstein and Mauterndorf. He also traveled to East Prussia for two weeks of stag hunting at his lodge, a sizable cabin made of huge tree trunks, with thatched roof jutting far out over the eaves, which lay deep in Rominten Forest, near the Lithuanian border.

In a white full-sleeved blouse under a leather jerkin, trousers stuffed into high boots, and at his broad leather belt a hunting knife in the shape of an old Germanic sword, he would set out into the forest each morning with his guests, his Jägers, and his Oberjägermeister. After supper, when the sun had gone down, he and the guests would assemble before the lodge, where the stags shot during the day had been laid out on the grass. A great bonfire of pine branches was lit; and in the illumination of its blaze, the Oberjägermeister ritually read out the bag and the names of those who had killed it. The Jägers, standing in the bright play of light, then lifted their curved, ancient hunting horns and sounded the *Halali,* the death of the stag, the age-old notes of the horns echoing back from the dark forest stillness.

From the wilds of Rominten the Reichsmarschall arrived back in Berlin to host a fête for Russian Foreign Minister Molotov. He put in a surprise appearance at his Paris art office to see how his advisers and experts were doing. He arranged the family Christmas gathering, where toasts were made to a victorious end to the war come spring. On his birthday he gave his yearly ball at the Prussian State Opera House. And soon thereafter he returned to his duties.

The war had dragged on, was growing more complex. In November, Mussolini had invaded Greece in a rash surprise move; the Italians had been defeated, and the English were now in Salonika, from which they could bomb the Rumanian oilfields. The Führer was faced with the question of whether or not to march to Salonika and drive out the English. This would mean an extension of the theater of war into the Mediterranean.

Each morning as the Reichsmarschall was driven through the Berlin streets to one or another of his offices, he was hailed by pedestrians and traffic policemen. Factories in the north of the city were sometimes hit and put out of commission for a day at the most, but it was residential Berlin the planes concentrated on, less for the minor damage meted out than to keep people from sleeping, to exhaust them, to wear down their morale. But the Berliners' morale was higher than it had been before the bombings; they finally felt a personal stake in the war, anger against the British toning up their spirit. And the winter was mild, they were on generous food rations, cinemas and theaters and nightclubs were going strong, soldiers back from defeated France brought home so much perfume that the city smelled like a hairdresser's salon. Only sleepless nights in the cellars disturbed the Berliners' sense of living in a victorious capital soon to check off its final triumph and a return to peace. If peace had been postponed from autumn to spring, that was how it was; in any event, spring would soon arrive. Meanwhile they cursed the irritating RAF, went on with their jobs and their lives and waved with enthusiasm whenever they caught sight of their Hermann driving by. All this he saw and was glad to see; even so, he preferred not to be reminded of the bombings, and no mention of them was allowed at Carinhall.

He dug into the work that had piled up in his absence. So familiar was he with the overlapping of his multitudinous jobs that he did not think it strange at all when, as Chief of the Four-Year Plan, he ordered a cut in payments to the relatives of Luftwaffe personnel, only to withdraw it as Chief of the Luftwaffe. There was nothing new in that kind of thing, but he found himself less patient than ever with details. Back into the hands of his subordinates went all but the largest matters.

He was having little success taking over commerce and industry in

France. After six months of battling with Ribbentrop, the Foreign Minister was winning out. The French themselves preferred to deal with the Foreign Minister's appointees, whom they rightly considered economic moderates, thereby avoiding the economic fate of Austria and Czechoslovakia, where the state-owned Hermann Göring Werke had incorporated private industry lock, stock and barrel.

In Germany itself the situation was not as radical; but the Ruhr industrialists, chafing under Göring's endless demands and restrictions, judged him little better than a Bolshevik. He had made himself clear as early as 1937 by stating publicly: "Just as I will be resolved to ignore the fate of individuals if the well-being of the community requires it, I shall not show weakness in placing the interests of the Volk above those of individual businesses."

He accused the industrialists of the crassest egoistic capitalism, and had even gone so far as to say they had a toilet-seat perspective on national affairs.

If France was a failure as far as the Hermann Göring Werke was concerned, in Poland all was different. There the Reichsmarschall had a free hand. Complete incorporation of Polish industry into the German economy was being achieved. Raw material, machinery, produce were all fed into Germany, along with human labor. Over a million Polish civilians and prisoners of war were now employed as agricultural and industrial workers, living in barracks or private rooms and receiving two-thirds the German wage. Unlike the Poles, who were forcibly recruited, laborers from occupied Western European countries were voluntary. They were paid better than the Poles and could mingle freely with the populace. Propaganda Minister Goebbels, who once again felt himself slipping into the background as his foreign propaganda powers were transferred by Hitler to the Foreign Office, was making the most of his domestic powers, coming down hard on the laborers from Poland. Every household in Berlin had received a leaflet warning against fraternization with Slav workers: "German people, never forget that the atrocities of the Poles compelled the Führer to protect our German people by armed force! The servility of the Poles to their German employers merely hides their cunning, their friendly behavior hides their deceit. Germans! The Pole must never be your comrade! He is inferior to each German comrade in his factory or his farm. Be just, but never forget that you are a member of der völkischer race!"

While Goebbels took care of the Poles' standing in the community, Göring took care of their allocation and distribution, as well as that of the Western European workers. As in the Great War, Germany was undergoing a blockade of food and raw material, but so far the blockade was ineffective because of steps previously taken. The main problem—always Germany's fundamental economic problem—was shortage of labor. Germany traditionally depended on seasonal foreign workers. Now they worked all year round, that was the difference, and it was necessary. With millions of German workers drafted into the armed forces or war labor forces, there was a dangerous dearth of workers on the land and in factories. If Germany was on its way to overcoming this problem by the use of foreign laborers, the difficulties involved sometimes seemed insurmountable to Göring.

There was the confusion and overlapping of offices in the sphere of labor in general. The Army handled drafting policies; the German Labor Front handled welfare and training of German workers; the Food Ministry handled agricultural labor; Himmler handled security and racial policies concerning foreign workers; even the German Housewives' Association had a voice in foreign labor matters.

There was the unavoidable fact that the more foreign laborers poured in, the more mouths there were that must be fed.

There were the private factory owners who, to assure themselves of a higher production rate than that of competing factories, continually inflated their labor requirements.

And there was the unbelievable fact that two hundred thousand German women remained employed as domestics instead of being put to war work.

But Hitler would not draw upon the womanhood of Germany to aid the war effort. He felt that it would have a demoralizing effect on the people. Above all, Hitler wished to maintain a peacetime standard of living. Consumer goods were always emphasized, unnecessary public works construction continued at the Führer's request, and German private business remained interested mainly in its own profits. Göring would have instituted a rigorous, large-scale mobilization of German workers and war output, but he understood that in the back of Hitler's mind was always the memory of the 1918 defeat, which had had its roots in the dissatisfactions of the home front, and that he was adamantly opposed to any such dissatisfactions arising again. Thus one had to work within the economic framework laid down by the Führer, with all its confusions and overlappings and half measures, because one had upheld the Führer principle from the start, had vigorously promulgated and solidified that principle, and although one possessed more autonomy than any other man in the high echelons of power, one was, oneself, a captive of that principle.

At the Air Ministry he found himself beset by more problems, grew short-tempered and was loud in his displeasure. Only when he was surrounded by the younger members of his staff—the Kindergarten, as Feldmarschall Milch caustically dubbed them—who were devoted to their Chief, who idolized him, who never argued with him, was he fully at ease.

Chief of Staff Jeschonnek was one of the Kindergarten members. Relatively young himself, he put a great premium on youth for its natural vigor and daring, and for being the age group in which National Socialism was most passionately upheld. It was a matter of deep pride to him that the Luftwaffe was called, unlike the two older armed services, "the Nazi service." The Chief of Staff preferred being with the younger men because he had difficulty impressing himself upon the senior Luftwaffe members, yet among the juniors he was not at home either, by reason of his heavy, humorless character. And he had no idea what to make of the mercurial Göring, whom he admired and wished to please, but in whose presence he felt himself more than ever rigid and charmless. Try as he would, he could not strike the right personal note with his Chief.

The one person Jeschonnek got on well with was his ultimate Chief. With his Führer he felt a sense of belonging, of being appreciated and understood. For this solitary young Generaloberst with his stolid countenance, his heavy rubbery lips that could never break into a spontaneous smile, the rapport he enjoyed with the greatest of all Germans living or dead, the wisest, the most brilliant, the most daring, was immensely gratifying and made up for much of the frustration he endured in his work.

For Göring, as the cool gray winter evolved into an early spring, and as it became increasingly clear that Hitler had permanently shelved all plans to invade England, there seemed no possibility of subduing the stubborn island.

Such a possibility had existed when the Gibraltar plan still had feasibility. The Reichsmarschall had been a strong exponent of the plan, which called for the bombing of Gibraltar and essentially a takeover of the Mediterranean, Britain's lifeline to her overseas empire. Hitler had begun feeling Franco out for permission to go through Spain, but Franco procrastinated with an answer. Time went by, and more time. The Reichsmarschall believed they should go through Spain with or without Franco's consent, the possession of Gibraltar being essential to knocking out Britain once and for all. But without Franco's cooperation, Hitler's interest in the plan had faded. His eyes were fastened on Russia.

The Führer had many reasons. Russia might at any moment tear up her friendship pact with Germany and make common cause with Britain. Russia was insidiously grabbing up territory she had no right to. Russia had always figured as the logical area in which the future population of Germany must be settled. Above all, Russia was the archfoe of Europe and the world. Did no one know how it had torn his soul to sign a pact with the Bolsheviks whom, from the last days of the Great War, he had vowed to destroy root and branch? Did no one remember the suicides among Party idealists on the day the pact was signed? Did no one know how that had weighed on him? That every moment of this Russian "friendship," which he had been forced into for strategic purposes, had been anathema to him? Now at last he would act freely, and God would stand behind him in this ideological scourge of humanity's foe.

When Göring and the generals pointed out the vastness of Russia and the impossibility of ever occupying such an area, when they spoke of the rash inadvisability of opening up a second front, they were reminded that the Russian Army was weak and primitive. It would be beaten in six weeks. After which Germany, with no worries at its rear, would turn around and finish off England.

At the end of March, before an audience of two hundred of his commanders, Hitler announced that the invasion of Russia would commence on June 22.

"I had planned on an earlier date, but it is now unfeasible in view of the necessity of sending troops to Greece and Yugoslavia. Yet Barbarossa cannot be much longer postponed. Now is the time, for no successor will ever exercise the authority I possess. No successor will ever accept the responsibility for unleashing such an invasion. I, and I alone, can stop Bolshevism before all Europe succumbs to it. The Bolshevik state must be destroyed, the Red Army annihilated. The war against Russia will be such that it cannot be fought in a knightly fashion. The struggle is one of ideologies and racial differences. It must be conducted with unprecedented, merciless, and unrelenting harshness."

Early April saw the attack on Yugoslavia, where constant aerial bombardment of Belgrade hastened the collapse of opposition. In Greece, German troops were fighting with powerful air support. In North Africa, where Feldmarschall Rommel was advancing on British-held Tobruk, large contingents of Stukas were in action. And over Britain, the bombing raids continued. Since the invasion of Norway a full year ago, the Luftwaffe had been given no respite whatsoever. And soon they were going to be asked to throw themselves into a war with Russia.

In early May the Reichsmarschall felt himself in need of another leave. With frayed nerves and a briefcase stocked with paracodeine pills, with a small retinue composed of a few adjutants, Herr Kropp and Nurse Gormanns, he took himself to quiet Veldenstein for a month.

Chapter 66

Generaloberst Udet was not surprised to receive a visit from State Secretary Milch. With the Chief gone, Milch was standing in for him, and taking advantage of it. During the Chief's protracted leave earlier in the year, the State Secretary had done a lot of sniffing, sniffing. Now suddenly he appeared, carrying his eternal ashtray and carefully tapping his cigar over it. His Feldmarschall's gold braid gleamed, but Udet did not think of him as Feldmarschall. An American magazine had recently described him as the German equivalent of an energetic U.S. businessman, and with this description Udet concurred. He asked the State Secretary to sit down, although the State Secretary was already sitting down without being asked. Udet rubbed the base of his skull, where he had begun to suffer from drilling headaches.

"You've been looking seedy, Udet. You'd better start pulling yourself together."

"And you'd better start keeping your nose out of my affairs."

The round face flushed crimson, but the neat small features remained impassive.

"I'm afraid that's not possible. I've recently heard of some things that must be cleared up."

The red-meat, drooping eyes of a bloodhound . . . no, they weren't red, they were piercing blue button eyes. It was his own eyes that were red.

Too much smoking, too little sleep. He rubbed them with nicotined fingers as the State Secretary began questioning him.

"How many department heads do you have reporting directly to you? Ten? Fifteen?"

"If you know, why bother asking?"

"Ten? Fifteen?"

Udet looked at him with weary loathing.

"Fifteen? As many as that? Have you actually that many department heads reporting to you? I demand to know. Ten? Fifteen?"

The battering words sent a glaze across Udet's inflamed eyes.

"Twenty-six," he sighed.

Astonished silence. Then the battering started in again.

"Everything turns to dust in your hands, Udet. And the main reason is clearly this grotesque number of departments. In the name of common sense, man, you must regroup your organization into three or four main sections. No more than four. Can't you see what a chaotic—"

"What I see is that you're taking advantage of the Chief's absence to further your own cause."

"It's not for my sake that I give you advice," said the State Secretary coldly, getting to his feet with his ashtray. "But you had better take it. You've been too long without it."

For some moments after his visitor had left, Udet sat kneading his throbbing head. Then, absently taking up a pen, he began making slow doodles on the desk blotter. They were circles, little balloons, many little balloons on a string which was held by nobody.

In Neuhaus, the following Sunday morning was peaceful and fragrant. Families who had allotments along the little River Pegnitz were out working in their vegetable and fruit plots, sleeves rolled up in the warm morning sun. Other families, on their way home from church, had stopped in at the Gasthaus for a second breakfast. Still others were starting off on their Sunday walk, closing behind them the heavy doors of their ancient houses, which all leaned perceptibly to one side. The rucksacked parents followed by the bare-legged children, the children followed by the circling, sniffing family dog, they promenaded down the cobbles in the forenoon quiet.

The calm was shattered by a car roaring past. They had time just to glimpse the Reichsmarschall and his chauffeur. The Reichsmarschall looked neither left nor right. Usually the chauffeur drove at a civilized speed down the twisting streets, and unser Hermann acknowledged with a smile or wave all those he passed. Not so today. The car scattered chickens and geese to either side as it blazed out of sight in the direction of the autobahn.

Göring was sweating in streams, despite the cool morning air that

rushed against his face. In his mind he continually went over the telephone message he had just received from Bodenschatz, who, as his
liaison with Hitler, was at the Berghof: "The Führer wants you to come
here at once, Chief. I cannot tell you why over the phone, I have strictest orders. He wants you to leave this instant." It was an unprecedented
order; and since it would take three hours to reach the Obersalzberg,
he would be three hours tormenting himself over the possible reason
behind it.

During those three hours much telephoning and discussion went
on at the Berghof, but most of the people there were unaware of it, all
houseguests and the Führer's "family" having been banished to an upper floor. When Herr Speer arrived from his little studio, bearing his
latest sketches of the triumphal arch to be erected in Berlin, he too was
bustled upstairs. "What in the world is going on?" he asked the photographer Hoffmann, who gave a mellow shrug. Fräulein Braun knew
nothing either, or only very little. "All I know," she said, "is that someone delivered a letter to him, and when he read it he gave a terrible
cry. Then we were all rushed upstairs."

"Like a flock of chickens," agreed the suave Hoffmann, with a
philosophical smile.

"And Bormann?" asked Speer, looking around. "Where is Herr
Bormann?"

"Come, come, Herr Speer. Bormann is not one of us chickens.
Bormann is down there holding his master's hand."

Speer walked over to one of the windows, his rolled-up drawings
under his arm. He had looked forward to discussing the triumphal-
arch plans with the Führer, since most of his work these days had to do
with factory buildings and plants. From down below there came a slamming of car doors, and he observed Ribbentrop hurrying up the broad
stone steps, his face very white, very worried. Shortly after, another car
drew up, this time bearing Goebbels. In his attempt to climb the stairs
swiftly, the Propaganda Minister ascended with more than his usual
awkwardness. His thin face was stony with apprehension. After another hour or more—Speer had sat down and visited with Fräulein
Braun—there was heard yet another car drawing up with all haste below. This time, going over to the window, he saw Göring bounding
bulkily up the stairs, his long lips drawn thin with tension.

Something catastrophic had obviously taken place. And it was curious, mused the architect, that each arrival looked anxious and guilty, as
if each was certain that he alone bore the blame for this terrible thing,
whatever it was, that had happened.

Speer's surmise was true in that each of the three, not knowing
why he had been summoned, nor that anyone but himself had been
summoned, believed the Führer was about to confront him with some
disaster incurred in his own departmental jurisdiction. None knew

what this disaster might be, but during their respective journeys their brains had churned with every dark possibility. It was therefore with a spontaneous heave of inner relief that each learned from a chalk-white, enraged Hitler that "Hess! Hess! Hess has flown to England!"

Relief was immediately blotted out by astonishment. "To England? Hess?"

The letter was flapped first in Ribbentrop's face, then in Goebbels's, and when Göring arrived, in his.

"Die verfluchte Luftwaffe again! It's your Luftwaffe that got him there!"

Aghast, Göring could only stare.

"Or the distance may have been too great," Hitler went on, pacing. "Can the English coast be reached from here? You're an airman, tell me!"

"What . . . what type of planes are they?" stammered the Reichsmarschall.

"Planes? Who's speaking of planes! How can the man fly more than one plane!"

The color returned to Göring's face. "Forgive me if I naturally pictured a heavy escort, mein Führer, having understood you to say that my Luftwaffe had gotten him there."

The slightly acidic edge was lost on the distraught Hitler, who slapped the letter in his hand. "It's one of your Messerschmitts, a 110. He says here he will have flown from Augsburg at six o'clock last night. That means he has been gone twenty hours already. I telephoned Messerschmitt and discovered that for months he has allowed Hess to use a 110 for practice flights. Practice flights for *what*? And the asshole answers that Hess was a flyer in the Great War. *I know that!* Well, he wanted to get himself back into flying shape. Into shape for *what*? Why, I believed it was just the patriotic urge of an ex-airman. Don't you know I expressly *forbade* Hess ever to fly again? I forbid *all* my chief lieutenants to take unnecessary risks! What's the use of repeating all this—Messerschmitt is an unmitigated idiot. The point is that I must know if it's technically possible for Hess to reach England. Messerschmitt says maybe, although the 110 has a limited range. I called Udet in Berlin, and he says it's unlikely. What do you say? What is your opinion?"

"Myself, I'd say he's probably got a fifty-fifty chance," answered Göring, using the English expression.

"So you're already speaking English!" Hitler flared up again, then fell silent. He who never allowed himself to be photographed while wearing his reading glasses, who in fact tried never to be seen with them on, had not removed them since he had read the first words of Hess's letter. Now, finally, abstractedly, he took the glasses off, hardly noticing that the ever-present Bormann gently removed them from his hand, carefully folded the stems, and placed them within easy reach.

There were tears in Hitler's eyes as he sat down. "To think that he could do it to me. My Hesserl . . . he whom I trusted with my whole soul. I tell you if he ever comes back I'll have him put in a madhouse or shot! He means to be taken to Churchill, he means to persuade him to stop fighting. He will guarantee the continuation of the British Empire if they will grant us a free hand in Europe. It is all here in the letter. It is exactly what I offered them eighteen months ago. But it was possible then, it is *not* possible now. Gott, doesn't he realize what he's doing? In the middle of a war he flies to the enemy camp! It's worse than the desertion of an army corps! Doesn't he realize he's handing the world a unique propaganda opportunity? *The Führer's Party Deputy defects to England!* And what if he gives away the invasion plans of Russia? . . . But no, he can't, he isn't privy to them."

"Surely he knows?" questioned Ribbentrop.

"He knows as much as you." Hitler shrugged.

Ribbentrop, whose crowning achievement had been the nonaggression pact with Russia, who for that achievement had been hailed by his Führer as the second Bismarck, had begun feeling increasingly less favored in recent months. Not only was his great pact vilified by Hitler as a temporary measure entirely alien to National Socialist ideology, but the Foreign Minister's power base was constantly shriveling as things diplomatic were crowded out by things military. He felt his Führer's offhand remark like a slap in the face.

"I suggest," Goebbels was saying, "that a communiqué be issued before the English have a chance to issue their own."

Göring gave a nod. "Perhaps to the effect that Hess is not in full possession of his faculties."

A sigh escaped Hitler's lips. He looked wistful. "Perhaps we should wait. Perhaps he has fallen into the sea . . . then nobody will know."

Then the dreamy hope passed; again he grew furious. "Churchill will use this incident shrewdly, you can depend on that sow! He will pretend either that Hess has gone over to their side, or that we are so weak we have sent out a peace feeler. Who will believe me when I say Hess didn't fly there in my name? That the whole thing isn't some sort of intrigue behind the backs of my allies? And what of our soldiers? If they think we're seeking peace with Britain, will they fight less hard? And how are we to state that the third man in the Reich is a *lunatic?*"

Toward evening, when those who had been banished upstairs were, with the exception of Fräulein Braun, allowed to descend, a certain calm had been restored. All that could be done had been done. Seven versions of a communiqué had been written. The final version, to be broadcast through the nation and published in all German newspapers, stated that Party Deputy Hess had commandeered an airplane against orders and disappeared. It was believed that he had crashed in some remote region. A letter left behind showed traces of a mental disturbance which justified the fear that Hess was the victim of hallucinations.

Herr Speer was dumfounded to learn of Hess's irrational act, but following his astonishment came a stronger emotion as he realized that Bormann, his *bête noire,* was next in line for Hess's position if the latter did not show up. Or even if he did show up, for how could a victim of hallucination be reinstated to the highest post in the Party?

The Führer looked aged and grieved, as if his faith in mankind had been shattered. There was obviously more to the disappearance of the loyal Hess than was being let on. Hess's aide, for instance, who had delivered the letter, had been immediately arrested. This Hitler admitted himself.

"I shall have him thrown in jail, and he can rot there as far as I'm concerned!"

Chapter 67

T HE next day, as Robert got his master out of his uniform into cord trousers, raw silk blouse and suede vest, he made no reference to the Reichsmarschall's abrupt departure the morning before. He never asked questions, even when he was very curious.

"You may as well know, since it will be in all the papers. Deputy Hess took a plane and disappeared."

"Disappeared? Deputy Hess?"

"Into thin air as far as is known. They say he had been acting strangely for some time. Well, when it comes to that," said the Reichsmarschall, going to the door, "he was always a bit strange. I remember a friend of mine saying, back in 'twenty-three, that you should watch out for a man who lives on lettuce leaves."

Robert smiled as the door closed. The Chief was certainly in a better frame of mind upon his return than when he had bolted off yesterday. He had seemed to expect a catastrophe. Often he seemed to expect a catastrophe. Often there was great tension in him. But less often when he was on leave. He was more his old self then, especially here at Veldenstein.

The valet hung up the uniform in the wardrobe, Veldenstein boasting no such modern convenience as a closet. Indeed, the bulk of the Reichsmarschall's clothes had to be hung in a storage room down the hall, a primitive arrangement. Veldenstein was primitive. Even the master bedroom here—walls damp to the touch, the angles of the room slightly off, as if pushed awry by the settling of time, and the old floorboards creaking when you walked across them. The room was not even terribly large for a master bedroom. Much of the floor space was taken up by a massive canopied bed, an exact replica of the one in the Reichsmarschall's bedroom at Carinhall. Above it hung a nude Diana by Rubens. The painting reached to the ceiling, for the ceiling was low. The only inherently interesting feature of the room was its windows, which looked out over a wonderful vista of fields and woods. Less wonderful, it gave one a jolt, was the view straight below: a sheer, dizzying drop down the jagged side of a cliff. Robert rearranged some things on the dresser, and looked around him again. Low-ceilinged, damp-walled, odd-angled, and creaking, it was nevertheless a room the Reichsmarschall loved.

But for Robert, Veldenstein took some getting used to. He was city, protocol, formality. There was no formality at Veldenstein, hardly any set rules, and practically nothing for him to do: no meetings or receptions to dress his master for, no medals to select, no agenda to keep. The Reichsmarschall's only activities at his burg were to see to his birds and farm animals and to go for shoots in the nearby forests.

Robert was not even certain how to dress here. Since the war's start, on trips with the Reichsmarschall he had worn the uniform of the National Socialist Flying Corps, apparently to give his presence a military justification. He was always glad on returning to Carinhall to change back into his usual formal attire. But here at Veldenstein formal attire was out of place. And so he wore a plain gray business suit, and felt yet more out of place. Nor did he know what to do with himself.

Going outside, he sat down on a bench with yesterday's newspaper. Nurse Gormanns, in her flowered dress, was taking one of her many walks. She also had little to keep her busy. Fortunately, the Chief's health always improved at Veldenstein; there was no need for her tray of pills, her hovering presence. She came walking over to him.

"Do come for a stroll, Herr Kropp, there is so much to see."

"Danke, I am fine where I am."

He watched her coolly as she went off. He resented that in the vaulted dining hall she often sat down beside him. She was too friendly and outgoing. She had made friends with the old couple that lived in the downstairs south wing of the manor, and with the big-booted, ham-fisted Schelling. He sat trying to enjoy what lay before him: the grassy courtyard, the flowering fruit trees, the view of the north wall, hung with scaffolding. The Reichsmarschall was having the crumbled parts repaired. Old Herr Schmidt stood among his flowers, bent over his cane. He rather liked the old man, because he was quiet. A good thing too, since one could hardly understand his dialect, though it wasn't as thick as Schelling's. Frau Schmidt, on the other hand, spoke a good German. But she spoke too much. And she acted as if she owned everything. "Have you seen our east view, Herr Kropp?" "Have you been down to our aviary?" "Are you enjoying our sun?" Our sun, indeed. And in the dining hall she and the old man sometimes ate with the Chief. At times even the crude Schelling could be seen eating in the dining hall. It was all informal, topsy-turvy, wrong, and he thought longingly of Carinhall, where order and elegance prevailed.

But as the days went by, Herr Kropp began to relax. He did not remove his coat jacket, although the weather was very warm for May, but he did stroll around the grounds, and even along the wooden walkways that had been built close to the tops of the walls.

"So you've finally relented! Aren't the views breathtaking?" This was from Nurse Gormanns, pointing into the distance with her strong forefinger with its square-cut nail.

"It is very pleasurable to walk here, Frau Gormanns, you were right in suggesting it." With a cordial touch to his nonexistent hat, he passed on. Even to Gormanns he was sociable. And it seemed to him that his growing pleasure in the visit, his restfulness and amiability, all derived from the Reichsmarschall's own increasing good spirits. One could not help but absorb tension when one was around it all the time, but the circles beneath his master's eyes were diminishing, as were the deep creases in the brow, and the swollen finger joints. The Reichsmarschall's tension was being replaced by his former good humor.

The capture of Crete put Göring in exceptionally fine spirits. He sensed only too deeply that the Führer blamed him for the failure in knocking out Britain, for the bombings of Berlin, and for the evacuation of Dunkirk, which in retrospect was seen as a disaster; nor had the Führer's sardonic remarks at the Berghof been lost on him; he had heard of the Führer's dissatisfactions from other sources as well, and that he had once even called him Herr Meier. But the Crete campaign was an incontestable success. Thanks to his Luftwaffe, the British had been expelled from the island in six brief days. German power now extended down the Balkans into the Mediterranean itself. He telegraphed Milch in Berlin to express his satisfaction in the good news.

But the next day Milch appeared at Veldenstein in person.

"It has been a great victory, Herr Reichsmarschall, but at a staggering cost. Both in men and material. We lost two hundred and seventy Junkers 52's—half our total Ju-52 fleet. Do you realize that the success in the Russian attack is going to be endangered because we will have only twenty-seven hundred first-line planes available? Why, even last year against England, we had twenty-six hundred planes!"

Göring, with a look of astonishment, sat down at his desk. "I don't understand," he said, taking up a sheaf of papers covered with figures. "According to Udet, at least fifteen hundred new planes are available."

"Udet is lying."

The following day, a Luftwaffe car deposited Generaloberst Udet at the foot of the paved walk that led up to the manor house. He had received orders to fly immediately from Berlin to report to Göring. Worriedly, he advanced up the walk and crossed the courtyard.

"General Udet," Nurse Gormanns informed Nikki, with whom she sat with coffee beneath a pear tree. Nurse Gormanns had a habit of explaining to her new friend the name and rank of every official visitor who appeared, and whereas in the past this would have annoyed Nikki very much, her new mellowness allowed her to respond with a gracious nod, even though the names meant nothing to her and she was not in the least interested. But on this occasion she narrowed her eyes and gave a delighted headshake.

"Udet! Well, I wouldn't have known him. It's years and years. Let me think . . . he visited a few times just after the war, when we lived in Munich. Just a twig of a boy, but such a hero. He and Hermann took walks. Ach, how they walked. And it rained. Ach, how it rained. Those were bad days in Munich, what with the Red government, and no coal or food, and the rain. I never liked Munich. He was a nice young fellow. Very artistic. He did a sketch of me, I remember. It was good, except that he got my nose too sharp. Ja, December of 1918 . . . and then at the wedding. That was the first Frau Göring, you understand. He came with a flock of girls. Quite the charmer, oh ja. Danced with every female there. Oh, ja, he danced with me. And I danced with Hermann too. Hermann was so happy that day. Ach, so long ago. Well, and so there is the little Udet again, but not so little."

"Tell me, Frau Schmidt, what was the first Frau Göring like?" asked Nurse Gormanns.

"She had dark hair. Rather round eyes. Very attractive."

"What I meant was not how she looked, but what she was like. I confess to being curious."

She was a charming person," replied Nikki, taking a sip of her coffee and ending the subject. For though she readily spoke of her and Hermann's shared past, indeed loved to do so, she would reveal nothing of an intimate nature. At a certain point she dropped the curtain.

Nurse Gormanns was too good-humored to be annoyed by the snub. She leaned back in her chair and breathed in the clear warm air. "It's going to be hot."

"Our late May is often hot. But we always have our little breeze." Nikki smiled at the leaves and blossoms stirring with delicate languor, and she too leaned back in her chair. She wore an ankle-length tweed skirt with a long-sleeved blouse buttoned to the neck, with a cameo at the throat. The cameo was of Queen Luise, and had been given her by Hermann's mother. She believed that her mistress, had she herself lived to be seventy, would have dressed in just this way.

"Listen . . ." murmured Nurse Gormanns. "Is it coming from the barn? It sounds like a bull. . . . No, it's coming from the house."

Nikki listened too. It was the sound of an enraged voice.

"The Reichsmarschall," whispered Nurse Gormanns, thinking of his blood pressure.

The roars came floating on the air from the study, whose windows must be open. No words could be deciphered; it was just an indistinct bellowing. From time to time it stopped—the silence apparently indicating Udet's side of the conversation—only to start in again. So it continued for fully twenty minutes as the two women sat without talking, their eyes lowered. Herr Schmidt down in the garden could hear it too. Even the workers on the north wall could hear, and kept turning their heads.

Presently General Udet emerged. His face shone with sweat. He stood still for a few moments, his fingers, as if detached from the rest of him, slowly turning his cap in his hands. Then, absently placing the cap on his head, he walked on across the courtyard and down the path to the staff car.

Inside the car he sat back and rubbed the base of his skull. The Chief had called him a liar, a bigmouth, an incompetent. He had struck the sheaf of aircraft figures with his hand and demanded an explanation. All the things that Udet had meant to bring up at their conferences but had kept postponing week after week, month after month, sinking at each conference into their habitual talk about the old days— all the things that he had meant to present coolly, rationally, in order, he was now forced to blurt out in a huge, hideous clot. The Chief slumped in his chair, only to burst into new invective. He's going to sack me, Udet had thought, but what had happened was even worse: he was told that from now on he would confer with Milch, that Milch would be investigating and reorganizing his affairs. It had stunned him. He had nodded, feeling very hot and nauseated, and gone out.

A few days later in Berlin, he said to Professor Heinkel, "They're all against me, Heinkel. The Iron Man is on leave. He's left me alone with Milch."

"Perhaps you will find him useful," suggested the patient Heinkel, to whom Udet brought many of his woes.

"Useful? In the Chief's absence Milch is now dealing with the Führer, and he will be only too anxious to see that my every fault is placed on the Führer's desk. I tell you, I can't deal with this persecution any longer."

"What you need is a good rest, my friend."

"That's impossible. Milch is already drawing up new plans. I must stay or he'll take over my job completely."

After the scene with Udet, Göring was in a bad temper all day. The next day he was morose and untalkative. The day after, he spent most of the afternoon in his study with his adjutants and Bodenschatz and Loerzer, and afterward was gloomy and preoccupied. It was clear to everyone that the restful vacation had ceased to be. And the following day, the dreadful bellowing could be heard once more from the study.

"General Kammhuber," Nurse Gormanns had informed Nikki earlier, as they strolled through the courtyard. "Commander of the night flight squadrons."

"Indeed," responded Nikki, pausing to wave at Hans, who was creaking along the second tier of gardens. The old man waved back with a smile.

And they saw each other only half an hour ago, thought Nurse Gormanns. It's touching, they're like young married people. Perhaps it's the air up here, so fresh and buoyant. If only it would would revive the Reichsmarschall, as it did when we first came.

Meanwhile, General Kammhuber had gone inside. He had been invited for lunch. The dining hall had been emptied of other diners for the occasion. He ate alone with the Reichsmarschall, who looked tired to the point of exhaustion. Bags hung under his eyes, and his hands were so swollen that his several rings appeared to cut cruelly into the flesh. He picked listlessly at his steamed trout, drank scarcely any of his wine. He had little to say. He talked desultorily of music, which surprised the general very much, for he did not think he had been summoned to discuss music.

"At Carinhall, I usually listen to the phonograph in the morning before dressing. Schubert, Beethoven, Auber . . ."

"Indeed," said the general.

"There is a new recording out of the *Eroica* . . . of course it's not the same as hearing it in the concert hall. You play the viola, don't you?"

"The cello, sir."

"Ah, the cello."

The conversation drifted away. Göring sighed, as if trying to find some other subject they could discuss. When they finally went into the study, the Reichsmarschall sighed again. But then his voice came out clipped, to the point.

"Kammhuber, I have called you here to tell you that the time to attack Russia has arrived. That is to say, the date is definitely set for the twenty-second of June. Dispositions are being made, and the requisite forces will now be transferred in readiness for action. I want you to begin with the withdrawal at once from Holland of sufficient night fighters to meet our needs at the Russian front, and for the protection of eastern Germany from any Red reprisals from the air. How many squadrons can you give me?"

Kammhuber stared at the heavy, pouched-eyed face. He was astonished by the Air Commander's ignorance of the night fighter situation.

"But Herr Reichsmarschall, I must point out to you that there are not enough night fighters in Holland to do the job they're supposed to be doing. RAF attacks are increasing, and we don't have enough planes to fight them off. What we need are *more* planes. We certainly don't have any to spare for an attack on the Russian front."

The Reichsmarschall's face suddenly flooded with red. He stepped furiously over to the general.

"Look, Kammhuber, I don't *want* this war with Russia! As far as I'm concerned it is the worst thing we could do—es ist *wirtschaftlich* falsch, *politisch* falsch, *militärisch* falsch! I've argued till my face is blue, now I wash my hands of the whole damned business, the whole war!" he shouted. "Do what you can, get half of your night fighters transferred—I can't be bothered about what happens anymore, I'm going upstairs!"

He flung from the room, slamming the door behind him as the general stared on in amazement.

Chapter 68

31 May, 1941

Dear Herr K,

I am writing in regard to R, whom I have not seen or heard from for more than two years. For over a year I observed her wish that I not try to find her, but finally I broke my word and ascertained her status. You will understand that with my husband's cooperation this was a simple procedure, a matter of his delegating some telephone calls. I learned where R lived, and that she had a work permit as an assistant to a well-known fashion designer. She appeared to be doing well, and I felt easier.

But in March, when the new work laws went into effect, I was anxious to know if her status had been changed. I did not want to make another official inquiry lest attention somehow be drawn to her, therefore I anonymously telephoned her place of employment and asked for her. When I was told that she would be with me in a moment I hung up, as I only wanted to know if she was still there. Last week I called again, but this time I was told that she was no longer employed there.

As I said before, I am hesitant to inquire a second time through the official channels that are within my reach, for fear of singling R out and inadvertently causing her some kind of difficulty. So I am turning to you in the hope that you will advise me as to the situation of your cousin. I re-

member well the several meetings we had in November of 1938, and am grateful for what we were able to do at that time. I see in the telephone directory that you are at the same address, and I hope that you are faring well. If you are ever in any kind of need, you must not hesitate to let me know.

Please use the following method in writing me. Send your letter to Fräulein Frieda Hauer, 14 Schillerstrasse, Berlin. She is a friend whom I visit when I am in Berlin. I will read the letter there. It is better that you do not send it to me here, as I suspect that my mail reaches me opened and resealed.

Tell R I want to help her in any way I can. Or perhaps it would be better not to say that, since she is so set against my help. Perhaps it could be arranged that I assist her anonymously. In any case, let me know where she is. I hope she is with you.

E.S.G.

Please destroy this letter.

2 June, 1941
Berlin

Dear Frau Göring,

I am caught between two urges—one to give you the information you ask for, and the other to abide by Rose's wishes. I must tell you first that even when she was living relatively near us, she very seldom visited. Her desire for anonymity amounted to an obsession. She lived an almost solitary existence. Even at work she hardly spoke to anyone. Incidentally, she did not work as a fashion assistant but as a cleaning woman. The designer, a friend of mine, hired her in that capacity but listed her as an assistant. Therefore Rose was in a secure work situation, since the fashion designer's enterprise is in the category of an "essential industry." In March, when the compulsory war labor law for Jews was passed, the studio was investigated but nothing came of it. Later—the mills of injustice apparently grind slowly—the place was investigated again, and it was discovered that Rose was working in a different capacity from that under which she was officially listed. I am glad to say no charges were brought against the designer who had so generously sheltered her. But I am sorry to say that Rose was obliged to take employment at a war plant and to change her place of residence.

I feel I cannot be more specific than that. I know Rose would not want it. I know too that if you were to send money anonymously, she would surmise the source and send it back. Her attitude is not directed toward you personally, Frau Göring, for whom I am sure her feelings will never change. It is the "connection," as she once described it to me. I think it must remain that way. But I can at least tell you that we had one of her rare visits recently, and that she was in good health and spirits.

As for myself, both because of my military record and because I am married to a gentile, I am in a "privileged" position, if I may use the distasteful term. But I thank you for your inquiry, and for your offer to help should the need ever arise. I too remember the work we engaged in after Kristallnacht, and will always be deeply grateful for the assistance you provided. How criminally sordid it is that since then things have only grown worse.

If anything should arise concerning Rose that I think you should know, I will write again to this address.

Respectfully,
Captain Max Korwan (ret.)

Chapter 69

GENERAL Kammhuber, happening to glimpse Göring in Paris one morning in early June, saw no indication of the malaise and turbulence that he had witnessed at Veldenstein. The Air Chief looked hale and energetic.

The Air Chief was on his way to brief the commanders of all the air units stationed in France. In one of the baroque palaces taken over by the conquerors to house their offices or serve as their military head-quarters—exquisite residences with pale-cream-and-gold interiors, with magnificently intricate wrought-iron balustrades, and each with its bronze bust of the Führer staring down from a square white pillar—the briefing took place.

"Gentlemen. As you know, the conquest of Crete proved a brilliant success. But Crete was only a dress rehearsal for the imminent invasion of the British Isles. The Battle of Britain thus far has been an overture to the final subjugation of the British enemy. This subjugation is to be effected by an immensely increased rearmament of the Luftwaffe and an intensification of the U-boat war, and will be brought to a con-clusion by the invasion itself."

The Air Chief spoke with a vigorous certainty that infected all who listened. But when he was finished, he took wing commanders Galland and Moelders aside and with an expression of beaming satisfaction asked what they had thought of his speech, then went on before they could reply, "There's not a grain of truth in it. I tell you this under the seal of greatest secrecy." He chuckled and rubbed his hands enthusiastically. "The whole speech is part of a well-planned bluff to hide the intentions of the High Command. Those real intentions are the imminent invasion of the Soviet Union."

Both young officers looked at him with astonishment. Then an expression of horror struck Galland's face.

"But a war on two fronts—that's absolutely the opposite of what the Führer told our squadron in December. That Germany must eliminate one enemy at a time, she must avoid a two-front war—"

He was cut off by an impatient headshake.

"The Führer cannot wage war against England with the full weight of our forces as long as our rear is threatened by a power that has offensive and hostile intentions toward us. We have no alternative. We must act now." The Reichsmarschall's voice once again took on its tone of vibrant enthusiasm. "The Red Air Force is numerically strong, but from the point of view of machines and personnel, it is hopelessly inferior. It would only be necessary to shoot down the leader of a flight for the remaining illiterates to lose themselves on the way home. We could shoot them down like clay pigeons."

"And England?" asked Galland.

"In two months the Russian forces will be crushed. Then we will throw all our strength to the west—and don't forget that our strength will be greatly enriched by the strategic resources of Russia."

Captain Moelders, a less vocal sort than his companion, had said nothing; but his face reflected the enthusiasm of his Chief, whereas Galland could not rid himself of his feeling of horror at the prospect of opening a second front against a new, unknown, gigantic enemy. Even as it was, the war had spread too far—North Africa, Yugoslavia, Greece . . .

"Moelders," the Reichsmarschall was going on, "in the first four weeks of the Russian campaign, you will go with your wing to the eastern front. After that," he said, turning to Galland, "you will go with your wing to relieve Moelders."

And with another injunction not to reveal what he had just told them, he dismissed the two men with the hearty, fatherly warmth for which he was generally known.

His master was greatly buoyed up, thought Robert upon the Reichsmarschall's return from the briefing. The valet drew the bath in the Hotel Ritz's magnificent marble bathroom, which was very similar to, if smaller than, the Reichsmarschall's own at Carinhall, got his master out of his uniform and sweat-dampened underclothes, listened to him splashing mightily, rubbed him dry with a scented Turkish towel, got him into a fresh uniform and handed him his cap, and all the while, as they had talked of one thing and another, he had been aware of the high spirits emanating from the large figure, which now strode briskly to the door.

"I shall be back at about four."

"Very good, sir."

Göring descended in the ornate elevator, *the invasion of Russia cannot be curtailed,* marched through the palatial lobby, *I must believe in its exigency,* stepped into his staff car, gave the chauffeur directions, *I must have no doubts, and I have none—we will defeat them in six weeks, eight at the most,* his eyes bright and assured. This morning, with a self-willed burst of vivid fantasy, and with the help of a double dose of his small white tablets, he had achieved a vigorously optimistic state of mind which remained with him still. But now, as the staff car drove through the sun-flooded Paris streets, across the Seine, and drew up before a building on the Quai d'Orsay, his radiant spirits divorced themselves completely from the invasion of Russia. Planes, guns, tanks, war—all had disappeared from his mind, leaving only the radiance. He bustled up the stairs.

His Paris art office held a half-dozen clerks and two managers, one real and one false. The real manager was Fräulein Limberger; but since National Socialist ideology did not permit women to hold positions in which they were above men, Göring had put in a false manager, a male, who was employed strictly to pass on her orders. It was to Fräulein Limberger the Reichsmarschall went. She was a severe-looking blonde in her early thirties, immensely efficient and knowledgeable; she kept all his records in connection with art, administered the finances involved, and was in charge of a large staff of librarians, photographers and art restorers.

The efficient young manager always noted the Reichsmarschall's radiant quality when he came into the office. It was because anything to do with art made him happy. And in her severe, humorless way, she was affected by his jollity, felt a flush in her cheeks and a softening in the set of her lips; yet no one knew better than she what a hard, shrewd, demanding employer he was. She had always heard that the swashbuckling Göring despised petty details; but when it came to art, he had to see every bill except the very smallest, he wanted receipts for everything, and he required that she give him a complete rundown of all that had taken place since their last meeting. He was happy, greedy, and mercilessly exacting. After forty-five minutes or an hour the efficient young manager was exhausted.

"Danke, Fräulein Limberger, keep up the good work!"

And Fräulein Limberger's cheeks flushed anew, she smiled, her wiltedness disappeared like that of a drooping flower put in water.

He bustled back down the stairs.

The staff car drove along the Left Bank, recrossed the shimmering

Seine and traversed the spacious Place de la Concorde, drawing up before the entrance of the Musée Jeu de Paume.

Just getting into another car as the Reichsmarschall got out of his was Dr. Rosenberg. The Party philosopher, with angry, glittering eyes, pretended not to see Göring. His fingers tapped furiously on his knee as he was driven off. He had arrived at the Jeu de Paume a few minutes before, only to be told that the museum was closed this afternoon to everyone but the Reichsmarschall. It was humiliating. He should have inquired ahead, knowing that whenever the Fat One was in town a private exhibit was held for him. Usually the place was filled with art dealers, high-ranking Wehrmacht officers, French collaborators. Sometimes the photographer Hoffmann was on hand taking pictures for the Führer to look over. Today everyone had been kicked out, the place was empty. "The Reichsmarschall has an appointment, Dr. Rosenberg." And it was he, Rosenberg, who administered the museum!

The forgotten man was now head of the Rosenberg Task Force for Occupied Territories—Einsatzstab Reichsleiter Rosenberg für die Besetzten Gebiete, or the ERR. After the fall of France he had asked Hitler for permission to search all French-Jewish libraries and archives in order to confiscate material which would be used in German institutions for National Socialist research and education. Permission was granted, and within the first few weeks he had already gathered together 55,000 rare and valuable books. Hitler had then enlarged the project to include Jewish art collections, and the ERR was born.

Such were the bureaucratic complications, however, that the ERR had no offices in Belgium or Holland; there the Enemy Property Control was already in effect. The only occupied territory besides France where the ERR had power was Poland. He had sent thirty German art historians to set up an office and check out whatever had not already been looted or burned. In Poland, outright stealing had been rampant, aided by an order from the Führer to the effect that no documentation need be made of what was taken from Polish subhumans—museums, churches, homes, all could be plundered or destroyed at will. Rosenberg's historians wrote him, for instance, that in the Kraków National Museum all European paintings had been stolen and the Polish paintings cut from their frames and nailed across the museum windows as blackout curtains. He did not believe, as Hitler did, that there was no such thing as Slav culture, history, art, and he had the ERR ship to German libraries the famous medieval Codex Suprasliensis of the Zamoyski family, and all the contents of the great Kraków Historical Library. Similarly, though Poles were supposedly incapable of creating artifacts of a high order, he instructed his staff to ship back the finest of what was left from the rampage of looting, and had now acquired for the Fatherland three exquisite altarpieces and several ecclesiastical vessels of wondrously wrought gold and silver.

But he had many more pressing things to deal with. His organization here in Paris was an enormous bureaucracy; there were endless matters to attend to, although the basic code was simple: art belonging to state museums or to Christians could not be touched; art belonging to anti-Nazi Christians or to Jews could be confiscated. Since there was no end of Jewish art collections in mansions, apartments, shops and galleries throughout France, there was no end of work. But the work went smoothly; the ERR was assiduous and effective. The only problem was that this hardworking and successful organization which he, Rosenberg, had created, which he headed, which bore his name, was squarely under the thumb of Göring.

The takeover had begun with the transportation difficulty. Enormous quantities of art had constantly to be shipped to the Fatherland, but only a few freight trains were made available. Complaints to the Führer came to nothing. Then it was that Göring had offered the use of Luftwaffe trains, trucks and planes, no strings attached. In fact, there were no strings attached, but from that moment on the Fat One ruled. Once he had established this transportation connection, he simply stepped in and hired ERR men as his representatives. How did one stop such a thing? Rosenberg did not know. The Führer had no time for him, and who else could he turn to? He wrote Göring that it was not proper to hire for one's own use people who already worked for someone else. He received a cordial letter in return which ignored the complaint entirely. And so it had somehow come to pass that Göring wielded greater influence in the ERR than he did himself. Few people on the outside knew this; even many people in the ERR were ignorant of it. But Rosenberg knew, and it made him feel gray inside. On days such as this, when he saw the fat brute in person, the grayness was replaced by fury.

But they rarely saw each other. They communicated through letters. Göring was always requesting something of him; he felt like an errand boy. Yet his replies were always dignified. Cooperative, but dignified. They expressed the dignity of a man who, however badly pushed around he might be, never lost sight of the fact that he was an idealist and consequently superior to his correspondent. The work of the ERR was done for the glory of the Fatherland; priceless treasures accumulated by greasy avaricious Jews were being taken from their hands and delivered to the Aryans; and it was true deliverance, for those great works of art had been demeaned and shamed by their Jewish ownership. They were meant to be owned by a race compatible with their own magnificence. Rosenberg did not make a pfennig off them. His salary was modest. He worked because he believed in his work. He knew that corruption existed in the ERR—rakeoffs, dirty deals—and he deplored it, but at least the crooks were small. What was intolerable was having to countenance Göring, a barefaced plunderer, a pirate, a greedy brute whose lust for art was so engorged you might have thought he was a throbbing lover rushing in to throw himself on real flesh. He did love nudes. And portraits. And battle scenes. And everything else. Everything. And all for himself.

Rosenberg's fingers were still beating an angry tattoo on his knee when the car drew up before his offices in the Hotel Commodore.

At the Jeu de Paume the Reichsmarschall was looking at paintings, etchings, pastels, enamels, sculptures in bronze, in marble, in wood, at Aubusson and Gobelin tapestries and carpets, at Chinese, Greek, Roman and Egyptian antiques. He drank a glass of champagne as he walked from one object to another. Champagne and elegant open-faced sandwiches were always set out for his private viewing, just as potted plants and fresh flowers in vases were always brought in. Two members of the Jeu de Paume staff followed the viewer at a respectful distance to answer questions if any were asked. Few ever were. The man had an eagle eye and an amazing store of knowledge. He finished his glass, and held it out from his side. It was refilled, and he resumed his viewing. He was engrossed, his eyes were slightly narrowed, lustrous with what they beheld. There was no sound in the room but the slow, heavy tread of his boots.

"So," he said at last, walking back to the table and chair that had been set out for his use. Seating himself, putting down his glass and pushing aside the sandwiches, he took a gray suede-bound notebook from his pocket. He was handed a hastily uncapped fountain pen. He began making his list. He always made his list on the spot. No returning a second day to muse further. No wavering at all, not even another glance at the collection. It was all there in his head, every item he had looked upon. And now he began listing what he wanted. It was called the G list, as distinct from the AH—the Adolf Hitler—list, which was compiled by the Führer's Paris advisers. The Reichsmarschall was not beyond adding items to his own list which he knew full well belonged on the AH list. He simply did it. And apparently the Führer never found out. In the business of art there was much room for confusion, mistakes, omissions. With rapid strokes of his pen, the Reichsmarschall filled his entire note page. He turned to a clean page and began filling that too. Then he turned to a third page and filled that too. Then he tore out all three pages and handed them to one of the staff members.

"They will be delivered to Carinhall at once, Herr Reichsmarschall."

"Send my office the bill as usual."

"Very good, Herr Reichsmarschall."

Then he took up one of the tiny sandwiches and swallowed it in a gulp, and got to his feet. He shook hands with the staff members, thanked them for their time, and strode from the building. His visits were always brief, intense, to the point. When he was gone the two staff members ate the rest of the sandwiches and drank the remaining champagne. They looked over the three-page list. The Reichsmarschall had spotted everything in the room that was of greatest value. Nothing had escaped him.

Outside, the Reichsmarschall climbed back into his staff car. He was very happy about the purchases he had just made, very happy to think of them gracing his own home, where he could drink in their beauty at any time, for as long as he wished. Almost Rosenberg, the Costermonger's Donkey, who shared his birthday but seemed much older despite his round adolescent face, his old enemy from twenty years back who had grown drab and gray, who lacked a thimbleful of true artistic knowledge or appreciation but had somehow blundered into the world of art—Rosenberg took up exactly five seconds of his thoughts as he was driven back to the hotel. It was late afternoon by now. Tomorrow his Paris visit would be over. In the morning he would return to Berlin, to the unfolding of the rest of the month, with its red-emblazoned 22nd.

Chapter 70

"At last, a proper war!" exclaimed General Jeschonnek as he got to his feet at the meeting's end. It was the final conference, held at the Air Ministry a week preceding the planned attack and attended by forty senior officers who had never before heard the young Chief of Staff express himself with such spontaneity. Jeschonnek himself seemed surprised, and his face at once settled back into its heavy cast. But his eyes remained lit. Lit also were the blue button eyes of Feldmarschall Milch, who, though burdened with doubts, felt a momentary fervor of enthusiasm based mainly on the assumption that Russia kept the bulk of her forces along her frontier, thus providing a possibility of defeating her there. General Udet, as he rose with his briefcase, was busy probing his ear with his finger. In addition to constantly kneading the base of his skull, he had begun this other activity of probing and pulling at his ears, deep within which there was a ringing, buzzing noise. As for Air Chief Göring, he had not attended the conference.

At one end of the little lake behind Carinhall, on a small dock for rowboats, houseguests in bathing costumes sat beneath beach umbrellas drinking gin and tonics—a concoction of their host—in the sizzling heat. Only a few guests had ventured into the chilly lake water, splashing with invigorated shouts that drifted faintly across the shimmering surface to the white wicker table on the terrace, where Emmy was having coffee with an actress friend from the Prussian State Theater. The table had its own beach umbrella, and in addition a small electric fan had been set up.

"Edda," she called, "for the last time, come and play here by the table where it's cool."

The child peered from the doorway of a perfect miniature chalet, a gift from her papa on her third birthday earlier in the month. The broad terrace before her scintillated in the heat.

"I'll have to run real fast!"

"Put your sandals back on, then you won't have to."

"Here I come!"

She tore across the burning flagstones, arriving at the table to hop up and down shaking her heat-stung bare feet. "Can I have this fork and spoon, Mutti?"

"Say hello to Frau Bergmann, dear."

"Guten Tag. Can I have this fork and spoon, Mutti?"

"But not to take back to the chalet where it's so hot." Emmy smiled, smoothing back the fine light brown hair. "Play with them here where it's cooler."

The small face resembled the mother's in its oval shape, but looked yet more like the father's, with his light blue-green eyes and his long-lipped mouth set at rather a distance from the nose, the rudimentary nose even showing the slight curve toward the end that distinguished his. She was a ravishingly pretty child, a fact which her mother intended to deal with sensibly.

"The fork is a prince and the spoon is a princess, nicht?" asked Frau Bergmann, with smiling, mock-serious eyes.

"Nein, one is a fish," the child replied, "and the other is a fish too." She disappeared with them under the table.

"My, but she looks like her father, Emmy. She's his exact image."

"Perhaps that will stop the talk," said Emmy dryly.

"Surely that's not still going on?"

"I suppose it will go on as long as Hermann has enemies. Will you have more coffee, Anna?"

"How peaceful it is here," sighed Frau Bergmann, sitting back with her refilled cup and looking out across the lake. "It's really like another world."

"Which is why I like it. I've bowed out a good deal from public life since Edda was born, you know. Special state functions, those can't be avoided, but everything else, all those Berlin receptions and teas—what a relief not to have to attend. I have more than enough to keep me busy here. But speaking of the outside world, tell me the news. Is there any decent gossip?"

"*In*decent, if that will do. Goebbels has gone off the straight and narrow, ja, I have it from a friend at UFA. Not an actress this time, just a secretary. And a very discreet business it is, oh, *very* discreet—except at home. Apparently he had the girl climb up through his window one night, can you imagine? And in the morning the little idiot left by the bedroom door. Magda practically bumped into her going down the hall."

"Dear, dear, is that woman never to have any peace?" asked Emmy, shaking her head.

"She looks very poorly. And she tries to hide it by using too much makeup, and that looks worse. But how could it be otherwise? On top of putting up with *him* year after year, she's hardly had a moment when she wasn't pregnant. From what I understand, every birth has been more difficult. They say the last one almost cost her her life, and that the doctors have forbidden her to have more. Well, tell *him* that. It seems that his goal is to populate all of Germany by way of poor Magda."

"I wonder she doesn't simply walk out on him."

"Except nothing is simple where politics are involved."

For a while they were silent in the hot, still air. The splashes and shouts of the swimmers came drifting across the little lake. From under the table they could hear, mixed with a silvery clinking on the cool flagstones, Edda's piping voice in murmured conversation.

"The child is a great one for fantasizing," Emmy confided to her friend.

Göring, at his bedroom window, smiled down at the sight of his wife and the two small bare feet sticking out from under the tea table and returned to the rococo desk on which lay his Hermann Göring Museum drawings. Wearing only a great pair of monogrammed silk underpants, with sweat trickling down his torso, he reseated himself before the papers. Unable to maintain his forced enthusiasm over the Russian invasion, he had grown more and more deeply involved with the plans for his museum. Receptacle of his collection, it would be constructed here on the grounds of Carinhall. On his death it would become the property of the state. His great art collection would be his bequeathment to the German people. Blotting his face and neck with his handkerchief, he took up a pencil and began sketching. Should the museum be simple, modern, like the Air Ministry building? Or more like Carinhall, so that it would fit into its surroundings? Or something classically Greek? What about a Viking structure, a great wooden building with a dragon's head at the top? But no, it must last, it must last forever. It must be of granite. That still left the architecture undecided. Modern? Greek? Baroque? The question was a happy one, and he sank down into it as a swimmer gliding down into cool, sunshot green depths.

June 22, the day of the attack, found him again home at Carinhall. Again it was hot, but today he was unable to sit half-naked over his museum plans. With Bodenschatz, Loerzer, and his adjutant, Colonel

Brauchitsch, he spent the day in his study taking telephone calls. The attack had begun an hour before dawn. Beneath the dark blue sky with its fading stars, in East Prussia, in Poland, in Rumania, from the sandy Baltic coast down two thousand kilometers to the Carpathian mountains, the calm was shattered by a thunder of cannon. By the time the sky began streaking with the colors of dawn, the three army groups were already flooding across the frontier in three mighty parallel streams, fleets of bombers and fighters roaring overhead. By nightfall two thousand Russian aircraft had been destroyed. Luftwaffe losses were light.

The RAF raids on Berlin continued sporadically through the summer of 1941, with minimal damage.

"Why don't they just drop one bomb on Horcher's?" Udet's mistress asked one August evening, as they sat at dinner in one of the private rooms. "Boom! Half the German leadership gone up in smoke."

No smile appeared on the face opposite. She realized it was a poor joke; how could Ernst enjoy a joke about the bombs falling on Berlin? But she was anxious to be amusing, to create a cheerful atmosphere, this being their farewell dinner. Tomorrow he was going away to enter a sanatorium for six weeks of rest. She wanted him to leave his worries behind, to take with him the memory of a pleasant, lighthearted evening. Then to come out with such an asinine joke. The truth was, his strain was beginning to tell on her, her brightness was forced, her own nerves were on edge, she often made stupid remarks from sheer jitteriness. She also needed a rest. His sanatorium stay would do them both good.

She was a handsome, auburn-haired divorcée who had been with him almost a year. Long ago, when she was a girl, she had fallen in love with his Heldenflieger postcard portrait. All through the Great War, she had kept it pinned to her bedroom wall, she had kissed it often, and dreamed of meeting him. When she did, twenty-five years later, she showed him the postcard. There could still be seen the little hole that had been made by the thumbtack. He was charmed; it was as if the youth in the portrait responded. And at the start they had been happy.

They turned to their consommé in silence.

"It's not Göring . . . the Chief blows his top, but he sticks by you. Last month when Milch told me to draw up an interim plan, I naturally took it to—"

"I've already heard about that several times," she murmured.

"—East Prussia and showed Göring. And Milch had the gall to order me to return immediately, I should show it to him before discussing it with the Chief. And Göring blasted him, said he'd damn well discuss the program with anyone he wanted to. Said Milch had better damn well learn how to cooperate with me . . ."

The loin of veal was served.

". . . but then he goes and sacks Ploch!"

"I know that. Göring fired your Chief of Staff. You have told me."

"It was bound to happen. Milch had drawn up a yard-long list of Ploch's deficiencies and kept sticking them under Göring's nose. All right, but Ploch could have been honorably posted away from Berlin if the Chief hadn't been in one of his moods—'There's the door, get out!' Sacked him. Sent him to the Russian front. Do you realize how humiliating that was for me?"

"I have told you I understand."

"It was all Milch's doing, that shitty bloodhound. He's got a nose like radar, he's decimating my staff!"

"Why don't you eat?" Her fingers around her knife and fork were tight.

He took up his fork, only to set it down again, press his hands to both ears, and probe them with his two forefingers, scratching and twisting as if he could somehow pull out the ringing and buzzing inside. It was not pleasant to watch, although one was sympathetic. The doctors were unable to help him. It was tension, they said. The headaches were also caused by tension, but the headaches he managed to dull with every drug on the market and with buckets of whiskey and cognac. He smoked like a smudge pot. Hardly slept. His eyes were bloodshot. And he seemed to have stopped seeing his barber entirely; his seal-brown fringe of hair stuck out scruffily over the back edge of his collar. His fingernails were not always clean.

She often thought of leaving him.

"They're all against me," he said, taking his fingers from his ears and tiredly rubbing his temples. "You're the only person I can talk to, Inge. The only person I trust."

Through her own tension there poured a renewed warmth of concern. "Then trust me, Ernst, when I say you'll feel better when you come back. You won't see things in this light."

"You think Milch's going to stand still while I'm gone?" he flashed at her. "He'll have my job by the time I get back. That's the whole point in sending me away."

"You know that's not true. You're being sent away because you're ill, because you need to rest. And everything will go much better when you return, you'll see."

"I don't know how . . . we're years behind schedule, we're short on spare parts. Damaged planes in Russia just sit there useless, for want of a few spare parts . . ."

In a last effort to salvage the evening, Inge said with determined cheer, "At all events, it's going well there in Russia. You can't dispute that."

"Ja, it's going well." He sighed. "The Red Army falls back, falls back. It's because they've got a lot of room to fall back in. They lose hundreds of thousands of men, but they just keep falling back across those endless plains, and they just keep replacing their losses with endless men."

"Well, as long as they keep falling back, that's all that counts. And when you return from your rest, you'll have regained your old energy for the victory over Britain."

"Maybe you're right," he conceded. "Maybe a rest will make a difference."

After that they spoke of Bubi, who was to stay with Inge.

"Shredded lettuce with his seeds. And remember to cover his cage at night. And you can give him a bit of carrot now and then."

"All on the list you gave me, sir." She sent him a smart salute across the table, and he laughed at himself. And the evening, after all, turned out to be a pleasant one.

As Generaloberst Udet checked into a military sanatorium on the Baltic coast, the subject of private sanatoriums, nursing homes, and similar institutions was under discussion in the office of Hitler's private Chancellery Chief.

It had happened that the Bishop of Münster, hearing mysterious talk of disappearing patients, had taken it upon himself to investigate. One Sunday morning he had stood up in his church and publicly revealed the top-secret program. "For being the bearers of so-called inferior genes, for being useless eaters, for possessing lives deemed unworthy of living, our regime has murdered crippled, retarded, and incurably ill persons in numbers I estimate to reach upward to one hundred thousand. And I say woe to the German people when not only can innocents be killed, but their slayers go unpunished!"

It was this extraordinary speech that was under discussion. A deputy from the Propaganda Ministry, sent by Goebbels, kept proposing that the bishop be summarily hanged until the Chancellery Chief turned on him contemptuously. "Doesn't your boss appreciate the importance of public opinion? I thought that was his job! This character is the most revered figure in Münster, in all Westphalia. Why do you suppose the Führer hasn't had him locked up a long time ago, always spouting off at the mouth? Because he carries too much weight. If we bring any punishment to bear on this loudmouth priest, we lose our hold on Westphalia. The Führer wants him assuaged." He gave an exasperated sigh. "The program is to be discontinued."

The others looked at him with disbelief.

"Officially halted. Above all and first of all in Westphalia. The

Führer wants the talk there stopped. Later on, we shall resume the program in other regions, but on a significantly reduced scale. Those are the Führer's orders."

And it was clear to both him and his listeners that the Führer was no longer deeply interested in the mercy-killing program, that his mind was occupied with other matters.

Army Group South had crossed the Dnieper, and after forty days of fighting had captured Kiev and was now progressing toward Kharkov. Army Group North, aided by the Finns, had captured Schlusselburg on Lake Ladoga, severing Leningrad's communications with the rest of Russia. And Army Group Center, having destroyed resistance at Smolensk, was pressing on to Moscow.

In October the rains began. Roads that had sent up clouds of dust now dissolved into marshes. Men were plastered with mud to their thighs, horses struggled to pull their caissons, heavy vehicles sank with engines whining. Even so, by late October, Army Group Center was within fifty kilometers of Moscow. Then the rain gave way to frost, the frost to snow.

For lack of long-range bombers, the Luftwaffe had had to leave untouched the Russian aircraft factories near the Urals. It was a grave and unalterable misfortune, though in all other ways the Luftwaffe's contributions to the swift victories in Russia were enormous. Great mobility was demanded of the short-range dive-bombers and fighters, and in the first months they had proved more than equal to their task. But aircraft losses inevitably accrued, and the replacements were insufficient. The fighting strength of the Luftwaffe was beginning to bleed away.

When Udet had returned from sick leave he had felt a new man. The headaches and the ringing in his ears were gone. His hair was trimmed, his fingernails were clean. He and Inge celebrated his return with another dinner at Horcher's.

But if he had not returned to a takeover by Milch, he had returned to something that appeared to him to be going in that direction. Although the State Secretary consulted with him, everything Udet said was overridden. Udet complained bitterly to Göring, but his Chief pointed out that unsparing steps must be taken to increase aircraft production. It was vital, every moment counted, he must put up with Milch's arrogance for the time being.

Then Milch went to the Chief with a list of Udetians who he felt were incompetents; they must all be dismissed. The State Secretary had already lined up new men for the vacancies, big names from Lufthansa and industry. Within days, Udet's planning chief was fired, and as the weeks went by, all the others were removed. The State Secretary was digging deep, dragging up things which he, Udet, had not even been aware of. His headaches returned, the buzzing, ringing noise started in again. It was intolerable to him that the State Secretary consulted with him, yet ignored his opinions. When Milch proposed that a certain von Gablenz be appointed the new planning chief, Udet reacted fiercely. "He's not my choice! I don't want him!" But Göring persuaded him. "He's the best man for the job, Ernst. That's all that counts. We must do everything we can to reorganize effectively."

When Ploch came home on leave from the eastern front in November, he and Udet spent an evening drinking at Udet's flat. The general's former Chief of Staff talked about the snow in Russia, the endless, howling, biting snow. "We don't know what it's like here," he declared in his liquor-thickened voice, shaking his head.

"I know what it's like," Udet said. "At least I know what it sounds like. I've got it here." He set his glass down and tapped both temples. "Between the ears. A howling, ringing, whistling noise. Never stops."

"You ought to see a doctor. Go see a doctor," Ploch said.

"I've seen doctors. I don't know, I don't know what I need. Maybe I need another rest." He drank the last of his cognac and refilled his glass.

"Well, you'll be getting a rest," Ploch told him, refilling his own glass. "Milch's sure to get you fired. It's only a matter of time."

Udet looked at him for a long moment, then gave a slow nod.

"I know. I've known all along. You think so too?"

"Gewiss. He's already got your job except in name. So you'll get your rest, old boy—"

"Don't call me old boy, you sow! I'm still your superior!"

But Ploch was too drunk to take notice. The evening had drawn into night, and the night was turning to early morning. Bottles and clogged ashtrays cluttered the small table between the two chairs. Udet got up unsteadily and made his way into the bedroom, where he put Bubi's cover over the cage. Then he went into the bathroom and emptied his bladder.

When he came back to the living room, Ploch was crawling on the floor looking for his shoes, which he had taken off. Udet flopped down into his chair. The jacket of his uniform was unbuttoned, the tie askew. He put another cigarette in his mouth and snapped on his lighter, but had trouble finding the tip of the cigarette. He gave up, shaking his head.

"They're all against me, Ploch. Even the Chief. He's turned against me too."

"That swine," mumbled Ploch, finding one of his shoes. "Göring's a swine."

"It was Milch's doing, Milch's behind everything. We used to be friends, but he was always against me . . . they all are, Ploch. You know it. You know I'm going to be sacked, you just said so, didn't you? You told me the truth."

"What time is it?" his companion asked, struggling into his shoes.

Udet focused his reddened eyes on the face of his old tin watch. "Almost four." The headache had started drilling at the base of his skull. He kneaded the area with his fingers, vaguely aware of Ploch weaving to the door.

He slept in his chair, woke, drank more.

I never wanted the bloody job . . . but to leave like this, covered with disgrace . . . but how could I have known what was going on? I had too much to handle, they put too much on my back. Hermann forced me into it. Why did I always do what he wanted? Shouldn't have trusted him, always against me, even in the old days . . . coming back with him after the Armistice, the bloody trains, fighting and pushing to get inside, had to break windows and climb in, and he gave me a boost—in you go!—and where did I land? In a toilet. A toilet! . . . He's shoved me down the toilet now, gone over to Milch.

With the howling, ringing, buzzing noise in his head, he went into his bedroom, changing into his pajamas and red silk bathrobe. He lay down on the bed to sleep the few hours before having to leave for work, then got up and let Bubi out of his cage, wandering after him into the living room. He felt slightly nauseated; his heart was beating rapidly. He began pacing, as if to walk off a sudden great sickened energy within him. Directing his paces to the den, he took his revolver from the desk drawer and checked to see that it was loaded. The great sickened energy took him with violent steps into the bedroom, where he threw the gun down on the bed and swept up from the night table a crayon he used for sketching. It was red; bits broke off from the pressure of his hand as he scrawled across the wall, *Iron Man, you have forsaken me!* and whipping his hand back, scrawled below, *Why did you put me in the hands of that Jew Milch?*

He turned, his eyes lighting on the telephone, and dialed a number as a breath of calm and hope invaded him.

"Inge? I know we quarreled, but—I know, I know it's been hard on you, I realize that—I know, I know, but . . . never mind, it doesn't matter . . . nein, there's nothing wrong . . . just that I can't stand the noise any longer. I can't stand it. Tell Pilli Körner he is to look after my will."

He dropped the receiver, the violent sick energy pouring back into him as he grabbed the revolver, pressed its muzzle with all his strength against his ringing temple, and snapped his forefinger back.

Chapter 71

I T was dark when the workers poured out from the armaments plant in Pankow, their footsteps ringing sharply in the clear frosty evening as they crossed the compound. Germans, Jews, Poles, they passed through the factory gates to queue up before frost-covered buses that would take them to streetcar stops or the S-bahn station. It was an area of factories, railroad yards, weedy lots, everything covered with a sheen of frost. The workers moved slowly, with orderliness, into the waiting vehicles. In an old coat and flat scuffed shoes, a gray knitted cap pulled down over her ears, Rose climbed into the dark interior and found a seat. Presently the door slammed shut and the bus rumbled crunchingly down the graveled road. Even in darkness the yellow cloth star, big as a dahlia, big as a manhole cover, burned through her coat front into her flesh.

Aboard the S-bahn train, as bright with electric light as the bus had been dark, she took hold of a strap and stood swaying with the sway of the train as it moved on. No one gave a second look at the star. In the two months that she had worn it, no one had paid it the smallest attention. And that was the strange thing, she thought: she was emblazoned yet no one seemed to see her, it was as if she did not exist. She had finally achieved anonymity. So had they all, all who wore the star. They were marked as invisible beings, and it was in this way that they stood out from everyone else.

Hanging on to the strap, head resting against her arm, she stood tiredly looking at the window before her. There was nothing to see except the blackout shade, but after eight months she knew by rote what was passing by outside: soot-blackened brick slums which would gradually give way to the center of the city; then they would cross the Spree, curve alongside the Reichstag Building, and clack on to Wilmersdorf and home, if it could be called that. An hour-and-a-half journey, three transfers.

A seat being vacated, she sank down into it with a sigh, taking up a folded newspaper that had been left behind. She stretched her sore feet inside her shoes, the bunched muscles in the small of her back, and felt a startledness at the sight of a familiar face looking out from a black border. Her eyes dropped to the print beneath it.

Generaloberst Ernst Udet, Luftwaffe Chief of Supply and Procurement, was killed this morning, Monday, the 17th November, 1941, testing a new aircraft. He died of his injuries on the way to the hospital. The Führer has ordered a state funeral for this officer who died in so tragic a manner while in the performance of his duty. In recognition of his magnificent achievements in the Great War, his sixty-two fighter victories, and of the great services he rendered in building up the Luftwaffe, the Führer will perpetuate Generaloberst Udet's name by bestowing it upon Jagdgeschwader 3.

Her eyes moved back to the coarse-grained gray of the photograph. His face was heavier than when she had last seen him, at some gathering at Carinhall. She had met him a few times there, she had liked his jauntiness, his cheerfully sardonic humor, but then she had stopped going to Carinhall, she had not seen Udet again, hadn't thought of him for years. She thought of him now, thought of those days of unbelievable ease and well-being, of that beautiful Christmas Advent party when the opera chorus had sung, and afterward she had recited before the great dazzling tree, a pearl diadem on her head.

The house in Wilmersdorf was a gray stucco middle-class building, fronted by a border of white-frosted shrubbery. She went up the steps unbuttoning her coat, and already had it off by the time she reached the door. Separated from the star, she immediately felt revived.

Inside, on the second floor, she opened the door of the flat she lived in: figures, voices, a sense of bumping elbows, the clatter of a dropped plate, the explosive flush of a toilet never given rest. There was a small living room and smaller kitchen, a small dining room where the men slept, a small bedroom where the women and children slept. The door to the bedroom could not be pushed open fully; it always banged up against one of the cots. She squeezed through, her face stinging from the cold outside. There was scarcely legroom among the cots and beds, you could have walked across them almost as across a single surface. The girl, Ida, did. She came bouncing across them now, landing at Rose's side as Rose added her coat to the other garments hanging bulkily from nails driven into the wall. The closet was crammed with boxes and suitcases. Boxes and suitcases were crammed beneath the cots.

"Fräulein Korwan, why do you dress that way for work?"

Rose took off her cracked leather gloves, her knitted gray cap, and stuffed them into the pocket of the old coat.

"What way?"

"Well, I don't know, like a peasant."

A loud snore issued from old Frau Leis, deep in one of her many naps. One of the younger children, with grinding and snorting noises, was pushing a toy truck around the tiny floor space.

"Not like a peasant," Rose said, squeezing alongside the cots to her own. "A proletarian."

Ida, who was about thirteen, and who had moved in with her parents only a few days ago, and who seemed to have chosen Rose as her heroine, followed her, walking across the cots.

"You don't have to. Nobody is forcing you to."

"That's why," Rose said, stretching out on the cot.

When someone forces you to do something, such as to stand all day trimming bits of metal on a conveyor belt, when they have not consulted you but taken you by the scruff of the neck, so to speak, and thrown you there, then you arrange it so that it is not you who are thrown there but someone else, someone who has no connection with you. They can never know who the real person is underneath, they can never touch that person because they cannot see her. No one forces me to dress like this except myself. It is my disguise, it is my own enforcement, it is my will operating within their dictates.

But she did not say this to Ida. "You're a great one for questions," she said instead.

Ida, sitting down opposite her crosslegged, Indian-style, gave a vivacious shoulder shrug of agreement. She was a small, slight girl with thick, kinky, unruly dark hair. She would not get away with much on the outside; there were no disguises for her. She was doubly trapped, by laws and by her looks. Her face was the map of Palestine. At the same time it was universally adolescent, rippling with mobility and spangled by rosy pimples. The vibrant hair was clamped down by two white enamel barrettes. She wore an unpressed blue pleated skirt and a pale beige sweater soiled gray along the ridges of its cuffs.

"What did you do before the compulsory war-labor law?"

"Does it occur to you that I'm trying to rest, Ida?"

"I bet you were a singer. You've got the voice of a singer."

"Singers very often have poor speaking voices."

"An actress then. An actress!"

Old Frau Leis, rumple-haired, deaf as a stone, climbed heavily from bed and made her way to a chair on which stood a chamber pot covered with a newspaper.

"An actress! Where? On the stage or in films?"

Rose stretched the full length of the cot, pressing the last of the tiredness from her bones, and did not reply.

"It's true what they say. They say you're very mysterious."

"I doubt if that's the word they use."

"Well," Ida confessed, through the fecal fumes drifting their way, "what they actually say is hochmütig."

"I'm not aloof. I just don't talk much."

"You talk to *me*."

"Because you're a pest. I have no choice."

One of the children came clattering in to drag his younger brother off to dinner. A yowling, having to do with the abandoned truck, vibrated against the walls until the door slammed shut. Rose noticed the older boy's navy-blue sailor coat lying face-up on the cot beside her. She reached over and picked it up.

"Look how big the star is," Ida said, shaking her head. "Wouldn't you think they'd make children-sized ones for children?"

It was very large on the small coat front, yellow, embroidered in black at its center with the word "Jude." It was sewn to the coat with close, tight stitches.

"I thought he was five," Rose said, laying the coat back.

"He turned six today. His mother lost no time sewing it on. She's a very nervous woman, Frau Stern, have you noticed? Her fingernails are bitten right down to the skin, they're all gnawed and bleedy-looking. Otherwise they're quite attractive hands."

Ida looked down at her own, raising them. "Once last year I painted my nails Chinese red. My parents were absolutely scandalized. 'This is going too far, my girl! Next thing it will be face powder! Eye shadow!' Oh, they were beside themselves, it was hilarious!" She broke into laughter, which decelerated into a sigh as her eyes moved around the room. Old Frau Leis was climbing back into bed, her lids already closed.

"What does it mean anyway, resettlement in the east?"

"Being settled in Poland in some sort of village, I suppose. Or maybe barracks. A community of some kind."

"That's what my parents say. They say if we're deported, at least we won't be squashed together like this. It would be our own community, and we would have room to move around in. I guess going off somewhere completely unknown is better than being stuck in this sardine can. I can tell you I was damned annoyed to have to leave my piano behind!" The worry that had settled on the girl's face was wiped clean by sparkling anger. She relished the adult phrase, and used it again. "Damned annoyed. I'm damned annoyed by the star, too. I can't get used to it. For one thing, it's a desecration, it shouldn't be used that way."

Rose nodded, although she did not feel similarly. To Ida and her parents the Star of David meant something; to her it was only a branding mark.

"Vati says I shouldn't complain about my piano. Vati says to look on the bright side, at least here we have a cellar to go down to during the raids. When we lived in our own flat, we couldn't go down with the rest. They all went down, oh very cozy, very nice, but we had to stay where we were. Once we went out into the building entryway because we thought it would be safer, but Vati got cut by flying glass."

Getting off the cot, Rose squeezed down beside it and pulled out an open cardboard box. From it she took out her good hat, her high heels, and her good wool dress, neatly folded. She changed out of her work dress into the other, then took the hairpins from her hair, shook it out, and with smoothing hands twisted it back into a roll, re-pinning it.

"You've got such pretty hair, Fräulein Korwan. But you don't brush it very much, do you? You should give it one hundred strokes every night. You give it only eight or nine. Usually nine. I've counted."

"Ach, du lieber," Rose sighed, stepping into her pumps.

"But your teeth you brush a lot. In the morning when it's still dark I hear you over at the basin, you brush them ten times as long as anyone else. They're really something, they're like pearls. Do you use a special toothpaste?"

"Baking soda."

"Baking soda? I'll try it too, then. I used to wear braces, everything got stuck under them, ugh! When I finally got them off this summer, Mutti gave me a party. Do you go a lot to parties?"

"There was a time when I did."

"It wasn't much of a party. We didn't want to make noise. At least here you don't have to tiptoe around afraid of the neighbors."

"There's not much tiptoeing here," Rose agreed, squeezing out from among the cots. Ida came bounding across them behind her, landing with a thud on the floor.

"Why do you wear that big watch?"

"Why don't you get back to your homework, Ida?"

The girl gave a vivid grimace. Her schoolbooks and papers lay on a small table where she had gladly abandoned them. It was a round-edged coffee table of cheap laminated wood on which stood, surrounded by a clutter of the occupants' possessions, a malfunctioning lamp in the form of a grinning brass Buddha with a lantern. It was the only table in the bed-crammed room. The walls, papered in pale pink with a white floral pattern, bristled with nails and thumbtacks from which hung the occupants' framed family photographs, there being no surface on which to stand them. The large window overlooking the street was hung with curtains dark with grime, the apartment having few enough washing facilities for the clothes of sixteen people, much less for curtains.

Ida had plopped down on the edge of a cot as Rose took down her good coat from the bulky row of hanging clothes. There was no star sewn on the coat. Ida looked on with admiration.

"It's wonderful how you break the curfew, Fräulein Korwan."

"It's not something to aspire to," Rose told her, buttoning the coat.

"Not wearing the star is dangerous. Wherever you go, it must be important."

Rose put on her small arc-shaped hat, arranging its tip just above one eyebrow.

"Where *do* you go?"

"You are the nosiest human being I have ever known, Ida."

There was an inrush of living-room noise as the door opened, banging against the side of a cot. Frau Müller, Frau Rosenthal, and Fräulein Stahl came squeezing in, shutting the door behind them. Now began the coming and going, the migration from one room to another, the terrible restlessness which would last until bedtime.

They moved down the narrow clothes-obstructed aisle, forming a clot with Rose. In her face she could smell Frau Müller's pungent red-cabbage breath. "You're asking for trouble," said Frau Müller, eyes flicking down and up from the coat front.

"It's her own neck," said Fräulein Stahl.

They pressed past her, to sit and talk for a while, to mend socks, or begin a game of dominoes—dominoes were all the rage in the building—before wandering out again. Frau Rosenthal, Ida's mother, told her to finish her homework. With a last shining look at the mysterious Fräulein Korwan, the girl jumped up on the cots and began walking back across them. "Be civilized, Ida!" her mother cried.

Rose went out into the living-room commotion. People eating at the table, playing dominoes there, sitting crammed on the sofa, talking, milling around the suitcases and boxes on the floor. A train-station waiting room. People were still cooking in the kitchen. Everyone cooked in relays. For all the noise and bumping of elbows, at bottom there was solid German order: schedules, rules, duties. Sometimes she wondered how she could bear it another moment—squeezing against others in the bedroom and kitchen, trying to get into the bathroom, maneuvering around belongings, listening to voices, voices, voices.

She closed the door on the noise. There were always a few people taking their evening stroll down the hall, since no one was permitted to go outdoors after eight o'clock. Downstairs she unlocked the front door and stepped into a bitter shock of cold. Her small arc of a hat was no protection against the frosty night, but she would not wear her beret or knitted cap, only her best. She clicked across the street, passed the to- bacconist's shop, turned the corner. With the house left behind, her feeling of entrapment faded. But the feeling had grown very strong these last two months. A month ago one thousand Berlin Jews had been transported to Poland for resettlement, two weeks ago another thousand. Rounding up people was a simple procedure, since they were all neatly branded and stuffed into specified housing, to wait with their suitcases. What would it be like, she wondered, to find yourself living in a village of barracks? Most likely a village of barracks that was a labor camp? They were supposed to be going as settlers, but who really knew? One thing she did know was that she would not be forced out of her country. But how she was to achieve this—that she did not know.

Nor did she know where she was going as she clicked along the blacked-out streets in her best clothes. The mysterious Fräulein Kor- wan, who dangerously broke the curfew and went dangerously starless in order to fulfill some important engagement, might take a tram to a cheap café near Prager Platz for a plate of sausage and potatoes. Or she might take a tram to the Kurfürstendamm and join the sidewalk nightlife. Or she might not take a tram anywhere. Often she simply walked, with no destination at all.

General Udet's funeral took place the following Thursday, all flags throughout the city flapping at half-mast in the bitter cold. From the Air Ministry where the body had lain in state in the Hall of Honor to the Invalidenfriedhof, where the burial would take place, the streets were lined with crowds who had come to pay their last respects. Rose stood among them, Thursday being her half day off from work. Ears freezing beneath the small arc of her hat, she looked out from among heads and shoulders as the cortège passed with a muffled rolling of drums, a cadenced thud of boots, a sound of clopping hoofs. Drawn by an armored vehicle, the gun wagon rolled slowly by. The coffin upon it, covered with a flag spanned by a black Iron Cross, had the strange, blindly upward look of all coffins. Rose followed the caisson with her eyes until it had passed, her gaze then falling on those who walked behind, Göring foremost. He was in a long military greatcoat, cap in hand. He walked heavily. His face looked gray. Then he too passed from sight.

In the small hours of the morning, Herr Kropp came down the stairs. He was not sure where he would find the Reichsmarschall, but instinct led him in the direction of his den.

The tragic air crash of General Udet had deeply affected the Reichsmarschall. And today had brought all the strain of a state funeral, the endless ceremonies, the long walk across the city. Herr Kropp had listened to the funeral proceedings on the radio. And had been stunned to hear that a second tragedy had taken place that very morning. The great young air ace Moelders, flying back from Russia to attend the funeral, had crashed and been killed just east of Berlin.

Under the door of the den was a faint gold line. Receiving no answer to his rap, he went quietly in. The Reichsmarschall was asleep in an armchair, his head to one side. Next to him stood a half-empty bottle of brandy and a glass. His military greatcoat hung over the back of the chair. He had unbuckled his belt, which hung loose around his great girth. Herr Kropp was not sure if he should wake him or let him sleep on where he was. The valet walked around the room, which was very cold. He paused before the Richthofen Squadron photographs on the mantelpiece, finding Udet's face. Young then. The Reichsmarschall too. He walked on in the lamplight, looking at the family photographs on the desk, the painting of the Reichsmarschall's first wife, the battle-stained *Ritter, Tod und Teufel*, the medallions of the young musician angels. The four small medallions were the only new thing in the room. The room never changed. From year to year, everything stayed exactly the same.

The Reichsmarschall was sleeping deeply, exhausted. Better to let him stay where he was than to disturb him.

Herr Kropp, thin and erect in his dark jacket and gray striped trousers, ascended the marble staircase with a clicking of footsteps that echoed through the sleeping house. In his room, he walked over to the window and stood there looking out. It was a matter of habit, like winding his clock. A thin crescent of moon hung over the forest's jagged peaks. There was a pale glitter of frost in the courtyard below, and on the bronze Indian brave, his arm flung back eternally with its spear. Herr Kropp stood listening to the keening of the wind, the only sound in the immense night silence of the forest.

Then, turning from the window, he took his clock up and wound it, setting the alarm for six.

Chapter 72

A few days later, a grand formal reception was held at the Leipziger Platz Palace for Count Ciano. On the surface the gathering appeared the same as before the war, but the cast of characters was different, many people had left the stage. The English were gone, and the most important of them, Sir Nevile, was said to be on his deathbed; the French were gone, gone the black waxed mustache and rapier wit of François-Poncet; there were no Russians standing off to one side, there were no Poles; the glum Attolico and his wife, with her startling originality and Garboesque voice, had been sent back to Italy. All these people who had been at the center of European affairs, whose names had rung with consequence, were recollections.

In their place was an increase of Japanese and Finnish dignitaries. There were more Rumanians and Bulgarians, and on this occasion there were of course many Italians. There were also faces dating back to the Weimar Republic and even before. Von Papen's, smooth and alert as always; after being ousted as Ambassador to Austria he had resurfaced as Ambassador to Turkey, where he had been ensconced ever since. And Baron von Neurath, home on leave from his duties as Reich Protector of Bohemia-Moravia, had also survived his fall. As for the baron's usurper, Foreign Minister von Ribbentrop, he was not to be seen. Göring did not invite Ribbentrop to his functions.

Frau Göring was dressed as a queen for the occasion. The Marschallin did not attend many affairs, but when she did she fulfilled her duties with a simple quiet charm at odds with the splendor of her official dress. Even so, the Marschall outshone her in a brilliant blue uniform with flaring gold lapels, across which was draped a necklace of butterfly-shaped garnets at whose end hung a gold eagle. In addition, he was covered with his stars and crosses and wore several of his huge rings. But his appearance was not in keeping with his mood. Genial and pleasant, he was nevertheless greatly subdued.

The guest of honor, in his white-and-green uniform glittering with gold braid, still held his head excessively high, but gone was the strutting and prancing, the overbearing flippancy. As well they might be, thought Dr. Schmidt, who as usual strolled around in his own thoughts, half listening to the background noise of voices and music. Ciano represented a country that had become a dragging liability. This grand reception in his honor was a hollow business, as hollow as the room's sparkling flow of chatter when you considered that just outside the satin-draped windows there was now a concrete bomb shelter dug beneath the garden.

Count Ciano was aware of his false position. Protocol demanded a reception, but he and his country were not respected. He disliked the Germans for that. He disliked them for forcing Italy into a war she was not prepared for. And if he could not blame them directly for Mussolini's rash and humiliating invasion of Greece, he blamed them indirectly, for the war was their doing. Nor had he been in good favor with Göring since Ribbentrop was awarded the Collar of the Annunziata after the signing of the German-Italian military alliance last year. No doubt feeling, with justification, that it was he, Göring, who had laid the foundation of the alliance, the big one had visibly winced and held back tears as he watched the Collar, Italy's highest decoration, presented to Ribbentrop; and ever since—even after he had finally managed to wangle a Collar for himself—he had treated Ciano with cold hauteur. But tonight was somewhat better. His host seemed softened, sad, kindly. Personal loss became him. Even so, the Count was not at ease. He went through the social gestures expected of him, but he was never free from the feeling that the reception was a piece of empty protocol, that Italy was despised and resented as a bungler; nor could he keep his thoughts from constantly returning to the growing chasm between himself and his father-in-law, who was so thoroughly pinned under Hitler's thumb.

Eventually, as the evening wore on, the Count was asked by his host to step out with him for a private talk. The last time they had had a private talk, Göring had taken him angrily to task for the Italian Army's failures, but Ciano doubted if tonight he would be so rudely attacked. The big one was too subdued, too abstracted.

As they went along hallways hung with tapestries lit like paintings, suddenly a large dog came toward them—no, not a dog, a half-grown lion. One had heard of this beast which had the run of the house. It was loping now, and reaching them sprang happily on its master, planting its big paws between the flaring gold lapels.

"You've met Caesar, haven't you, Count?" asked the Reichsmarschall, as if it were one of the guests who had come up to them, while at the same time scratching the round furry ears and giving the muzzle a smacking kiss.

"I have not had the honor," replied Ciano dryly. "I hope I am not required to kiss him too."

"Nein, nein," sighed Göring, as if momentarily aware of the ludicrous picture he presented, yet giving the muzzle another smacking kiss before setting the animal down. "Some people are afraid of Caesar," he said as they continued along the hallway, "but they have no reason to be. He is allowed to leap only on me. Other people would be knocked down."

It was true, thought Ciano as his host opened the study door, it would take a great deal to knock down this solid, bulging block of a man, who just now was shaking into his palm a couple of small white pills. He had been in the habit of doing this for some years now; perhaps, like his Führer, he was subject to indigestion. They were walking over to a pair of deep crushed-velvet armchairs, around them beautiful old wood carvings, paintings on easels, magnificent tapestries. How gorgeous was every room in the Reichsmarschall's Berlin residence, yet, thought Ciano, how they paled in comparison with the grandeur of Carinhall. He wondered how a country almost socialized could tolerate such pomp—the houses and castles, the lavish dinners and parties, the fleets of motorcars, the array of picturesque uniforms. But the Germans seemed to love him for it. In Italy he was not loved. He seemed to believe that his flamboyance—one thought of the extraordinary coat he wore on his latest visit to Rome, ankle-length, all of sable, a cross between a motorist's garb of 1906 and what a high-grade prostitute might wear to the opera—was a southern attribute which would make him fit right in with his Latin allies; but he was in fact considered too militaristic, too cold and Prussian and overbearing. Not that Italians could stomach anyone German, Prussian or otherwise.

They had sat down. The Count expressed his deep regret over the air-crash death of General Udet, causing tears to fill the blue-green eyes.

"It was a great blow. A great blow to the Luftwaffe, and a great personal blow. I can only say what I said in my funeral oration, that I have lost my best friend."

Presently, inevitably, they got onto the subject of Libya, and the Count was relieved not to hear the Italian forces berated. "Together we will shortly clean up North Africa. As for the Russians, I am convinced that we will defeat them by this coming spring. By summer Britain will lay down her arms . . ."

Then, drawing toward him a cut-crystal bowl that stood on the table, a bowl which the Count saw was filled with precious gems, he began running his fingers through them, lifting the gems and dropping them with little clicking sounds. They appeared to be opals, amethysts, rubies, brethren to the rings on the broad fingers that sifted through them. Ciano looked on with fascination. He had heard that the Reichsmarschall sometimes had his aides bring him a vase filled with gems, that he would count them, line them up, mix them, and repeat this procedure many times, happily absorbed. But he was not so elaborate tonight. Nor did he appear happy. Rather he was grave, thoughtful. He talked about the food situation in Greece.

"I am thinking of appealing to Roosevelt for help. Then if Roosevelt refuses to send aid, the blame for Greek starvation will be his." He accompanied this with a smile, which faded again into graveness. "On the other hand," he went on, digging his fingers into the bowl, "we cannot worry unduly about the hunger of the Greeks. It is a misfortune which will strike many other people besides them. For instance, in the camps for Russian prisoners of war, after having eaten everything possible, including the soles of their boots, they have begun to eat each other, and what is more serious, they have also eaten a German sentry. In the coming year, between twenty and thirty million persons in Russia will die of hunger. Perhaps it is well that it should be so, for certain nations must be decimated. But even if it were not, nothing can be done about it. It is obvious that if humanity is condemned to die of hunger, the last to die will be our two peoples."

Ciano listened to the clicking of the gems as they dropped one upon the other. The quietly spoken words had sent a chill through him. Had they been spoken by Hitler or Goebbels, harshly, defiantly, he would not have felt the same chill; but one admitted to oneself, despite one's treatment by Göring this last year, that he was the most human of the German chiefs. One did not expect these terrible words from his lips; in public speeches perhaps, as Hitler's mouthpiece, but not in private conversation. Words spoken almost indifferently, with a kind of lazy, museful hardness, not so much as an eyeblink in prophesying the deaths of thirty million people by starvation; and even worse, a touch of dry humor when mentioning the Russians eating a sentry . . . he had not really been grave at all, or rather, in his graveness was an undercurrent of irony, of something like philosophical doubt, almost as if he were mocking the Party line, subtly, very subtly . . . or was one seeing shades of meaning where none existed? The eyes of the big one gave no clue; he was going on now to the subject of France, of General Weygand's removal.

At length they rejoined the other guests in the reception hall, which was filled with the string quartet's strains of *Die Zirkusprinzessin*, by Kalman, a Jewish composer whose works were banned in Germany but not in Göring's residences. He played what he wanted. The guests, in dress uniform or evening clothes, the women in sparkling necklaces and fashionable gowns from Paris, had settled down at little gilt tables for supper. Dr. Schmidt, over a forkful of salmon mousse, observed that the Count appeared more at ease.

The German losses in Russia were great, but their greatness spoke of greatness. Army Chief of Staff Halder read over the German casualty reports from the Russian front—100,000, 80,000, 250,000—and slapped them down with a beaming look. "Finally we've got some real casualties," he said to his adjutant, giving a virile hand tap to the papers. "How many did we lose in France, a hundred thousand all told? It was child's play. And they played at it like children. I saw with my own eyes a detachment of motorcycles simply drive off the road and take a shortcut through a field. Can you imagine such a slipshod occurrence in the Great War? Bumping across a field like schoolboys on holiday! France was too easy for them, like cutting through butter. But now they're up against a real enemy. Now they fight as German soldiers should. Seriously. Great losses, but greater victories. It was time they were forced to show their mettle! My faith is restored."

But the enemy was not only the Red Army, it was also the weather, which was turning into the severest winter Russia had known since weather records were kept. The Germans were not equipped with winter uniforms, Hitler having envisioned victory before the necessity for warm clothing arose. Even so, poorly outfitted as they were against the wolfish cold, flanks of Army Group Center penetrated the suburbs of Moscow in early December.

Then they were pushed back. At the same time, from Rostov, Feldmarschall Rundstedt led the first full retreat in the war. In a rage, Hitler cashiered him, and General Guderian as well. There followed a blanket sacking of the top brass in the east, and finally, bitterly disappointed by his generals' pusillanimity, the Führer sacked his Commander in Chief of the Army, assuming personal command himself.

Führer, Chancellor, Commander in Chief of the Wehrmacht, now Commander in Chief of the Army—the very last crack had been closed.

Chapter 73

WIND-DRIVEN sleet swept outside the windows of Göring's Air Ministry as he sat waiting for Milch, who arrived punctually, ashtray in hand, to make the long echoing walk to the massive desk. An attitude of cordiality now existed between the two men, for cooperation was necessary if the Luftwaffe was to be bailed out of its difficulties. But both knew that behind Milch's cordiality lay triumph, and that behind Göring's lay frustration. He had not clipped his deputy's wings back in 1938 with the idea of their sprouting again bigger than ever, but that was exactly what was happening, Milch being the only man who could carry out the job of resurrection.

"Well, how much more have they dug up?" the Air Chief asked glumly as his deputy sat down.

"Of course, it will be weeks before the investigation is completed," Milch answered, setting his ashtray on the polished desk top and tapping his cigar over it. "Hundreds of people are still being interrogated, down to the lowest clerks. But I can inform you of this much. Udet's office has cost us thousands of unbuilt fighter aircraft."

Göring's hand slammed down flat on the desk blotter, where the fingers drummed furiously.

"What they dished up was nothing but rubbish," Milch went on. "For instance, they had a special department drawing up programs in multicolored graphs and diagrams—green, yellow, blue—which no one understood, least of all the people who had prepared them. It was a complete misuse of funds. It was total self-deception and fantasy."

At this Göring's fist banged down on the desk. "Never have I been so deceived—so bamboozled—so cheated as by that office! It has no equal in history!"

Milch nodded in agreement as his Chief pushed his chair back and strode over to a window, where he stood with his broad back turned, hands clenched at his sides.

It is your own fault, the deputy said to himself. It would never have happened if you had allowed me access to Udet. Now you see the results.

When Göring spoke again, his voice was quieter. "Udet tried. It wasn't his fault. It was the fault of Ploch and the others."

Inevitably the Chief's eyes would be glistening with tears. Hardly ever did he speak Udet's name without this happening. Milch himself, though sorry about the suicide, was always impatient with the Reichsmarschall's swimming eyes, a time-consuming luxury.

"If only he had come to me earlier . . ."

He *did* come to you. He came to you every day. But all the two of you ever did was chew the fat over your old Heldenflieger feats. That was your fault, not his. Your fault alone. You were his superior. Why didn't you once get down to brass tacks? What a wretched waste those talks were. Everyone seems to forget that I too did some flying in the Great War, but I have never wasted valuable time sloshing about in nostalgia. . . .

Göring came heavily back to the desk, his eyes moist, and sat down again.

"So," said Milch, carefully stubbing out his cigar end in his ashtray, "now that the United States is in the war, we're going to have to—"

"They only know how to manufacture razor blades and refrigerators, they don't have a baboon's idea of war industry. Besides, their fight's not with us, it's with Japan, and so far they've made a miserable showing."

"Aren't you being overly sanguine?"

"In any case, it will be a year at least before they're capable of joining forces with England against us."

"That's about my own reckoning. We must make every moment count. We're going to have to increase aircraft production enormously by the time of the spring offensive in Russia."

"And for that you have my fullest support, as you know."

But in late January of the new year, Hitler canceled the absolute priority which he had accorded aircraft production six months earlier and turned to in-depth rearmament of the Army.

The blow sent Göring to his bed with inflamed joints and swollen glands. When he returned to the Air Ministry, his joints still aching, he received the judge advocate whom he had appointed to head the investigation of the Air Armaments Office. The advocate came with his final report.

"May I say at the start, Herr Reichsmarschall, that I don't feel charges should be brought against Ploch and the others. No one would benefit by a public prosecution except perhaps the enemy, for whom it would provide a welcome scandal. In addition, it would undermine the people's faith in the Air Ministry."

Göring gave a silent nod.

"What is more," the advocate went on, "the blame falls on General Udet's shoulders. The investigation proves conclusively that it was not a matter of the general's having delegated too many tasks to his subordinates, but of his failing totally to provide leadership. He offered not a shadow of leadership. He neglected his duties in an almost criminal fashion. He—"

To the astonishment of the advocate, his listener suddenly put his face in his hands, breaking into sobs, his shoulders heaving. "I am grateful—grateful for his death!"

The advocate rose from his chair, horribly ill at ease. "Perhaps the Reichsmarschall would rather we discussed the report at some later date."

"Nein . . ." Gaining control of himself, the Reichsmarschall shook his head. "Now."

Later in the day when he spoke with Loerzer in private, he was still in a highly emotional state. "I curse him! I tell you I'm grateful for the fate that pressed the gun into his hand! When I think of the opportunities that were missed because of him! Listen, two years back I issued a specification for a wooden aircraft. Time went by, I heard nothing. Finally I asked Udet what had become of it. He said it was technically unfeasible. I took him at his word, I assumed that he had thoroughly looked into the possibilities of manufacturing a wooden fighter aircraft. Today the advocate showed me the minutes from the conference concerning my directive. Udet wasn't even there. One of his technical advisers passed judgment in two seconds flat. There in black and white it stood before my eyes: 'Of course there is no question of manufacturing such rubbish.' *Rubbish!* It's why today we have nothing like the superb RAF Mosquito! I tell you I curse him! He has set us back five years! And now with the Führer's decision to cancel Luftwaffe rearmament priority—" He broke off, pushing his fingers agitatedly through his hair.

"But what about this idea concerning Todt?" asked Loerzer. "That might be the answer to many of our problems."

Göring sighed, giving a nod. Dr. Todt, Minister of Armaments and Munitions, was having difficulties with his job for lack of coordination in his dealings with the three armed services. A single coordinating director, a kind of overlord of all the services, was needed to alleviate the constant armaments confusion that existed. Milch had already talked with Todt, hinting that he, Milch, would be the best man for the post. It now remained to be seen if the suggestion had taken hold.

"We shall find out the end of next week," Göring said. "Milch has made an appointment to talk with him again at that time."

"You will have returned from Goldap by then?"

"I should be back by the middle of next week."

The following day the Reichsmarschall left in his private train for Luftwaffe headquarters in East Prussia.

Headquarters were situated at Goldap, only a few kilometers from Göring's hunting lodge. In winter the lodge was unused except when the Reichsmarschall visited headquarters, at which time a cook, maid and manservant were installed to see to his and his retinue's needs. The interior of the lodge was simple, rustic and comfortable. Outside, all was silent, white with snow.

"What's the use of inspecting headquarters and visiting airfields," Göring said to Colonel Brauchitsch, his aide, over breakfast, "when we're stymied at the source? It's essential that an armaments overlord be appointed. But the question is, will Todt accept Milch?"

"When is Milch to see him?"

"Friday next."

They were interrupted by the ringing of the telephone, which was brought over to the table by the manservant. Göring took up the receiver, and as he listened an expression of shock passed over his face. He gave a nod or two, said a few brief words, and hung up.

"He won't be seeing him Friday, he's dead."

"Dead? Milch dead!"

"Not Milch, Todt. Killed less than an hour ago in an air crash. Listen, this is excellent, this changes everything." He rose energetically from the table, tossing down his napkin. "Robert, bring my coat! We'll leave at once for Wolfsschanze, Brauchitsch. I'll have the Führer appoint me Todt's successor. That will eliminate the entire problem of an armaments overlord!"

They arrived an hour and a half later at Hitler's East Prussian headquarters, where Göring was immediately given entry to the Führer's office. "I have just heard the news, mein Führer," he said as he strode over to him where he stood with his architect, Speer. "May I offer my deepest condolences. It is a very sad loss, a very sad and very grave loss. But if I may point out the practical side: it would be best if I were to take over Reichsminister Todt's assignments within the framework of the Four-Year Plan. This would do away with the frictions and difficulties which we have had in the past as a result of overlapping responsibilities. It would be much—"

"I have already appointed Todt's successor. Herr Speer here has assumed all of Dr. Todt's offices as of five minutes ago."

Göring looked as if he had received a physical blow. His eyes flicked to the young architect, to whom he managed a small nod of acknowledgment; then, unable to mask his anger and disappointment, he said curtly to Hitler, "You will understand if I do not attend Todt's funeral. You know the battles I had with him. I don't wish to be present."

"On the contrary, you must be present. It wouldn't do if by absenting yourself from a formal act of state in his honor, your disagreements with him became public knowledge. You must attend."

The Reichsmarschall's nostrils had widened. His mouth was clamped. He unclamped it. "As you wish, mein Führer."

When he rejoined Brauchitsch, he flung himself into the seat beside him. "He has appointed Speer."

"Who? Speer . . . you don't mean that architect of his? But that's astounding. What in God's name can he know about armaments?"

"My question exactly," muttered Göring, and fell gloomily silent as they were driven through the streets of neat barracks beneath tall pines. It began to snow as they left Wolfsschanze behind and entered open country. "There still remains the need for an armaments overlord for the three services. Milch will now be discussing this with Speer instead of Todt. And there is this to say for Speer. He is not the hardheaded bull that Todt was. You can see by his face that he's weak."

A few days later, in Berlin, Speer was summoned by Göring to his Four-Year Plan office. He found the Reichsmarschall cordial, even friendly.

"I remember well the harmony that existed between us, Herr Speer, when you were the architect of my Berlin residence. I sincerely hope this harmony will not change. I had a written agreement with Dr. Todt, and a similar agreement is being prepared for you. I shall send it to you for your signature. The agreement stipulates that in your procurement for the Army you will not infringe on the areas covered by my Four-Year Plan."

Speer nodded, but said nothing. It seemed to him, since the Four-Year Plan embraced the entire economy, that his hands would be completely tied if he abided by Göring's arrangement.

"In any case," Göring went on, "you will learn more during the course of tomorrow's conference with Milch and others."

When Speer left the office he felt anxious about the conference to be held the next day. He felt anxious in general. Everyone had been astounded by his appointment, and no one had been more astounded than himself, though he was not at all averse to accepting the extraordinary promotion. He had long since ceased to be a simple architect, and at Hitler's behest had taken on construction responsibilities in the Todt Organization, discovering in himself a native talent for planning and organizing. Still, what did he, an architect and builder, know about armaments? No one could possibly have faith in him, no one except Hitler. Hitler being back in Berlin, he went to him and expressed his feeling of insecurity.

He felt better afterward. If any problems arose during the meeting, he was to interrupt the proceedings and tell everyone to go over to the Chancellery. There Hitler would say whatever was necessary.

Thus the newly appointed Reichsminister of Armaments felt more at his ease the next day when the conference hall at the Air Ministry began to fill. Everything went smoothly until Economics Minister Funk stood up, looking rumpled as usual, as if he had just climbed out of bed, and turned to Feldmarschall Milch.

"It is clear that we are all in essential agreement that there must be one man to coordinate decisions. The only remaining question, therefore, is who the man should be. Who would be better suited for the purpose, my dear Milch, than you yourself, since you have the confidence of our revered Reichsmarschall? I therefore believe I am speaking in the name of all when I ask you to take over this office."

Speer suddenly turned to Milch, who sat next to him, and whispered hastily in his ear: "The conference is to be continued at the Chancellery. The Führer wishes to say a few things."

Milch hesitated only a moment, then quickly raised his hand, palm out. "I am greatly honored, Dr. Funk, but I cannot accept."

At which Speer got to his feet and announced that the discussion would be continued at the Chancellery, where the Führer wished to speak to them. The flurry of surprise that went through the audience made it clear to the new minister that he was starting from an immensely stronger position than his predecessor had ever known.

At the Chancellery the members of the conference were directed into the Cabinet Room, the "sacred room"—to be received there inevitably made a deep impression on anyone so honored, or so intimidated. Hitler immediately took the floor, Speer at his side. Ignoring entirely the question of an armaments overlord, he held forth for more than an hour, speaking in general terms except when he brought up Göring. "This man cannot look after armaments within the framework of the Four-Year Plan. It is essential to separate the task from the Four-Year Plan and turn it over to Reichsminister Speer."

Again a flurry of amazement went through the audience.

"I appeal to you to cooperate fully with Reichsminister Speer. I ask not only cooperation from you, but fair treatment. Treat him like a gentleman!"

What precisely were Speer's tasks, the Führer, as was his predilection, did not clearly state. But what he had made absolutely unequivocal was his personal backing, which was worth its weight in gold. And during the next few days, as Minister Speer began taking up his new duties, he found that within the wildest limits he could do practically as he pleased.

It was not more than a week before he was summoned to Carinhall. He arrived punctually at eleven o'clock after a long automobile ride, only to be kept waiting in the reception hall. Again and again he consulted his watch as he wandered up and down the immense room, looking at the magnificent tapestries without seeing them. He hated the waste of time and had grown irritable when at last his host appeared, wearing a satin dressing gown. They greeted each other coldly. It was clear to the visitor that Göring was extremely angry, although he held his anger in until they had entered his large official study and sat down at his desk. He roughly pushed some papers across the desk top to Speer.

"Why did you not invite me to the meeting you held yesterday?" he asked loudly, with bitterness. "Here are your organizational plans, with attached notes by Milch and the ministerial director of my Four-Year Plan—agreed! Agreed! They agree with everything! They were there, why wasn't I?" Suddenly he got to his feet and began pacing the room, frantic with agitation. "My deputies are spineless wretches! By giving their signatures, they've made themselves your underlings for all time to come! And this without even asking me!" He swung around and returned to the desk, giving it a blow of his fist. "I will not tolerate this eating away of my power! The whole manpower section taken out of my hands—nein! I'll go at once to the Führer and resign as Chief of the Four-Year Plan!"

Both knew that this step would not be accepted by Hitler because of political consequences, but Göring was so wrought up that there was no question that he was prepared to slap down his resignation papers on the Führer's desk.

It would be no loss if you resigned, Speer said to himself. You may have pushed the Four-Year Plan with supreme energy at the beginning, but you must realize by now that you're generally regarded as distinctly averse to solid work. You take up too many ideas, you see nothing through, you hold too many jobs. And it's obvious that you would rather spend your time with your paintings than with any of these jobs.

But aloud he expressed himself diplomatically, having no desire to make an enemy of the formidable and violent Reichsmarschall. "I assure you, Herr Reichsmarschall, that the new arrangement will in no way infringe on your position as head of the Four-Year Plan. I am willing to become your subordinate and to carry out my work within the framework of the Four-Year Plan."

At this, Göring looked at him suspiciously.

"I shall draw up a decree," Speer went on, "appointing myself Chief Representative for Armaments within the Four-Year Plan."

Göring seemed mollified. "Stimmt. Do that. Then bring it to me and I'll sign it."

This procedure was carried out, but a few weeks later it became clear to the new Armaments Minister that, given Göring's reduced powers, they were not sufficient for Speer's own work. He therefore asked the Führer to sign another decree: *The requirements of the German economy as a whole must be subordinated to the necessities of armament production.* In view of the usages of the authoritarian system, this decree of Hitler's amounted to handing Speer dictatorial powers over the entire economy.

Göring was once more laid low by an eruption of his ailments. The glaring March sky sent a cold harsh light through the windows. He asked Robert to draw the curtains around the canopied bed.

"Speer?" he murmured, his eyes closed. "That housebuilder . . . that juvenile nonentity? *Speer?*"

The new Armaments Minister was stimulated by the scope and challenge of his job, and just as eight years ago he had stood intoxicated by the grandiosity of his Nuremburg stadium, twice the length of the Baths of Caracalla, he now went about intoxicated by the grandiosity of his new tasks. He went about quietly, with the well-bred, studious expression that had always characterized him, a tall, youngish, unassuming man giving no outward indication that he was rapidly becoming one of the strongest leaders in the Reich. It was said that the Führer looked upon him as his principal spokesman, his trusted adviser in all economic matters. An official of the Wehrmacht's Armaments Office reported: Speer is the only one who can say anything. He can interfere in any department. He already disregards all other departments. We must join the Speer Organization and pull together, otherwise Speer will go his own way.

Soon after the selection of a Plenipotentiary General for Manpower—the Gauleiter of Thuringia, Sauckel—Speer received the necessary decree from Göring: *My manpower sections are hereby abolished. Their duties, recruitment and allocation of manpower, regulation for labor conditions, are taken over by the Plenipotentiary for Manpower. The Plenipotentiary will be directly under me. In case of ordinances and instructions of fundamental importance, report is to be submitted to me, in advance.* Speer was satisfied by the decree, the last two sentences being sheer rhetoric. Nothing would be directly under Göring except on paper.

Two months after having taken up his new duties, Speer realized that some kind of central authority must be established to direct the allocation of raw materials. He discussed the matter with Milch, and they decided they would together form a Central Planning Commission. As usual it was necessary to have Göring's formal agreement, and the two set out to Carinhall in order to procure it. The countryside, which had been blossoming with the colors of spring, was being pounded by a dark wintry rain that had swept in just after the bombing of Lübeck three days before, as if to sadly commemorate the destruction of the beautiful old Hanseatic port. No German city had heretofore been worked over as intensively as this small medieval town. In addition to ordinary high-explosive bombs, liquid incendiary bombs had been used. In one night the town had been devoured by flames.

Minister Speer was grieved by the irreplaceable architectural losses. Feldmarschall Milch was beset by the realization that the British had finally achieved a truly tangible success. Both knew they would find the Reichsmarschall in no pleasant mood.

He looked tired. In one of his velvet dressing gowns, deep russet in color and decorated with a large ruby brooch, he took them into his study, where they set forth their idea of establishing a Central Planning Commission. He was unwilling to discuss it. He reminded the two men of a horse running around and around inside a fenced-in field as he talked of one thing after another which had no direct bearing on the subject at hand—a useless exercise which gradually came to an end, the horse slowing, stopping, understanding that it would get nowhere. They set forth the suggestion again. He answered that he was not in favor of it. They remained firm, strong with the stamp of the Führer's support, and finally he agreed with a silent nod, adding, almost shyly, "Could you possibly take my friend Pilli Körner? Otherwise he will feel sad at the demotion."

Driving back through the rain to Berlin, the two men further discussed their project. They had acceded to Göring's wish that they include Körner. It had placated the Reichsmarschall a little, and in any case Körner would have no say whatsoever, since their own two votes would always outweigh his one.

In reprisal for Lübeck, the Luftwaffe bombed the old seaside town of Exeter. In reprisal for Exeter, the British bombed the old port city of Rostock. In reprisal for Rostock, the Luftwaffe bombed the famous Regency town of Bath. These reprisal raids on both sides took on the name "Baedeker attacks," since their purpose was not practical but psychological—the destruction of historical sites where tourists had flocked for centuries, the wiping out of magnificent architecture that represented the very soul of the nation's past and pride. After Bath, however, the Luftwaffe abandoned its reprisal attacks as too costly. At the same time, the RAF Marshal reported to his staff: The attacks against Lübeck and Rostock brought the total acreage of bombing devastation in Germany up to 780 acres, which about squares our account. We shall now turn to a new form of attack: area bombing on a grand scale. In the past we have used at the most only 230 planes. We shall now use a thousand.

On the morning of May 31, at his East Prussian headquarters, Hitler was sitting at his daily conference with his military and naval spokesmen. He listened quietly as the naval liaison told him of the trouble German shipping had run into off the coast of Africa. He then listened to the Army spokesman's report on the great battle raging around Kharkov. He then looked over at General Jeschonnek and asked for the Luftwaffe report.

Bodenschatz, who as Luftwaffe liaison officer to the Führer was present, noticed that the Youngster's hands were nervous as he took up his papers.

"I am waiting," said Hitler.

"Cologne, mein Führer. There was an RAF attack on Cologne last night. A pretty heavy attack."

"How heavy?" Hitler asked coldly.

"According to preliminary reports, we estimate that two hundred enemy aircraft penetrated our defense. The damage was rather heavy . . . we are still waiting for final estimates."

"You are still waiting for final estimates," Hitler repeated quietly, almost softly, then his voice accelerated to an enraged shout. "And the Luftwaffe thinks there were two hundred enemy aircraft! The Luftwaffe has probably been asleep last night! But I have not been asleep— I stay awake when one of my cities is under fire! And I thank the Almighty that I can rely on my Gauleiters, even if the Luftwaffe deceives me! Let me tell you what Gauleiter Grohe of Cologne has to say—listen to me and listen carefully! There were a *thousand* or more English aircraft! Do you hear? A thousand, twelve hundred, maybe more!"

He sat back furiously in his chair. Jeschonnek's face had paled. Hitler's eyes moved angrily around the room. "Herr Göring of course is not here," he said with biting sarcasm. "Of course not."

At this, Bodenschatz slipped from the room and made a telephone call to Veldenstein, where Göring had gone for a week's stay. "Chief, you'd better come. There's trouble."

"Cologne?" came the voice at the other end of the wire.

"Very bad. Very bad. They used over a thousand aircraft."

"A thousand? But I have here a staff report saying there were two hundred. . . . Never mind, I'll leave at once."

Three hours later, he stepped into the conference room at Wolfsschanze and went up to the Führer to shake hands with him. Bodenschatz shuddered with vicarious humiliation as Hitler ignored the outstretched hand, simply ignored it—in front of junior officers he was cutting his Reichsmarschall dead; he might as well have turned his back. Göring lowered his hand uncertainly.

"I have come, mein Führer, to . . . I understand there was a discrepancy in the reports."

The Führer made no response. A sense of excruciating embarrassment filled the room. Jeschonnek, caught between his loyalty to his Führer and his loyalty to his Air Chief, kept his eyes painfully lowered. The Führer turned to the officer to whom he had just been speaking and continued the conversation where it had been left off. After a few moments Göring turned and left the room, Bodenschatz following.

"I'm terribly sorry, Chief. I had no idea this would happen. I thought it would be best if you came."

"Of course it was. It was the right thing."

They walked through the snowy grounds toward the Reichsmarschall's quarters. Except for Keitel and Jodl, who were always with the Führer, only the Reichsmarschall had private quarters at Wolfsschanze. It was a great honor to be the only Wolfsschanze outsider with one's own home away from home. But as they approached the small timbered building surrounded by pines, the Chief looked at it unseeingly. His face still bore an expression of bewilderment. He stopped and turned to his old friend.

"He refused to shake my hand, Karl."

Chapter 74

IN the days before it had become circumspect not to disturb their neighbors, Ida had been inordinately attached to her piano—not that she was a very good pianist, her repertoire consisting of two Strauss waltzes drastically simplified for beginners, which she had committed inaccurately to memory; but if her renditions were littered with wrong notes they were, to her parents' distress, more than compensated for by an ear-shattering brio. One of these two Konzertstücke of hers was the first thing she heard as she jumped down from the train to the platform. It was being played by a band she couldn't see for the press of people, but the sound bounced and sparkled through the whole place, turning the noise and confusion into a holiday outing. "It's 'Künstlerleben,'" she shouted over the noise to her mother, who didn't answer as she squinted around in her travel-crushed suit, dark with sweat under the arms. "It's 'Künstlerleben,'" Ida told her again, without response. "'*Künst*lerleben'!" "Ja, ja, 'Künstlerleben,'" her father muttered, wiping his forehead with his handkerchief.

Her parents were both worn out and irritable from the trip, a miserable journey, far worse than she could have imagined. After the first ten minutes in the sway and rattle and bumping of the boxcar she had begun to long for the dreary Wilmersdorf apartment; after twelve hours of the stifling heat, the thick smell of many people's sweat, the much worse smell of the overflowing slop pot behind a rigged-up curtain, the bickering, the short tempers, her own maddened squirms because she was wedged in, cramped, sweaty, hungry, sore in every bone—after twelve hours she could not think of a solitary thing worth being resettled for, not even the fact that in Poland there would be no air raids. But just then the clattering wheels had begun to slow, and presently the train came to a stop and they were climbing out in a blaze of evening sunlight. Open summer air, band music, the miserable journey left behind on the tracks. Wiping her face with her arm, she looked up at the vast expanse of sky, at the big dusty chestnut trees whose leaves stirred in the flashing brilliance of "Künstlerleben." But Mutti and Vati remained frowning in the sunlight, rubbing their sore backs, arguing over a misplaced string bag. Finally they picked up their suitcases. She already stood with hers in the jostling mass of disembarking, milling passengers, a thousand at least. No one seemed to know what to do or where to go.

"Ida, where's your sweater!"

"I don't know, Mutti, it got lost."

Her mother gave a furious, exasperated headshake—as if anyone needed a sweater in this heat. Her father, his usually smooth-brushed gray hair disheveled, was trying to keep the three of them together in the confusion.

A loudspeaker crackled through the air. "Achtung! Achtung!" And again: "Achtung! Achtung!" as the voices and movement diminished. "Damen und Herren, you have arrived at the work camp of Auschwitz. You will be employed here according to your abilities. Skills most in demand are those of carpenters, masons, mechanics and heavy equipment drivers. For men unskilled in these areas there will be field work. Families will remain together. You will be housed in living quarters with cooking facilities. Your luggage will be delivered to your living quarters after you have undergone regulation disinfection and showers. Leave your luggage on the platform and proceed to the north end of the platform. Vehicles there will take you to the bathhouse. To mitigate disorder we ask that you form up in two rows, five abreast in each."

"A labor camp," Vati said through his teeth.

"Does it come as a surprise?" Mutti asked angrily.

Ida could see clusters of gray-clad SS men standing alongside the platform with briefcases and clipboards, the same scene as in Berlin early this morning, at the railway yard. She could also see the camp band now, a small group in suits and ties, their instruments flaring in the orange sun. They had stopped playing during the announcement; now they started up again with "La Cucaracha."

"When they say field work, Erich, what do they mean?" Mutti asked.

"I don't know. Digging ditches, carting stones."

"Couldn't you tell them you're a carpenter? After all, you did make those cabinets for the summer house."

"I don't know. I suppose I could."

"And they were done to perfection, Erich. Absolute perfection."

"I wouldn't go that far."

"No, it's true. Absolute perfection."

Ida could tell that her mother was trying to make up for her quick temper. It was her way. She wasn't one to apologize.

"What about disinfection?" Ida asked. "What does that mean, Vati?"

"Delousing."

"De*lousing*!"

"Must you always scream!" snapped Mutti, putting her hands to her ears.

"But phew—lice. Who's got lice?"

"People who've been stuck in filthy boxcars for half a day," said Vati. "And then they play music for us. Why must they play this damned music?"

"La Cucaracha" gave way to a fox-trot as the two broad lines began moving along the platform. Ida would have liked them to play "Künstlerleben" again, but she supposed they would have to use up their whole repertoire before they started over, and that wasn't likely, since the lines were moving at a steady pace. Now and then an SS officer motioned for someone to step out and go to the right, but it didn't hold up the rest of them. Very soon she saw the end of the platform. A tango was playing as they climbed up into one of six or seven open trucks, the others already full. When theirs was filled, the trucks set off along a gravel road as the tango faded away.

More dusty chestnut trees lined the road. She could only glimpse their tops, being short and squeezed among tall adults even more tightly than in the boxcar. Her revitalized spirits began to droop in the crammed, bouncing vehicle so reminiscent of the long train journey. But the ride was brief, they were soon climbing down.

Everything seemed speeded up now; she had time only to glimpse a big thatch-roofed farm building with a sign saying *Disinfection,* a couple of smaller wooden buildings, SS men with dogs, before she and Mutti were hurried off with the other women. "Women and children to the left! Men to the right!" She couldn't even see Vati's rumpled gray hair among the swarm of men being directed to the right, everything was going so fast.

"Don't lag so, Ida!" Her mother jerked her along by the hand.

Ida protested under her breath. Throughout the whole trip Mutti had been after her, never had her mother been so annoyed with her as today, and she hadn't even done anything. But as they entered the wooden building marked *Damen,* her preoccupation with her abuse was scattered by the sight of previous truckloads of women, old, young, children among them, standing around stark naked. Her eyes blinking with startled embarrassment—she had envisioned dressing rooms, little stalls—she blundered after her mother to a wooden bench. Her mother began unbuttoning the jacket of her gray pinstriped suit. All the women they had streamed in with were getting out of their clothes. The worst thing of all was the presence of men, three or four of them who walked around explaining where to hang their clothes, where to put their shoes, what the procedure was after they came back from the bathhouse. They looked like the band members, they were dressed the same way. At least they didn't stare or act interested. But still, they were men.

"Get on with it, Ida!"

Slowly she pulled her wrinkled, dusty dress over her head, followed by the sweaty cotton slip. Then grievously, her face flaming, she eased out of her undershirt, revealing her small secret breasts for all the world to gawk at, and sitting down on the bench squirmed out of her pants, quickly crossing her legs.

"For heaven's sake, Ida! Hang up your things, memorize the peg number so you can find them afterward!"

"What number?" she mumbled, standing up in her terrible nakedness, somehow getting her clothes on a peg. Her mother took her by the hand. She did not look at her mother, she did not want to see her naked. Everyone was going to the door, a great mass of pale backs and behinds. She felt suffocated by nakedness, and suddenly no longer shamed and self-conscious, as if that were a small thing already far in the past, but crushed by a feeling of something terribly wrong in so much nakedness. Out they walked into the dusty gold evening light, SS guards and officers standing along the path looking at them.

She felt her mother's arm clasp her protectively to her side, so tightly that it hurt her ribs, and in the painfully crushing embrace she sensed all her mother's sharpness of the entire day, it was the sharpness of terror. There was no sound as they walked along the sun-warmed dirt; everyone had grown absolutely silent. Inside the farm building they were handed towels and bars of soap. They went inside a large whitewashed shower room, many, many women, filling most of the room, standing crowded together with their towels and bars of soap. "Shall I take out my barrettes, Mutti?" she asked. Her mother put her hand to her daughter's head, touching the wild hair that sprang up from under the two white barrettes. "It's pretty dirty," Ida said faintly. "It's all the dust."

Suddenly their menfolk came pouring in through the door as naked as themselves, everything crammed and confused and horrifying as the door slammed shut and the lights went out.

Chapter 75

OBERGRUPPENFÜHRER Heydrich had been busy for eleven years, ever since he had joined the SS. But since the invasion of Poland in 1939, his activities had increased enormously, step by step. First he had been put in charge of the Einsatzgruppen which liquidated the Polish intelligentsia. With the invasion of Russia, the duties of his Einsatzgruppen had expanded to the execution of all men, women and children who for whatever reason might appear suspect as partisans, all government officials, and all Jews. It was during this time that he had received an order signed by the Reichsmarschall, as every important order was signed, directing him to effect a final solution to the Jewish problem by organizing a total resettlement in Poland of all European Jews. This solution, as Himmler subsequently explained to him, would not be actual resettlement but would be a matter of bringing the Jews to the slave labor camps already existing. Those unable to work would be disposed of through gassing, the German euthanasia program having yielded much valuable information regarding the use of gas for extermination purposes. Execution by means of firing squads was clumsy, time-consuming and expensive. Zyklon B was both efficient and more cheaply produced than bullets. Heydrich was to organize and oversee the entire project, which needless to say would be top-secret.

Busier than ever before, he nevertheless found time to keep up his special files on the top men in the Reich. In the Göring folder, for instance, he worked forward from the protracted sexual relations of Göring's mother with the Jew Epenstein, through Göring's morphine addiction in Austria, Italy and Sweden, to the subversive inclinations of his brother (or possibly half brother) and the religious meddlesomeness of his two Catholic sisters, to his wife's surreptitious activities on behalf of Jewish friends, as well as Göring's own role in these activities, to the shady side of his gargantuan and complex finances—the forays into staying tax evasion proceedings against some firm which would then reciprocate lavishly; the continual monetary contributions, or hopeful bribes, from various industrialists; the priceless birthday gifts extracted from cities and organizations . . . Göring's file was particularly thick and bulging, like the man himself, but all the files were interesting. There were some twenty of them, including one on Himmler. There was even one on Hitler. For it was not inconceivable to Heydrich that he might one day usurp both his chiefs.

Meanwhile, he had added to his other posts that of Reich Protector of Bohemia-Moravia. Appointed by Hitler, who had ousted Neurath for the feebleness of his administration, Heydrich went to Prague to take up the challenge of growing unrest. Using every terror tactic in the SS book, earning himself the sobriquet "the Butcher of Prague," he restored order in a short time. Then, being the highly intelligent man he was, he did a complete turnabout: raised food rations, opened the luxury spas to the workers, instituted social security schemes. He had only to sit back in Hradčany Castle and watch the unfolding of the results: cooperation, political apathy.

As the months passed, the exiled Czech government in London concluded that if hatred of the German occupiers was to be intensified, if the people were to be induced to resist, reprisals must be provoked. An extreme step must be taken to unleash German brutality. If Reich Protector Heydrich was assassinated, German countermeasures would be more than sufficiently brutal to stimulate resistance. Consequently, two Czech officers in exile, trained by the English in sabotage and guerrilla tactics, were flown to Bohemia in a British long-range aircraft and dropped by parachute near Prague.

It took the Reich Protector eight long agonizing days to die of his wounds, after which reprisals went into effect. More than a thousand people were summarily shot; and since there were rumors that the assassins had been harbored in the village of Lidice, every male in the village over the age of twelve was executed, every woman sent to a concentration camp, every child sent to a Lebensborn home to be raised by the state, and every stick of the village set afire and burned to an ash, so that not a single trace of Lidice remained. After this, an active Czech resistance came into being.

Heydrich's associates were not cast down by his death. "Thank

God that sow's gone to the butcher" was the response of most. To one degree or another, everyone who had known him—and everyone who had known him had feared him—was relieved. Göring was greatly relieved, but only for a while. For what difference did Heydrich's death really make? Himmler still held the SS reins, and the SS would continue to encroach upon power wherever it could.

Berlin sweltered in the late-summer heat wave of 1942, but when the head of the SS Foreign Intelligence Service entered Göring's Air Ministry office he found it pleasantly cool, the mugginess from outside dispersed by the room's vast dimensions. He was certain that nothing else about the visit would be pleasant.

The SS Gruppenführer began the long echoing walk to the desk at the far end. Not long ago he had been sent to Carinhall bearing unwelcome news: Himmler was to take over the Reichsmarschall's spying organization, the Göring Forschungsamt. He had been astonished by Göring's response: the Reichsmarschall had dug his hand into a cut-crystal bowl filled with gems, had fingered them, gazed at them, until he seemed almost in a trance. The Gruppenführer had sat silently, watching with fascination, until with an abstracted gesture he was dismissed. How smoothly the unpleasant task had gone. But since then it had become clear that the Reichsmarschall harbored a strong dislike of him, associating him with the painful news he had imparted that day at Carinhall. In the Reichsmarschall's various Berlin offices, without his gems nearby to soothe him, he treated the Gruppenführer with open hostility. And now today, for the second time, the Gruppenführer was bearing unwelcome news.

He felt he had been walking for kilometers. The long echoing servantlike trek to the solitary, imperious figure struck him as a scene out of date. The impression pleased him, became a shield against the insultingly cold reception he would soon undergo. What, after all, was the Reichsmarschall? Nothing more than a vehicle for the transmission of the Führer's orders. Or if that was overdoing it, at least he no longer stood where he had. For people who knew things, the Reichsmarschall had been slipping very badly. A displaced figure, whose bustlingly sporadic requests had to be catered to. Bringing him the special report on American war production was an empty formality, a waste of time.

The big beringed hand took the folder. The unfriendly face settled into an expression of studiousness.

Sitting down across the desk from him, the Gruppenführer, with rigidly composed features, mentally read the contents of the folder: an annual steel production of ninety million tons; rapid development of the United States Army Air Force . . .

The studious expression had begun to harden. A page was turned.

Blotches of red were appearing on the forehead and cheeks. Suddenly the eyes flashed up.

"Everything that you have written here is total nonsense! You should have your mental condition examined by a psychiatrist!"

The Gruppenführer was struck speechless by the insult. His face flooded with red as his folder was slapped shut and sent skidding across the polished desk top.

"Get out of here with this crap!"

His fingers stiff with outrage, the Gruppenführer got his folder into his briefcase, zipped it with difficult jerks and began the long, echoing journey back to the great double doors.

Glowering after him until he was finally gone, the Reichsmarschall pushed back his throne of a chair and paced over to the window to stand staring out across the heat-hazed city, his hands gripped behind him. After looking at his watch, he raked his fingers through his hair and stamped off to preside over a meeting of commissioners for the occupied territories.

"God knows you were not sent to work for the welfare of the populations, but to squeeze the utmost out of them so that the German people may live! It makes no difference to me if you say your people are starving! It seems to me to have been a relatively simple thing in former days—it used to be called plundering! It was up to the party in question to carry off what had been conquered! Today things have become more genteel, but in spite of that I intend to plunder, and to do it thoroughly!" He stopped to glare at the commissioners seated around the table. "Gentlemen, I have a very great deal to do and a very great deal of responsibility. I have no time to read letters and memoranda informing me that you cannot supply my requirements, I have time only to ascertain whether the commitments are being fulfilled! I will get what I demand from you; and if you cannot manage it, I will set up agencies that will get it out of you whether you like it or not!"

In bad humor, he left the Air Ministry early. The streets he was driven through were blanched of color by the heat. The trees along the sidewalks stood motionless, dusty. Occasionally there came into view a construction site where a bomb-damaged building was being repaired. He sat back and closed his eyes.

At Carinhall, having been got out of his sweat-drenched uniform by Robert, he took a cooling shower and presently emerged from the house in a loose dressing gown of pale blue silk. He crunched along the flower-bordered gravel path, gazing at the grounds where his bronze statues had been augmented by carved French cupids, Greek satyrs, marble busts of ancient Romans, Renaissance sundials, huge alabaster vases. Arranged among shrubbery, gracing lawns, they did not seem to him at all out of place in their northern setting of pines and firs. He filled his eyes with them. The air was clear, hot, resinous, still. He breathed deeply of it as he walked, feeling the earlier part of his day fade like mist in the sun. He would have tea with Emmy on the terrace, and play with little Edda. Later he would work with his museum drawings. And in the evening, the most beautiful time of day in late summer, he would take his walk down to the mausoleum, to Carin. He would return along the edge of the lake, its water reflecting the gold-and-apricot evening sky. Then he might sit again with his museum drawings. There would be guests for supper, and afterward a film. Or instead of a film, perhaps they would just sit out on the terrace and enjoy the warm, still summer night.

Chapter 76

T HE nights became less peaceful that autumn. RAF raids on Berlin grew more numerous, and the bombers sometimes made their thunderous way there over Carinhall. The very night, in late November, that Thomas von Kantzow arrived for a visit, as he sat at a late supper with Hermann, Emmy and Hermann's sister Olga, a servant came in and quietly announced:

"They're on their way, Excellency."

Hermann nodded, and continued eating. Olga, who had been talking, resumed her conversation.

"You, of course, know how it is," she said to Thomas.

"The cold. The cold, yes."

Despite her fifty-odd years, Olga had volunteered as a Luftwaffe nurse and had been sent to Russia. Her experiences were horribly fresh in her mind, especially that of the Russian winter.

"It was possibly even worse in Finland," she said to him, "although I cannot imagine it."

"Cold is cold," he answered briefly, smiling for the sake of politeness. He wished she would speak of something else. No doubt Hermann wished the same, for Russia meant Stalingrad: after seven weeks of savage battle, the German Sixth Army had penetrated the city, fighting from house to house, only to have their supply lines cut off by the enemy. The entire Sixth Army was surrounded.

Hermann moved back the sleeve of his robe and looked at his watch.

"We shall have time for dessert."

Dessert, a variety of cheeses glistening from gold foil and several beautifully polished red apples set among imported plums and figs, was partaken of leisurely.

"When do they arrive?" Thomas asked with mild curiosity.

"We were telephoned from Wittenberg—that gives us a good half hour," Hermann told him. He was extremely heavy, mammoth in his quilted emerald-green robe. His face was sallow and tired-looking, though he appeared to be in good spirits. "We'll have our coffee and liqueur down there," he said at length, and the party rose from the table.

They walked down the hallway to an elevator, new to Thomas. The lights in the house were being turned off. They stood in darkness a moment before the elevator doors opened. When they stepped out, it was into a small luxurious flat, well lit, comfortable and inviting. "You think you're upstairs, nicht?" Hermann asked with a clap to his stepson's shoulder. "Come, I'll take you on the tour. Olga, come too, you didn't see everything last time."

They were shown the air-conditioning installation, the all-electric kitchen with its well-stocked refrigerator and wine cellar, the rose-tiled bathroom, the bedroom with its large soft bed covered with a silken eiderdown, and the nursery, where Emmy was just turning out the light. With her was the nursemaid, who had apparently come down with little Edda at the first signal. They went quietly from the darkened room, the nursemaid then departing for the adjacent house-staff shelter. In the kitchen, a servant had begun preparing coffee. Presently he rolled in a tea wagon laden with coffee things and liqueurs and, with a bow, left the room. Emmy began serving from the silver service, as Hermann looked over the liqueur bottles. Olga had again begun telling about Russia.

". . . they're so badly frozen that when a limb is amputated, there is scarcely any blood . . ."

Before Thomas's eyes there appeared a frozen limb separated from its frozen torso, the severed end a marbled whorl of hard, dark red like a frigid end cut of meat at the butcher's. If his own limbs were amputated, this is how they would look. He didn't have to go to Russia to get frozen. At thirty, he was permanently refrigerated—going to his job each day, sitting late into the night with a book and bottle, occasionally undertaking a safe little affair. One day he would come to the end of his life. If he had been religious, he might have hoped to be reunited with his mother; but he was not religious, he would be reunited with nothing. Even so, he had no fear of death. It would be a relatively even exchange. As he sat sipping his coffee, he knew that if this room here began to shake under RAF bombs, he would feel no distress for himself. But of course the room would not shake, its whole point was that it was so deep in the earth that nothing could affect it. The planes must be overhead by now, or nearly. On the other hand, they might already have passed. There was no way of telling. Except for Olga's voice, one heard only a deep, underground, artificial silence, in which the air-conditioning unit hummed with an eerie earnestness.

Hermann had sat listening to his sister with all his earlier cheeriness gone, as if something brightly forced had ebbed from his face. Emmy, too, had lost her sunniness. But when the Russian tales were over, she made an attempt to lift spirits.

"Do you know what I'm going to do when we've won the war? I'm—"

"Why can't you realize we're not going to win this war?" Hermann cut her off. "We're losing in Africa! We're losing in the Mediterranean! Now Stalingrad is lost! The war is already lost, even if the Führer refuses to recognize the fact! Why can't you realize that?"

For Thomas, these words came as no great shock. Nothing ever came as a great shock. But Olga's eyes widened and stared, while Emmy, putting her hand to her cheek as if slapped, broke into tears. Hermann took her in his arms, and he too was crying. They sat together, weeping silently, in the low eerie hum of the air conditioner.

The bombers that had just roared over Carinhall were within minutes of Berlin. In an underground shelter similar to the Görings', Frau Goebbels and the nursemaids had tucked the children in. The younger ones had not wakened at all, and the older ones had gone right back to sleep, for which she was thankful. She turned out the light and went into the living room with the two nursemaids, who said goodnight and went on to the servants' section of the shelter.

The living room took on an intense emptiness with their departure. She walked over to an armchair and sat down, opening a silver cigarette box at her side. Her face, heavily made up, was drawn, hollow beneath the cheekbones. She lit a cigarette, sat back, exhaled. She said in a flat tone, "There is actually no need for us to come down here."

Her husband, sitting nearby, raised a brow to indicate that he had heard, but did not look up from his writing.

"We're far enough away from the city not to. No one else out here bothers to take cover."

"We've been over all that," he murmured, still writing.

She sat listening to the unnatural silence of the room. Tomblike. When her husband was away, she never disturbed the children because of an air raid. The noise was distant, muted; they slept right through it.

It was a pity to rouse them, bundle them into their bathrobes, take them down and down in the elevator to this miserable place. Sometimes they had difficulty getting back to sleep.

"It upsets the children. It puts ideas in the heads of the older ones. Helga is already talking about the war."

"What do you mean, already?" murmured her husband. "It's been going on for a third of her life."

"I try to protect them from the war."

"That is unrealistic."

She shrugged, and examined her fingernails. There was something in her husband's attitude, a satisfaction in going below. He liked being down here in this concrete hole, which was what it was however much it might be disguised as a flat. He liked the idea of everyone running for shelter, he wanted the war to be as terrible, as frightening, as extreme as possible.

But these thoughts faded for lack of stimulus. She had little interest in him, the sight of him made her tired, he bored her unutterably, he was like a dreary roommate whom one was chained to. Fortunately there were times of separation when she could forget him for days, sometimes weeks. For he was very busy. Predictably, he had grown ever busier as the war left him with less and less to do. War was a bad time for a man of words. Hectically, frantically, he kept trying to make himself as indispensable as the military, but he was not succeeding. There had been that period before the war when the Führer had valued him again, and they had seen a great deal of the Führer and it had been like the old days, those vivid, beautiful, gold-dusted days; but gradually, as the war went on, everything had gone back to the way it had been when the Führer seemed to lose sight of them, to forget them. And Josef was unable to stop it. All he could do was thrash about in his activities, touring the country, sticking his nose in everywhere, holing up for days at the ministry. With no results. The Führer had lost sight of him. He was a frantic little man kicking up dust.

Frau Goebbels stubbed her cigarette out and crossed to her bedroom. Inside it the absence of windows was even more pronounced than in the living room. She sat down at the dressing table and carefully began creaming her face. As pancake makeup, mascara and lipstick were transferred in greasy smears to balls of tissue, the face in the mirror emerged worn with poor health. She was not disturbed by the fact that her loss of radiance must please her husband, who no longer need feel blotted out in her presence. Not that there remained much of him to be blotted out, frantically running in circles, and sexually as well. Admittedly, the sight of the little secretary sneaking from his room had come as a profound shock, for to her discredit she had forgotten his predictability during his long period of faithfulness. But the shock had been salutary. Sharp, clean, final. Finally final. An abrupt amputation. And she had felt an unexpected amusement as she realized, for the first time, that anyone wholly predictable was in some inexplicable way ludicrous. She had even teased him about the affair until she grew bored by the subject. When the little secretary had left him to marry her fiancé, Josef had been shaken, no mistress ever before having walked out on him; and predictably he had set up his turnstile again; and predictably it was turning faster than ever, like the pages he sat scribbling and turning over in the next room.

Her husband turned over a page and continued writing. It was not his diary he was working on, though he had kept a diary since his youth. The early ones had throbbed with love affairs, burned with poetry, wept with Weltschmerz; but gradually they had grown less intimate until he was writing solely about the official world he inhabited, and now he dictated his entries each morning before the day's work began. But he felt the lack of an outlet for his innermost thoughts, and from time to time would scrawl out a kind of letter to himself, copious, unvarnished, afterward rereading and tearing up the confidential pages.

. . . I disapproved of the war, I knew the F would soon listen only to his generals & that it would be very hard for me. Borne out. The roar of tanks & guns has silenced the art of Goebbels. But now is when I should perhaps gather my breath, for I will come into my own again only when the generals have proved themselves inadequate to their tasks. In which case I must make a *radical* change—

Switch to steely factuality. Propaganda must abandon its former euphoria & address its audience in sober terms. We must compensate for the failure of the military, must become the *driving force* behind total mobilization of Germany's resources. *Total war*—

The people must feel fear & hatred as they've not yet felt it. Black fear, infernal hatred. They have had it too easy, in part our own fault for mollycoddling them. No more. They will hear the truth & will have no protection against it except to work harder for the war effort. In this we will be aided by the bombings. Things are getting hot for them, this is what we must make use of. An entirely *new* approach—

Also as regards the F—his bond with the people must be preserved. But his appearances grow fewer as he becomes more wrapped up in military matters. A new tack must be used, maybe along these lines: the F has almost disappeared behind his mighty tasks—the indelible furrows written on the

F's face by endless days of work & endless nights without sleep—the F a historical figure—utterly great & utterly lonely—

But I may be leaping ahead of myself. Who knows which way the war will go? Yet if it is going to get better, it is certainly first going to have to get worse. Defeat at Stalingrad a likelihood. Would provide a first-rate platform for total mobilization. Begin now thinking in terms of its use as an emotional rallying point. Have everything ready to go if & when it happens. Nationwide mourning, round-the-clock radio speeches. All stops pulled: German people, you must face the disaster of Stalingrad as you must face the bombing of your cities—the war can be won only by a people that rises above all adversity—only through iron determination & ceaseless effort & every kind of sacrifice—only by a people who exert themselves *totally*—

"If you can hear 'em, don't worry."

"Why?"

The long, descending wail ended in a muffled thud, like a giant kiss blown. The light bulbs flickered, went out, came back on.

"Why?" the child asked again in its piercing voice. "Why, Oma?"

But the old woman, sitting pressed against Rose, only yawned, disclosing old ridged teeth with gaps.

"Why? Why, Oma?"

Whether it was a boy or girl, Rose could not tell. Bundled up, a hood over its head. The nose ran unattractively. The voice stabbed through the noise like an icepick.

"Why, Oma? Why?"

"Shut up, or I'll give you one you'll remember!"

The child swung its head around as flak soldiers came running along the concrete floor, their hobnailed boots adding to the cavernous din of the Zoo Bahnhof bunker, the city's largest. Hundreds of people were sitting and lying throughout. Many had brought suitcases and blankets, and had set up households for the night. Multitudinous voices mixed with the shrill crying of children. From the bunker roof came staccato bursts of antiaircraft artillery. Suddenly there was another long wail, followed by a muffled blast. Swinging its head back, the child in the hood began tugging at the old woman's coat.

You see, if you can hear them falling it means they're a distance away. That's why your grandmother says that if you can hear them not to worry. Because with a direct hit you don't hear anything. But she doesn't want to talk, she wants to sleep. You should try to sleep too. Just don't start crying or she'll give you a smack. Or maybe I will.

The child had stopped its useless coat tugging and pushed a finger deep into one round nostril of its running nose. Absorbedly, as if entering a trance, it began digging for treasure.

Please, please don't do that.

"Use a handkerchief!" The command came from an elderly man, stout, well dressed, who was lodged against the offender. "Why?" asked the child in its shrill voice, uncertainly removing its finger. "Why?" came the piercing voice again. The old man took the child's coat sleeve and pressed it to the small nose. "Use it!" But the child hastily resumed its activity, as if diving back to some form of holy self-communion. The old man, glaring through his spectacles, turned his face away.

I agree, it's worse agony to see a nose being picked then to be drawn and quartered. Why don't you move? I would, but for me it's not a good policy. You too maybe? A curfew breaker? Left your star at home? Your papers in a drawer? So here is the best spot in the bunker for us. Hemmed in, not easily gotten to if a police patrol comes checking. So worm yourself in where it's most closely packed, noisier, smellier, but safer. And the old woman's head on my shoulder, very nice, providential. Mouth hanging open. Snoring. Poor old thing, who would want to disturb her, or her loving daughter so patiently supporting those adenoidal blasts? Ja, here is the best place for the likes of you and me. But you're moving after all. Creaking, puffing, getting stiffly to your feet. Auf Wiedersehen then, Herr Free to Move Where You Please. No Jew obviously. Too fat and well dressed in any case. I hope another nose-digger finds you and destroys you.

The old woman's deadweight head was heavy. It was swaddled in a brown kerchief with fringes. From beneath her coat poked the hem of her nightgown, and beneath this were the pant legs of men's trousers. Her gnarled hands, with black-rimmed fingernails, lay upturned in her lap. The passion of her snores bespoke nights of interrupted sleep.

What am I supposed to do, feel sorry because you're old? Be thankful you're still drawing breath. Not everyone is lucky enough to reach their sunset years. Walther, for instance. What would you have done to help Walther? Why don't you stir yourself and do something for that miserable grandchild of yours? It's frantic. Has to anchor itself in its own matter to find relief. Disgusting.

The light bulbs cast a dim, shadow-striated illumination over the massed shapes throughout the bunker. Sitting on suitcases, on the concrete, some rolled up in blankets trying to sleep in the din. Women, children, men past draft age. Everyone bundled up against the cold. Some eating bread and sausages from their net bags. Some laughing here and there, mostly young girls. Unable to control high spirits.

Why was I stunned? Considering its routineness. There when I left for work, not there that night. Where is Ida? Frau Stern playing dominoes with Fräulein Stahl. I wait to hear them say in the bathroom, downstairs. But naturally that's not what they say. Why stand there stunned, it was routine. A week later the Sterns' turn. Und so weiter. And so I live in solitude again, isn't that what I wanted? No noise, no bumping elbows, no cabbage breath in the face. Cots and suitcases and clutter gone. Notices for them all. Remaining: the Müller couple and myself. War workers, exempt from deportation.

Thank God the child has stopped its digging. Curling up alongside battle-ax Oma. Round as a sowbug. Don't lie there with your eyes darting. Anyone as warm as you should damn well be able to sleep. They're all packed up like Eskimos. Granny here in her winter coat. Old, has seen plenty of use, but a real winter coat like all the coats down here. No forced surrender of blankets and winter coats for the troops at the Russian front. But what was the surrender of blankets? That much less to lug to Poland. Forbidden the use of public rest rooms? Drink less. Public transportation? Walk. Wine, cigarettes, newspapers, magazines? There's always dominoes. Food restricted to cabbage, potatoes, black bread? Meat's not good for you anyway. But none of this disturbs the Berliners' sleep. That's left to our British visitors. I should welcome them as saviors. Those in the house do. In the cellar when the light flickers, I can feel their satisfaction, although I can't share it. But I can resent you bundled up sausage-chewers on behalf of my cellarmates. You're all oversized sowbugs littering the floor. The filthy planes are going at it a long time tonight. At home in the cellar they're blessing each thud. If I'm not part of them, even less am I a part of you down here. Part of nothing. I endure. Use window drapes for blankets. Mend my clothes, wear newspaper under them. Each morning put cardboard inside the shoes. Get on the S-bahn, show my travel permit, travel to work. Work, travel back. Eat dinner. Every morsel of black bread, to preserve the health. Once a fortnight, for the soul's health, snip the threads from the star and go out after curfew. Must be careful, must preserve myself. But the question gnaws like a rat: preserve myself for what?

The clatter of flak left off like an arm dropping to rest. There would be a lull of thirty minutes, forty, before the next wave of planes. The children's whining and crying faded, people got up and stretched, others used the opportunity to dig into sleep. The heavy head on Rose's shoulder snored on. She took her shoulder away, the head jerked up, eyes opening confusedly. Small eyes, gummy with old age. A great yawn, exposing all the dreadful teeth. Then a radiant smile. Comradely gratitude. On the old woman's lap the child in the hood, the nose-digger, was crawling, fussing, pulling a button, seeking attention, until a cuff to the side of the head silenced it.

The huge metal bunker door was being opened. Rose pressed in among the others who were leaving, people like herself who had been caught on the street, others who had come to stay the night but could not keep from hurrying home to check their apartments before the next wave. She stood in the freezing night air, which was filled with the smell of burning and the high-low, high-low wail of fire trucks. Forty minutes would see her to her doorstep if she walked close to a run.

Chapter 77

23 November, Monday. Carinhall. What Hermann said in the shelter last night may be true, but the war goes on and so does he: called away today to Hitler's hdqts in East Prussia, left at noon.

E: A shame your visit with Hermann is cut off like this.

K: But you and I shall have a good visit.

Lies slide from my tongue like snow water. We no longer have good visits, E and I, in the sense of ordinary. Something deferential in her manner toward me, as one finds at funerals. Of course she converses, we converse as always, but in some impalpable way, and quite unconsciously, I'm sure, she defers to what I have become.

Hermann lacks the acuteness of her instincts. Because I attained the stature of a hero he feels I attained something indestructible, something iron-hard and rich in sustenance, which can never alter or be taken away. Something as real as any internal organ, more real, tucked away behind the breastbone like a hard shining kernel, inviolable, immortal, remaining when the rest will have turned to dust.

Evening. Went into his den. There was a time when I wouldn't have, but everything has grown easy. Step into someone's sanctuary—what difference from stepping into someone's front hall? Turned on the desk lamp. Same caramel-colored lampshade that I wrote under that day seven, eight years ago. Same array of framed faces, same small porcelain soldiers and antique dagger letter opener. The rest of the house is in a constant state of change, things renewed, improved, new artifacts brought in, but the den does not change. Old Fritz and his two greyhounds on the mantelpiece, the sword in its scabbard hanging above. The Richthofen Squadron photographs, most of the faces under the turf by the war's end—for Udet the same fiery crash, only postponed twenty-five years. A sound of wind whistling around and around in the fireplace.

I remember how the fire roared that night when I made my stand to save the world. The flames reflecting on Hermann's face. My racing heart, the damp prickling of my palms. The heroic leap, the mighty verbal avalanche—ten minutes, fifteen—at the end drained, drained, and blissful, as if I beheld in my damp palm, opening my hand, the one clear, flawless diamond each life is promised at least once.

I walked over and stood before Mother's painting. The smile, the mountain peaks, the honeymoon spot. *Alpine Rapture* I had labeled it years ago, my little lemon twist of irony always at hand, and always one remove from understanding itself. For what I say now is: at least I had her at the end. It is easy to say now, but for a decade I could not face it, could not think of it except with an overwhelming sense of guilt toward Hermann. Yes, it was I who told Mother of your telegram, I who got you out of the house and out of the country, I who made sure she would die without you. That you weren't there has always tormented you. Many times I have wanted to tell you, to relieve my conscience. But now I no longer have a conscience.

Everything has become easy for me. I walked around the den. The same Scandinavian throwrugs, the pendulum clock ticking in the corner. On the wall behind the desk, the old print of *Ritter, Tod und Teufel*, spotted, waterstained, crossed with rusty fold lines from its sojourns in the blood-spattered feldgrau knapsack, the soldier who did his duty, the knight with his long spear frightened not by death, tempted not by the devil, amen. And something new after all, though very old, four small paintings the size of saucers. Child angels each playing an ancient musical instrument. Beautiful, luminous faces.

24 November, Tuesday. Tea in the Viking Room this afternoon with Emmy, Olga and a Frau B. Her husband is Hermann's only personal friend in the Party. Mother had a poor opinion of Party wives, called them pushy upstarts, but this one was only tedious.

Frau B: Our war with Russia is more than a war, it is the greatest ideological contest since the ancient wars of religion.

O: I would it *were* a war of religion in the old sense. Religion in Germany has been crushed to death.

E: Olga, a beet sandwich? (Because she's not sure of the servants? Of Frau B? Anyway, Hermann's relatives always say the wrong thing.)

Frau B: Russia is our true test. Don't you agree, Herr von Kantzow?

K: Of course. (True test of what? For what?)

O: When I think that this time last year we stood fast from the Arctic to the outskirts of Cairo, from the Atlantic to the suburbs of Moscow . . .

(Said with a mixture of nostalgia and bitter determination. Are you thinking of Hermann's black outburst in the bunker? No, you're not thinking at all. If you were thinking, you would realize that a German victory will be a National Socialist victory. You're like the generals. You fight for Germany, not the regime. But Germany and the regime have become one and the same.)

Frau B: It is in Russia that we will stand or fall.

O: Thomas here has also had experience with the Russians.

Frau B: So I understand, Herr von Kantzow. In the Finnish War. The Russians took a dreadful beating at the start, didn't they?

K: A dreadful beating. (At least a dozen I can personally account for in very close quarters, their faces as clear as yours.)

Frau B: They have manpower, but they haven't the training.

O: I assure you they have the training. They're not the clods they were three years ago.

Frau B: Then your opinion is what, Frau Riegele?

O: My opinion counts for nothing. I was only a nurse. I can only say that we must fight on, and we must win.

Frau B: And you, Herr von Kantzow, what is your opinion?

K: The same.

(My opinion, if I could be said to entertain any idea as strong as an opinion, is that the only victor will be the iron framework. This escapes you, Frau B, as it seems to escape everyone. If Hitler wins, the iron framework wins. If the Allies win, the iron framework wins. The iron framework will be the victor. The true test was lost a long time ago, Frau B, when Germany was seen as a surface of blazing sunlight; but that sunlight was really ice, and under it lay fathomless black water. Those with eyes should have seen that Germany would create the most horrifying drama the world has ever known, that Germany would become a monstrosity.

The conversation finally turned to other things. To please Emmy I stayed to the end. I counted the hunting horns, the white hides of slain polar bears, the bright tassels hanging in fringes from the old Norse rugs on the wall.

In Jeschonnek's eyes was a veiled accusation: you should have been here to argue. Of what use are you six hundred kilometers away in Carinhall?

Göring's face was ruddy from the bitter cold outside. He crossed the room to where the Führer stood, the same spot where he had stood eight months before with the freshly appointed, freshly anointed Speer at his side; the same spot where he had stood after the bombing of Cologne and refused to shake hands. Today there was a handshake. The matter in question was immediately taken up.

"Your Chief of Staff here is not in favor of the idea."

"I have not said that, mein Führer," protested Jeschonnek, who in fact had not expressed his doubts aloud, his Prussian reserve and the awe in which he held his Führer both having militated against argument. "I did not say that I—"

"You did not say it but it is clear. I want to know your opinion, Reichsmarschall. Can it be done?"

"What you informed me of in your dispatch, mein Führer, this plan to supply the Sixth Army by air, to fly in five hundred tons of material a day for some four months—we are speaking here of providing for a quarter of a million men daily: a hundred and fifty tons of food, three hundred tons of fuel, fifty tons of ammunition—"

"I am not asking to hear what I have already told you. I am asking if you can do it."

"This task you propose would require at least eight hundred transport planes. The Luftwaffe has only seven hundred and fifty all told. And of these, more than three hundred are supplying Rommel in North Africa."

"Can bombers be adapted for transport purpose?"

"They can be, but—"

"Then it must be done. The Luftwaffe must support my armies at Stalingrad until my panzer formations can break through and relieve them. Listen to me! If you gather together all available transport planes, including Lufthansa civil planes, in addition to a sufficient number of bombers, we can keep Stalingrad supplied. I also happen to know that you have kept a wing of Heinkel 177s in training for the spring offensive. You can tell them that spring has arrived. They can finish their training in Russia."

Jeschonnek's eyes were moving back and forth between the two speakers. He saw Göring wince.

"But the Heinkel 177—this is our answer to the American Flying Fortress. It wasn't built to fly milk cans—"

"I want everything committed. Everything! And all I want to know from you is if it can be done! Can you supply Stalingrad or not?"

Jeschonnek's eyes moved from the granite visage of his Führer to the tense features of his Chief. His Chief was not being asked, he was being commanded. But what if he were to shake his head in the negative? What if he were to say no? No, mein Führer, it would very likely fail. Did his silence indicate the mighty building up to such a head-shake?

"My Luftwaffe can do it. Depend on it, mein Führer."

Chapter 78

In the middle of December 1942, panzer forces made an attempt to rescue the Sixth Army, although the Sixth Army's commander dared not order his men to break out to meet them, since this could be construed as a form of retreat. Retreat from Stalingrad was forbidden by the Supreme Commander. And even if the trapped army had tried to break out, it was now so badly weakened that the effort would likely have been fruitless. In the event, the rescuing forces were crushed before they neared the city.

The airlift had also failed. Only a fraction of the needed supplies were getting through. The airlift continued nevertheless, at enormous cost to planes and pilots, as the temperature steadily dropped. By the end of December, it had plummeted to thirty below zero.

At Hitler's East Prussia headquarters, General Bodenschatz unhappily awaited Göring's arrival. He had telephoned to Carinhall the day before: "You had better return at once, Chief. He wants you." Since the beginning of the airlift, the general had delivered this message at least three times, and each time Göring was yanked back for another tongue-lashing. What was most painful to Bodenschatz was to hear Hitler refer to the Chief, in front of whoever happened to be present, as "this Göring fellow, this fat, well-fed pig!"

As the Chief entered the room, one could see his features composing themselves to meet the onslaught: a tightening of the long lips, a narrowing of the eyes.

"This is your doing, you incompetent—seventeen more planes down! I asked for an airlift, not a series of air crashes! Your pilots are cowards, idiots—the dregs of the Wehrmacht!"

Afterward, Bodenschatz walked with his Chief across the snowy compound. The blasting voice, issuing less than an arm's length from its recipient, with flecks of the famous spittle flying, had lasted a quarter of an hour. Göring's facial armor had shown chinks—minute twinges, brief eyeblinks—but it was now recomposed to meet whatever looks were directed their way as they crossed the compound. From generals down to junior officers, everyone at Wolfsschanze knew of the abusive tirades; they were one of the juicier topics of conversation. The Chief crunched through the snow with hard, military steps.

But inside his quarters, his rigid features sagged. "Seventeen more," he murmured, sinking down at his desk.

Bodenschatz gave a silent nod. The toll in transport planes was now over five hundred.

The big shoulders began to shake silently. Then a sound of sobbing filled the room as the Chief sat rocking back and forth over his desk.

"By rights, this should have been the grandest celebration of them all."

"I think it will be fine, Robert."

"Perhaps," assented the valet, giving a final straightening touch to the lapels of his master's dinner jacket. But a person's fiftieth jubilee was one of the great occasions of a lifetime. Considering that the Reichsmarschall's other, lesser birthdays had been celebrated by the Opera Ball, it seemed a letdown that the most important one of all was to be marked only by a reception.

"Perhaps," he murmured again.

"You're a terrible creature of habit, Robert," the Reichsmarschall scolded him, turning around to the dresser and taking up his vial of pills, of which he now consumed some eighty a day. "In any case, it's just a wartime measure. After the war I will resume my Opera Balls." Shaking out a few of the pills, he clapped them into his mouth and moved over to the cheval glass, where he stood looking at himself. He did not appear very happy on this great occasion. "Come on," he said dryly, "you can watch me make my grand entrance."

The valet followed him to the staircase, where the Reichsmarschall shot his cuffs and, with his dry, unsmiling expression, descended the stairs. Guests came streaming from the reception hall to greet him, a hubbub of congratulations filled the air, and the stout, black-clad figure was borne away to the center of his celebration.

He let himself be consumed by the moment, shaking hands and smiling, then beaming. Emmy's face before him—he kissed her, bent down and kissed little Edda all in blue, lifted her in his arms. The reception hall was ablaze with flowers, their perfume mixing with the happy voices around him; and beyond the hall, filling not two rooms but three, more gifts than ever before, such was the specialness of one's fiftieth birthday, a great milestone in a man's life—furniture, foods, paintings, three life-size medieval statues, a Sèvres service of three thousand pieces, a solid-gold, diamond-encrusted reading lamp, and, despite everything, the Führer's yearly gift, on this occasion a fine morocco desk set, and gifts that could not even fit into a room, such as the French hunting lodge dismantled in France and sent to Germany where he would erect it on one of his estates—more and greater tributes than he had ever before known.

While at that same moment in Berlin his subordinate, Milch, in the ultimate insult to his Air Chief, was packing for a trip to the Russian front, Hitler having decided that if anyone could reorganize the airlift and save the situation at Stalingrad, it was assuredly not Göring but his deputy.

The deputy's plane descended in a mid-January gale to the Fourth Air Force base in Taganrog, three hundred kilometers from the battered industrial city of Stalingrad, a bombed, shelled, pockmarked sprawl of buildings and factories stretching alongside the frozen Volga, a door-to-door battleground that had taken on the static, sacrificial overtones of Verdun, a tomb, perhaps, for the entire Sixth Army, the mightiest phalanx ever advanced by Hitler's Germany, now trapped for two long winter months and having battled for five. Stalingrad, a place whose name alone had become the object of the battle, a symbolic name that had mesmerized the Supreme Commander, as if forming in him a spellbound rigidity of pure will.

The next morning, Milch, apprised of the situation, set off for the airfield, but on the way met with a violent automobile accident. Two men were killed, he himself rushed by ambulance to a field hospital. In less than three hours, with a serious head injury and high temperature, his broken-ribbed torso encased in plaster, weak from loss of blood, he was carried back aboard the Fourth Air Force command train, where he demanded to be propped before the telephone and radio. His blue button eyes were sharp with pain and organization.

He began a siege of orders. Day after day, as the snow raged outside, his bruised body throbbing, his ashtray crammed with cigar ends, hardly skimming the long advice-packed telegrams arriving from Göring, hardly taking time to eat, he issued commands. By the end of the week his voice was hoarse and he had achieved the seemingly impossible.

He had rushed prefabricated huts to the most severely immobilized airbases where fifty-mile-an-hour gales blew; where the planes were enveloped in huge snowdrifts with engines frozen solid, where no shelter existed for the hundreds of airmen who huddled on the blizzard-swept field like snowmen, brain-dulled, demoralized, useless. He had seen to it that under penalty of death the cold-start procedure for engines was used, finding no amusement in the explanation that most of the crews, having arrived directly from Africa, had not even heard of the cold-start procedure. When he learned that one of the first containers unloaded and opened at Stalingrad, back in November, had held a supply of condoms and black pepper, he ordered an immediate check of the present cargos; and on being informed that some of the sacks contained only fishmeal, he requested that the victualing officer be hanged. At Stalingrad itself the problems had been worse. After Pitomnik airfield was captured, another field, Gumrak, had been hastily prepared. It had minimal ground organization, was disorderly, badly equipped, lacking even flares for night landings, so that the planes were forced to drop their supply loads into the darkness. He had demanded that flares be set out at Gumrak; if they had none, then improvise—use truck lights, tank lights, anything. Gumrak now had a flare path of ten tank lights. In addition, the daylight landings were being met with improved organization. After only a week he was able to write in his daybook: "Today 30 Heinkels landed at Gumrak carrying ammunition, gasoline, foodstuff and medical supplies."

Gumrak fell the next day. Another landing ground was improvised, but the planes were wrecked as they came in, crashing through bomb craters under the snow. It was bitterly clear to Milch, and to everyone, that there could be no further landing of supplies at Stalingrad. The men of the Sixth Army were told that they could write one last letter home. A Heinkel was dispatched to the airfield, made a dangerous but successful landing, and took off again with seven bulging mail sacks. Soon after the plane had disappeared into the gray sky, the airfield was overrun by Russians. Pocket by pocket, street by street, the city was being retaken by its own.

From the command train at Taganrog, Milch kept the organization of the airlift under tight control. Ever more supplies were being flown in. Peak efficiency had been reached. But because the planes were unable to set down, their cargos had to be parachuted into the void. The supplies were meant to settle in the city's Red Square, where Sixth Army headquarters was located, but poor visibility and high winds combined to land most of the containers in the broken, snow-filled tops of the surrounding buildings, tall blackened ruins from which they could not be retrieved.

On January 29, the day before the tenth anniversary of the National Socialist seizure of power in 1933, there arrived from Germany a dozen fighter aircraft requested by Milch. He ordered that on the following day there must be German fighters seen over Stalingrad; the reputation of the Luftwaffe in the eyes of the German Army was at stake.

At dawn of the 30th, the fighters were over the city. Far below, fires raged around Red Square. By late morning Russian troops were closing in on Sixth Army headquarters.

That same day at Veldenstein, Nikki turned on the radio and sat back in her armchair with her knitting. It was a cold, clear afternoon, wind howling outside the windows. The courtyard was an expanse of brilliant white, the tower roofs wore dazzling white caps. From the radio, the full-bodied virile voice had begun to speak. She leaned across and turned the volume up above the noise of the wind.

". . . the toughness of the struggle has increased gigantically, and you must not forget that Germany is standing guard on all fronts— from the North Cape to Biscaya, from Africa to the Volga. On all fronts Germany fights, and bleeds, but also wins . . ."

Her husband came in from the kitchen, where he had been sorting winter apples. The entire apartment smelled of apples. Bent over his cane, he eased himself into the chair opposite hers and gave a nod at the glowing cat's eye of the radio. They never listened to the radio. Only when Göring made a speech did Nikki turn it on.

"'Tis him?" he asked, squinting to hear better, for he was growing deaf.

"The tenth-anniversary speech. Let me turn it higher for you."

"Nein, seems it's getting louder now."

The voice, in fact, had risen to shouting volume.

". . . every German in a thousand years will remember the name Stalingrad with sacred shivers, knowing it was there that Germany put the final stamp on her final victory! *The law commands it!* The law of warfare which is nothing but the nation's will of survival! Whether a soldier falls and sacrifices his life in Africa or Russia, it is all the same! His sacrifice is always for the life of the nation! The sense of struggle is only freedom or destruction! It would have to be a total idiot who could imagine that we could somehow come to an 'arrangement' . . ." The last word was said in French, "arrahnjemah," which the couple did not understand; they only understood, as the voice went on, sometimes shouting so that the radio seemed to jangle, sometimes chopping along with a hoarse, growling, chewing intensity, that this speech was different from all his others.

The voice suddenly dropped, became hushed, solemn.

". . . My belief . . . in Germany's victory . . . is unconquerable . . ."

And rose in a shattering blast, a veritable scream.

"*Ten years* the Führer has led us from *victory* to *victory*! Out of the deepest *despair*, out of *chaos* and *hopelessness*—and I *know*—I *know* the Führer is now leading us to the *final,* the *ultimate* victory!"

Nikki leaned across and clicked off the dial. The green cat's eye slowly faded. The room was quiet except for the keening wind outside.

"It recollects me of that day with General Udet," Hans remarked at length, smoothing his great white mustaches as if they had been blown askew by the voice.

"Hermann has always had a temper," Nikki said, taking up her knitting. "No one would argue about that."

But both knew that temper did not describe the violent voice of this afternoon. There had been something completely unfamiliar in it, something pushed to the extreme, overspent, which made them uneasy, silent. All that could be heard in the little room, smelling of apples, was the click of knitting needles and the wind howling around the corners of the burg.

Chapter 79

NEWS bulletins on the radio were always preceded by the majestic, stirring chords of Liszt's *Preludes,* but on February 2 there was heard instead a long, funereal roll of muffled drums.

"Stalingrad ist gefallen."

Newspapers bordered in black carried pages of small black crosses, so many crosses that the pages themselves appeared black. Bereaved wives and mothers, hitherto forbidden to wear even black armbands, were issued special ration coupons for the purchase of mourning clothes. All places of entertainment were closed for three days. Bells tolled from morning till night.

"I should like my words to be a message from my innermost heart to yours, and I will therefore clothe my remarks in holy earnestness and perfect frankness," a Sportpalast audience of fifteen thousand was told by Minister Goebbels. "Through this tragic blow of fate, you, the German people, have been purified to the depths of your being. You have stared into the hard and pitiless face of war, and you know the cruel truth. . . . The schooled and disciplined German people can bear to know the truth. That Stalingrad has fallen. That the Red Army has gone over into an offensive. That the assault from the steppes has been loosened with a fury which surpasses human and historical imagination. That our ancient and honorable continent is directly threatened. That two thousand years of constructive work by Western humanity is in danger. . . . The masses of tanks attacking our eastern front are the result of a quarter century of social misfortune of the Bolshevik nation, and behind the attacking Bolshevik divisions we already see the Jewish extermination commandos. What would be the result of Bolshevik-capitalist tyranny? Bolshevization of the Reich. Liquidation of our entire intelligentsia and leadership class. Forced labor battalions for the Siberian tundra. Terror, the specter of mass starvation, total anarchy. No country but Germany is capable of resisting the Bolshevik divisions of motorized robots. The German Army and its allies are the only conceivable bulwark. Thus there is only one choice: a Bolshevik Europe or a Europe under Axis protection. Thus total war is the need of the hour. We must act quickly and radically, or else it will be too late. Today the radical is just radical enough! Today the total is just total enough! Therefore let there be an end to any bourgeois squeamishness! The time has come for us to take off our kid gloves and bind our fists!"

He stopped, drowned out by passionate applause. He had worked like a slave on the speech, and knew it to be a masterpiece. He waited, his face perspiring in the hot lights.

"All of us here today, children of our people, welded together with the people, will swear to stake our priceless blood on what we most deeply cherish. All difficulties will be overcome by the power of the masses, by militance of thought and action, by revolutionary drive. It is every German's duty to bear misfortune and overcome it. A people that performs this duty is unconquerable!"

Again he was drowned out by roaring enthusiasm. As he went on, he was obliged to stop every few minutes to allow for the massive response. By the time he grew near the end of the speech, people were standing on their chairs, men had ripped off their neckties and were waving them. Never before had the Sportpalast been witness to such scenes of passionate rejoicing.

"You, my audience," he cried, "represent the nation at this moment. For the benefit of our enemies in foreign countries who are listening on the radio, I wish to ask you ten questions which will demand a sacred oath. The first is this: "Do you possess the will to total war?" The hall could hardly contain the mighty surge of affirmation. "Do you believe in Germany's victory?" Again the long, long, long roar. "Are you willing to fight?" And again. It was like listening to a pounding waterfall. "Are you willing to work harder and produce more?" And again. "Have you absolute faith in the Führer?" And again, an even longer roar, filled with cries of "Führer command, we will obey!" "Do you accept your obligation to give the military everything it needs for victory?" And again the massive roar. "Do you accept the necessity of labor service for women?" And again. "Do you accept the most radical measures against slackers and profiteers?" And again. "Do you accept the necessity of making equal demands on all Germans behind the lines, and the fact that anyone who detracts from the war effort will lose his head?" And again the frenzy of affirmation, in which the speaker stood wet-faced in the heat of the lights, having held forth for two hours without so much as a sip of water, his brilliant dark eyes going around the panorama of cheering, stomping, embracing figures; and although among them was a hefty claque of supporters, trusted functionaries ordered to dress in civilian clothes and bolster enthusiasm, there was clearly no need for bolstering. Even journalists from neutral countries had leaped up from the press platform again and again, applauding wildly. He had created a hysteria of ecstasy. And filling his lungs one last time, he cried out his finale: "Now, people, arise! And let the storm winds blow!"

When he left the platform, his shirt was wringing wet. He often lost two or three kilos during the course of a speech, so great was the energy he burned up. This time he had probably lost even more. He was exhausted, utterly drained, utterly satisfied. "What an idiocy!" he said to his entourage, smiling and mopping his face. "If I had asked them to jump from the fourth floor of the Columbia House they would have done it."

All that evening he felt a sense of rapture. It could not be diminished even when he learned that the Führer had been in conference at the time of the speech and had thus been unable to listen. The Führer would listen to the rebroadcast the next morning. But the next morning was too early for the Führer. He always slept late, and he slept through the rebroadcast.

Goebbels's high spirits were nevertheless sustained by the world's reaction: the speech occupied the front pages of newspapers around the globe. Never before, he felt, had any speech created such a sensation. Even his cool and uncommunicative wife admitted that the speech had moved her deeply.

But gradually the exultation wore away. By the time the Führer finally looked at the text of the speech, deeming it a psychological and propagandistic masterpiece, Goebbels had come back down to earth. The Führer's comment was gratifying, but the Führer was not putting the masterpiece into effect. No actual steps toward total war were being taken. Only the same small, pointless steps that had been taken since the inception of the Committee of Three for Total War. It was at Goebbels's urging that the Führer had set up the committee; but though the Propaganda Minister had hoped to be appointed its head, he was not appointed at all. The Führer's three appointees were Bormann, Keitel and Lammers, his deputies for Party, Wehrmacht and State. Goebbels had been given only an advisory role. He had felt great bitterness over this, and had hoped his Sportpalast speech would move the Führer to reassess the importance of total war, and reassess his, Goebbels's, own place in its execution. But nothing had been achieved.

He was frustrated in another sphere as well. As Gauleiter of Berlin, he found it intolerable that his territory was infested with more Jews than any other corner of the entire Reich. For months he had pressed Hitler, in vain, to deport all those who remained in the city. "There are still thousands upon thousands of Jews in Berlin," he had dictated for entry in his diary, "and despite the heavy blows dealt them, they are still insolent and aggressive. It is exceedingly difficult to shove them all off to the east because a large part of them are at work in the munitions industry, and Jews are evacuated by family only. This is a thing which is unbearable. I shall try to get the order canceled and at least try to get their families deported." But bureaucracy had stood in his way. Jews were deported by family only: this was how it was, and must remain. Then deport the armaments workers themselves, he had urged the bureaucrats, and be rid of both the workers and their families. But the workers were vital to the war effort, he was told. This, of course, he knew, and urged that foreign workers be brought in to replace them—this was the obvious solution to the problem. The alternative of foreign workers was naturally being explored, he was told, but no conclusion had yet been reached. He had cursed the inordinate thoroughness of the German mind. It was only now, in February of the new year, that he was able to dictate, with a sense of things going well at least in one area: "The Führer expressed his decision that all Jewish people under all circumstances have got to be taken out of Berlin. We can get 250,000 foreign workers. The Jews can now be easily replaced."

At a clash of cymbals, she walked onto the bright stage of the Weimar Theater. Wearing a heavy brocade gown and towering powdered wig, she began speaking her lines, which fell soundlessly from her lips. The audience was exceedingly noisy, and was throwing a barrage of brown apple cores at her while the orchestra played Schönberg's *Gurre-Lieder*—melodious, otherworldly, a tender river of song that she would have liked to float on, to sleep in, to be carried away by like a clean, polished piece of driftwood, but again came the clash of cymbals and her eyes fluttered open to the wall by her bed.

She felt feverish, blurred; all she wanted was to sleep. Before dawn she had risen and dressed for work as usual, but, with a splitting head and a throat like sandpaper, she had crawled back under the drapes she used for blankets and sunk again into heavy oblivion. Which she wanted back, groggily pulling the drapes over her head to block out the strange sound of voices and cymbal clashes, which she suddenly realized was a slamming of doors in the hallway mixed with shouts, cries, and a heavy thud of boots.

She felt a strange, voluptuous sense of peace, of deliverance, of the end of trying, yet at the same time her body was acting on its own, rolling off the bed onto the floor, where it thrashed around with indecision, scrambling under the bed and then barging back to seize the coat and handbag, diving under, dragging her under with a flashing sense of the futile and embarrassing, rolling her through gloom and dustballs and smashing her against the wall as the door swung open.

She could see two pairs of black boots and a pair of baggy civilian trouser legs. The trouser legs belonged to the porter, who spoke. "Three armaments workers. A woman in this room, a married couple in the other, all out at their jobs. No children or other family."

As abruptly as they had come, they disappeared, leaving the door open. She heard them go into the Müllers' room and come out again, thudding across the living room to the hallway door. It slammed behind them.

She lay staring out at her horizontal view of the room: chair legs, table legs, cold morning light the color of pearl. Was it early morning, or late? Was it afternoon? Then there might be an air raid, the night raids had been joined by daylight raids, why shouldn't there be one? But hoping for a raid was useless. Things were going very fast here, the boots had been hurried, the commotion she lay listening to was hurried—a grand sweep, a grand entrance onto the Weimar stage, something about Schönberg, why did she have such irrelevant thoughts? Her mind was a whirlpool. All she wanted was to stay pressed against the wall, but her body was pulling her away, was hastily crawling with the coat and bag from the shadowy dust beneath the bed, getting her up, pushing her over to the window, where she looked down at the commotion in the street. Shouts of command breaking through a hubbub of questions and cries from the tenants being loaded into two trucks, no suitcases, no coats or hats, very fast, very rushed. A tall bald old fellow from the first floor, walking snaillike with his two canes, was seized and flung inside with such violence that his bones must have been fractured. She swung around and stood frozen. Then once more her body was moving on its own, frantically busying itself with the coat front star, one hand reaching for the razor blade on the low table with its tarnished Buddha lamp, the other holding the material fast, threads being slashed away.

Then put the coat on, take your bag. The hallway noise is gone. Do something. They'll be coming back for a final search. Move. Get out.

All this her body told her, and she obeyed. Without another glance at the bedroom, she walked out of it. In the empty hallway she walked to the back stairs, went down into the courtyard, walked around the back of the adjoining building, and came out on the front sidewalk into a knot of onlookers who were being approached by an SS man vigorously enjoining them to go on about their business, which she did, continuing down the street and turning the corner.

Then she was aware of everything. The bitter cold of the air, trams clanging by. Her raw throat and aching head. The racketing of her heart, the shaking of her hands. Her legs kept walking, they felt like stilts, unsteady, conspicuous. But no one looked at her, she was just a woman in a shabby coat going out to shop or visit. She turned her head as she realized the two trucks were driving by. Covered trucks, characterless, with no indication of crammed interiors or fractured bones. Standing still, she watched until they had passed from sight, feeling such exhaustion, such heaviness of heart, that it seemed unbelievable that people were hopping from trams, riding bicycles, walking along talking together. She moved on slowly among them, free, unpursued, headed nowhere.

Chapter 80

Oɴ the evening of that day, the tall glossy-haired Speer and the round rumpled Funk were ushered into one of the rooms of Goebbels's Berlin palace. The residence was immense, elaborate, and had recently become gloomy, for in order to set an example of total war austerity the Propaganda Minister had had its public rooms closed and most of the light bulbs removed. He rose to greet his guests in a darkness offset only by a shaded lamp, and after liveried servants had brought sandwiches, coffee and French cognac, of which he did not partake, he renewed an earlier discussion. It concerned the possibility of using Göring's powers as Chairman of the Reich Defense Council to stiffen the home front. The problem was that the council was inactive to the point of nonexistence, as Göring had done nothing to tap its resources. Yet the Defense Council was an instrument through which one could make radical decisions, a body by which one could transfer political leadership away from the Committee of Three to a policy of total war. If one revived Göring's prestige and made use of his name in activating the Defense Council, then with the Reichsmarschall as a popular figurehead, Goebbels as deputy chairman, Speer beside him, and around them a select group of colleagues, the council could effectively put the Committee of Three—and specifically Bormann—on ice.

"Everything goes through Bormann," he complained bitterly. "Since the Führer abandoned politics for his work as Commander in

Chief, one can no longer influence him politically. I can't even report the most urgent political measures in my area. Everything goes through Bormann."

"The committee has provided Herr Bormann with a rather strong base," Speer agreed in his quiet manner, sipping his coffee.

"It's clear that we'll get no support from him or Lammers or Keitel—every effort we've made toward increased armaments production has been bogged down in meaningless details. Our only hope is to form a body to usurp the committee's powers, and the Reich Defense Council is clearly that body. But if we're going to activate it, we're first going to have to activate Göring."

"Except," put in Funk, raising a humorous eyebrow over his cognac, "this may not be the most propitious time for you to approach him, Herr Goebbels."

Goebbels gave a shrug of his slight shoulders. His only successful austerity measure to date was to shut down Berlin's luxury restaurants, and Göring's only recent sign of life was his protest against the closing of Horcher's. Göring had seen to it that the restaurant remained open. Goebbels had hired demonstrators to smash the windows. Göring had fumingly yielded.

"I am willing to forget personal differences in the best interests of the nation, Herr Funk. I can only trust the Reichsmarschall to feel the same."

Still, at the end of the discussion, it was decided that Speer should approach Göring first, and he should do so as soon as possible.

"I shall fly to the Obersalzberg tomorrow," Speer said. "I understand that he's down there on one of his vacations." And he added: "One of his longer ones." Still curled up licking his wounds. After Stalingrad Hitler had refused to have his name even mentioned in his presence.

"Actually," said Funk, as they rose from their chairs in the dim light, "I believe the Reichsmarschall will welcome your suggestion. In fact, he is bound to."

Getting up from a nap in the bedroom of his chalet, the Reichsmarschall rubbed his face, kneaded his scalp, and frowned at his watch. Speer had telephoned earlier to ask if he could come by at three o'clock for a talk "of great importance to you, Reichsmarschall," which phrase the Reichsmarschall repeated in a mutter as he walked heavily across the room to the bureau. In the wintry light, his mirrored face looked at him colorless as lint, except for a ruddy patch on either cheekbone, nor was the glow a natural and healthy one, but only the residual flush from the overlarge meal he had consumed before lying down. Taking a brush to his rumpled hair, he smoothed it back from his dead-white forehead, and for a moment lost himself in the reflected motions of his hand—in the gleamings and sparklings from his jeweled watch, his rings, his fingernails lustrous with clear lacquer—then, putting down the brush, he eased his stockinged feet into his slippers and tiredly descended the stairs to his study.

Minister Speer came walking briskly down from the Berghof. Spring in this year of 1943 was late in coming to the Obersalzberg—snow still lay in glaring patches under a sky of silvery white, and the air was like ice water, pure and invigorating. He had not been to Göring's mountain home before. Apparently, he saw, it was one of the Reichsmarschall's few residences of a normal size. A rustic wood-and-stucco chalet, it adhered in style to the southern tradition, even to the large wooden crucifix above the balcony. One had, of course, heard of the swimming pool, the only pool on the mountain. In winter Göring used it as an ice rink. The rink stood empty. The entire place imparted a feeling of deepest solitude, heightened by an awesome view—a truly exceptional panorama reaching from the Hoher Göll in the east to the Untersberg in the northwest. Typically, the big one had built his house on what was probably the best location on the Obersalzberg.

The young Armaments Minister was received courteously, but with eyes as cold as the cold outside. It was clear that the Reichsmarschall expected another infringement of some sort. The man's mind had gotten into a rut of negativity. You could see it in the lethargic step, in the very color of his face, pasty and unhealthy, with cheeks which—unbelievably—he had seemingly tried to brighten with rouge. Also astonishing were his fingernails, very obviously lacquered. But the velvet robe, the enormous ruby brooch, the visitor was already familiar with, as well as the handful of uncut gems withdrawn from the robe pocket as they sat down. These the Reichsmarschall let glide through his fingers as he sat listening, his pallid face ill-humored and suspicious.

But as Speer explained the Propaganda Minister's proposal, he felt himself aided by the atmosphere of the study. It was a simple room, with low bookcases on which stood a few small art objects, its walls graced with a modest number of paintings, only one of which, a portrait of a dark-haired woman, was of any size. With its green-tiled Bavarian stove and cozy flowered curtains, the room had an intimate feeling not present in the great study at Carinhall. Perhaps it would help create a sense of understanding between them.

And after a time, Göring seemed to stir a little from his melancholy cocoon, his deep-carved frown gave way somewhat. Gradually he began asking questions, whose answers he met with a certain degree of receptivity. But then came a slow, blunt, retroactive headshake. He didn't welcome any proposal from Goebbels. He was still angry over the Horcher affair. Hiring thugs to smash windows—he was to ally himself with someone like this?

In the best interests of the nation, countered Speer, and he began to work on this theme. Finally, appealing to his host's vanity, putting him in the driver's seat as it were, he suggested that the Reichsmarschall request that Goebbels fly down at once from Berlin in order for the Reichsmarschall to confront him with questions that he, Speer, had been unable to answer. This suggestion also required a fair amount of labor before it was accepted. But he was at last granted the consent he sought, and after some further conversation he left for the Berghof to telephone Goebbels. Returning from seeing his guest out, Göring allowed his pleasure to spread across his face. He was thoroughly fascinated by the project and delighted that they had thought of him. But he was disinclined to show agreeableness too quickly. Let them work at it.

The following day, after Goebbels had arrived at the Berghof, he and Speer drove down to the chalet. The distance was not far, but to walk when not necessary was anathema to the man whose gait was so noticeably uneven. He was in a shining mood, his fine dark eyes gleaming with the task that lay before him. Getting out of the car, he flicked his cigarette away and, in his long, coffee-colored leather overcoat that reached the ground, pegged energetically ahead of his companion to the door of the torpid one.

As they entered the study, Speer saw that Göring appeared better rested today, his face less haggard, less pasty. And when he shook hands with Goebbels it was with no sign of hostility. The battle for his cooperation was very likely half won already. And why not? The Reichsmarschall had everything to gain and nothing to lose. That was true of all three of them.

As had been agreed beforehand, the Armaments Minister withdrew after a few minutes, allowing the two to talk alone.

Goebbels was gratified that his host had relinquished his personal animosity in the greater interests of the nation; and as he spoke, he felt a growing warmth for his old comrade sitting across from him, old Speck und Eier—beefy and bally—as the workers had used to call him, the strongarm, the fist, and the supremely effective salon politician as well. Side by side they had worked in those days, side by side they must work again, he must infuse with ardor this heavy, haggard figure in its peculiar getup, voluminous green satin robe, big ruby brooch . . . and lacquered fingernails? But that was how he was, one had to accept his idiosyncrasies, they even had a certain charm about them . . . and the Minister's voice resonated with sincerely felt friendship and goodwill, and with the expressed hope of Germany's victory, which would be inestimably aided by the activization of the Reich Defense Council . . .

Suddenly impatient with playing hard to get, Göring interrupted with a few frank words stating the keenness of his interest. "I want to hear every aspect of this proposal," he concluded, and he felt the future opening up once again, for himself, for Germany, and at the same time he felt the power of the past, of the old days, the old fight, the old comrades. Goebbels here, who had used to come for Christmas at Wilmersdorf those years ago when the big battle was finally getting into gear . . . they had grown far apart in recent years, but now they would be rejoined in a supreme effort to win the war, and he felt a rush of warmth toward the small familiar figure leaning forward in his chair.

"You know as well as I, Herr Göring, that the Führer has aged fifteen years in this last year. For that reason we must become his strongest personal support. One can't stand by any longer and see how he's so weighed down with worries big and small he can hardly breathe. The cause is greater than any of us. The men who helped the Führer win the revolution will now have to help him win the war."

"They weren't bureaucrats then, they must not be bureaucrats now."

"If in reactivating the Defense Council, you can surround yourself with a group of courageous, upright and loyal men, Herr Göring, such a group would be able to relieve the Führer of most of the chores, setting him free again for his high mission of leadership. He would certainly approve of such a situation, since it would make his tasks much easier for him."

"This is true. Everyone does as he pleases because there's no strong authority anywhere. The Party goes its own way and won't have anybody interfere. And it's not only the Party—there's not one honest and trustworthy personality among the generals. They create difficulty after difficulty for the Führer; they continually try to unload their mistakes onto him. To his face they're naturally friendly, but in their hearts they think quite differently. We should be on our guard, Herr Goebbels, we've got very few friends among them. Jodl especially. They all try to play us off against each other. Whereas this should be a time for unity, because we know our enemy in the east will remain strong. Gott, where does Bolshevism keep getting its weapons and soldiers! This is what I keep asking and asking myself. But perhaps the question isn't important—the essential thing is that it still has them, and always manages to get more."

"Exactly. And it is why our war potential must be used to the limit."

"I agree entirely. We can effectively meet the Soviet war potential only with sweeping measures."

"My hope is that we will be able to get started immediately. Once we succeed in transferring the political leadership from the Committee of Three to the Defense Council, we will be over the hump."

When after four hours Herr Speer was called back into the study, he found the two men unwearied by their talk. Quite the opposite, and Göring especially. There would be no need to activate the big one, he was already activated, walking back and forth with elastic briskness, rubbing his hands together at the prospect of the battle about to begin.

"We'll take care of these Three Wise Men from the East! We'll go to work with a driving power that will put in the shade anything that has ever existed!"

He radiated a kind of flooding light, an almost palpable conviction and passion. Reseating himself with a limber adroitness of his great bulk, he went on to condemn Ribbentrop. Ribbentrop must also be taken care of.

"I blame him entirely for the fact that Spain wasn't brought over to our side. German foreign policy should have found some way of bringing Franco into our camp so that we could have got to Gibraltar. But Ribbentrop made no real effort, or with England either. He never made an earnest attempt to achieve a *modus vivendi* with England. This man is entirely responsible for our lack of an active foreign policy."

"He's incapable of finding a political solution to our sorry military predicament," Goebbels agreed, "and the Führer is incapable of seeing through him. He sees through Ribbentrop as little as he sees through Lammers—"

"Lammers!" exclaimed Göring, springing up from his chair again. "Lammers is always putting a word in edgewise and torpedoing me from below the waterline. If I allowed the Defense Council to become inactive, it was because Lammers torpedoed my efforts by constantly butting in and reporting to the Führer. But this is going to end right now! I am going to see to it, gentlemen!"

"It isn't only Lammers," Speer put in quietly. "It's Bormann as well. Bormann seizes every opportunity to undermine your prestige, Reichsmarschall. I've observed his tactics at close range. He's doing everything in his power to annihilate you in the eyes of the Führer."

"But we're going to open the Führer's eyes about Bormann and Lammers," said Goebbels. "If each one of us supports the other to the Führer, we'll soon be on top of the situation and can form a solid fence around him."

"Stimmt!" Göring replied with a vigorous nod, again rubbing his hands together. "Stimmt!"

"This is going to work," Goebbels said jubilantly as they got into the car. "He's really come back to life. I haven't seen him like this for a long time."

"He was completely his former self," Speer agreed as he turned on the ignition, and paused for a thoughtful moment, acknowledging the force of the Reichsmarschall's personality. The Reichsmarschall's former self was not exactly what they had had in mind in reactivating him, it was rather more than they had had in mind . . . however, they would have to cross that bridge when they came to it.

From the window of his study, the Reichsmarschall stood watching the car drive away. Its red taillights disappeared behind the trees, leaving everything silent, still. The great mountain range to the west was a majestic black silhouette against the deepening blue, in which a few brilliant stars had emerged. He stood looking out for a long while, feeling one with the splendorous night, stronger, calmer, happier than he had for months, for years, and if they thought they were merely going to make use of his name and position, if they thought he was going to settle for that, they were very badly mistaken.

The chief difficulty, prominent in the minds of all three men during the discussion but not alluded to, was Göring's poor standing with Hitler, whose sanction for the activization of the council would be necessary. It was tacitly understood that Goebbels's formidable powers of persuasion would make the Führer look less harshly upon his Air Commander. To that end Goebbels flew the following week, with Speer, to the Führer's headquarters in the Ukraine.

But the interval had been unkind. Not only had Essen been badly bombed, but Berlin had suffered its worst raid to date. They found the Führer in no mood to be approached on the subject of Göring. Quietly putting aside their proposal until a more favorable time, they sat late into the night discussing other matters with their Chief, only to be interrupted with the news that Nuremberg had just been hit by a heavy raid, and to witness General Bodenschatz, whom Hitler had ordered pulled out of bed, undergo a violent tongue-lashing in place of the Reichsmarschall.

"I'm afraid," Goebbels said to Speer as they walked to their own quarters, "that it's getting to be five minutes to midnight for Göring."

Even so, Goebbels was not willing to give up. Returning to Berlin, he had further meetings with Göring. Then bad blood cropped up when the Reichsmarschall made a heated attack on Milch—and indirectly on Speer—in connection with the labor program. Meanwhile, Goebbels felt out the Führer again and found him still intractably critical of the Air Commander, at which point he decided that the person he had better try to work with was Bormann.

There was no more talk about the Reich Defense Council.

Chapter 81

IT was a morning in April, a particularly summerlike morning, with a vast blue sky from which, if one were to look down, one could see the gargantuan metropolis of Berlin sprawled in an endless complex of varicolored tiny roofs along streets like long intersecting shoelaces. Scattered gray-brown patches showed where bombed buildings had been roped off amid the sinuous sparkling of rivers and canals. Here was the moving glint of early-morning traffic, there the thin black centipede of a curving train, and throughout everything the squares and puzzle pieces of parks gleaming upward in vivid green, the largest being the Tiergarten, shaped like a three-pronged emerald crown. Out on his morning walk beneath the park's glossy leaves, a thin high-shouldered man in tweed knickerbockers and jacket glimpsed coming in his direction a woman who seemed in a fleeting, peripheral way to be familiar.

A pair of habit-clad horseback riders cantered by with a creak of leather. In some places in the park, trees had been shattered, the earth scooped out in craters, but there was no bomb damage in this area. The trees overhead trilled with birds, the air was already buoyant. Swinging an amber-knobbed stick, the man walked with a precisely energetic step, his bearing erect and military, on his seamed face the perpetual faint severity of a man in whose shoulders and back pieces of shrapnel were still working themselves out after a quarter of a century.

Suddenly he paused with a squint of astonishment at the woman on the path, who had paused too, and was turning around.

"Rose!" He hurriedly strode forward, thrusting his stick under his arm, his whole face beaming as he clasped his cousin's hands. "But how can this be? You said in your letter—but you're still here?"

"Apparently," she said. "How are you, Max?"

"I? As you see," he answered genially, "always the same." But his astonished pleasure at seeing her was erased by her strange manner, and by the fact that she had clearly wished to avoid him. "But you, Rose—what in the world has happened?"

"Nothing," she said. "I'm very well."

She looked exceptionally well. The thinness of undernourishment had left her face, her beautiful hazel eyes were clear, well rested. She looked almost like the Rose of days gone by, except that her hair was darker, duller, apparently a wig. She wore a handsome gray-and-white plaid coat, and her shoulder bag and shoes appeared to be new. What she was doing in Berlin he could not fathom. After the sudden roundup of Jewish armaments workers and their families, he and his wife, desperately worried, had had word from Rose. She wrote that she had not been taken, that she had money and papers and was leaving for southern Germany, where arrangements had been made for her to stay with the family of friends. That was more than a month ago, and here she stood in the middle of the Tiergarten.

"Let's sit down." He took her by the elbow. "What is all this about? Why haven't you been in touch?"

"There's nothing to talk about," she said, hanging back.

There was a metallic jangling as an elderly couple emerged from around the corner of the path walking a Scotch terrier on a leash, its license tags clinking.

"'Morgen, Herr Korwan."

"'Morgen, Herr Nagel, Frau Nagel." He touched his cap with his gloved hand. "The fine weather continues."

"Indeed it does."

The strollers passed on, the dog trotting with short passionate steps in the morning freshness.

He lowered his voice to a whisper. "Don't aggravate me, Rose. You have always aggravated me."

"And I don't want to aggravate you any further."

"We're going to sit down here and talk."

"If you must," she sighed.

They sat down on a bench, he in his contained, high-shouldered way, remaining as erect as when standing. He clasped his hands over the amber knob of his stick. He had on gray pigskin gloves worn thin along the sides and at the fingertips. Inside his shoes, the toes of his socks were neatly mended. He looked at his cousin's clear-skinned, impassive face, on which large dapples of sunlight moved.

"Well then?"

"Well then," she said, with the hint of a shrug. "Well then, I escaped the Fabrik Aktion by chancing to stay home that morning with a sore throat. When the SS came to the house I got out the back. Then I stayed in train stations. In one I bought an envelope and stamp and wrote you. I wrote what I did because I didn't want you and Lotte to worry."

"It wasn't true?"

"There were no arrangements. No money, no papers. A couple of marks and the clothes I stood in."

"But why in God's name didn't you come to us?"

"Why? Harboring a Jew is punishable by death." She shrugged.

"You know we would have been more than willing to take that risk! We could have helped you. I could have gotten you papers. You know I've got contacts. I've helped many—you know that."

"Why argue, that's how it was."

He gave a shake of his head, wondering whether she might have suffered some kind of mental breakdown.

"You've been living in train stations all this time? How do you eat without money? How do you get your clothes?"

"I haven't resorted to prostitution." She smiled. "Nor to collaboration."

"That had not crossed my mind."

She said no more. She sat looking at the trees.

"Well then, how? How do you manage?"

"Nicely enough. After the big raid, at least. I got caught in it walking to the Lehrter Bahnhof. You never dared stayed too long in one station, so every night I walked to another—"

"And you could have been with us!"

"—and during the big raid a building front came down on me. Only something must have landed to form a pocket, a beam of wood maybe, I don't know. I woke up in a hospital and not a scratch. They let me stay two days because of the throat, it was badly infected by then. The room was warm, the bed was comfortable, I got injections and three meals a day. A nice joke, ja? When I left I took a coat off the rack in the waiting room, nobody noticed. The one I had on was no good at all."

He narrowed his eyes at the coat, everything in his Prussian soul rising up against the thought of thievery.

"It gets worse. I told you you wouldn't like it."

"Never mind if I'll like it," he said sharply.

"I eat in restaurants. It's quite simple to do. But first I had to have a bag, to look presentable. My old one was lost in the raid. And some decent-looking shoes too. So I went into a department store and took what I needed. Nobody noticed. Nobody ever notices anything. In a restaurant I sit down and order a meal, and when I'm done I walk out without paying. Nobody ever notices."

He suppressed his burning disapproval. It would have done no good anyway. There was something so distant about her, it was as if she could not be touched.

"Life has become very simple. I had been sleeping in bombed-out buildings, but now that it's warm I sleep here in the Tiergarten. In the morning I wash at the Zoo Bahnhof. That's where I'm going now."

"Do you realize what you're telling me? That you sleep out in the open? With the bombings? Are you out of your mind?"

"I'm not the only one. Do you know how many people there are who live like this?"

"I do know, but the difference is this. You don't have to. You could have come to us at any time."

"Dear Max," she sighed. "What you don't understand is that it doesn't matter. Whatever I do or don't do, however I turn, I'm spared. I roll under a bed, and they walk out. I come out on the street smack into an SS man, and he tells me to go on about my business. A building falls on me, and I'm unhurt. Not only unhurt, but at the hospital they cure my throat and feed me. I steal and no one notices. I eat without paying and no one notices. I sleep in the Tiergarten and not a bomb falls near me, night after night, and all I've got to show for it is a fresh complexion and dirty hair."

His eyes moved to the dull, dead-leaf brown that had been russet, so altered that he had thought it was a wig.

"Listen to me, Rose," he said carefully. "The thing to do is to get you out of here. And that is very simple. We get up and we leave. We go to the house. And you will have a bath. That's a nice thought, ja? Steaming water, bath salts, and afterward clean clothes. Lotte has everything you would need. And you will stay with us. You will eat with us. You will sleep in a bed at night."

"No, now that I've told you what you wanted to know, I'll be going."

"That's quite impossible," he said, carefully laying his hand on her coat sleeve. "We've hardly talked yet."

"Haven't we? It seems to me that we've talked a long while."

"Ten minutes."

There was a silence. "How is Lotte?" she asked.

"Very well." He paused. "She would love to see you, Rose. It's only a few blocks' walk."

"I know how far it is."

He had to fight down his urge to argue and advise. Disapproval had always interlaced his sincere fondness for her. The careless quality of her life, always losing things, never on time, the endless love affairs—she was too much the gypsy to meet his high standards of conduct. He had always acted as the kind but stern adviser, but when she had begun to change utterly, when from the most gregarious pleasure seeker she had become solitary, sober, obsessed with the single theme of existing unnoticed, of living like a mole until the wretched situation had finally passed—this change, in which there was much admirable strength, had had nothing to do with his advice. He had in fact counseled a milder, better-balanced attitude, a less extreme approach. He should have realized then, those many months back, that she was entering some mental area where she could not be followed or understood. Now he thought of the unwashed skin and rank clothes beneath the handsome coat, the seemingly wigged head that lay each night on dirt and leaves, the long elegant fingers, none too clean, that lifted things from racks and counters, her wandering, aimless days and nights until finally, like a sleepwalker looking for death, she would be spared no longer.

"But what of—what was his name? The one at Sachsenhausen, the young man. It was for him as well as for yourself."

"Walther," she said. "Walther was a bore."

His face froze with distaste. If she had said a child molester or ax murderer, it could not have sounded more obscene.

"I mixed Walther up with what happened to him. The tragedy with the man. It took a long time before I understood that. Walther himself would have praised me for facing reality, he was always lecturing me on reality. He said I lived in an illusion. So the Walther illusion has ended. I'm giving reality its due."

"Nevertheless, I see that you're still wearing his watch."

"I've always worn a watch."

"He would have wanted you to go on," he said with frustration.

"Go on? Where?"

"You know what I mean. But to wander about like this until your chances give out—"

"It's all chance. All chance. Think, Max, if I had married my gentile Bodo, it would be completely different. I would be as privileged as you."

"I'm to feel guilty for that, I see. Perhaps I should go to the Gestapo and say, 'Kindly declassify me as being married to a gentile and send me off to a labor camp in Poland'? Quatsch. I'm thankful I'm in a position to help those less fortunate—"

"Those you persuaded by the hundreds not to emigrate."

"I said what I thought was right at the time. No one can see into the future."

"We lived in an illusion."

"I'm getting a little tired of your repeated use of that word."

"An illusion around a hallucination. The hallucination was real, and the illusion was that it wasn't."

"What is real is that you're sitting here wanted by the Gestapo, with no money, no papers, nowhere to go, and that my apartment is five minutes away. You can discuss philosophy there!"

"The same pictures on the walls, the same sheet music on the piano . . . and you come in from your walk, and everything is the same, except that your gloves have gotten a little seedy, and Lotte has to stand in queues. But otherwise . . . rugs, furniture, pictures, the same as always. Your Pour le Mérite in its same place in the desk drawer, or bureau drawer, or wherever you keep it, or do you wear it under your shirt next to your heart? And the vases filled with flowers from our good German soil, and the beloved old songs . . . why would I want to go back to that Dreck? There comes a time when the stupidity finally goes—"

"When the whole brain goes, apparently—"

"Everything goes when you get tired enough. Even my teeth are going."

"Rose, listen to me, if you realize you're not thinking clearly—"

"I didn't say that. Everything has to go before you can think clearly. First Walther went. Then the people in the house went. And then Germany went. During the raids I began to realize I didn't care if the country was bombed flat, with all its flowers and music and history. And so Germany was gone for me too, and then there was nothing left at all."

"You are rolling in self-pity, Rose."

"Do you think Germany wants your loyalty? If you were young enough to serve again, they wouldn't touch you with tongs."

"It's not the Army itself."

"It's not the Army. It's not anyone. It's just him. Well, try going up to that old couple with the dog you just said hello to. Tell them you're a Jew. Do they know you're a Jew? Tell them you've got no place to go, no food, no money, see if they keep smiling. Their eyes will take on an empty look. You don't exist. All you'll see is their backs as they walk off."

"You seem to forget that I work with people who take in Jews— those people are gentiles."

"I don't forget. I can guess how many."

"We live in a terrorist state—what do you expect? You say you think clearly, but everything you say is totally unrealistic."

"Do you think so? When the bombs fall, do you ever consider that you belong to the tradition that has brought us to this? The marching, the might, the holy nation. I belonged to it too, but you yet more, and you've never stopped. God knows why, when they have excluded you from tradition. I'm glad I was excluded. I'm glad because it opened my eyes. The right of the nation, the glorious panorama of history, when history is nothing but a filthy river of blood."

"You have become an intellectual."

"I wasn't meant to think. I was meant to lead an easy animal life, that was my talent. I never asked to think. It was forced on me. Now I think so clearly that there's nothing left at all."

"Rose, I want you to listen to me. I want you to come with me to the house. I want you to come now."

"The house. The only tradition you have is inside those four walls of yours. That's all they've left you with, and you don't even know it. They took half your shoulders and back, and you're still thanking them for it."

In the silence that followed, she rubbed her forehead tiredly. "I didn't want to say these things, Max. I didn't want to hurt you."

"Indeed, indeed you haven't," he replied with his severe, contained look, trying to smile.

"I didn't want to talk at all. I have to go now," she said, getting up from the bench.

"You can't just walk off," he protested, rising too.

She lifted her hand to his cheek. "Stay well, my dear Max."

"You can't," he said again, putting a restraining hand around her wrist. "I won't allow you."

She stood quietly as he envisioned himself trying to keep her. He had no grip to speak of. With his hollowed, cratered back and shoulders, his wizened upper arms, he could not even hold back a dog on a leash if it decided to run. All his effort, and it was enormous, continual effort, went into holding himself erect.

He took his hand away, and watched as she walked on down the path, the plaid coat disappearing as she went around the curve.

He stood without moving for several moments, then, getting his body into gear for the remainder of the walk, he turned and continued in his original direction, no longer briskly, not swinging his cane, eventually emerging onto the street into the sound of trams and automobiles, newspaper hawkers, bustling morning footsteps, and was lost from sight in the stream of people, as the sun continued its slow journey over the great, mute city below.

Chapter 82

By midsummer, North Africa had been lost. The Allies had invaded Sicily. The Kursk offensive in the east had failed. In Germany, the bombing raids had continued but had not accelerated. It was believed that they would. Berlin prepared for disaster.

Although Hitler was strongly urged by Milch to sack and replace his Air Chief, he would not do this. Even apart from the impression it would create in enemy nations, it would cause serious loss of prestige in the eyes of the people and the Party. But Hitler's wrath continued unabated, and Göring's wrath was equally great, and both found their mark in Jeschonnek. The Youngster was the man between, receiving on one side Hitler's outbursts over Luftwaffe failures, and on the other Göring's resentment of his underling's close association with the Führer. Having borne the brunt of Hitler's fury, standing stiff, chalk-white, he would then undergo further enraged assaults in Göring's company. Even worse, whenever he appeared with his Air Chief before the troops, he was reduced to the lowliest recipient of orders. "Write this down! See to that!" The Youngster, now forty-four, looked exhausted and worn. He had begun to suffer excruciating stomach cramps as disasters and defeats accumulated more rapidly, as the Luftwaffe was bled nearly white. Even worse than the psychological battering he received from his two Chiefs was his knowledge that he himself was partly responsible for the ghastly state of the Luftwaffe. Not everything could be blamed on Göring. He himself had failed to tell Hitler that the Air Force could not fight a protracted war, he himself had agreed to leave fighter production at a low figure, had overestimated the Ju-88, underestimated the Anglo-American air menace, had not realized the need for adequate air defense and, most damning of all, had not spoken up against the Führer's idea of using the Luftwaffe as a shuttle service at Stalingrad. For the first time he began to understand that the war might be lost, and that he was in part responsible. Sickened by the possibility of defeat, tortured by Luftwaffe worries, fearful that he had lost his Führer's trust, he nevertheless had moments in which he believed there was still hope of turning the tide by making a frank report to the Führer of the Luftwaffe's many ills, by broaching to him the lack of organization at the top, by clearly stating his difficulties with Göring—that he was not allowed to discuss anything with him, that he was treated like an errand boy. But when his secretary urged him to take this step, he shook his head at her. "I cannot. Perhaps you could, but I cannot. I cannot go against Göring—I am a soldier." The stomach cramps grew worse. He now placed all his hopes in the secret V-weapons being made at Peenemünde.

Goebbels had issued a decree that women and children be evacuated from the city, but when the first saturation raid came it was not on Berlin.

Hamburg was bombed around the clock for ten solid days. When the bombing ceased, General Bodenschatz was sent by his Chief to bring back a personal report. Shaken to his core, the general returned to Wolfsschanze, where Göring awaited him.

"The reckoning is that some two hundred thousand high-explosive and incendiary bombs were dropped, and as many as five thousand phosphorescent canisters. The resultant fire storms were beyond anything that could be imagined—inferno winds like cyclones, streets melting, people consumed on the spot . . . shriveled to practically nothing, the bodies of ten adults could be loaded onto one wheelbarrow. There is no way yet to establish the death toll, but half the city—the second-largest city of the Reich—is entirely destroyed."

Two days later, young Fighter Commander Galland of the skeptical eyes and thick black mustache reminiscent of a pirate's, always at odds with his Chief and with the entire running of the Luftwaffe, arrived at Wolfsschanze, where he and other air leaders had been summoned for a conference. He found Göring in a frame of mind entirely unexpected. The shock of Hamburg, far from having sent him deeper into accusatory outbursts, seemed to have shaken him free of recrimination and faultfinding. He was quiet, steely, objective. All his thoughts were directed to one end: radical reorganization of air defense.

"Another Hamburg must never happen. Germany's threatened cities must be protected at all costs."

Reorganization of air defense, absolute priority of the air industry and an enormous increase in fighter production—these were the demands of the hour. In turning from offense to defense, from bomber to fighter emphasis, Göring was turning completely around. It was clear that for once he had accepted the truth of a situation and was prepared to let go of his own—and Hitler's—long-held opinions. Galland realized, too, that everyone in the room—Milch, Jeschonnek, officers of the General Staff, commanders of air fleets—had stripped themselves of personal and departmental disagreements in a common will to put the defense of the Reich above all else. Every man present was in the fullest and most determined accordance with Göring, and he with them. Never before had Galland witnessed such resolute cooperation among those responsible for the leadership of the Luftwaffe. When the measures had been thoroughly discussed, Göring rose immediately and with his senior aide-de-camp went to the Führer's bunker for the necessary permission to go ahead.

Half an hour later he came back through the door staring in front of him, said not a word, and went into the adjoining room, closing the door behind him.

They stared after him, then turned to the aide-de-camp for some explanation. The aide was so greatly upset that his tale was chaotic, but its essence was that a heated discussion had taken place during which the Führer had rejected every suggestion put to him. They were stunned. As Göring himself had realized the absolute necessity of regaining and assuring air power, understanding that any other course would be insane, so, surely would the Führer. They had hardly absorbed the aide-de-camp's shattering report when Göring's voice called from the other room. He wanted Galland. And Peltz, General of Combat Fighters.

The two men stepped inside to find that the Air Chief had broken down completely. He was seated at his table with his head buried in his arms, not weeping, as he was sometimes said to do, but moaning, moaning as one who is undergoing some excruciating physical pain, as if his legs had been torn off or his arms crushed. Now and then as the two men stood in helpless, burning embarrassment, they could hear through the terrible moans some indistinguishable, hopeless-sounding word or phrase. After a time, the Air Chief leaned back heavily in his chair. His face was drained of color. He looked up at them with dull eyes.

"You are witnessing my deepest moments of despair. The Führer has lost faith in me, he rejected every suggestion I put to him. He said the Luftwaffe has disappointed him too often . . . to go from the offensive to the defensive was out of the question. But he would give the Luftwaffe one last chance to rehabilitate itself."

With sinking hearts, Galland and his companion waited to hear what this chance might consist of.

"A resumption of air attacks against England. But this time on a larger scale." He gave a weary sigh. "Attack. Terror can only be smashed by counterattack. The Führer said this was always how he had dealt with his political enemies."

"But that is entirely—" Galland began.

"Nein . . . I realize my mistake. The Führer is always right. He is always right." And above the dull, tired eyes, the eyebrows slowly knotted. "Our strength must now be concentrated on dealing the enemy in the west such mighty retaliation blows that he will not risk another Hamburg. As a first measure in the execution of his plan, the Führer has ordered the creation of a leader of the attacks on England."

Suddenly he rose to his feet with enormous command, his eyes narrowed and hard.

"Oberst Peltz! I herewith appoint you assault leader against England!"

Go back in time, but where? This is the important thing that I have got to figure out. We think time can be measured by small metal hands . . .

"What small metal hands?"

Why is she answering? Did I speak aloud?

"A big metal hand, that I understand. Last night I dreamed I was caught in one. It was a hand made of iron. The joints of the fingers and thumbs worked on hinges, evidently well oiled. I was on the palm, this iron palm, you see, trying to scramble off. And the fingers slammed down around me with a terrible clang, iron on iron."

"Literary," Rose said. "Very literary. Too symbolic."

"Isn't that the nature of dreams?"

Rose's cellmate, who had arrived at Berlin's Grosse Hamburger Strasse Deportation Center only that afternoon, was a small young woman with a massively structured nose. Below it were small rosebud lips, above it heavy-lidded dark eyes. Her skin had the unhealthy pallor of someone who had not been outdoors for a long while. But in the darkness she was only a gray form. She went over to the window, which was barred, and stood looking out. "It was a portent," she said. "By this afternoon I was here."

The gray form went back to the cot and sat down again. In the room were two cots and two bunks. Rose lay on one of the lower bunks, her head resting on her folded plaid coat.

What is time? How can we believe it is measured by these small metal hands? . . . Why is she putting that blanket in her mouth, is she trying to eat it? . . . Or calendars. Things to do with sun and moon, seasons, days and nights. The watch obediently ticks away, believing that it's measuring something, but time is somewhere else. . . . She's clamping her teeth on the blanket, pulling it hard, her teeth will break. Mine wouldn't have once, but they've gotten bad . . . suddenly in the Zoo Bahnhof mirror there were little serrated edges, little black caries. This is evidence that time can't be measured by clocks and calendars . . .

"No good," the girl murmured. She bent over and began pulling the blanket frayingly back and forth across the sharp corner of the steel cot.

Because overnight my teeth started to go, which by ordinary standards of time should have taken many years, if ever. It was like one of those speeded-up films of plants shooting from seed to leaves and flowers in twenty seconds.

There was a long sound of cloth ripping. "My cousin was interrogated here last autumn. He was questioned about a fellow war worker who had disappeared."

"Your cousin," said Rose.

"They kept him three weeks before releasing him. During that time he came down with influenza, and they put him in the infirmary."

My cousin, I spoke with him when? Days ago? Months? It was spring, so it must have been three or four months ago, maybe more. This is why I know time is somewhere else than in clocks and calendars. How long ago did I see Max when all the days and nights since have been the same, forming one single day and night until I came here, and now wherever time is going, it's going fast . . .

"What I recall him saying"—there was another long sound of ripping, she was tearing the blanket—"was that the infirmary window had no bars."

"Melodramatic," said Rose. "Too melodramatic."

"Isn't that the nature of escape?"

And looking out from under the bed, those black boots . . . that moment spanned hours. And the sound of bones fracturing in the van . . . a noise that never ends inside my head. This is where time is, it's inside us . . .

"The next room is full," the girl said. "And the one next to that, and the one next to that. Six women in each. We're the last two. They may wait to fill this room before they start deportation, or they may not. That depends on how many men there are. I counted twenty-one when we were let into the corridor tonight, but some may have stayed in their rooms. This means there are altogether forty-one people here and possibly more. A woman I spoke with in the corridor said the minimum number for a deportation load is now fifty. From a thousand it's come down to fifty. We're very close to fifty, if not already there. I estimate two more days at the most."

She talks so much. She talks as much as Walther, and has the same kind of logic.

"How long do you say you've been here? Three days?"

"Three, four. I don't know," Rose said.

"How did it come about with you?"

"A catcher. The porter where I used to live. He saw me on the street and turned me in."

"I never went out, but this morning I did. In spite of the dream, I went out and it happened. I never went out before, but I had to have fresh air."

A storeroom behind a bookcase maybe, or the corner of an attic. Dare not show the face, not with that nose. A classic *Stürmer* face. Except for the skin—swarthiness drained to dead white. Always inside, maybe months, maybe years . . .

"In the corridor I heard a man talking," the girl said as her hands began to move in the darkness, braiding the strips of blanket together.

"I know the one. I've heard what he says."

All gassed to death as soon as they arrive, and their bodies burned to ash in ovens . . . but is this something that can happen in the world? It is. I know that it is.

"He once heard it over the radio, an English broadcast," the girl went on in the dark. "But it must have been enemy propaganda. Mustn't it have? How can one believe such a thing?"

She is crying. But if you would halt time, you need only put memory in its path like a boulder. A boulder that you are inside of, as in a chamber of light, forever. But the question is, where shall I cast back to? Ringelblumen orange and yellow in the sun when I was small? Nein, that stands for nothing. But what stands if not that? If not that, what stands? Who is this, anyway, in her chamber of light? A child fed on the dupe's diet of sacred soil and heroes? Nein, an actress, she was a stage actress. Or was it a cleaning woman? Nein, she was a thief. I can't remember. Was she a Jew, a non-Jew? A friend of the powerful, who ate rotten potatoes? A great lover of men, or a dry stick lying alone? I don't know, I don't know who she is, except that she liked Nusstorten . . . must I leave her in all eternity with only that, a Nusstorte?

In the morning there was a smell of vomit. The girl had put her finger down her throat. And she had rubbed her face against the sharp corner of the cot, raising red welts. She had wound the braided rope around her waist and hips under her dress, giving the dress a bulky look.

"They won't notice that. They'll only notice the vomit and my face. I'll be sent to the infirmary. Since I went out yesterday, my parents and husband have had no idea of what has become of me. I won't let them wonder forever. I won't disappear into—into what the man in the corridor said."

All nose now, a nose like granite hewn with jackhammers from the side of a cliff. But pathetic. Doesn't she realize they've probably barred the window since her cousin was there?

"I didn't sleep, but I gave myself a dream anyway to cancel out the other. It was the dream of an air raid. I need one tonight for confusion."

"And if there isn't?"

"There will be."

"That rope under your dress. You'll have to undress."

"They don't put you in hospital gowns. You think they take that trouble for Jews? You lie in your clothes. This is what my cousin said."

"What if there are other patients? You would implicate them."

"I have to hope no one else is there. Listen to me, if I'm going to do this I can't look on the dark side like you." She gave a slight nod of her head. "The guards." She stood listening to the sound of boots in the corridor. She looked at the vomit on the cot, her fingertips touching her welts, testing them.

She was sent up to the infirmary, and Rose with her in case the disease was contagious.

There were no other patients in the room. The window was unbarred. They were not asked to change into hospital gowns. The nurse did nothing for them and went out: deportees who would be gone very soon anyway. They lay on the beds, each under a sheet. The girl talked.

She talks as much as Walther, and is as dark as Ida.

Night fell. The sound of the air raid sirens started in. "You see," the girl said, getting up from the bed. She lifted the skirt of her dress and unwound the rope. "I'll wait until the planes come over." She sat down on the edge of the bed with the coils of rope in her hand. Then she got up and arranged the blankets in a hump, so that it would seem she was asleep under them.

Like a bad play.

"Will you come?" the girl asked, sitting down again.

Two stories, three? And if we should fall from the rope? And if we did make it to the ground, guard dogs turned loose if we're seen? And even if the whole thing did work, only to have to begin again?

"No," she said.

Presently there came the noise of antiaircraft, and a drone that grew into a roar. The girl got up and resolutely walked to the window, where she secured the rope around a pipe running beneath it. Pushing open the window, she threw out the coils and leaned her head after them. "The rope goes most of the way," she said, turning. "Not far to drop from it, maybe less than a story. You won't change your mind? All

right. Tell them you were asleep, you saw nothing. You won't be implicated." Sitting down on the sill, she swung her legs over and took hold
of the rope. A moment later she had disappeared, leaving only the
rectangle of night sky crossed by searchlights.

A scraping of door bolts sounded through the din from outside,
sending Rose from her bed and across the room to the open window.

The window, I should have shut it—

Before she reached it, a flashlight beam swept in from the door.
She heard the nurse's startled cry, then the beam swept away with a
shout down the hall for the guard. "Go on!" she hissed to the dangling,
descending figure, hair spread in the wind. "Go on!"

If I shut the window they'll see the rope around the pipe anyway.
Coming now, thuds, thuds, don't let him look down. Make him think
it's you, get on the sill, get your legs over, take hold of the rope, but it's
high, so high—hold on to it, let yourself down just enough so he can't
see past you. He's got hold of my arms, make him work, make him
work just long enough . . .

An abrupt slackening of the rope in her straining hands told her
the girl had dropped from its end. There was no outburst of barking
dogs let loose. A few moments more would see her into the trees behind the building. A few moments? A few centuries in this terrible
noise so high, so high, I wonder he doesn't let me fall, but they've got
their head count. Leaning out and pulling, pulling. Is she gone? Let
him pull me in, wrapping my arms around his neck, pressed jaw to jaw,
his rotten subhuman face. And suddenly, with a smile breaking like
light, knowing this was the memory to have forever, the only one, she
scraped her feet up against the bricks of the building and thrust herself
out into the air, pulling him with her, a glimpsed horrified mask, two
figures plummeting through the calamitous dark to the concrete walk
below.

In Italy, in July of 1943, Mussolini was deposed at a meeting of the
Fascist Grand Council, his son-in-law being one of those voting against
him. The Duce's arrest and imprisonment indicated that Italy would
withdraw from the Axis, thus requiring occupation by large German
troop units badly needed elsewhere. In Sicily, German and Italian
troops were being beaten back. In Russia, the Red Army had recaptured Belograd, Zolochev and Karachev. In Germany itself, intermittent bombings of Hamburg continued, with increasingly heavy attacks
on other cities. The new air offense against England was got under way
with little effect and severe losses. In mid-August, Kharkov was retaken
by the Russians. Two days later, Axis resistance ended in Sicily. And on
the same day, in Germany, the Americans mounted a heavy raid on the
ball-bearing industries at Schweinfurt and Regenburg, while that night

six hundred RAF aircraft bombed the rocket research center at Peene-münde.

At Luftwaffe headquarters in East Prussia, the news of the Peene-münde bombing was learned early the following morning. The report was handed to Chief of Staff Jeschonnek, who read it without expression. He then got up from his desk and went back to his room, although the daily situational conference was about to start.

Jeschonnek's chief adjutant waited a quarter of an hour to accompany him to the conference. Finally he asked the secretary to telephone and find out if he was coming.

"He says he is coming directly," the secretary said, putting the receiver down. Still he did not appear. Another ten minutes went by. The phone rang; it was Jeschonnek. "He says that you should go on over," the secretary said, again putting the receiver down.

The adjutant left as ordered, but the secretary felt a sense of apprehension. As she worked, she looked now and again down the hallway to Jeschonnek's door. The Chief of Staff never missed the daily situational conference. Despite the worries that tormented him, despite the stomach cramps which even from that stolid face one knew were unbearable, the Chief of Staff did not miss the daily conference. After a while she took it upon herself to telephone him again. She could hear the phone ringing in his room—eight, nine, ten times—but there was no answer. Finally she got up and went down to the door, but her rapping went unanswered. Hesitantly opening the door, she saw him lying on the floor by the bed, his eyes fixed on the ceiling of the small spartan room. As she came inside, she observed, with a sense of distance and unreality, that his service revolver lay on the floor beside him. It was strange that she had heard no shot; perhaps it had occurred just as she scraped her chair back to get up. On the tightly made bed there lay a sheet of paper, a rectangle of white on the austere gray, which she looked down at. *I can no longer work with the Reichsmarschall. Long live the Führer!* She saw that other notes littered the usually tidy table. The room was very still, very warm. From behind his right ear, blood was forming in a small shiny pool on the floor. Only then did her numbness dissolve, and she ran headlong into the hallway.

Chief of the General Staff of the Luftwaffe Generaloberst Hans Jeschonnek had succumbed to a long illness, ran the newspaper and radio reports. The Youngster was buried with honors and replaced by General Korten.

Imprisoned in the Apennines, Mussolini was rescued by a squad of glider-borne SS men sent by Hitler and taken to the north of Italy, where he tried to refound a sovereign government. The Allies had already invaded the Italian mainland; a month later Italy declared war on Germany. The Russians had recovered Smolensk and Dnepropetrovsk. In early November Kiev fell to them.

Later that month, exactly two years to the day since Udet's suicide, the disaster which Berlin had awaited took place, the heaviest if shortest raid the city had yet undergone, an unrelieved bombardment which seemed a concentration of all noise in the universe to those squeezing their palms like suction cups to their ears as they sat in their inadequate and shaking cellars. But outside the cellars and bunkers the mammoth noise separated itself into its components: blockbusters detonating, walls crashing, plate glass shattering, the stuttering and roaring of antiaircraft artillery, shrapnel bouncing off tin roofs like hailstones. Everything was lit by the moving dome of searchlights, by red projectiles of tracer bullets, blinding flashes of cannon bursts, shooting flames of incendiary bombs. The green glow of phosphorescent canisters poured down walls or spilled along streets, turning to inextinguishable streams of fire that licked among twisted tram tracks and burned among explosions of concrete and earth shooting into the night sky, and seeped in fiery rivulets down celler steps to engulf the wooden doors of the shelters.

Three nights later there was another raid of equal intensity, and the night after that another, and another each week throughout December, into the fifth year of the war.

The new year of 1944 was cold in northern Italy, wet, with sweeping winds. In the outskirts of Verona, in a field within the walls of an old fortress, five chairs had had their legs thrust securely into the damp ground. Five men, one of them Count Ciano, in a drizzle-darkened raincoat and gray hat, were being taken leave of by a priest. The priest's black robes flapped in the wet wind as he solemnly crossed the field to a group of twenty Italian militiamen with rifles, four or five German officers who had set up newsreel cameras, and a doctor with a black bag.

Holding his chin high, as had always been his wont, with a jaw-clenched whitened look of concentration, the Count with the others turned around as ordered and straddled his chair. In accordance with Italian law, traitors were shot in the back.

Only one thing might erase the stigma of this moment. All his thoughts were concentrated on this erasure as he turned his shoulders and head as far around as he could, the wind battering his hat, and looked squarely at the militiamen raising their rifles and taking aim.

The commander brought his arm down.

Chapter 83

I<small>N</small> the courtyard of the Air Ministry building, inside which twenty-seven bomb-damaged offices were under repair, the long gray open Mercedes, flying the Reichsmarschall's standard, received its passenger to a flurry of salutes and banged heels. The car door was shut behind him and the chauffeur eased the purring vehicle through the warm late-spring air toward the entrance. It was the end of an ordinary day. The Reichsmarschall seldom appeared at the Air Ministry, but the rarity of his visits had themselves become expected, ordinary.

The car moved into the traffic of the altered city. The hotels Kaiserhof, Eden and Bristol were blackened husks. Many ministries had been leveled, as well as the old French and Italian embassies. In Grunewald and Wilmersdorf entire blocks lay in ruins. The Zoo Bahnhof had been hit, and the Charlottenburg and Hallensee stations. Along the Kurfürstendamm, the scars culminated in the Kaiser Wilhelm Gedächtnis Kirche, a massive Romanesque landmark of which there remained only the central part and one charred and broken spire. Beneath the spire, the hands of the round clock stood permanently stunned at twenty-six minutes past ten. Traffic was being rerouted from streets flooded by broken water mains and sewer pipes.

Beyond the northern outskirts, the car gained speed through flat greening fields and dark stands of pines. Presently it turned off the highway onto the narrow road canopied by arching trees. Barreling through the aquarium-green light that alternated with radiant bursts of sun, it zoomed past the SS checkpoint without stopping, finally slowing down inside the driveway gates, passing through sun-flooded gardens and statuary and turning into the courtyard, where the great double doors were already being opened. The Reichsmarschall climbed from the car, filling his lungs with the pine-scented sunny air, and with eager steps passed inside.

Germany has begun to crumble in fire and billowing smoke, but once he is inside his forest, his driveway gate, his door, the outside world vanishes as if by the fall of a stage curtain. That world of gathering doom and personal failure, horribly and inextricably mixed, is suddenly a stage set behind him, while before him lies all that is real.

Collecting has become his primary passion—bronze Apollos, stone saints, gold Empire soup tureens, priceless tapestries, ancient armor, beautiful lace, antique furniture, and paintings, paintings, paintings. There are those who say few greater art plunderers in all history have existed, and on most days he is not averse to accepting this accolade, for he believes in history, is part of history, and since the beginning of history the plundering of art by conquerors has been an accepted part of war, has indeed been its most civilized offshoot. But on other days, in a more Prussian mood—perhaps remembering the Prussian troops in the War of Liberation, freezing in winter rather than cut woods not belonging to them—he concentrates on the fact that he loots nothing, but makes honorable if small payment for every piece of art that crosses his threshold.

Whichever mood is in the ascendance, that of Renaissance prince or *bon soldat,* he takes extreme joy in walking through the halls of Carinhall, a tour he makes at least twice a week, gazing at and pausing before the heavy gilt-framed pictures that now hang in three and four tiers, sheathing the walls—Titians, Dürers, Rubenses, Cranachs, Rembrandts, Velázquezes, van Dycks, Memlings, Raphaels, Bouchers, from France, Holland, Poland, Yugoslavia, Italy, their imperishable beauty reaching far inside him, causing a deep intoxication that spreads through his veins with the knowledge that his is the greatest private collection in the world, and that it is his bequeathment to his nation. It is his monument, his immortality. On his sixtieth birthday, in January of 1953, he will present the completed Hermann Göring Museum, filled with all its treasures, to the German people. And he passes on, pausing for long moments before a mighty, mythical scene from Rubens, a noble quattrocento visage, a glowing fall of Cranach drapery, before glowing skies and mountain peaks, glowing jewellike colors wherever the eye settles. And if among the magnificence there hang some worthless daubs, insipid watercolors and academic still lifes thrown in with a trade or received as gifts from unsophisticated admirers, they have their unglanced-at place on the walls because the passion to fill these walls is almost as great as the passion for the highest and finest. To fill, to cover everything, to overwhelm. The desk in his official study is now laden with so many alabaster statuettes and silver and gold bibelots that on the infrequent occasions when a conference is held and a map spread out, the treasures must first be pushed aside to make room.

Like many monarchs of old, he prefers the company of women. His wife and little daughter, his wife's niece and sister, his own sisters Olga and Paula—these compose the loyal and loving little court he most enjoys, and he spends much of his time in the center of their warmth and good cheer. Neither war nor politics are brought up. Olga has had some difficulty suppressing her inclination to discuss the war, but her brother's lack of response has taught her the pointlessness of such talk.

The talk usually revolves around personalities and daily doings. In good weather, walks are taken around the lake or in the gardens. The child skips ahead, then runs back to walk with her father, putting her hand in his. The child is especially dear to him.

A routine has long since been established regarding air raids. A telephone call is made to the weather bureau in the morning; if a stream of bombers overhead seems unlikely, the Reichsmarschall may go off on a shoot. This remains one of his greatest pleasures, the fresh forest coolness of morning, the lowering shafts of sunlight in late afternoon; and the variousness beneath one's steps, pine needles, fallen oak leaves, ferns, dry grass, wet marshland; the smell of earth, dogs, cordite; and the camaraderie, the excitement, and the kill itself with the hunting horns lifting in ancient chorus over the slain beast, a sound unchanged for a millennium; and the long trek back from the heart of nature, the sense of achievement and bodily exertion, the glowing satisfied beating of the heart's blood.

On the tennis court he is less enterprising, altogether less active, in fact almost inert, playing by his own eccentric rules. In white ducks, a hairnet over his head to keep his long hair from falling in his eyes, he stands in one spot on the red clay court and swats the ball only if it comes directly to him. "What are you trying to do, make me run all over?" he demands if the ball lands out of reach, and no amount of explanation can change him. He plays in order to lose weight, but he loses no weight.

His attempts to do so have in fact fallen off almost completely. He eats more than ever and more often than ever. Dr. Ondarza and Nurse Gormanns fear that his excessive poundage, combined with his age, will result in heart trouble. Erratic heartbeats have already been detected. In addition, his insomnia is much worse, the painful swelling of his lymph glands recurs more often, as does the debilitating inflammation of his joints, and he is now consuming some hundred paracodeine pills a day. His face, never prone to the beefiness of his body but luxuriously padded and smooth and florid, has for a long while been pallid and worn, the resplendent blue-green eyes looking out from above heavy, deep-cut pouches grayish in color. He looks ill, and is ill, but no amount of exhortations on the part of his doctor and nurse can make him cut down on his food or to smoke fewer cigars or to resume his exercises in the basement gymnasium, and since his word is law, they can only hover about uselessly.

The Reichsmarschall's morning schedule has changed somewhat. He continues to rise from his canopied bed at half past six, and to listen to the gramophone records his valet selects to match his morning's mood, and to sip a cup of coffee as he sits reading; but his reading no longer includes the stacks of domestic and foreign newspapers, underlined in red and blue by his staff, which he so avidly went through in the past. His reading consists entirely of art books. Nor, when he has had his bath, and has been shaved and manicured, and has been got into his clothes by the valet, and has consumed his large breakfast downstairs, does he drive off to meet the demands of his many offices. Instead, he returns to his sitting room, where he receives his art agents, his jewelers, and his tailors, in that order.

When Herr Kropp's alarm clock rings at six, he rises and bathes and dresses with his usual smooth alacrity. He glances out the window at the courtyard, at the early-morning sky, and when he has folded his white silk handkerchief into his breast pocket he goes to the door, glancing at the large painting of Carinhall that hangs beside it. The painting is not bad, but it has no artistic value, and he knows it. The painting is a trade-off from his master. For Herr Kropp had come into a very fine if small seventeenth-century Dutch landscape in Amsterdam, where he had admired it in an art dealer's shop only to have the dealer, hoping for Göring's goodwill, press it upon him. Much surprised by his good fortune, Herr Kropp had brought the painting to his master and asked if he had been right in accepting it. "Of course. Of course you must keep it," he was told, but there was a gleam in the Reichsmarschall's eyes that made Herr Kropp wonder how long he would remain in possession of it. Indeed, soon after, he was presented with the Carinhall view in exchange for the little jewel of a landscape, nor did the Reichsmarschall make any attempt to hide his delight in this transaction which brought yet another small treasure to him.

Herr Kropp takes a philosophical view of the incident. Of course, he would like to have kept the Dutch painting, now ornately framed and hanging between a Ruisdael and a Hals in the reception hall, but in matters of art his master has lost his bearings. He is like an alcoholic drunk not on liquor but paintings. One cannot take it personally.

Herr Kropp enters the bedroom to find his master already up. In his white terry-cloth robe, which he will wear to the bath, he sits in an armchair, reading. They exchange a few morning words. Herr Kropp telephones to the kitchen for the coffee to be sent up. He draws the drapes back from the windows and goes to the cabinet of gramophone records to make his choice for the morning concert. After putting on the record, Herr Kropp runs the bath and puts out towels. The bathroom has undergone changes over the years; its tile has been replaced by green marble, its silver-plated fixtures by gold. One wall is at present in the process of being inset with floor-to-ceiling panels of heavy green glass etched with gracefully stylized gulls and leaping sea waves. The workmen's tools lie in one corner. Workmen are forever busy at Carinhall, enlarging, adding, embellishing. There is a folk saying that Herr Kropp thinks of: when the house is finished, death comes.

After the Reichsmarschall has had his bath, after he has been shaved, his face massaged, his finger and toenails seen to, and the barber and manicurists have gone, the valet helps him into a fur-trimmed cocoa-brown velvet robe. The fur trim is something new. The Reichsmarschall puts his feet into a newly made pair of slippers, heavy with brocade. He selects his rings for the day. Herr Kropp twists them onto the great plump fingers with difficulty, but gently. Then the diamond-cluster brooch, which alternates with the ruby brooch and the one of lapis lazuli. Sometimes he wears all three. Herr Kropp reminds himself that the Vikings also ornamented themselves lavishly.

During the day the Reichsmarschall will change his clothes many times, not because of his sweating, which requires only two or three changes, but for the sheer sake of variety—hunting costumes, riding costumes, leisure costumes, and costumes that cannot be categorized, such as that which he always wears to tour his paintings, consisting of wine-red velvet jacket worn with frilled silk blouse, wine-red velvet knickerbockers, and shoes with golden buckles. Herr Kropp gets him in and out of these outfits as often as seven times a day, and each time his master walks from the room in his latest attire, Herr Kropp knows that he is taking on a role that will distract and soothe him only until the next one seems better.

He retires late, as always, beneath the life-size nude of Europa, and sleeps poorly, as always. He rises at half past six, the drapes are drawn, and the daily routine begins once more. Day after day, week after week. His official life has virtually ceased.

*   *   *

But sometimes, as if galvanized, he will suddenly have himself dressed in his uniform and race off to the Air Ministry. From his great refuge in the forest, he reenters the world of gathering darkness in a state of agitation, flushed and tempestuous.

"Execution! I order execution!"

General Bodenschatz, who has submitted to his Chief a court-martial sentence against an airman, looks at him with astonishment.

"Five years?" Göring roars on. "Five years for cowardice in the face of the enemy? I order execution!"

"But, Chief, this is only a boy. He is seventeen."

"Execution!"

The Reichsmarschall slashes out the verdict with his pen, writes in his own, and scrawls his signature. But Bodenschatz has no sooner left the room with the death sentence in his hand than he is called back.

"Let the court's original verdict stand," he is told curtly.

He becomes furious with his Chief of the Operations Staff for disagreeing with him on some point. The veins on his temples swell like ropes. "You are trying to sabotage the Luftwaffe! You are a traitor!" he cries, his fingers suddenly curling as if to strangle the amazed general, to whom he comes pounding so close that the great belly presses against him. "You are a traitor! A traitor!" The staring general wonders what he should do if the hands go around his neck. Should he give a good knee-kick to the belly before it can happen? The situation is so preposterous it is almost comical, yet he is white-faced with insult. Swinging on his heel, he leaves the room and writes out his resignation.

When the resignation is received by Göring, it is sent back with an apology. "I regret my impetuousness. I assure you of my complete confidence." The general accepts the apology, but he cannot forget the swinish rudeness of his superior.

He and Milch barely speak. He expresses his feelings to Bodenschatz, employing his favorite and well-worn definition of his second-in-command. "What is this Milch, anyway? A fart out of my asshole!" His agitated face, with the heavy pouches beneath the eyes, turns red with anger as he goes on. "First he wanted to play the part of my crown prince—now he wants to be my usurper!" But he knows he is using the wrong tense, for to all intents and purposes the usurpation has already come to pass. The ground has already slipped from under his feet. The Luftwaffe, the economy—everything. Everything has been taken from him.

*   *   *

He visits bombed ruins. On one occasion a photographer snaps his picture as he climbs out of the car. His brow is furrowed, his eyes are lifted in a narrowed, painful gaze at the shattered buildings. His long lips, which with the years have followed a tendency to curve down at the corners, are slightly parted and drawn in a sickly-looking gash across his face. His hat is in his hand, and his hair has an unkempt look, with several long strands escaped from the rest and hanging to one ear. Even his uniform, though not rumpled, has a rumpled appearance. It is as if the savaged, gray, rubbled spirit of the place has physically entered his being and made him part of it. The click of the camera captures this phenomenon, but a few moments later when it clicks again the Reichsmarschall embodies encouragement, strength, good cheer. His face is sober, yet lit with warm geniality. His hair seems suddenly sleek and proper, though the strands still hang. His uniform no longer seems rumpled, but as if in a moment's space has been freshly pressed. The people are coming to him, they whose homes have been destroyed, who have lost loved ones; and their faces beam with courage and resolution as he shakes their hands and talks with them. He is sympathetic, kindly, and there is humor too, of an earthy, human kind, and at the same time there is about him a dynamism, an inspiring quality of determination and perseverance. They press around him, they squeeze his hand, they clap his shoulder, they assure him they can and will carry on. He takes time with each of them, and when he leaves they say to one another, "Der Dicke is a good sort. Der Dicke cares. There are those who don't." They follow him to the car and stand waving as he drives off. He thinks: They should be throwing rotten vegetables at me.

He is moved and heartened by their loyalty. The people at any rate have not turned against him. He is still theirs, and they are still his. But their suffering is his too, and he thinks of those faces he has just been with, in their surroundings of smoldering, eviscerated buildings, and he feels again only the pain and sickness of heart that he felt on lifting his eyes to the ruination. There will be no surcease, only more raids. And those faces, flickering one by one through his mind, will, many of them, soon or late, go down under flaming debris. But it is not a picture that can be of any use to a soldier. Individual faces are a poet's luxury. A poet may plumb tragic depths through the doomed individual's smile and eyes, but the soldier must keep to the anonymous if he is to remain a soldier. Distance is freedom of action. Faces become small, indistinct, they turn to statistics. So it has always been and so it must always be. The Reichsmarschall's thoughts have moved on to other things within a few blocks.

*   *   *

When he learns that Milch has incurred the Führer's special wrath over the jet aircraft snaggle, he is jubilant. It appears that his old enemy who pisses ice may soon be put on ice. It appears that the Führer may actually fire him for his part in the Luftwaffe's development of the jet as a fighter, rather than the "blitz bomber" the Führer had wrongheadedly demanded and is now angrily insisting on producing. The Reichsmarschall discusses the Milch situation with General Loerzer, Chief of Personnel and second only to Göring himself in his blackmarket dealings, receiving truckloads of hard liquor, wines, tinned foods, silk stockings and perfume from occupied countries. The Reichsmarschall expresses his great satisfaction in his State Secretary's imminent downfall. But the satisfaction grows dampened by the knowledge that even if he wished to protest this great change in the organization of his Luftwaffe, he would not be given voice. After a few moments he abruptly turns the conversation elsewhere.

But these trips from Carinhall are sporadic, each one like a sudden shooting spark. He works hard for hours, studies reports, sees people, holds conferences, and then is gone. Berlin will not see him again for weeks.

The Mercedes passes from the environs of the city. Dust, smoke, rubble are left behind. The Luftwaffe is left behind, the advances from the east, and the inevitable, oncoming Allied invasion in the west. Here is the aquarium green alternating with bursts of sunlight, and here through the gates of the drive is the house that holds all that is real.

Chapter 84

THE grass was turning with autumn, the fruit trees and big elms were all shades of gold. In the far distance beyond the west wall of the burg, the sky was streaked with the white vapor trails of enemy bombers. Hans Schmidt, leaning on his cane, was watering the geraniums by the manor door, limited to this small activity now that it was too difficult for him to get down into the garden, and especially to get back up again. The last time he had labored up the path was two weeks ago, after Schelling had persuaded him to come for a drive. It would do Herr Schmidt good, he said, he was going over to Palden for manure. Unfortunately, in the Palden village square they were hanging a Polish worker. Hans used a zinc watering can, tipping it slowly, watching the little stream splatter down through the leaves and soak into the dark earth.

He stoops so badly now, and is always full of pain, his wife said to herself. She sat knitting on a nearby bench, a ball of blue yarn on her lap. What is it supposed to be? she wondered. A scarf? A pot holder? It's already too big for a pot holder. Schelling should bring in the apples tomorrow, all over the ground. Nuremberg half gone. Maybe it's a sweater. In the old days I used to sit out here knitting and I could see the Frau Reichskommissar leaning from one of the upper windows watering the geraniums. She always liked to water the window plants herself. I could hear her humming. The sunlight fell on her face. The allotments are gone, Frau Kloppmann wrote. Came home from work and she found them gone—houses, sheds, neighbors, only a crater. Schelling said they hanged a young Polish worker in Palden for lying with a female of the Reich. Hans won't talk about it. The bomber trails are clouding together now, they make the whole sky gray. But it's not Hermann's fault. It's that one—oh that he should survive a time bomb stuck right next to him, when everyone else is dying by the thousands. The Pole was maybe fifteen, Schelling said. Palden where I was born. The Frau Reichskommissar always watered the window plants herself. That time when I saw the two moths flying backward I remembered how it frightened me, and I told her, and she said it was imagination. The Frau Reichskommissar was usually right about everything, but that time she wasn't right. The Great War, we called it, but what should we call this one? All our beautiful old cities going under. Our towns, even our villages.

"Are you tired?" she asked as her husband, finished with his watering, stiffly lowered himself onto the bench beside her clicking needles.

"A bit, mayhap."

They sat looking at the sky beyond the west wall, where the long vapor trails of the enemy bombers had dissolved into each other, turning the distant blue to gray.

"I wonder sometimes, what of the Bang child these days."

"Her, Minna? Why, she's out leading the troops."

"More likely dead."

"Come, Hans. Many people in Nuremberg aren't dead."

"Aye."

In the silence there came the sound of a horse neighing down by the barn. Sparrows rustled in the leaves of the trees.

"Hermann's father always liked to sit here on this bench. You could always see him in his black quilted morning jacket. He never removed it, even when the weather was very warm. But not that old Hurenbock, Epenstein. Epenstein had no sense of propriety."

"Na," Hans said, "when you can still get after Epenstein, I know you're all right, Nikki."

She smiled at him, her needles clicking.

After a while, when the shadows had lengthened, she put the shapeless piece of knitting into her satchel, and they took their afternoon walk through the grass of the courtyard.

The morning was cold and foggy as Nikki walked down the steep cobbled streets to where the little Pegnitz ran, and she continued along the path at its side. The river was banked by mossy wooden planks and old stone walls. Here and there it widened and went meandering around small islands of trees, their long trunks reflected in the motionless water. She went on through the dripping woods, the path choked with dark leaves. Beyond the woods stretched a plowed brown field where kerchiefed women stood in the fog, piling turnips into a wooden cart. Between the field and the cemetery stood a border of chestnut trees, their crowns lost in the dense gray. She pulled open the creaking cemetery gate and walked until she arrived at the new part, where most of the headstones were surmounted by the Iron Cross in marble. Her husband's headstone was plain. The mound of earth was still new, had not yet settled. The keeper had removed the browning wreaths and sprays that had covered it.

"I brought these from the garden," she said, withdrawing a bunch of purple stock from the net bag she carried. "There are still some left, even this time of year."

In the silence she lay them on the ground and found a jar. She filled it with water from a faucet and brought it back. With her red bony hands, she arranged the flowers in it and set it softly before the headstone. A cough that went into pneumonia so fast it was almost as if he had willed it. She understood. She had not even been surprised. But that had not helped her grief. Her eyes burned as she bent down and brushed fallen leaves from the soil. She straightened up and stood for a while, then went back the way she had come.

She walked with her sharp nose thrust forward, a manner that had intensified with the years. Beneath the woolen scarf wrapped around her head, her long thin gray braid was twisted in its tight, neat knot. Under her loden cape, her cameo brooch of Queen Luise was fastened as always to the front of her blouse. She walked back through the dripping woods and along the motionless river, up the steep, misty streets of the village, up higher yet along the ancient dirt road and through the burg's great wooden gates with their brass nailheads, up higher yet through the tiers of gardens, and into the long manor house, into her silent apartment with its faint smell of gathered apples.

I should have gone with them, Frau Kloppmann realized. For sure I should have gone with them.

She sat up in the dark, on the edge of the sofa that served as her bed, kneading the roll of fat under her chin as if that would somehow lessen the noise. The housing project where she lived with her nephew's widow and two small children had no cellar; whenever the siren started up they had to bump the baby carriage down three flights of stairs and run five blocks, carrying their suitcases, pushing the carriage before them in a swarm of other project residents to a public shelter. And each time they had to run faster, for it seemed each time the interval between the sirens and the raid was shorter. Her niece-in-law was young, thin, and could go like a demon; whereas Frau Kloppmann was round, short-legged, and not so young. She was tired to the bone. The thought of another pounding, gasping race, and her always falling far behind, had made her give an uncertain shake of the head tonight when the sirens started.

"Maybe I'll just stay. What do you think? Should I?"

"Up to you, Auntie," was the brief reply. The child and infant were briskly deposited in the carriage. The door slammed shut.

Frau Kloppmann lay back on her pillow with a sour look. And presently the rumbling began, growing nearer as she sat up on the side of the sofa kneading the roll of fat under her chin. It grew extremely near, like huge blossoming shocks opening in a direct line toward her, and suddenly from directly above there came an intense, plummeting shriek, a downward howl of growing, irresistible, savage force.

"Jesu Maria!" she cried, gripping the blanket with both hands.

An explosion threw her across the room as all the furniture jumped up and came down with a clatter, followed by a ragged crash of objects hitting the linoleum. Then there was silence, in which the building, with faint creakings, settled back into itself.

Frau Kloppmann lay in her wrinkled slip, blinking for a while, covered with fallen plaster. Presently she got unsteadily to her feet, feeling her forehead with her fingers where it had struck the floor. Furniture every which way, jagged pieces of window glass driven into the door, the linoleum a mess of shattered glass, broken lamps and pictures. It was some moments before she realized she could see everything so clearly because the room was lit by a reflection of flames. Stepping around the glass, she went to the empty window, where she saw, through clouds of dust, a beating sheet of fiery orange. It was the other housing-project building just across the walk. She felt the enormous heat on her face and chest, in her ears was a steady, beating roar, embers and sparks came flying in the wind, and looking up at the roof of her own building she saw that it had already caught and was burning.

In the tiny kitchen she rummaged through the tins and boxes that littered the floor, coming up with the squat bottle of cherry brandy her niece kept hidden in the back of the cupboard. It was unbroken. Pulling out the cork, she took a long gulp. Her niece would have been enraged. "Makes no difference now," she said, setting the bottle down and returning to the other room. The brandy had given her strength. "I'd better save what I can," she said, trying to think what her niece would need most. "Only what she's got between her legs." She gave a bitter grunt. Even before he was killed, even while writing those wifely love letters to the front. "Well, I cramped her style good, what with taking over the sofa." Anyway, there was no time to think of saving anything. Sparks had ignited the drapes, they were withering up. Hurriedly she pulled her dress on, yanking it down around the slip she used as a nightgown. All her clothes had gone up in the blast that had destroyed her house. Her niece could provide her with no nightgown. She had none big enough, she said.

Frau Kloppmann stuffed her feet into her shoes, grabbed her coat and bag, and picked up her air raid suitcase, which was filled not with her things, since she had nothing, but with the children's. Muttering "Ach, ach," she crunched across the linoleum in the orange beating light, and at the door turned around for a final glimpse of the small perishing room. Her nephew's picture hung wildly crooked on the wall. Going back, she dropped all that she held and reached up with both hands to straighten it. The cluster of dark oak leaves had fallen from the top of the frame; she found it on the floor and replaced it carefully. Uniformed, smiling, resolute, he looked out at her in the beating light. She touched her fingers to the glass, then gathered up her things and made her way out.

The girl came wheeling the carriage back in the wan light of early morning. Everyone was returning from the shelter, standing around looking at the two big smoldering heaps. Frau Kloppmann gave the girl the suitcase with the children's things. Where will you go? she asked her. Somewhere, the girl said. She did not ask Frau Kloppmann where she would go.

Frau Kloppmann felt momentarily sorry for herself. Her Kurt was dead. Her husband, at his age and with his back, had been drafted. Their house, with everything in it, had been wiped out. Three days a week she had to contribute to the war effort by bicycling across town to a factory where she pasted labels on jars of ersatz marmalade. She was not a good cyclist and wobbled from side to side. On several occasions she had fallen down. Now, in addition to old bruises, she had a lump on her forehead where she had struck the floor last night. No one cared about her or wanted her.

Then her native buoyance reasserted itself. She would go to Burg Veldenstein. She kissed Kurt's two babies in the carriage, shook her niece-in-law's indifferent hand, and got onto her bicycle. Swaying and wobbling, she set off down the street.

In a way it was a comfort to be at the end of your rope. It made everything simple. You had no choices left. After she was bombed out of her house she wouldn't have thought of going to the Schmidts', because she had a relative she could stay with. But now there was nothing left but Burg Veldenstein or getting a bombed-out certificate and being squeezed into the barracks of a camp for the homeless. She would do that when she had rested up at Veldenstein and come back, but she couldn't face it this morning, she was too tired. Tired in her brain, her eyes, her bones. Pedaling was hard work, but at least it required no thought. Just go east. Smoke from the raid filled the gray early-morning sky. There was the usual acrid smell, the usual gritty film of brick dust on her lips. She concentrated on her pedaling, trying not to wobble and fall down.

It wasn't long before she had to get off and rest, standing behind the handlebars panting and wheezing. Around her fires were still crackling, rescue workers still digging. It was piercingly cold, and she was shaking as she climbed back on and continued east. On the busier thoroughfares she was careful not to be bumped by other, better cyclists, people on their way to work, their lunches in briefcases. Gradually her exertion warmed her, she began to sweat. When she stopped again to regain her breath she took off her kerchief, sending flakes of plaster from her tight permanent to her shoulders. She sighed, looking around her. She had to make better time than this if she wasn't going to be caught in the daylight raid. After a night bombing there was often another during the day, around noon, when the sky had cleared of smoke. Climbing on again, bulging roundly from the saddle, she pushed on in the direction of Veldenstein, friends, rest, pumping grindingly along the streets. She was beginning to think the whole idea had been a poor one. How could she possibly cycle all the way to the burg when she couldn't even make her way out of the city?

Other people ride bicycles without any trouble, look at them. Probably I should lose weight, but I was born that way. It hasn't got anything to do with food. I haven't had a decent meal in two years and I'm still fat. I wish I had my bearings better. That can't be the stadium over there—no, the stadium's way back by the park. If it's still there at all. That year I bought my cartwheel hat, that was the best year. There was never anything like it—the drums, the marching, the flowers flying, something so beautiful, so strong and high. I've got to rest again, my calves are killing me. No sign of outskirts yet, seems the city just goes on and on. What's left of it.

But in time, persevering over the handlebars, she found herself in the suburb of Erlangstegen, and shortly after in open country. It was an unremarkable landscape, fields of scrubby brown grass, clumps of leafless December trees. But gazing around her, she realized how long it had been since she had seen anything like it. Fields, trees, no sound except the long twittering of a bird now and then.

The follow-up raid came on time, in late forenoon as she pumped across a stone bridge over the little Pegnitz and took a road alongside the tracks toward Rückersdorf. She had never heard the noise from far off before, it sounded like distant rolling thunder. Pumping alongside a freight train that had stopped, she was startled to see the engineer jump down from the locomotive and three or four people leap from a boxcar—apparently locals who had caught a ride—as a piece of the distant thunder detached itself and grew suddenly brain-splitting. Explosions rocked the ground, dirt and stones flew up in a line alongside the train wheels. Four fighter-bombers swooped up into the air and out of sight. Frau Kloppmann had fallen down, but she bounced to her feet and ran as fast as she could, scuttling behind the others into a field as the fighters turned and came back, again swooping low over the train, this time with a direct hit on the locomotive; and again they roared off, two of them turning and coming back, soaring down over the scattered, flat-lying forms below. Frau Kloppmann, breathless from her run, wheezed into the crook of her arm until a line of bullets ripped through the back of her coat.

One of the three people unscathed, an old handyman with a twisted nose, walked Frau Kloppmann's bicycle all the way back to his village, too shaken to ride, and gave it to his wife. Hers having fallen apart in most of its departments, she was able to put it to good use.

Chapter 85

"I should think they could, don't you, Engelchen?"

"Could what?" he asked, absently chewing a thin slice of whole-wheat bread.

"Take the ponies out this afternoon."

He emerged from his thoughts.

"Gewiss," he agreed, sending a smile across the breakfast table at his wife. "Go for a good ride," he told the children, who gave vent to a small cheer. Quite small, as they were too mannerly to make loud noises at the table.

Sipping her coffee, Frau Quandt thought how familiar was the rosy domestic scene. "Engelchen." Smiles across the table. It was just like the last reconciliation, except that this time both had changed greatly, especially Magda. Her gauntness made you think of the refugees moving in clots along the roads, although in her case it derived from plaguing illnesses rather than lack of food. A severe inflammation of the trigeminal nerve was her present affliction. Under her meticulously applied makeup, the facial muscles could be seen contracting with pain as she chattered with the children. The governess poured herself another cup of the good rich coffee, Goebbels's two personal assistants tried to eat rapidly in order to keep up with him. He was unusually silent today as he mechanically chewed his food. His dark hair had grown gray-flecked at the temples; the deep lines around his mouth looked incised by a knife. His intense abstractedness this morning made Frau Quandt wonder if it had failed, the great counteroffensive unleashed last week, accompanied by the Propaganda Minister's ardent broadcasts assuring the people that the tide would now unquestionably turn. Had this last desperate surge become yet another catastrophe?

"Nein, nein, stay and finish," he told his assistants as he scraped back his chair. Coming around the table, he kissed his wife on the cheek, said a few playful words to the children and went to his study. On the rare occasions that he was able to leave Berlin, he always brought part of his staff along and carried on with his ministry work. He had arrived last night, and would leave again tonight. He would not be able to stay for Christmas tomorrow.

It was a peaceful place for Christmas, the Lanke estate at Bogensee. Situated farther away from Berlin than Schwanenwerder, it lay far from the path of bombers. Magda and the children had been at Lanke since October. They had arrived the same day the Red Army broke through into East Prussia.

Frau Quandt sat relishing her coffee. Magda's food remained patriotically plain, but the excellent coffee had never been replaced by ersatz. Aromatic, full-bodied, strong, it revived the very soul. If everyone in the nation could somehow be provided with one cup of real coffee a week, she thought, it might result in more miracles than all the weapons combined.

The two assistants rose and excused themselves.

"It's beginning to clear," announced one of the children.

Beyond the windows, the sagging dark clouds seemed to be shifting. The children went on with their breakfast. They were all so unobtrusive, so well mannered, and so alike in their precocious intelligence and unusual beauty that one sometimes forgot how different they were from each other underneath, each one a complete, small individualist.

"Could we go right now?" they asked. "Could we go now and not wait?"

"Why not?" Their mother smiled at them. "But wait, wait! Finish your breakfast first."

A few minutes later they hurried off, followed at a dignified pace by the governess.

Magda lit a cigarette over her coffee. She sat looking out at the clearing sky. "Do you suppose we will have a thaw?" she asked.

"I don't know. We might."

"It's been dreadfully cold."

Frau Quandt was not to be put off by pointless talk.

"Have you written Günther yet?" she asked.

She was answered by a small shake of the head, which made Frau Quandt shake her own. Her brother-in-law, Magda's first husband, had offered to provide a refuge for the children by taking them into his home in the Schwarzwald. They would be safe from the bombings—who knew how long Bogensee would remain unscathed?—and they would be safe from the end when it came.

"You know that you're going to have to think about it," she persisted quietly.

"I have thought about it," Magda said, her face undergoing a spasm of pain. "I am going to write him that they will come."

"The offer is for you too, Magda. You know it is," she said with some insistence. "Surely you plan to go with them."

"I cannot. I cannot leave Josef. I have already told you that."

"I don't understand you—never in a thousand years will I understand you. There is no reason on God's earth that you should stay with him."

"There's no point in discussing it!" Magda cut her off sharply, and in the abrupt silence drew deeply on her cigarette. Her long fingers, very thin, were faintly yellowed by nicotine.

And was it Josef whom she could not tear herself from? Frau Quandt wondered as she sat looking across the table at her. For all Magda's "Engelchens" that had blossomed anew since his restoration to the heights, for all her revived and loving smiles, was her refusal to leave him really for him, or was it for the gray-jacketed bosom with its Iron Cross which he had now been reclasped to, and she along with him?

"I'm sorry, Ello," she sighed, turning to her friend with a look of conciliation in her haggard eyes. "I didn't mean to shout."

"That doesn't matter," Frau Quandt said sadly. "That doesn't matter at all."

Goebbels's zoom back to the heights had taken place after the assassination attempt that summer. The whole affair was squashed flat in twelve hours. Even if the bomb at Wolfsschanze had succeeded in killing Hitler, the plotters' failure to take immediate steps in Berlin would probably have doomed their plan of overthrowing the regime. Hours had slipped by in a miasma of broken communications, chance strokes of ill fortune, and general confusion.

"What dilettantes, what dolts!" Goebbels later told his associates. "They had an enormous chance—why didn't they seize the radio stations and spread the wildest lies? They put guards in front of my door, but it didn't occur to them to cut off my telephone. What idiots to let me go right ahead and telephone the Führer and plan the countermove entirely! To hold so many trumps and botch it—what beginners!"

"The German nation," he had broadcast five days after the attempt, "has every reason to draw from the events of July twentieth an even greater certainty of the coming victory of our just cause, which is under God's protection. I am convinced that there is no misfortune and no danger which in the end will not turn out in our favor." In this hour-long speech the Propaganda Minister scaled the very peak of his talents, turning the murder attempt into a God-given sign that the Führer was meant to survive and lead his people to victory, and going from there to the certainty of victory by announcing measures for total war. "Yesterday the Führer issued an order that the whole of public life must be adapted in every respect to the requirements of total war. The comprehensive tasks connected with this gigantic reorganization will be put into the hands of a Reich Plenipotentiary for Total War. At the request of the Reichsmarschall, the Führer has entrusted this task to me, and has appointed me Reich Plenipotentiary for Total War."

Vested at last with plenary power, he threw himself into his new work, introducing a sixty-hour week for war industries, conscripting women into factories, ordering all males under and over draft age, from sixteen to sixty, to serve in the Volkssturm, setting up training centers for boys under sixteen to learn to use bazookas and to man antiaircraft guns, forbidding train travel, closing down theaters and nonessential stores, suspending the printing of magazines, merging newspapers, and organizing the beating of malcontents. Everyone responded to the lash of his authority. Goebbels controlled Germany, while Hitler controlled the war.

Nothing had ever escaped his need to be well informed. Unlike Hitler, he listened to foreign broadcasts, and listened assiduously. Unlike Göring, he carefully read every report that was submitted to him. He despised the Reichsmarschall for refusing to read depressing military reports. He himself was furious if anyone tried to minimize a military failure or obfuscate something that had gone wrong. "How can you influence the public," he would demand, "if you don't even know what you've got to deceive them about?"

With his new powers he expressed himself more freely.

"We've wiped out the Jews—the next thing is to wipe out the aristocrats. They constitute an alien element in the state, and since they marry only among themselves they intensify their degenerate proclivities. Like the Jews they will never cease to cultivate their own caste. They must be annihilated, men, women, children. Root and branch."

The relatives of the conspirators had been sent to concentration camps. While Goebbels approved the dispersal of these upper-bourgeois and noble families, he was vexed that the punishment did not extend beyond immediate families, to aunts, uncles, cousins, nieces, nephews. The totality he would have liked to see was missing. He was better pleased with the uniformity of selection applied to the arrest and incarceration of the several thousand persons implicated in the conspiracy, regardless of whether the implication was so remote as to constitute not even a gossamer thread. A clean sweep could not be discriminatory.

And he was in full agreement with the special punishment of the ringleaders themselves, those representatives of the officer class whom he not only loathed for their act against the Führer but despised as muddle-headed, idle gossips. To be strangled slowly by a deep-cutting thin hempen noose suspended from a butcher's hook was appropriate in the extreme. He readily carried out the Führer's request that a movie camera record the experience of the first batch—the convulsive jerkings, the darkening faces—and had the film rushed to headquarters for the Führer's viewing. But he was far too realistic to suppose, as did the Führer, that the film would meet with general enthusiasm. When it was run before an audience of Luftwaffe officers, they got up and left, as Goebbels could have predicted. The film was then recalled and not shown again. By that time the attempted assassination, in any case, was fading from prominence in the increasing turmoil and stress of the war.

The Allied invasion of France in June of this year, though expected, had been a horrible blow, but the offensive the Germans were planning in the Ardennes was to be the huge stroke that would change everything. The columns waiting to attack through the snowy, craggy region stretched back into Germany for 180 kilometers. Goebbels intensely predicted its victorious outcome, although the previous month he had already ordered ministry documents systematically pulped to prevent them from falling into enemy hands. Over the radio and in his newspapers he poured out his fiery words—a decisive battle, a new turn in the road, ultimate victory—and sent the hopes of the populace soaring. But, after only a few days, it appeared that the battle was lost, and as he sat at his desk in the study at Lanke, he continued to feel the deep sense of dismay that had invaded him yesterday upon learning the bad news. His two assistants, joining him, looked as if they were ashamed of having harbored such high hopes.

"We shall have other opportunities," he told them. "This is not our last!"

As they drove back to Berlin that night, after he had taken leave of his wife and children, he adjusted himself to the failure of the offensive. At least the battle would drag on for a while, upsetting the enemy's timetable for advance into the Reich. And the Reich would keep fighting. Between himself and Minister Speer, he on the human front, Speer on the industrial, they had kept Germany going much longer than might have been hoped. It was extraordinary that despite the increased violence of the bombings, armaments production now towered over the figures attained three years ago in relatively untroubled conditions. The fighting would go on. Speer ground out the metal, he,

Goebbels, inflamed the spirit, and the Führer's will guided them both and all.

There had been a time when the Führer's will had not guided him, when doubts had assailed him, when he had undergone a crisis of faith. After Stalingrad he had believed the war would be lost entirely if it continued on two fronts; and since the Western powers were implacable, it seemed to him that a separate peace should be made with Russia and all Eastern Europe surrendered to her. But to Hitler, giving up the eastern territories would be tantamount to ideological ruin. It was extremely hard for Goebbels, as a dispassionate realist, to watch a whole building go up in smoke for the sake of ideology, when with the use of some cold practical good sense one might save at least part of the building. Hitler's bullheadedness in this matter had badly undermined Goebbels's belief in the Führer's genius, as had his continued reluctance to establish a total war economy, his reasons dating back to the Great War. The Führer's eyes were always riveted on the past. He was narrow, inflexible, unimaginative. Yet each time he saw the Führer in person, and talked with him, all his faith came rushing back—only to dissolve later, leaving him in mental anguish. Was he himself the true author of Hitler's infallibility? Was this godlike figure which he had promoted for the consumption of the public actually his own concoction? A legend which he had created? A myth? And he remembered the novel he had written in his youth, with its haunting line "The greater and more towering I make God, the greater and more towering I am myself." Did I make him? he asked himself. Is there nothing, then, except myself? Only that? Only emptiness? And he regained his faith as directly as a starving man who shoves food in his mouth. The pain was soothed, the terrible emptiness inside him was filled.

With more fervent dedication than ever he worked to keep the Führer's image Olympian, to make it even greater than it had been, so that it would tower as a beacon above the black smoke of a hopeless war.

If the war could not be won, it could at least be fought totally, savagely, to the end, a supreme spectacle of destruction unequaled in history. And such were the Minister's talents that he could toil almost without rest, day and night, for ultimate victory, while at the same time foreseeing only absolute ruin.

He rose at six and usually worked until midnight, frequently interrupted by the necessity to go down into the ministry bomb shelter, where he continued his duties as the walls resonated with the blasts from above. He took little time to eat, gave himself no relaxation, and when he was driven home late to his palace, through five or six blocks of ruins, it was to continue working for another hour or more before turning out the light. He seldom read anything that was not concerned with the war, nor for many years had he opened a novel or volume of poetry, his early fear of being regarded as a bourgeois intellectual having eaten into his habits. That he had once actually laid flowers on the grave of Annette von Droste-Hülshoff seemed a gesture by someone else, a youth of seventeen, his soul aquiver with romantic yearnings, his adolescent heart simultaneously breaking with melancholy and pulsating with joy. How worshipfully he had placed those flowers—the need to worship, how great a drive is the need to worship. He had memorized every line of her work . . . *It lies so still in the light of dawn, as peaceful as a pious conscience . . . deep surge, deep surge of ecstasy, when the cloud dissolves in the blue . . .* but the poems came back to him only in fragments . . . *false, false, always false, his eyes are so distorted that the whites are in front . . . a huge form, growing more and more gigantic, see it step from the tops of the oak trees, moonbeams trembling in its limbs . . . and last of all, I saw myself being drawn into the pores of the earth, like smoke . . .*

Chapter 86

THERE were not many cars in the courtyard, Feldmarschall Milch saw as he parked. That meant that the birthday party was small, which was fitting. An icy blast of wind struck him as he got out, jerking the boars' and stags' heads along the wall. On the drive from Berlin across the flat iron-gray countryside the wind had dealt fierce thuds to the Feldmarschall's car. The drive was north, then east toward the forests. The forests stretched to the horizon. Beyond the horizon the Russians advanced inexorably across Poland.

Cast out into the dark by his Führer—an action readily acceded to by his Air Chief—Milch had since worked under Emperor Speer, very much under, his career virtually at an end. He remained loyal to his Führer, made a point of getting on with Speer, but toward Göring felt only deepest resentment. That he was showing up uninvited for the Air Chief's birthday was somewhat surprising to himself as he plowed through the bitter wind and went inside. Certainly there was an element of shrewdness in the gesture, since a display of goodwill might protect the single post he still held in the Air Ministry; but there was also the urge to act as a reminder, like the skeleton at the banquet, of the fact that the approaching catastrophe might have been avoided if Göring and his ministry clique, his vermin, had not eternally plotted against him and worked for his downfall.

"My congratulations, Herr Reichsmarschall."

Huge, sallow, dressed in a silver-gray uniform, the Reichs-marschall, summoned from the dining room, brusquely shook hands with his ex-deputy, astounded and angry to see him. He had not been invited. He was not wanted. In addition, the Reichsmarschall had only that morning sent off a letter dismissing him from the last Air Ministry post he held. The ex-deputy's blue button eyes were cold, his rosebud lips were curved in a smile, his cheeks were flushed pink. The Reichsmarschall turned rudely.

"You may as well come in."

They walked across the dining room toward the banquet table. Al-though the party consisted of no more than a dozen people, one could see that they were being served a feast of enormous extravagance. The Reichsmarschall gave a shrug as they walked, their heels ringing on the marble.

"The Göring family has always enjoyed a good table. Why deny ourselves now? We'll all be getting a shot in the neck very soon."

Milch saw that it was hardly necessary to play the skeleton at the banquet. A sense of doom hung palpably over the table, despite the ordinary light conversation he sat down to. But it was not a generalized sense of doom he was interested in, it was all the accusations he burned with, his cheeks bright pink as he looked around him. Broad-nosed Loerzer was of course present, and Bodenschatz the Devoted, minus the finger or two he had lost in the conspirators' explosion . . . the explosion had killed Jeschonnek's replacement, General Korten, a good man, Korten . . . bad luck Göring hadn't stood there instead, since Hitler refused to throw him out . . . he would throw out spectacular Milch but not useless Göring—Milch, who might have saved the Luft-waffe through his organizational genius, but not Göring and his filthy clique . . .

So ran the Feldmarschall's thoughts as he began partaking of the birthday feast, a coldly, ironically smiling figure. The Reichsmarschall's gaze rested from time to time on his old enemy with the round icy eyes, the paranoiac smile, the pink flush of supersensitivity . . . he had been flushing pink for years like a machine constantly going off and on, the cherub cheeks burning at every criticism, every real or imagined slight, every obstacle put in the way of the ferocity of his ambition. Well, those cherub cheeks could now burn to the end.

The chandeliers shed their sparkling light on the Botticellian tape-stries, on the lofty windows that looked out on the darkening little lake and windswept forest, and on the small group that sat eating at the long banquet table. There was claret, burgundy, champagne, and duck and venison, and many other dishes, including the last of the *pâté de fois gras* from France, the last of the salmon from Danzig, and the last of the caviar from Russia.

*   *   *

At the Zinna Forest Station two weeks later, Emmy and little Edda, Cilly, Frau Gormanns and Göring's two sisters boarded a special train that would take them south to Berchtesgaden.

Soon after, the evacuation of the art works began. Trucks rolled out of the courtyard bound for the Potsdam bunker which would serve as a refuge for the treasures until they could be sent south. One great shipment went by train to Neuhaus, where, at the little brick station, the contents were unloaded from the boxcars into trucks and driven up the steep cobbled streets to Burg Veldenstein. There they were packed into the underground shelter and throughout the rooms and hallways of the manor house until it looked like a storage depot. Frau Schmidt was not on hand either to protest the clutter or welcome the magnificence which was Veldenstein's due. On a night late the previous November, having unwound her braid, gotten into her nightgown, and climbed into her side of the empty bed, she had turned her head on the pillow as usual, to lie looking at the sky through the east window until she fell asleep. Up here so high, the wind never rested. A thousand years it had been sweeping and booming against this east wall, sweeping the fog along like a river, and the snow, and the rain, and on clear nights scouring the stars, so that they shone unbelievably. The stars over Veldenstein were always brighter than anywhere else. To the old familiar sound of the wind, she fell asleep, and toward morning her heart stopped.

Nikki's death had followed her husband's by three weeks. The Reichsmarschall was saddened, yet among so many deaths, the quiet passing of the aged couple seemed a thing at least natural, right, somehow even good.

At Carinhall the rooms grew increasingly bare. Period furniture thinned, carpets were rolled up and tied, tapestries taken down from walls. Thousand-piece porcelain sets were packed in excelsior, the more valuable books were hauled from the library in fifty cases. Throughout the house was a ringing of hammers as crates were nailed down.

"You fighter pilots have let down your country again and again!" an enraged, metallic voice came blasting out over an airfield loudspeaker. "You have conducted yourselves as cowards and shirkers! In this hour of crisis is it too much to ask that you finally try to find some courage within yourselves? Sacrifice must be made! Sacrifice is demanded!" The Reichsmarschall had recorded this furiously derogatory speech and had disks sent to the remaining area stations with orders that they be played throughout each day at intervals. Hardly more than an officer or two carried out the command even minimally; for the rest, the disks were flung aside to gather dust.

At Carinhall, Emmy had organized and worked hard and long at a system of aiding bombed-out Berlin families, sending them clothing—drawn largely from the stockpiles of the Luftwaffe, which in effect had ceased to exist—and food parcels; but she had not been outside her home for months, and had no real sense of her country's devastation by bombs. The train trip changed that, leaving her grateful for the peace of the Obersalzberg, steeped in silence, the snow covering everything like a vast, pristine pillow. There was little to do in the chalet but sit and wait. Sometimes she thought of the old days, of Weimar, of Rose. It was almost two years since Herr Korwan had written that Rose had got out of Berlin and was safe in Bavaria, where friends had taken her in. But where in Bavaria? Emmy wondered. Munich? Nuremberg? Both had been terribly bombed. Yet why need it be a city? Perhaps Rose's friends lived in the country, somewhere remote. Often she had wondered if Rose was still safe, but the letter she had written Herr Korwan last year had gone unanswered. His address was in an area of Berlin said to be demolished.

No matter if she thought of the past, it all came back into the present. Although Hermann called from Carinhall every night, she had no idea when, if ever, they would see each other again.

"Everything the Führer says about the Luftwaffe is one long indictment of Göring," Goebbels dictated for his morning's diary entry. "Yet he says he cannot afford to make a sweeping change of personnel. He says Göring is totally inadequate and incompetent but no successor can be found, and even if one were, no successor can be nominated." The Propaganda Minister sat back in his chair with a scowl. Protecting the Reichsmarschall's reputation in the eyes of the public was still a firm stand of the Führer. The Führer had even begun to speak well of Göring on occasion, if only retrospectively. For as the present grew increasingly bleak, the Führer's thoughts tended more and more in the direction of the old days. Not long ago he had said nostalgically, "Göring was the best SA leader I ever had. They were a shitheap when Göring got them. He made soldiers of them." Rare as this kind of admiring talk was, and little effect as it had on the Führer's attitude toward the present-day Göring, the Propaganda Minister was not pleased with such misplaced sentimentality. He sat forward, continuing.

"Göring is no National Socialist but a sybarite, and certainly no disciple of Frederick the Great. It is a pity that the Party is represented by Göring, who has as little to do with the Party as a cow with radiology. Bemedaled idiots and vain coxcombs have no place in our war leadership. I shall not rest until the Führer has put this in order. He must change Göring inside and out or show him the door. For instance, it is grossly bad style for the senior officer of the Reich, in the present wartime situation, to strut about in a silver-gray uniform. The Führer is glad that Göring's wife has moved to the Obersalzberg, because she was a bad influence on him. Anyway, Göring's whole family entourage is not worth a row of beans. It encouraged instead of restrained his tendency to effeminacy and pleasure-seeking. By contrast, the Führer has high praise for the simplicity and purity of my family life."

The fact that Göring had been shown the door in all ways except in the retention of his titles did not placate the Minister. No quarter should be given anyone who fell short in his duty to total war. He dictated a few harsh sentiments about the generals, referred cautiously to Himmler, whom he admired for his radical methods—he had done a monumental job with his extermination camps—but despised for his unartistic soul and secretly feared for his ubiquitous and insidious powers, then went on to the Führer, of whom he spoke with intimacy, relishing their trust and closeness, and not failing to record every word of praise from his lips. Also, for the first time he was becoming popular with the people, for whom he continually left his pressing work to visit in person. "I was amazed at their excellent spirit. Nobody cries, nobody complains. Sometimes I have the impression that the Berliners are in a religious trance. Women come up to me and put their hands on me in blessing, imploring God to preserve me. Show these people small favors, and you can wrap them around your finger."

Sitting at his massive desk, sometimes snapping his fingers impatiently if his words rushed out too fast for the stenographer to follow, he drew the morning's dictation to a close. Getting up, he walked back and forth in silence. His face showed deep strain. New lines had been carved by the horrific bombing of Dresden. He planned to propose to the Führer that all Allied airmen in captivity be executed in reprisal for the mass murder of civilians in terror bombings. Private problems also had their place in his thoughts. His wife, whom he had tried to persuade to evacuate with the children, had instead moved from Lanke back to Schwanenwerder. He must try again to make her understand that here in Berlin he would very likely meet his end. That must not be the children's fate, she must go westward with them, they would not be harmed by the Allies. They must leave, and soon.

Sitting down again, he returned to his work as the freezing wind swept along the street outside with its craters and boarded-up windows and mountains of rubble. His was the only ministry building still intact.

Almost Rosenberg never figured in the Propaganda Minister's diary entries these days. Almost Rosenberg was as obscure as a sick owl after three years as Reichsminister for the Eastern Occupied Territories, appointed to this seemingly weighty office by Hitler in order to get him out from underfoot. Although he was ostensibly responsible for the civil administration of the Baltic states, Belorussia and the Ukraine, his powers actually extended nowhere. He was forced to compete with Speer and Sauckel over the labor force, and to fight long and hard and unsuccessfully with the Propaganda Ministry for control of broadcasting and filming in the east. He carried no authority with the Werhmacht, the SS or the police, Himmler in fact being empowered to direct Rosenberg's subordinates on all matters of security. He failed on all sides, beaten down by stronger personalities, including even his own deputies. He struggled on for three years before at last accepting his fate and resigning, his bleak letter of inquiry to Hitler—"I beg you, my Führer, to tell me whether you still require my services, or if I should yield to the assumption that you no longer consider my activities necessary"—having gone humiliatingly unanswered.

He felt that no one had answered him in these three years, no one had listened to him. Admittedly he was the exponent of an eastern policy sharply divergent from the one practiced, believing that these people—who cherished no love for Russia, who had greeted the invading Germans as liberators—should be treated humanely, granted a degree of self-government, and won over as allies in the fight against Russia. He had done what he could to bring about a more moderate program, had tried to diminish the worst ferocities, and although unable to find the courage to protest to Hitler himself, had more than once joined with the Wehrmacht to write scathing letters to OKW Chief of Staff Keitel on the harsh treatment of Russian prisoners of war. But neither as an administrator nor as a moderation seeker did the Party theoretician achieve anything. His Ostministerium slid out of his hands as relentlessly as had his ERR in Paris, until, with little left but his title, he had resigned in the autumn, since then keeping to himself, unvalued, bitter, with heavy recourse to drink.

In the eastern occupied territories, autumn's rain had turned to winter's snow, which lay spread across the land in a heavy blanket. Then came a sudden thaw, gushings and gurglings followed by a steeper plunge of temperature that froze the landscape to dazzling, diamondlike ice. And in the supernatural clarity of the night there might have been heard, out in the woods or in some field, the ghost of an inconsolable scream, a wraithlike note from months or years back, struggling up through the frozen soil into the starlit night. One, ten, a hundred, a hundred thousand, a million, two million machine-gunned in rows or bludgeoned to death like rabbits, from Latvia to the south Ukraine, Jews, Slavs, toppling into hewn ditches. And tracts of land surrounded by barbed wire where Russian prisoners of war had cropped the grass like cattle, devoured their dead, and were found by their advancing compatriots frozen to blue marble in inextricable heaps.

As the onrushing Red Army broke through into Poland and fought its way westward, hectic activities took place in the extermination camps. The Reichsführer SS believed it wise, particularly in view of his hopes to make a negotiated peace with the Western Allies, to erase all evidence of what had taken place. The previous summer he had sent body-burning specialists to do away with the camps' mass graves, enormous pits that had been used for the dead before crematoria had been built. The earliest of these pits had created problems, for the soil above the bodies turned a dark spongy red, spreading a stench of indescribable foulness and polluting wells and ponds through cadaveric poisoning. These early graves had had to be cleared out and the bodies burned. Subsequent graves had been dug to a much greater depth. But now these graves too, for different reasons, had to be excavated. The specialists directed prisoners in digging away the dirt and bringing up the pestilentially offensive contents with the aid of iron hooks, piling the corpses on wooden platforms surrounded by logs, drenching them with gasoline, and setting fire to them. It was a frustratingly slow procedure owing to the many thousand corpses that had to be dealt with, and to the poor flammability of corpses three and four years old. This was a difficulty which did not confront the specialists who were sent to camps where crematoria had never been built. Here among older corpses were those more recent, and these unaged corpses, still possessing a layer of fat, burned well and also saved on fuel, for if the floor of the cleared pit was redug at a slant and the bodies were piled back in and set fire to, the fat flowed downward and could be scooped up in buckets to be flung back over the burning flesh in a hissing conflagration that soon took on the beating whiteness of a furnace.

The last sparks from this giant project did not die until autumn, after which new sparks began flying from the massed belongings of the dead—clothes, umbrellas, dentures, baby carriages—which were dragged out daily from the storehouses and piled in great pyramids. By late January, when the Russians arrived, gas chambers and crematoria had been blown up and all prisoners capable of walking had been herded on foot through the snow toward distant railways. The survivors were ordered into open flatcars headed for the concentration camps of Germany. Only a fraction of the original thousands arrived alive, there to die among others as diseased and emaciated as themselves while winter froze its way on toward spring.

Chapter 87

A few minute blades of grass had broken through the shattered pavement before the Arms Ministry, thrusting themselves up from bared brown dirt among chunks of gray cement. Though it was daylight the sky was darkened by smoke and falling ashes, requiring Minister Speer to light his office with a pair of candles. The electricity was out, as was all the glass in the windows, allowing the bitter cold from outside to pass freely through the room where he sat working in overcoat and gloves.

At the end of the day he climbed into his white sports car and drove out from the side entrance of the partially collapsed ministry, maneuvering around rubble with a fleeting thought of the pillared Baths of Caracalla. The frosty evening air was acrid with smoke and along the streets fire trucks and rescue workers sent up a clamor, yet there was the aura of seeming quiet that always prevailed between bombings, an illusion of silence created by the withdrawal of the mammoth, relentless pounding. Nothing could stop the single ferocious will of the Führer that had prolonged this lost war, and was now intent on total annihilation. Speer had considered killing him.

It had taken the Armaments Minister a very long time to accept that the war was lost. Immersed in production figures, efficiency, achievement, his speeches ringing with faith in wonder weapons, in ultimate victory, his every action directed toward the continuation of the war, he had only recently seen that it was all useless. He had become a sudden possessor of perspective. And so he had thought to introduce poison gas into the above-ground ventilator of the Chancellery bunker which now served as the Führer's headquarters. But faced by insurmountable practical difficulties, he had let the idea come to nothing. He had had to make do with efforts to thwart the Führer's scorched-earth policy, whose administration he was in charge of. Efforts to influence the Führer were useless; the Armaments Minister's new attitude toward the war had cost him Hitler's confidence, and he was treated coolly by Hitler and with open hostility by Goebbels and Bormann. These were the Führer's bosom companions, his consorts in extremism, his two final lieutenants. They would have died too if he had accomplished his ventilation idea. But had he actually meant to see it through, to kill Hitler? It had been more of a fantasy, although the times were drenched in murder. Not just warfare, but murder on a staggering scale.

He was driving through the industrial part of the city now. The factories that were left were still going strong. He knew the production output of each, the number of workers that each employed. The figures were all there in his head: so many Germans, so many Polish, French, Dutch civilians, so many Russian prisoners of war. But this mental ticking-off was automatic, purposeless, since he was not in the area on business but only to pass through. As the outskirts were left behind, the cold rushing night air took on the purity of open country. Behind the speeding car the dull red sky over Berlin gradually grew distant.

Under that sky the factory workers had another hour to go before the night shift took over. The foreign workers were distinctly bonier than their German counterparts, poorly dressed and shod, many given to deep rattling coughs, but in the gargantuan slave labor program there existed every degree of treatment from the paternalistically benign to the starkly inhuman. In Berlin no treatment quite compared to that of the Krupp Works in Essen, where the imported labor marched ten kilometers to work each morning, rag-wrapped feet leaving trails of blood and pus, and returned each evening to a dinner of dirty soup into which the fleas fell from their scabbed and swarming heads to be overlooked in the slurping exigency of hunger.

He parked in the courtyard, turning the ignition off. A crystal moon hung overhead, shedding pale light on the great sloped roofs of the house. What would the mujiks, not more than fifty or sixty kilometers to the east now, make of this rustic Taj Mahal? he wondered. Göring, so he understood, had concentrated his parachute division around the estate, apparently determined to stay on until the last possible moment.

It was not necessary to inform Göring of his plans. Reporting to Göring was an empty formality usually taken care of by a memo, if at all. To come in person and disclose a decision which it was highly inadvisable to mention to anyone—this Speer could not account for in himself as he crossed the courtyard. Perhaps he had a desire to unburden himself generally, and Göring was at least a realist, it was not like talking to the others. But he wondered what his reception would be. He, Speer, the usurper, showing up on the doorstep of the man who had been left his rank and possessions as an act of charity. Probably he should not have come.

He waited in the entryway as a servant telephoned upstairs to Göring. The entryway was bare. Through the door into the grand reception hall he saw a denuded vastness.

Presently the Reichsmarschall came down the staircase in one of his hunting costumes, suede jerkin barely encompassed by a broad belt from which hung a dagger in a jeweled scabbard. Never before had he reached such proportions. The neck bulged, the flabbed chins obscured his collar. He looked ill, deathly tired, but he was not hostile.

They went into a small, partially furnished sitting room, where one servant made a fire while another brought a tray of venison cold cuts and a bottle of Château Lafite-Rothschild. The intimacy that Speer had worked so hard to establish two years ago, on the Obersalzberg, seemed to come of its own tonight. Perhaps it was only because of Göring's weariness. Whatever the cause, his barriers were down.

"Wonder weapons," Speer said. "Goebbels hammers it into them day and night. Wonder weapons. Ultimate victory. But he thinks only of Götterdämmerung. They are all to go down in roaring flames."

"Goebbels," Göring said with a dismissive shrug. "Goebbels is his foot."

"No doubt. But the point is that the people must not be sacrificed further. And this brings me to the reason for my visit, Herr Göring. I have been ordered to do things which I plan not to carry out."

Göring waited, an eyebrow lifted.

"There is no fuel left in Berlin or the other cities. Or only enough for one of two functions: either it goes to the factories to continue manufacturing armaments, or it goes to the hospitals and bakeries for the needs of the people. The Führer has ordered me to give priority to the factories. I have decided to disobey him."

Göring continued looking at him for several moments.

"Mein lieber Herr Speer," he said at length, "I appreciate your point, but where would we end if this habit of countermanding orders should prevail? That sort of thing would spread, and soon you too would be left without any authority."

"I only know that we're now at a point where we must think solely of the nation's survival."

"But surely you can't break your word to the Führer and go against him behind his back?" Göring asked sharply. "Report sick! Or go abroad!"

"But this would defeat my purpose, don't you see?"

Göring's small burst of vitality ebbed away. He shrugged, taking a sip of his wine. Speer was silent for a time.

"I have come to feel a great disappointment in the Führer."

Göring nodded, gazing at the burning logs. "I have often felt the same," he said. "But it's easier for you. You joined him much later than I, and you can free yourself all the sooner. I have much closer ties with him. Many years of common experiences, of struggles, have bound us together . . . and I can no longer break loose."

Later they walked in the park beside the house. The crystal moon had risen in the dark blue passageway of the RAF, which, in an hour or two, would be thundering over. They walked in silence, the Reichsmarschall's tread slow, hands joined behind his back. "Until the fighting ends," he said abruptly, "I must stand by the Führer." Speer gave a small fatalistic nod. He had been wrong to disclose his decision. He would now be reported back to Hitler. "What comes after that . . ." Göring gave a heavy shrug. "For myself, I suppose I can count on a certain degree of friendliness from the Americans. Their press has always treated me favorably, much more so than any other German leader. Also, I have economic ties. Deterding, General Motors . . ."

The unpleasant odor of egomania and self-interest caused Herr Speer not to reply, although had he probed his motives for turning against Hitler, for disobeying his orders, he might have seen that he himself was looking toward the Allied-controlled future, that in part he was guided by the hope of setting himself above the stigma of the inner circle. They came around from the park into the courtyard, where they shook hands by the car. His companion's face in the moonlight, sallow, bloated, seemed to him a picture of degeneracy.

"Incidentally, Herr Speer, you don't have to worry . . . I may be many things, but a denouncer I am not."

Chapter 88

AT night before winding his clock, and in the mornings after dressing, Herr Kropp stood as always looking out the window for a few moments, and these days he was more than ever aware of the silence of the forest. In contrast to the sirens of Berlin, the hasty clatter down the stairs of the palace bunker as the bombs began to fall, and the drive home later through the gray, skeletal, expiring city with its smoke and beating flames that never cleared, in contrast to this, the eternal stillness of the forest seemed to hold something imperturbable, otherworldly.

And the enormous silence of the forest was repeated in the silence of the house. But the silence of the house held a different quality. It was as if the stone and wood embodied tension, as if the long-gathering doom pressed down on the roof, against the walls, clenching itself around these empty rooms that echoed as you passed through them.

He could not escape the thought that his master was something like the house. His master had been scooped out, hollowed, was nothing but hollowness and tension, and had been for a very long time. There were periods of frenzied activity from which he emerged more exhausted and depressed than before. Everything he said was weary, suspicious, bitter.

"Those dunghills . . ."

"That sewer . . ."

"I am taking note of everyone who pisses on me, or just lifts a leg . . ."

"Bormann thinks he can blacken me to the Führer. What can that sow do? His brains are in his scrotum."

And each time he returned from a scene with the Führer, drained of color, pouring with sweat, he had to sit down for half an hour in order to calm his nerves.

"It's downright mental prostitution," he had once uttered after such a scene, and had suddenly buried his face in his hands. "I wish I were dead. I wish I were dead."

His helplessness was like a sickness, and all his sicknesses had broken out in force—the high blood pressure, the heart palpitations, the swelling of the lymph glands, the agonizing pain in the old wounds, in the joints, and even in his face something was breaking out: the size of small peas, two wartlike excrescences under the skin had grown noticeable. The doctor said they were nothing, but to Herr Kropp they were part of the Reichsmarschall's body. And the more debilities he broke out with, the more flesh he accrued, so that he was almost elephantine—he puffed when he went up the stairs, and had to pause every few steps to get his breath. The more vividly and exotically he dressed, the more jewels he covered himself with, the more it seemed to Herr Kropp that the massiveness of his body, and the sicknesses that tormented that body, and the jewelry and gorgeous raiments in which he encased it, all existed around a hollowness, that he was no more than a shell, a husk, and that this had been so for a very long time.

In the evenings Herr Kropp took a tray into the den, the only room in the house that had not yet been dismantled. That was to be left to the very last. The Reichsmarschall had a fire going in the fireplace these cold spring nights. He sat by a lamp in one of his satin robes, sometimes reading, sometimes resting with his eyes closed. In this room from his past which had never changed, he himself had grown lined, warted, coarse, sagging.

In all these thoughts, Herr Kropp passed no judgment. As he had been the soul of loyalty in the days of his master's glory, he was the soul of loyalty to the massiveness and sickness and jewelry that was left.

The wolfish cold abated. Rain began spattering in the courtyard, then splashed in torrents that lasted till the end of day, when birds sang in the clear, dripping sunset. Now in the mornings Herr Kropp saw enormous white sculpted clouds moving across a clear blue sky. He began taking walks outside. Where a few green needles had poked from the ground, there suddenly appeared deep, springy, vivid grass, caught everywhere with pale Michaelmas daisies. Everything was all at once drenched, permeated with spring. Wood doves warbled from budding trees, the silken surface of the little lake shone with skipping sunlight, the air was alive with the resurgent tang of pine.

It was just at this time, simultaneously, that a Russian scout car was spotted in the region, and that the Reichsmarschall's paratroop division was ordered away to man the line south of Berlin.

Many friends and relatives of the Goebbelses had fled from Berlin to Schwanenwerder during the past few weeks. All were dismayed to see Frau Goebbels and her children depart one morning for the city. She was going to visit her husband, who could no longer leave his duties to see her and the children. This seemed to her guests rash and foolhardy, but Frau Quandt was more than dismayed. She stood in the doorway, white to the lips, as her friend and the six children climbed into two open touring cars.

"We are going there to stay," Magda had told her the night before, very calmly. "I will certainly not leave Josef now. I will die with him and the Führer."

The rest of the horrifying conversation Frau Quandt remembered only in scraps. Josef wanted the children taken to safety to the west, but she, Magda, could not allow that. The children were too good, too lovely, for the world that lay ahead. "We will all die," she had said, "but by our own hands, not those of the enemy." And with her enormous calm, she had removed the fingers of Frau Quandt clutching her arm, had kissed her and said goodbye.

She still looked very calm as she sat down in the first of the two cars, arranging the youngest on her lap. For weeks, for months, she had been a nervous wreck. Two operations on the trigeminal nerve had failed to reduce the pain and facial spasms, which had been joined by an abnormal suppuration of the salivary glands, so that she had constantly to gather and swallow her spittle. But this morning, as last night, her eyes, her voice, her gestures were serene. Frau Quandt understood that the decision had brought her a kind of numbed peace. She herself, in the doorway, stood unable to breathe as she lifted her hand in response to the children's waves.

The two big open touring cars rolled down the flower-bordered drive onto the road to Berlin, where they were forced to make their way slowly through crowds of refugees from East Prussia and Pomerania, past laden wagons and straining horses, around overheavy baggage dumped on the roadside. Beyond the sparkling Havel, a great darkness of smoke hung over the capital, while the battering of Soviet heavy artillery came rumbling through the air like the thunder of a spring storm.

In Berlin, at his palace, which he had been working out of since the ministry had received a direct hit, Goebbels was addressing his staff on a subject close to his heart. It was the recently released color film *Kolberg*, a lavish and magnificent reenactment of Gneisenau's and Nettelbeck's victorious efforts to save the beleaguered city of Kolberg from Napoleon's troops.

"In a hundred years' time, gentlemen, they will be showing another fine color film describing the terrible days we are living through. Don't you want to play a part in this film, to be brought back to life in a hundred years' time? Everybody now has the chance to choose the part which he will play in that film. I can assure you it will be a fine and elevating picture. And for the sake of this prospect, it is worth standing fast. Hold out now, so that a hundred years hence the audience does not hoot and whistle when you appear on the screen."

Those he addressed moved their eyes to one another in amazement, not knowing whether to break into laughter or oaths. The Minister, very pale, with burning, intense eyes, with his quick, hobbled walk, went from the room.

In his private apartments he had earlier gathered together his personal papers in several boxes. At the old-fashioned tile stove in the corner, Goebbels's aide began helping him feed in letters, pages of notes, a photograph of the Minister as a child in a sailor suit, his confirmation picture, his grammar-school report cards, each memento crisping, blackening, flying up in sparks. The Minister suddenly paused, looking at a large glossy photograph in his hands.

"Now, there is a beautiful woman," he murmured, showing it to the aide, who recognized the dark-eyed, smiling face as Lida Baarova's.

The Minister stood looking at it several moments longer, then tore it across.

"Into the fire with it."

In his gray military greatcoat, his visored cap on his head, frowning and trying to smile, the Reichsmarschall went from one to the next of his foresters, who stood in a row before him, shaking hands with each and saying a few words of farewell.

Herr Kropp, in his uniform of the National Socialist Flying Corps, standing with three of the Reichsmarschall's aides and his four bodyguards, waited by the cars and trucks in the courtyard of Carinhall. Before taking leave of his foresters, the Reichsmarschall had made his last tour of the house and had walked down to the mausoleum by the edge of the little lake, where he had stayed for an hour. Now it only remained for them to leave.

The Reichsmarschall walked into the courtyard, frowning and silent. He gave a look at the boars' and stags' heads staring before them in the fresh, pine-scented air, at the naked Indian brave on his horse, his arm drawn back eternally with its spear, at the steep thatched roofs, and with a curt gesture of his head walked to the gray Mercedes.

Herr Kropp got in behind the wheel, there was a slamming of car

doors, and the two cars, followed by the trucks, drove out of the courtyard.

On their departure, engineers from Göring's paratroop division
began going through the rooms, soaking the beautiful woodwork and
velvet drapes with gasoline. They had already placed twenty-two mines
throughout the building, from basement to attic, and one in the
mausoleum.

Late in the afternoon a tremendous blast shook the forest. The
great feudal mansion split in two and came raining down in broken
boards.

When a day later Russian troops passed through the region on
their march to Berlin, they came upon what appeared to be the remains of an intense bombing raid. Fragments of masonry and smoldering, blackened boards littered a great area by the shores of a little lake,
sending small spirals of smoke into the sunny air.

Chapter 89

Two days later the vehicles drew up before Göring's Obersalzberg chalet. He climbed tiredly from his car, then hurried forward as the door flew open and the child came racing to him, her mother a few steps behind. He enfolded them in an emotional embrace as Herr Kropp began unloading the luggage, taking out first the large suitcase containing Germany's entire supply of paracodeine pills.

Greeting the other occupants of the house, including Nurse Gormanns, whose face betrayed dismay at his unhealthy appearance, the Reichsmarschall tried without great success to answer their questions. "I spoke to the Führer a few days ago on his birthday, but I don't know what is going to happen. If he is going to come here, he will have to leave Berlin very soon."

And there rose before him Berlin at midday: sunlight blocked by rust-colored dust and acidic black smoke, truckloads of eastern refugees caught in debris-clogged streets, soldiers of fourteen running past in greatcoats that scraped the ground, a frantic clangor of fire trucks mixing with the ponderous *ohhhh voooom, ohhhh voooom* of Soviet artillery, and then the blackened shell of the Chancellery. He had entered the Chancellery garden with its steel-reinforced, SS-guarded bunker door and been let into a passageway whose floor was covered with water laid over by boards, then down into the concrete warren to the small crowded conference room where the Führer was seated at the map table. It was horribly awkward to express congratulations on this birthday, but the Führer seemed not to notice; no doubt he had been the recipient of such awkwardness all day.

The discussion in progress concerned the necessity of his leaving Berlin at once if he was to carry on the fight from the Obersalzberg. The city was almost surrounded. The only open route, to the south, might become inaccessible at any moment.

On the Führer's feldgrau jacket were small grease stains, evidently the result of the unsteadiness of his hand when he ate. His hands lay clasped and trembling before him on the table. For months his hands, along with one leg, had been afflicted by this tremor, which had grown extremely noticeable, as if he suffered from palsy. He was enormously aged, temples grizzled, eyes covered by a film of mental and physical exhaustion. Bent, shriveled, with a voice that had grown hoarse and low, he nevertheless projected the absolute authority of old.

"I have decided that the battle for the city will be fought street by street. If it is necessary to shift military headquarters to the Obersalzberg, then do it. But I cannot call upon the troops to undertake the decisive battle for Berlin if at the same time I withdraw. I shall leave it to fate whether I die here or fly to the Obersalzberg at the last moment."

When the Reichsmarschall asked whether he should send his Chief of Staff south or if he should go himself, the Führer answered with an indifferent shrug, "You go." And later, when they shook hands goodbye, the Führer muttering a few words and turning to other things, the Reichsmarschall could hardly believe that this empty parting might mark the last time they ever saw each other.

Now at the chalet, he sank into lethargy, waiting for the end.

On the second day his Chief of Staff arrived from Berlin with the news that Hitler was determined to die in the bunker, and that he had said, although not officially, that the Reichsmarschall could carry out negotiations better than he.

The Reichsmarschall was neither flattered, knowing the contempt in which Hitler held peace negotiations, nor pleased. His adjutants agreed that it was a low trick to indicate a step without command or clarification. As the Führer's legal successor—unless the successorship had long since been turned over to Bormann—was he to act now? Was he to interpret the Führer's decision to remain in the beleaguered city as a situation requiring his successor to take over? Or was he to infer that he should wait to act until the Führer was dead? Was the Führer in fact alive or dead? And if the Führer was still alive, how could the Reichsmarschall send a message asking: Shall I act now or wait until you're dead? And what about Bormann, his deadliest and most active enemy—what if Bormann had been appointed successor?

A discussion with another old enemy, Lammers, Chief of the

Chancellery for Political Affairs, who was also on the Obersalzberg, revealed that the decree of successorship had not been altered since it had been drawn up.

That still left the difficult message to be written. If Hitler was alive, the Reichsmarschall wanted his approval to act on his own. If Hitler was not alive, if there was no return message by ten o'clock that night, he would go ahead with negotiations. Laboring over one draft after another, he finally completed a message both clear and tactful and dispatched it by radio. He also sent messages to Ribbentrop and Keitel to report to him as soon as possible unless they received contrary instructions from the Führer.

A little past noon, Minister Speer came down into the bunker, Bormann, his *bête noire*, at once materializing at his side to ask him if he would try to persuade the Führer to fly south to the Obersalzberg before it was too late. Bormann clearly did not wish to stay here and die, and his imploring manner brought a strong sense of satisfaction to the young Minister, who walked on wearily to Hitler's quarters. He had been traveling for ten hours by car and plane from Hamburg—the pilot setting down before Brandenburg Gate—on the sudden and overwhelming urge to see the Führer one last time.

The visit was flat. When he confessed that he had never carried out his scorched-earth orders, the Führer's eyes filled with tears at the betrayal, but he said nothing. It was as if everything was beyond him now, a remoteness had settled into the sagging, colorless face. He did not order execution for having disobeyed a Führerbefehl, nor did he show a shade of warmth in the knowledge of the perilous flight into Berlin that had been made for his sake.

Speer went back out into the corridor, with its rusty brown walls seeping moisture in places, and was passed by Bormann stepping hurriedly to Hitler's open door with a radio message in his hand. "Mein Führer! Göring is launching a coup d'état!" Hitler took the communication, reading it without response; but a few minutes later there was another message from the Reichsmarschall, this time addressed to Ribbentrop. "It's clear that he is engaged in treason, mein Führer! Already he is sending telegrams to members of the government and announcing that he will assume your office at ten o'clock!"

Looking in from the door, Speer saw that this time Hitler was violently shaken from his disinterest.

A light snow had begun to fall on the Obersalzberg when the Reichsmarschall was brought a return radio message from the Führer.

YOUR CONDUCT AND STEPS TAKEN BY YOU ARE A BETRAYAL OF
MY PERSON AND THE NATIONAL SOCIALIST CAUSE. I AM IN

FULL POSSESSION OF MY FREEDOM OF ACTION. I FORBID ANY
FURTHER STEPS.

HITLER

He was still stunned by the accusation of betrayal when a second
message arrived.

YOUR CONDUCT DESERVES DEATH. IN VIEW OF YOUR PAST SER-
VICES I ALLOW YOU THE OPPORTUNITY TO RELINQUISH ALL
YOUR OFFICES AND TITLES ON THE PRETEXT OF ILLNESS.

HITLER

And he was still reeling from this when, as evening fell, a sound of
vehicles and voices took him to his study window, from which he saw
that the house was being surrounded by SS.

A few minutes later, with Robert trying to bar their way with his
body, the two senior SS commanders of the Obersalzberg area entered the room, revolvers drawn, and arrested him on charges of high
treason.

Herr Speer stayed on in the bunker as evening turned to night
and night to early morning. For a long while he had been unable to
leave because of a heavy RAF raid above, but even afterward he had
remained, unable to bring himself to depart until he had said a final
farewell to Hitler. It was four in the morning now, although down
here, in this harsh electric glare, there was no difference between day
and night. He passed a pair of generals, some adjutants, SS orderlies—
with the exception of Goebbels and Bormann, everyone of the highest
rank had left.

He stood before the tremulous, terribly aged man to whom he had
dedicated his life twelve years before, and began to say goodbye.

"So you're leaving? Good," muttered the Führer. "Auf Wiedersehen."

Climbing up the bunker stairs, he knew that the Führer's final
coldness was due to his, Speer's, halfhearted offer to remain at his side.
So feebly spoken, so lukewarm. It would have been better if he had
said nothing. He felt deepest shame, yet at the same time he experi-
enced an inner rush of thankfulness to be coming out of this catacomb
where Frau Goebbels lay in her bed suffering from heart attacks, her
husband walked about expressing himself on eternal glory, Fräulein
Braun sat in her room sipping champagne, and the Führer vacillated
between suicide and eleventh-hour faith in illusionary armies.

Confined to his room under house arrest, unable to communicate
with his family or adjutants, without access to his pills, the ex-

Reichsmarschall passed the hours in physical and mental torment. It could not be the Führer, he told himself, it had to be Bormann. But whether the Führer or Bormann, the punishment for high treason was death. It was the final, the foulest blow, to die as a traitor. The grinding pain in his hip and leg, pains everywhere, stomach cramps, all due to the sudden cut-off of his pills, were almost a blessing in that they distracted from the immeasurably worse mental pain.

On the morning of the third day a sudden sweeping roar grew out of the gray sky, followed by the hurried ring of boots, the door flung open, the SS herding him and everyone else down into the cellar as the mountain rocked with explosions.

High above the snow-striated glaciers and snow-patched slopes, coming for a full hour in wave after wave, three hundred RAF bombers rained down tons of explosives on the small squares of buildings that marked Hitler's mountain retreat. When the last planes roared out of sight, the entire plateau was cratered like the moon.

From the cramped cellar of the chalet, captors and captives made their way outside, united in shock. A bomb that had hit the swimming pool had torn away half the house. For a while they all stood together in the throbbing silence. Then the captors took up their positions again. Just before the bombing, they had received a radio message from Reichsleiter Bormann.

THE POSITION IN BERLIN IS MORE TENSE. IF BERLIN AND WE SHOULD FALL, THE TRAITOR OF 23 APRIL MUST BE EXTERMINATED. MEN, DO YOUR DUTY. YOUR LIFE AND YOUR HONOR DEPEND ON IT. BY ORDER OF THE FÜHRER.

BORMANN

"And you—why have you worked with me? Now you'll have your little throats cut! But when we step down, let the whole earth tremble!"

Although nerves were at the breaking point, Goebbels was generally calm. Intense, but perfectly in control. What he had just snapped at his two aides was followed by a contemptuous shrug of his narrow shoulders. He went off to work on his newssheet, *Der Panzerbär,* while his wife, sitting at a table in the corridor with one of Hitler's two secretaries, conversed about ordinary things, as if she were in her own living room. She had recovered from her hysterical breakdown of the first day. Fashionably turned out now in the one dress she had brought with her, midnight-blue with snowy collar and cuffs, elegantly ankle-length, with every wave of her blond hair perfectly in place, her gaunt face very discreetly made up—the Führer disapproved of cosmetics—she presented a serene and dignified appearance. Only her constant swallowing, caused by the disorder of her salivary glands, betrayed the unbearable tension within.

When the secretary said goodnight and went to lie down—she and the other secretary slept outside the Führer's door in sleeping bags—Frau Goebbels realized that it was two o'clock in the morning. Time was completely scrambled down here in this glaringly lit cave, with its walls of brown rust or battleship gray, its smell of damp cement, mustiness, coming death.

Swallowing, she took herself along the corridor toward the concrete stairs leading to the first level, hoping that she would not run into Fräulein Braun. The woman's presence was insufferable.

In the morning she rose exhausted, having been unable to sleep, but was determinedly cheerful as she went into the children's room to help them dress. With no maid or governess, she had taken up this task herself, gladly but not well. It seemed sometimes, when she buckled a shoe or combed a skein of silken hair, that her fingers melted, lost all strength, that she could not breathe. The two secretaries helped her, and she was grateful. She was also grateful that the children were in good spirits. They played ball in the corridors, explored the maze of tiny rooms; and when the walls shook, she told them that it was caused by the rescuing troops who were growing near, and that in a few days, when victory was won, they would all fly to the Obersalzberg with Uncle Führer. This thought gave them much pleasure, for they had never been in an airplane.

One day an aviatrix appeared. Unbelievably, she had managed to fly into the city with General von Greim, whom the Führer appointed the new Commander in Chief of the Luftwaffe. The aviatrix was very famous, and very kind. She played with the children and taught them how to yodel in the Tyrolean fashion. Then she and the new Luftwaffe chief were gone, too, but not before witnessing a tremendous scene by the Führer, which she had described to Frau Goebbels.

"It was terrible, terrible. There was a radio message that Himmler had offered to surrender Germany unconditionally to the Western powers. I happened to be there in the corridor when it came. The Führer was beside himself with anguish and fury—he raved about Göring, said that he had always known he was corrupt and degenerate, a drug addict, he had ruined the Luftwaffe, ruined everything, then had the gall to try to replace him, he said he always knew that Göring was at heart a traitor. 'But Himmler, der treue Heinrich!—and now he has betrayed me too!' he said. 'Hess left me. Speer is gone. Göring has betrayed me. And now Himmler. There are no disappointments or betrayals that I have not experienced! Nothing is spared me! Nothing!' It was dreadful to hear him in such torment."

They all fall away, Frau Goebbels had said to herself as she listened. One by one they fall away, but we shall not fall away.

Whenever her resolution ebbed, when her heart palpitations returned, and the facial spasms grew worse, and the suppuration of the salivary glands became unbearable, she took from the bureau in her room the Führer's Golden Party Badge and called back the moment when he had risen from his desk, stooped, shaking, ill, this crushed, expiring great man, and with his own hands pinned the badge to her jacket. Under the dull glaze of exhaustion, his eyes looked into hers as strong as ever, those eyes of immense depth and life, as if you could drown in them, and in them was a glow of gratitude, of love that spoke of a bond everlasting. The concrete cubicle they had stood in, with its cold gray walls, had for an instant expanded in a vastness of light, become sheer radiance.

And this, when she tenderly closed her hand around the badge, was what sustained her.

While above the tiny room in which Frau Goebbels sat, above the ten meters of concrete and soil, above the ruin of the Chancellery still relentlessly cannonaded, the air was choked with phosphorus fumes and hot ashes. The falling ashes had covered what had once been the wild back gardens that stretched to Hermann-Göring-Strasse, trees and bushes and blooms now metamorphosed to a field of craters and rubble. A few blocks beyond, the enemy had reached the Tiergarten. Volksturm troops fought savagely, but were falling back as they had been falling back for days, their numbers slashed away from hour to hour.

Through the confusion of refugees and retreating troops that clogged the road south of Salzburg, a small convoy of cars and trucks with an SS motorcycle guard gradually came clear as it left the valley and began climbing. The convoy had been on the road for a day and a half, crawling from traffic jam to traffic jam on a trip that would normally have taken two hours. Göring was in the first car, alone except for his captors—his adjutants had been taken to the SS barracks near Salzburg—relatives and servants in the following cars, luggage and possessions from Carinhall in the three trucks bringing up the rear.

Sitting next to Göring, the SS commandant was in the grip of the chaos that had surrounded them on the roads. Everything was breaking up. He was under orders to execute his prisoner when Berlin and the regime fell, but when Berlin fell—and perhaps it had already fallen—who would be left in power to see if the order had been carried out? Why kill Göring now, at the very end? What purpose would it serve? It was not as if he, himself, believed Göring was a traitor. But the order had been given. The commandant brooded over this matter as the car slowly maneuvered the ice-covered mountain road. He was not sure that it was a good idea to be going to Mauterndorf, the Reichsmarschall's Austrian residence, but there had been no choice after the Obersalzberg house had been wiped out and they were forced to move into a mine entrance. Men, women, children, everyone crowded in, no beds, no water. Three days had been enough, they had to go elsewhere. Now like refugees themselves, they had been on the clogged roads for thirty-six hours. He rubbed his eyes, widened them, tried to keep them open.

The former Reichsmarschall, in a travel-creased gray uniform, his heavy jaws unshaven, sat looking from the car window at the steep meadows passing by. In the late-afternoon sun they were a vivid, burning green-gold, with long violet shadows from trees and cows running down them like ribbons. The air was clear, windy, and grew windier as they mounted.

At the top of the pass everything was crude, savage, wild—blinding masses of snow, boulders big as houses, coarse brown grass whipping, the sky immense, just as when he had come to this height the first time, in Pate's big open carriage.

Dr. Goebbels raised his champagne glass to the newly married couple, smiling his frank, attractive smile, which was his best feature. He was sincerely happy for his Führer, and he was glad that the woman who would die at the Führer's side, this fluffy-haired nonentity in her black taffeta gown, would not enter upon the historic suicide as insignificant Fräulein Braun but would be raised to the stature of Frau Hitler. And he felt satisfaction in the dramatic setting of the marriage, the extreme contrast between the champagne, the phonograph music, the bride's radiant face, and the continual shaking of the bunker walls beneath the last convulsions of the city.

While Frau Goebbels, her facial spasms and her swallowing severe, was able to produce gracious words only by remembering that this woman was capable of offering up but one single life. Frau Hitler she might be, but it was not in her power to make the tormenting, the overwhelming sacrifice of a mother, which only she, Magda, could make.

The rest of that day and the next, Frau Goebbels kept very much to her room. She did not know if she would learn by way of a shot ringing out, or by her husband coming to tell her, or by a sudden instinctive certainty within herself. It was the latter: as if all at once she knew of the scraping, shuffling footsteps on the concrete stairs at the far end of the lower bunker, of the struggle of several men carrying a heavy burden.

Goebbels stood below, watching with narrowed, moist eyes as the three SS guards labored upward with the Führer's still-warm body. Behind them, the lighter body of the bride was being carried by the Führer's chauffeur. As the Führer's body was borne higher and higher up the stairs toward consumption by a funeral pyre, the familiar black trousers and one sleeve of the feldgrau jacket were all that Goebbels could see. Then he too began the climb, to help with the burning of the two bodies.

Twenty-four hours later, he and his wife prepared for their own departure. After doing the thing which had to be done—he had gone into an empty room and waited, his head in his hands—his wife had returned ashen, red-eyed, wringing her hands until it seemed she would break all the bones in them.

Frau Goebbels had not stopped thinking of what she had done for the space of a second, but finally she accepted it as unalterable. The doped chocolates, the anguished wait for them to take effect . . . the little teeth were crisp against her fingers, the jaws opened effortlessly. She had laid the capsule between the back teeth, then gently brought the jaws together, crushing it. She smoothed back the fine hair each time, and kissed the beloved lips, which emitted a bitter almond scent.

Afterward, she went to her room, where slowly she pinned the Führer's Golden Party Badge to her coat front. She drew on the coat, buttoned it, smoothed the collar and returned to her husband, who had put on his long uniform overcoat. Around his neck was a white silk scarf. He adjusted his gold-braided hat and drew on his gloves, carefully smoothing each finger. In her hand was a capsule, in his coat pocket a revolver. He gave her his arm, like a cavalier, and together, in silence, they walked past the closed door of the children's room, down into the lower bunker and to the concrete stairway where Goebbels's adjutant and chauffeur stood waiting with the cans of gasoline. The couple paused before the stairway, then resolutely, if slowly, leaning a little toward each other, they began mounting the steps.

At Mauterndorf the sun rose over the mountain peaks, touching the gray valley below with gleams of morning. Unable to sleep, Göring stood at his window, looking out as the trees and meadows came clear. Putting on a robe, he walked through the sleeping castle into the courtyard with its rustic, splashing fountain and paced in the fresh air under the observation of two SS guards with carbines. He was not permitted to go farther than the courtyard.

The radio was his only contact with the outside world. He had already heard the announcement that he had resigned from all his offices because of a serious heart condition. He had heard that Mussolini was dead, that German forces in Italy had unconditionally surrendered, that Munich had been taken.

This morning after breakfast, he and his wife sat down again by the radio. Because of the mountains the reception was poor, and they had to listen carefully through the static. ". . . People of Germany, we ask you to stand by for a most grave and important announcement," issued a scratchy voice, followed by the crackling of somber music. "Yesterday, on the thirtieth of April, fighting Bolshevism to the end, the Führer fell in Berlin . . ."

He felt a sudden weakness in all his bones: not shock, or sorrow,

but overwhelming strangeness. "He's dead," he murmured, getting up
slowly and going to the window. "He's dead, Emmy." He stood looking
out the window for a long moment, then said with bitterness, "Now I'll
never be able to vindicate myself. I'll never be able to convince him that
I was loyal to the end."

The next day Berlin fell. He kept to his room, in a state of deepest
despair as Germany's total collapse grew near. And Veldenstein, he
thought, was Veldenstein still standing . . . or had those walls, after
surviving a millennium of wars, been laid waste by the ferocious bombings of these final weeks? Destruction and defeat saturated his
thoughts. But after a few days, with access to his paracodeine pills, and
with the realization that his SS guards were growing negligent and preoccupied with their own fate, his spirits began to revive. On the morning that a Luftwaffe signal unit came tramping across the little wooden
bridge and liberated him from his unmindful captors, he entered a
state of extreme euphoria. At once he sent off a radiogram to Admiral
Dönitz, whom Hitler in his last moments had designated his successor.

> . . . I HAVE JUST LEARNED THAT YOU INTEND TO SEND JODL TO
> EISENHOWER WITH A VIEW TO NEGOTIATING. I BELIEVE THAT
> IN THE INTERESTS OF OUR PEOPLE IT IS IMPORTANT THAT I
> ALSO OFFICIALLY APPROACH EISENHOWER. MY SUCCESS IN ALL
> IMPORTANT NEGOTIATIONS ABROAD, WHICH THE FÜHRER AL-
> WAYS ENTRUSTED ME WITH BEFORE THE WAR, IS SUFFICIENT
> GUARANTEE THAT I CAN CREATE THE PERSONAL ATMOSPHERE
> APPROPRIATE FOR JODL'S NEGOTIATIONS. MOREOVER, BOTH
> GREAT BRITAIN AND AMERICA HAVE PROVED THROUGH THEIR
> PRESS AND RADIO THAT THEIR ATTITUDE TOWARD ME HAS AL-
> WAYS BEEN MORE FAVORABLE THAN TOWARD OTHER GERMAN
> POLITICAL LEADERS. AT THIS MOST DIFFICULT HOUR, NOTH-
> ING SHOULD BE NEGLECTED WHICH MIGHT ASSURE THE FU-
> TURE OF GERMANY.
>
>   GÖRING, REICHSMARSCHALL

Lack of response did not deter him. "I'll go to Eisenhower myself,"
he told his wife. "I don't need Dönitz. I'll put myself in touch with the
Americans and they'll set up the meeting. Robert, we're packing!"

Herr Kropp had not seen his master in such soaring spirits for
years. Although he was a physical wreck, and was chewing his pills
without stop, there was about him a radiance that belied his sickly pallor, and Herr Kropp was glad to take fire from this resurgence of the
old vitality. He even chided him, most happily, on the old subject. "If
you're going to negotiate the peace, sir, you had better get a haircut
first. You look as if you'd just come off a desert island."

"So I have." The Reichsmarschall smiled, bustling around the room. "So I have. A desert island for too many years. But now that's all changed. And I shall see that we're given an honorable peace, and honorable terms. I shall see that Germany is treated justly."

By noon the luggage had all been reloaded, everyone was ready. "One last thing," the Reichsmarschall said, going over to one of the trucks. He knew that his art treasures were lost to him; two loaded freight trains stood in a tunnel near Berchtesgaden, probably being looted this very minute, the rest stored in salt mines near Salzburg. Of the art works he had with him in the trucks there were a few he wanted to give into special safekeeping—a Roger van der Weyden Madonna, a Burgundian primitive, and Memling's luminous little quartet of musician angels. These he put with his wife's personal possessions, then the convoy that had climbed over the Tauernpass a week before started back along the same route to meet up with the American Army.

The roads were even more chaotic now, clogged with tanks, trucks, horse carts, civilians, soldiers on foot, all churning up dust in the suddenly warm spring weather. Whenever the Reichsmarschall was recognized, soldiers fired their last round of ammunition into the air and came crowding up to shake hands with him through the car window, crying "Heil der Dicke!" after him as the car moved on.

It was near Radstadt, in a traffic entanglement, that the first Americans were sighted. The Reichsmarschall climbed out of his car in the clamorous, dusty air and returned the salute of an officer who was rapidly approaching him through the noise and confusion. In his blue-gray uniform he stood immense and straight, wearing only three decorations: the Iron Cross, the Golden Air Medal and, around his neck on its black-and-gray ribbon, his Pour le Mérite.

Chapter 90

O F the scavenger birds attracted to Nuremberg, ravens were the most numerous. They were at their thickest on holy property, in the open ruins of churches and adjacent remains of old graveyards. They also had a predilection for the few trees still standing along the Pegnitz, on whose branches they clustered so heavily as to appear a black foliage. Others perched in gapped rows along broken walls, or gazed through the stillness from pyramids of debris. In the hot summer months following the war's end in May of 1945, the smell of death had been overwhelming; even now in the rainfalls of March, almost a year since the end, there still existed a strong claim by the Nurembergers beneath the rubble, a putrid sourness shot through with the tang of quicklime.

Most of the correspondents and trial staff were lodged in the former Hotel Reichsparteitag. The badly damaged building had been hurriedly patched up for occupancy, so hurriedly that some doors still opened out into space; nor had there been time to put down other rugs in place of those patterned with interlocking Hakenkreuze, or to substitute new knives and forks for those with their engraved Hakenkreuz-Adler embellishments. To the hotel occupants it seemed there was no escape from the doomed men in the Palace of Justice dock, escape neither from the past nor the present. Two extra cocktail bars had been built off the lobby, but despite these, despite entertainers flown in from Paris—singers, jugglers, mimics—nothing could efface the sense of death that had been and of death to follow. Liquor flowed, feverish romances were struck up, the singers sang and the jugglers juggled, and each night the artificial activity beat on into the small hours, after which the dead silence of the hotel joined the dead silence surrounding it.

Each morning the occupants climbed into limousines, jeeps and military buses to jolt over the two kilometers of cleared road that separated the hotel from the Palace of Justice. There—and they had done this for more than a hundred days already—they sat down to endure seven solid hours of listening. Their ennui had grown to crushing proportions, but it began to dissipate as the testimony of the defendants, beginning with that of the chief war criminal, grew near. Everyone felt a renewal of interest and alertness in anticipation of Göring's taking the stand.

The weekend, however, intervened. As always it was dull. It was also wet. People wandered around the hotel lobby, they sat drinking in the three bars, a few showed new arrivals the sights. The eternal crowd of beggars stood in the drizzle outside the entrance, patient and well behaved, waiting to surge forward at the sight of a flicked cigarette butt. Today, Sunday morning, the beggars watched a small group come out through the revolving glass doors, behind which could be glimpsed the heated, chandelier-lit interior. The group walked past, no one smoking, no one throwing a butt, and set off across the rubble. Why anyone would want to leave the hotel those who stood shivering outside did not know.

The members of the group put up umbrellas as they crunched along. There was not much to see, it was all the same. They passed a thread of smoke rising from the debris, some cave family cooking their meal. They passed a house sheared in two, still inhabited, canvas hung across the gaping rooms. A few fronts of buildings stood perfectly intact, with nothing behind them. These the group avoided because, as the newcomers were told, they had a habit of collapsing without warning. Indeed, as the visitors passed in the vicinity of one they heard something like a sigh—perhaps set off by their footsteps—and the ancient half-timbered building front disintegrated before their eyes, fell down in an avalanche of bits and pieces with a resounding crash and a high sweep of dust into the wet air, after which everything was again silent.

They walked on to St. Lorenzkirche, standing as a landmark in the surrounding flatness. Though the church was roofless, partially caved in, its great arched doorway was untouched, and here they stood like tourists before the carved Gothic stonework. Once in a while, the newcomers were told, the cathedral bell could be heard—perhaps it was a priest still living in the ruin who pulled the rope, or scavenging children, or perhaps it was imagination. They loitered, wanting to hear Sunday bells. Then because of the dampness and cold, because of the smell, because of everything, they began their slow way back under their umbrellas. Suddenly from behind them there came a peal, and they turned to see hundreds of ravens flapping up from inside the roofless structure, flapping and cawing as the bell pealed again, and, as the reverberations died, settling in their flapping, cawing hundreds in the adjacent graveyard.

He woke to silence. For a while he lay looking at the guard's face that looked at him from behind the wire mesh window in the door. It was a young face, impassive beneath its khaki cap. The jaws worked slowly, revolvingly, on a wad of chewing gum.

"What time?" the prisoner asked in English.

The guard gave a look at his watch. "Quarter past three."

The prisoner adjusted his head on the folded trousers that served as his pillow and closed his eyes. He lay listening to the steady spattering of rain against the celluloid of the cell window, but the sound did not put him to sleep. His eyes opened again. Tonight, when he needed his rest most, he was unable to sleep except in snatches. Tonight he found it hard to sustain the flat, mummylike position required. His fingers, stiffened by the cold, drummed on the blanket. Illumined by the lamp set at its oblique angle behind the wire mesh, the blanket was the color of pumice stone, as was everything in the cell, everything as clear as if drenched in moonlight.

After five months he was no longer disturbed by the absence of darkness at night, or the absence of light in the morning. The cell's gray tones had become his accustomed environment. Only when he entered the courtroom each day did he realize the dimness in which he lived. The first time he had stepped inside the courtroom he had felt blinded, not only by the brilliant lighting but by a rush of blood to his head, by such a heightening of strain and excitation that for a moment he was not even aware that he was walking forward.

Then he had been aware of everything—faces, tables, spaciousness, above all spaciousness—a vastness of light and life pouring in as he walked the few steps to the front of the prisoners' dock, the others following, and sat down at the end of the bench. His eyes, even before adjusting to the brightness, were moving rapidly around the room.

The four Allied flags stood furled against the opposite wall, before them the judges' table, as yet unoccupied. A battery of prosecutors, defense lawyers, court stenographers, and to the right the international press section. Some of the correspondents had equipped themselves with opera glasses or binoculars, all of which were trained on his face. That was as it should be. Inside a large glass cubicle set into the opposite wall stood a bevy of photographers and newsreel men. Hence the glaring brightness of the lights around the dock, so strong it was already creating an uncomfortable heat. One would get used to that. To the left of the dock, behind a long glass partition, sat a line of interpreters with headsets and microphones: the proceedings were to be translated simultaneously into four languages. He picked up the earphones beside him, but of course nothing had yet begun. Impatiently he put them down and swung around on the bench for a look at the others.

He knew from the exercise yard the appearance of each, but he was not prepared for the collective jolt. Exceptions, to be sure, but the overwhelming effect was drabness, bentness, gloom. Rising halfway from his seat, he sent a blistering glower down the two rows of men. Some responded with a hostile look, most straightened up at once. That done, he again occupied himself with the chamber before him. It was the principal courtroom of the Palace of Justice, a building connected with the jailhouse by an enclosed catwalk which only a few minutes ago they had filed through, handcuffed, under guard, a dim wooden tunnel with a few chinks of daylight like diamonds. At the end was an iron door, unlocked and opened by a double guard with carbines. Here in the courtroom the guards were in their Sunday best: white helmets, white belts, looped gold lanyards. Seven stood at the back of the dock, a dozen more were posted throughout the room. Heavily bomb-damaged and hastily repaired, the room was a contrast between the old original dark-paneled walls and a renovated interior whose furnishings, modern and angular, were of pale reddish-blond wood. Covering the entire floor was a thick beige carpet. No sound was made as people walked across this carpet or chairs were pulled out. All that could be heard was a dim murmur of voices and a continual rustling of paper.

The strain of waiting was growing unbearable. As his eyes roved and darted he was constantly clearing his throat, which felt cobwebbed by the long solitude of his cell. Not only the heat of the lights made him wipe his forehead, but strain, the pressure of energy screwed to battle pitch. Under the now too large, sagging tunic of his dove-gray uniform, stripped of its rank and insignia, the sweat trickled from his armpits.

The bailiff's voice rang out: everyone rose. The judges filed in and took their places at the long polished table, two seating themselves before the Russian flag, two before the British, two before the American, two before the French. The Russians were in uniform, all the others were black-robed except for the presiding judge, who was in crimson robes—a bald, middle-aged Englishman with a heavy, precise face, who, without further ado, raised his gavel and brought it down.

The reading of the general indictment began.

"The United States of America, the French Republic, the United Kingdom of Great Britain and Northern Ireland, and the Union of Soviet Socialist Republics versus Hermann Wilhelm Göring, Rudolf Hess, et cetera, defendants . . ."

He sat listening to the voice coming through his earphone, to words he had studied so often in his cell that he knew them almost by heart. After a while, impatiently kneading his brow, he realized that the entire indictment was going to be read, a hundred and thirty pages. The sound of the voice droning in his earphones became like that of a fly buzzing against a pane of glass, stupefying. When it finally ended four hours later, and earphones were removed throughout the room, there was an audible sigh, a weary stretching of legs on the beige carpet, a resettling in chairs. Then the earphones were all put on again. He straightened his tunic, which clung to his damp sides, and once more cleared his throat in preparation for his speech. But what now followed was the reading of the individual indictments.

Gott, will it never end! he thought.

Another hour passed before the individual indictments had been read and at last the presiding judge addressed the court in a dry, withered, precise voice. "I will now call upon the defendants to plead guilty, or not guilty, to the charges against them. They will proceed, in turn, to a point in the dock opposite the microphone." There was a short pause, then: "Hermann Wilhelm Göring."

He heard the ring of his boots on the dock floor as he made his way past knees and feet. He took hold of the cold metal rod of the microphone and cleared his throat a final time. He felt the words mounting from his very loins. "Before I answer the question of the high court as to whether or not I am guilty—"

"I informed the court that the defendants were not entitled to make a statement. You must plead guilty or not guilty."

For a moment he did not speak at all, his knuckles whitening around the metal rod. Then he brought out with rapid harshness: "I declare myself in the sense of the indictment not guilty!" Returning to his place he sat down furious, flushed, crossing his arms. The calling of the defendants proceeded.

"Rudolf Hess."

His seatmate rose with an absent expression and went with his hunched, scuttling walk to the microphone, where he gave a loud, preoccupied "Nein!" and came back. "That will be entered as a plea of not guilty," the presiding judge said, rapping his gavel at a ripple of amusement going around the room. "If there is any disturbance in court, those who make it will have to leave the court." He went on to the next name. "Joachim von Ribbentrop."

Ribbentrop stood up and went to the microphone. "I declare myself in the sense of the indictment not guilty."

"In the absence of Ernst Kaltenbrunner, the trial will proceed against him, but he will have a chance to respond when he is sufficiently well to be brought back into court. Wilhelm Keitel."

A moment later Keitel's voice was heard over the microphone. "I declare myself not guilty!"

"Alfred Rosenberg."

"I declare myself in the sense of the indictment not guilty."

"Hans Frank."

"I declare myself not guilty."

"Wilhelm Frick."

"Not guilty!"

"Julius Streicher."

"Not guilty."

"Walther Funk."

"I declare myself not guilty."

"Hjalmar Schacht."

"I am guilty in no respect!"

"Karl Dönitz."

"Not guilty."

"Erich Raeder."

"I declare myself not guilty."

"Baldur von Schirach."

"I declare myself in the sense of the indictment not guilty."

"Fritz Sauckel."

"I declare myself in the sense of the indictment, before God and the world and my people, not guilty."

"Alfred Jodl."

"Not guilty. For what I have done, or had to do, I have a pure conscience—before God, my conscience, and my people!"

"Franz von Papen."

"I declare myself not guilty at all."

"Arthur Seyss-Inquart."

"I declare myself not guilty."

"Albert Speer."

"Not guilty."

"Konstantin von Neurath."

"I answer the question in the negative."

"Hans Fritzsche."

"As regards this indictment, not guilty."

With the last words from the last defendant, the dock was again silent. It had now remained silent for four months.

Silent except for those times when he had to listen to some small-time Party official testifying for the prosecution, some putrid cipher out to save his own neck; then he could not restrain himself from a carrying utterance of "Schweinehund!" At first the presiding judge had brought his gavel down sharply at these interruptions, but as the days passed, he seemed to grow weary of doing this.

Often he studied the presiding judge's face, trying to assess it. Intelligent, impassive, not a great deal of vitality. The two Russians were inscrutable, but one knew what was behind their eyes. He watched the prosecutors, listened to them carefully, came to conclusions about their strengths and weaknesses. Sometimes he sat looking at the journalists, many of whom he knew with a nostalgic stirring of old times, and all of whom—busily jotting down his mood of the day for the edification of the world, whether he seemed jolly, contemplative, irascible—had a refreshing effect on his spirit.

But usually he was profoundly, crushingly bored, as was everyone. When it was necessary to be alert he took copious notes, scribbling on a notepad held on his knee. When it was not necessary to be alert he turned off his earphones, feeling an abrupt shift in unrealities as the buzzing metallic voice of the interpreter was supplanted by a spectral atmosphere. The thick carpet absorbed every footstep, every cough, even the words of the person speaking, so that they were faint, as if coming from a great distance; and the speaker usually looked at no one but kept his eyes on the paper he read from, with a resultant sense of unconnectedness, almost of purposelessness, of words endlessly diffusing in a vacuum.

With his elbow propped on the partition before him, cheekbone in the heel of his hand, he would sit looking at the pale reddish-blond wood just under his eyes, studying its grain and the fine white granules of powder that still came seeping in from the rubble outside. Or in a heavy-lidded gaze he would watch the rolls of transcript steadily emerging from under the stenographers' fingers and slowly coiling in piles on the beige carpet. Sometimes he surreptitiously read a book or folded newspaper, as did all the defendants. If one was not covert enough, the guards would notice and the reading material was removed. Only Herr Hess was allowed to read, as if his utter indifference to his surroundings somehow overcame the rules. Hour after hour, with his big black eyebrows knitted, he remained deeply absorbed in his pages, whether they were those of a geography text or Grimm's fairy tales. Even when the testimony behooved the defendants' closest attention, Herr Hess read on, sometimes laughing aloud or muttering a comment as he turned a page. It was humiliating to have this mental wreck present. Nor for other reasons did he like sitting on the same bench as Kaltenbrunner, Heydrich's successor; or Frank, former Governor General of occupied Poland; or Streicher. But at least the sex-obsessed Streicher, looking more pop-eyed every day, provided you with an inner laugh when you considered the strict sleeping regulations; no wonder he was pop-eyed, unable to get at his privates for five months now. On the other hand, not so amusing. It was all frustration. Physical, verbal, and every other kind.

One of his greatest frustrations was that he could not be with the others during the noon break. At the trial's start he had eaten with the rest of them in a small room down the hall at tables whose tablecloths were a spread of old newspapers. Even under the noses of the eternal guards, it was the greatly looked-forward-to social hour. He enjoyed conversing with those he was on friendly terms with—von Neurath, von Schirach, Keitel, Funk—and in holding forth throughout the room, pounding home his views and putting starch back into spines. But then the Allgegenwärtige, the Omnipresent One—their private name for the prison psychiatrist—began making a point of sitting with them, and very soon the prison commandant ordered defendant Göring to be returned to his cell each noon to eat in solitude. From then on it was only at Sunday chapel, or in the exercise yard, or during lulls in court, that he was able to communicate with his fellow prisoners.

From time to time he would look around the dock, ready to pounce visually on anyone who sat too slumped. He was always struck by the preponderance of identical suits. These were a pallbearer's shade of dark blue, issued *en masse* to those who had been captured without appropriate clothing. The suits fit poorly, and created a felonious look when combined with the dark glasses often worn against the strong lights. Some of the prisoners were in their own clothing, most conspicuously von Papen in his natty pinstripes and Hess in his bulky English tweed. He himself, Feldmarschall Keitel and General Jodl were in uniform. But whatever was worn, it looked crumpled within an hour. Each night the clothes were collected from the cells to be spotcleaned and pressed, but after so many months of sitting, the wrinkles had grown permanent. A scruffy, neglected look prevailed, in keeping with the ashen complexions of the faces. There was unity in their appearance, if in nothing else. Many had never laid eyes on each other until finding themselves fellow prisoners. Others had known each other only too long, too well, and sat sucking bitterly on old grievances. And all the while the transcripts kept feeding out from under the stenographers' fingers, slowly coiling on the thick beige carpet. At the end of eight hours it was a gargantuan relief to stand up and stretch one's cramped legs, to turn away from the hot glare of the lights. Even so, he always felt the keenest reluctance to leave, for the room had become the center of his existence.

His eyes had again come to rest on those of the guard, trained on him through the mesh, jaws still working.

"Hau doch ab, du Armleuchter," he muttered irritably, bunching up the trousers under his head, then returning his arms to his sides.

Do you really think I'd try to kill myself tonight? What are you, feeble-minded? Of course, it's not your choice to stand there, I realize that. What's that phrase they keep handing around the courtroom like a piece of dirty toilet paper, orders are orders? Still, you should give yourself a break tonight. Read a magazine, take a nap.

His eyes moved to the small table at the foot of his cot, where documents and notes lay in stacks. His lawyer had urged him to take his notes with him on the stand, but he intended to rely on memory. He was confident that he would not lose his thread, even though what he had to say would take at least three days. Nor did he fear he would be ordered to compress his testimony. On the contrary, every word would be hung on raptly. The courtroom had waited as long to hear him as he had waited to be heard.

Everything on the table was palely illumined. Stacks of paper, dark squat bottle of ink, the sponge and piece of soap, the big meerschaum pipe, his three small photographs in their dark frames. He closed his eyes again and tried to sleep, listening to the rain spattering against the celluloid of the window.

Chapter 91

GUARD'S *report this morning was that prisoner had bad night,* wrote the young intelligence captain, the prison psychiatrist, known as der Allgegenwärtige. *Poor sleep, restless. I went into his cell shortly before he was taken to ct. rm. but saw no sign of fatigue. Like warhorse champing at the bit. Would-be spruce appearance, maroon scarf tucked smartly into collar of sagging tunic. Told him he looked tense. He said of course he was tense getting up on stand after sitting in silence for 4 mo's, & added: But I still don't recognize the authority of this ct. Like Maria Stuart I can say that I can only be tried in a ct. of peers.*

Very much the martyred nobleman about to enter the stage for the last act. Went on in same imperious tone: anything that happened in our country does not concern you in the least. Our state policies are our own business. Bringing the heads of a sovereign nation before a foreign ct. is a presumptuousness unique in hist. I told him it was also unique that the issues at stake here go to the root of civilized existence. Also reminded him that no one was forcing him to take the stand. But naturally he wld take the stand, has thought of nothing else for 4 mo's. Strode eagerly forward as guards opened door.

P.M. No conversation to report. Went into cell & found him sitting in semidarkness, had asked guard not to turn on light. Had also sent back supper untouched. Asked him why. Said he was too wrought-up to eat. Asked why he didn't want light on, but wldn't answer. Clearly wished to be left alone. Savor triumph in solitude. 6 hrs of nonstop testimony, to be continued tomorrow. He shld be forced to compress. Granted this is the ct's first coherent & inside pict of the steps leading to Nazi takeover, but he's making propaganda all the way. Cunning, shrewd, smoothly sardonic, weaves in subtly damning remarks abt the democracies as he goes his endless digressive route, & the ct sits spellbound. All I can say is that he'd better be torn apart in cross-exam, or everything the ct has built up these last 4 mo's will be undone.

Visited some of the others: Rosenberg, Frick, Streicher, Frank, Hess. The Old Fighters. All in nostalgic mood, even muddled Hess. All forgetting past diff's with G, all united in his recapitulation of their glorious early struggle. Rosenberg actually used the wds: glorious early struggle.

3 days of uninterrupted testimony. Looked in on him tonight. Sat on cot puffing big Bavarian pipe, blankets wrapped around legs which are paining him, cell very damp & cold, rain battering against window. Very tired from strain. Anticlimax. His big moment over. In brooding, cynical mood. Said empire of Ghengis Khan, the Roman Empire, & even the British Empire hadn't been built on principles of humanity but have won respected place in hist. I said the world was growing too sophisticated to regard war & murder as signs of greatness. He said this was sentimental idealism of an American who cld afford such self-delusions after America had hacked its way to rich living space by revolution, massacre & war. Clearly will tolerate no maudlin sentimentality to crab his entrance into Valhalla.

He also spoke of Hess, worried abt his mental condition, can't remember from one day to the next. Said what a farce if he testifies. I told him Hess's memory wasn't completely gone. In fact I cld have cited a conversation between Hess & G himself last wk, told me by ct guard. Have appt'd members of ct guard who understand German to report all overheard conversations between prisoners & between prisoners & counsel. The exchge was trivial but showed Hess's intermittent grasp of past. Turned to G & said: Look at you, Herr Göring, all the fancy food you ate & fine wines you drank & what good did they do you? Here you sit. G replied: Well look at you, Herr Hess, you never enjoyed a damn thing and here you sit too. Hess turned away annoyed. It's obvious he has clear moments if few & far between. G thinks he's partly faking but not much. Worries abt mental state of others too, esp Ribbentrop & Frank. Still hoping for united front when the others begin testifying, but doubts it will happen. Said: None will conduct himself as impressively as I have.

Von Papen's cell: That is the Göring of the early days, when he was still reasonable. But when he stated that outside of my charming personality I contributed nothing to the Party, I must tell the ct that not only did I not contribute anything but tried to take away!

Von Neurath's cell: Was pleasantly surprised by G's line of defense, esp his taking responsibility for all his actions. But then as usual Neurath got onto his bête noire, Ribbentrop.

Von Ribbentrop's cell: Came to ct today with collar unbuttoned, no tie,

*cheek twitching, even more bewildered look than usual. I called attn to lack of tie
& he told me wearily that his collar was too tight. Subconsciously feels noose
tightening around neck. Have often observed him rubbing back of neck. I sent
someone for tie, told him he cld wear it without buttoning collar. Tonight in cell
I asked what he thought of G's testimony. But no interest, unable to concentrate.*

*Funk's cell: Göring is a strong personality, Schacht too. They are strong
personalities. But the rest of us—I assure you I don't have the stuff for heroism.
I didn't then & I don't now. Maybe that is the trouble . . . but I often wonder
what I wld have done if I had known about those things . . . those atrocities. He
began to weep.*

*Speer's cell: Said he was moved in spite of himself by G's speech because it
was obviously his swan song. Called it gripping. Added that he looked forward
to seeing him cut down to size by Jackson's cross-exam.*

*Frank's cell: I am pleased that Göring took responsibility for all his actions.
But it is going to be interesting when Jackson gets up to cross-examine him, ha
ha, ha! The representative of Western democracy and the last Renaissance figure, ha, ha, ha! Now Göring has his wish at last, standing up as No. 1
spokesman for the Natl. Soc. regime—what's left of it. But I must say I'm
pleased at the way he is conducting himself. I told him yesterday it was too bad
he wasn't thrown in jail for a yr a few yrs ago, ha, ha, ha! Every sentence
interjected with the high-pitched hysterical laugh that characterizes his speech
more & more.*

Each day during the chief war criminal's testimony, judges had
made diary notes, and pens had jotted away in the international press
section:

". . . Göring is the man who has really dominated the proceedings,
and that, remarkably enough, without ever uttering a word up until
the moment he went into the witness box. That in itself is a very remarkable achievement. . . . He has followed the evidence with great
intentness when the evidence required attention, and slept like a child
when it did not; and it has been obvious that a personality of outstanding, though possibly evil qualities, was seated there in the dock. . . .
Nobody seems to have been prepared for his immense ability and
knowledge, and his thorough mastery and understanding of the captured documents."

". . . Göring's stream of words sweep away all the Germans' legal
efforts and false pleas to save him, and themselves, which preceded
him in court. What he offers his judges is no mea culpa but a dissertation on the techniques of power. . . . There was considerable surprise,
though there should not have been, that behind his fancy tailoring, his
fat, and his medals, he had one of the best brains of a period in history
when good brains were rare. On the stand he is malicious and disturbing. He pointed out that only rich nations could afford the luxury of
democracy, with its wasteful political squabbles and parliamentary inef-

ficiencies, so he and his Führer had aimed at the economy of single power for poor Germany. . . . He said he probably didn't understand freedom, but he nevertheless had freed German workers from both the strikes and the lockouts that bother the democracies in their liberty. . . . He cited the Communist Party and the Catholic Church as two flourishing institutions that operate on his theory of one-man, totalitarian rule. . . . Then he began on the sellout of Europe, country by country."

". . . If this leader of the surviving Nazis could be exposed and shattered, and the purposes and methods of the Nazi government revealed in their horrible crudity, then the whole free world would feel that this trial had served its supreme purpose. But if that design should fail, then the fears of those who thought the holding of any trial would be a mistake would be in some way justified."

". . . Arrogant, crafty, intelligent, the defendant has obviously enjoyed himself as he held the courtroom spellbound these three days. And if he is not cut down to size in Jackson's cross-examination, everything the court has built up in these four months will be undone."

". . . The cross-examination had not proceeded for more than ten minutes before it was evident that Göring was the complete master of Mr. Justice Jackson. Suave, shrewd, adroit, capable, resourceful, he quickly saw the elements of the situation, and as his confidence grew, his mastery became more apparent."

". . . With one of the worst cases in history to defend, Göring is doing a remarkably good job. From the moment he first spoke from the witness box, and now even more under cross-examination, he has impressed everyone with his skill, his self-control, and not least his personal courage."

". . . Despite Jackson's great ability and powers of exposition, he seems to have no conception of how to put forth with simplicity and power the great issues which he had earlier spoken of so eloquently. Standing with his thumb hooked under his suspender strap, he had the unfortunate air of a righteous Inquisitor, both accusatory and patronizing, although this soon changed. . . . Time and again he was brought up short by unexpected answers, found himself coolly corrected on facts he had wrong, at one point throwing down his earphones in a rage."

". . . With Göring having bested Mr. Justice Jackson, the whole fate of the trial hangs in the balance."

But here the courtroom's anxiety began to subside. As the deputy chief British prosecutor took over, it was clear that he was both a smoother and more cautious interrogator than Jackson; moreover, he had learned from Jackson's mistakes in handling the defendant. The defendant was allowed no opportunity to make capital of the prosecution's weaknesses, but was instead taken into areas where there was no way out: the pillory of occupied nations, the use of forced labor, the destruction of the Jews.

The defendant put up a dogged fight, but his moment of triumph was over.

Said angrily: They lay everything *at my door! —Well isn't that what you want? You've taken full responsibility for everything. Arming the nation. Annexing Austria. Taking over Czecho. Planning & waging aggressive war. — Don't make me laugh, since when is planning & waging aggressive war a crime? This whole trial is built on charges without legal precedent. No international law exists that prohibits & penalizes the planning & waging of aggressive war. If such a law existed, yr Russians wld be sitting in the dock for invading Poland. It's a perpetration of fraud. I know & you know & the ct knows you can't try anyone according to laws made after the fact. I've said all this before, but I'll say again that I worked for peace, but when war came I did my best to ensure victory. As for Austria, I did that alone. It was a righteous action, & I stand behind it. I stand behind rearming Germany, I rearmed it until it bristled! I also admitted freely that I took what Germany needed from the occupied countries, & that I requisitioned foreign labor to man the factories. But I will* not *be blamed for these mass murders! Anyway it's all propaganda. —You still don't believe what you've seen in the Russians' atrocity films? —Anybody can make an atrocity film if they take corpses out of their graves & then show a tractor shoving them back in again. These were the Russians' own atrocities on the Germans!*

It's very clear that he will accept being punished as a German patriot but not as a war criminal, & will go to any lengths of self-deception to prevent it.

Says he's glad Hess didn't take the stand. Said Ribbentrop's so far gone he's practically dead already. Was pleased with Keitel: soldierly & straightforward.

But if ever a move backfired, it was Kaltenbrunner's decision to use the Auschwitz commander as a defense witness. His idea was apparently to prove thru the commandant's testimony that the camp was such a closely guarded secret that even he, Kaltenbrunner, cld not have known of it. His hope was not only smashed, but the description of the camp's function was like the opening of a floodgate of blood & ashes that filled the whole ct rm to the ceiling.

G's hope for a united front has crumbled. Says the other defendants are turning into squirmers & double-crossers. Asked him tonight what he thought of Speer's testimony. Furious response: If there was to be any denunciation of the Führer, I was the one who had the right! I was the one who was hated & ordered shot! Where does Speer get off denouncing him when he was favored right up to the end? I am the one who had the right to denounce Hitler on the stand, but I wldn't do it because of the principle. Do you think I have any personal love for Hitler? But I swore my loyalty to him, & when I give my oath of loyalty I cannot break it. I had a hell of a time keeping it too, I can tell you, but I cld never plot behind his back with poison gas! —But don't you know that history & yr people wld think better of you if you had said on the stand that you kept yr oath to Hitler, but he betrayed you & the German people? —You have no understanding of German tradition! It has not always been easy for German heroes, but they kept their loyalty just the same. Let those who belong to the future think differently. Anyway, you can't expect me at the age of 53 to suddenly chge my entire concept. Gott im Himmel, how cld Speer stoop so low! To tell a rotten thing like that on the stand just to save his rotten neck! I died of shame listening to him! To think that a German cld be so rotten just to prolong this filthy life, just to piss in front & crap from behind for a little longer! Do you think I give that much of a damn about this filthy life? For myself I don't give a damn if I get executed, or drown, or crash in a plane, or drink myself to death, but there is still a matter of honor in this rotten life!

It was July when the last defendant stepped down from the stand. The courtroom's weariness was heavy as the defense summations began. When they ended, in August, the defense of indicted National Socialist organizations started in. The room was hot and close. The visitors' gallery had grown half empty. The newspaper correspondents seldom moved their hands with rapidity across their notebook pages. Everything was the same as nine months ago, when the trial had begun. Dust from the remains of Nuremberg still gathered on every surface. Transcripts still coiled in piles at the stenographers' feet on the beige rug. Papers were still being shuffled, marked, endlessly read from. Horror testimony continued to be given and atrocity films shown. There were the same doomed, sallow faces in the dock. Everything was the same except that the sense of death, death that had been and death that would follow, suffocated the room.

"Here in this enlarged photograph from Yugoslavia you will observe a number of heads on the ground, mostly adults' but also children's. Observe the sign the Germans have stuck next to them. 'Spring fruit!' Evidently it was spring."

"In the Mauthausen camp, hundreds of us lay near death in unheated barracks in the dead of winter, on rotten straw never renewed, so that a stinking liquid formed in which worms and maggots crawled."

"An attempt was apparently made to burn this film, but enough remains for our purpose. We will run it for you at half speed." How slowly they come, unearthly, like a floating ballet inside the burned edges of the film. Walking naked and white so slowly through slow clubbings and kickings, some falling slowly to the ground. One young girl, very pretty, and apparently because very pretty, is helped to her feet by an officer, but only so that she can be clubbed to the ground again, the film rattling to its end of charred cellulose.

On the second day of September, court was adjourned until the judges' verdicts should be pronounced a month hence. The weather had grown cool. The windows of the cells, whose thick gray celluloid had glowed like pearl in the sunlight from outside, now modulated to squares of opalescent stone. The faint dampness of the cells, hovering throughout summer, bloomed in floor and wall and in the grain of the oaken doors. By the time the days had crawled to the middle of September, the prisoners' breath was visible before them.

Like the others he's only thinking of one thing right now, the first visit of wives & children tomorrow. After 1½ yrs the prisoners are in a state of intense anticipation. Except Keitel & von Papen, who refuse to be seen by their wives in circumstances they consider degrading.

G agrees the circumstances are degrading. Spoke of his stepson in Sweden who writes him as often as is allowed, said the stepson had wanted to take the stand as a witness in his defense. Said he was deeply moved, but cld not allow it. Wanted no one in his family mixed up in this gangster trial, as he calls it.

But to speak with his wife for the last time, didn't care how degrading the circumstances were. Said his greatest agony when first imprisoned at the interrogation center was not knowing what had become of her & the child. Spoke bitterly of being kept in dark. Was finally told they were in American prison camp. Later was told they had been released, were living near Neuhaus. Today he said again how grateful he was that I'd gone to see them. Added his usual sarcasm: of course I know your professional inquisitiveness was primarily involved. Still, I was deeply grateful. To know they were all right, & to have a letter brought back from them, that was a beautiful day.

Didn't tell him then & haven't told him since the full details, as Frau G insisted upon it. Cld say it was a hut in the woods, but not that it was without heat or water. Wasn't to mention they had very little to eat, one chge of clothing. Everything confiscated, including Burg Veldenstein. Was used as a billet for Sudeten refugees, now locked up, empty, untended. Not to tell him that. Only that it's still standing. South wall damaged by bombs, but the rest untouched. Tell him the burg still stands.

Said he feels keyed up about tomorrow but in control of himself, only afraid that at the sight of the child he might break down. Told him too bad he hadn't thought of that yrs ago.

Until the end of September the prisoners and their families were allowed a daily half-hour visit through the grilles of the partitioned conference room. At the beginning, the experience was one of extreme joy, but as the days passed a sense of terrible strain grew, and grew to such unbearableness that when the final visit was over, it was felt by both prisoners and families to be a mercy.

Chapter 92

THE sounds that had characterized the opening of each day's courtroom session—murmurous voices, papers being shuffled—were not to be heard on the morning of October 1. As the door at the back of the dock opened and the prisoners came filing in to sit down for the last time, the room was totally silent.

The presiding judge, his dry, precise voice showing the strain of the occasion, called the name of the first defendant. In his faded, voluminous Luftwaffe uniform, a pair of dark glasses over his eyes, the defendant rose from the bench.

"From the moment he joined the Party in 1922 and took command of the street-fighting organization, the SA, Göring was the adviser and the active agent of Hitler, and one of the prime leaders of the National Socialist movement. As Hitler's political deputy he was largely instrumental in bringing the National Socialists to power in 1933, and was charged with consolidating this power and expanding German armed might. He created the Gestapo and he created the first concentration camps, relinquishing them to Himmler in 1934. That same year he conducted the Röhm purge, and later he engineered the sordid proceedings which resulted in the removal of von Blomberg and von Fritsch from the Army. In the Austrian Anschluss he was, indeed, the central figure, the ringleader. The night before the invasion of Czechoslovakia, at a conference with Hitler and President Hácha, he threatened to bomb Prague if Hácha did not submit. He commanded the Luftwaffe in the attack on Poland and throughout the aggressive wars that followed. He made plans for the spoliation of Soviet territory long before the war on the Soviet Union.

"Göring persecuted the Jews, particularly after the November riots, and not only in Germany but later in occupied territories as well. His own utterances, both at that time and in his court testimony here, show that his interest was primarily economic—how to get their property and how to force them out of the economic life of Europe. Although their extermination was in Himmler's hands, Göring was far from disinterested or inactive, despite his protestations from the witness box.

"There is nothing to be said in mitigation. For Göring was often, indeed almost always, the moving force, second only to his Leader. He was the leading war aggressor, both as political and military leader. He was director of the slave labor program, and the creator of the oppressive program against the Jews and other races, at home and abroad. All these crimes he has frankly admitted. On some specific cases there may be a conflict of testimony, but in terms of broad outline, his own admissions are more than sufficiently wide to be conclusive of his guilt. His guilt is unique in its enormity. The record discloses no excuses for this man. We find him guilty on all four counts of the indictment."

The reading of the verdicts was followed by the midday break, after which the sentencing was to take place, each man to be brought into the dock alone. As the court reconvened after the break, the prisoners were kept downstairs under guard. In the event that aid might be needed as each was brought back from his sentencing, a doctor and nurse were present. Inside the waiting elevator, two guards stood posted with a stretcher and straitjacket.

Finally someone called: "They're ready!"

The first defendant was handcuffed to a guard and taken into the elevator. He had removed his dark glasses. The ride, which he had taken some two hundred times since the trial began, was short, efficient, the elevator doors opening onto the dock.

The guard unlocked his handcuffs. He stepped out into the glare of the courtroom, receiving a pair of earphones from another guard. He put them over his head and braced himself for the words, taking a deep breath through his nostrils. But he heard no words. The presiding judge spoke without sound. With an abrupt motion, the prisoner indicated that something was wrong with his earphones and took them off. In the enormous silence he stood waiting for an excruciating span of moments as the earphones were examined, the defect rectified.

Once more he put them over his head, once more braced himself. This time the words came through clearly.

"Defendant Hermann Wilhelm Göring, on the counts of the indictment on which you were convicted, the International Military Tribunal sentences you to death by hanging."

In order to observe the prisoners' reactions to their sentences, the Allgegenwärtige planned to meet each of them as they were returned, one by one, to their cells. He was waiting in the cell of the first as the prisoner entered. The Allgegenwärtige observed that his face was dead-white, his eyes stared straight ahead.

"Death," he said, sitting down on his cot and picking up a book. The Allgegenwärtige observed that his breathing was growing hard, his eyes were moist.

"Please leave me by myself."

Throughout that afternoon, every quarter of an hour, the footsteps of a returning prisoner and his guards rang out in the corridor, until eighteen of the twenty-one prisoners had been returned to their cells. The three men who had been acquitted—von Papen, Schacht and Fritzsche—had been moved elsewhere during the midday break.

For a time the corridor was silent. Then there was a commotion of doors being unlocked and opened, of guards' voices, and of collective footsteps, as those who had not received the death penalty were removed to cells on the second floor. Seven prisoners climbed up the winding metal stairway: Hess, Raeder and Funk with life sentences; Speer and von Schirach with twenty years; von Neurath with fifteen; Dönitz with ten. The ascending clatter of their feet on the metal steps echoed through the corridor below, which then fell silent again.

Within three days the judges, the prosecution staff, and almost everyone else who had been involved in the everlasting trial had departed from Nuremberg with haste and relief.

Has filed an appeal that, as an officer of the German armed forces, he be executed by firing squad. Apart from that his main concern is for wife & child. Asked abt the other 10 condemned. Says he can hear Sauckel weeping, says he leaves 7 young children. Says why shld Sauckel be given death and Speer not, when Sauckel only carried out Speer's forced labor orders? Says it's because Sauckel didn't pull Speer's double-crossing stunt on the stand. I told him it was apparently beyond his powers of conception that Speer might be a man sincerely penitent. He said it was.

Wanted to know when they wld be informed as to the date the sentences wld be carried out. Told him they wld not be informed.

*   *   *

Sharp mood swings. Generally quiet & fatalistic, but sometimes breaks into defiant talk abt invalidity of jdgmnt by foreign ct, etc, & on to his usual heroic-legend ideas. But appears to me to be fighting down intense depression.

Informed Göring, Keitel & Jodl that their appeals for execution by firing squad have been refused.

Prisoners allowed a last visit with their wives today. G appeared composed when I visited him tonight, but guard told me he had returned from visit a broken man. Told guard he wasn't afraid to die, what he was afraid of was to have to live another day.

I found him sitting on his cot reading, blankets wrapped around legs against the cold. Said old wounds were painful, but that was one pain he didn't mind. Asked him what his book was. Effi Briest, German novel abt 19th century Prussia. Said he expected sentences wld now be carried out very soon.

Guards complain that the prisoners keep asking them when sentences will be carried out. Guards wld like to know themselves. After 2 weeks it's getting too much for their nerves. Anxious to have it over.

"Glieshübler gave a quite unusually delightful smile and was encouraged to put down his hat—far too tall for his size—which he had hitherto been twirling in his hand. 'Yes, dear lady, that is true.'

"'Oh, I can understand,' she said. 'I've heard about the consuls that—'"

A sound of tapping made him pause in his reading. It was an erratic sound, stopping, starting, which seemed to be in the cell with him, in the walls. Then he realized it was not tapping, but a faint, distant sound of hammering, of carpentry, coming from the direction of the prison gymnasium.

His eyes returned to the page before him, but he had lost his place. Nor had he been absorbing the words he read. He began reading the page over again. In the indescribable silence that had hung over the cellblock these last two weeks, only the wind could be heard, day after day, night after night, intermittently rattling the celluloid of the window. And now the sound of the gallows being erected. He put his book aside as the guard behind the wire mesh adjusted the lamp to its oblique angle at half past nine. Along with the sporadic rattling of the window, the faint clatter of hammering went on throughout the night.

This morning the prisoners' attorneys came for a final visit. After that the American chaplain made his rounds. He said G seemed lower than usual, which was not surprising in view of things to come. G asked for the last rites, but the chaplain was forced to refuse him. Said he cld not administer the Lord's Supper to him because in previous talks G had denied the divinity of Christ. Furthermore, he had denied the fundamentals of the Christian Church tho claiming he was a Christian because he had never stepped out of the church. The chaplain beseeched him to surrender his heart & soul to his Savior, but he wld not. He became more discouraged when the chaplain insisted he cld not meet Edda, his daughter, in heaven, if he refused the Lord's way of salvation. Said he was saddened not to be able to give him the Sacrament, but cld not have done so in good faith.

Afternoon. Have taken leave of the prisoners.

In spite of the day's tension, the ordinary routine was maintained. The prison librarian came with books that had been asked for, and took back those that had been finished. At three o'clock the usual mugs of ersatz coffee arrived. Some of the condemned were kneeling in prayer on the stone floors of their cells. Others paced, or lay on their cots, staring at the ceiling. Still others sat at their tables, writing.

The prisoner in Cell No. 5 came over and took the coffee mug from the shelf beneath the wire-mesh portal and returned with it to his table. Sitting down, he rewrapped the blankets around his legs and continued writing. Pausing now and again to take a sip of coffee, he wrote most of the afternoon. Then, sitting down on the cot, he took up his book.

The guards outside the doors were aware of the extraordinary silence. The silence had bothered them more than anything these last two weeks. Today it was unbearable. Only a sound of sobs, issuing from a couple of the cells and echoing faintly down the corridor, disturbed the absolute stillness.

Then as evening fell, a sense of activity suddenly began to gather. All the lights in the corridor were switched on as bright as day. From outside could be heard a sound of cars arriving.

"Through a narrow gap in the dunes, they could see the beach and the pier. The November sun, already quite wintry, cast its pale glow on a sea still rough from the storm. There was a heavy swell. Now and again a great gust of wind carried the spray almost to where they were sitting. It . . ."

He put the book down as the doctor entered with a guard. The doctor took his pulse and gave him a white powder to drink with water if he felt his nerves needed calming. They spoke a few words, and shook hands.

The door was slammed shut, there was a clangor of bolts and locks. The guard's face reappeared behind the mesh.

"What time?" the prisoner asked in English.

The guard looked at his watch. "Ten past nine."

He sat down again at the small wobbly table. From a folder he withdrew three sealed envelopes. One was unmarked, and contained a manifesto to the German people. The other was addressed to the prison authorities. The third was addressed to his wife. He propped the three envelopes against his bottle of ink. He sat listening to the wind striking in hard gusts against the gray celluloid of the window. He looked at the flaked, dingy wall before him, at the long smear of greasy dirt above his cot. His eyes moved to the half-finished mess tin by his elbow, the sponge and sliver of soap, the matchbox containing one button.

Turning his head aside from the gaze of the guard, he drew toward him the three small photographs in their dark blue leather frames. Emmy and little Edda. Mutter and Vater. Carin. He looked at each one for a long moment, then got up and prepared for bed.

When he had gotten into his dark blue silk pajamas, he folded his prison fatigues and put them aside. He brought his mess tin, his pen and his dark glasses over to the door and handed them through the portal to the guard. Then he went over to the toilet in its shallow recess in the wall and emptied his bladder, bending over afterward to swiftly dislodge the metal container from its porcelain groove. Returning to his cot, he got under the blankets, lying on his back with his arms exposed, in the required position, the container in his loosely curled right hand. A few minutes later the lamp was turned to its oblique angle for the night. It was his supposition that the sentence would be carried out at midnight.

His mind felt curiously empty. After a while he twisted off the cap of the container with the fingers of his right hand, feeling the capsule lying smooth on his palm. You can decide that I will die, he said to the watching eyes, but not the way I will die.

"What time?" he asked aloud.

"Twenty past ten."

The minutes were going by much faster than he had realized. He lay listening to the wind outside, banging against the gray celluloid of the window. His heart was beating rapidly, his lips were dry. After a while he brought his hand up and rubbed his face, at the same time sliding his palm across his mouth before returning his arm to the blanket. The capsule lay smooth and cold on his tongue. He eased it between his back molars. His heart pounded in his throat, his mind was suddenly like the shade of a window rolling up again and again, a different scene flashing before him each time—pamphlets fluttering down from the clockwork figures of a Rathaus, faces fluttering down, the silver flick of a fish, mass graves, dead cities, great flag-bearing columns marching to drums and music, sunlight streaming. He lay still a moment longer, then brought his teeth violently together as the wind swept against the window, as it swept through the dark grounds of the burg, calmed for a moment, then rose again, rushing through the four window slots of the tower.

Afterword

ALL the named characters in the book are real except Nikki and Hans Schmidt, and the minor figures of Schelling, Frau Kloppmann, Walther, Ida, Dr. Weinblatt, Minna Bang and Max Korwan. Rose Korwan was an actual person, an obscure provincial stage actress and friend of Emmy Göring, who died at Auschwitz. When she entered the book as a peripheral character, I used her real name; and when, later, she developed into a major character, I retained the name. Many aspects of her life as described herein are imagined, and have no known connection with the actual person who was Rose Korwan. I have also taken imaginative license in bringing Thomas von Kantzow's life and personality into fullness.

Carin Göring's and Thomas von Kantzow's diaries are fictitious vehicles which incorporate actual occurrences; some of Carin Göring's letters are used in her diaries. The psychiatrist's daybook at Nuremberg is a combination of fictional and factual elements. Colonel Jodl's diary entry is factual, as is Goebbels's. Goebbels's long note to himself is taken from statements he made to his staff.

Göring's letter to his parents, the one to his mother-in-law and the first sentence of his letter to Thomas von Kantzow are factual; the letters between him and his brother Karl are fictional, as are those between him and Putzi Hanfstaengl, with the exception of his 1937 letter to Hanfstaengl, which is reconstructed from a description of the letter's contents in Hanfstaengl's memoir; Göring's letter to Hitler is reconstructed from Göring's description of its contents at Nuremberg. The letters of Göring's mother to Hermann von Epenstein are fictional. Carin Göring's letter to her sister is fictional; her letters to Thomas von Kantzow incorporate sections of her actual letters. Olga Riegele's letter to her sister is fictional, as are Frau Ballin's letter to Göring, Colonel Jeschonnek's letter to his parents, Rose Korwan's letter to Emmy Göring, and Emmy Göring's and Max Korwan's exchange of letters. The contents of all the letters are based on historical or personal facts.

Documents, reports, speeches, newspaper items, telegrams, and radio announcements are factual. Göring's book, *Germany Reborn,* is factual. With three exceptions—the scene in which Hitler and Göring first meet, the scene among Hitler, Göring, and Himmler after the Röhm purge, and the scene between Hitler and Blomberg during the Rhineland invasion—Hitler's words, whether spoken in official context or in private conversation, are actual.